中国分析哲学　2009

■ 中国现代外国哲学学会分析哲学专业委员会 编

中国分析哲学

ANALYTIC PHILOSOPHY IN CHINA 2009

2009

ZHEJIANG UNIVERSITY PRESS

浙江大学出版社

中国分析哲学

常务编委：江　怡　　　　执行编委：蒉益民

学术委员会（按姓氏笔画为序）

王　路（清华大学）
刘晓力（中国人民大学）
朱　菁（中山大学）
朱志方（武汉大学）
江　怡（北京师范大学）
张庆熊（复旦大学）
张志林（复旦大学）
邹崇理（中国社会科学院）
陈　刚（华中科技大学）
陈　波（北京大学）
陈亚军（南京大学）
陈嘉映（首都师范大学）
胡新和（中国科学院研究生院）
徐向东（北京大学）
盛晓明（浙江大学）
蒉益民（中国社会科学院）
韩东晖（中国人民大学）
韩林合（北京大学）
魏屹东（山西大学）

Analytic Philosophy in China

Editor in Chief: **Yi Jiang**, *Beijing Normal University*
Executive Editor: **Yimin Kui**, *Chinese Academy of Social Sciences*

卷首语*

江 怡

2009 年，对当代分析哲学来说是一个重要的年份：分析哲学的奠基人弗雷格的奠基性著作《概念文字》发表 130 周年、分析哲学的主要创始人之一维特根斯坦诞辰 120 周年、维也纳学派在中国的传人洪谦先生诞辰 100 周年、分析哲学的主要创始人之一罗素访华 90 周年、分析哲学的早期主要代表维也纳学派发表宣言《科学的世界概念：维也纳学派》80 周年。在这个特殊的时候，回忆分析哲学在中国的百年历史，我们会发现，分析哲学带给中国哲学的不再是一种理解哲学性质的看法，更重要的是如何处理哲学问题的方法；哲学分析的方法对中国哲学来说不再是一种舶来品，而是变成了研究中国哲学的一种必不可少的基本方法。进入 21 世纪以来，分析哲学在中国哲学界以及整个学术界的声音和影响正在逐渐增强，重视哲学分析的作用已经成为当代中国哲学家们的普遍共识。正是在这样的思想条件下，《中国分析哲学》应运而生了：她将成为中国哲学家们以分析的方式讨论思想理论的重要平台，成为中国哲学家形成和提出自己创造性思想的孵化器，成为中国哲学家与西方哲学家共同交流的重要途径。

我们知道，哲学分析方法在中国哲学中的占位，经历了几代哲学工作者的努力。张申府先生、张岱年先生最早介绍维也纳学派哲学时，就把这种哲学首先理解为哲学分析的方法，指出这样的哲学分析与唯物辩证的方法可以相辅相成，共同贡献于中国哲学事业的发展。冯友兰先生曾在中国哲学史著作中反复强调逻辑分析对中国哲学研究的重要性，金岳霖更是积极倡导以分析的方式处理中国哲学中的基本问题。他不仅通过分析建立了自己的知识论体系，弥补了中国传统哲学中的空白，而且用分析的方法讨论中国传统哲学的"道"概念，最终确立了自己的哲学信念。洪谦先生作为维也纳学派的中国传人，将毕生贡献给了分析哲学事业，他不仅大力宣传维也纳学派的分析精神，而且积极推进逻辑实证主义哲学的发展。沈有鼎、周礼全等逻辑学家更是以逻辑分析的方法深入研究中国传统哲学中的逻辑思想，整理出了具有中国传统特色

* 本文的最初版本发表于《社会科学报》（上海）2009 年 9 月 3 日第 5 版，题目为《反思分析哲学中国百年》。

的中国逻辑学。进入新世纪之后，当代中国哲学家们全面深入地推进了分析方法在哲学研究中的重要作用，通过分析阐述、对话交流等方式讨论了英美分析哲学在早中晚等各个时期的发展，涉及逻辑经验主义、批判理性主义、科学哲学中的历史主义、逻辑实用主义等众多内容，形成了国内外思想交流的共同平台。

特别值得注意的是，意识到澄清概念意义和分析命题意义的重要性，已不仅是我国分析哲学研究者的大力提倡，而是已经成为我国当代哲学家们的普遍共识，比较明显地表现在西方哲学史研究和中国哲学史研究中。20 世纪 90 年代以来，我国西方哲学史研究发生了一些重要变化，其中之一就是对"存在"概念意义的澄清。围绕着对这个概念意义的理解，哲学家们形成了不同的解释阵营。一种意见认为，我们以往误解了西语中的"Being"一词，用"存在"概念翻译这个词，导致我们与西方哲学拉开了距离，所以应当恢复这个西语的本来意义，即"是"。但另一种意见则认为，"Being"一词在西语中原本就有"存在"的意义，所以无须改变原译名的用法，否则只会导致更多的混乱。还有意见认为，我们可以在不同的语境中使用不同的译名，不必在所有的情况采用统一译名。这场争论表面上看，涉及的是翻译问题，实际上关系到如何理解西方哲学，即通过对西方哲学概念意义的澄清，深入讨论西方哲学的重要问题。在中国哲学研究中，张岱年先生的《中国古代哲学概念范畴要论》（1982）开启了用分析的方法处理中国哲学概念的先河。当代研究者们（特别是港台学者）更加关注用逻辑的方法论证中国传统哲学命题的意义分疏，取得了许多重要成果，例如对《墨经》的研究。如今，越来越多的中国传统哲学的研究者认识到，对传统哲学概念的辨析，不仅可以有助于我们更好地揭示传统智慧的内容，而且有利于我们重构中国哲学的论证关系。2009 年 6 月在华东师范大学举行的"中国哲学与分析哲学国际学术研讨会"，就集中反映了这样一种共识。

如果说当今西方哲学家把分析哲学的遗产主要归结为哲学分析的方法，那么，围绕着如何认识和使用这种方法，20 世纪的中国哲学家们曾展开了各种思想论战，引发了当代中国哲学的不同发展路径。在西方分析哲学中，哲学分析方法的精髓在于以科学探究的方式追求语言意义的清晰和严格。但正是这种对哲学的科学态度，遭到了坚持哲学以追求道德理想为目标的中国哲学家们的强烈反对，由此形成了 20 世纪 20 年代到 30 年代在中国哲学界发生的"科玄之战"。同时，在强调经验证实的分析方法与提倡社会革命的政治理想之间，也发生了影响后世的"问题与主义之争"。冯友兰先生虽然大力宣传逻辑分析对中国哲学的重要意义，但他在新理学的体系建构中却没有坚持运用这种方法，而是强调形而上学在新理学中的决定作用，由此造成了他与洪谦先生在 20 世纪 40 年代的一场学术公案。这些思想论战虽然表面上针对不同时期的不同问题，但实际上都关系到中西不同思维方式之间的交锋，其实也是我们长期简化地理解西方哲学的结果，即把西方哲学看做与中国哲学截然不同的、铁板一块的一种思维方式。当今的中国哲学家们已经认识到，即使当代西方哲学家们也会对哲学的性质持有不同的理解，以何种方式讨论哲学问题就变成了哲学流派分野的主要依据。由于冯友兰、金岳霖等哲学家早已指出，中国传统哲学严重缺乏逻辑分析，因而大力提倡和运用分析方法讨论中国哲学，自然就成为当今中国哲学家们推进哲学发展的重要内容。

反思分析哲学在中国的百年历史，我们可以从正反两个方面理解哲学分析方法对中国哲学研究的重要意义。一方面，严格的逻辑分析使我们清楚地看到了中国思想传统中的明显缺陷，哲学史研究从以往对"经史子集"的经典引证，走向了对哲学概念的体系建构；而中国哲学学科的确立，正是按照西方哲学模式对中国传统经典文本进行义理分梳的逻辑结果。但另一方面，完全按照西方哲学的模式建构中国哲学，又使得我们失去了中国传统思想中的"天人之道"、"人世之道"；而由此带来的中国哲学研究中的缺失，往往被归咎于逻辑分析方法的运用。不幸的是，在当代中国哲学研究中，哲学分析方法总是被看做西方哲学思维方式的典型代表，因而，在任何一次中西哲学争论或冲突中，分析哲学总是遭到"野蛮的"（即武断的）攻击。然而，这完全是对分析哲学及其哲学分析方法的误解。

概括地说，分析哲学的特征主要表现在这样几个方面：首先，它与现代逻辑具有非常密切的关系。至少在分析哲学诞生之初，现代逻辑就被看做哲学研究的主要手段，而且，早期的分析哲学家大多都是根据现代逻辑从事哲学分析活动；虽然某些分析哲学家并没有强调逻辑分析方法的重要作用，但逻辑的观念和基本逻辑思想完全深入到分析哲学家的具体工作之中。其次，分析哲学与当代哲学中的"语言的转向"有着密切关系，甚至有哲学家认为，它正是这种转向的必然结果；而且从时间上看，语言转向的发生与分析哲学的诞生几乎是同时出现的，因此，分析哲学注定是以语言分析为主要对象的。再次，"分析哲学"的名称就标明了这种哲学的分析性特征，即以分析作为哲学研究的基本方法，无论是逻辑的分析还是概念的分析；而且，这样的分析并非与综合方法完全对立，因为分析哲学家们大多都是经验主义者，因而他们处理的问题恰恰是需要归纳综合的经验内容，所以，分析作为一种哲学研究方法，在分析哲学的视野中，与综合方法并非背道而驰，而是相得益彰。当然，以上概括并未完整地阐明分析哲学的基本特征。事实上，分析哲学的魅力正在于，我们总是在哲学分析的活动中不断发现这种哲学为我们开启的新视野。

我们希望，《中国分析哲学》的出版能够为中国哲学事业的发展贡献绵薄之力；我们更希望，我们对分析哲学的研究以及对哲学分析方法的运用，能够为中国哲学屹立于世界哲学之林作出更大的贡献！

目　录

专文

Probability and Danger　　◆ Timothy Williamson　·1

逻辑哲学

Contradiction and the Structure of Unity　　◆ Graham Priest　·35

拒斥克里普克和索姆斯反对描述论的论证　　◆ 陈波　·44

一个刻画理解、知识与信念的逻辑 UKB　　◆ 李小五　·82

广义量词的单调性及其检测方法　　◆ 张晓君　郝一江　·101

逻辑的经验性与先验性——从蒯因到冯契　　◆ 晋荣东　·114

心灵哲学

现象概念与物理主义　　◆ 黄益民　·130

经验的现象特征与表征主义　　◆ 王华平　黄华新　·145

下向因果何以存在？

　　　　——兼评金在权对下向因果的消解　　◆ 陈晓平　·160

Defending Evidentialism　　◆ Zhongwei Li　·173

A Thought-Experimental Investigation into Replication　　◆ Jun Luo　·189

知识论证和 Frank Jackson 的表征主义回应策略　　◆ 刘玲　·217

语言哲学

Semantics without Metaphysics　　◆ Chienkuo Mi　·227

限定摹状词的指称性使用与语义学的边界　　◆ 任远　·281

概念的合用及合用度

　　　　——以维特根斯坦《哲学研究》为视角　　◆ 陈常燊　·295

道德哲学

斯特劳森论道德责任　　◆ 徐向东　·307

知识、道德和政治：欧克肖特的洞见和盲点　　◆ 郁振华　·330

维特根斯坦研究

维特根斯坦的遗稿：道路或背景？　　◆ 楼巍　·350

后期维特根斯坦哲学研究评析　　◆ 徐弢　·362

人物与事件

回忆洪谦教授　　◆ 洪汉鼎　·377

维也纳学派在中国的命运　　◆ 江怡　·386

缅怀彼得·斯特劳森爵士

　　　　——写在斯特劳森诞辰 90 周年之际　　◆ 林允清　·404

中山大学分析哲学读书会状略　　◆ 刘小涛　·416

编后记　·420

Contents

Special Essay

Probability and Danger ◆ *Timothy Williamson* · 1

The Philosophy of Logic

Contradiction and the Structure of Unity ◆ *Graham Priest* · 35

Refuting Kripke and Soames' Arguments against Descriptivism ◆ *Bo Chen* · 44

A Logic UKB for Understanding, Knowledge and Belief ◆ *Xiaowu Li* · 82

The Monotonicity of Generalized Quantifiers and Its
 Test Methods ◆ *Xiaojun Zhang & Yijiang Hao* · 101

The Aposteriority and Apriority of Logic——from Quine to Fengqi ◆ *Rongdong Jin* · 114

The Philosophy of Mind

Phenomenal Concepts and Physicalism ◆ *Yimin Kui* · 130

Phenomenal Character of Experience and
 Representationalism ◆ *Huaping Wang & Huaxin Huang* · 145

How does Downward Causation Exist? A Comment on Kim's Elimination of
 Downward Causation ◆ *Xiaoping Chen* · 160

Defending Evidentialism ◆ *Zhongwei Li* · 173

A Thought-Experimental Investigation into Replication   ◆ *Jun Luo*   · 189

Knowledge Argument and Frank Jackson's Representationalism Response   ◆ *Ling Liu*   · 217

The Philosophy of Language

Semantics without Metaphysics   ◆ *Chienkuo Mi*   · 227

The Referential Use of Definite Descriptions and the Boundary of Semantics   ◆ *Yuan Ren*   · 281

The Usability and Its Limit of a Concept——From the perspective of Wietgenstein's
　　Philosophical investigation   ◆ *Changshen Chen*   · 295

The Moral Philosophy

Peter Strawson on Moral Responsibility   ◆ *Xiangdong Xu*   · 307

Knowledge, Morality and Politics: A Critical Examination of
　　Michael Oakeshott   ◆ *Zhenhua Yu*   · 330

Studies of Wittgenstein

Wittgenstein's Nachlass: road or background   ◆ *Wei Lou*   · 350

A Critical Analysis of later Wittgenstein's *Philosophical Investigation*   ◆ *Tao Xu*   · 362

People and Events

A Recollection for Professor Tscha Hung   ◆ *Handing Hong*   · 377

The Fate of Vienna Circle in China   ◆ *Yi Jiang*   · 386

In Memory of Sir Peter F. Strawson—written on the 90th anniversary of
　　his birth   ◆ *Francis Yunqing Lin*   · 404

A Survey of the Reading Group on Analytic Philosophy in Sun Yat-sen
　　University   ◆ *Xiaotao Liu*   · 416

Postscript   · 420

Probability and Danger[*]

◎ Timothy Williamson

　　University of Oxford

Abstract: The lecture concerns the epistemological structure of situations in which many small risks add up to a large one. Examples include the Lottery Paradox, the Preface Paradox, and recent puzzles about quantum-mechanical blips. Such situations pose a threat to the principle that competent deduction is a way of extending our knowledge ('multi-premise closure'), since it seems that most of what counts as knowledge by everyday standards involves such small risks, and that competently deducing the conjunction of many such items of knowledge from the conjuncts takes us to a conclusion that is too risky to constitute knowledge. Thus we seem to face a dilemma between scepticism and abandoning multi-premise closure. I argue that the dilemma is false. In extreme cases, knowledge and chance come radically apart: one can know truths that have a high chance of being false (but aren't). More generally, I argue that the ordinary distinction between safety and danger has a structure that is modal rather than probabilistic, and satisfies closure and factiveness conditions analogous to those for knowledge. It can be modelled using a notion of close possible worlds. This conception of safety is used as an analogy for knowledge, and leads to a closeness-based interpretation of possible worlds semantics for epistemic logic. To avoid the notorious problem of logical omniscience—that according to the standard semantics everyone knows all the logical consequences of what they know, even without performing any deductions—a relation of epistemic counterparthood between formulas is introduced, which both solves other problems for a safety conception of knowledge and formally articulates the idea that how much one's knowledge is closed under deduction depends on one's logical competence.

Keywords: Knowledge; safety; probability; epistemic logic; logical omniscience; lottery para-

----

　　* This is The 2009 Amherst Lecture in Philosophy Williamson gave in 2009. The Amherst Lecture in Philosophy each year brings a distinguished philosopher to Amherst College for a public lecture. Thanks to Professor Timothy Williamson for contributing his lecture essay to our volume for the first time in print. ——editor.

dox; preface paradox

1. Much of recent and not-so-recent philosophy is driven by tensions, or at least apparent tensions, between common sense and natural science—in the terminology of Wilfrid Sellars, between the manifest image and the scientific image of the world. These tensions arise most saliently in metaphysics and the philosophy of mind, but are far from confined to those branches of philosophy. In this lecture, I will discuss one specific form they take in contemporary epistemology.

Central to common sense epistemology is the distinction between knowledge and ignorance. Knowledge is not usually conceived as coming in quantifiable degrees: we do not ask and could not answer 'To what degree does she know where the station is?'.[1] By contrast, a continuum of numerical degrees of probability is central to contemporary natural science. The point is not merely that a framework of probabilities has to some extent displaced a framework of knowledge and ignorance in the scientific image of cognition. Worse, probabilistic reasoning seems to destabilize common sense conceptions of knowledge. As so often, we cannot just blandly assert that the manifest image and the scientific image are both fine in their own way, but useful for different purposes. We face *prima facie* conflicts between them which seem to imply that if the scientific image is accurate, then the manifest image is radically misleading. We have to do the hard work of analysing the apparent conflicts in detail, to determine what their upshot really is.

Elsewhere, I have argued that the sort of probability most relevant to the epistemology of science is probability on the evidence, and that the evidence is simply what is known; thus knowledge is a precondition, not an outdated rival, of probability in science (Williamson 2000). I have also shown that much of the supporting argument for that conclusion is robust even when recast in probabilistic form (Williamson 2008). But those arguments do not entitle us to ignore specific probabilistic considerations that seem to undermine common sense epistemology. This lecture concerns one such threat to a non-probabilistic conception of knowledge.

2. Why is deduction useful? The obvious answer is that it is a way of extending our knowledge. It is integral to that answer that extending one's knowledge in this way depends on the temporal process of

---

[1] For discussion of the (un)gradability of knowledge ascriptions see Stanley 2005: 35 – 46.

carrying out the deduction, for one knows more after doing so than one did before. Moreover, one cannot expect to obtain knowledge thereby unless the deductive process involves forming a belief in the conclusion. This suggests a principle along the following lines, now often known as 'Multi-Premise Closure' (Williamson 2000: 117):

MPC   If one believes a conclusion by competent deduction from some premises one knows, one knows the conclusion.

Here competence is intended to stand to inference roughly as knowledge stands to belief. One can no more hope to attain knowledge of the conclusion by less than competent deduction than one can hope to attain it by deduction from premises of which one has less than knowledge. But competence does not require knowledge that the deduction is valid, otherwise the attempt to use MPC to explain how deduction extends knowledge would involve an infinite regress of knowledge of the validity of more and more complex deductions (Carroll 1895). MPC is closer to the dynamics of cognition than is the static principle that one knows a conclusion if one believes it, knows it to follow deductively from some premises, and knows the premises.

At first sight, there is no tension between MPC and a scientific account of cognition. Mathematics is essential to science, and its main role is to extend our knowledge by deduction.

Perhaps some fine-tuning is needed to capture exactly the intended spirit of MPC. Nevertheless, some such principle seems to articulate the compelling idea that deduction is a way of extending our knowledge. I will not discuss any fine-tuning of MPC here. Nor will I discuss challenges to MPC that are closely related to traditional sceptical puzzles, for instance where the premise is 'That is a zebra' and the conclusion is 'That is not just a mule cleverly painted to look like a zebra'. It is generally, although not universally, agreed that such examples do not refute a properly formulated closure principle for knowledge. [1]Even if we start by answering the question 'Do the spectators know that that is a zebra?' in the affirmative and then the question 'Do they know that it is not just a mule cleverly painted to look like a zebra?' in the negative, once that has happened and we are asked again 'Do they know

---

[1]   The example is of course from Dretske 1970; the other classic version of such a challenge to closure is Nozick 1981. For critical discussion of such objections to closure see Vogel 1990 and Hawthorne 2005.

that it is a zebra?' we are now inclined to answer in the negative. Thus the supposed counter-example to closure is not stable under reflection.

The probabilistic threat to MPC starts from the truism that many acceptably small risks of error can add up to an unacceptably large one. The most obvious illustration is a version of the Lottery Paradox (Kyburg 1961). Suppose that for some positive real number δ a risk of error less than δ is acceptable. Then for any suitably large natural number n, in a fair lottery with n tickets of which only one wins, for each losing ticket the statement that it will lose has an acceptably small risk of error, but all those statements together logically entail their conjunction, which has a probability of only $1/n$—the structure of the lottery being given—and *a fortiori* an unacceptably large risk of error. This does not constitute a clear counter-example to MPC, since one can deny that the premises are known: even if a ticket will in fact lose, we do not know in advance that it will; we only know that it is almost certain to. But can we legitimately treat knowledge of lotteries as a special case?[1] For example, does not a scientific study of human perception and memory show that even in the best cases they too involve non-zero risks of error? If we reacted to the Lottery Paradox by insisting that knowledge requires zero risk of error, that requirement seems to constrain us to denying that there is human knowledge by perception or memory, and more generally to force us into scepticism. Even beliefs about our own present mental states seem to carry some non-zero risk of error. But if knowledge of our contingent circumstances is unobtainable, the distinction between knowledge and ignorance loses most of its interest.

A version of the Preface Paradox helps make the point vivid (Makinson 1965). Suppose that I compile a reference book containing large quantities of miscellaneous information. I take great care, and fortunately make not a single error. Indeed, by ordinary standards I know each individual item of information in the book. Still, I can reasonably acknowledge in the preface that since almost all such works contain errors, it is almost certain that mine does too. If I nevertheless believe the conjunction of all the individual items of information in the book (perhaps excluding the preface), the risk of error in that conjunctive belief seems so high that it is difficult to conceive it as knowledge. Thus MPC seems to fail, unless the standard for knowing is raised to sceptical heights.

One advantage of the objection to MPC from the Preface Paradox over the generalization from the Lottery Paradox is that it avoids the unargued assumption that if a true belief that a given ticket will lose

---

① See Hawthorne 2004 for discussion.

fails to constitute knowledge, the reason must be just that it has a non-zero risk of error. For whether a true belief constitutes knowledge might depend on all sorts of factors beyond its risk of error: for example, its causal relations. By contrast, the objection from the Preface Paradox makes trouble simply by conjoining many miscellaneous items of what by common sense standards is knowledge; it does not depend on the subject matter of that putative knowledge.

The common sense epistemologist seems to face a dilemma: either reject MPC or become a sceptic. The first horn is not much better than the second for common sense epistemology. If deduction can fail to extend knowledge, through the accumulation of small risks, then an explicitly probabilistic approach seems called for, in order to take account of those small risks, and the distinction between knowledge and ignorance is again sidelined, just as it is on the sceptical horn.

However, the argument for the dilemma is less clear than it seems. It trades on an unexamined notion of risk. It treats risk as a probabilistic matter, but what sort of probability is supposed to be at issue? The problem does not primarily concern the agent's subjective probabilities (degrees of belief), for even if the agent has perfect confidence in every conjunct and their conjunction, that does not address the worry that the risk of error in the conjunction is too high for the agent's true belief in it to constitute knowledge. Nor do probabilities on the agent's evidence do the trick. For since the probability of any item of evidence on the evidence of which it is part is automatically 1, the probability of any conjunction of such items of evidence on that evidence is also 1. But whatever exactly the items of evidence are, some variant on the Preface Paradox will arise for them too. This may suggest that risk should be understood as a matter of objective probabilities (chances), at least for purposes of the argument.

In a recent paper, John Hawthorne and Maria Lasonen-Aarnio have developed just such a chance-based argument. [1]It can be adapted for present purposes as follows. Assume, with common sense, that we have at least some knowledge of the future. For example, I know that my carpet will remain on my floor for the next second. Nevertheless, as an instance of quantum indeterminacy, there is a non-zero chance, albeit a very small one, that the carpet will not remain on the floor for the next second, but will instead rise up into the air or filter through the floor. Now suppose that there are n carpets, each in a situation exactly like mine. Let pi be the proposition that the ith carpet remains on the floor for the

---

[1] See Hawthorne and Lasonen-Aarnio 2009. I have omitted various subtleties from the argument that are not of present concern; my reply in Williamson 2009 pays more attention to them.

next second (for expository purposes, I write as though from a fixed time). Suppose also that nothing untoward will in fact happen, so all those propositions about the future are true:

(1) $p_1, \ldots, p_n$ are true.

We may assume:

(2) Each of $p_1, \ldots, p_n$ has the same high chance less than 1.

We may also assume, at least to a good enough approximation, that the carpets and their circumstances do not interact in any way that would make the chances of some of them remaining on the floor depend on the chances of others doing so; the n propositions about the future are independent of each other in the sense that the chance of any conjunction of them is simply the product of the chances of the conjuncts. In brief:

(3) $p_1, \ldots, p_n$ are mutually probabilistically independent.

For large enough n, (1), (2) and (3) together entail (4):

(4) The chance of $p_1 \& \ldots \& p_n$ is low.

Imagine that one is in a good position to monitor each carpet. One believes of each carpet that it will remain on the floor, competently deduces the conjunction of all those propositions from the conjuncts and thereby comes to believe that all the carpets will remain on the floor:

(5) One believes $p_1 \& \ldots \& p_n$ by competent deduction from $p_1, \ldots, p_n$.

We may treat (1) – (5) as a relevantly uncontentious description of the example. A further plausible claim about the example is that one knows of each carpet that it will remain on the floor, in much the way that I do with my carpet:

(6) One knows each of p_1, ..., p_n.

A plausible general constraint is that one cannot know something unless it has a high chance of being true:

HC One knows something only if it has a high chance.

Unfortunately, relative to the uncontentious description of the example (1) – (5), (6) forms an inconsistent triad with MPC and HC. For (5), (6) and MPC together entail (7):

(7) One knows p_1 &... & p_n.

But (4) and HC together entail the negation of (7):

(8) One does not know p_1 &... & p_n.

Holding (1) – (5) fixed, we must give up at least one of (6), MPC and HC. Which should it be?

Although giving up (6) permits us to retain both MPC and HC, it amounts to scepticism, at least with respect to knowledge of the future. If we remain anti-sceptics and retain HC, we must give up MPC, and face the consequent problems. Later, I will assess the third option, giving up HC in order to combine anti-scepticism with MPC, and argue that it is much more natural than it sounds. Before doing so, however, I will explore some probabilistic aspects of the argument in more detail.

3. According to some philosophers, the principle of bivalence fails for future contingents. On their view, p_i is neither true nor false in advance, because the chancy future is a mere range of possibilities until one of them comes to pass. Thus examples of the kind supposed are impossible, because (1) is incompatible with (2): p_i cannot be simultaneously true and chancy. Presumably, on this view, since p_i cannot be true in advance, it also cannot be known in advance. Thus (6) is denied, as well as (1). This is a form of scepticism with respect to knowledge of the future, but its motivation is quite

specific; it does not threaten to spread into a more general scepticism. Truths about the past are supposed to have chance 1. This view of the future makes the argument uninteresting. However, since I accept bivalence for future contingents—they are true or false in advance, whether or not we can already know which—I will not try to defuse the argument in that way. I accept $(1) - (5)$ as a description of a genuine possibility.

Nevertheless, the resort to objective chance in the argument is curious. For, on the face of it, the problem does not depend on objective chance. For example, suppose that the observer is isolated for the relevant second, unable to receive new perceptual information about the fate of the carpets. At the end of that second, the relevant propositions have become straightforward truths about the past. But the same epistemological problem seems to arise: belief in the conjunction p_1 &... & p_n still seems too risky to constitute knowledge, even though the risk is not a matter of objective chance. More generally, the Preface Paradox seems to raise the same problem, irrespective of the specific subject-matter of the conjoined propositions. Even if our universe turns out to be deterministic and devoid of objective chance, we still face situations in which many acceptably small risks of error in the premises accumulate into an unacceptably large risk of error in the conclusion. Although posing the problem in terms of objective chances makes it especially vivid, it also makes its underlying nature harder to discern. Perhaps we need a kind of probability that is less objective than objective chance, but more objective than probability on the evidence, in order to capture the relevant notion of risk.

Whatever the relevant kind of probability, it should obey the standard axioms of the probability calculus, and we can make some points on that basis. The starting point for the problem is that if δ is any positive real number not greater than 1, there are deductively valid arguments each of whose premises has a probability greater than $1 - \delta$ but whose conclusion has a probability not greater than $1 - \delta$. Any such argument has at least two premises. For the probability axioms guarantee that when a conclusion follows deductively from a single premise, the probability of the conclusion is at least as high as the probability of the premise, and when a conclusion follows deductively from the null set of premises, the probability of the conclusion is 1 (because it is a logical truth). The problem therefore seems to be essentially one for *multi*-premise closure (MPC), and not to arise for single-premise closure:

SPC   If one believes a conclusion by competent deduction from a premise one knows, one knows the conclusion.

On further reflection, however, that is not a satisfying result. For what seems to be a version of the same problem arises for single-premise closure too (Lasonen-Aarnio 2008). The reason is that the process of deduction involves its own risks. We are no more immune from errors of logic than we are from any other sort of error. The longer a chain of reasoning extends, the more likely it is to contain mistakes. One might even know that in the past one made on average about one mistake per hundred steps of reasoning, so that a chain of one's reasoning a thousand steps long is almost certain to contain at least one mistake. Suppose that one knows p, and does in fact carry out each step of the long deduction competently, thereby eventually arriving at a belief in q. By repeated applications of SPC, one knows each intermediate conclusion and finally q itself (surely carrying out the later steps does not make one cease to know the earlier conclusions). But the same worry as before about the accumulation of many small risks of error still arises.

Of course, we can still ask probabilistic questions about the process of deduction itself. For example, what is the probability that the conclusion of an attempted deduction by me is true, conditional on the assumption that the premise is true and the attempted deduction contains a thousand steps, each with an independent probability of $1/100$ of containing a mistake? The difficulty is to know *which* probabilistic questions to ask. The question just formulated abstracts from the identity of the premise and conclusion of the attempted deduction, but not from its length. Why should that be the relevant abstraction? After all, the reasoner usually knows the identity of the premises and conclusion quite well. If we specify their identity in the assumption, and the attempted deduction is in fact valid, then the conditional probability is 1 again, and the risk seems to have disappeared. This, of course, is an instance of the notorious reference class problem, which afflicts many theories of probability. [1]But it is of an especially pressing form, because the apparent risk can only be captured probabilistically by abstracting from intrinsic features of the deduction and subsuming it under a general reference class.

None of this shows that probability does not have an essential role to play in the understanding of risk; surely it has. However, when probabilities are invoked, much of the hardest work will consist in the prior analysis of the issues that explains why one reference class rather than another is relevant. When epistemological risk is at issue, the explanation will be in epistemological terms; invo-

---

[1] See Hájek 2007 for a recent discussion.

king probabilities to explain why a given reference class is the relevant one would merely postpone the problem.

4. In thinking about the epistemological problem of risk, it is fruitful to start from a conception of knowledge as safety from error. I have developed and defended such a conception elsewhere. ①I do not intend it to provide necessary and sufficient conditions for knowing in more basic terms. Without reference to knowing, it would be too unclear what sort of safety was in question. Rather, the point of the safety slogan is to suggest an analogy with other sorts of safety that is useful in identifying some structural features of knowledge.

For comparison, think of David Lewis's similarity semantics for counterfactual conditionals. Its value is not to enable one to determine whether a counterfactual is true in a given case by applying one's general understanding of similarity to various possible worlds, without reference to counterfactuals themselves. If one tried to do that, one would almost certainly give the wrong comparative weights to the various relevant respects of similarity. Nevertheless, the semantics gives valuable structural information about counterfactuals, in particular about their logic. Likewise, the point of a safety conception of knowing is not to enable one to determine whether a knowledge attribution is true in a given case by applying one's general understanding of safety, without reference to knowing itself. If one tried to do that, one would very likely get it wrong. Nevertheless, the conception gives valuable structural information about knowing. ②③The considerations that follow are intended in that spirit.

There seem to be two salient rival ways of understanding safety in terms of risk. On the 'no risk' conception of safety, being safe from an eventuality consists in there being no risk of its obtaining. On

---

① See Williamson 1992 and 2000: 123 – 130. For a related notion of safety see Sosa: 1996, 2000 and 2007.

② See Lewis 1973: 91 – 5 and 1986: 52 – 5 for his conception of similarity. At Lewis 1986: 41 (reprinted from Lewis 1979) he writes: 'Analysis 2 (plus some simple observations about the formal character of comparative similarity) is about all that can be said in full generality about counterfactuals. While not devoid of testable content—it settles some questions of logic—it does little to predict the truth values of particular counterfactuals in particular contexts. The rest of the study of counterfactuals is not fully general. Analysis 2 is only a skeleton. It must be fleshed out with an account of the appropriate similarity relation, and this will differ from context to context.' Lewis then makes it clear that, in the latter task, we must use our judgments of counterfactuals to determine the appropriate similarity relation.

③ An example of structural information about knowledge that can be extracted from the safety conception is anti-luminosity: only trivial conditions obtain only when one is in a position to know that they obtain (Williamson 2000: 96 – 109). For replies along these lines to some critics of the safety conception see Williamson 2009.

the 'small risk' conception of safety, being safe from an eventuality consists in there being at most a small risk of its obtaining. The two conceptions disagree on whether a low but non-zero level of risk excludes or implies safety. Each conception of safety combines with a general conception of knowledge as safety from error to yield a more specific conception of knowledge. The safety conception of knowledge and a 'no risk' conception of safety jointly imply a 'no risk of error' conception of knowledge. The safety conception of knowledge and a 'small risk' conception of safety jointly yield a 'small risk of error' conception of knowledge.

At first sight, the 'no risk of error' conception of knowledge imposes an unrealistically high, infallibilist standard on human cognition that leads to scepticism, and in particular forces rejection of (6) while allowing retention of both MPC and HC. From the same perspective, the 'small risk of error' conception of knowledge seems to impose a more realistically low, fallibilist standard on human cognition that avoids scepticism, and in particular permits retention of (6) as well as HC while forcing rejection of MPC. This makes the 'small risk of error' conception of knowledge look the more attractive of the two, even though its rejection of MPC is initially unpleasant and makes the usefulness of deduction harder to explain.

One immediate problem for the 'small risk of error' conception of knowledge is that, unrevised, it is incompatible with the factiveness of knowledge: only truths are known. If p is false, you don't know p, even if you believe that you know p. For if the risk of error is small but not nonexistent, error may still occur. Although one could revise the 'small risk of error' conception of knowledge by adding truth as an extra conjunct, such *ad hoc* repairs count against a theory.

In order to decide between the two safety conceptions of knowledge, it is useful to step back from epistemology and consider the choice between the corresponding conceptions of safety in general. By reflecting on the non-technical distinction between safety and danger, especially in non-epistemological settings where we have fewer theoretical preconceptions, we can see the epistemological issues from a new angle. After all, the distinction between safety and danger is not in general an epistemological one. For example, whether one is safe from being abducted by aliens is a completely different question from whether one knows or believes that one will not be abducted by aliens.

5. Here are two arguments about safety that seem to be valid, when the context is held fixed between premises and conclusion:

Argument A$_{\text{safety}}$

Premise   S was shot.
_____

Conclusion   S was not safe from being shot.

Argument B$_{\text{safety}}$

Premise 1   S was safe from being shot by X.

Premise 2   S was safe from being shot by Y.

Premise 3   S was safe from being shot by Z.

Premise 4   S was safe from being shot other than by X, Y or Z.
_____

Conclusion   S was safe from being shot.

On a 'small risk' conception of safety, neither argument is valid. Indeed, the corresponding arguments explicitly about small risks do not even look particularly plausible:

Argument A$_{\text{smallrisk}}$

Premise: S was shot.
_____

Conclusion   S's risk of being shot was not small.

Argument B$_{\text{smallrisk}}$

Premise 1   S's risk of being shot by X was small.

Premise 2   S's risk of being shot by Y was small.

Premise 3   S's risk of being shot by Z was small.

Premise 4   S's risk of being shot other than by X, Y or Z was small.
_____

Conclusion   S's risk of being shot was small.

In the case of argument A$_{\text{smallrisk}}$, it is obvious that one may be shot even if one's risk of being shot is small. In the case of argument $B_{smallrisk}$, it is almost equally obvious that many small risks may add up to a large one.

By contrast, on a 'no risk' conception of safety, both arguments are valid. ①The corresponding arguments explicitly about the absence of risks look compelling:

Argument A$_{norisk}$

Premise: S was shot.

_____

Conclusion   S was at some risk of being shot.

Argument B$_{norisk}$

Premise 1   S was at no risk of being shot by X.

Premise 2   S was at no risk of being shot by Y.

Premise 3   S was at no risk of being shot by Z.

Premise 4   S was at no risk of being shot other than by X, Y or Z.

_____

Conclusion   S was at no risk of being shot.

These results strongly suggest that we ordinarily think of safety according to a 'no risk' rather than a 'small risk' conception. Given the ease with which we classify the 'small risk' arguments as invalid, it is quite implausible that we have a 'small risk' conception of safety but are unable to work out its consequences for A_{safety} and B_{safety}. But then, if the 'no risk of error' conception of knowledge commits us unwittingly to epistemological scepticism, presumably the 'no risk' conception of safety likewise commits us unwittingly to the analogue of scepticism for safety in general, the view that we are

_____

①   Argument A_{norisk} would be invalid if 'no risk' were equated with 'zero risk' in a probabilistic sense, for events of probability zero can occur. This holds even if infinitesimal probabilities are allowed (Williamson 2007). In quantitative terms, the 'no risk' conception is not the limiting case of the 'small risk' conception. The 'zero risk' conception of safety is intermediate between the 'no risk' and 'small risk' conceptions; it does validate argument B_{safety}. I do not discuss it at length here because it is a hybrid that combines many of the features of the 'no risk' and 'small risk' conceptions that each side objects to in the other's view.

virtually never safe from anything. Alternatively, in order to avoid such generalized scepticism, it might be held that, contrary to appearances, arguments A_{safety} and B_{safety} are in fact invalid. Either way, we turn out to be radically mistaken about the nature of safety, in one case about its structure, in the other about its extent. Nor is any explanation of our radical misconceptions in the offing.

Those are unattractive hypotheses. Fortunately, we are not forced to choose between them, for we have been considering too narrow a range of theoretical options. An alternative is to retain the 'no risk' conception of safety, while understanding the quantification it involves as restricted to eventualities that occur in possible cases close to the actual case. Since safety varies over time, closeness should do likewise. To a first approximation, one is safe in a possible world w at a time t from an eventuality if and only if that eventuality obtains in no world 'close' to w at t. Call this the 'no close risk' conception of safety. ①

Given that every world is always close to itself, the 'no close risk' conception of safety validates arguments A_{safety}. If S was shot in a world w, then S was shot in a world close to w at any given time t, namely w itself, and so is not safe in w at t from being shot. Without need of any such special assumptions about closeness, the 'no close risk' conception of safety also validates argument B_{safety}. For if the premises hold in w with reference to a time t, then S was not shot by X in any world close to w at t, S was not shot by Y in any world close to w at t, S was not shot by Z in any world close to w at t, and S was not shot other than by X, Y or Z in any world close to w at t, so S was not shot in any world close to w at t; thus the conclusion holds in w with reference to t.

On the 'no close risk' conception, safety is a sort of local necessity, and closeness a sort of accessibility relation between worlds in a possible worlds semantics for modal logic. A_{safety} generalizes to the T axiom schema $A \rightarrow \Diamond A$ of modal logic (whatever is is possible), which corresponds to the reflexivity of the accessibility relation. B_{safety} generalizes to the K principle that if $(A_1 \& \ldots \& A_n) \rightarrow B$ is valid, so too is $(\Box A_1 \& \ldots \& \Box A_n) \rightarrow \Box B (n \geqslant 0)$, which holds for any accessibility relation. Together, the two principles axiomatize the modal system KT (also known as T).

Within this framework, the substantive task remains of specifying closeness as informatively as we can in terms of appropriate respects of similarity, perhaps in context-dependent ways, just as with Lewis's possible worlds semantics for counterfactual conditionals. Later I will discuss closeness for the

---

① See Sainsbury 1997, Peacocke 1999: 310 – 28 and Williamson 1992, 1994: 226 – 30 and 2000: 123 – 30 for such ideas.

special case of epistemological safety. For safety in general, I will confine myself to a few brief remarks about closeness and chance.

We should not take for granted that all worlds with a non-zero physical chance in a world w at a time t of obtaining count as close to w at t. Of course, that condition holds vacuously if individual worlds are so specific that each of them always has zero chance of obtaining, but then the point must be put in terms of less specific possibilities, where a possibility is a set of worlds and obtains if and only if one of its members does. We should not take for granted that all possibilities with a non-zero chance in a world w at a time t of obtaining contain worlds that count as close to w at t. Perhaps, for example, some possibilities may involve such large deviations from w in overall trends (short of strict physical laws) that no world in them counts as close to w at t. Not all worlds with the same laws of nature as w that branch from w only after t need count as close to w at t.

Recall the case of deterministic worlds, whether or not the actual world is one of them. Let w be such a world. If whatever does not happen in w was always safe in w from happening, then the distinction between safety and danger has no useful application to w. In w, if you play Russian roulette and get away with it, you were always perfectly safe. That is not the distinction the inhabitants of w need for practical purposes. They need one on which playing Russian roulette counts as unsafe, whether or not you get away with it. Presumably, the idea will be something like this: if you play Russian roulette in w at t and get away with it, you are unsafe in w at t because in some world w^* relevantly but not perfectly similar to w, you play Russian roulette at t and do not get away with it. The standard for sufficient similarity must be set reasonably high, otherwise almost everything will count as unsafe, and again the distinction will not be the one the inhabitants of w need for practical purposes.

Such a distinction between safety and danger, based on similarity rather than chance, is available in indeterministic worlds too. Even when objective chance is present, it does not automatically 'capture' the distinction. But that does not mean that chance is irrelevant to safety either. For chance can help constitute similarity, both directly through similarity in chances and indirectly through probabilistic laws in virtue of which some further respects of similarity carry more weight than others. But the resultant distinction between safety and danger will not be a directly probabilistic one, because it will have the structural features characteristic of the 'no close risk' conception of safety. In particular, it will validate the arguments A_{safety} and B_{safety}.

In practice, we may expect this non-probabilistic conception of safety to diverge dramatically from a probabilistic conception in at least a few cases, by arguments of a similar form to B_{safety}. Although one can construct formal models in which safety entails a high chance without entailing chance 1 (Williamson 2005: 485 −6), it is unclear that all the relevant cases can be modelled in that way. For instance, if we bracket the epistemological aspect of the example of the n carpets considered earlier, we may simply ask whether we are safe from the ith carpet's not remaining on the floor. By hypothesis, nothing untoward will in fact happen; all the carpets will remain on the floor. For any given i a positive answer is plausible; moreover, it would be implausibly *ad hoc* to give a positive answer for some numbers i and a negative answer for others. But if for all i $(1 \leqslant i \leqslant n)$ we are safe from the eventuality that the ith carpet does not remain on the floor, then by an argument of a similar form to B_{safety} we are safe from the eventuality that not every carpet remains on the floor. The latter eventuality will not in fact obtain, but for large enough n it has at the relevant time a very high chance of obtaining.

Although this is hardly a comfortable result, the defender of the 'no close risk' conception of safety may be able to live with it. For if we suppose that we are not safe from the eventuality that not every carpet remains on the floor, we cannot consistently suppose in addition that for each carpet we are safe from the eventuality that it does not remain on the floor; the B_{safety}-style argument seems valid even when we deny its conclusion. Thus we infer that for at least one carpet we are not safe from the eventuality that it does not remain on the floor. But since the carpets are all on a par, we conclude that for no carpet are we safe from the eventuality that it does not remain on the floor. Thus denying that we are safe from the eventuality that not every carpet remains on the floor would push us towards the analogue of scepticism for safety, a view on which almost nothing is safe and the distinction between safety and danger becomes useless in practice.

At this point, the probabilist may be inclined to comment: if that is how the 'no close risk' conception of safety works, we are better off without it. Why not simply take advantage of modern technology, and use a probabilistic conception of safety instead?

Undoubtedly, when we have a well-supported probabilistic model of our situation, it is often more prudent to use it than to rely on a 'no close risk' conception of safety. Lotteries and coin-tossing are obvious examples. Of course, a probabilistic model will help us little if it is computationally intractable. In practice, even for lotteries and coin-tossing, we are hardly ever in a position to calculate the quantum mechanical chances, even to within a reasonable approximation. The standard probabilistic models of lotteries and coin-tossing were developed long before quantum mechanics. Their utility does not depend on whether our world is indeterministic. Not only do the models ignore eventualities such as the coin landing on its edge or the lottery being rigged; they need not even approximate the objective chances on a specific occasion. A coin that comes up heads about half the time may nevertheless have an objective chance of 10% or 90% of coming up heads when I toss it right now.

In practice, we must take most of our decisions without the help of a well-supported probabilistic model of our situation. ①Am I safe from missing my train if I walk to the station? In answering the question, I do not attempt to calculate with probabilities, let alone objective chances. If I did, I could only guess wildly at their values. Moreover, in order to make the calculations, one needs numerical values for the levels of interdependence between the different risks, and I could only guess wildly at their values too. If the result of the calculation was at odds with my non-probabilistic judgment, I might very well adjust my estimates rather than my non-probabilistic judgment. ②

We need a conception of safety that we can apply quickly in practice, on the basis of vague and impoverished evidence, without making probabilistic calculations. ③The 'no close risk' conception of safety meets that need. Since it validates B_{safety}-style arguments, it permits us to make ourselves safe from a disjunction of dangers by making ourselves safe from each disjunct separately, and to check that we are safe from the disjunction by checking that we are safe from each disjunct in turn. That way of thinking assumes a closure principle for safety that the 'no close risk' conception can deliver and the 'small risk' conception cannot. The chance of the disjunction is much higher than the chance of any disjunct, but if each disjunct is avoided in all close cases, so is their disjunction. The price of such a practically tractable conception of safety may be that we count as safe from some dangers that have a high chance of obtaining.

Someone might object that safety in this sense cannot be relied on, for when one is safe from being shot even though one has a high chance of being shot, one has a high chance of being simultaneously shot and safe from being shot. But that is a fallacy. The 'no close risk' conception of safety validates argument A_{safety}. If one is safe from being shot, one is not shot; every world is close to itself. Necessarily, if one had been shot, one would not have been safe from being shot. Even though one has a high chance of not being

---

① Even if we have well-defined credences (degrees of belief) in the relevant propositions and they satisfy the probability axioms, that is not what is meant by having a well-supported probabilistic model. As already explained, credences are too subjective for purposes of the distinction between safety and danger.

② I have anecdotal evidence that this happens when the safety of nuclear power stations is being estimated.

③ Compare Gigerenzer et al. 1999.

safe from being shot, one is in fact safe from being shot. High chance events do not always occur; that includes safety events. Of course, we sometimes think that we are safe when in fact we are not, but we have no reason to expect ourselves to be infallible about safety, or anything else.

A different objection to the 'no close risk' conception of safety is that it makes safety ungradable, whereas in fact it is gradable—it comes in degrees. It does so even when what is at issue is someone's being safe from a specific danger at a specific time, the proper analogue of someone's knowing a specific truth at a specific time. For example, we can sensibly ask how safe someone is from being shot, or say that he is safer from being shot by X than from being shot by Y. However, the mere fact that the 'no close risk' conception of safety avoids reliance on a probability threshold does not entail that it makes safety ungradable. It treats safety as a local modality, a restricted sort of necessity. Possibility and necessity do not involve a probability threshold, but they are in some sense gradable. For example, we can sensibly ask how possible or necessary it is to keep children in sight at all times, or say that it is more possible or necessary to do so with children than with cats. ① There are several ways in which the grading might work. It might concern the proportion of close worlds in which the eventuality obtains, just as a glass two-thirds full is fuller than a glass one-third full even though neither is full; call that the 'proportion view of graded safety'. Alternatively, it might concern the distance from the actual world of the closest worlds in which the eventuality obtains; call that the 'distance view of graded safety'.

Here is an example to illustrate the difference between the two views of graded safety. Your opponent is throwing a die. All six outcomes obtain in equal proportions of close worlds. In the actual world, she will throw a five. On the proportion view of graded safety, you are no safer from her throwing a six than you are from her throwing a five, since the proportion is 1/6 in both cases. But you are safer from her throwing a five than you are from her throwing a number divisible by three, since the proportion is 1/6 in the former case and 2/6 in the latter. By contrast, on the distance view of graded safety, you are safer from her throwing a six than you are from her throwing a five, since she throws a five in the actual world, and no counterfactual world is as close to the actual world as the actual world is to itself. You are not safer from her throwing a five than you are from her throwing a number divisible by three, for the same reason.

I will not attempt to decide between the two views of graded safety here. Each is compatible with

---

① Googling the strings 'more possible than', 'more necessary than', 'how possible is' and 'how necessary is' yields tens of thousands of examples in each case.

the 'no close risk' conception of safety. Each has its advantages and disadvantages. They make grading carry different sorts of information. Perhaps we use both, in different situations. For present purposes the moral is just that grading safety does not undermine the 'no close risk' conception.

The conception of probability as obeying the mathematical principles of the probability calculus goes back only to the mid-seventeenth century. ①The distinction between safety and danger is far older. No wonder it works according to different principles. But it is no mere survival from pre-modern thinking. It has a distinctive structure of its own that fits it to serve practical purposes for which a probabilistic approach is infeasible. We need both.

6. It is time to return to epistemology, and apply the 'no close risk' conception of safety in general to knowledge in particular.

As with safety in general, we may expect the difference in structure between knowledge and high chance to produce dramatic divergences between them in cases specially designed for that effect, such as those constructed by Hawthorne and Lasonen-Aarnio. The alarm that such cases can induce may be lessened by reflection on other examples in which knowledge and high chance come apart. A lottery is about to be drawn. Each ticket has chance $1/n$. Let Lucky be the ticket that will in fact win ('Lucky' is a name, a rigid designator). Lucky has the same chance of winning as any other ticket, namely $1/n$. But we know in advance that Lucky will win. ②Of course, the tricky linguistic features of such examples make room for manoeuvres that are not available in more straightforward cases, such as the conjunction about the n carpets. Nevertheless, the example shows that any connection between knowledge and high chance would have to be established by very careful argument, not taken as obvious. The present hypothesis is that high chance is not a necessary condition on knowledge; HC fails.

One point of disanalogy between knowledge and safety emerged in the previous section: safety is gradable; knowledge is not. Although we have little difficulty in thinking of some knowledge as 'more

---

① Hacking 1975 is the classic work on the emergence of such a mathematical conception of probability. Although subsequent scholarship has modified his account in various ways, they do not concern us here. When I spoke on this material in California, I got an unintended laugh by referring to the mid-seventeenth century as 'recent'.

② Such examples are of course applications of the account of the contingent *a priori* in Kripke 1980 to objective chance in place of metaphysical necessity. For such applications see Williamson 2006 and Hawthorne and Lasonen-Aarnio 2009.

solid' or 'less shaky' than other knowledge, we do not find it natural to express such comparisons by modifying the word 'know' with the usual linguistic apparatus of gradability. This might be a serious objection to a semantic analysis of 'knowledge' in terms of 'safety'. But that is not the project. Rather, the aim is to use safety, in the ordinary sense of 'safety', as a model to help explain the underlying nature of knowledge itself, in the ordinary sense of 'knowledge'.

Clearly, A_{safety}-style arguments correspond to the factiveness of knowledge: if something is so, nobody knows that it is not so. Similarly, B_{safety}-style arguments look as though they should correspond to some sort of multi-premise closure principle.

However, if knowing p is simply being safe from error in the sense of being safe from falsely believing p, the 'no close risk' conception of safety does not automatically predict a multi-premise closure principle such as MPC. For example, suppose that I know p, I know $p \rightarrow q$, and believe q by competent deduction, using modus ponens, from those premises. Thus I am safe from falsely believing p, so p is true in all close worlds in which I believe p, and I am safe from falsely believing $p \rightarrow q$, so $p \rightarrow q$ is true in all close worlds in which I believe $p \rightarrow q$. Without extra assumptions, it does not follow that q is true in all close worlds in which I believe q. For, although modus ponens preserves truth, there may be close worlds in which I falsely believe q on utterly different grounds, without believing p or $p \rightarrow q$. Thus I do not count as safe from falsely believing q, and so do not count as knowing q.

Such examples are not genuine counter-examples to MPC. I can know q when I believe q on good grounds, even though I might easily have falsely believed q on different grounds. I may know that the Prime Minister was in Oxford today, because I happened to see him, even though he might easily have cancelled, in which case I would still have had the belief, on the basis of the newspaper announcement which I read this morning.

One way to handle such cases is by explicit relativization to bases. For example, suppose that I am safe from falsely believing p on basis b, and safe from falsely believing $p \rightarrow q$ on basis b^*. Thus p is true in all close worlds in which I believe p on basis b, and $p \rightarrow q$ is true in all close worlds in which I believe $p \rightarrow q$ on basis b^*. Let b^{**} be the basis for believing q which consists of believing p on basis b, believing $p \rightarrow q$ on basis b^*, and believing q by competent deduction from those premises. Then in any close world in which I believe q on basis b^{**}, I believe p on basis b and $p \rightarrow q$ on basis b^*, so p and $p \rightarrow q$ are true, so q is true. Thus I am safe from falsely believing q on basis b^{**}.

However, talk of the 'basis' of a belief is much less clear when applied to non-inferential beliefs. In effect, fixing the 'basis' of a belief seems to boil down to requiring some given level of similarity to the actual world in respects relevant to that belief. This suggests that we may be able to reach a tidier and more perspicuous treatment by rolling all such similarities into the overall relation of closeness between worlds. This relation will vary both with the agent and with the time. For simplicity, those two dimensions will be kept fixed and tacit in the formal treatment to come. The idea is that when one knows p 'on basis b', worlds in which one does not believe p 'on basis b' do not count as close; but knowing 'on basis b' requires p to be true in all close worlds in which one believes p 'on basis b'; thus p is true in *all* close worlds. In this sense, the danger from which one is safe is p's being false, not only one's believing p when it is false.

The simplest formal realization of this idea is a standard possible world semantics for epistemic logic (Hintikka 1962). The formal language is just that of the propositional calculus, augmented with a single unary sentential operator **K**, read 'one knows that'. A model is a triple $< W, R, V >$ where W is a set, whose members we informally conceive as worlds, R is a binary relation (a set of ordered pairs) between members of W, which we informally conceive as the closeness relation between worlds, and V is a function from worlds to sets of atomic formulas, which we informally conceive as the atomic formulas true at the given world. All the epistemology in the model is packed into the relation R; informally, $< w, w^* > \in R$ if and only if w^* is epistemically possible in w, in the sense that whatever the agent knows in w is true in w^*. In the present setting, epistemic possibility is conceived as a form of closeness. Relative to a model of this form, the truth of a formula **A** at a world $w \in W (w \models \mathbf{A})$ is given a recursive definition of the usual sort; it is displayed here for purposes of later comparison:

$w \models \mathbf{p}$ if and only if $\mathbf{p} \in V(w)$, for atomic **p**

$w \models \mathbf{A} \mathbf{\&} \mathbf{B}$ if and only if $w \models \mathbf{A}$ and $w \models \mathbf{B}$

$w \models \neg \mathbf{A}$ if and only if not $w \models \mathbf{A}$

$w \models \mathbf{KA}$ if and only if for all $< w, w^* > \in R$, $w^* \models \mathbf{A}$

Informally, one knows something if and only if it is true in all close worlds. Formulas $\mathbf{A}_1, \ldots, \mathbf{A}_n$ are said to *entail* a formula **C** if and only if with respect to every model $< W, R, V >$ and $w \in W$, if $w \models \mathbf{A}_1, \ldots, w \models \mathbf{A}_n$ then $w \models \mathbf{C}$ (for $n = 0$ this just requires that $w \models \mathbf{C}$). Thus entailment is truth-preservation at all worlds in all models.

Since R is interpreted as closeness, a reflexive relation, we are only interested in models in which R is reflexive. As usual, this secures the factiveness of knowledge: **KA** always entails **A**.

Although the semantic clause for **K** does not include a separate belief condition, this does not imply that the intended interpretation permits knowledge without belief. Rather, that interpretation can wrap belief up into the epistemic relation R, so that if the agent does not believe **A** at w, w will have R to some world w^* at which **A** is false, so the agent will not count as knowing **A** at w either. The same goes for other putatively necessary conditions on knowledge.

The notorious problem for the standard possible worlds semantics for epistemic logic is that it validates multi-premise closure in far too strong a form. From the structure of the models, independently of any constraints on R, we have this form of logical omniscience (for $n \geq 0$):

LC If $\mathbf{A}_1, \ldots, \mathbf{A}_n$ entail **C** then $\mathbf{KA}_1, \ldots, \mathbf{KA}_n$ entail **KC**.

This corresponds to the closure condition on safety under the 'no close risks conception'. Thus if one knows some simple truths, one knows any logical consequence of them, no matter how complex and hard to derive. In particular, one automatically knows any logical truth. Similarly, on the corresponding semantics for doxastic logic, if one believes some things, one believes any logical consequence of them, no matter how complex and hard to derive. In particular, one automatically believes any logical truth. Unlike MPC, LC imposes no restriction to cases in which one has carried out the deduction, or even to those in which one has contemplated its conclusion. Out of the frying pan into the fire!

Possible worlds semantics for knowledge attributions has found some diehard defenders, usually amongst those who want to treat the objects of propositional attitudes as sets of possible worlds. [1]As al-

---

① For a sophisticated and qualified defence of such a view of knowledge and belief attributions see Stalnaker 1984: 71 – 99 and 1999: 241 – 73. It is not always appreciated that the account in Lewis 1996 is of this type; indeed, since Lewis's accessibility relation is an equivalence relation, his account validates not only logical omniscience but the very strong epistemic logic S5, with the theorems $\mathbf{KA} \rightarrow \mathbf{KKA}$ and $\neg \mathbf{KA} \rightarrow \mathbf{K} \neg \mathbf{KA}$. The idea that in deduction we gain only the metalinguistic knowledge that a sentence is true is both hopelessly implausible and *ad hoc*, for example as applied to scientific knowledge, and in any case does not work as a defence of logical omniscience, since the agent typically knows in advance of making the inference elementary semantic facts which, combined with the rest of the agent's knowledge, already entail the truth of the sentence; thus, given logical omniscience, the agent knew in advance of making the inference even that the sentence was true.

ready indicated, simple probabilistic accounts of knowledge have similar problematic consequences for *single*-premise closure, since if p entails q, the probability of q is at least as high as the probability of p, even if no one has performed the deduction. When we are studying how deduction *extends* knowledge, such accounts are far too indiscriminate. In particular, if—as here—we are treating knowledge simply as a relation to an object, then we must individuate the objects of knowledge finely enough to permit them to be distinct even when logically equivalent, so that an agent can know p without knowing q, even though q is logically equivalent to p. For these purposes, we cannot regard the objects of knowledge as simply sets of possible worlds.

7. A possible solution to the problem of logical omniscience is suggested by a related problem for a safety conception of knowledge. Suppose that S believes a complex truth p of first-order logic only on the say-so of his utterly unreliable guru. Surely S does not know p, even though p itself is perfectly safe from falsity.

The natural response is to note that although S could not have falsely believed p, S would just as easily have believed some false counterpart p^* which his guru might easily have intoned instead of p. The suggestion is that knowing p requires safety from the falsity of p and of its epistemic counterparts. The counterpart p^* is close to p in a way analogous to that in which a world w^* may be close to a world w. ①

We must coordinate counterparthood between different formulas. For consider a different agent who is credulous and undiscriminating with atomic formulas but scrupulously respects logical relations. Suppose that her counterparts for atomic q in worlds w^* and w^{**} are atomic q^* and q^{**} respectively; then her counterparts for $\neg q$ in w^* and w^{**} are $\neg q^*$ and $\neg q^{**}$ respectively. She would never treat $\neg q^{**}$ as the negation of q^* in w^* or $\neg q^*$ as the negation of q^{**} in w^{**}.

We can handle these complexities by replacing the two-place relation R in the models by a three-place relation (for which 'R' will also be used), consisting of triples $<w, w^*, \mathbf{f}>$, where w and w^* are worlds as before but $\mathbf{f}$ is a function mapping all formulas of the language to formulas of the language. The idea is that $\mathbf{f}(\mathbf{A})$ in w^* is a counterpart of $\mathbf{A}$ in w, and that w^* is close to w under the

① For the use of epistemic counterparts at the propositional level in safety-style epistemology see Williamson 1994: 231 –4 and 2000: 101. Hintikka also proposed using counterparts in the semantics of quantified epistemic logic, although for individuals rather than formulas and in a quite different way from that envisaged here (Hintikka 1970).

counterpart mapping **f**. In modelling the example just given, one imposes the special constraint that **f** $(\neg\mathbf{A}) = \neg\mathbf{f}(\mathbf{A})$ for all formulas **A** and triples $<w,\ w^*,\ \mathbf{f}>$ in R.

The semantic clause for **KA** must be modified in accordance with the use of epistemic counterparts. The new version is:

$w \models \mathbf{KA}$ if and only if for all $<w,\ w^*,\ \mathbf{f}> \in R,\ w^* \models \mathbf{f}(\mathbf{A})$

No other changes in the models are needed, at least for present purposes. Call the new models *refined*.

Here is a toy example to show how knowledge can fail to be closed under even very elementary inferences in refined models. Let W contain a single world w, and R consist of all triples $<w,\ w,\ \mathbf{f}>$ such that $\mathbf{f}(\mathbf{p}\ \&\ \mathbf{p}) = \mathbf{p}\ \&\ \mathbf{p}$, where **p** is a fixed atomic formula and $\mathbf{p} \in V(w)$, so $w \models \mathbf{p}$ and $w \models \mathbf{p}\ \&\ \mathbf{p}$. By the constraint on **f**, $w \models \mathbf{K}(\mathbf{p}\ \&\ \mathbf{p})$. But there is a function **f** such that $\mathbf{f}(\mathbf{p}) = \neg\mathbf{p}$ and $<w,\ w,\ \mathbf{f}> \in R$, so not $w \models \mathbf{f}(\mathbf{p})$, so, by the semantic clause for **K**, not $w \models \mathbf{Kp}$. Thus the agent's knowledge in the model is not even closed under the elementary deduction from **p** **&** **p** to **p**. Indeed, one can easily check that **p** **&** **p** is *all* that the agent knows in the model.

For unrefined models, we required R to be reflexive—to contain $<w,\ w>$ for every $w \in W$—so that **KA** would entail **A** (the factiveness of knowledge). To achieve the same effect in refined models, we require R to contain $<w,\ w,\ \mathbf{1}>$ for every $w \in W$, where **1** is the identity function such that $\mathbf{1}(\mathbf{A}) = \mathbf{A}$ for every formula **A**: every formula is a counterpart of itself in the same world. Call refined models meeting this constraint *reflexive*. In such models, if $w \models \mathbf{KA}$, then $w \models \mathbf{1}(\mathbf{A})$, so $w \models \mathbf{A}$.

If we wanted to insist that a formula must be its sole counterpart with respect to the original world, we could add the constraint that $<w,\ w,\ \mathbf{f}> \in R$ only if $\mathbf{f} = \mathbf{1}$. Toy models with only one world like that above would then have to be replaced by models with several worlds. Although that could easily be done, for simplicity we may continue to allow R to contain triples $<w,\ w,\ \mathbf{f}>$ in which $\mathbf{f} \neq \mathbf{1}$.

Some more general results illustrate the complete failure of logical omniscience in refined models. The logic of reflexive refined models has a sound and complete axiomatization in which the only axioms are truth-functional tautologies and formulas of the form $\mathbf{KA} \rightarrow \mathbf{A}$ and modus ponens is the only rule of inference: the models impose no special features on knowledge beyond factiveness. No disjunction of disjuncts of the form **KA** is valid in all reflexive refined models: there is no set of formulas at least one of which must be known. Nor does knowing some formulas entail knowing any other formulas in reflexive refined formulas, provided that the formulas do not contain **K** (of course factiveness entails theorems such as **KKA→KA**). All these results are proved in the appendix.

If one wants to guarantee some elementary forms of closure, one can easily do so by adding further constraints on refined models, but they are not intrinsic to the very structure of the semantics.

If we wanted to, we could even recover logical omniscience in a special class of refined models. Given an unrefined model $<W, R, V>$, we can define a corresponding refined model $<W, R\#, V>$ that 'behaves in the same way', where the members of $R\#$ are just the triples $<w, w^*, \mathbf{1}>$ such that $<w, w^*> \in R$. One can easily check by induction on the complexity of a formula **A** that **A** has the same truth-value at any world in $<W, R\#, V>$ as it has at that world in $<W, R, V>$. Thus refined models in effect include the original unrefined models as a special case. Consequently, whatever is valid on all refined models is also valid on all unrefined models (but not *vice versa*). Only the inclusion of functions other than **1** makes refined models behave differently from refined ones. Given any refined model $<W, S, V>$ such that for all worlds w, w^*, $<w, w^*, \mathbf{f}> \in S$ only if $\mathbf{f} = \mathbf{1}$, we can define a corresponding unrefined model $<W, S\hat{\ }, V>$, where $<w, w^*> \in S\hat{\ }$ if and only if $<w, w^*, \mathbf{1}> \in S$. Then any formula has the same truth-value at any world in $<W, S\hat{\ }, V>$ as it has at that world in $<W, S, V>$. In fact, $S\hat{\ }\# = S$ and $R\#\hat{\ } = R$. Call refined models of the form $<W, R\#, V>$ *effectively unrefined*.

Refined models permit the definition of an analogue of competent deduction. The analogue is not a diachronic relation, because far more complex models would be needed to capture changes in safety over time. Rather, it captures a form of synchronic epistemic dependence of a conclusion on premises. The analogue is called *safe derivation*. Given a refined model $<W, R, V>$ and a world $w \in R$, the definition is this:

C safely derives at w from $\mathbf{A}_1, \ldots, \mathbf{A}_n$ if and only if

whenever $<w, w^*, \mathbf{f}> \in R$, if $w^* \models \mathbf{f}(\mathbf{A}_1), \ldots, w^* \models \mathbf{f}(\mathbf{A}_n)$ then $w^* \models \mathbf{f}(\mathbf{C})$.

We must first check some useful properties of safe derivation. The first is that it preserves truth at any given world in any given reflexive refined model:

Fact 1. In refined reflexive models:

If **C** safely derives at w from $\mathbf{A}_1, \ldots, \mathbf{A}_n$ and $w \models \mathbf{A}_1, \ldots, w \models \mathbf{A}_n$ then $w \models \mathbf{C}$.

The reason is simply that since the model is reflexive by hypothesis, $< w,\ w,\ \mathbf{1} > \in R$, so if $w \models \mathbf{1}(\mathbf{A}_1),\ \ldots,\ w \models \mathbf{1}(\mathbf{A}_n)$ then $w \models \mathbf{1}(\mathbf{C})$, in other words, if $w \models \mathbf{A}_1,\ \ldots,\ w \models \mathbf{A}_n$ then $w \models \mathbf{C}$. More interestingly, safe derivation preserves *knowledge* at any given world in any given refined model, reflexive or not:

Fact 2. In refined models:
If $\mathbf{C}$ safely derives at w from $\mathbf{A}_1,\ \ldots,\ \mathbf{A}_n$ and $w \models \mathbf{KA}_1,\ \ldots,\ w \models \mathbf{KA}_n$ then $w \models \mathbf{KC}$.

For if $< w,\ w^*,\ \mathbf{f} > \in R$ then $w^* \models \mathbf{f}(\mathbf{A}_1),\ \ldots,\ w^* \models \mathbf{f}(\mathbf{A}_n)$ because $w \models \mathbf{KA}_1,\ \ldots,$ $w \models \mathbf{KA}_n$, so $w^* \models \mathbf{f}(\mathbf{C})$ because $\mathbf{C}$ safely derives at w from $\mathbf{A}_1,\ \ldots,\ \mathbf{A}_n$; thus $w \models \mathbf{KC}$. Fact 2 is the analogue of MPC for refined models: knowledge is closed under safe derivation.

In models that correspond to the original unrefined ones, safe derivation collapses into knowledge of the material conditional with the conjunction of the premises as antecedent and the conclusion as consequent:

Fact 3. In effectively unrefined models:
$\mathbf{C}$ safely derives at w from $\mathbf{A}_1,\ \ldots,\ \mathbf{A}_n$ if and only if $w \models \mathbf{K}((\mathbf{A}_1\ \&\ldots\ \&\ \mathbf{A}_n)\rightarrow\mathbf{C})$. ①

The proof is trivial. In other refined models that criterion can fail in both directions. Here are two toy examples. As before, for simplicity, W contains a single world, w, and $\mathbf{p} \in V(w)$. First, let $\mathbf{f}(\mathbf{p}\rightarrow\neg\neg\mathbf{p}) = \neg\mathbf{p}$ and $\mathbf{f}(\mathbf{A}) = \mathbf{A}$ for every formula $\mathbf{A}$ other than $\mathbf{p}\rightarrow\neg\neg\mathbf{p}$, and $R = \{\ < w,\ w,\ \mathbf{1} >,$ $< w,\ w,\ \mathbf{f} >\ \}$. Then at w $\neg\neg\mathbf{p}$ safely derives from $\mathbf{p}$, because both formulas are held constant by the functions in R and they are both true at w. But it is not the case that $w \models \mathbf{K}(\mathbf{p}\rightarrow\neg\neg\mathbf{p})$, since $\mathbf{f}$ maps that conditional to a formula false at w. Thus the equivalence fails from left to right. Conversely, let $\mathbf{g}$ $(\neg\neg\mathbf{p}) = \neg\mathbf{p}$ and $\mathbf{g}(\mathbf{A}) = \mathbf{A}$ for every formula $\mathbf{A}$ other than $\neg\neg\mathbf{p}$, and $S = \{\ < w,\ w,\ \mathbf{1} >,\ < w,$ $w,\ \mathbf{g} >\ \}$ and consider the model $< W,\ S,\ V >$ instead of $< W,\ R,\ V >$. Then $w \models \mathbf{K}(\mathbf{p}\rightarrow\neg\neg\mathbf{p})$, because the functions in S hold $\mathbf{p}\rightarrow\neg\neg\mathbf{p}$ constant and it is true at w. But $\neg\neg\mathbf{p}$ does not safely derive at w

---

① Define the conjunction of a null set of formulas as a given tautology; then fact 3 holds even when the premise set is null.

from **p** in this model, for $w \models \mathbf{g}(\mathbf{p})$ but not $w \models \mathbf{g}\ (\neg\neg\mathbf{p})$. Thus the equivalence fails from right to left. Indeed, knowledge is not preserved, for $w \models \mathbf{Kp}$ but not $w \models \mathbf{K}\neg\neg\mathbf{p}$. The same points can be illustrated with more realistic models, but they would be far more complex.

Although safe derivation is not equivalent to knowledge of a conditional, it is a knowledge-like condition, as one can see by comparing its definition with the semantic clause for **KA**. Indeed, **A** is known at a world if and only if it safely derives at that world from the null set of premises. Unlike knowledge of a conditional, safe derivation in refined models is exactly the knowledge-like condition that gets one from knowledge of the premises to knowledge of the conclusion. We might say that safe derivation means that one makes a 'knowledgeable' connection from premises to conclusion, rather than that one knows the connection.

Safe derivation requires an epistemic connection between premises and conclusion, not a logical one. This is already clear in effectively unrefined models. For example, suppose that **p** is known at a world in such a model. Then for any formula **A**, the conditional $(\mathbf{p} \leftrightarrow \mathbf{A}) \rightarrow \mathbf{A}$ is also known at that world, since it follows from **p**. Thus **A** safely derives from $\mathbf{p} \leftrightarrow \mathbf{A}$ at the world, even though **A** is logically independent of $\mathbf{p} \leftrightarrow \mathbf{A}$.

Although safe derivation does not require a logical connection between premises and conclusion, it nevertheless possesses the core structural features of a relation of logical consequence—those that hold of all formulas, irrespective of their composition. These features are the Cut Rule (a sort of generalized transitivity), the Rule of Assumptions (reflexivity) and the Thinning Rule (monotonicity):

Fact 4. The Cut Rule holds in refined models:
if **C** safely derives at w from $\mathbf{A}_1, \ldots, \mathbf{A}_m$ and
D safely derives at w from $\mathbf{B}_1, \ldots, \mathbf{B}_n,$ **C** then **D** safely derives at w from $\mathbf{A}_1, \ldots, \mathbf{A}_m,$ $\mathbf{B}_1, \ldots, \mathbf{B}_n.$

Fact 5. The Rule of Assumptions holds in refined models:
A safely derives at w from **A**.

Fact 6. The Thinning Rule holds in refined models:

if C safely derives at w from A_1, ..., A_m then

C safely derives at w from A_1, ..., A_m, B_1, ..., B_n.

The proofs of facts 5 and 6 are trivial. To prove fact 4, suppose that C safely derives at w from A_1, ..., A_m and D safely derives at w from B_1, ..., B_n, C in some model $< W, R, V >$. Let $< w, w^*, f > \in R$. If $w^* \models f(A_1)$, ..., $w^* \models f(A_m)$, $w^* \models f(B_1)$, ..., $w^* \models f(B_n)$ then $w^* \models f(C)$ because C safely derives at w from A_1, ..., A_m, so $w^* \models f(D)$ because D safely derives at w from B_1, ..., B_n, C. Thus D safely derives at w from A_1, $\cdots$, A_m, B_1, ..., B_n, as required. At this level of generality, safe derivation has the same structure as deductive consequence, even though neither implies the other.

To see how constraints on the relation R correspond to closure properties of safe derivation, consider the case of conjunction. Call a function f *relevant* at a world w in a refined model $< W, R, V >$ if and only if $< w, w^*, f > \in R$ for some $w^* \in W$. When the logical properties of conjunction are 'transparent' to the agent's cognitive system at a world w, $f(A \& B) = f(A) \& f(B)$ for all formulas A and B and functions f relevant at w: the counterpart of a conjunction is the conjunction of the counterparts of its conjuncts. One can easily check that this implies that the introduction and elimination rules for conjunction hold for safe derivation at w: $A \& B$ safely derives at w from A and B and each of A and B safely derives at w from $A \& B$. Thus knowledge at w is closed under both conjunction introduction and conjunction elimination; one knows a conjunction if and only if one knows the conjuncts.

Of course, it is far more plausible that knowing a conjunction requires knowing the conjuncts than that knowing the conjuncts requires knowing the conjunction; one may fail to put two pieces of knowledge together. [1]However, we should not conclude from this that we need models in which the conjuncts always safely derive from the conjunction, although the conjunction need not safely derive from the conjuncts. Safe derivation is a sufficient but not necessary condition for knowledge to be closed under the given argument. For an agent who has considered the conjuncts separately but not together, and knows the conjuncts but not the conjunction, the conjuncts may not safely derive from the conjunction any more than the conjunction safely derives from the conjuncts. Nevertheless, although the case is a counterexample to the closure of knowledge under conjunction introduction, it is no counterexample to the

---

① On the putative closure of knowledge under conjunction elimination see Williamson 2000: 276 – 83.

closure of knowledge under conjunction elimination, precisely because it is not a case of knowing the conjunction. We can model this idea by imposing the weaker constraint that when $w \models \mathbf{K(A\ \&\ B)}$, $\mathbf{f(A\ \&\ B) = f(A)\ \&\ f(B)}$: the counterpart of a known conjunction is the conjunction of the counterparts of its conjuncts, but the counterpart of an unknown conjunction need not be. This weaker constraint implies that $w \models \mathbf{K(A\ \&\ B)}$ only if $w \models \mathbf{KA}$ and $w \models \mathbf{KB}$ without implying the converse. It achieves this effect without requiring $\mathbf{A}$ and $\mathbf{B}$ always to safely derive from $\mathbf{A\ \&\ B}$; they do so when the conjunction is known, but may fail to do so otherwise.

A crude, simple way for a model to meet the weaker constraint without meeting the stronger one (that $\mathbf{f(A\ \&\ B) = f(A)\ \&\ f(B)}$ unconditionally) is for it to divide all formulas into two groups, *considered* (by the agent) and *unconsidered* (by the agent), relative to each world. If $\mathbf{A\ \&\ B}$ is considered at w, then $\mathbf{f(A\ \&\ B) = f(A)\ \&\ f(B)}$ for every function $\mathbf{f}$ relevant at w. If a formula $\mathbf{C}$ is unconsidered at w, then $\mathbf{f(C)}$ can be anything, in other words, every formula $\mathbf{D}$ is $\mathbf{f(C)}$ function $\mathbf{f}$ relevant at w. Consequently, only considered formulas are known, for if $\mathbf{C}$ is unconsidered at w then for some function $\mathbf{f}$ relevant at w $\mathbf{f(C) = C\ \&\neg C}$, so for some world $w^* < w$, $\langle w^*,\ \mathbf{f}\rangle \in R$ and not $w^* \models \mathbf{f(C)}$, so not $w \models \mathbf{KC}$. Hence if $w \models \mathbf{K(A\ \&\ B)}$ then $\mathbf{A\ \&\ B}$ is considered at w, so $\mathbf{f(A\ \&\ B) = f(A)\ \&\ f(B)}$. Thus such models meet the weaker constraint, even though they violate the stronger one with respect to unconsidered formulas. So knowing a conjunction implies knowing the conjuncts in models of this type. But knowing the conjuncts does not imply knowing the conjunction in them, for the conjuncts may be separately considered even though their conjunction is unconsidered. Thus we obtain the asymmetry between conjunction introduction and conjunction elimination in a fairly natural way.

None of this poses any problem for the applications of conjunction introduction that were used to raise the problem in section 2. The conjunctions there *are* considered. On the present view, they just are examples that make vivid the radically non-probabilistic nature of knowledge.

These elementary examples suggest that refined models provide a useful safety-inspired framework for analysing the epistemology of inferential relations. No doubt there are subtleties that they cannot capture, but they have enough flexibility for most purposes. Of course, the intended interpretation of the relation R has been described only in a highly schematic way. That is hardly surprising, for the whole nature of knowledge is packed into that interpretation. There is still plenty of work to do even at this abstract structural level.

8. A scientific epistemology needs both a distinction between knowledge and ignorance and a continuum of epistemic probabilities. The latter does not induce a collapse of the former, despite their great structural differences. But it is easier to make structural generalizations about knowledge and about probability than to predict how either of them will apply to individual cases. That is where common sense may be in for a few surprises.

Appendix

Let $\sum$ be the logic axiomatizable with all truth-functional tautologies and all formulas of the form **KA→A** as its axioms and modus ponens as its rule of inference. We write $\vdash_\Sigma$ **A** to mean that **A** is a theorem of $\sum$.

Proposition 1. $\sum$ is sound and complete for the class of reflexive refined models.

Proof: Soundness is obvious (using reflexivity for **KA→A**). For completeness we use a version of the canonical model construction from modal logic. Let W be the set of all maximal $\sum$ – consistent sets of formulas. Define the epistemic depth of a formula **A**, ed(**A**), recursively: if **A** is atomic, ed(**A**) = 0; ed(¬**A**) = ed(**A**); ed(**A & B**) = max { ed(**A**), ed(**B**) }; ed(**KA**) = ed(**A**) + 1. Let R consist of all triples $< w,\ x,\ \mathbf{f} >$ such that $w \in W$, $x \in W$, f is a total function from formulas to formulas, and for every formula **A**: (1) **KA** $\in w$ iff **Kf(A)** $\in x$ and (2) ed(**A**) = ed(**f(A)**). R is obviously reflexive. Let $V\ (w)$ be the intersection of w with the set of atomic formulas. Relative to the reflexive refined model $< W,\ R,\ V >$, we prove that for every $w \in W$ and formula **A**, $w \models$ **A** iff **A** $\in w$ by nested induction on ed (**A**) and within that on the complexity of **A**. The only interesting case is the induction step for **KA**. Suppose that for all $w \in W$ and formulas **A** such that ed(**A**) ⩽ n, $w \models$ **A** iff **A** $\in w$. Let ed (**A**) = n. Suppose that **KA** $\notin w$. Now $\vdash_\Sigma$ ¬(**A &** ¬**A**) and $\vdash_\Sigma$ **K(A &** ¬**A)** →(**A &** ¬**A**), so $\vdash_\Sigma$ ¬**K(A &** ¬**A)**. Since w is $\sum$ – consistent, **K(A &** ¬**A)** $\notin w$. Moreover, ed(**A &** ¬**A**) = ed(**A**). Thus if **f** is the function such that f(**A**) = **A &** ¬**A** and **f (B)** = **B** for every other formula **B**, then $< w,\ w,\ \mathbf{f} > \in R$. Since not $w \models$ **A &** ¬**A** (= **f(A)**), not $w \models$ **KA**. For the converse, suppose that **KA** $\in w$. Let $< w,\ w^*,\ \mathbf{f} > \in R$. Then **Kf(A)** $\in w^*$ by definition of R. Since $\vdash_\Sigma$ **Kf(A)** →**f(A)** and w^* is a maximal $\sum$ – consistent set, **f(A)** $\in w^*$. But ed(**f(A)**) = ed(**A**) = n by definition of R, so by induction hypothesis, $w^* \models$ **f(A)**. Thus $w \models$ **KA**. This completes the induction. As usual, if not $\vdash_\Sigma$ **A** then ¬**A** $\in w$ for some

$w \in W$, so not $w \models \mathbf{A}$, which gives completeness.

Proposition 2. Not $\vdash_{\Sigma} \mathbf{KA_1} \vee \ldots \vee \mathbf{KA_m}$ for any formulas $\mathbf{A_1}, \ldots, \mathbf{A_m}$.

Proof: Consider a model $< W, R, V >$ in which R contains all permissible triples $< w, w^*, \mathbf{f} >$. Pick $w \in W$. For any formula $\mathbf{A}$, $< w, w, \mathbf{f} > \in R$ for some function $\mathbf{f}$ such that $\mathbf{f(A)} = \mathbf{A} \,\&\, \neg\mathbf{A}$. Since not $w \models \mathbf{A} \,\&\, \neg\mathbf{A}$, not $w \models \mathbf{KA}$. Hence not $w \models \mathbf{KA_1} \vee \ldots \vee \mathbf{KA_m}$. Hence not $\vdash_{\Sigma} \mathbf{KA_1} \vee \ldots \vee \mathbf{KA_m}$ by soundness.

Proposition 3. Let $\mathbf{A_1}, \ldots, \mathbf{A_m}, \mathbf{B_1}, \ldots, \mathbf{B_n}$ be $\mathbf{K}$ – free formulas. Then

$\vdash_{\Sigma} (\mathbf{KA_1} \,\&\ldots\&\, \mathbf{KA_m}) \rightarrow (\mathbf{KB_1} \vee \ldots \vee \mathbf{KB_n})$ iff either $\mathbf{A_1} \,\&\ldots\&\, \mathbf{A_m}$ is a truth-functional contradiction or for some i, j $\mathbf{A_i} = \mathbf{B_j}$.

Proof: Suppose that $\vdash_{\Sigma} (\mathbf{KA_1} \,\&\ldots\&\, \mathbf{KA_m}) \rightarrow (\mathbf{KB_1} \vee \ldots \vee \mathbf{KB_n})$ but $\mathbf{A_1} \,\&\ldots\&\, \mathbf{A_m}$ is not a truth-functional contradiction. Then $\mathbf{A_1} \,\&\ldots\&\, \mathbf{A_m}$ is true under some assignment of truth-values to atomic sentences; let X be the set of atomic sentences true under that interpretation. Construct a model $< W, R, V >$ by setting $W = \{ w \}$ for some w, $V(w) = X$, and $< w, w, \mathbf{f} > \in R$ iff for $1 \leqslant i \leqslant m$, $\mathbf{f(A_i)} = \mathbf{A_i}$. By choice of V, $w \models \mathbf{A_1} \,\&\ldots\&\, \mathbf{A_m}$. Thus for $1 \leqslant i \leqslant m$, if $< w, w, \mathbf{f} > \in R$ then $w \models \mathbf{f(A_i)}$, so $w \models \mathbf{KA_i}$, so $w \models \mathbf{KA_1} \,\&\ldots\&\, \mathbf{KA_m}$. Since the model is reflexive and $\vdash_{\Sigma} (\mathbf{KA_1} \,\&\ldots\&\, \mathbf{KA_m}) \rightarrow (\mathbf{KB_1} \vee \ldots \vee \mathbf{KB_n})$, by soundness $w \models \mathbf{KB_1} \vee \ldots \vee \mathbf{KB_n}$, so for some j, $w \models \mathbf{KB_j}$. Let $\mathbf{f(B_j)}$ be a contradiction and $\mathbf{f(A)} = \mathbf{A}$ for every other formula $\mathbf{A}$. If $< w, w, \mathbf{f} > \in R$ then $w \models \mathbf{f(B_j)}$, which is impossible. Hence $< w, w, \mathbf{f} > \notin R$, which must be because $\mathbf{B_j}$ is some $\mathbf{A_i}$. Conversely, suppose that $\mathbf{A_i} = \mathbf{B_j}$. Then trivially $\vdash_{\Sigma} (\mathbf{KA_1} \,\&\ldots\&\, \mathbf{KA_m}) \rightarrow (\mathbf{KB_1} \vee \ldots \vee \mathbf{KB_n})$. Finally, if $\mathbf{A_1} \,\&\ldots\&\, \mathbf{A_m}$ is a truth-functional contradiction then $\vdash_{\Sigma} \neg (\mathbf{A_1} \,\&\ldots\&\, \mathbf{A_m})$; but $\vdash_{\Sigma} (\mathbf{KA_1} \,\&\ldots\&\, \mathbf{KA_m}) \rightarrow (\mathbf{A_1} \,\&\ldots\&\, \mathbf{A_m})$ since $\vdash_{\Sigma} \mathbf{KA_i} \rightarrow \mathbf{A_i}$ for each i, so $\vdash_{\Sigma} \neg (\mathbf{KA_1} \,\&\ldots\&\, \mathbf{KA_m})$ and therefore $\vdash_{\Sigma} (\mathbf{KA_1} \,\&\ldots\&\, \mathbf{KA_m}) \rightarrow (\mathbf{KB_1} \vee \ldots \vee \mathbf{KB_n})$.

Note

This paper is the written version of my Amherst Lecture in Philosophy, delivered at Amherst College on 5th March 2009. Earlier versions of the material were presented to colloquia at Sheffield University, the University of Southern California, Stanford University, a discussion group in Oxford, an

Arché workshop at the University of St. Andrews, and the memorial conference for Peter Lipton at the University of Cambridge, where Paul Dicken was the commentator. It develops a theme from my reply (in Williamson 2009) to a paper by John Hawthorne and Maria Lasonen-Aarnio (Hawthorne and La-sonen-Aarnio 2009). It has benefited greatly from discussion on all those occasions. Particular thanks are due to Amherst College for the invitation to deliver the lecture.

Bibliography

［1］ Carroll, L., 1895, 'What the tortoise said to Achilles'. *Mind* 4: 278 – 280.

［2］ Dretske, F., 1970, 'Epistemic operators'. *Journal of Philosophy* 67: 1007 – 1023.

［3］ Gigerenzer, G., Todd, P. M., and the ABC Research Group (eds.), 1999, *Simple Heuristics That Make Us Smart*. Oxford: Oxford University Press.

［4］ Greenough, P., and Pritchard, D. (eds.), 2009, *Williamson on Knowledge*. Oxford: Oxford University Press.

［5］ Hacking, I., 1975, *The Emergence of Probability*: *A Philosophical Study of Early Ideas about Probability*, *Induction and Statistical Inference*. Cambridge: Cambridge University Press.

［6］ Hájek, A., 2007, 'The reference class problem is your problem too'. *Synthese* 156: 563 – 585.

［7］ Hawthorne, J., 2004, *Knowledge and Lotteries*. Oxford: Clarendon Press.

［8］ Hawthorne, J., 2005, 'The case for closure', in Steup and Sosa 2005.

［9］ Hawthorne, J., and Lasonen-Aarnio, M., 2009, 'Knowledge and objective chance', in Greenough and Pritchard 2009.

［10］ Hintikka, K. J. J., 1962, *Knowledge and Belief*. Ithaca, N. Y. : Cornell University Press.

［11］ Hintikka, K. J. J., 1970, 'Objects of knowledge and belief: acquaintances and public figures', *The Journal of Philosophy* 67: 869 – 883.

［12］ Kripke, S. A., 1980, *Naming and Necessity*. Oxford: Blackwell.

［13］ Kvanvig, J. (ed.), 1996, *Warrant in Contemporary Epistemology*. Lanham, Md. : Rowman & Littlefield.

［14］ Kyburg, Jr, H. E. *Probability and the Logic of Rational Belief*. Middletown: Wesleyan University Press.

［15］ Lasonen-Aarnio, M., 2008, 'Single-premise deduction and risk', *Philosophical Studies* 141: 157 – 173.

［16］ Lewis, D. K. 1973. *Counterfactuals*. Oxford: Blackwell.

Lewis, D. K. , 1979, 'Counterfactual dependence and time's arrow'. *Noûs* 13: 455 – 476. Reprinted with postscripts in Lewis 1986.

[17] Lewis, D. K. , 1986, *Philosophical Papers*, *Volume II*. Oxford: Oxford University Press.

[18] Lewis, D. K. , 1996, 'Elusive knowledge'. *Australasian Journal of Philosophy* 74: 549 – 567.

[19] Makinson, D. C. , 1965, 'The paradox of the preface', *Analysis* 25: 205 – 207.

[20] Nozick, R. , 1981, *Philosophical Explanations*. Oxford: Oxford University Press.

[21] Peacocke, C. A. B. , 1999, *Being Known*. Oxford: Clarendon Press.

[22] Roth, M. , and Ross, G. (eds.), 1990, *Doubting*. Dordrecht: Kluwer.

[23] Sainsbury, R. M. , 1997, 'Easy possibilities', *Philosophy and Phenomenological Research* 57: 907 – 919.

[24] Smith, Q. (ed.), 2008, *Epistemology: New Essays*. Oxford: Oxford University Press.

[25] Sosa, E. , 1996, 'Postscript to "Proper functionalism and virtue epistemology" ', in Kvanvig 1996.

[26] Sosa, E. , 2000, 'Contextualism and skepticism'. *Philosophical Issues* 10: 1 – 18.

[27] Sosa, E. , 2007, *A Virtue Epistemology: Apt Belief and Reflective Knowledge*. Oxford: Clarendon Press.

[28] Stalnaker, R. C. , 1984, *Inquiry*. Cambridge, Mass. : MIT Press.

[29] Stalnaker, R. C. , 1999, *Context and Content*. Oxford University Press.

[30] Stanley, J. , 2005, *Knowledge and Practical Interests*. Oxford: Clarendon Press.

[31] Steup, M. , and Sosa, E. (eds.), 2005, *Contemporary Debates in Epistemology*. Oxford: Blackwell.

[32] Vogel, J. , 1990, 'Are there counter-examples to the closure principle?', in Roth and Ross 1990.

[33] Williamson, T. , 1992, 'Inexact knowledge'. *Mind* 101: 217 – 242.

[34] Williamson, T. , 1994, *Vagueness*. London: Routledge.

[35] Williamson, T. , 2000, *Knowledge and its Limits*. Oxford: Oxford University Press.

[36] Williamson, T. , 2005, 'Replies to commentators'. *Philosophy and Phenomenological Research* 70: 468 – 491.

[37] Williamson, T. , 2006, 'Indicative versus subjunctive conditionals, congruential versus non-hyperintensional contexts'. *Philosophical Issues* 16: 310 – 333.

[38] Williamson, T. , 2007, 'How probable is an infinite sequence of heads?' *Analysis* 67: 173 – 180.

[39] Williamson, T. , 2008, 'Why epistemology cannot be operationalized', in Smith 2008.

[40] Williamson, T. , 2009, 'Replies to critics', in Greenough and Pritchard 2009.

概率与危险——2009 年阿姆赫斯特哲学讲座
蒂莫西·威廉姆森

牛津大学

摘　要：本次讲座关注多个小风险累加至一个大风险这种情况的认识论结构。此类例子包括彩票悖论、序言悖论，以及最近有关量子力学光点的难题。这种情况对适当的演绎是扩展我们知识（即"多前提的闭合性"）的一种方式这个原则构成了威胁，因为大多数能以日常标准被认定的知识都涉及这些小风险，以至于从对众多包含这类知识的项通过适当的演绎得到的合取会把我们带向一个太不牢靠从而不能构成知识的结论。因此我们似乎面临着怀疑论与放弃多前提的闭合性之间的二难困境。我认为，这个困境是虚假的。在极端情况下，知识和机会从根本上是彼此分开的：一个人可以知道有很高的几率为假的真理（但并不为假）。我认为，更一般地说，通常关于安全与危险之间的区别有一个模型上的、而不是概率上的结构，它满足与知识条件相类似的闭合性和事实性条件。它可以通过使用闭合的可能世界的概念被模型化。这种安全观被当做知识的一个类比，并导致了对认知逻辑的可能世界语义学的一种基于闭合性的解释。为了避免逻辑全知——即按照标准语义学，每个人都知道他现在知识的所有逻辑后承，甚至无须进行任何演绎——这一臭名昭著的问题，本文引进了诸公式之间在认识上的对应性关系，从而既解决了知识的安全性概念问题，也正式地阐明了这一观点，即一个人的知识在演绎下的闭合性在多大程度上依赖于其逻辑能力。

关键词：知识；概率；风险；逻辑全知；安全性；认知逻辑；彩票悖论；序言悖论

Contradiction and the Structure of Unity

◎ **Graham Priest**

Universities of Melbourne and St. Andrews

Abstract: The paper discusses the question of what it is that makes a collection of parts a unity, and not a mere congeries. The answer given is that it is the *gluon* of the collection, an entity with contradictory properties. The gluon achieves the unity by being identical with each of the parts. This account requires a formal theory of identity according to which is it is non-transitive. This matter is reserved for a separate paper.

Keywords: Frege; Russell; Bradley; unity of the proposition; unity; gluon; dialetheism; non-transitive identity

Unless an object is utterly simple, it has parts. The parts are not a congeries, but are structured so as to produce a whole. But how do they do so? Answers to this question soon lead to difficulties and contradictions. I will argue that they are best handled by an appropriate conception of identity. The key notion here will be that of a *gluon*, and, in particular, the way that this behaves with respect to identity.

Frege on the Unity of the Proposition

Let us start with what might at first appear to be rather a trivial issue: Frege on the unity of the proposition. [1]Consider the sentence 'Sortes homo est'. The sentence is constituted by a noun-phrase, 'Sortes', and a verb phrase, 'homo est'. According to Frege, the sentence expresses a proposition (thought), that Socrates is a person, and the proposition is constituted by the referents[2]of the two

---

[1] On which, see Priest (1995), 12.2.

[2] Actually, senses. The referents combine to make a truth value, not a thought. But the same problem arises for senses. I simplify for the sake of perspicuity.

parts of the sentence. 'Sortes', like all noun phrases, refers to an object, the person Socrates, *s*. 'Homo est', like all verb phrases, refers to a concept, *c*, that of being a man. But the proposition is not just a congeries of its two parts, *s* and *c*. Somehow these cooperate to form a unity. But how?

Frege's answer was that concepts are radically different from objects. Unlike objects, they are "unsaturated", radically incomplete. The concept referred to by 'homo est' has a "gap" in it, which is plugged by the object referred to by 'Sortes' to produce a single object. Note the form of words here:

(*) The concept referred to by 'homo est' has a "gap" in it.

The notions of being unsaturated, of having a gap, and so on, are of course metaphorical. This is not in itself a problem: literal explanation must give out somewhere. But what is a problem is that Frege's account drives him straight into a contradiction. The expression 'the concept referred to by "homo est"' would, for all the world, appear to refer to a concept. But it is a noun-phrase. It therefore refers to an object, not a concept. And objects and concepts are *in toto mundo* different: the latter are unsaturated; the former are not.

Frege was well aware of the matter. His solution was to insist that, despite appearances, the description in question does refer to an object, not a concept; but he was aware that this put him in a difficult situation. He says:[①]

> I admit that there is a quite peculiar obstacle in the way of an understanding with my reader. By a kind of necessity of language, my expressions, taken literally, sometimes miss my thoughts; I mention an object when what I intend is a concept. I fully realize that in such cases I was relying on the reader who would be ready to meet me half-way-who does not begrudge me a pinch of salt.

But Frege underestimated the problem. If he is right in his insistence that the description refers to an object, this undercuts his whole explanation of the unity of the proposition. Merely reflect for a moment on (*). This is now simply false.

---

① Geach and Black (1953), p. 54.

Unity

This is all well known-and frequently ignored as a minor puzzle. Moreover, the problem can be avoided entirely by rejecting Frege's theory of meaning. But the problem is just, in fact, a special case of a much more general one concerning unities, which cannot be avoided in such a simple way. Let me explain the general problem.

Things have parts. A computer has components, a country has regions, a history has epochs, a piece of music has notes, an argument has statements, and so on. What is the relationship between a thing and its parts? For a start, the thing is more than the simple sum of its parts. Thus, one can have the materials to build a house, but until the house is built it does not exist. The parts of the house are not sufficient: they have to be arranged in a certain way. Similarly, a piece of music has to have its notes related to each other in the right way. And an argument has to be structured into premises and conclusion. Thus, an object is more than the sum of its parts.

What is this more? We might call it the structure, form, or arrangement of the parts. Exactly how to understand what this is, is a sensitive matter. Conceivably, it may be a different sort of thing in different cases: what constitutes the unity of a house is likely to be different from what constitutes the unity of an argument. And what constitutes the unity in any of these cases is, very likely, itself a contentious issue. In the case of a house, for example, is it the geometric shape; is it the causal interactions between the bricks; or is it the design in the mind of the architect? Never mind. Whatever structure is, it is something that binds the parts into a whole. But now we have a contradiction. The structure is, after all, *something*, an object. We can refer to it, think about it, quantify over it. On the other hand it cannot be an object. If it were, the collection of the parts *plus* the structure would be just as much a congeries as the original collection of parts. So the problem of binding would not be solved. In Frege, note, the role of binding is played by the concept. It is therefore that which occupies this contradictory role.

Let me put the problem in abstract terms. Take any thing, object, entity, with parts, p_1, ... , p_n. (Suppose that there is a finite number of these; nothing hangs on this.) A thing is not merely a congeries of parts: it is a unity. There must, therefore, be something which constitutes them as a single thing, a unity. Let us call it, neutrally, the *gluon* of the object, g. Now what of this gluon? Ask whether it itself is a thing, object, entity? It both is and it isn't. It is, since we have just talked about it, referred to it, thought about it. But it isn't, since, if it is, $p_1, \ldots, p_n, g$, constitute a congeries, just as much as the original one, and we still have no account of what constitutes the unity of the object.

We have, then, an aporia. Whatever it is that constitutes the unity of an entity must itself both be and not be an entity. It *is* an entity since we are talking about *it*; it is *not* an entity since it is then part of the problem of a unity, not its solution.

The Aporia

Faced with this aporia, we have essentially four options:

1. We can say that there are no gluons.

2. We can reject the arguments to the effect that a gluon is an object.

3. We can reject the arguments to the effect that it is not an object.

4. We can accept the contradictory nature of gluons. Whilst, no doubt, there is much to be said about the matter, the prospects in cases 1 – 3 look bleak.

In the first case, there are no complex unities, which seems quite false: I am such a unity. And even if we suppose that there are no such unities, there certainly appear to be; that is, there are unities in thought. This means that the mind constitutes unities——as, perhaps, for Kant. But in this case, there are gluons. These are mental entities, but they fall foul of the aporia in the usual way. At the other extreme, one might suppose that there are unities, but that they have no parts, and hence that there are no gluons. This is a desperate move. It runs in the face of the common sense observation that, if someone steals the keyboard of my computer, it is then missing an essential part (etc.). ①

In the second case, we must insist that the gluon is simply not an object. But this seems wildly implausible: we can refer to it, quantify over it, talk about *it*. Anything we can think about is an object,

① Bradley, who we will meet in a moment, had an extreme case of this sort of position. There is just one thing, the Absolute, with no parts; all appearance to the contrary is simply illusion. Even if we take everything we experience to be illusory, however, the position does not really avoid the problem. If my motor bike is not a *real* object, it certainly appears to me to be such. There are, therefore, objects, unities, in thought, and we are back with the problem of what makes these thought objects unities.

a unity, a single thing (whether or not it exists). There seems little scope here.

In the third case, we can suppose that the gluon is just a plain old object. But then we are bereft of an explanation of the unity of an object. How could we even have had the impression that any object *could* constitute the unity of another bunch of objects? Only because of the habit of taking the unity for granted. We write 'Sortes homo est' and the rest is obvious. But putting 'Sortes' and 'homo est' next to each other does not do the job; it is just produces a list of two things. When we think of the two as cooperating, the magic has already occurred.

Let us assume, then, that gluons are contradictory, that is, dialetheic, objects.

The Regress

So far so good. But we still have the question of how a gluon binds the parts (including itself) into a whole. Its being inconsistent does not immediately address this question——though, one might now suspect, inconsistency is going to play some role. To move towards an answer to the question, which will also bring us to the notion of identity, let us ask why, if the gluon is simply an object, it cannot bind together the parts. One consideration is a regress argument as old as Plato's *Parmenides*.

At one stage in his career, Russell was much concerned with the question of the unity of the proposition, and one possibility he considered was that it was the copula, 'is', that binds the constituents together. So, in Fregean terms, there is just one concept, which is the copula. [1]He then explains why the copula cannot be on a footing with the other constituents: [2]

It might be thought that 'is', here, is a constant constituent. But this would be a mistake: 'x is α' is obtained from 'Socrates is human', which is to be regarded as a subject-predicate proposition, and such propositions, we said, have only two constituents [Socrates and humanity]. Thus 'is' represents merely the way in which the constituents are put together. This cannot be a new constituent, for if it were there would have to be a new way in which it and the two other constituents are put together, and if we take this way as again a constituent, we find ourselves

---

[1] A discussion of this view, in the context of its regress, is given in Gaskin (1995).

[2] Eames and Blackwell (1973), p. 98.

embarked on an infinite regress.

Russell is using an argument used earlier to great effect by Bradley. Again addressing the problem of the unity of the proposition, Bradley starts by supposing that a proposition has components A and B. What constitutes them into a unity? A natural thought is that it is some relation between them, C. But, he continues:[1]

> [we] have made no progress. The relation C has been admitted different from A and B... Something, however, seems to be said of this relation C, and said, again, of A and B... [This] would appear to be another relation, D, in which C, on one side, and, on the other side, A and B, stand. But such a makeshift leads at once to the infinite process... [W]e must have recourse to a fresh relation, E, which comes between D and whatever we had before. But this must lead to another, F; and so on indefinitely... [The situation] either demands a new relation, and so on without end, or it leaves us where we were, entangled in difficulties.

And Bradley is, in fact, aware that this is not just a problem concerning the unity of the proposition. It is much more general. Thus, in discussing the unity of the mind, Bradley writes:[2]

> When we ask 'What is the composition of Mind,' we break up that state, which comes to us as a whole, into units of feeling. But since it is clear that these units, by themselves, are not all the 'composition', we are forced to recognise the existence of the relations... If units have to exist together, they must stand in relation to one another; and, if these relations are also units, it would seem that the second class must also stand in relation to the first. If A and B are feelings, and if C their relation is another feeling, you must either suppose that component parts can exist without standing in relation to one another, or else that there is a *fresh* relation between C and AB. Let this be D, and once more we are launched off on the infinite process of finding a relation between D and $C - AB$; and so on forever. If relations are facts that exist *between* facts, then what

---

[1] Allard and Stock (1994), p. 120.

[2] Allard and stock (1994), pp. 78 – 79.

comes between the relations and the other facts?

We can state the regress problem generally in terms of gluons, thus: Suppose that we have a congeries of parts, a, b, c, ... , and that one is puzzled as to what constitutes their unity. Suppose one attempts to explain this by the postulation another object, the gluon, g. Then invoking g simply adds an extra element to the melange. If one is puzzled by the unity in the first case, one should be puzzled by the supposed unity of the extended collection in the second. Thus, e. g. , instead of the congeries of the physical parts of a house, we now have the congeries of [parts plus configuration]. More generally, we have the parts of an object plus the relationship between them——or the *action* of the relation, or the *fact* that they are so related. How is this any better? To use a metaphor (suggested to me by Steward Candlish): if one has to join two links of a chain together, it helps not one whit to say that one does this by inserting a connecting link.

How to break the regress? The regress is generated by the thought that g is distinct from a, b, c, d, etc. If this is the case, then there is room, as it were, for something to be inserted between g and a, etc. Or to use another metaphor, there is a metaphysical space between g and a, and one requires something in the space to make the join. Thus, the regress will be broken if g is identical to a. There will then be no space for anything to be inserted. Of course, g must be identical with b, c, d, and so on, for exactly the same reason. Thus, g is able to combine the parts into a unity by being identical with each one (including itself). The situation may be depicted thus:

$$
\begin{array}{ccccc}
 & & b & & \\
 & & \| & & \\
a & = & g & = & c \\
 & & \| & & \\
 & & d & &
\end{array}
$$

It should be immediately obvious that the notion of identity in question will not behave in the way that identity is often supposed to behave. In particular, the transitivity of identity will fail. We have $a = g$ and $g = c$, but we will not have $a = c$. It might be doubted that there is any such coherent notion, or that if there is, it is not really one of identity. These concerns cannot be set aside lightly, and the only way to assuage them is to provide a mathematical theory of identity that provides what is required. That is a topic for a separate paper.

References

[1] Allard, J. W. , and Stock, G. (eds.), 1994, *F. H. Bradley*; *Writings on Logic and Metaphysics*, Oxford: Oxford University Press.

[2] Eames, E. , and Blackwell, K. (eds.), 1973, *Collected Papers of Bertrand Russell*, *vol. 7: Theory of Knowledge*, London: Allen and Unwin.

[3] Gaskin R. , 1995, 'Bradley's Regress, the Copula and the Unity of the Proposition', *Philosophical Quarterly* 45, 161 – 80.

[4] Geach, P. , and Black, M. (trans.), 1952, *Translations from the Philosophical Writings of Gottlob Frege*, Oxford: Basil Blackwell.

[5] Priest, G. , 1995, *Beyond the Limits of Thought*, Cambridge: Cambridge University Press; second (extended) edition, Oxford: Oxford University Press, 2002.

矛盾与整体的结构

格拉汉姆·普利斯特

澳大利亚墨尔本大学/英国圣安德鲁斯大学

摘　要：除了极简单的对象，每一个对象都由部分构成。但问题是，一个事物与其部分的关系如何呢？显然，一个对象超出了其所有部分之总和。这些部分并非简单堆积，而是有结构的，从而产生一个整体。但是，这些对象是如何形成整体的？这个问题的答案很快导致困难和矛盾：不管构成一个实体的单位是什么，它必须既是又不是一个实体。它是实体，因为我们正在谈论它；它并非实体，因为它只是一个整体的问题之部分，而不是其解决方案。

本文从一个看似微不足道的问题开始：弗雷格对命题整体的论述。但问题在于，弗雷格对此的解释陷入一个矛盾之中。我要论证说，这个矛盾能由一个适当的同一性概念得到最好的处理。这里的一个关键概念将是"胶"，尤其从其同一性表现方式来看。而且，通过拒绝弗雷格的意义理论，这个问题可以完全得到避免。关于整体，不能以这样一个简单的方法避免。显而易见的是，有问题的同一性概念将不会以通常被假定的同一性方式去表现，尤其是同一性的传递将失败。或许应当怀疑并没有这么融贯的概念，或者即使有，也不是真正的同一性概念。我们不能对这些问题掉以轻心，缓和它们的唯一的方法是提供数学上的同一性理论，它能提供所要求的东西。

关键词：对象；结构；命题单位；弗雷格；同一性

拒斥克里普克和索姆斯反对描述论的论证*

◎ 陈 波

北京大学外国哲学研究所

摘 要：本文批判性地考察了克里普克为反驳关于名称的描述论，并确证名称不同于摹状词所构造的三个著名论证：认知论证、语义论证和模态论证，以及他所提出的关于严格指示词的直观测试。本文还批判性地考察了索姆斯为维护模态论证所构造的那些论证。所得出的结论是：克里普克和索姆斯的那些论证都不成立，都基于某些虚假的预设或严重的错误之上；克里普克的整个严格指示词理论及其各种推论并没有得到很好的辩护和证成。

关键词：严格指示词；模态论证；认知论证；语义论证

一、引 言

索尔·克里普克（Saul Kripke，1940— ），20 世纪后半期逻辑学和分析哲学领域的一位天才人物，他本人及其学说在某种意义上构成一个传奇。

1970 年，克里普克在普林斯顿大学作了题为"命名与必然性"的三次讲演，其讲演稿先作为论文发表（1972），后作为单本书印行（1981）。《命名与必然性》（*Naming and Necessity*，以下缩写为 *NN*）在 20 世纪后半期的分析哲学中发挥了关键性的影响力，其主要影响范围在语言哲学、形而上学、知识论和心灵哲学领域，也扩散到其他哲学领域。从方法论上讲，该书有如下特点：

（1）它所使用的最基本的概念工具就是"可能世界"和"反事实条件句"：假如某个个体不同于它在现实世界中的情形，它会怎么样……克里普克强调，所有的反事实设想都是从现实世界中的个体及其状况出发的，并且是从我们自己实际所使用的语言出发的："记住，我们是用我们的语言，而不是用人们在那种情形中会使用的语言来描述这种情形的。因此我们必须使

* 本文属于国家社会科学基金重点项目"当代西方语言哲学研究"（批准号 07AXZ003）和教育部人文社会科学基金项目"虚拟对象的名字及其指称理论"（批准号 09YJA720003）的成果。

用与在现实世界有同一指称的'长庚星'和'启明星'这些词语……"（*NN*，109n）

（2）它所依赖的最基本的论证手段就是克里普克本人的直觉："当然，有些哲学家认为，某个事物具有直观内容并不是支持它的很有说服力的证据。我自己却认为，直观内容是支持任何事物的非常重要的证据。归根结底，我确实不知道，对于任何事物来说，人们还能以某种方式获得何种比这更有说服力的证据……"（*NN*，42）克里普克在该书中提出的很多重要观点并没有得到严格论证，没有被深入细致地探讨。在很多情形下，他所给出的只是一个轮廓和纲要。

（3）该书所批判的靶子是名称的描述理论①，后者有不同的表述版本，我这里将其要点归结如下：1）名称都有涵义和所指，或者说，都有内涵和外延；2）名称的涵义是由关于名称所指对象的一个或一簇描述给出的；3）名称的涵义是识别名称的所指的依据、标准或途径，或者说，名称的涵义决定名称的所指；4）名称的所指是外部世界中的对象。

（4）该书至少发展了如下四个理论：

（i）语言哲学理论，起源于如何处理同一替换原则在模态语境中的失效。克里普克提出，"给出名称的意义"和"确定名称的指称"是两个不同的问题；并且，"名称如何指称对象？"与"我们如何确定名称的指称？"也是两个不同的问题，关于前者他提出了严格指示词理论，关于后者他诉诸肇始于初始命名仪式的传播名称的因果历史链条。然后，他把如此得到的关于专名的理论扩展到自然种类词，认为它们也像专名一样，是严格指示词，通过因果历史链条得到传播。

（ii）形而上学理论，其中包括：关于可能世界的温和实在论，克里普克认为可能世界只不过是现实世界的可能状况、可设想的情形、反事实的情形；"跨越世界的同一性"和"跨越世界的识别"这样的问题和提法是不合法的，它们源自于过于认真地看待"可能世界"这样的比喻性说法，把它们看做是处在现实世界之外的遥远"行星"或"国家"；他还发展了一种本质主义观点：本质就是在所有可能世界中保持不变的东西，或者说，本质属性就是必然属性；并且，起源（origin）或物质构成（material constitution）构成个体的本质；内部结构（internal structure）构成自然种类的本质。

（iii）知识理论。克里普克认为，"必然"和"偶然"属于形而上学，描述事物的存在方式

---

① "description"一词在本文中有不同的翻译，其本义就是关于对象的描述，故多数地方用"描述"；但是，当与名称并列使用了，还是按照习惯，使用"摹状词"这一译法；我认为，"摹状词"这个译法很雅致。"descriptivist theory of names"就是把名称理解为关于名称所指对象的一个或一组描述的理论，译成"名称的描述理论"，旧译"名称的摹状词理论"并无错误，只是人们对术语有不同的偏好和选择。

或存在状况;"先验"和"后验"属于知识论,描述知识获得的途径和方式;"分析"和"综合"与语言的意义有关,属于语言哲学;它们分属于不同的领域,可以发生重叠和交叉,例如有"先验偶然命题",如"巴黎标准尺是一米长";后验必然命题,如"启明星=长庚星",以及各种关于理论同一性的陈述。

(iv)心灵哲学理论。克里普克提出了一个论证,以反对心灵哲学中的同一论唯物主义:每一个精神事实都等同于某个物理事实,例如身体或大脑的某种物理状态。他认为,捍卫这种同一性的唯一途径是诉诸后验必然的同一性,例如"疼痛是对中枢神经的刺激"。但由于存在如下可能性:有疼痛而没有对中枢神经的刺激,或有对中枢神经的刺激而没有疼痛,所以这样的论断甚至不是必然的,当然更不是后验必然的。

我本人至少对前三个理论持有系统且严重的异议,认为它们是建立在下述虚假的预设之上的:①给出名称的意义与确定名称的指称,以及名称如何指称对象与我们如何识别名称的所指,这样的问题可以截然分开。②从反事实谈论中可以引出严格指示词。③如果名称真有意义的话,它们的意义必须唯一确定,并且必须是确定其所指的充分必要条件。④事物的本质与事物的其他性质之间没有关联,至少可以相互独立。我认为,这些预设都可以受到质疑和挑战。我本人将主要通过反驳这些预设来反驳克里普克的严格指示词理论及其各种推论。我打算撰写一系列论文(目前计划8篇左右),对他的名称理论及其各种推论提出系统性挑战。

(5)不过,我认为,《命名与必然性》一书的最大贡献,在于凸显了语言活动(如命名)的社会性和历史性,提出了很多原创性的观点和论题,从而在20世纪后半期的西方哲学中引起极其广泛的关注,并得到了很多哲学家的认同,其观点在很多哲学领域中得到扩散和发酵。

＊　　＊　　＊　　＊　　＊　　＊

克里普克提出了"指示词"(designator)这一概念,它首先包括专名(proper name)和摹状词(description),前者如一个人的名称,一座城市的名称,一个国家的名称。后者是通过摹写一个对象的独有特征来指称该对象的短语,如"亚历山大的老师","美国第一任总统"。其次包括通名(general name),其中有各种各样的种名,如"牛"和"虎";物质名词,如"水","黄金"和"黄铁矿";一些描述自然现象的语词,如"热"、"光"和"疼痛";以及一些谓词,如"热的","大声的","红色的"。

在克里普克之前,最有影响的名称理论是弗雷格和罗素所主张的描述论,以及维特根斯坦、塞尔等人所主张的更精致的版本——簇描述论。克里普克按照他的理解重新严格表述了簇描述论:

（1）对每一个名称或指称表达式'X'来说，都有一簇与之相应的特性，即特性族 φ 使得 A 相信'φX'。

（2）A 相信，其中一种特性或几个特性的某种结合，唯一地标示某个个体。

（3）如果 φ 的大多数或加权的大多数为唯一的对象 y 所满足，则 y 就是'X'的所指。

（4）如果表决不产生任何唯一的对象，那么'X'就无所指。

（5）"如果 X 存在，则 X 具有 φ 的大多数特性"这个陈述被说话者先验地认知。

（6）"如果 X 存在，则 X 具有 φ 的大多数特性"这个陈述表达了一个必然真理（用说话者的个人习语说）。

（C）对于任何成功的理论来说，说明都不能是循环的。在表决中使用的各种特性本身都不准以最终无法消除的方式包含指称的观念。（*NN*, 71）①

克里普克解释说，"（C）不是一个论题，而是其他论题必须满足的条件。换句话说，不能以某种导致循环的方式，即某种无法导致任何独立地确定指称的方式，来满足论题（1）至（6）。"（*NN*, 71）② 并且，其中论题（1）—（4）是基本的，（5）和（6）只不过是它们的推论："而论题（5）和（6）其实只不过是说，一个经过深思熟虑的说话者理解了这条关于专名的理论。由于懂了这个理论，他就看出论题（5）和（6）是真的。"（*NN*, 73）

如此表述的簇描述论就成为克里普克的批判靶子。为了反驳把名称在语义上等同于摹状词

---

① 在克里普克的上述表述中，我宁愿把"说话者 A"换成"语言共同体 A"，因为当我们讨论名称的涵义和所指的时候，我们是在语义学层面说话，只考虑被某个语言共同体赋予语言表达式的公共涵义和公共所指，并不考虑被某个特定的说话者所赋予它们的特殊意涵和特殊所指。并且，我还宁愿把"特性"（properties）一词换成"描述"（description），因为当我们讨论名称的"意义"（属于主观的或认识的领域）时，"特性"一词容易让人想到客观事物本身的性质，这是一种客观的东西。

② 我本人赞成克里普克所提出的论题 C。确实，某些描述论者为了给出能够唯一地确定名称所指的摹状词，而给出了明显循环的说明。除克里普克本人提到的涅尔（W. Kneale）外，蒯因是另一个例子。蒯因提议，为了消除一个名称，在找不到合适的摹状词的情况下，可以把该名称人为地摹状词化：例如，把"柏伽索斯（Pegasus）"表述为"那个是柏伽索斯的东西"，"那个柏伽索斯化的东西"，然后按罗素消除摹状词的办法把该名称消除掉。（参见涂纪亮、陈波主编：《蒯因著作集》，中国人民大学出版社，2007 年，第 4 卷，第 18—19 页）一般而言，描述论者为了确定像"亚里士多德"这样的名称的所指，必须求助于一个或一些描述，如"亚历山大的老师"。但问题是：后面的描述中又包括新的名称，这些新名称的指称又如何确定呢？如此追问下去，将导致无穷倒退，或者将导致循环说明。我认为，为了避免这种困境，描述论者必须补充一个环节：从一开始，绝大多数物理对象必须被实指地命名，即在那些对象在场的情况下伴随实指动作给它们命名。没有这个初始环节，描述论者无法摆脱"自我循环"的困境。正是克里普克的论题 C 及其相关评论，使我这个坚定的描述论者意识到了这一点。

的描述论，并论证他本人的"名称是严格指示词，大多数摹状词是非严格指示词"的观点，克里普克提出了三个论证：认知论证、语义论证和模态论证①。其中，对论题（2）和（5）的否认构成所谓的"认知论证"，对论题（3）和（4）的否认构成所谓的"语义论证"，对论题（6）的否认等等则构成所谓的"模态论证"。索姆斯指出，"除非这些论证能够得到答复，否则，将没有什么机会去推荐描述论。"（Soames，2002，21）我同意这样的论断，将在下面仔细地回应克里普克的这三个论证，也将仔细地回应索姆斯本人所提出的维护模态论证的那些论证（参见 Soames，1998），并由此引申出一些重要的结论。②

二、对克里普克的认知论证的批评

如前所述，对论题（2）和（5）的否认构成克里普克反对描述论的"认知论证"。

克里普克论述说，论题（2）之所以不成立，是因为：（i）常常很难非循环地给出足以确定名称所指且满足唯一性条件的描述。例如，若确定"西塞罗"所指的描述是"谴责喀提林的人"，其中又包含名称"喀提林"；若再确定后者所指的描述是"被西塞罗谴责过的人"，就会出现循环。若确定"爱因斯坦"所指的描述是"发明相对论的人"，其中名称"相对论"的所指又如何确定？依靠"那是爱因斯坦的理论"这个描述或另外的描述吗？这就很难避免循环，从而会违反克里普克所提出的合理性条件 C。（ii）其实，名称的所指不是用描述词确定的。某个人听说了"费因曼"这个名称，尽管他关于费因曼这个人所知甚少，没有能够唯一地标示出费因曼的任何描述，他仍然能够像其他人一样使用"费因曼"这个名称去指称费因曼这个人。（参见 *NN*，80—82）

克里普克接着说，上面的论题（5）也常常是假的：

论题（3）和（4）的真实性是一种经验的"偶然的事情"，对此说话者几乎不可能先验地认知。这就是说，另一些原理实际上决定了说话者的指称，该指称与被论题（2）至（4）所决定的东西相吻合这一事实也是一件"偶然的事情"，对此我们无法先验地认知。仅在某些罕见的情况下，通常是在初始命名的情况下，论题（2）至（5）才全都是真实

① 如此归纳和总结最早是由萨蒙提出的，参见 Salmon, N. , 1982, *Refenrence and Essence*, Oxford：Basil Blakwell, pp. 23 – 31.

② 在本文中，为了避免不必要的复杂，不涉及所谓的"空专名"问题，即不讨论名称所提到的事物是否"存在"的问题。因而，本文中所谈到的名称都有所指，所谈到的事物都是现实存在的，至少假定是如此。

的。(*NN*, 78)

论题（5）说，"如果 X 存在，那么 X 具有 φ 中的大多数特性"这个陈述对于 A 来说是先验地为真。请注意，即使在论题（3）和论题（4）凑巧成真的情况下，一个典型的说话者也很难像该理论所要求的那样，先验地知道它们是真实的。(*NN*, 87)

上面的论述构成克里普克反对描述论的"认知论证"，概述如下：

假如关于名称的描述论是正确的，那么，相应的摹状词就构成名称的意义或其意义的一部分。于是，一个其主词是名称、其谓词是相应的摹状词（描述）的陈述，例如"亚里士多德是《形而上学》一书的作者"，就应该是一个先验为真的陈述，不依赖于任何历史的或经验的发现。但实际情形并非如此。因此，关于名称的描述论在认知事实上出错。

我同意克里普克的说法：论题（5）是假的；但我不认为，从一个表述良好的描述论中可以推出论题（5）。还有，我认为，在认知论证及其他论证中，克里普克隐含地利用了一个假设：如果名称有意义的话，其意义必须保持确定不变。因为他指责关于名称的描述论的一个重要理由，就是名称并不与一个或一簇描述严格同义。既然要求描述与名称同义，其先决条件只能是：名称本身有意义，并且其意义还保持确定不变。否则，一个本身的意义很不确定、常在变化的名称，另一个东西（摹状词）如何与它保持严格同义？我将证明，这个假设是错误的，根本不成立。

假如我们拥有一部关于名称意义的完善的和确定不变的辞典，其中给出了一个名称（例如"亚里士多德"，"牛津"，"虎"，"DNA"）的全部含义（描述），那么，相对于这样一部辞典，以该名称作主词、以刻画其含义或部分含义的描述词作谓词的句子，例如，"亚里士多德是《形而上学》一书的作者"，"牛津因一所世界著名大学而知名"，"虎是一种动物"，"DNA 是……"就是分析的，人们可以先验地知道它们为真。因为，通过查阅该辞典，我们就能够知道它们是真的，而不必诉诸任何经验手段。不过，这里必须指出：首先，即使这些句子的分析性和先验性，也是相对于那部预先给定的辞典而言的，仅仅具有相对的意义；其次，我们没有、也不可能有这样一部完善的辞典，现实的辞典都是对于我们的语言活动的描述、报道、精释、校正，因而都具有经验的起源和经验的内容。并且，我们对于语言（包括名称）的使用是变动的，因为我们的生活处在变化的过程中，语言（包括名称）的对象处在变化的过程中，我们对这些对象的认识也处在变化的过程中，于是语言（包括名称）的意义也处于生长、变化的过程中。这就是我们要不时地更新我们的辞典和百科全书的原因。因此，语言（包括名称）不可能有确定不变的意义。[1]

下面举"牛津"和"DNA"（脱氧核糖核酸）这两个名称为例，确证我刚刚陈述的观点。其中，"牛津"原先是一个专名，后来演变成为一个名称家族；"DNA"是科学名词，后者类似于克里普克频繁使用的"H_2O"，"分子运动"，"对中枢神经的刺激"等等。

据称，牛津（Oxford）最早是人们赶牛群（ox）过河的一个渡口（ford），它恰好位于英国中部的中心位置，处于南北方向和东西方向的贸易通道的交汇处。泰晤士河和查维尔河的卵石滩为人们提供了干燥的定居地，于是在这里形成了最初的市镇——牛津镇。《盎格鲁—萨克逊编年史》（公元 912 年）首次称它为 Oxnaforda。1086 年的《英国土地志》记载，当时的牛津有 1 018 所房子，为英国当时的第六大城市，排在伦敦、约克、诺里奇、林肯和温切斯特之后。1167 年前后，英国学生被禁止进入巴黎大学，于是，选址牛津开办学校。1224 年左右，牛津大学有了首任校长——林肯主教罗伯特·格罗斯泰特（Robert Grosseteste，约 1168—1253）。随着牛津大学在欧洲迅速成名，这里聚集的人口也越来越多，牛津镇变成了牛津市。后来，英国政府设立牛津郡（Oxfordshire），目前的辖区面积 2 605 平方公里。1355 年，牛津大学的学生与牛津市民发生激烈冲突，导致 63 名学生倒在血泊之中。其中一部分师生逃至剑桥，在那里开办了剑桥大学。随着牛津大学在世界范围内声誉日隆，各种以"牛津"为招牌的东西也流行开来，如牛津果酱、牛津鞋、牛津包、牛津蓝、牛津灰、牛津画框、牛津口音、牛津单位、牛津植物、牛津运动、牛津条例，当然还有各种牛津人物，牛津大学出版社，《牛津英语词典》等等。[2] 现在，"牛津"实际上已经成为一个"名称家族"，"牛津市"和"牛津大学"构成该家族的核心。这个名称家族有共同的起源，有连续的演变历史，并且有共同的核心意义。假如像克里普

---

① 苏珊·哈克（Susan Haack）有说服力地论证了意义的生长，这不仅指语词获得新的意义，而且指它们丧失了某些旧含义，以及铸造新词去表达新的概念和区分。她一般性地断言："一门自然语言是一个有机的活物。在一个漫长的时程中，一门语言（如拉丁语）可以生出好几种不同的新语言，并最终落入废弃不用和死亡的下场。并且，所有的自然语言缓慢地——有时候并不是那么缓慢——转换、改变和适应：借用其他语言的词语，借用科学家、士兵、水手、法官、官僚等等的专门行话；把一度活跃的隐喻转用于新的目的，或者把它们驯化成为令人舒服的陈词滥调；把玩新的习语、时髦语、俗语和口号。""我认为，意义的生长远比新近的哲学主流所承认的显眼得多；但是，并非如激进派所假定的那样，它对合理性构成妨碍；相反，它对合理性所要求的认知灵活性有所助益。"（参见 Haack，2009）

② 参见彼得·扎格尔，2005，《牛津：历史和文化》，朱刘华译，中信出版社；以及 *Oxford English Dictionary*，Second edition on CD-Room（Oxford University Press，2009）中关于"牛津"的众多辞条。

克所说的那样，专名都是严格指示词，那么"牛津"这个名称究竟严格指称什么呢？指原来那个渡口吗？但该渡口的确切位置已经不为人知；或者，转指牛津镇、牛津市、牛津郡、抑或牛津大学？如果像克里普克所说的那样，名称都是无意义的直接指示词，那么，我们上面关于"牛津"这个词写下的所有这些句子算什么呢？难道它们不能帮助我们更好地理解"牛津"这个词吗？我们通常是把这些句子视为"牛津"这个词的意义或其意义的一部分，除开它们之外，我们确实也不知道还有任何称得上是"牛津"这个词的意义的东西。

苏珊·哈克相当仔细地考察了生物学中从"蛋白质"（protein）到"DNA"和"RNA"（核糖核酸）这些概念的演变史。"Protein"来源于希腊语"protos"，意思是"第一"，大约在1844年进入科学词汇之列。如这个术语表明的，protein长期被认为具有第一位的生物学重要性。1869年，有人发现了不同于protein的物质，当时被叫做"nuclein"；1889年，有人提纯nuclein，得到"nucleic acid"（核酸）；后来进一步发现，nucleic acid含有ribose sugars（核糖，缩写为"ribo"）和一个hydrogen（氢）分子（缩写为"deoxy"），于是有了后来流行的名称"deoxyribonucleic acid"（缩写为DNA，出现于1944年）。此后，科学家又分辨出A－DNA、B－DNA、Z－DNA等。在发现DNA的结构之后，先前被叫做"pentose nucleic acid"的东西在1948年变成了"ribonucleic acid"（核糖核酸，缩写为RNA），指包含ribose uracil作为结构成分的各种核糖核酸，其用途在于控制细胞活动。后来，科学家又区分出"messenger RNA"（信使RNA）和"transfer RNA"（转录RNA）、"mtDNA"等等。

苏珊·哈克作出结论说：

> 如此简述的这段历史表明了某些东西，后者与科学家的下述过程有关：调整和重新调整他们的术语，并且转换和改编现存词语的意义，以便造出一个更好地表征新材质的真正类型的术语。"protein"一词已经失去了第一位重要性的暗示；"核糖核酸只能在细胞核中发现"也不再是分析句；旧词"nuclein"最终已经分步骤地被"DNA"代替了；"DNA"本身已经获得了新的复杂内涵，并且生出了新的、更精细的术语后嗣；如此等等。在《梅里亚姆—韦伯斯特辞典》中，"DNA"的定义证实了这样一点：这个词确实如皮尔士所说，已经"在使用和经验中""获得了信息"；知识经过某种类型的沉淀，成为它的意义：
>
> DNA... ［deoxyribonucleic acid（脱氧核糖核酸）］：各种核酸中的任何一种，特别地位于细胞核中，在许多生物那里是遗传的分子基础，由双螺旋构成，双螺旋由嘌呤和吡多胺之间的氢键聚合在一起，由包含脱氧核糖和磷酸盐的不同链接的两根链条向内旋转。
>
> 某些人可能会反驳说，韦伯斯特的定义把"DNA"的意义混同于关于"DNA"所知道

的东西；并且，把该定义按其表面价值看做是在简单地给出该术语的意义，就是误把重要的生物学发现——DNA 是遗传物质，它有双螺旋结构，等等——表征为分析真理。理所当然，我不否认这些是主要的生物学发现；我也不否认，在作出这些发现之时，DNA 是遗传物质，它是一种双螺旋等等，并不是"DNA"意义的一部分。还有，该反驳选错了目标。因为我的论题部分地是意义随知识的生长而生长；这既意味着"'X'的意义"和"我们所有的关于 X 的知识"之间的区分是一种人为的区分，也意味着"分析的"最好理解为"分析的，若假定那些词语在时间 t 的意义"的省略说法（这最后一个想法应该不会令人吃惊："a simple truth is silly sooth"在现代英语中毫无意义；但在莎士比亚时代却是分析句，当时"silly"意味着"simple（简单）"，而"sooth"——如在"soothsayer"中——意指"truth（真理）"）。（Haack，2009）

苏珊·哈克的上述分析和断言是我所赞同的。

从以上两个例子中，我引出如下结论：(i) 名称所指的对象本身处于生长和变化的过程中；(ii) 我们关于名称所指对象的知识也处在生长和变化的过程中；(iii) 我们关于名称所指对象的得到公认的知识被辞典编撰者收入辞典，构成相应名称的意义；(iv) 仅仅相对于这样一部辞典，关于该名称的有些陈述才是分析的和先验的；(v) 但由于辞典本身是我们关于对象的经验知识的总结，因此，辞典具有经验的起源和经验的内容；(vi) 因此，刻画名称意义的相应陈述不在任何绝对的意义上是分析的和先验的；(vii) 因此，克里普克反对描述论的认知论证不成立。

三、对克里普克的语义论证的批评

克里普克对（簇描述论的）论题（3）和（4）的否认构成他反对描述论的"语义论证"，概述如下：

> 假如关于名称的描述论是正确的，即一个名称与相应的一个或一簇摹状词严格同义，那么，名称的涵义就应该是确定其所指的充分必要条件，或者说唯一性条件。也就是说，若任一对象满足与名称相应的一个或一簇摹状词，则该对象就是该名称的语义所指（涵义对于确定所指的充分性）；或者，任何不满足相应的一个或一簇摹状词的对象，就不是相应名称的语义所指（涵义对于确定所指的必要性）。但实际情形并非如此。因此，描述论在语义事实上出错。

克里普克先用"反例"挑战论题（3），因为有可能出现这样的情况：通常与名称 x 关联的一簇描述 φ 的大多数或绝大多数为唯一对象 y 所满足，但 y 却不是 x 的指称。这是在挑战涵义对于确定所指的充分性。他论述说，名称"哥德尔"通常与摹状词"形式算术的不完全性的证明者"相关联。但我们完全可以设想这样的反事实情形：哥德尔有一位名叫"施密特"的好友，后者证明了形式算术的不完全性，但不幸早死，其手稿落到了哥德尔手里，他就用自己的名义将这些手稿发表了，于是获得了"形式算术不完全性的证明者"的名声。但实际上，该摹状词的语义所指是施密特。如果"哥德尔"与摹状词"形式算术的不完全性的证明者"同义，难道它的语义所指也变成了施密特吗？克里普克指出，并非如此，"哥德尔"还指哥德尔这个人，但"形式算术的不完全性的证明者"却指施密特这个人。他继续论述说，这样的情形并非总是虚构的，现实中就有现存的例子。例如，人们通常把皮亚诺说成是"发现了几条说明自然数序列性质公理的人"，但实际上，更早作出这种发现的人却是戴德金；有许多人误以为爱因斯坦既是"相对论的发明者"又是"原子弹的发明者"，但后一描述是错误的，发明原子弹的并不是一个人，而是一群人；许多人把哥伦布说成是"第一个认识到地球是圆的的人"，"第一个发现美洲新大陆的人"等等，但其中有些描述是错误的，另外的人满足这些描述，但这些人并不是"哥伦布"的语义所指，"哥伦布"仍然指称哥伦布这个人。所以，一个名称的语义所指并不就是满足相应的一个或一组描述的人，名称并不与那些描述同义。

我认为，克里普克的这个论证中隐含一个假设，即"名称或摹状词如何指称对象"这个问题仅仅是名称和对象、语言和世界之间的关系，与使用名称、描述和语言的"我们"无关。例如，满足"形式算术的不完全性的证明者"这一描述的人事实上是施密特，它就指施密特，尽管"我们"用它指哥德尔，但我们的用法是错误的。我对克里普克这一假定持有严重的异议。在我看来，名称、描述不会自动与对象发生关系，语言不会自动与世界发生关系，是作为名称、描述或语言的使用者的"我们"让名称、描述与对象以及语言与世界发生如此这般的关系。当我们讨论语义学问题时，我们并不是不考虑语言的使用者，而是不考虑语言的个别使用者对语言附加的某些特殊意涵，而只考虑语言共同体对语言所加予的公共意涵，即被载入语言词典里面的那些意涵。当我们讨论语用学问题时，我们还要考虑特殊的语言使用者对语言所附加的与话语语境密切相关的特殊意涵，这与说话者的意向、各种语境因素或背景条件密切相关。克里普克自己就说过：

　　一般而言，我们的指称不仅取决于我们自己所想的东西，而是依赖于共同体中的其他成员，依赖于该名称如何传到一个人的耳朵里的历史，以及诸如此类的事情。正是遵循这

样一个历史，人们才了解指称的。（NN，95）

我认为，当克里普克构想"哥德尔/施密特/形式算术的不完全性的证明者"这样的反例时，他完全忘记了他刚才所说的话。我只能对克里普克说：你的这个例子是完全臆造出来的，没有被我们的语言共同体所接受，没有进入关于哥德尔的因果历史链条，因此，我们仍然认为，"形式算术的不完全性的证明者"指称哥德尔这个人，而不指称施密特这个人。你在这件事情上弄错了！另外，假如你所设想的情形被我们的语言共同体所确认，那么，我们会切断名称"哥德尔"与摹状词"形式算术的不完全性的证明者"之间的关联，该摹状词会与名称"施密特"建立新的关联，因而其语义所指就是施密特这个人；而名称"哥德尔"也许会与一个新的摹状词——"那位在形式算术不完全性的证明上偷窃别人成果的臭名昭著者"——建立关联，成为后者的语义所指。至于你所提到的那些现实的"反例"，其情形与此类似：关于皮亚诺、爱因斯坦、哥伦布这些人，重要的不是他们本身做了什么，而是我们的语言共同体认为他们做了什么，只有得到语言共同体确认的那些事情或描述才能构成相应名称的涵义，而那些没有得到语言共同体确认的描述，不会进入关于这些人物的"正史"，也不会成为相应名称的涵义或部分涵义。所以，你所构想的那些虚构的或现实的"反例"，实际上不构成反例，"涵义决定所指"的原则仍然成立。

簇描述论的论题（4）断言，"如果表决不产生任何唯一的对象，那么'X'就无所指。"克里普克对此作了两点评论：（i）表决可能产生不出唯一的对象，因为描述是不充分的，可能有不止一个对象满足那个或那些描述。例如，很多人关于西塞罗所知道的也许仅仅是"著名的古罗马演说家"，关于费因曼所知道的仅仅是"一位物理学家"，显然这些描述不能决定唯一的所指。（ii）表决可能产生不出任何对象，即没有任何对象满足所给出的那些描述中的全部或大多数，例如有《圣经》学者断言，《圣经》所谈到的约拿是一个真实的历史人物，但关于他的谈论或描述几乎全都是错误的，那些描述是关于一个真实人物的虚假描述，但"约拿"这个名称仍然指称约拿这个人，尽管他不满足《圣经》上关于他的那些描述；还可以设想，摩西可以不做《圣经》上归于他的所有事情或大多数事情，但不能由此推出摩西不存在，或"摩西"这个名称没有所指。所以，克里普克有时候说，描述论者不能对"摩西存在"和"摩西不存在"这样的句子提供合适的分析。假如他的以上说法成立，则作为名称涵义或部分涵义的描述对于确定名称所指来说就是不必要的；因此，他是在挑战涵义对于确定名称所指的必要性。

不过，我认为，克里普克的上述挑战又失败了。因为，关于像"苏格拉底"、"西塞罗"、

"摩西"、"孔子"这样的历史人物的名称，我们真正关心的是历史典籍、历史文献关于它们的所指对象的种种描述，我们不可能直接接触这些历史人物，我们关于他们的种种信息都是由这些描述得来的；对于我们来说，真正重要的不是"苏格拉底"、"孔子"这些名称在历史上本来指谁，而是满足与这些名称相关的那些描述的人是谁，我们真正关心的是由这些描述"建构"出来的对象。至于克里普克本人所设想的，那个没有做过《圣经》上关于摩西的那些事情的人，他爱把他叫做什么就叫做什么，也可以仍然叫做"摩西"，但肯定不是《圣经》上所说的那个摩西，我们只关心后一个摩西，对前一个摩西，我们不关心、不在乎！克里普克所设想的那个没有做过历史记载中关于亚里士多德所做过的任何事情的人，他爱把他叫做什么就叫做什么，我们也不在乎！我们真正在乎的，是"活"在我们的历史典籍中、"活"在我们的文化传统中的苏格拉底、亚里士多德、孔子这些人。假如后来发现的历史文献证据，证明我们先前接受的关于历史人物的某些描述弄错了，或者先前的描述很不充分，可以大大增补，这种"更正"和"增补"也需要得到我们的语言共同体的认可，进入我们关于这些名称的"因果历史链"。否则，它们就不构成相应名称的意义，也不能用来确定相应名称的指称！改用克里普克的话，关于一个名称的意义和指称，在很大程度上不取决于我们单个人怎么想，而取决于该名称如何传到我们这里的整个历史，取决于我们的整个语言共同体。确定名称的意义和所指的活动是一种社会的、历史的活动！

如前所述，克里普克在反驳描述论、论证名称不同于摹状词时，反复强调的一个重要理由是：假如名称有涵义的话，其涵义必须是确定其所指的充分必要条件，或者说唯一性条件。但摹状词不能提供满足这一条件的涵义，因此，名称从根本上说无涵义，是纯粹指示性的严格指示词。我将论证，克里普克的这些说法又是错误的。

首先，克里普克把描述论的重要原则——"涵义决定所指"——解释为要求名称的涵义提供确定其所指的充分必要条件，是对该原则的误解或曲解，不成立。

"涵义决定所指"这一原则最早是由弗雷格提出来的，他关于专名涵义的相关论述可概括如下：（i）专名的涵义是其所指对象的呈现方式。一个专名只有表达了某种涵义，才能指称某个对象；一个专名究竟指称哪个对象，取决于相应的对象是否具有该专名的涵义所描述的那些特征或性质。这表明，专名的涵义是识别其所指对象的依据、标准、途径。反过来，专名的所指并不决定其涵义，由所指的同一不能推出涵义的同一，因为同一所指可以由不同的涵义所决定。例如，同一个三角形既可以称为"等边三角形"，也可以称为"等角三角形"。（ii）专名的涵义由描述其所指对象的特征的摹状词给出，同一个专名的涵义可以用不同的摹状词来表示，这等于说，对同一个专名的涵义可以有不同的理解。"只要所指保持同一，涵义的这种变化是可以容忍的……"（Frege，1892，p. 153n）（iii）由于自然语言的不完善性，其中一个专名可能对应于不止一种涵义（歧义性），还存在有涵义无所指的专名，例如"奥德赛"，"离地球最远的天体"，"最小的快速收敛级数"，"发散的无穷序列"等等。弗雷格提议，在自然语言中，只要一个名称在同一个语境中有同样的涵义，人们就应该感到满意；当遇到一个没有所指的名称时，我们就人为地指定它的所指，例如 0 或空类。

从弗雷格的论述中，我们可以得知：（i）名称的涵义是确定其所指的充分条件。这就是说，只要给定一个涵义，我们就能找到与该涵义相应的所指；若在现实世界中找不到，就人为地为它指定一个所指，即 0 或空类。由此保证，所有名称都有由其涵义确定的所指。（ii）名称的单个涵义却不是确定其所指的必要条件。因为，弗雷格允许对名称的涵义有不同理解，只要这些涵义都能确定其所指就行。这意味着，这些涵义中的任何一个对于确定所指来说都不是必要的，即使缺失其中某一个涵义，其他的涵义也能够确定其所指，因此我们仍然可以说：涵义决定所指。所以，当克里普克把涵义解释为确定所指的充分必要条件时，他至少违背或误解了弗雷格的原意。

其次，当克里普克指责名称的涵义不能提供确定其所指的充分必要条件时，就隐含地预设了：我们有可能提供确定名称所指的充分必要条件。否则，指责人们没有去做一件他们不可能做到的事情有什么意义？很显然，这一预设也是假的，因为寻求确定名称所指的充分必要条件，就等于寻求对名称的所指对象作完全充分的描述，这种描述因而能够长期保持不变。但我们在原则上不可能做这样的事情，也不可能得到这样的描述！克里普克自己就谈到，关于名称如何指称对象，他本人只是提出了一种比描述论"更好的描述"，却不想把它发展成为一个理论，不想给出一组适用于像指称这类词的充分必要条件，因为"人们可能永远也达不到一组充分必要条件"。（*NN*，94）

所以，克里普克反对描述论的语义论证不成立，因为它底层所隐含的那些假设是错误的！

四、对关于严格指示词的直观检验和精确定义的批评

在进入克里普克的模态论证之前，先讨论一下他的"严格指示词"概念。

克里普克把所有指示词分为两大类：严格的和非严格的。一般来说，专名是严格指示词，大多数摹状词是非严格的指示词。在指称对象的方式上，通名与专名类似，都是严格指示词。他的"严格指示词"概念起源于这样的语言直觉：我们可以对现实世界中的个体作各种反事实

的谈论。例如，亚里士多德本来是如此这般，但我们完全可以设想，亚里士多德不是如此这般，而是如此那般，他甚至没有做过他在现实世界中所做过的所有那些事情，但即使如此，我们仍然是在谈论现实世界中那个被我们叫做"亚里士多德"的个体，是在谈论有关他的种种反事实的情形，而不是在谈论有关别人的某些情形。

关于严格指示词和非严格指示词的区分，克里普克提出了两个说明：一个是直观测试，另一个是精确定义。先看他的直观测试：

> 譬如，我们可以说，太阳系行星的数目可能会不同于事实上的那个数目，举例来说，可能只有七颗行星。我们可以说，双焦点透镜的发明者可能会是事实上发明了双焦点透镜的那个人之外的某个人。虽然我们不能说，81 的平方根可能会不同于事实上的那个数目，因为该数恰好必定是 9。如果我们把这种直观测试应用于像"理查德·尼克松"这样的专名，它们似乎在直观上就会显现为严格指示词。（*NN*，175－176）

> 在这些讲演中，我所主张的直观论题之一就是：名称是严格指示词。这些名称看起来肯定能满足我在上面提到的那种直观测试：虽然一个不是 1970 年美国总统的人有可能是 1970 年的美国总统（例如，汉弗莱就有可能如此），但是，没有任何一个不是尼克松的人有可能成为尼克松。（*NN*，48）

于是，我们有下面两种很类似的直观测试：

直观测试 I
d 是非严格指示词，当且仅当，d 可能不是 d。
d 是严格指示词，当且仅当，d 不可能不是 d。

直观测试 II
d 是非严格指示词，当且仅当，d 之外的某个个体可能是 d。
d 是严格指示词，当且仅当，没有 d 之外的个体可能是 d。

举例来说，"1970 年的美国总统"是非严格指示词，因为 1970 年的美国总统有可能没有当选 1970 年的美国总统，而是另外某个人（例如汉弗莱）当选 1970 年的美国总统；反之，"尼克松"则是严格指示词，因为尼克松不可能不是尼克松，没有尼克松之外的任何一个人有可能是尼克松。

由于这两种直观测试的类似性，限于篇幅，我下面只分析直观测试I。我认为，上面的表述很不严格，因为名称必须是某个对象的名称。对上述表述作改进（为了方便后面的讨论，加上序号）：

直观测试 I′

（i）d 是对象 o 的非严格指示词，当且仅当，d 可能不是 d。

（ii）d 是对象 o 的严格指示词，当且仅当，d 不可能不是 d。

问题是：作为（i）和（ii）的定义项，"d 可能不是 d"、"d 不可能不是 d"中的"d"究竟代表什么？它们相同吗？我认为，至少有两钟不同的解读方法。

相同的读法，又分"形而上学读法"和"语义学读法"。

形而上学读法：在（i）和（ii）的定义项中，两个 d 是相同的，都表示对象。于是，"d 可能不是 d"就是假的，因为一个对象不可能不是它自身；而"d 不可能不是 d"则是真的，因为它仅仅表示一个对象的自我同一。但问题是：这与名称和对象之间的命名、指称关系有什么相干？更明确地说，我们如何从一个形而上学论断"一个对象必定自我同一"过渡到一个语言哲学命题"一个名称是一个对象的严格指示词"？

语义学读法：其中的两个 d 是相同的，都表示名称。于是，"d 可能不是 d"是假的，因为违反使用名称时必须遵守的同一律；"d 不可能不是 d"则是真的，因为它仅仅表示一个名称的自我同一。类似的问题是：这与名称和对象之间的命名、指称关系有什么相干？我们如何从一个逻辑命题"一个名称必定与自身同一"过渡到一个语言哲学命题"一个名称是一个对象的严格指示词"？

不同的读法，又分"稍微不同读法"和"完全不同读法"。

稍微不同读法：这也是一种形而上学读法。例如，把"d 可能不是 d"读为：指示词 d 所指称的对象可能不具有摹状词 d 所刻画的那种性质，例如"1970 年的美国总统有可能没有当选 1970 年美国总统"，其中"1970 年美国总统"作为主词，指称一个特定的人，即尼克松这个人；作为谓词，则表示他所具有的某种抽象性质（如具有1970年的美国总统身份）。在这样的解释之下，（i）变成："'1970 年美国总统'不是尼克松这个人的严格指示词，当且仅当，尼克松这个人有可能没有 1970 年的美国总统身份"。这在直观上是成立的，但类似的问题仍然存在：

（i）的被定义项涉及名实关系，而定义项仅仅涉及对象的存在状态。怎么能够接受这样的定义？！

并且，按上面的方式，（ii）的定义项"d 不可能不是 d"不再成立，因为它至少可以解读为：指示词 d 所指称的对象不可能不具有摹状词 d 所刻画的那种性质，例如"亚里士多德不可能不是亚里士多德"，其中"亚里士多德"作为主词，指称一个特定的人，即亚里士多德这个人；作为谓词（"不是亚里士多德"）的构成成分，则表示某种抽象的性质：例如，不是亚里士多德实际所是的那个人，或者，不具有亚里士多德实际所有的那些性质。在这样的解释之下，"我本来可以不是我"这类说法也是可以成立的，即我本来有机会不成为现在的我，即没有我现在所有的身份或状态，而具有某些别的身份或状态。按这种解释，"亚里士多德不可能不是亚里士多德"这类说法就是假的。

完全不同的读法，即（ii）定义项中两个 d 一个表示对象，一个表示名称。本来就应该如此，因为（ii）的被定义项涉及名称和对象之间的关系，故其定义项也要涉及这种关系才行。但如此一来，该定义项就不再成立，因为对象 d 当初完全可能不用名字 d，而用另外的名字；即使最初用了名字 d，后来也可以改名或换名。

因此，克里普克的下述说法使我迷惑不解：

> 在这些讲演中，我将基于直观去论证，专名是严格指示词，因为，虽然这个人（尼克松）可能没有成为总统，但他不能不成其为尼克松（虽然他有可能不叫"尼克松"）。（*NN*，49）

在论证"亚历山大的老师"是非严格指示词、"亚里士多德"是严格指示词时，克里普克说：

> 当有人观察到，亚历山大的老师可能不曾教过亚历山大（在这种情形下，他就不会是亚历山大的老师），这些事实既说明"亚历山大的老师"在模态语境中能够有辖域的区别，也说明它不是一个严格指示词。另一方面，亚里士多德有可能不是亚里士多德却不是真的，虽然亚里士多德有可能不被叫做"亚里士多德"，就像 2×2 有可能不被称作"4"一样［……］。而且，尽管在某些情况下亚里士多德不曾教过亚历山大，但是，这些情况并非是他原本不是亚里士多德的情况。（*NN*，62n）

　　既然严格指示词涉及名称和对象之间的命名、指称关系，对象自身的本体论状况（如它不可能不是它自身）就是完全不相干的，而怎么样去命名或指称一个对象才是真正相关的。但克里普克反复强调前者，完全漠视后者。使人（至少是像我这样的人）迷惑不解！①

　　我的结论是：克里普克关于严格指示词的直观测试行不通，其中存在一个不合法的过渡，即从"一个对象不可能不与自身同一"这个形而上学论断，过渡到一个语言哲学命题"一个名称是一个对象的严格指示词"。这一过渡是建立在克里普克的哲学直觉之上的，他并没有对它给出严格的哲学论证。② 所以，说得夸张一点，克里普克的"严格指示词"概念的提出，实际

---

　　① 我认为，对于回答我对直观测试的上述批评——即如何从一个形而上学论断合法地过渡到一个语言哲学命题？——来说，索姆斯的下述解释和说明是不切题的：

　　"为了适当地理解亚里士多德是严格指示词这个论题，人们必须清楚地理解下面两个论断是如何协调的：

　　（i）名称亚里士多德是严格指示词。于是，对于这个世界的所有状态 w 而言，名称亚里士多德都指称在 w 中或位于 w 或相对于 w 的同一个个体，即亚里士多德这个人。

　　（ii）亚里士多德叫做'亚里士多德'，这并不是必然真理。于是，有可能发生的情况是：名称亚里士多德并不指称亚里士多德，这意味着：存在某个世界状态 w，使得下述断言在 w 中或位于 w 或相对于 w 是真的：名称亚里士多德并不指称亚里士多德。

　　因为克里普克将会第一个主张，这两个断言都是真的。这可能看起来使人迷惑不解，因为它们有可能看起来是不一致的。事实上，它们并非如此。"

　　索姆斯对此解释说："说话者在 w 中用 n 指称什么样的个体，对于确定下述一点来说是关键性的：二元关系——指称——相对于 w 可以应用于名称和对象的何种有序偶？名称 n 指称对象 o 当且仅当说话者在 w 中用 n 去指称 o，这一说法相对于 w 是真的。于是，（ii）所说的是，存在世界状态 w 使得说话者在那些世界状态中并不使用'亚里士多德'去指称亚里士多德。这与（i）所作的下述断言是相容的——即是说，当我们的话语被看做是对无论什么样的世界状态的描述时，名称'亚里士多德'，如我们在现实世界的此时此地所使用的那样，指称亚里士多德这个人。"（Soames，2002，pp. 317 – 318）

　　据我理解，索姆斯的意思是：我们就用"亚里士多德"这个名称去指称被我们在现实世界中叫做"亚里士多德"的那个人，尽管这个人可以处于各种各样的可能状态中，这些状态可能非常不同于他在现实世界中的状态，尽管处于这些可能状态下的人们也有可能不把他叫做"亚里士多德"，这都没有关系，这并不妨碍"亚里士多德"这个名称的严格性。即使索姆斯的这些解释是对的，也并不说明克里普克的直观测试是奏效的或可行的。这是两个不同的问题。

　　② 在《命名与必然性》一书的"序言"中，克里普克提到："我们必须区分三个不同的论题：（1）同一的对象必然是同一的；（2）严格指示词之间的真实的同一性陈述是必然的；（3）在实际语言中我们所谓的'名称'之间的同一性陈述是必然的。（1）和（2）都是独立于自然语言的（自明的）哲学逻辑论题。它们是相互关联的，尽管（1）是关于对象的论题，而（2）是元语言论题［用严格指示词替换全称量词，从（1）可以粗略地'推导'出（2）。……］"这表明，克里普克已经意识到，形而上学论题（1）和语言哲学论题（2）是有区别的，并且他认为，（2）是用严格指示词替换全称量词从（1）粗略地推导出来的。不过，既然推导过程要用严格指示词去替换全称量词，那就表明：我们需要先有关于"严格指示词"的独立定义，而不能直接诉诸所谓的"哲学直观"，从形而上学论题直接过渡到语言哲学论题。

上源自于他的一个基本错误：混淆形而上学和语义学；我在另文①中将证明，他所提出的有些惊人的哲学论题，也系统地依赖于"严格指示词"这一概念的歧义性：有时候把它用在所指称的"对象"的意义上，有时候把它用在作为"指示词"的身份上。

不过，除了关于严格指示词的直观测试之外，克里普克还提出了它的精确定义，有两种稍微不同的说法：

> ……当我使用严格指示词这个概念时，我并不意谓着，被指称的那个对象必定存在。我的意思只是，在所谈论的那个对象确实存在的任何可能世界中，在该对象将会存在的任何情况下，我们用所提到的那个指示词指称该对象。在该对象不存在的情况下，我们应该说，那个指示词没有所指，所谈论的那个被如此指称的对象不存在。(*NN*, 173)

> 如果一个指示词在每一个可能世界中都指示同一个对象，我们就称之为严格指示词。否则，就称之为非严格的或偶然的指示词。当然，我们并不要求那些对象在所有可能世界中存在。……一个必然存在物的严格指示词可以叫做强严格指示词。(*NN*, 48)

> 我说，一个专名严格地指示其所指对象，甚至在我们谈论该对象并不存在的反事实情形时也是如此。(*NN*, 21n)

上述两种定义方式的差别在于：当在一个可能世界中没有相应的对象时，一个严格指示词是否仍然有其所指。据报道，克里普克本人曾在给一位哲学同行的信中解释说，对于一个名称在所谈论的对象不存在的世界中是否仍然指称该对象这一问题，他的态度是中性的，不持特别的立场。(参看 Fitch, 2004, xiii)

我们权且接受这种解释。于是，我们有下面的定义：

> 一个指示词 d 是一个对象 o 的严格指示词，当且仅当，(1) d 在 o 存在的每一个可能世界中都指示 o；(2) 在设想 o 不存在的可能世界中，d 仍然指示 o。

> 若一个指示词 d 指示一个在每个可能世界中都存在的对象 o（必然存在物），则 d 是一个强严格指示词。

---

① 参见陈波，《存在"先验偶然命题"和"后验必然命题"吗——对克里普克的知识论的批评》。

对于这样的精确定义，我有如下两点评论：

（1）精确定义与产生"严格指示词"概念的语言直观有冲突，其冲突之点在于：我们能否对虚构个体作反事实谈论？

按照克里普克反复强调的语言直观，我们可以对一个现实个体，例如亚里士多德，作各种反事实谈论：他可能不是这样，而是那样……这意味着，名称 n 对模态词"可能"取宽辖域，用符号表示：

①[n]◇(¬Fn∧Gn∧...)

如果我们也可以对虚构个体，如福尔摩斯，作反事实的谈论，那么，情况必定是：模态词"可能"本身取宽辖域，名称 n 则相对于该模态词取窄辖域，用符号表示：

②◇(¬Fn∧Gn∧...)

这里，①和②的区别在于：①是 *de re* 模态，关于一个现实个体的反事实谈论；②是 *de dicto* 模态，述说一个语句或命题是必然真还是偶然真，其中对名称 n 究竟是指称一个实存个体还是虚构个体，并没有特别的要求。这就是说，在 *de dicto* 模态中，名称 n 既可以指称一个实存个体，也可以指称一个虚构个体。[①] 显然，①和②之间有重要区别。

上面那个精确定义，似乎对严格指示词究竟是指称一个实存个体还是虚构个体，并没有明确的规定。因为，即使一个名称在现实世界中没有所指，它也可以在它有所指的所有可能世界中指称其所指对象，因而仍然是一个严格指示词。不过，克里普克所强调的有关严格指示词的语言直观，却只是对一个现实个体作反事实谈论："当我说一个指示词是严格的，在所有可能世界中指示同一件事物时，我的意思是说，正像在我们的语言中所使用的那样，当我们谈论非真实的情形时，它代表那件事物。"（Kripke，1981，77）显然，"那件事物"指一个现实个体。索姆斯表述的原则 GR 也证明了这一点：

> 我们认为亚里士多德是一个严格指示词，是因为我们相信由原则（GR）所表达的东西：

---

① 早在中世纪，欧洲逻辑学家就区分了 *de dicto* 模态 和 *de re* 模态。*de dicto* 模态是关于句子或命题的模态，是用模态词修饰一个完整的句子或命题，简称"从言模态"，例如◇p，◇(Fa)（可能 a 是 F），□∀xB(x)。从言模态既可涉及实存个体，也可涉及纯粹想象的个体，或虚构个体。在从言模态中，模态词本身取宽辖域，其中的名称或摹状词则取窄辖域。*de re* 模态是把模态词插入一个句子或命题中间，修饰其主词和谓词的联系方式，简称"从物模态"，例如 (◇F)a(a 可能是 F)，∃x□B(x)。从物模态断言实存个体可能具有或必然具有某种性质，它要求所述说的个体必须存在。在从物模态中，模态词本身取窄辖域，其中的名称或摹状词取宽辖域。

GR　存在某个个体 x，使得对于每一个可能世界 w，"亚里士多德是一位哲学家"这个命题在 w 中是真的，当且仅当，"x 是一位哲学家"在 w 中是真的……对于使用名称亚里士多德所表达的其他命题，情况也如此。(Soames，2002，25)

反之，允许对一个虚构个体作反事实谈论，这样的说法是很奇怪的，也与我所理解的克里普克关于可能世界的观点相冲突。因为他认为，只有一个真实的世界，这就是我们面前的这个世界，其他可能世界只不过是现实世界的各种可能状况、各种可设想的情形、各种反事实的情形。同样的道理，当我们对现实个体作反事实谈论时，并不是在谈论别的纯可能的或虚构的个体，而仍然是在谈论那些现实的个体。他根本不承认"跨越世界的个体"或"跨越世界的同一性"这类提法的合法性，认为它们源自于对可能世界话语的误解。根据这种看法，严格指示词似乎必须是现实个体的指示词，这就与那个精确定义所说的严格指示词不一致，因为后者至少允许有些严格指示词是非实存对象的指示词。①

（2）即使接受关于严格指示词的精确定义，我也认为，关于严格指示词的谈论，可以归结为 de re 模态，或者说，归结为对相应指示词的使用②，即关于现实对象的谈论，与该对象叫什么名字无关。在下一节，我将详细证明这一点。

基于上面的定义，克里普克强调指出，名称是严格指示词；除少数例外，大多数摹状词都不是严格指示词，因为摹状词并不给出名称的意义，并不与名称严格同义，而只是偶尔被用来确定名称的所指。因此，"给出名称的意义"与"确定名称的所指"是两件不同的事情。

五、对克里普克的模态论证的批评

克里普克对（簇描述论的）论题（6）的否认等等构成他反对描述论的"模态论证"，概述如下：

如果关于名称的描述论是正确的，一个名称在语义上被同义地定义为一个或一簇摹状

---

① 不过，这个问题很复杂，牵涉到如何在严格指示词的框架内说明所谓的"空专名"问题，克里普克在牛津大学所作的约翰·洛克讲演"指称和存在"（1973 年）中系统地处理了这个问题，我将另文探讨。
② 我认为，名称和摹状词都有使用与提之分：名称或摹状词的"使用"是指用它们去指称外部世界中的一个对象；对它们的提及则是谈论该名称或该摹状词本身；例如，"上海"这个名称指称上海这座城市，这里带引号的"上海"被提及，带着重号的上海被使用，后者指一个语言外的对象。（在本文中，当要强调名称与对象的区别时，带引号的是名称，底下带着重号的是对象）

词，那么，该名称和相应的摹状词就应该有相同的模态身份（modal profiles）和语义作用，以该名称做主词、以该摹状词做谓词的句子就应该是必然的。举例来说，假如"亚里士多德"被同义地定义为"亚历山大的老师"，下面的句子就应该是必然的：

（1）亚里士多德是亚历山大的老师。

但是，在反事实谈论中，（1）可以为假。因为可以设想这样一种情景：亚里士多德从未做过教师，当然也就没有做过亚历山大的老师，而是另外某个人做了亚历山大的老师。但即使在这种情况下，我们还是在谈论亚里士多德这个人没有做过那些事情的情形，亚里士多德仍为亚里士多德，但亚历山大的老师却是某个另外的人。因此，关于名称的描述论在模态事实上出错。（参见 NN，61－63，74－76）

但是，我认为，克里普克的上述论证不成立。因为，假如采用他证明"双焦点透镜的发明者是美国第一任邮政部长"也表示一个对象（即富兰克林）的自我同一的方法（参见 Kripke，1971，166），我也可以证明："亚里士多德是亚历山大的老师"也表示对象的自我同一，因而是一个必然命题。因为该句子等于说："恰好有一个人 x 是亚里士多德，恰好有一个人 y 满足'亚历山大的老师'这个描述，x＝y，并且，必然地 x＝y。"若用"a"代表"亚里士多德"，用"the F"表示摹状词"亚历山大的老师"，用"∃!y(y＝the F)"表示"只有唯一的对象 y 满足摹状词'亚历山大的老师'"，则"亚里士多德是亚历山大的老师"的必然性可以表示如下：

（2）$[a][\text{the F}]((a＝亚里士多德)\wedge \exists!y((y＝\text{the F})\wedge(a＝y)\wedge \Box(a＝y)))$

这里的关键在于：名称和摹状词都相对于模态词取宽辖域。我们可以把这种方法加以推广，去解释克里普克的"严格指示词"概念，去解释那些人们通常提到的关于名称的描述论的"反例"。

人们通常认为，下面两个句子有不同的真值，至少可以取不同的真值：

（3）亚里士多德有可能不是亚历山大的老师。

（4）亚历山大的老师有可能不是亚历山大的老师。

并由此证明，名称和摹状词有不同的模态身份和语义作用，关于名称的描述论不正确。不过，如果（3）和（4）中的名称和摹状词都相对于模态词取宽辖域（de re 模态），也就是对名称和摹状词都采用使用读法，强调其指称对象的功能，那么，它们的意思分别是：

（5）恰好有一个人是亚里士多德，他可能不是亚历山大的老师。

（6）恰好有一个人满足摹状词"亚历山大的老师"，他可能不是亚历山大的老师。

可以分别用符号表示成如下的公式：

（7）［a］（（a＝亚里士多德）∧∃!y（（y＝the G）∧◇（a≠y）））

（8）［the G］（∃!y（（y＝the G）∧◇（y≠the G）））

（7）和（8）显然都是真的，故（3）和（4）有同样的真值！

人们之所以认为，至少在有些可设想的情形下，（3）真而（4）假，是因为他们把名称"亚里士多德"理解为指称一个特定的人，即现实世界中的亚里士多德这个人；而认为摹状词"亚历山大的老师"并不指称一个特定的人，而是指称某种抽象的性质，这种性质在不同的可能世界中可以被不同的个体所具有，即该摹状词在不同的可能世界中有不同的所指。这显然不是我们在现实世界中使用摹状词的情况。例如，当我们使用"美国第一任总统"这个摹状词时，我们就是用它指称现实世界中的华盛顿这个人，而不是指在其他可能的情形下有可能成为美国第一任总统的那个人或那些人；当我们使用"模态逻辑的完全性定理的证明者"这个摹状词时，我们就是用它指现实世界中的克里普克这个人，而不是指在其他可能的情形下有可能证明模态逻辑完全性的其他人。如果从指称的角度着眼，摹状词也能够被严格化，因而也是所谓的"严格指示词"，只不过要加上一个被省略了的限定"在@ 中"。（请注意，这个@ 仅指我们面前的这个现实世界，不指其他任何可能世界；更明确地说，@ 不是索引性的。）由于我们总在@ 中说话，没有必要总提到@，故在话语中将其省略。当我们做各种反事实谈论时，我们已经超出现实世界而进入到其他可能世界之中，于是要把省略的限定@ 加进来："@ 中亚历山大的老师"，后面这个词已经像专名"亚里士多德"一样严格化了，它固定地指称现实世界中亚里士多德这个人，并且在任何可能世界中都指称这个人！

我还认为，所有关于严格指示词（包括名称和严格化的摹状词）的谈论，都可以归约为 de re 模态①，即关于现实对象的谈论。这是关于对象如何存在的理论，与该对象有什么样的名字无关。在我看来，至少模态谓词逻辑是关于对象如何存在的形而上学理论，只不过是用逻辑的技术手段建构出来的；它与语言哲学无关，特别是与名称理论无关，正像一阶逻辑与名称理论无关一样。极而言之，我们完全可以不用名称，而用纯粹的实指动作，来完成反事实谈论：

"这个对象在现实世界中是如此这般，但我们完全可以设想：它有可能不是如此这般，而是如此那般……"

克里普克赞同卡普南（David Kaplan）的观点，认为像"这"、"那"、"我"、"你"、"它"等指示代词都是严格指示词。（参见 NN，10n，28n）我对此表示怀疑。我认为，伴随实指动作

---

① 这一点是由达米特最先提出来的（参见 Dummett，1981，Appendix to Chapter 5："Note on an Attempted Refutation of Frege"，pp. 111 – 151，特别是 pp. 127 – 128）。

的指示代词，凸显出我们正在谈论处在我们面前的那个现实对象，因为我们不能用实指动作去指称一个不存在的东西；而在反事实谈论中，可以用指示代词代替名字，也凸显出我们正在谈论的是我们面前的现实对象，正在对这个现实对象作各种反事实设想。在这样的反事实谈论中，我们可以用这个名字去称呼它，也可以用另外的名字去称呼它，并且在不同的反事实情形下还可以用不同的名字去称呼它，就像我们可以用很多不同的名字去称呼同一个现实对象一样。例如，鲁迅除了本名"周树人"之外，据说还用过 180 多个笔名。这说明，在作反事实谈论时，名字是一个无关紧要的变量，根本上就没有进入这个情景或故事中！①②

综上所述，名称作为所谓"严格指示词"的使用，可以化归于非严格的名称相对于模态词取宽辖域，也就是关于特定的现实个体的谈论。并且，假如有所谓"严格指示词"的话，大多数摹状词也能够被严格化，成为严格化的摹状词，固定地指称现实世界中的一个特定个体，并且在所有可能世界中都固定地指示该个体。因此，我们仍然无法将名称与摹状词严格区别开来，也没有理由否认名称可以释义为相应的摹状词的缩写。我可以由此断言，克里普克的模态论证不成立，他并没有成功地反驳关于名称的描述论！

克里普克在《命名与必然性》的序言中对严格性可以归约为 *de re* 模态的说法有所回应（参见 *NN*，5 - 13）。他说，即使我们完全不用模态词来作反事实谈论，"名称是严格指示词、摹状词是非严格指示词"这一点仍然可以显露出来。看他的例子：

(9) Aristotle was fond of dogs.

根据其描述理论，罗素会把（9）理解为下面的（10）：

(10) The last great philosopher of antiquity was fond of dogs. ③

克里普克说，（9）表述了两种情形：一种是真实的情形，在这种情形下，（9）的真值条件是：亚里士多德这个人喜欢狗；另一种是反事实的历史进程，它在某些方面类似于真实的进程，但在其他方面却不同。既然在设想一种反事实的情形，亚里士多德之外的某个人当然可以成为

---

① 亨迪卡等人也认为，"更一般地说，重要的是要认识到，如果限定了跨界识别的标准，模态和内涵语境的量化完全有意义，这一点与人们关于名称和其他单称词项，以及它们与其所指称的个体的关系所可能想到的东西完全无关。丝毫没有必要去假定任何特别的'严格指示词'的类别。就给定的可能世界类而言，如果单称词项'b'是一个'严格指示词'，这在该语言内可以用量词表达为：

(8)（∃x）*N*(b = x ）"（参看 Hintikka and Sandu, 1995, 250 - 251）

② 阿里夫·阿赫默德也指出，即使完全不提到严格指示词，而只提到相关的对象本身，也能够谈论用严格指示词谈论的那些事情。参见 Ahmed, 2007, 26 - 28。

③ 这两个例句之所以直接用英语，是因为它们在英语中涉及虚拟语气，表示一种假想的情形。由于汉语中没有虚拟语气，直接翻译成汉语句子，至少会对它们的意义有所遗漏或扭曲。

"古代最后一位伟大的哲学家",于是(10)中的那个摹状词就可以适用于亚里士多德之外的对象,这另一个对象的存在状态(如是否喜欢狗)就会决定(10)的真假。于是,(10)的真值条件就可能与(9)的有所不同。因此,名称"亚里士多德"与摹状词"古代最后一位伟大的哲学家"的语义作用有所不同,前者是严格指示词,后者是非严格指示词。

我认为,克里普克的上述回应有两个问题:(i)他从使用的角度去理解"亚里士多德"这个名称,即它所指称的对象——现实世界中的亚里士多德这个人;而仅从字面意思本身去理解摹状词"古代最后一位伟大的哲学家",将其理解为一个漂浮在不同可能世界之间、能够被不同世界中的不同个体所满足的一个描述;如果也从指称的角度去理解该摹状词,现实世界中满足这个描述的就是亚里士多德这个人,因此它所指称的也是亚里士多德这个人。因此,(9)和(10)有同样的真值条件!(ii)尽管(9)和(10)表面上不含模态因素,但是,当克里普克为说明名称与摹状词有不同的语义作用而设想这样的反事实情形——即亚里士多德之外的某个人成为古代最后一位伟大的哲学家——时,他就是在设想一种可能的情形,模态因素已经牵涉其中。

为了反驳把严格性归结于名称和摹状词相对于模态词取宽辖域,克里普克还给出了另外的论证。为了保持前后一致,还是用前面的例子(3)和(4),关于它们,除了 *de re* 读法外,还有 *de dicto* 读法:

(11)亚里士多德不是亚历山大的老师这一点可能是事实。

(It might have been the case that Aristotle was not the teacher of Alexander.)

(12)亚历山大的老师不是亚历山大的老师这一点可能是事实。

(It might have been the case that the teacher of Alexander was not the teacher of Alexander.)

这里,没有名称和摹状词相对于模态词取"宽辖域"(*de re* 模态)的问题,两个句子中的名称和摹状词都取"窄辖域"(*de dicto* 模态)。于是,按前面的办法,(11)和(12)可以分别表示成:

(13) $\diamond((a=\text{亚里士多德})\wedge\exists!y((y=\text{the G})\wedge(a\neq y)))$

(14) $\diamond\exists!y((y=\text{the G})\wedge(y\neq\text{the G}))$

显然,(13)表达一个真理,而(14)却表达一个谬误或矛盾,永远为假。克里普克由此断言:名称和摹状词有不同的模态身份,这一点与名称和摹状词相对于模态词取什么"辖域"无关。(参见 *NN*, 13, 61–62)

我仍然认为,克里普克的上述分析不正确,同样有两个理由:(i)他反复强调,当我们从事反事实谈论时,我们是从我们的世界和我们的语言出发的,例如当我们说"亚里士多德可能会怎么样"时,我们仍在谈论现实世界中被我们叫做"亚里士多德"的那个人,尽管别的可能世界中可以不把他叫做"亚里士多德";同样的道理,当我们谈论"亚历山大的老师"时,我们也是在谈论现实世界中满足这一描述的那个人,我们的语言共同体公认这个人就是亚里士多德,而不是任何别的可能满足这一描述的人,更不是另外的某个可能世界中的某个另外的人。于是,(12)变成了(15):

(15) @ 中亚历山大的老师不是亚历山大的老师这一点可能是事实。

我们只能把(15)表示成下面的公式:

(16) $\exists!y((y = \text{the G}) \wedge \Diamond(y \neq \text{the G}))$

显然,(16)也表达一个真理,与(13)完全一样!就像现实世界中的一位父亲可以不是一位父亲一样,因为完全可以设想,他没有结婚,或者结婚了但没有孩子或不想要孩子。否则,一位现实世界中的父亲就必然成为一位父亲,而这种说法是荒谬的。

(ii)即使克里普克的上述分析成立,也没有反驳"严格指示词可以归于 *de re* 模态"的说法,除非 *de dicto* 模态中的名称也是严格指示词(至少按我的理解,克里普克确实这样认为,参见 *NN*,6)。而这一点是可以受到质疑的(参见上一节对严格指示词的精确定义的质疑)。

至此,我作出结论:克里普克关于名称和摹状词具有不同模态身份的分析,以及他对关于这种分析的责难的回应都不正确!

六、对索姆斯维护模态论证的批评

1998 年,索姆斯(Scott Soames)发表论文《模态论证:宽辖域和严格化的摹状词》一文,对反驳模态论证的两个重要理由进行再反驳。① 他给出了两大论证,一个反驳用宽辖域分析去反驳克里普克的模态论证,一个反驳用严格化的摹状词去反驳该论证。但我下面将证明,这两个再反驳都不成立。

I. 反驳名称和摹状词对模态词取宽辖域的论证不成立

如前所述,所谓"严格指示词"就是专名相对于模态词取宽辖域。如果摹状词也相对于模

---

① Soames, Scott, 1998, "The Modal Argument: Wide Scope and Rigidified Descriptions", *Nous* 32: 1, 1–22. 此文经小幅改写后,作为其专著 *Beyond Rigidity: The Unfinished Semantic Agenda of Naming and Necessity* (Oxford University Press, 2002) 中的第二章(第18—55页)。

态词取宽辖域，那么，专名和摹状词的语义作用就是一样的。因此，没有必要引入所谓的"严格指示词"去解释反事实谈论，并且也不能据此把名称和摹状词严格区分开来。实际上，名称和摹状词都是非严格的指示词，并且仍然可以把名称看做是相应摹状词的缩写，关于名称的描述论仍然是正确的。

我认为，描述论的一大优势是：能够很好地解释，当 a 和 b 是专名时，为什么"a = b"能够传达"a = a"所没有的新语义内容；并且，它也能很好地解释下面两个信念句之间的差别：

（1）比尔相信启明星是启明星。

（2）比尔相信启明星是长庚星。

尽管启明星 = 长庚星，即它们的所指相同，但涵义（由相应的摹状词给出）不同，若比尔不知道这一点，则他会根据逻辑相信"启明星是启明星"，而不相信"启明星是长庚星"，于是就发生了（1）真而（2）假这样的事情。

索姆斯不同意上述分析，为了反驳它，他构造了一个基本论证，转述如下：

基本论证

如果名称"n"的语义内容由摹状词"the G"给出，那么，由语句"如果 n 是 F，则某物既是 F 又是 G"所语义表达的命题，就是由语句"如果 the G 是 F，则某物既是 F 又是 G"所语义表达的命题。于是，我们有前提 1：

P1. "如果 n 是 F，则某物既是 F 又是 G"这个命题 = "如果 the G 是 F，则某物既是 F 又是 G"这个命题。

我们再增加一个明显为真的前提 2：

P2. "如果 the G 是 F，则某物既是 F 又是 G"这个命题是必然真理，即：

$$\square[\ ([\text{the } x:Gx]Fx) \rightarrow \exists y(Fy \wedge Gy)\ ]$$

很清楚，从 P1 和 P2 可以合逻辑地推出 C：

C. "如果 n 是 F，则某物既是 F 又是 G"这个命题是必然真理，即：

$$\square[\ (Fn \rightarrow \exists y(Fy \wedge Gy))\ ]$$

根据名称 n 在语义上等于摹状词 the G，并且 the G 相对于模态词 $\square$ 取宽辖域，C 就被释义为 C'：

C'. The G 使得命题"如果它是 F，则某物既是 F 又是 G"这个命题是必然真理，即：

$$[\text{the } x:Gx]\square[\ (Fx \rightarrow \exists y(Fy \wedge Gy))\ ]$$

但从 P1 和 P2 却推不出 C'，而按宽辖域分析，C 恰好就是 C'，因此，从 P1 和 P2 也应该推不出 C。于是，宽辖域分析就使一个明显有效的推理（从 P1 和 P2 到 C）变成无效推理（从 P1 和 P2 到 C'）了。因此，宽辖域分析不正确。（参见 Soames，2002，25 –31）

对于索姆斯的基本论证，我有如下三点评论：

1. 从 P1 和 P2 本来就推不出 C。首先，P1 所陈述的两个命题相等（同一）是什么意思？等号两边的命题在形式上肯定不相等，因为一个含有名称，另一含有摹状词；即使名称的涵义由摹状词给出，说这两个命题相等，是说它们的真值相等还是说别的？索姆斯没有交代清楚。这也情有可原，因为蒯因早已论证，"意义同一性"，"内涵同一性"或"命题同一性"的条件是非常难以规定的。① 其次，由两个命题相等是否就可以断定：它们在模态语境中可以相互替换？反正我们知道，当两个名称或摹状词的所指对象相等时，它们在模态语境中是不能随便替换的，否则会由真前提得出假结论：引用蒯因的著名例子，由"行星的数目 = 9"和"9 必然大于 7"，不能推出"行星的数目必然大于 7"。② 为了保证同一替换在模态语境下成立，同一必须强化成必然同一，即（x = y）→□（x = y）。于是，要从 P1 和 P2 推出 C，P1 本身必须强化成 P1′：

P1′ □（"如果 n 是 F，则某物既是 F 又是 G"这个命题 = "如果 the G 是 F，则某物既是 F 又是 G"这个命题）

这就是说，从原来的 P1 和 P2 推不出 C！

2. 原来的 P1 之所以成立，是因为还有一个隐含前提，即名称的含义由相应的摹状词给出，用符号表示，即"n = the G"，它才是真正的前提 1，原来的 P1 是由它通过同一替换派生出来的。所以，基本论证的真正结构是：

P1″ n = the G

P2. "如果 the G 是 F，则某物既是 F 又是 G"这个命题是必然真理，即：

$$□[([the\ x:\ Gx]Fx)→∃y(Fy∧Gy)]$$

从 P2 再根据 P1″做同一性替换，即用 n 替换 P2 中的摹状词 the G，得到 C：

C. "如果 n 是 F，则某物既是 F 又是 G"这个命题是必然真理，即：

$$□[(Fn→∃y(Fy∧Gy))]$$

---

① 参见蒯因，2007，《经验论的两个教条》，载涂纪亮、陈波主编：《蒯因著作集》，中国人民大学出版社，第 5 卷，第 29—50 页。

② 参见涂纪亮、陈波主编，2007，《蒯因著作集》，中国人民大学出版社，第 5 卷，第 131 页。

如前所述，P2 含有模态词□，而模态语境下的同一替换要成立，同一必须强化成必然同一，于是，P1″变成下面的 P1‴：

P1‴　　□（n ＝ the G）

如此一来，既然名称 n 与摹状词 the G 必然同一，那么，若名称 n 是所谓的"严格指示词"，则摹状词 the G 也是严格指示词。在模态语境下，两个严格指示词当然可以相互替换。这再次说明，仅从原来的 P1 和 P2 推不出 C，该推理本来就是无效的！

3. 论断 C 和 C′并不相同。既然基本论证要用到隐含前提"n ＝ the G"，于是，名称 n 与摹状词 the G 在语句中的语义作用就是一样的：如果 n 在一模态语句中相对于模态词取宽辖域，则 the G 也相对于模态词取宽辖域；如果 n 相对于模态词取窄辖域，则 the G 也相对于模态词取窄辖域。不可能像在索姆斯的基本论证中那样，名称 n 在论断 C 中相对于模态词取窄辖域，而摹状词 the G 则在 C′中相对于模态词取宽辖域。

达米特早就指出，所谓"严格指示词"就是名称相对于模态词取宽辖域；用我自己的话说，就是针对一个现实个体作各种反事实谈论。并且，索姆斯自己也强调指出："关键之点在于下述断言：语句'亚里士多德是一位哲学家'在一个世界（状态）w 中的真值，取决于我们在现实世界中叫做亚里士多德的那个人在 w 中是不是一位哲学家……我们认为名称亚里士多德是严格指示词的最终根据，就是我们确信：存在某个个体 x，使得对于每一个可能世界（或状态）w，命题'亚里士多德是哲学家'在 w 中是真的，当且仅当，在 w 中 x 是一位哲学家，其他命题的情况与此类似。"（Soames，2002，24）按此道理，既然名称 n 在论断 C 中是严格指示词，则它相对于模态词取宽辖域，比照 C′的写法，C 应该写成：

C″　　［n］□［（Fn→∃y（Fy∧Gy））］

正像从 P1 和 P2 推不出 C′一样，从 P1 和 P2 也推不出 C″。这再次说明，从 P1 和 P2 到 C 的推理是无效的，在这一点上索姆斯弄错了，其错误的根本原因在于：对名称 n 和摹状词 the G 的模态辖域的处理不一致：当 n 取窄辖域时，却要求替换 n 的 the G 总取宽辖域。若照此办法，索姆斯所说的该论证的简化版本也不成立：

（i）　α ＝ β

（ii）　α 是一个必然真理

（iii）　β 是一个必然真理

索姆斯规定 α 必须不含名称，因而其中必定含有摹状词 the G 或指示代词，而 β 中则含有名称 n。于是，(ii) 和 (iii) 可能具有下面的形式：

(ii)′ □[([the x：Gx]Fx)→∃y(Fy∧Gy)]

(iii)′□[(Fn→∃y(Fy∧Gy))]

其中，摹状词 the G 在 (ii)′中相对于模态词取窄辖域，即 (ii)′为 *de dicto* 模态；若规定 (iii)′中的名称 n 必须替换为宽辖域的摹状词，则 (iii)′必须分析为：

(iii)″　[the x：Gx]□[(Fx→∃y(Fy∧Gy))]

从 (i) 和 (ii)′中同样推不出 (iii)″。索姆斯的分析方法也会使一个本来有效的推理变成无效的！因此，索姆斯的基本论证不成立，它不能从宽辖域分析中拯救克里普克的模态论证。

索姆斯还构造了反对宽辖域分析的论证 2，简述如下：

论证 2

P1. 比尔断定：如果 n 存在，则 n 是 F。

P2. "如果 n 存在，则 n 是 F" 是一个必然真理。

C. 比尔断定了一个必然真理。

在 P1 中，规定 F 是 n 所指对象的本质属性，也就是 n 必然具有的特性。既然如此，P2 肯定是真的。并且，从 P1 和 P2 能够合逻辑地推出论断 C。上述论证可以符号化为：

P1′. 比尔断定 [that：n 存在→Fn]

P2′. [the x：Gx]□[x 存在→Fx]

C′. ∃p [比尔断定 p 且 p 是必然真理]

索姆斯论证说，由于名称 n 的涵义由摹状词 the G 给出，并且摹状词相对于模态词取宽辖域，于是 P2 被符号化为 P2′。由于 P2′并没有断定比尔所断定的那个命题是必然的，而只是断定了开语句 "x 存在→Fx" 对于满足摹状词 the G 的所有个体都必然为真，因此，从 P1′和 P2′不能推出 C′。这表明，对摹状词的宽辖域分析会使一个直观上有效的推理（从 P1 和 P2 到 C）变成无效的推理（从 P1′和 P2′到 C′）。因此，宽辖域分析不正确。

我对论证 2 的评论是：当我们反驳克里普克的模态论证时，我们并不是把名称和摹状词的所有出现都解释为相对于模态词取宽辖域（即 *de re* 模态），而不承认它们的有些出现也可能取窄辖域（*de dicto* 模态）。而只是说，当名称作为所谓的 "严格指示词" 出现时，其出现必须解释为宽辖域；既然相应的摹状词给出名称的含义，该摹状词的出现也应该解释为宽辖域。更明确地说，在模态语境中，名称和摹状词相对于模态词的辖域应该相互一致和吻合：若其中一个取宽辖域，则另一个也取宽辖域；若一个取窄辖域，则另一个也取窄辖域。论证 2 的问题是：对名称 n 和摹状词 the G 的模态辖域（通常把"断定"、"知道"、"相信"等也看做是一类特殊的模态词，即"认知模态词"）的处理不一致：n 在 P1 中取窄辖域，而 the G 在 P2 中取宽辖域。如果 the G 在 P2 中也像 n 在 P1 中那样取窄辖域，则从 P1 和 P2 到 C 的推理就是有效的；如果 n 在 P1 中也像 the G 在 P2 中一样取宽辖域，则从 P1 和 P2 到 C 的推理就是无效的（下面讨论存在概括问题时，也会涉及这一点）。所以，索姆斯的论证 2 也不成立。

此外，索姆斯还构造了反对宽辖域分析的论证 3，简述如下：

论证 3

4. 必然地，如果比尔断定（相信）n 是 F 且 n 是 F，则比尔断定（相信）某些真的东西。

5. 必然地，如果比尔断定（相信）n 是 F 且比尔断定（相信）的一切都是真的，则 n 是 F。

从直观上看，论题 4 和 5 表达的几乎都是自明之理。但索姆斯认为，根据摹状词的宽辖域分析，4 和 5 分别符号化为：

4′. ［the x：Gx］□［比尔断定（相信）［that：［the y：Gy］Fy］∧Fx→∃p（比尔断定（相信）p∧p 是真的）］

5′. ［the x：Gx］□［［比尔断定（相信）［that：［the y：Gy］Fy］∧(p)［比尔断定（相信）p→p 是真的］→Fx］

索姆斯指出，这种符号化导致两个问题：（1）4′和 5′分别断定了现实世界中有唯一一个个体具有 G 所表达的性质，但 4 和 5 中却没有这样的意涵，其中的专名可以指称在现实世界中不存在的个体，如比尔所幻想的某个个体，或他所知道的其他虚构个体，即专名可以是空专名。（2）可以构造 4′和 5′的反例，证明它们为假，其中的摹状词 the G 是非严格指示词（详见 Soames，2002，39），而 4 和 5 却是日常语言中明显为真的句子。因此，对摹状词的宽辖域分析不正确。

我认为，索姆斯的上述论证不成立，其主要问题在于：对名称 n 和摹状词 the G 的模态辖域的处理前后不一致：在对命题 4 和 5 的直观理解中，名称 n 取窄辖域，这意味着 n 可以指称一个不存在的但比尔相信它存在的对象，也就是说，n 可以是一个空专名；但在其符号化分析中，相应的摹状词 the G 却取宽辖域，这意味着：必须有唯一一个现实对象满足描述词 G。如此一来，名称 n 的含义还能由摹状词 the G 给出，名称 n 和摹状词 the G 还能够有相同的含义和相同的指称吗?!

Ⅱ. 反驳名称作为严格摹状词的论证不成立

索姆斯还反驳了对克里普克的模态论证的另一种描述论挑战：把摹状词本身严格化，从而成为严格化的摹状词，进而认为名称与严格化的摹状词同义。其具体策略是引入"*actually*"（现实地）算子，关于这个算子，索姆斯解释如下：

> 从句法上说，"*actually*"与一个语句或公式相结合，形成一个更复杂的语句或公式。从语义上说，"*actually*"是一个索引词，像"我"、"此时"、"这里"一样。由于这一点，它的内容——即它对包含它的语句所表达的命题的贡献——随话语语境的不同而变化。（Soames，2002，40）

必须指出，为了强调对一个摹状词的使用（即其指称功能），我在前面引进了"@"这个符号，去固定该摹状词的语义所指，或者说把该摹状词严格化，例如"@ 中亚历山大的老师"固定地指称现实世界中亚历山大的老师，而这个人就是亚里士多德。不过，我的@与索姆斯提到的"*actually*"算子至少有以下两点重要区别：

（1）我用"@"固定地指称我们身在其中的这个现实世界（the actual world），或者说这个真实的世界（the real world）。而"*actually*"算子却是索引性的，随说话者所在的世界不同而不同。例如，假如说话者在柯南道尔所虚构的那个小说世界中说话，那么"现实世界"就是指那个小说世界，索姆斯用"A_w"表示这种索引性的现实世界。我不同意这种处理方法，因为诚如克里普克所言，我们只有我们面前的这一个世界，即现实世界，其他的"可能世界"只不过是某种比喻说法，相当于现实世界的各种可能状况，各种可设想的情形，各种反事实的情形，最好把它们叫做"现实世界的可能状况"。于是，在克里普克那里，在众多的"可能世界"中，现实世界（包括现实个体）具有特殊的地位。我赞同克里普克的上述看法，只允许"@"指称我们生活于其中的这个世界，而"@ 中 F"则指称在@ 中唯一满足摹状词 F 的那个个体，并且它也将在所有可能世界固定地指称那个个体。在这个意义上，"@ 中 F"是一个严格化的摹状词，如果有所谓的"严格指示词"的话。

（2）索姆斯提到的"*Actually*"算子可以被置于一语句之前，如"*Actually* S"："只要 S 是真的，*Actually* S 就是一必然真理。"（Soames，2002，40）并且，该算子可以使一个摹状词严格化："只要限定摹状词 *the x：Fx* 在现实世界中指称个体 o，严格化的摹状词 *the x：actually Fx* 就在 o 存在的所有可能世界中都指称 o（并且绝不指称任何别的东西）。"（Soames，2002，40）相反，我所引入的 "@" 不是语句算子，不能用来修饰语句；它只是一个地点副词，即 "在现实世界中"，在一摹状词前面加上它之后，例如 "@ 中亚历山大的老师"，就使一个有可能漂浮在不同的可能世界之间，在这些世界中指称不同个体的摹状词严格化了，它固定地指称现实世界中唯一满足描述词 F 的那个个体，并且在所有的可能世界中都固定地指称那个个体。从指称的角度讲，这样的严格化摹状词，例如 "@ 中亚历山大的老师"，与相应的名称，例如 "亚里士多德"，总是指称同一个个体。在这个意义上，名称与相应的摹状词同义。

索姆斯指出，把名称等同于被 "*actually*" 严格化的摹状词的做法面临一些困难（参见 Soames，2002，41–42），他自己还构造了如下一个论证，试图证明：用如此方法去反驳克里普克的模态论证是行不通的：

P1. 有可能相信亚里士多德是一位哲学家而不相信有关现实世界 A_W 的任何东西。特别地，存在这样的世界 W^*，其中认知者相信亚里士多德是一位哲学家，对于 A_W 却不相信其中有任何东西是 F，所以对于 A_W 也不相信其中那唯一是 F 的东西是一位哲学家。

P2. 必然地（一个人相信那个现实的 F（the actual F）是一位哲学家，当且仅当，对于现实世界，他相信其中那唯一是 F 的东西是一位哲学家）。

C1. 并非必然地（一个人相信亚里士多德是一位哲学家，当且仅当，那个现实的 F 是一位哲学家）。

P3. 如果在语境 C 中所使用的名称 "亚里士多德" 的内容等同于也在语境 C 中使用的摹状词 "那个现实的 F" 的内容，那么，(i) 由 "亚里士多德是 G" 和 "那个现实的 F 是 G"（所表达的命题）的内容就会是同一的；(ii) 由 "α 相信亚里士多德是 G" 和 "α 相信那个现实的 F 是 G" 所表达的命题就会必然等值；(iii) C1 就会是假的。

C2. 在一个语境中所使用的名称 "亚里士多德" 的内容，与在该语境中所使用的摹状词 "那个现实的 F" 的内容并不相同。

即是说，从前提 P1 和 P2 可以推出结论 C1，再加上前提 P3 后可以推出结论 C2。

我对这个论证的评价是：它把太多的东西牵扯进来，从而把事情弄得非常复杂化，因而不能证明任何东西。其中牵扯的东西至少有：模态词 "必然" 和 "可能"；认知模态词 "相信"；名称作为严格指示词；摹状词作为严格指示词；名称与严格化的摹状词同义，等等。甚至克里普克本人也承认，即使在信念语境中，仅仅"名称作为严格指示词"这一点就会遭遇难以克服的困难（puzzle）①。而索姆斯的论证牵涉如此之多的复杂项目，它能够证明什么呢？即使退一步承认他的归谬论证的结论是正确的，由于该论证至少隐含地利用了三个明显陈述的前提以及五个暗中利用的前提，它能够逆推上去否定什么呢？没有逻辑的理由认为，它恰好否定了名称与摹状词同义这一条，而不是其他七条。并且，我认为，该论证在前提中假设人们可以对作为严格指示词的名称和严格化的摹状词持有不同的信念，这等于说"名称作为严格指示词不同于严格化的摹状词"，再由此证明名称作为严格指示词不同于严格化的摹状词。这里明显有"窃题"（循环论证之一种）之嫌，即把要证明的东西预先安置在前提中。实际上，索姆斯的假设是不成立的。既然名称是严格指示词，它在所有可能世界（信念世界是可能世界之一种）都指称同一个个体；既然严格化的摹状词也在所有可能世界中指称同一个个体，若再假设名称与严格化的摹状词同义，则它们的语义作用也相同，就再也不可能出现如他的前提 P1 所说的那种情况：人们对名称和相应的严格化摹状词持有不同的信念！

索姆斯还提到所谓的"唐纳兰测试"（Donnellan's test）。考虑下面两个句子（我做了一些变动）：

①Ralph believes that t is a spy.

②Ralph believes that（the x：*actually* Fx）is a spy.

这里，①说"拉尔夫相信 t 是一位间谍"，其中"t"是专名；②说"拉尔夫相信（the x：*actually* Fx）是一位间谍"，其中"the x：*actually* Fx"是严格化的摹状词。

据说，唐纳兰认为，从①加上"存在 t 所指称的个体"可以引出如下结论：

③存在某个个体 x 使得拉尔夫相信 x 是一位间谍。

但索姆斯认为，从②中却不能引出类似的结论，因此，名称与摹状词在信念语境中的作用不同。

我这里不去追究唐纳兰关于①和②究竟说了些什么，只给出我自己对①和②的解释。如果按我前面所述的那样，把"*actually*"算子理解为"@"（固定地指称我们面前的这个现实世界），那么，②中的摹状词"the x：*actually* Fx"就固定地指称现实世界中满足描述词 F 的那个现实对象，于是②只允许一种解释：摹状词 the x：*actually* Fx 相对于认知模态词"相信"取宽辖域：

---

① 参看 Kripke，1979。当然，他还认为，这个困难也适用于关于名称的描述论，并非为直接指称论所独有。

④〔the x：*actually* Fx〕Ralph believes that（the x：actually Fx）is a spy.

它说，关于摹状词 the x：*actually* Fx 所指称的那个现实个体，拉尔夫相信他是一位间谍。显然，从④中也可以引出存在性断言③。

相反，如果按索姆斯所述的那样，"*actually*"算子是索引性的，取决于说话者处在哪一个可能世界：说话者所处的那个世界就是"现实世界"。那么，若说话者恰好处在这个真实的世界，②就相当于④，仍可引出存在性断言；反之，若说话者处在某个非真实的可能世界中，则②是说：关于在非真实的可能世界中的那个个体，拉尔夫相信他是一位间谍，由此不能引出存在性断言。

不过，这样一来，①也允许两种不同的解释：

（i）名称 n 相对于认知模态词"相信"取宽辖域：

⑤〔n〕Ralph believes that t is a spy.

它说，关于名称 t 所指称的那个现实个体，拉尔夫相信他是一位间谍。显然，从⑤也可以引出存在性断言。

（ii）名称 t 相对于认知模态词"相信"取窄辖域，那么，①并不必然表示：关于一个现实个体，拉尔夫相信他是一位间谍，因为信念句中的名称 t 既可以指现实个体，也可以指称比尔想象中的个体，或其他虚构个体，例如"福尔摩斯"或"孙悟空"。从如此解释的①不能推出存在性断言③。但如果规定，即使在信念句中，任何名称也都是所谓的"严格指示词"，那么，对①就只有一种解释，那就是⑤。于是，从④和⑤都可以引出存在性断言③。

因此，从①能否引出存在性断言③的问题，就取决于我们把①解释为拉尔夫关于一个现实个体拥有一个信念，还是他关于一个虚构个体拥有一个信念。也就是说，①是有歧义的，允许两种不同的解释。对①的这种理解似乎更合乎直观，也更可理解。①

七、结　语

在本文中，我仔细地、批判性地考察了克里普克所提出的关于严格指示词的直观测试，以及他所构造的三个著名论证：认知论证、语义论证和模态论证，这些论证旨在反驳关于名称的

---

①　当我完成本文之后，才知道 David Sosa 在"Rigidity in the scope of Russell's theory"一文（Noús, vol. 35，no. 1，pp. 1 – 38）中阐述了对 Soames 论证的批评，其批评与我在本文中阐述的批评在主旨上类似，细节上不同。详细说明这些同异，只能留待另文。

描述论，并确证名称是严格指示词，大多数摹状词是非严格指示词。我也批判性地考察了索姆斯为了维护模态论证、反驳对该论证的挑战所构造的那些论证。我得出的结论是：克里普克和索姆斯的那些论证都不成立！

克里普克的认知论证隐含地假设了：如果名称有意义的话，其意义必须保持确定不变；我们有可能获得关于名称意义的一部完善辞典。但我通过考察"牛津"和"DNA"这两个名称的演变史，引出如下结论：（i）名称所指的对象本身处于生长和变化的过程中；（ii）我们关于名称所指对象的知识也处在生长和变化的过程中；（iii）我们关于名称对象的得到公认的知识被辞典编撰者收入辞典，构成相应名称的意义；（iv）仅仅相对于这样一部辞典，关于该名称的某些陈述才是分析的和先验的；（v）但由于辞典本身是我们关于对象的经验知识的总结，因此，辞典具有经验的起源和经验的内容；（vi）因此，刻画名称意义的相应陈述不在任何绝对的意义上是分析的和先验的；（vii）因此，克里普克反对描述论的认知论证不成立。

克里普克的语义论证隐含地假定了："名称或摹状词如何指称对象"这个问题仅仅是名称和对象、语言和世界之间的关系，与使用名称、摹状词和语言的"我们"无关。我证明，这一假定是错误的：名称、摹状词不会自动与对象发生关系，语言不会自动与世界发生关系，是作为名称、摹状词或语言的使用者的"我们"让名称、摹状词和语言与对象和世界发生如此这般的关系。关于一个名称的意义和指称，在很大程度上不取决于我们单个人怎么想，而取决于该名称如何传到我们这里的整个历史，取决于我们的整个语言共同体。确定名称的意义和所指的活动是一种社会的、历史的活动。只有得到我们的语言共同体确认的关于名称所指对象的描述，才能进入相应名称的涵义之中。并且，把名称的涵义解释为确定其所指的充分必要条件，也是对描述论的重要原则——涵义决定所指——的误解和曲解，其中隐含着一个虚假的预设：我们有可能对名称的所指对象作完全充分的描述。

克里普克关于严格指示词的直观测试，从一个形而上学论断"一个对象必定自我同一"过渡到一个语言哲学论题"一个名称是一个对象的严格指示词"，但这种过渡是不合法的，有混淆形而上学和语义学之嫌。他所谓的"严格指示词"可以归结为（非严格的）名称相对于模态词取宽辖域，也就是关于现实个体的谈论，与该对象叫什么名字无关；并且，对于大多数摹状词而言，通过给它们加上一个限制词"在现实世界（@）中"，它们就分别固定地指称我们的现实世界中的一个特定对象，并且在所有可能世界中都固定地指称这个对象，这些摹状词也被严格化了，仍然可以把名字看做是相应摹状词的缩写。因此，克里普克的模态论证不成立。

此外，索姆斯所构造的那些维护模态论证的论证也不成立，后者是基于某些严重的错误之上，主要在于他对名称和摹状词的模态辖域的处理不一致：在模态语境中，他允许名称既取窄辖域又取宽辖域，却要求替代名称的摹状词总取宽辖域。这就等于说，名称与摹状词在模态语境中的作用不相同，他把要证明的结论预先安置在前提中，至少犯有"窃题"（循环论证之一种）的谬误。

我的总结论是：克里普克的整个严格指示词理论及其各种推论并没有得到很好的辩护和证成。我将由此展开对克里普克的严格指示词理论及其各种推论的系统性质疑和批判，并由此发展我本人所主张的关于名称的"因果历史的描述论"，以及一种新的本质主义观点——本质相对性学说。这是后话。

参考文献

［1］Ahmed，Arif，2007，*Saul Kripke*，London，UK：Continium.

［2］Dummett，Michael，1973，"Appendix to Chapter 5：Note on an Attempted Refutation of Frege，" in his *Frege：Philosophy of Language*，New York，NY：Harper & Row，First edition，1973；Second edition，1981. 本文相关注释页码为第二版页码。

——1981，"Chapter 9 and Appendix 3，" in his *The Interpretation of Frege's Philosophy*，London，UK：Duckworth.

［3］Fitch，G. W，2004，*Saul Kripke*，Durham，UK：Acumen Publishing Limited.

［4］Frege，Gottlob，1892，"On Sinn and Bedeutung"，in *The Frege Reader*，edited by Michael Beaney，Oxford，UK：Blackwell Publishers，1997，pp. 151 – 171.

［5］Haack，Susan，2009，"The Growth of Meaning and the Limits of Formalism：Pragmatist Perspectives on Science and Law，" forthcoming，URL = < http：//www. as. miami. edu/phi/assets/haack/growth% 20of% 20meaning,% 20pragmatist% 20perspectives% 20June% 2024% 202008. doc > .

［6］Hintikka，J. and G. Sandu，1995，"The Fallacies of the Theory of Reference"，*Syntheses*，Vol. 104，pp. 245 – 283.

［7］Hughes，Christopher，2006，*Kripke：Names，Necessity，and Identity*，New York，NY：Oxford University Press.

［8］Kripke，Saul，1971，"Identity and Necessity，" in *Identity and Individuation*，edited by M. K. Munitz，New York，NY：New York University Press，pp. 135 – 64. Reprinted in *Meaning and Reference*，edited by A. W. Moore，New York，NY：Oxford University Press，1993，pp. 162 – 191. 在本文的引文注释中，该文被缩写为 IN，所注页码为重印处页码。

——1977，"Speaker's Reference and Semantic Reference，" *Midwest Studies in Philosophy*，Vol. 2，pp. 255 – 276.

——1979，"A Puzzle about Belief，" in *Meaning and Use*，edited by A. Margalit. (Boston，MA：Reidel，1971)，pp. 382 –409.

——1980，*Naming and Necessity* (Paperback Edition, Oxford, UK：Blackwell Publishing, 1981). 在本文的引文注释中，该书被缩写为 *NN*。若引文注释出现"*NN*，10n"，表示引文出处是在该书第 10 页脚注中。[克里普克，2001，《命名与必然性》，梅文译，涂纪亮、朱水林校，上海译文出版社]

[9] Putnam，Hilary，1975，"The Meaning of 'Meaning'，" in his *Philosophical Papers*：*Volume* 2，*Mind*，*Language and Reality*，Cambridge，UK：Cambridge University Press，pp. 215 –271.

[10] Salmon，Nathan，1982，*Reference and Essence*，Oxford，UK：Basil Blackwell.

——1986，*Frege's Puzzle*，Cambridge，MA：MIT Press.

[11] Searle，John，1983，"Chap. 5：Proper Names and Intentionality，" in his *Intentionality*，Cambridge，UK：Cambridge University Press.

[12] Soames，Scott，1998，"The Modal Argument：Wide Scope and Rigidified Descriptions，" *Nous*，Vol. 32，pp. 1 –22.

——2002，*Beyond Rigidity*：*The Unfinished Semantic Agenda of Naming and Necessity*，New York，NY：Oxford University Press.

——2003，"Part 7：Saul Kripke on Naming and Necessity，" in his *Philosophical Analysis in the Twentieth Century*，Vol. 2，Princeton，NJ：Princeton University Press，2003，pp. 333 –460.

——2008，"Reference and Description，" in *The Oxford Handbook of Contemporary Philosophy*，edited by F. Jackson and M. Smith，New York，NY：Oxford University Press，pp. 397 –426.

[13] Sosa，David，2001，"Rigidity in the Scope of Russell's Theory"，*Noûs*，Vol. 35，No. 1，pp. 1 –38.

[14] Stanley，Jason，1997，"Names and Rigid Designation，" in *A Companion to the Philosophy of Language*，edited by Bob Hale and Crispin Wright，Oxford，UK：Blackwell Press，pp. 555 –585.

Refuting Kripke and Soames' Arguments against Descriptivism

Bo Chen

Institute of Foreigh Philosophy, Peking University

Abstract：This paper challenges systematically Kripke's three well-known arguments, i. e. , epistemic argument, semantic argument, and modal argument, which aim to establish that descriptions are not synonymous with names, and to defeat the descriptivism about names. Moreover, It also criticizes carefully Soames' defense of Kripke's modal argument. Its conclusions are that all of Kripke and Soames' arguments are untenable, which based either on some false presuppositions or some mistakes; there's no justification to advocate Kripke's theory of rigid designators as well as its consequences.

Keywords：rigid designators; epistemic argument; semantic argument; modal argument

一个刻画理解、知识与信念的逻辑 UKB

◎ 李小五

中山大学哲学系逻辑与认知研究所

摘　要：相对一个智能主体，对命题的理解是一个重要的认知概念。本文首先直观讨论理解的一般逻辑特性以及它与知识和信念之间的关系，然后给出包含理解、知识和信念作为模态算子的语言和语义。其次，我们提出一个刻画这些模态算子的系统 **UKB**，给出它的证明论的一些结果，然后证明 **UKB** 的框架可靠性和框架完全性。最后，我们证明 **UKB** 的一个扩充系统相对这样的语义有模型可靠性和模型完全性。

关键词：理解；知识；信念；框架可靠性；框架完全性

第一节　引　　论

本文我们要研究的对象是智能主体（intelligence agent）。我们所谓的智能主体是指具有类似人那样的智能的主体。智能主体的知识和信念（简称为知信）是经典认知逻辑已经刻画得比较多的两个重要的认知概念。它们通常被看做是表述智能主体的认知状态的概念。例如，Kφ 和 Bφ 可以分别表示命题（语句）φ 是主体的知识和信念。还有一个重要的认知概念，经典认知逻辑似乎没有注意到，那就是理解。理解也是一个表述主体认知状态的概念。在我们看来，主体理解 φ 就是主体知道 φ 的意义。那么，如何在经典认知逻辑中刻画理解概念，从而揭示理解与知信的关系？本文尝试做这样的工作。

我们的智能主体是理想状态下的主体。例如，它遵循关于理解的必然化规则［参见后面的 3.3（5）］。此规则是从公理 KB、BU 和关于知识的必然化规则推得，所以这种理想性来自于我们对主体关于知识的理想性要求。但我们不希望这样的主体具有完美的理解能力：能理解所有的语句从而做到大彻大悟。一般人的理解能力总是不完美的。

类似对知信概念的处理，本文我们也把理解看做是一个模态算子。用 Uφ 表示智能主体理解 φ。那么 Uφ 有些什么逻辑特性呢？下面我们先来作一些直观的讨论。

逻辑主要研究联结符的逻辑含义。这里的联结符指的是布尔联结符（可以解释为真值函数）和模态算子。所以我们下面的讨论围绕联结符展开。

1. 主体总能理解恒真和恒假这两个概念。用语形表示就是主体能理解恒真式"φ 或并非 φ"和恒假式"φ 且并非 φ"。这两个公式逻辑学家通常视为 0 元联结符。

2. 主体理解一个命题 φ 自然也应该理解 φ 的否定，反之亦然。用公式来表示就是：$U\varphi \leftrightarrow U\neg\varphi$。它的直观意义是：理解 φ 当且仅当理解 φ 的否定。换句话说，知道 φ 的意义等于知道 φ 的否定的意义。

3. 那么理解与知信是什么关系呢？通常我们认为 $K\varphi \to B\varphi$ 应该成立，即主体总是相信自己知道的东西，或者说，知识就是信念。顺着此思路，我们认为 $B\varphi \to U\varphi$ 也应该成立，即主体总是理解自己相信的东西，或者说，信念就是理解。除非愚昧，主体应该理解自己相信的东西，从而理解自己知道的东西：知识总是理解的。

4. 智能主体应该具有反思能力。不仅对知信来说如此，对理解来说也应该如此。所以我们应该有 $U\varphi \to UU\varphi$ 和 $\neg U\varphi \to U\neg U\varphi$。实际上，我们应该加强到 $U\varphi \to KU\varphi$ 和 $\neg U\varphi \to K\neg U\varphi$。

5. 若主体理解两个命题 φ 和 ψ，则它自然也就应该理解这两个命题的二元布尔复合命题"φ 且 ψ"、"φ 或 ψ"、"若 φ 则 ψ"和"φ 当且仅当 ψ"。这个原则可以称为**理解的由简致复原则**。例如，下列公式就是此原则的一个特例：

(C_U)　$U\varphi \wedge U\psi \to U(\varphi \wedge \psi)$。

这里自然出现的一个问题：主体是否也应该遵循**理解的由复致简原则**？也就是说，下面的公式是否成立：

$U(\varphi O\psi) \to U\varphi \wedge U\psi$，其中 $O \in \{\wedge, \vee, \to, \leftrightarrow\}$。

考虑

(M_U)　$U(\varphi \wedge \psi) \to U\varphi \wedge U\psi$。

乍一看主体应该遵循此原则。但实际上不然。假设在当下语言的范围内，主体有一个命题 φ 无法理解（否则它具有完美理解能力）。据 M_U 我们有

(#)　$U(\varphi \wedge \neg\varphi) \to U\varphi$。

虽然主体不理解 φ，但它总该理解 φ∧¬φ！这样据（#），它理解 φ，即主体理解它不理解的东西。矛盾。

这里实际有两种理解：对单个命题的理解和对某种特殊的联结符组合的理解。用上面的例子来说，就是 $U\varphi$ 和 $U(\varphi \wedge \neg\varphi)$。像 φ∧¬φ 和 φ∨¬φ 的意义应该是固定的，而且我们都知道，所以即使我们不知道 φ 的意义也应该知道 φ∧¬φ 和 φ∨¬φ 的意义。若我们要刻画的主体连这些

都不理解，那么它也太没有智能了。

据上面的讨论，我们大概能接受下面的命题：

$$¬(φ∧ψ↔φ∧¬φ)∧U(φ∧ψ)→Uφ∧Uψ。$$

这里 $¬(φ∧ψ↔φ∧¬φ)$ 表示 $φ∧ψ$ 不是矛盾命题。相对经典逻辑，上述公式等价

$$(RM_U) \quad φ∧ψ∧U(φ∧ψ)→Uφ∧Uψ。$$

令 RM_U 中的 $ψ$ 是 $¬φ$。从直观上说，只有在不可能世界（状态）中，主体才理解它不理解的东西。所以，这种情况对我们无害。

我们下面的工作就是要建立一个逻辑来刻画单个智能主体的知信与理解及其相互关系，为此我们要给出适合的语义和系统来表述上面我们提到的几点要求。

本文以下提到但未定义的概念和记号，请参见李小五的 [1]。

第二节　语言与语义

令 $PV: = \{p_1, \ldots, p_n, \ldots\}$ 是一个由可数多个命题变元组成的集合。

定义 2.1

（1）**认知语言** L 是由以下规则给出的全体公式 $φ$ 的集合：

$φ: = p | ¬φ | (φ∧ψ) | Kφ | Bφ | Uφ$，其中 $p ∈ PV$。

（2）任给 $φ, ψ∈L$，我们引入下列缩写：

$(φ∨ψ): = ¬(¬φ∧¬ψ)$，

$(φ→ψ): = (¬φ∨ψ)$，

$(φ↔ψ): = ((φ→ψ)∧(ψ→φ))$，

$⊤: = (p_1∨¬p_1)$，

$⊥: = ¬⊤$，

$φ_1∧\ldots∧φ_n: = ⊤$，其中 $n = 0$。⊣

说明：下面我们总是省略一个公式最外面的括号。至于一个公式内部的括号，我们根据下面符号左强右弱的结合力来省略：

$¬, K, B, U, ∧, ∨, →, ↔$

我们还规定同类联结符满足右向结合原则，因此 $φ_1→\ldots→φ_n$ 表示 $φ_1→(φ_2→(\ldots→φ_n)\ldots)$。

任给集合 X，我们总用 $℘(X)$ 表示 X 的幂集。

定义 2.2

（1） L 的**框架**是一个四元组 (W,R,S,N)，其中

$W \neq \varnothing$ 是一个状态集；

R 是 W 上的一个二元关系使得下列框架条件成立：对所有 $w,u,v \in W$，

（自返性） wRw，

（欧性） wRu 且 $wRv \Rightarrow uRv$；

S 是 W 上的一个二元关系使得下列框架条件成立：对所有 $w,u,v \in W$，

（持续性） $\exists x \in W(wSx)$，

（传递性） wSu 且 $uSv \Rightarrow wSv$，

（欧性） wSu 且 $wSv \Rightarrow uSv$；

N 是从 W 到 $\wp(\wp(W))$ 中的映射使得下列框架条件成立：对所有 $w \in W$ 和 $X \subseteq W$，

（全性） $W \in N(w)$，

（补等性） $X \in N(w) \Leftrightarrow W - X \in N(w)$。

此外，R，S 和 N 还满足下列框架条件：令 $R(w) = \{u \in W \mid wRu\}$ 且 $S(w) = \{u \in W \mid wSu\}$，

（知信关联性） $S(w) \subseteq R(w)$，

（信解关联性） $S(w) \subseteq X \Rightarrow X \in N(w)$，

（解知正关联性） $X \in N(w) \Rightarrow \forall u \in W(wRu \Rightarrow X \in N(u))$，

（解知负关联性） $X \notin N(w) \Rightarrow \forall u \in W(wRu \Rightarrow X \notin N(u))$。

（2） L 的**模型**是一个五元组 (W,R,S,N,V)，其中 (W,R,S,N) 是一个框架，V 是从 PV 到 $\wp(W)$ 中的一个映射。我们也称 V 是 (W,R,S,N) 上的一个**赋值**。

（3） 令 Frame 是所有框架组成的类，Model 是所有模型组成的类。⊣

说明：R 和 S 的规定，除了信解关联性，都是通常逻辑学家公认的。

$N(w)$ 直观表示：主体在状态 w 中理解的所有命题都在 $N(w)$ 中。通常称 N 是邻域映射。

定义 2.3（真值集定义） 令 $M = (W,R,S,N,V) \in$ Model。对于每一个 $\varphi \notin$ PV，相对于 M，如下递归定义 φ 的**真值集** $V(\varphi)$：对所有 $w \in W$，

（1） $w \in V(\neg\varphi) \Leftrightarrow w \notin V(\varphi)$，

（2） $w \in V(\varphi \wedge \psi) \Leftrightarrow w \in V(\varphi)$ 且 $w \in V(\psi)$，

（3） $w \in V(\mathrm{K}\varphi) \Leftrightarrow R(w) \subseteq V(\varphi)$，

（4） $w \in V(\mathrm{B}\varphi) \Leftrightarrow S(w) \subseteq V(\varphi)$，

（5） $w \in V(\mathrm{U}\varphi) \Leftrightarrow V(\varphi) \in N(w)$。⊣

易证下列引理:

引理 2.4　令 $(W,R,S,N,V) \in \text{Model}$。则

(1) $V(\neg\varphi) = W - V(\varphi)$;

　　$V(\varphi \wedge \psi) = V(\varphi) \cap V(\psi)$;

　　$V(\varphi \vee \psi) = V(\varphi) \cup V(\psi)$;

　　$V(\bot) = \varnothing$,　　$V(\top) = W$。

(2) $V(\varphi) \cap V(\varphi \to \psi) \subseteq V(\psi)$。

(3) $V(\varphi \to \psi) = W \Leftrightarrow V(\varphi) \subseteq V(\psi)$。

(4) $V(\varphi \leftrightarrow \psi) = W \Leftrightarrow V(\varphi) = V(\psi)$。$\dashv$

第三节　系统与证明论

本节我们要给出一个刻画理解和知信的系统, 并推出一些我们想要的东西。

定义 3.1　**认知系统 UKB** 定义如下:

(Taut) 全体重言式的代入特例,

(K_K) $K(\varphi \to \psi) \to K\varphi \to K\psi$,

(K_B) $B(\varphi \to \psi) \to B\varphi \to B\psi$,

(T_K) $K\varphi \to \varphi$,

(D_B) $\neg B\bot$,

(4_K) $K\varphi \to KK\varphi$,　　　　　　(知识的正反思)

(4_B) $B\varphi \to BB\varphi$,　　　　　　(信念的正反思)

(5_K) $\neg K\varphi \to K\neg K\varphi$,　　　　(知识的负反思)

(5_B) $\neg B\varphi \to B\neg B\varphi$,　　　　(信念的负反思)

(N_U) $U\top$,

(NE_U) $U\varphi \leftrightarrow U\neg\varphi$,

(KB) $K\varphi \to B\varphi$,　　　　　　(知总信)

(BU) $B\varphi \to U\varphi$,　　　　　　(信总理解)

(4_U) $U\varphi \to KU\varphi$,　　　　　(理解的正反思)

(5_U) $\neg U\varphi \to K\neg U\varphi$,　　　(理解的负反思)

(MP) φ, $\varphi \to \psi / \psi$。

（RN_K） $\varphi/K\varphi$，

（RE_U） $\varphi\leftrightarrow\psi/U\varphi\leftrightarrow U\psi$。⊣

定义 3.2 φ 是 **UKB** 的**内定理**，记为⊢φ，如果 φ 在 **UKB** 中有一个形式证明，即存在一个公式序列 φ_1，…，φ_n 使得对每一个 $1\leq i\leq n$，φ_i 是 **UKB** 的某个公理的代入特例，或者 φ_i 是通过 **UKB** 的规则从它前面的公式得到。⊣

引理 3.3 下面是 **UKB** 的导出规则和内定理：

（1）$\varphi_1\wedge\ldots\wedge\varphi_n\rightarrow\varphi/K\varphi_1\wedge\ldots\wedge K\varphi_n\rightarrow K\varphi$，

　　$\varphi_1\wedge\ldots\wedge\varphi_n\rightarrow\varphi/B\varphi_1\wedge\ldots\wedge B\varphi_n\rightarrow B\varphi$。　　　（证明如通常）

（2）$\varphi\leftrightarrow\psi/K\varphi\leftrightarrow K\psi$，　　$\varphi\leftrightarrow\psi/B\varphi\leftrightarrow B\psi$。　　　（据（1））

（3）（**等价置换定理**）$\psi\leftrightarrow\theta/\varphi\leftrightarrow\varphi(\theta/\psi)$，

　　　　　　　　　　其中 $\varphi(\theta/\psi)$ 表示用 ψ 替换 φ 中 θ 的若干出现得到的公式。

（4）$K\varphi\rightarrow U\varphi$。　（据公理 KB 和 BU）

（5）$\varphi/B\varphi$，　　$\varphi/U\varphi$。　　（据规则 RN_K 和公理 KB 以及 BU）

（6）$U\perp$。　（据公理 N_U 和 NE_U）

（7）$U\varphi\rightarrow BU\varphi$，$U\varphi\rightarrow UU\varphi$。　　（据公理 4_U，KB 和 BU）

（8）$\neg U\varphi\rightarrow B\neg U\varphi$，$\neg U\varphi\rightarrow U\neg U\varphi$。　　（据公理 5_U，KB 和 BU）

（9）$K\varphi\vee K\neg\varphi\rightarrow U\varphi$。　　（据（4）和 NE_U）

（10）$K\varphi\rightarrow U\varphi\wedge\varphi$。　　（据（4）和 T_K）

（11）$U\varphi\leftrightarrow KU\varphi$，$\neg U\varphi\leftrightarrow K\neg U\varphi$。　　（据 4_U，5_U 和 T_K）

证明：证（3）：据 RE_U 和（2），且施归纳于公式 φ 的结构，详细证明如通常。⊣

说明：从 **UKB** 推出来的东西在我们看来很自然地刻画了理解这一概念。

下面我们用 L_0 表示用 PV 中的原子公式和布尔联结符 $\neg$，$\wedge$ 如上构成的全体公式的集合，用 PC_0 表示 L_0 表述的经典命题演算：PC_0 = 用 L_0 表述的全体重言式 + MP。我们来研究 **UKB** 与 PC_0 的关系。我们要证明前者可以协调地退化为后者。

定义 3.4

（1）定义从 L 到 L_0 的**翻译映射** t 如下：

$t(p)=p$，　　对所有 $p\in PV$；

$t(\neg\varphi)=\neg t(\varphi)$；

$t(\varphi\wedge\psi)=t(\varphi)\wedge t(\psi)$；

$t(K\varphi)=t(B\varphi)=t(\varphi)$；

$t(\mathrm{U}\varphi) = \top$。

（2）对每一公式 $\varphi \in \mathrm{Form}$，称 $t(\varphi)$ 是 φ 的 t - **翻译**。⊣

据上面的定义，易证

$t(\varphi \vee \psi) = t(\varphi) \vee t(\psi)$，

$t(\varphi \rightarrow \psi) = t(\varphi) \rightarrow t(\psi)$，

$t(\varphi \leftrightarrow \psi) = t(\varphi) \leftrightarrow t(\psi)$。

定义 3.5 令 **S** 和 **T** 是两个公理化系统。

称 **S** 能 t - **退化**为 **T**，当且仅当 **S** 的所有内定理都能 t - 翻译为 **T** 的内定理。⊣

定理 3.6 **UKB** 能 t - 退化为 $\mathbf{PC}_0$。

证明：易证

（1）若 φ 是 **UKB** 的公理，则 φ 的 t - 翻译是 $\mathbf{PC}_0$ 的内定理；

（2）若 R 是 **UKB** 的规则，则 R 的 t - 翻译是 $\mathbf{PC}_0$ 的导出规则。

所以

（3）若 φ 是 **UKB** 的内定理，则 φ 的 t - 翻译是 $\mathbf{PC}_0$ 的内定理。⊣

定义 3.7 称系统 **S** 是**协调系统**，当且仅当，不存在 φ 使得 φ 和 $\neg\varphi$ 都是 **S** 的内定理。⊣

定理 3.8 **UKB** 是协调的。

证明：我们知道 $\mathbf{PC}_0$ 是协调。假设 **UKB** 不协调，则存在 φ 使得 φ 和 $\neg\varphi$ 都是 **UKB** 的内定理，则据上面的定理，$t(\varphi)$ 和 $\neg t(\varphi)$ 都是 $\mathbf{PC}_0$ 的内定理，矛盾于 $\mathbf{PC}_0$ 的协调性。⊣

第四节　框架可靠性定理

定义 4.1（有效性定义） 令 $F = (W,R,S,N) \in \mathrm{Frame}$ 和 $M = (W,R,S,N,V) \in \mathrm{Model}$。

（1）φ 在 M 中有效，记为 $M \vDash \varphi$，$\Leftrightarrow V(\varphi) = W$；否则记为 $M \nvDash \varphi$。

（2）φ 在 F 上有效，记为 $F \vDash \varphi$，$\Leftrightarrow$对 F 上的每一赋值 V，$V(\varphi) = W$；否则记为 $F \nvDash \varphi$。

（3）规则 $\varphi_1, \ldots, \varphi_n / \varphi$ 相对于 M 保持有效性$\Leftrightarrow$

$V(\varphi_1) = \ldots = V(\varphi_n) = W \Rightarrow V(\varphi) = W$。⊣

如通常易证：

引理 4.2 令 $(W,R,S,N,V) \in \mathrm{Model}$。则

（1）$V(\neg\varphi) = W - V(\varphi)$，

$V(\varphi \wedge \psi) = V(\varphi) \cap V(\psi)$，

$$V(\varphi \vee \psi) = V(\varphi) \cup V(\psi),$$

$$V(\perp) = \varnothing, \qquad V(\top) = W_\circ$$

(2) $V(\varphi) \cap V(\varphi \rightarrow \psi) \subseteq V(\psi)$。

(3) $V(\varphi \rightarrow \psi) = W \Leftrightarrow V(\varphi) \subseteq V(\psi)$。

(4) $V(\varphi \leftrightarrow \psi) = W \Leftrightarrow V(\varphi) = V(\psi)$。⊣

定义 4.3 令 **S** 是一个系统, 且令 **C** 是一个框架类。

(1) 称 **S** 相对 **C** 是**框架可靠系统**, 当且仅当, **S** 的内定理在 **C** 的所有框架中有效。

(2) 称 **S** 相对 **C** 是**框架完全系统**, 当且仅当, 在 **C** 的所有框架中有效的公式是 **S** 的内定理。⊣

定理 4.4 (框架可靠性定理) UKB 相对 Frame 是框架可靠的。

证明: 任给框架 $F = (W, R, S, N)$ 和 F 上赋值 V。

只须验证 **UKB** 的每一公理相对 $M = (F, V)$ 有效且推理规则相对 M 保持有效性。

验证公理 N_U: 据定义 2.2 的框架条件 "全性", 任给 $w \in W$, 有 $W \in N(w)$, 所以据 $V(\top) = W$ (见 4.2) 和真值集定义, 有 $w \in V(U\top)$。

验证公理 NE_U: 据定义 2.2 的框架条件 "补等性", 任给 $w \in W$, 有

$$V(\varphi) \in N(w) \Leftrightarrow W - V(\varphi) \in N(w),$$

所以据 $W - V(\varphi) = V(\neg\varphi)$ 和真值集定义, 有

$$w \in V(U\varphi) \Leftrightarrow w \in V(U\neg\varphi),$$

从而有 $w \in V(U\varphi \leftrightarrow U\neg\varphi)$。

验证公理 KB: 据定义 2.2 的框架条件 "知信关联性", 易证 $w \in V(K\varphi \rightarrow B\varphi)$。

验证公理 BU: 据定义 2.2 的框架条件 "信解关联性", 任给 $w \in W$, 有

$$S(w) \subseteq V(\varphi) \Rightarrow V(\varphi) \in N(w),$$

所以据真值集定义易见 $w \in V(B\varphi \rightarrow U\varphi)$。

验证公理 4_U: 据定义 2.2 的框架条件 "解知正关联性", 任给 $w \in W$, 有

$$V(\varphi) \in N(w) \Rightarrow \forall u \in W(wRu \Rightarrow V(\varphi) \in N(u)),$$

所以据真值集定义, 有

$$w \in V(U\varphi) \Rightarrow \forall u \in W(wRu \Rightarrow u \in V(U\varphi)),$$

再据真值集定义易证 $w \in V(U\varphi \rightarrow KU\varphi)$。

验证公理 5_U: 据定义 2.2 的框架条件 "解知负关联性", 任给 $w \in W$, 有

$$V(\varphi) \notin N(w) \Rightarrow \forall u \in W(wRu \Rightarrow V(\varphi) \notin N(u)),$$

所以据真值集定义和2.4，有

$$w \in V(\neg U\varphi) \Rightarrow \forall u \in W(wRu \Rightarrow u \in V(\neg U\varphi)),$$

再据真值集定义易证 $w \in V(\neg U\varphi \rightarrow K \neg U\varphi)$。

验证规则 RE_U：设 $\varphi \leftrightarrow \psi$。则 $V(\varphi) = V(\psi)$，所以任给 $w \in W$，有

$$V(\varphi) \in N(w) \Leftrightarrow V(\psi) \in N(w),$$

所以据真值集定义，有 $w \in V(U\varphi \leftrightarrow U\psi)$。

其余公理和规则的验证如通常。⊣

第五节　完全性定理

定义 5.1

令 **S** 是一个系统，且令 w 是公式集。

（1）称 w 是 **S－一致集**，当且仅当，对所有有穷序列 $\varphi_1, \ldots, \varphi_n \in w$，有

$\nvdash_S \neg(\varphi_1 \wedge \ldots \wedge \varphi_n)$。

（2）称 w 是**极大集**，当且仅当，对所有 $\varphi \in L$，$\varphi \in w$ 或 $\neg\varphi \in w$。

（3）称 w 是 **S－极大一致集**，当且仅当，w 既是 **S－一致的又是极大的**。

（4）称 **S** 是**一致系统**，当且仅当，**S** 的全体内定理的集合 Th(**S**) 是 **S－一致的**。⊣

说明：在不致混淆之处，我们省略上述记号中的下标 **S** 和参数 **S－**。

引理 5.2　**UKB** 是一致的。

证明：假设 **UKB** 不一致。则 Th(**UKB**) 不一致，所以存在 $\varphi_1, \ldots, \varphi_n \in$ Th(**UKB**) 使得

⊢ $\neg(\varphi_1 \wedge \ldots \wedge \varphi_n)$。

另一方面，因为 $\varphi_1, \ldots, \varphi_n \in$ Th(**UKB**)，所以易证

⊢ $\varphi_1 \wedge \ldots \wedge \varphi_n$。

据定义3.7，**UKB** 不是协调的，矛盾于定理3.8。⊣

因为 **UKB** 是 **PC₀** 的扩充，所以如通常证明①，我们有下列结果。

引理 5.3　令 w 是公式集。

（1）φ 属于每一以 w 为子集的极大一致集，当且仅当，存在 $\varphi_1, \ldots, \varphi_n \in w$ 使得

⊢ $\varphi_1 \wedge \ldots \wedge \varphi_n \rightarrow \varphi$。

―――――――――――――――

① 参见李小五 [1]。

（2）若 w 是极大一致的，则

$\neg\varphi\in w\Leftrightarrow\varphi\notin w$,

$\varphi\wedge\psi\in w\Leftrightarrow\varphi\in w$ 且 $\psi\in w$,

$\varphi\vee\psi\in w\Leftrightarrow\varphi\in w$ 或 $\psi\in w$,

$\varphi\in w$ 且 $\vdash\varphi\rightarrow\psi\Rightarrow\psi\in w$,

$\varphi\in w$ 且 $\varphi\rightarrow\psi\in w\Rightarrow\psi\in w$。

（3）$\mathrm{Th}(\mathbf{UKB})\subseteq w$。

（4）（**Lindenbaum–引理**）每一一致集都可以扩充为一个极大一致集：若 u 是一致集，则存在极大一致集 v 使得 $u\subseteq v$。

（5）若 $\nvdash\varphi$，则存在极大一致集 u 使得 $\varphi\notin u$；

若 $\nvdash\varphi\rightarrow\psi$，则存在极大一致集 u 使得 $\varphi\in u$ 且 $\psi\notin u$。⊣

定义 5.4 $|\varphi|:=\{w\mid w$ 是极大一致集使得 $\varphi\in w\}$。⊣

引理 5.5

（1）$|\neg\varphi|=W-|\varphi|$，其中 W 是所有极大一致集的集合，

$|\varphi\wedge\psi|=|\varphi|\cap|\psi|$,

$|\varphi\vee\psi|=|\varphi|\cup|\psi|$,

$|\bot|=\varnothing$, $|\top|=W$。

（2）$|\varphi|\cap|\varphi\rightarrow\psi|\subseteq|\psi|$。

（3）$|\varphi\rightarrow\psi|=W\Leftrightarrow|\varphi|\subseteq|\psi|\Leftrightarrow\vdash\varphi\rightarrow\psi$。

（4）$|\varphi\leftrightarrow\psi|=W\Leftrightarrow|\varphi|=|\psi|\Leftrightarrow\vdash\varphi\leftrightarrow\psi$。

证明：据上一引理易证。⊣

定义 5.6 令 w 是公式集。

$K^-w:=\{\varphi\mid K\varphi\in w\}$, $B^-w:=\{\varphi\mid B\varphi\in w\}$。⊣

引理 5.7 令 w 是极大一致集。则

（1）$K\varphi\in w\Leftrightarrow$任给极大一致集 u，若 $K^-w\subseteq u$，则 $\varphi\in u$。

（2）$B\varphi\in w\Leftrightarrow$任给极大一致集 u，若 $B^-w\subseteq u$，则 $\varphi\in u$。

证明：（1）"$\Rightarrow$"：设 $K\varphi\in w$。任给极大一致集 u 使得 $K^-w\subseteq u$。易见 $\varphi\in u$。

"$\Leftarrow$"：设

① 任给极大一致集 u，若 $K^-w\subseteq u$，则 $\varphi\in u$。

这意味 φ 属于每一以 K^-w 为子集的极大一致集。据 5.3，存在 $\varphi_1, \ldots, \varphi_n \in K^-w$ 使得

② $\vdash \varphi_1 \wedge \ldots \wedge \varphi_n \rightarrow \varphi$。

据引理 3.3，有

③ $\vdash K\varphi_1 \wedge \ldots \wedge K\varphi_n \rightarrow K\varphi$。

因为 $\varphi_1, \ldots, \varphi_n \in K^-w$，所以 $K\varphi_1, \ldots, K\varphi_n \in w$，因此据③和引理 5.3，有 $K\varphi \in w$。

同理可证（2）。⊣

定义 5.8

（1）定义 **UKB** 的**典范框架** (W, R, S, N) 如下：

① $W = \{ w \mid w \text{ 是极大一致集} \}$；

② $wRu \Leftrightarrow K^-w \subseteq u$，对所有 $w, u \in W$；

③ $wSu \Leftrightarrow B^-w \subseteq u$，对所有 $w, u \in W$；

④ $\mid \varphi \mid \in N(w) \Leftrightarrow U\varphi \in w$，对所有 $w \in W$ 和公式 φ。

（2）定义 **UKB** 的**典范模型** (W, R, S, N, V) 如下：(W, R, S, N) 是 **UKB** 的典范框架，且

⑤ $V(p) = \mid p \mid$，对每一 $p \in \mathrm{PV}$。⊣

说明：

（1）**UKB** 的典范框架相对 **UKB** 来说不是唯一的，因为如上定义的邻域映射不是唯一的：当 $X \subseteq W$ 且不存在 φ 使得 $\mid \varphi \mid = X$ 时，这样的 X 可以加入 $N(w)$ 也可以不加入。

（2）据引理 5.2，**UKB** 是一致的，所以 W 是非空的。

定理 5.9（典范模型基本定理） 令 (W, R, S, N, V) 是 **UKB** 的典范模型。

（1）$\varphi \in w \Leftrightarrow w \in V(\varphi)$，对每一 $w \in W$ 和公式 φ。

（2）$\mid \varphi \mid = V(\varphi)$，对每一公式 φ。

证明：

（2）从（1）易得。所以只须证（1）。施归纳于 φ 的结构。

句符的情况据定义 5.8 的⑤。

布尔联结词 ¬ 和 ∧ 的情况如通常所证。

令 $\varphi = K\psi$。则

$\varphi \in w \Leftrightarrow K\psi \in w$

$\quad\quad\quad \Leftrightarrow R(w) \subseteq \mid \psi \mid \quad\quad\quad$ 据引理 5.7 和定义 5.8

$\quad\quad\quad \Leftrightarrow R(w) \subseteq V(\psi) \quad\quad\quad$ 据归纳假设

$$\Leftrightarrow w\in V(\mathrm{K}\psi) \qquad\qquad 据真值集定义$$

$$\Leftrightarrow w\in V(\varphi)。$$

令 $\varphi=\mathrm{B}\psi$。则同理可证。

令 $\varphi=\mathrm{U}\psi$。则

$$\varphi\in w \Leftrightarrow \mathrm{U}\psi\in w$$

$$\Leftrightarrow |\psi|\in N(w) \qquad\qquad 据定义 5.8$$

$$\Leftrightarrow V(\psi)\in N(w) \qquad\qquad 据归纳假设$$

$$\Leftrightarrow w\in V(\mathrm{U}\psi) \qquad\qquad 据真值集定义$$

$$\Leftrightarrow w\in V(\varphi)。\dashv$$

定理 5.10　令 $M=(W,R,S,N,V)$ 是 **UKB** 的典范模型。则对每一公式 φ，有
$M\models\varphi\Leftrightarrow\vdash\varphi$。

证明：

$$\vdash\varphi\Leftrightarrow|\varphi|=W \qquad\qquad 据引理 5.3$$

$$\Leftrightarrow V(\varphi)=W \qquad\qquad 据上一定理$$

$$\Leftrightarrow M\models\varphi \qquad\qquad 据有效性定义 4.1。\dashv$$

定义 5.11　令 (W,R,S,N,V) 是 **UKB** 的典范模型，且令 $X\in\wp(W)$。
称 X 是一个命题 $\Leftrightarrow$ 存在 $\varphi\in L$ 使得 $|\varphi|=X$。$\dashv$

引理 5.12　令 (W,R,S,N,V) 是 **UKB** 的典范模型，且令 $X\in\wp(W)$。则
X 是一个命题 $\Leftrightarrow W-X$ 是一个命题。

证明：设 X 是一个命题。则存在 $\varphi\in L$ 使得 $|\varphi|=X$。再据 5.5，

$$W-X=W-|\varphi|=|\neg\varphi|,$$

所以 $W-X$ 是一个命题。

设 $W-X$ 是一个命题。则存在 $\varphi\in L$ 使得 $|\varphi|=W-X$。下证

(#)　$X=|\neg\varphi|$。

易见

$$w\in X\Leftrightarrow w\notin W-X \qquad\qquad 据集合论基本事实$$

$$\Leftrightarrow w\notin|\varphi| \qquad\qquad 据 |\varphi|=W-X$$

$$\Leftrightarrow w\in|\neg\varphi|。 \qquad\qquad 据 5.3$$

据 (#)，易见 X 是一个命题。$\dashv$

定义 5.13 定义 **UKB** 的**适当结构**（proper structure）$M^* = (W,R,S,N,V)$ 如下：

（1） $W = \{w \mid w$ 是极大一致集$\}$；

（2） R 和 S 如 5.8 定义；

（3） 对任意 $w \in W$，$N(w) = N_1(w) \cup N_2(w)$，其中

$N_1(w) = \{\mid \varphi \mid \mid$ 存在 $\mathrm{U}\varphi \in w\}$，

$N_2(w) = \{X \in \wp(W) \mid X$ 不是命题$\}$；①

（4） $V(p) = \mid p \mid$，对每一 $p \in \mathrm{PV}$。$\dashv$

说明：易见适当结构对一个系统来说是惟一的。

引理 5.14

令 $M^* = (W,R,S,N,V)$ 如上定义。则 $F^* = (W,R,S,N)$ 是 **UKB** 的典范框架。

证明：据定义 5.8，只须证：对所有 $w \in W$ 和公式 φ，

$$\mid \varphi \mid \in N(w) \Leftrightarrow \mathrm{U}\varphi \in w.$$

令 $\mathrm{U}\varphi \in w$。据上一定义，$\mid \varphi \mid \in N_1(w)$，所以 $\mid \varphi \mid \in N(w)$。

令 $\mid \varphi \mid \in N(w)$。据上一定义，易见 $\mid \varphi \mid \notin N_2(w)$，所以 $\mid \varphi \mid \in N_1(w)$。则存在 $\mathrm{U}\psi \in w$ 使得 $\mid \psi \mid = \mid \varphi \mid$。据引理 5.5，有 $\vdash \varphi \leftrightarrow \psi$。据 $\mathrm{RE_U}$，有 $\vdash \mathrm{U}\varphi \leftrightarrow \mathrm{U}\psi$。所以据 5.3，对所有 $w \in W$，

$$\mathrm{U}\varphi \in w \Leftrightarrow \mathrm{U}\psi \in w.$$

再据 $\mathrm{U}\psi \in w$，有 $\mathrm{U}\varphi \in w$。$\dashv$

定理 5.15（**框架完全性定理**） **UKB** 相对 Frame 是框架完全的。

证明：据上一引理，F^* 是典范框架。所以为了证明 **UKB** 相对 Frame 是框架完全的，据定理 5.10，只须证明 $F^* \in \mathrm{Frame}$，为此只须证 F^* 满足定义 2.2 的框架条件。

如通常易证 R 满足自返性和欧性，S 满足持续性、传递性和欧性，且 R 和 S 满足知信关联性。下面我们来验证涉及邻域映射的框架条件。任给 $w \in W$ 和 $X \subseteq W$。

验证全性：据引理 5.3，公理 $\mathrm{N_U}$ 在 w 中，所以 $\mathrm{U}\top \in w$，因此据 5.13，$\mid \top \mid \in N_1(w)$，所以 $\mid \top \mid \in N(w)$，再据 5.5，$W \in N(w)$。

验证补等性：任给 $X \in N(w)$。要证 $W - X \in N(w)$。

情况 1 $X \in N_1(w)$。则据 5.13，存在 $\mathrm{U}\varphi \in w$ 使得 $\mid \varphi \mid = X$。据 5.3，公理 $\mathrm{NE_U}$ 在 w 中，因此 $\mathrm{U}\neg\varphi \in w$，所以 $\mid \neg\varphi \mid \in N_1(w)$，因此据 5.5，$W - \mid \varphi \mid \in N_1(w)$，所以 $W - X \in N(w)$。

---

① 易见 N 是从 W 到 $\wp(\wp(W))$ 中的映射。

情况 2 $X \in N_2(w)$。则 X 不是命题。据 5.12，$W - X$ 也不是命题。因此 $W - X \in N_2(w)$，从而 $W - X \in N(w)$。

任给 $X \in W$ 使得 $W - X \in N(w)$。要证 $X \in N(w)$。

情况 1 $W - X \in N_1(w)$。则据 5.13，存在 $\mathrm{U}\varphi \in w$ 使得 $|\varphi| = W - X$。据 5.12 的证明，我们有

(#) $X = |\neg\varphi|$。

因为 $\mathrm{U}\varphi \in w$，所以据公理 $\mathrm{NE_U}$ 有 $\mathrm{U}\neg\varphi \in w$，所以 $|\neg\varphi| \in N_1(w)$，因此据 (#)，$X \in N_1(w)$，所以 $X \in N(w)$。

情况 2 $W - X \in N_2(w)$。则 $W - X$ 不是命题。据 5.12，X 也不是命题。因此 $X \in N_2(w)$，从而 $X \in N(w)$。

验证信解关联性：任给 $X \in W$ 使得 $S(w) \subseteq X$。要证 $X \in N(w)$。

情况 1 X 是一个命题。则存在 $\varphi \in L$ 使得 $|\varphi| = X$。所以 $S(w) \subseteq |\varphi|$。再据 5.7，有 $\mathrm{B}\varphi \in w$，再据公理 BU 有 $\mathrm{U}\varphi \in w$，所以 $|\varphi| \in N_1(w)$，因此 $X \in N(w)$。

情况 2 X 不是命题。则 $X \in N_2(w)$，从而 $X \in N(w)$。

验证解知正关联性：任给 $X \in N(w)$ 和 $u \in W$ 使得 wRu。要证 $X \in N(u)$。

情况 1 X 是一个命题。则存在 $\varphi \in L$ 使得 $|\varphi| = X$。所以据 $X \in N(w)$ 和引理 5.14 的证明，易见 $\mathrm{U}\varphi \in w$，再据公理 $\mathbf{4_U}$ 有 $\mathrm{KU}\varphi \in u$，因此据 wRu 有 $\mathrm{U}\varphi \in u$，所以 $|\varphi| \in N_1(u)$，因此 $X \in N(u)$。

情况 2 X 不是命题。则 $X \in N_2(u)$，从而 $X \in N(u)$。

验证解知负关联性：任给 $X \notin N(w)$ 和 $u \in W$ 使得 wRu。要证 $X \notin N(u)$。

因为 $X \notin N(w) = N_1(w) \cup N_2(w)$，所以 $X \notin N_1(w)$ 且 $X \notin N_2(w)$。据后者，X 是命题，所以存在 $\varphi \in L$ 使得 $|\varphi| = X$。但据前者，$|\varphi| \notin N_1(w)$，因此 $\mathrm{U}\varphi \notin w$，所以 $\neg\mathrm{U}\varphi \in w$，再据公理 $\mathbf{5_U}$ 有 $\mathrm{K}\neg\mathrm{U}\varphi \in u$，因此据 wRu 有 $\neg\mathrm{U}\varphi \in u$，所以 $\mathrm{U}\varphi \notin u$，因此 $X \notin N_1(u)$。因为 X 是命题，所以 $X \notin N_2(u)$。最终我们有 $X \notin N(u)$。$\dashv$

第六节   UKB 的一个扩充系统

我们认为本文开头提到的 $\mathrm{C_U}$ 和 $\mathrm{RM_U}$ 的直观意义很自然，但我们目前还没有找到使它们完全的框架条件，所以下面我们给出 **UKB** 的一个扩充系统并证明它相对某个模型类是模型可靠和模型完全的。

定义 6.1　**系统 UKB$^+$是在 UKB** 中加入下列公理得到的系统：

(C_U)　$U\varphi \wedge U\psi \rightarrow U(\varphi \wedge \psi)$，

(RM_U)　$\varphi \wedge \psi \rightarrow U(\varphi \wedge \psi) \rightarrow U\varphi \wedge U\psi$。　　（受限单调公理）⊣

说明：UKB$^+$是一个比较全面的系统，因为它不仅描述了理解算子 U 和初始布尔联结符¬以及∧的关系，而且还描述了 U 和经典知识算子 K 以及 B 的关系。

定理 6.2　下面是 **UKB$^+$**的内定理：

（1）$U\varphi \wedge U\psi \rightarrow U(\varphi O\psi)$，其中 $O \in \{\vee, \rightarrow, \leftrightarrow\}$。

（2）$\varphi \wedge \psi \rightarrow (U(\varphi \wedge \psi) \leftrightarrow U\varphi \wedge U\psi)$。

（3）$K(\varphi \wedge \psi) \rightarrow U\varphi \wedge U\psi$。

证明：（1）据公理 C_U 和 NE_U，有 $U\varphi \wedge U\psi \rightarrow U \neg (\neg\varphi \wedge \neg\psi)$，所以

$U\varphi \wedge U\psi \rightarrow U(\varphi \vee \psi)$。

再据 NE_U，有 $U\varphi \wedge U\psi \rightarrow U(\varphi \rightarrow \psi)$。因此

$U\varphi \wedge U\psi \rightarrow U(\varphi \rightarrow \psi) \wedge U(\psi \rightarrow \varphi)$。

因此据 C_U，

$U\varphi \wedge U\psi \rightarrow U((\varphi \rightarrow \psi) \wedge (\psi \rightarrow \varphi))$。

因此 $U\varphi \wedge U\psi \rightarrow U(\varphi \leftrightarrow \psi)$。

（2）据公理 C_U 和 RM_U。

（3）据公理 T_K 和 3.3（4），有

$K(\varphi \wedge \psi) \rightarrow \varphi \wedge \psi \wedge U(\varphi \wedge \psi)$。

再据 RM_U，有 $K(\varphi \wedge \psi) \rightarrow U\varphi \wedge U\psi$。⊣

说明：（1）表示：若理解两个子命题，也就理解它们的复合命题。这就是理解的由简致复原则。

定义 6.3　令 $M = (W, R, S, N, V) \in$ Model。

（1）称 M 是 **UKB$^+$**－模型，当且仅当下列**模型条件**成立：对任意 $w \in W$ 和公式 φ 和 ψ，

（交闭性）$V(\varphi), V(\psi) \in N(w) \Rightarrow V(\varphi) \cap V(\psi) \in N(w)$；

（受限单调性）$w \in V(\varphi) \cap V(\psi)$ 且 $V(\varphi) \cap V(\psi) \in N(w) \Rightarrow V(\varphi), V(\psi) \in N(w)$。

（2）所有 **UKB$^+$**－模型组成的模型类记为 Model（**UKB$^+$**）。⊣

如前易证：

定理 6.4　**UKB$^+$**是协调的。⊣

定义 6.5　令 **S** 是一个系统，且令 C 是一个模型类。

（1）称 **S** 相对 **C** 是**模型可靠系统**，当且仅当，**S** 的内定理在 **C** 的所有模型中有效。

（2）称 **S** 相对 **C** 是**模型完全系统**，当且仅当，在 **C** 的所有模型中有效的公式是 **S** 的内定理。⊣

定理 6.6（模型可靠性定理） UKB$^+$ 相对 Model(UKB$^+$) 是模型可靠的。

证明：任给框架 $F = (W, R, S, N)$ 和 F 上赋值 V。

只须验证 UKB$^+$ 的每一公理相对 $M = (F, V)$ 有效且推理规则相对 M 保持有效性。

验证公理 C_U：据定义 6.3 的模型条件"交闭性"，任给 $w \in W$，有

$$V(\varphi), V(\psi) \in N(w) \Rightarrow V(\varphi) \cap V(\psi) \in N(w),$$

所以据 $V(\varphi) \cap V(\psi) = V(\varphi \wedge \psi)$ 和真值集定义，有

$$w \in V(U\varphi) \text{ 且 } w \in V(U\psi) \Rightarrow w \in V(U(\varphi \wedge \psi)),$$

从而有 $w \in V(U\varphi \wedge U\psi \rightarrow U(\varphi \wedge \psi))$。

验证公理 RM_U：据定义 6.3 的模型条件"受限单调性"，任给 $w \in W$，有

$$w \in V(\varphi) \cap V(\psi) \text{ 且 } V(\varphi) \cap V(\psi) \in N(w) \Rightarrow V(\varphi), V(\psi) \in N(w),$$

所以我们有

$$w \in V(\varphi \wedge \psi) \text{ 且 } w \in V(U(\varphi \wedge \psi)) \Rightarrow w \in V(U\varphi \wedge U\psi),$$

从而有 $w \in V(\varphi \wedge \psi \wedge U(\varphi \wedge \psi) \rightarrow U\varphi \wedge U\psi)$。

其余公理和规则的验证同于定理 4.4 的相应验证。⊣

定理 6.7（模型完全性定理） UKB$^+$ 相对 Model(UKB$^+$) 是模型完全的。

证明：据定理 5.10，为了证明 UKB$^+$ 相对 Model(UKB$^+$) 是模型完全的，只须证明如同 5.13 定义的 M^* 属于 Model(UKB$^+$)。

只须证 M^* 满足定义 6.3 的模型条件：任给 $w \in W$ 和公式 φ 和 ψ。

验证交闭性：据 5.9，只须证

$$|\varphi|, |\psi| \in N(w) \Rightarrow |\varphi| \cap |\psi| \in N(w)。$$

设 $|\varphi|, |\psi| \in N(w)$。则据 5.13，存在 $U\varphi, U\psi \in w$。据 5.3，公理 C_U 在 w 中，因此 $U(\varphi \wedge \psi) \in w$，所以 $|\varphi \wedge \psi| \in N_1(w)$，因此据 5.5，$|\varphi| \cap |\psi| \in N_1(w)$，所以 $|\varphi| \cap |\psi| \in N(w)$。

验证受限单调性：据 5.9，只须证

$$w \in |\varphi| \cap |\psi| \text{ 且 } |\varphi| \cap |\psi| \in N(w) \Rightarrow |\varphi|, |\psi| \in N(w)。$$

设 $w \in |\varphi| \cap |\psi|$ 且 $|\varphi| \cap |\psi| \in N(w)$。易见 $\varphi \wedge \psi \wedge U(\varphi \wedge \psi) \in w$。再据公理 RM_U，$U\varphi \wedge U\psi \in w$，所以 $|\varphi|, |\psi| \in N_1(w)$，因此 $|\varphi|, |\psi| \in N(w)$。⊣

说明：我们可以把定义 6.3 的模型条件改写为下列框架条件：对任意 $w \in W$ 和 X, $Y \subseteq W$,

（交闭性）X, $Y \in N(w) \Rightarrow X \cap Y \in N(w)$；

（受限单调性）$w \in X \cap Y$ 且 $X \cap Y \in N(w) \Rightarrow X$, $Y \in N(w)$。

易证 **UKB⁺** 相对加入上述框架条件的框架类的可靠性。但如何证明相应的框架完全性还需要进一步研究。

考虑

(RT_U) $UU\varphi \rightarrow U\varphi$。

看起来这是一个很自然的公式，但把它加入上述系统会得到

$\neg U\varphi \rightarrow \neg UU\varphi$。

另一方面，据 3.3（8）和 NE_U，有

$\neg U\varphi \rightarrow UU\varphi$。

由此易得 $U\varphi$。这样，主体又具有完美理解能力！这说明我们的逻辑有一定的局限性：5_U 和 RT_U 不能同时纳入一个系统。

除了知识与信念，主体的愿望（desire）和意图（intention）通常也用模态算子 D 与 I 以及关于它们的公理和规则来刻画。那么 $D\varphi$，$I\varphi$ 和 $U\varphi$ 是什么关系？这也值得我们研究。我们认为，至少 $D\varphi \rightarrow U\varphi$ 和 $I\varphi \rightarrow U\varphi$ 相对智能主体应该成立。

我们上面对理解的解释（刻画）只是一种解释。还有许多其他的解释。有一种比较有意思的解释是：理解一句话就是知道说话者说这句话的意图。如果主体 A 说 φ 的意图可以用 $I_A\varphi$ 来表示，则主体 B 理解 φ 就可以用下面的公式来表示：

$U_B\varphi \leftrightarrow K_B I_A\varphi$。

这样我们可以在带意图算子的多主体认知逻辑中给出对理解的一种解释。①

除了命题（语句）可以作为理解的对象，还有许多东西可以作为理解的对象。例如，主体和活动，因为我们常说"我理解你"，"我理解他做此事"这样的话。当然，后者可以进一步分析为"我理解他为什么做此事"，从而分析为"我理解他做此事的理由"。而前者也可以进一步分析为"我理解你的心思"，"我理解你的处境"，等等。

如果我们把理解这一概念看做是中文的懂这一概念（有时它们确实可以互相替代），我们甚至还可以考虑"他理解模态逻辑"，"他不理解数学"那样的命题。

如何用逻辑来刻画这样的理解，在我们看来，是一个很有意思的工作。

---

① 上述公式的一个特例是 $U_B\varphi \leftrightarrow K_B I_B\varphi$。

参考文献

［1］李小五,《模态逻辑》,2005,中山大学出版社。

［2］R. Fagin,J. Y. Halpern,Y. Moses and M. Y. Vardi,1995,*Reasoning about Knowledge*,The MIT Press.

［3］李小五,何纯秀,"一个刻画理解的认知逻辑",西南大学学报（社科版）,2009 年第 5 期。

A Logic UKB for Understanding, Knowledge and Belief

Xiaowu Li

Sun Yat-sen University

Abstract: Understanding a proposition for a rational agent is an important epistemic concept. In this paper, we first discuss intuitively general logical characteristics of understanding, and the relation among it, knowledge and belief, and thus give a language and a system containing them as modal operators. Secondly, we present the system **UKB** for the operators, give some results of its proof theory, and then we prove the frame soundness and frame completeness of **UKB**. Finally, we prove the model soundness and model completeness of an extension of **UKB**.

Keywords: understanding; knowledge; belief; frame soundness; frame completeness

广义量词的单调性及其检测方法①

◎ 张晓君　郝一江
中国社会科学院

摘　要：本文主要以 Stanley Peters 和 Dag Westerståhl 的著述（2006）为基础，探讨广义量词的单调性及其检测方法，旨在为自然语言的逻辑处理等诸多方面提供不同的研究视角和研究方法，从而拓展逻辑推理的思路。首先，简要介绍广义量词的相关概念。其次，给出广义量词各种单调性的定义和特点。最后，给出广义量词单调性的两大类检测方法：自然语言检测法和数字三角形法。在介绍数字三角形方法的基础上，笔者对其表述方式作了一些改进，并对广义量词的单调性与数学中的单调性进行了比较。

关键词：广义量词；限定词；单调性；类型为 $\langle 1 \rangle$ 的量词；类型为 $\langle 1, 1 \rangle$ 的量词；自然语言检测法；数字三角形法

许多计算机科学中的问题可以通过把它们限制到有限模型中用数理逻辑的方法来加以解决，这是导致有限模型论成为数理逻辑的一个独立发展分支的主要原因之一。虽然一阶逻辑能够处理诸多问题，但是仍然有很多问题需要、甚至只能依赖于更强大的逻辑来加以解决。比如：在多项式时间内可计算性问题就是在不动点逻辑中的有序结构上的可定义性问题。"在可控的方式下通过广义量词的方法是增强一阶逻辑的表达力的方法之一"（Jarmo Kontinen, p. 1）。也就是说，为了提升一阶逻辑的表达力，为计算机能够更好地处理自然语言而引入了广义量词。来自于一阶逻辑的两个标准量词——全称量词和存在量词被看做是广义量词。从 1957 年 Mostowski 开始研究基数量词这种新量词以来，人们对广义量词的研究兴趣与日剧增，1966 年 Lindström 对广义量词中的 Lindström 量词概念给出了形式化的定义。广义量词理论不仅适用于标准量词，而且使得非标准量词的定义和表达成为可能，它提出了量词的一些重要的语义普遍特征以及有关的语义现象，其中单调性就是最重要的语义现象之一。

---

①　本文由北京市哲学社会科学"十一五"规划项目（06BaZX022）资助。

一、广义量词的相关概念

（一）广义量词与限定词的概念

在一阶逻辑中，量词一般是指全称量词（用"∀"来表示）和存在量词（用"∃"来表示）。一阶逻辑中的量词对应自然语言中的量化表达式。比如："someone is sad"、"there are hens"、"somebody is taller than John" 中的 "someone"、"there" 和 "somebody" 对应的是存在量词。这三个语句的逻辑形式分别是 "∃x(Human(x)∧ Sad(x))"、"∃xHen(x)" 和 "∃x(Human(x)∧ Taller than(x, John))"。其中 '∃x' 的意思是 "there is an x such that…（存在一个 x 使得……）" 或者 "there is at least one x such that…（至少存在某个 x 使得……）"。另外，"all boys are happy"、"every girl loves her mother"、"each book is old" 中 "all"、"every" 与 "each" 对应的是全称量词。这三个语句的逻辑形式分别是 "∀x(Boy(x)→Happy(x))"、"∀x(Girl(x)→Love(x, her-mother))" 与 "∀x(Book(x)→Old(x)'"。因此，"∀x" 的意思是 "对每一个 x 来说，……成立)"。当然，把语句翻译成逻辑形式时，还有其他方法，读者可参见 Makoto Kanazawa（p. 6）和 Patrick Saint-Dizier（p. 557）。在逻辑中："some"、"a"、"the" 对应的是存在量词，"every"、"all"、"each" 对应的是全称量词。

根据 Gamut 的观点，我们可以把对名词短语的语义分析看做〈1〉类型的广义量词（generalized quantifiers），即可以看做是集合的性质（Gamut 1992，p. 227）。比如：*one* boy、*two* eggs、*some* books、*most of* students、*any* pen、*several* girls、*many* women、*few* news、*no* man、*my* books、more students *than* teachers、*half of* workers 都是广义量词。也就是说，广义量词是指整个名词短语，而 "限定词" 是指名词短语中的量化词项。前面广义量词的例子中的斜体部分表示的就是限定词。

在广义量词理论的初期，大部分研究者都对名词短语和它所包含的限定词加以区分，他们认为：广义量词除了包括一阶逻辑中的全称量词（∀）和存在量词（∃）外，还包括由限定词 a, an, the 或其他量化关系指称所形成的名词短语 NP，广义量词是指整个名词短语。后来随着研究的深入，研究者们发现，广义量词的主要性质与限定词的主要性质几乎是一致的，所以，更多的研究者越来越趋向于把名词短语和限定词都看做是广义量词。

（二）类型为 〈1〉 的量词与类型为 〈1、1〉 的量词的概念

量词的类型主要是根据其集合论运算中的论元来进行划分的。

"类型为 〈1〉 的量词"指其论元是一个集合，是"表示集合的性质的量词"（Stanley Peters and Dag Westerståhl，p. 12），比如：everyone、nobody、everyone、everything 是类型为 〈1〉 的量词。

"类型为 〈1，1〉 的量词"是"表示集合之间的二元关系的量词"（Stanley Peters and Dag Westerståhl，p. 12）。比如：every、exactly three、an even number of 是类型为 〈1，1〉 的量词。

在自然语言中，限定词所表示的量词大多数是类型为 〈1，1〉 的量词，但也有量词带有两个或更多个论元，它们是类型为 〈1，1，1〉 及其以上的量词。比如：more…than…、twice as many…as…、proportionately more…than…等量词。

Kasia Jaszzolt 认为"广义量词都是两个集合之间的关系"（p. iii）。在自然语言中确实有许多这样的量化表达式例子，下列表达式中的斜体表示量词，A、B、C 是集合，$|X|$ 是集合的基数。比如：

All $(A, B) \Leftrightarrow A \subseteq B$

Some $(A, B) \Leftrightarrow A \cap B \neq \varnothing$

No $(A, B) \Leftrightarrow A \cap B = \varnothing$

Most $(A, B) \Leftrightarrow |A \cap B| > |A - B|$

Not-all $(A, B) \Leftrightarrow A \cap B \neq A$

exactly-four $(A, B) \Leftrightarrow A \cap B = 4$

at-most-seven $(A, B) \Leftrightarrow |A \cap B| \leqslant 7$

the-eight $(A, B) \Leftrightarrow |A| = 8$ 且 $A \subseteq B$

all-but-five $(A, B) \Leftrightarrow |A - B| = 5$

between-three-and-six $(A, B) \Leftrightarrow 3 \leqslant |A \cap B| \leqslant 6$

at-least-half-of-the $(A, B) \Leftrightarrow |A \cap B| \geqslant 1/2 \cdot |A|$

just-finitely-many $(A, B) \Leftrightarrow$ 存在一个自然数 n，使得 $|A \cap B| = n$

但是，笔者认为，Kasia Jaszzolt 的"广义量词都是两个集合之间的关系"这一观点只适合类型为 〈1，1〉 的量词。之所以 Kasia Jaszzolt 的观点得到了许多人的理解和接受，是因为自然语言中绝大多数量词是类型为 〈1，1〉 的量词。然而，自然语言还有更多类型的量词。对于类

型为〈1，1，1〉的量词来说，广义量词指的是三个集合之间的三元关系，因为根据类型为〈1，1，1〉的量词的定义可知，该类量词有三个论元，比如：

more…than… （A，B，C）$\Leftrightarrow$ ｜A∩C｜ > ｜B∩C｜

proportionately more…than… （A，B，C）$\Leftrightarrow$ ｜B｜ · ｜A∩C｜ > ｜A｜ · ｜B∩C｜

以此类推，对于类型为〈1，1，…，1〉（n 个 1）的量词来说，广义量词指的是 n 个集合之间的 n 元关系，因为根据该类量词的定义可知，该类量词有 n 个论元。还有其他类型的量词，比如类型为〈1，2〉的相互量词 each other，等等。

一般说来，广义量词理论是外延性的语义理论。一方面是因为它"只使用外延模型 M = 〈E，［ ］〉"，其中 E 是个体的集合，而 ［ ］ 是把外延解释指派给表达式的一个解释函数。例如：量词 "every boy" 可以解释成 "［every boy］$_E$ = { X⊆E｜［boy］⊆X }"。

二、广义量词的单调性

在自然语言中，常常存在这样一种现象：有些命题能够从另一个命题推出，而另一些命题却不能够从另一个命题推出。例如：

（1） a. Some boys ran quickly. $\Rightarrow$Some boys ran.

　　　b. Some boys ran. $\not\Rightarrow$ Some boys ran quickly.

（2） a. No boy ran$\Rightarrow$No boy ran quickly.

　　　b. No boy ran quickly. $\not\Rightarrow$ No boy ran.

（3） a. Exactly three boys ran quickly. $\not\Rightarrow$ Exactly three boys ran.

　　　b. Exactly three boys ran. $\not\Rightarrow$ Exactly three boys ran quickly.

我们把（1）中的"Some boys"叫做"向上单调的（*upward monotone*）"量词，把（2）中的"No boy"称之为"向下单调的（*downward monotone*）"量词，把（3）中的"Exactly three boys"称为"非单调的（*non-monotone*，既不向上单调也不向下单调的）"量词。一个量词如果是向上单调或向下单调，我们就说这个量词具有单调性。笔者在对相关文献进行综合整理后，给出以下几种单调性的定义：

（一）类型为〈1〉的量词的单调性

令 A，B 是集合，E 是我们所讨论的论域，"⊆"是包含关系（是……子集）。

定义 1　类型为〈1〉的量词 Q_E 是向上单调的（记作 Mon↑）当且仅当：若 $Q_E(A)$ 且 A

$\subseteq B \subseteq E$，则 $Q_E(B)$。

定义 2   类型为 $\langle 1 \rangle$ 的量词 Q_E 是向下单调的（记作 Mon↓）当且仅当：若 $Q_E(A)$ 且 B $\subseteq A \subseteq E$，则 $Q_E(B)$。

在自然语言中，大多数类型为 $\langle 1 \rangle$ 的量词要么向上单调，要么向下单调。比如：all N，every N，many N，at least six N，infinite N 和 more than two-fifths of N 等量词是向上单调的；at most six N，less than three-sevenths of N 这些量词是向下单调的；an even number of N，exactly four N，between five and nine N，not exactly five N 这些量词是非单调的，也就是说，既不向上单调，也不向下单调。

（二）类型为 $\langle 1, 1 \rangle$ 的量词的单调性

类型为 $\langle 1, 1 \rangle$ 的量词可能只在一个论元上具有单调性，也可能在两个论元上都具有单调性，还有可能在两个论元上都不具有单调性。又因为"每个具有驻留性[1]和扩展性[2]且类型为 $\langle 1, 1 \rangle$ 的的量词等价于某个类型为 $\langle 1 \rangle$ 的量词 Q 的亲缘量词 Q^{rel}"[3]（Stanley Peters & D. Westerståhl，p. 141），所以研究类型为 $\langle 1, 1 \rangle$ 量词的单调性时，可以通过研究类型为 $\langle 1 \rangle$ 的局部量词的亲缘量词的单调性来实现。

定义 3   若 $Q_E(A, B)$ 且 $B \subseteq C \subseteq E$ 蕴涵 $Q_E(A, C)$，我们就说这个量词是右单调向上的，记作 mon↑。例如：

(4) All students left early. $\Rightarrow$All students left.

(5) Most girls laughed loudly. $\Rightarrow$Most girls laughed.

(6) At least four boys were dreaming. $\Rightarrow$At least four boys were asleep.

(7) Both men walked. $\Rightarrow$Both men moved.

---

[1]   1981 年 Keenan 提出了驻留性（conservativity）的概念。一个类型为 $\langle 1, 1 \rangle$ 的量词 Q 满足驻留性 C_{ONSER} 当且仅当，对任意的论域 E 和任意的 $A \subseteq E$，$B \subseteq E$，$Q_E(A, B) \subseteq Q_E(A, A \cap B)$。

[2]   扩展性也叫"论域独立性"，大致说来，当论域被扩展时，该广义量词所刻画的关系不会改变。一个类型为 $\langle 1, 1 \rangle$ 的量词 Q 满足扩展性 E_{XT} 当且仅当 对任意的满足 $E \subseteq E'$ 的论域 E，E'，任意的 A，$B \subseteq E$，则 $Q_E(A, B) \Leftrightarrow Q_{E'}(A, B)$。

[3]   亲缘量词定义：如果 Q 是类型为 $\langle n_1, n_2, \cdots, n_m \rangle$ 的量词，那么 Q 的亲缘量词 Q^{rel} 的类型是 $\langle 1, n_1, n_2, \cdots, n_m \rangle$，对所有的 $A \subseteq E$ 且 $R_i \subseteq E_i^n$，其中 $1 \leqslant i \leqslant m$，定义 $(Q^{rel})_E(A, R_1, R_2, \cdots, R_m) \Leftrightarrow Q_A(R_1 \cap A_1^n, R_2 \cap A_2^n, \cdots, R_m \cap A_m^n)$。如果 Q 是类型为的 $\langle 1 \rangle$ 量词，那么它的亲缘量词的定义是：对所有的 $A \subseteq E$，$(Q^{rel})_E(A, B) \subseteq Q_A(A \cap B)$。

在语句（4）中，Q = all，A = ［students］，B = ［left early］，C = ［left］，B⊆C 且 Q(A，B) 蕴涵 Q(A，C)。由定义 3 知，all 是右单调向上的量词。（5）、（6）、（7）中的 most、at least、four、both 都是右单调向上的量词。

定义 4　若 $Q_E(A，B)$ 且 C⊆B⊆E 蕴涵 $Q_E(A，C)$，则量词 Q_E 是右单调向下的，记作 mon↓。例如：

（8）No students left. ⇒No students left early.

（9）Not all girls laughed. ⇒Not all girls laughed loudly.

（10）At most four boys were asleep. ⇒At most four boys were dreaming.

（11）Less than half of the women smoked. ⇒Less than half of the women smoked cigars.

根据定义 4，no、not all、at most four、less than half of the 都是右单调向下的量词。

我们可以类似地给出↑mon（左单调向上）、↓mon（左单调向下）、↓mon↑（左单调向下且右单调向上）、↑mon↓（左单调向上且右单调向下）的定义。比如：

定义 5　若 $Q_E(A，B)$ 且 C⊆A 蕴涵 $Q_E(C，B)$，而且若 $Q_E(A，B)$ 且 B⊆D 蕴涵 $Q_E(A，D)$，则我们就说 Q_E 是一个左单调向下且右单调向上的量词，记作↓mon↑。

（三）任意类型的量词的单调性

定义 6　一个在论域 E 上的类型为 $\langle n_1，\cdots，n_m \rangle$ 的量词在第 k 个论元上（1≤k≤m）是向上单调的，当且仅当，若 $Q_E(A_1，\cdots，A_m)$ 且 $A_k⊆A'_k⊆E^{n_k}$ 则

$Q_E(A_1，\cdots，A_{k-1}，A'_k，A_{k+1}，\cdots，A_m)$。

定义 7　一个在论域 E 上的类型为 $\langle n_1，\cdots，n_m \rangle$ 的量词在第 k 个论元上是向下单调的，当且仅当，若 $Q_E(A_1，\cdots，A_m)$ 且 $A'_k⊆A_k⊆E^{n_k}$ 则 $Q_E(A_1，\cdots，A_{k-1}，A'_k，A_{k+1}，\cdots，A_m)$。

并非所有的广义量词都具有单调性。例如：exactly four boys 就是非单调〈1〉类型的量词，我们可以用下面的实例来加以说明：

（12）Exactly four boys were asleep ⇏ Exactly four boys were dreaming.

（13）Exactly four boys were dreaming ⇏ Exactly four boys were asleep.

由定义 1、2 可知，exactly four boys 既不单调向上，也不单调向下，所以它是非单调量词。

三、广义量词单调性的检测

通过对相关文献的综合，笔者认为，目前对广义量词的单调性的检测方法主要分为自然语

言检测法和数字三角形法两大类。

（一）自然语言检测法

自然语言检测法的基本思想是把要检测的量词放在具体的语言环境中来对其单调性加以判断。很多量词的单调性可以同时采用多种方式来加以判断。该方法在实施的过程中所采取的方式大致又可以分为以下两种。

1. 语句辨别法。即把所考察的量词放在实际的语境中来进行检测。简单说，对类型为 $\langle 1 \rangle$ 的量词来说，如果当论元的范围被扩大（或缩小）时，含有该量词及其论元的语句还成立，我们就说该量词是向上（或向下单调的）；而对类型为 $\langle 1，1 \rangle$ 的量词而言，如果当一个量词的右（或左）论元的集合被扩大（或减小）时，含有该量词及其论元的语句还成立，就说这个量词是右（或左）单调向上（或向下）的。读者可以参见前面的例句（4）–（13）。

2. 动词辨别法。也就是通过 Gamut 所提出的单调性检测方法来进行检验。

向上单调的检测："若 $[VP_1] \subseteq [VP_2]$，则 NP $VP_1 \vDash$（蕴涵）NP VP_2"（Gamut，p. 233）。例如：

（14）At least two-fifths boys were dreaming. $\Rightarrow$At least two-fifths boys were asleep.

由检测 1 可知，at least two-fifths boys 是向上单调的量词。

向下单调的检测："若 $[VP_1] \supseteq [VP_2]$，则 NP $VP_1 \vDash$（蕴涵）NP VP_2"（Gamut，p. 235）。例如：

（15）Neither John nor Ann smoked. $\Rightarrow$Neither John nor Ann smoked cigars.

由此检测可知，neither John nor Ann 是向下单调的量词。

（二）数字三角形法

该方法就是根据量词所对应的数字三角形来进行判断。通过数字三角形来表示量词的单调性是 van Benthem 于 1984 年提出来的。笔者认为，此方法因其直观明了而得到了大家的普遍接受和传播，并在传播中对这种方法进行了不断的完善。该方法的大致思想如下：利用数字三角形来表示或证明类型为 $\langle 1 \rangle$ 的量词的同构闭包[①]或者类型为 $\langle 1，1 \rangle$ 的量词的驻留性、扩展

---

　① 同构闭包表达了这样一种思想："只有结构是重要的，而个体对象、集合、或关系都无关紧要。也就是说，在逻辑语言中，如果一个语句在一个模型中是真的，那么该语句在所有的同构模型中是真的。"（Stanley Peters and Dag Westerståhl，p. 95）

性和同构闭包性质以及这两种类型的量词的单调性。

在介绍广义量词的数字三角形画法之前，我们先定义一个基数间的二元关系 Q 如下：（1）如果类型为 $\langle 1 \rangle$ 的量词 Q 满足同构闭包性 Isom，那么对任意的基数 k、m，可定义：$Q(k, m) \Leftrightarrow$ 存在论域 E 且 A $\subseteq$ E，使得 $|E - A| = k$，$|A| = m$ 且 $Q_E(A)$；（2）如果类型为 $\langle 1, 1 \rangle$ 的量词 Q 满足驻留性、扩展性和同构闭包性，那么对任意的基数 k、m，可定义：$Q(k, m) \Leftrightarrow$ 存在论域 E 且 A，B $\subseteq$ E 使得 $|A - B| = k$，$|A \cap B| = m$ 且 $Q_E(A, B)$。这里的 k、m 是自然数，也可以是无穷基数。相反地，"给定基数之间的任意一个二元关系，就存在唯一的类型为 $\langle 1 \rangle$ 的量词与之相对应"（Stanley Peters and Dag Westerståhl，p. 96）。

所以，在有限论域 E 中，类型为 $\langle 1 \rangle$ 量词与类型为 $\langle 1, 1 \rangle$ 的量词可以看做自然数之间的二元关系，即笛卡儿积 N×N 的子集。在数字三角形中，以序对（0，0）作为它的顶点。对类型为 $\langle 1 \rangle$ 的量词 Q，给定有限论域 E，且 A $\subseteq$ E，令 $|E - A| = k$，$|A| = m$；对类型为 $\langle 1, 1 \rangle$ 的量词 Q，给定有限论域 E，且 A，B $\subseteq$ E 令 $|A - B| = k$，$|A \cap B| = m$。若序对（k，m）具有二元关系 Q 的性质，在数字三角形中就用"＋"来表示，若序对（k，m）不具有二元关系 Q 的性质，在数字三角形中就用"－"来表示（Stanley Peters and Dag Westerståhl，p. 160）。笔者认为这可以简单地理解成，对类型为 $\langle 1 \rangle$ 的量词的数字三角形而言，在"＋"号处，表示 $Q_E(A)$ 在它所对应的（k，m）这一序对处成立，在"－"号处，表示 $Q_E(A)$ 在它所对应的（k，m）这一序对处不成立。而对类型为 $\langle 1, 1 \rangle$ 的量词的数字三角形而言，在"＋"号处，表示 $Q_E(A, B)$ 在它所对应的（k，m）这一序对点处成立，在"－"号处，表示 $Q_E(A, B)$ 在它所对应的（k，m）这一序对处不成立。根据以上这些说明，可以画出图 1 这样的数字三角形。

$$
\begin{array}{ccccccc}
 & & & (0, 0) & & & \\
 & & (1, 0) & & (0, 1) & & \\
 & & (2, 0) & (1, 1) & & (0, 2) & \\
 & (3, 0) & (2, 1) & & (1, 2) & & (0, 3) \\
 (4, 0) & (3, 1) & & (2, 2) & & (1, 3) & (0, 4) \\
(5, 0) & (4, 1) & (3, 2) & & (2, 3) & (1, 4) & (0, 5) \\
(6, 0) & (5, 1) & (4, 2) & (3, 3) & (2, 4) & (1, 5) & (0, 6)
\end{array}
$$

图 1：数字三角形

其中，由（0，0）、（1，0）、（2，0）、（3，0）、（4，0）、（5，0）、（6，0）所形成的这条边叫做数字三角形的左边界，由（0，0）、（0，1）、（0，2）、（0，3）、（0，4）、（0，5）、（0，6）所形成的这条边叫做数字三角形的右边界，通过（0，0）的水平线叫第 0 阶层，通过（1，0）和（0，1）的水平线叫第 1 阶层，通过（n，0）、（n−1，1）、…、（n−m，m）、…、（1， n－1），（0，n）的水平线叫第 n 阶层。

根据以上的说明，笔者可以给出 not all 的数字三角形并对其进行分析。

图 2：not all 的数字三角形

由 not all 的数字三角形可知，除了右边界全是"－"号以外，其他地方全是"＋"号。读者可以用一个实例"Not all students walked in the garden"来理解 not all 的数字三角形的画法。这是类型为〈1，1〉的量词，它表示的是 students 所组成的集合 A 与 walked in the garden 所组成的集合 B 之间的二元关系。第 0 阶层表示论域为空集，学生也为空，该语句不成立，所以 not all 的（0，0）序对处对应的是"－"号；而第 1 阶层表示论域里只有一个个体，该阶层的（1，0）序对表示 $|A－B|=1$，$|A\cap B|=0$，此时该语句成立，所以 not all students 在（1，0）序对处对应的是"＋"号；同样的道理，第 1 阶层的（0，1）表示 $|A－B|=0$，$|A\cap B|=1$，此时该语句不成立，所以 not all 在（0，1）序对处对应的是"－"号；由（0，0），（0，1），（0，2），（0，3），…，（0，n－1），（0，n）所形成的数字三角形的右边界中，$|A－B|=0$，$|A\cap B|=|E|$，这时该语句都不成立，所以 not all 的数字三角形除了右边界全是"－"号外，而在其他地方 $|A－B|\neq0$，$|A\cap B|\neq|E|$，此时该语句都成立，在这些序对处对应的是"＋"号。由 not all 的数字三角形的特点可知，not all 是左单调向上且右单调向下的（↑MON↓）。因为若某个广义量词 Q 是 MON↓，那么，若（k，m）具有二元关系 Q 的性质（即在序对（k，m）用"＋"号），那么与（k，m）在同一阶层且紧接（k，m）的左边的所有序对（k＋i，m－i）∈Q（其中1≤i≤m），即在每一序对（k＋i，m－i）处用"＋"号。又因为若某个广义量词 Q 是↑MON，那么，若序对（k，m）具有二元关系 Q 的性质（即在序对（k，m）处用"＋"号），且 $k\leq k'$ 且 $m\leq m'$，则（k′，m′）也具有二元关系 Q 的性质，即这些序对处对应的都是"＋"号。

在 Stanley Peters 和 Dag Westerståhl 所给出的数字三角形的简图（p. 176）中，只有左边界、右边界、"●"和"→"。笔者对他们的简图进行了改进，只保留了"→"，而把"●"换成"＋"，因为从任意一个"→"之后且有"＋"的地方开始，所对应的结论都是成立的；并且在"－"之后也引入了"＋"号，表示在箭头所示的方向上，没有"－"，只有"＋"。通过

图 3、图 4 这两个简图的对比，读者可以看出，改进之后的简图能够更加清楚直观地说明问题。笔者简图中的 "+" 表示（k，m）所对应的序对具有二元关系 Q 的性质，也即表示含有该量词的表达式在该序对处成立；箭头的方向表示只有 "+" 号的方向，此时 "+" 所对应的序对具有二元关系 Q 的性质；西南方向的直线表示左边界，东南方向的直线表示右边界。

例如，我们来探讨一下前面定义 5 所给出的右单调向上且左单调向下（$\downarrow$ mon $\uparrow$）的量词在数字三角形中的特点。

根据定义 5，右单调向上且左单调向下的量词可以形式化地表示如下：

如果 Q(k，m) 且 k≠0，则 Q(k−1，m) 且 Q(k，m−1) 且 Q(k−1，m+1)；

通过归纳可得，如果 Q(k，m) 且 k′≤k 且 m′≤m 且（1≤i≤k），则 Q(k−i，m+i) 且 Q(k′，m′)。

换句话说，如果右单调向上且左单调向下的量词 Q 的数字三角形在（k，m）点对应的是 "+" 号，那么对 k′≤k 且 m′≤m 的所有序对点（k′，m′）对应的都是 "+" 号，而且与（k，m）处于同一阶层且紧接（k，m）的右边的所有序对点（k−i，m+i）对应的都是 "+" 号。此时，从（k，m）点对应的 "+" 号出发的分别向西北方向延伸和正东方向延伸后与左边界和右边界所形成的四边形区域内的所有序对点对应的都是 "+" 号。此类量词的数字三角形可以通过简图 3 或简图 4 来表示。

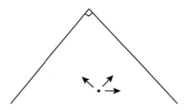

图 3：由 Stanley Peters 和 Dag Westerståhl 的方法给出右单调向上且左单调向下量词的数字三角形简图

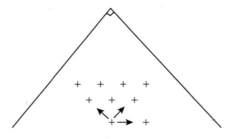

图 4：笔者改进后所得的右单调向上且左单调向下量词的数字三角形简图

对图 3 和图 4 进行对比不难看出，笔者改进后的数字三角形的简图比由 Stanley Peters 和 Dag Westerståhl 给出的数字三角形的简图显得更加直观明了。箭头的起点由"●"换成了"+"，表明延伸的是"肯定"而不是"否定"，并且添加延伸的"+"，使得延伸的方向更加明确。而且我们可以根据量词的数字三角形的特点来判断其单调性，也可以根据量词的单调性来画出它所对应的数字三角形。

最后，笔者还想说明以下两点：

第一点是，广义量词的单调性与数学中的单调性是有区别的。首先，二者的概念有区别。当我们说某个类型为 $\langle 1, 1 \rangle$ 的量词 Q 具有左（或右）向上（或向下）的单调性是指该量词所讨论的左（或右）**论元的集合被扩大（或缩小）**时，含有该量词的**语句仍然成立**。当我们说某个类型为 $\langle 1 \rangle$ 的量词具有向上（或向下）单调性时，是指当这个量词的唯一论元集合被扩大（或缩小）时，含有该量词的语句依然成立。而在数学中，当我们说某个函数 f(x) 具有向上（或向下）单调性，是指当 **x 的值增大（或减小）**时，**f(x) 的值也随着变大（或减小）**。其次，二者所对应的图形有区别。具有单调性的类型为 $\langle 1 \rangle$ 或 $\langle 1, 1 \rangle$ 广义量词在数字三角形中所对应的全体序对（k，m）所组成的图形是**由或像等腰三角形、或像四边形或像其他多边形、或水平向左、或水平向右的离散的点组成**。而在数学中，具有向上（或向下）单调性某个函数 f(x) 所对应的全体序对（x，f(x)）在笛卡儿直角坐标系中所组成的图形是些**具有向上（或向下）趋势的离散的点、直线或曲线**。

第二点是，在自然语言中，绝大部分的广义量词都是类型为 $\langle 1 \rangle$ 的量词或类型为 $\langle 1, 1 \rangle$ 的量词，数字三角形主要用于判断这两种类型的量词的单调性。而具有更加复杂类型的量词，比如类型为 $\langle 1, 1, 1 \rangle$ 的量词和类型为 $\langle 1, 2 \rangle$ 的量词的单调性能否通过数字三角形的特点表现出来？如果能，它们的数字三角形有什么特点？如果不能，能否通过把这些复杂类型的量词化归为类型为 $\langle 1 \rangle$ 的量词或类型为 $\langle 1, 1 \rangle$ 的量词，然后通过对后者的数字三角形的特点进行研究来表现前者的单调性？这些都有待于我们进一步探讨。

参考文献

［1］Gamut, L. T. F, 1991, *Intensional Logic and Logical Grammar*, University of Chicago Press, pp. 222 –245.

［2］Jaszczlot, Kasia, 2007/2008, "Quantified Expressions", University of Cambridge, 3 Oct. 2008 < http：//www. mml. cam. ac. uk/ling/courses/ugrad/p_5. html >, pp. i – vi.

［3］Kanazawa, Makoto, 1993, "Dynamic Generalized Quantifiers and Monotonicity", Stanford University, 25 Nov. 2008 < www. illc. uva. nl/Publications/dgq. pdf >, pp. 1 –37.

［4］Kontinen, Jarmo, Zero-One Law and Rational Quantifiers, staff. science. uva. nl/ ~ katrenko/stus06/ images/kontinen. pdf, pp. 1 – 12

［5］Peters, Stanley and Dag Westerståhl, 2006, *Quantifiers in language and logic*, Claredon Press · Oxford, pp. 1 – 191.

［6］Ruys, Eddy and Yoad Winter, 1997, "Background on Generalized Quantifier Theory", 3 Oct. 2008. < www. helsinki. fi/esslli/courses/readers/K18/K18 – 2. pdf > , pp. 1 – 11.

［7］Saint-Dizier, Patrick, 1988, "Default Logic, Natural Language and Generalized Quantifiers", 1RISA – INRIA, 25 Nov. 2008. < www. aclweb. org/antholgy-new/c/c88/c88 – 2117. pdf > , pp. 555 – 561.

The Monotonicity of Generalized Quantifiers and Its Test Methods

Xiaojun Zhang and Yijiang Hao

Chinese Academy of Social Sciences

Abstract: This essay, mainly based on the work of Stanley Peters and Dag Westerståhl (2006), is to explore the monotonicity of generalized quantifiers and its test methods. The purpose of this study is to provide different research methods and angles for natural languages handled by logics as well as for other fields, and to expand train of thought in logical inferences. Firstly, some concepts correlated with generalized quantifiers are briefly introduced in the essay. Secondly, several definitions of monotone quantifiers and their corresponding characteristics are given in details. At last, the two test methods of the monotonicity of generalized quantifiers are analyzed by the writers, that is, the method in natural languages and that in number triangles. On the basis of introducing the latter, the authors improves its illustrative way and compares the monotonicity of generalized quantifiers to that in mathematics.

Keywords: generalized quantifiers; determiners; monotonicity; type $\langle 1 \rangle$ quantifiers, type $\langle 1, 1 \rangle$ quantifiers; the test method in natural language; the test method in number triangles

逻辑的经验性与先验性——从蒯因到冯契[*]

◎ 晋荣东

华东师范大学

摘　要：蒯因经验论的逻辑观既没有阐明逻辑与经验发生联系的具体途径，也没有解释最小伤害准则何以造成了逻辑的先验性。基于概念摹写与规范现实的双重作用，冯契对此进行了更为全面和深入的考察。主要表现在：区分了"逻辑"所包含的思维逻辑、逻辑原则与逻辑理论诸种含义；论证了思维逻辑的经验起源与自然赋予的统一，以及逻辑原则的经验性与先验性的统一；为证成具体逻辑理论的描述性与规范性的统一指明了方向。

关键词：逻辑；经验性；先验性；蒯因；冯契

引　言

虽然蒯因（W. V. Quine）对所谓"经验论的两个教条"进行了众所周知的批判，但其哲学立场本质上仍然是经验论的。在逻辑观上，为了证成"逻辑的可修正性"这一论题，他从 20 世纪 50 年代就开始关注逻辑与经验的关系。在《经验论的两个教条》一文中，蒯因指出，在我们的知识或信念的整体中，无论是地理学和历史学的最偶然的事件，还是原子物理学的抑或甚至是纯数学和逻辑的最深刻的法则，都是人为的织造物。它们只是沿着边缘同经验（experience）相接触。换个比喻说，整个科学就像是一个力场，其边界条件就是经验。[①] 在《逻辑哲学》一书中，他进一步强调了逻辑的经验特征（empirical character）：与自然科学中最普遍、最系统的方面近似，逻辑也以间接的方式为观察所支持，因为它加入了一个有组织的整体，后者

　＊　本文的主要内容曾以相同题目发表于《华东师范大学学报》（哲学社会科学版）2009 年第 2 期，并在第五届全国分析哲学研讨会（2009·杭州·梅城）上宣读。论文的撰写受到了教育部人文社会科学重点研究基地重大项目（07JJD720045）与上海市哲学社会科学规划课题（2007BZX002）的支持，在此谨致谢忱。

　①　参见 W. V. Quine, 1963, *From a Logical Point of View*, second edition, New York：Harp Torch Books, p. 42.

虽远在其经验边缘之上，却仍与观察相一致。① 如同力场外缘跟经验的冲突将导致力场内部的重新调整，当知识或信念遇到顽强不屈的经验时，某些陈述的真值就必须予以重新分配。而作为处于知识或信念整体最核心地位的陈述，即便是像排中律这样的逻辑法则（the logical law of the excluded middle）也逃脱不了这样的命运，"没有任何陈述是不容修正的"②。

不过，对于逻辑的修正，蒯因认为必须持慎之又慎的态度，"假使针对逻辑的如此深入的修正很少被提出来的话，其原因是相当清楚的，即最小伤害准则（maxim of minimum mutilation）。这一准则足以解释系于逻辑和数学真理之上的必然性的气派。"③ 按蒯因的整体主义知识论，此所谓最小伤害，指的是对现存理论或假说的修正应该尽可能与先前信念保持一致，以不超过必要为益。这也就是他与 J. S. 尤里安（J. S. Ullian）在《信念之网》中论及的一个理论或合理的假说应当具有的保守性（conservatism）：为了说明那些人们提出假说来加以说明的事件，这样的假说可能不得不与人们先前的某些信念相冲突，但是这种冲突应该越少越好。④ 在他看来，最小伤害准则对于保持知识或信念整体的稳定、避免科学体系的振荡和崩塌至关重要。它不仅有助于解释逻辑真理和数学真理的必然性，而且"简单性的最大化与伤害的最小化，正是科学借以证明其未来预见之正确性的准则"⑤。

诚如麦迪（Penelope Maddy）所说，蒯因的如上论述堪称经验论的或自然主义的逻辑观的典范："逻辑位于信念之网的中心；它远离感觉经验，但凭借其在所有我们成功的理论建构中所起的作用而得到广泛确认；就像其他理论一样，逻辑是后验的（a posteriori），但考虑到最小伤害准则，它对于修正又有着最大的抵抗力；于是，逻辑从表面上看甚至在事实上又是先验的（a priori）。"⑥ 不过在笔者看来，尽管蒯因在论及逻辑的可修正性时已经触及了逻辑与经验的关系问题，并对日后的相关讨论产生了深刻的影响，但他其实并没有给予逻辑的经验性以充分的

① 参见 W. V. Quine, 1986, *Philosophy of Logic*, second edition, Cambridge：Harvard University Press, p. 100.

② W. V. Quine, *From a Logical Point of View*, p. 43.

③ W. V. Quine, *Philosophy of Logic*, p. 100.

④ 参见 W. V. Quine and J. S. Ullian, 1978, *The Web of Belief*, second edition, New York：McGraw-Hill Inc., p. 66.

⑤ W. V. Quine, 1992, *Pursuit of Truth*, revised edition, Cambridge：Harvard University Press, p. 15.

⑥ Penelope Maddy, 2002, "A Naturalistic Look at Logic", in *Proceedings and Addresses in the APA*, vol. 76：2, pp. 61 – 90. "a posteriori" 与 "a priori"，本文译作"后验的"与"先验的"。也有学者将其译作"后天的"与"先天的"，参见尼古拉斯·布宁、余纪元编著，2001，《西方哲学英汉对照辞典》，人民出版社；康德，2004，《纯粹理性批判》，邓晓芒译、杨祖陶校，人民出版社。或译作"验后的"与"验前的"，参见康德，1991，《纯粹理性批判》，韦卓民译，华中师范大学出版社。

证成，即没有具体阐明逻辑与经验发生联系的途径和方式。另一方面，无论是蒯因本人还是麦迪都没有深入解释当逻辑面对经验挑战时所采取的最小伤害准则何以又使得逻辑具有了一种先验性。

值得注意的是，较之蒯因的论说，当代中国哲学家冯契在 20 世纪 70 年代末 80 年代初已经对逻辑的经验性与先验性这一论题进行了更为全面和深入的考察。冯契（1915—1995）师从金岳霖、冯友兰、汤用彤等人，长期在华东师范大学任教授，著述结集为《冯契文集》（10 卷），在 20 世纪中国分析哲学的谱系中占有重要的地位。他对逻辑的经验性与先验性的考察主要集中于《逻辑思维的辩证法》与《认识世界和认识自己》这两部著作。前者是他于 1980—1981 年为硕士研究生授课的讲课记录稿，后者是 1990—1994 年在青年教师和博士生讨论班开设讲座的记录稿。本文试图在蒯因工作的基础上，重建冯契的相关论证，揭示其洞见，点明其盲点，以期有助于我们对逻辑的经验性与先验性的进一步思考。

一、概念澄清："逻辑"的多重含义

蒯因所说的"逻辑"，即"对于逻辑真（logical truths）的系统研究"[1]，主要指演绎逻辑。作为逻辑真的载体，一个语句为逻辑真当且仅当一切具有它那种语法结构的语句都是真的，因此逻辑是真和语法这两部分的合成物。以此为前提，当蒯因在论及逻辑的可修正性或逻辑的经验特征时，"逻辑"一词主要就是指逻辑真语句集，更确切地说，主要是指基本的逻辑法则，如排中律、矛盾律、二值原则，等等。[2]

冯契对逻辑的经验性与先验性这一论题所进行的更为全面和深入的考察，首先表现在对"逻辑"一词在实际使用中的多重含义予以了澄清。

（一）思维的逻辑与逻辑学

冯契指出，"逻辑本来也是自在之物，人们开始是自发地遵循逻辑进行思维，后来才逐渐意识到了，通过'反思'来考察逻辑学问题。"[3] 作为一种自在之物，思维的逻辑是客观存在着的东西，不以人的主观意志为转移，表现着人的思维活动的内在本质，并通过逻辑思维的各种

---

[1] W. V. Quine, *Philosophy of Logic*, p. vii.

[2] 参见 W. V. Quine, *From a Logical Point of View*, p. 43, 以及 *Philosophy of Logic*, pp. 80 – 94.

[3] 冯契，1996，《逻辑思维的辩证法》，华东师范大学出版社，第 66 页。

形式、结构和规律而显现其作用。而逻辑学则是对人的思维中固有的逻辑的自觉掌握。简单地说，作为对思维逻辑的反思与研究，理论形态的逻辑研究的是思维形式及其规律。

思维的逻辑与逻辑学的区分非常类似于皮尔士（Charles S. Peirce）在自发逻辑（*logica utens*）和自觉逻辑（*logica docens*）之间所作的区分。按皮尔士之见，每一个推理者对于什么是好推理都有某些一般性的看法，即自发逻辑。这些看法先于通过研究推理而得到的知识，是人们作为推理者本身所拥有的本能、习惯等自然能力。换言之，在构造有关推理的理论之前，人们就已经懂得并且在运用推理了。另一方面，通过对推理的系统研究而获得的那些能最有效地增进知识之方法的理论，就是自觉逻辑。① 从内涵上看，冯契所说的思维的逻辑，其实就是皮尔士所说的自发逻辑，而逻辑学则是自觉逻辑。

（二）形式逻辑与辩证逻辑

对于逻辑学或自觉逻辑，冯契进一步区分了形式逻辑和辩证逻辑。在他看来，逻辑学的对象是思维形式及其规律。在人们通过概念、判断、推理等思维形式来把握世界的过程中，为了交流思想和如实反映对象，概念必须和客观对象相对应，所以思维形式有相对静止状态，逻辑思维必须遵守同一律。对思维的相对静止状态进行反思，撇开内容把思维形式抽象出来进行考察，这就有了形式逻辑。

相异于部分逻辑学家对辩证逻辑合法性的否定，冯契在逻辑观上持一种多元论的观点，认为辩证逻辑也是逻辑学的一种合法形态。简言之，人们为了把握现实的变化发展，概念必须是对立统一的、灵活的、能动的。对思维的辩证运动进行反思，密切结合认识的辩证法和现实的辩证法来考察思维形式的辩证运动，就有了辩证逻辑。②

（三）基本的逻辑原则与具体的逻辑理论

在蒯因的术语使用中，"逻辑法则"（logical laws）与"标准逻辑"（orthodox logic）、"变异逻辑"（deviant logics）等的所指是不同的。前者指的是排中律、矛盾律、二值原则等基本的逻

---

① 参见 C. S. Peirce, 1931, *Collected Papers of Charles Sanders Peirce*, Cambridge, Mass.：Harvard University Press, Vol. 2, §186–189, §204–205. "*logica utens*" 和 "*logica docens*"，也有学者将其译作 "非形式论证" 与 "形式论证"，如尼古拉斯·布宁、余纪元编著，《西方哲学英汉对照辞典》；或者译为 "常识逻辑/实践逻辑/日常逻辑/本能逻辑" 与 "学院逻辑/理论逻辑/逻辑科学"，如彭漪涟、马钦荣主编，2004，《逻辑学大辞典》，上海辞书出版社，第 151 页。

② 参见冯契，《逻辑思维的辩证法》，第 227 页。

辑法则，后两者则是指那些基于对逻辑法则之起作用方式的不同理解而建构出来的不同的逻辑演算系统。

与此类似，冯契也对基本的逻辑原则和具体的逻辑理论这两者进行了区分。他不仅深入研究了作为知识经验之必要条件的形式逻辑的同一原则（或同一律）、辩证逻辑"以得自现实之道还治现实"的基本原则，而且明确提及了形式逻辑和辩证逻辑在其历史发展过程中实际出现的不同的理论形态。如黑格尔曾说 19 世纪的形式逻辑"像用碎片拼成图画的儿戏"，理应受到"蔑视"、"嘲笑"，但冯契认为 20 世纪"现代数理逻辑有了很大的发展，形式逻辑成了一个严密的系统，本身是一个有机整体，不是碎片拼成的图画，决不是儿戏"①。

要言之，在逻辑的经验性与先验性的论题语境中，蒯因实际论说的逻辑仅仅相当于冯契所说的基本的逻辑原则，思维的逻辑与具体的逻辑理论并没有进入其论说范围。而冯契对思维的逻辑、基本的逻辑原则与具体的逻辑理论三者所作的明确区分，预示着他对逻辑之经验性与先验性的考察将从"逻辑"一词所指的上述三个层面上具体展开。

二、理论前提：概念的双重作用

"概念的双重作用"是冯契考察逻辑的经验性与先验性的理论基础，它源于金岳霖提出的"意念对所与的摹状与规律"的思想。② 金岳霖认为，知识就是以抽自所与的意念还治所与。而作为人类用以收容和应付所与的最主要的工具，抽象活动既有摹状作用，也有规律作用。与此相应，作为抽象活动之所得，抽象的意念同样既有摹状成分，也有规律成分。意念无摹状则不能规律，无规律也不能摹状。③ 对于这一思想，冯契给予了高度的重视。首先，他认为金岳霖克服了休谟的经验论、康德的先验论的缺点，用意念具有摹状和规律双重作用来说明知识经验就是以得自所与（经过抽象）来还治所与，比较辩证地解决了感觉与概念的关系问题。其次，为了更接近人们现在的语词使用习惯，他又对金岳霖的术语作了必要的修正，把意念的摹状与规律修改为概念的摹写与规范，并明确将此二者规定为概念对现实对象具有的双重作用。

按冯契之见，相对于对象来说，一切概念都有摹写现实和规范现实的双重作用。所谓摹写

---

① 冯契，《逻辑思维的辩证法》，第 235 页。
② 参见金岳霖，1987，《知识论》，商务印书馆，第 354—416 页。
③ 摹状与规律，金岳霖最初称为"形容"和"范畴"。如"我们底范畴都是概念，而我们底概念有两方面的作用：一方面是形容作用，另一方面是范畴作用。"参见金岳霖，1987，《论道》，商务印书馆，第 7 页。此外，他在《知识论》中对意念与概念、意念图案与概念结构也作了区分。

（description），是指概念作为思维形式，乃是对现实对象的特性或本质的反映；通常是以语言文字为工具，借助意念图案中的抽象结构即概念间的关联来反映现实。而所谓规范（prescription），则指概念是具体事物的规矩、尺度，即可以用概念来衡量、辨认和说明具体事物。就二者的关系说，概念的规范作用和摹写作用是不能割裂的，只有正确地摹写才能有效的规范，也只有在规范现实的过程中才能进一步更正确地摹写现实。仅从表述上看，冯契与金岳霖在此并没有什么不同。不过，有见于金岳霖对意念的理解还不是彻底的辩证法，注重更多的是对人类知识经验作静态的分析，冯契立足实践唯物主义的辩证法，对金岳霖的思想作了进一步的引申和发挥。他认为，以得自经验者（概念）还治经验，便是有"知"。但是，知与无知的矛盾一直难分难解，因此概念并不是一次抽象就能完成的，它还有一个从前科学概念到科学概念，从低级阶段的科学概念到高级阶段的科学概念的发展过程。在这个过程中，"概念既摹写现实又规范现实，所以人的整个知识经验无非是'即以客观现实之道，还治客观现实之身'。摹写与规范反复不已，概念越来越深入事物的本质，而经验越来越因经过整理而秩序井然。这种根源于经验，反映事物本质而秩序井然的知识就是科学知识。"①

在此基础上，冯契借助后验性与先验性这对范畴对"概念的双重作用"作了进一步的解说。从哲学史上看，康德曾经区分了两种认识，一种是独立于经验的先验知识，一种是以经验为基础的后验知识。② 与康德割裂先验与后验不同，冯契认为，从概念对所与、理论对经验的关系来说，理论和概念都具有后验性，也都具有先验性。就前者说，概念、理论（由反映概念间联系的普遍命题所表示）总有其被动性，即思维之所得正来自经验，摹写必须是对现实的如实摹写。③ 从后者看，当人们把概念和理论作为规矩、尺度来整理经验，赋予经验以秩序时，这些概念和理论又总是先于当前的具体经验。至此我们不难看出，尽管康德所说的"*a priori*"，冯契将其译作"先验的"，但这两个语词的用法已经有了本质的区别。康德强调的是知识不依赖于经验并且无须由经验来确立真理，而在冯契这里，"先验性指普遍概念独立于在其适用范围内的特殊事例、特殊时空关系。"④

与摹写作用、后验性相关联，冯契认为，"概念若是科学的，则又必然与事实经验有巩固

_____

① 冯契，《逻辑思维的辩证法》，第 64 页。

② 参见 Immanuel Kant，1992，*Lectures on Logic*，translated and edited by J. Michael Young，Cambridge，U. K.：Cambridge University Press，p. 252.

③ 从"后验"这一汉语词语的字面含义看，指的是后于经验；就其理论实质，强调的是概念、理论以现实本身为依据，离不开经验。鉴于此，笔者在本文中对"后验性"与"经验性"这两个术语不作区分。

④ 冯契，1996，《认识世界和认识自己》，华东师范大学出版社，第 210 页。

的联系，它反映的是现实事物间的本质的联系，故也有其内在性。"① 尽管不同于个体的存在，事物之间的本质联系仍具有不可否认的现实性和实在性，而现实的和实在的总有其时空秩序，因此无论是自然史、社会史的历史法则，还是物理、化学、生物等的规律，其内容都包含有时空尺度或适用的时空范围的规定。这就是说，概念和理论总是内在于事实经验之中，有其特殊的时空范围的限制。而与规范作用、先验性相联系，概念和理论又具有超越性。从概念和理论思维的角度看，感性认识到抽象认识的飞跃，正表现在抽象知识不受特殊时空限制，不受个体和事实的时空界限的限制。如"人"的概念不受张三、李四等特殊个体的时空关系的限制，无论古代、今人或是中国人、外国人，都可用"人"的概念加以规范。质言之，思维形式本质上具有不受特殊时空限制的超越性，因此它才能有效地规范现实。

历史地看，在概念和理论的摹写作用、后验性、内在性与规范作用、先验性、超越性这两个序列的关系问题上，经验论者对前一序列予以了较多的重视，但由于片面强调知识来源于经验，对科学抽象不能作出正确解释，否认概念和理论可以摹写事物的本质，往往贬低了概念和理论的先验性与超越性，贬低了它们规范现实的作用。另一方面，先验论者虽然对后一序列给予了更多的关注，但由于对规范作用作了片面理解，过分强调概念和理论赋予经验以秩序，割断了它们与感觉经验的联系，往往否认概念和理论摹写现实的作用，当然也就否认了它们的后验性与内在性。有鉴于此，冯契再三强调，"规范和摹写是统一的，先验和后验是统一的，越是正确地摹写就越能有效地规范，越是有效地规范，就越是正确地摹写，二者相互促进，相辅相成。"②

三、思维的逻辑：经验起源与自然赋予的统一

关于思维逻辑的起源，经验论者倾向于在客体中寻找思维逻辑的运演结构的根源，认为思维形式是对客体加以直观的产物。如洛克就指出，那些具有逻辑性质的复杂概念，都是由简单观念机械组合而成，而后者主要来源于对外物的直接感知。③ 先验论者则把注意力转向逻辑与主体的关系，强调主体是逻辑形式的诞生地，思维结构为主体所固有的。例如，康德所说的作为知性思维形式的范畴，无非就是先验框架的同义语。

---

① 冯契，《认识世界和认识自己》，第 188 页。
② 冯契，《认识世界和认识自己》，第 166 页。
③ 参见洛克，1991，《人类理解论》，关文运译，商务印书馆，上册，第 132—133 页。

　　有见于经验论者和先验论者在解决思维逻辑的起源问题上的局限，黑格尔另辟蹊径，提出了"行动的推理"（syllogism of action）这一概念，① 认为行动、实践即是逻辑的推理、逻辑的式，从而以思辨的方式猜测到了"行动本身包含逻辑"这一观点。列宁吸收了黑格尔思想的合理因素，进而把认识史与社会实践结合起来，提出了"逻辑起源于社会实践"的观点："人的实践经过亿万次的重复，在人的意识中以逻辑的式固定下来。这些式正是（而且只是）由于亿万次的重复才有着先入之见的巩固性和公理的性质。"② 这就是说，思维的逻辑既不是直观的产物，也不是主体的先天形式，而是社会实践重复积淀的结晶。

　　如果说列宁主要是通过把社会实践导入认识论从而在原则上科学地解决了思维逻辑的起源问题，那么皮亚杰（Jean Piaget）借助对儿童心理演变过程的实证研究，则从个体认识发生的微观角度对列宁的思想作了具体的论证。皮亚杰认为，思维逻辑的运演结构起源于主体的活动，"逻辑的根源必须从动作（包括言语行为）的一般协调中去探求"③。最初，儿童只能通过本能的反射来适应世界，如吮吸、注视、抓握等。这些动作的特点是身体的某部分直接与客体相联系，彼此缺乏联系。随着儿童活动的发展，动作之间开始有了协调，如对某些动作加以联合或分解，对它们进行归类、排序，使其发生相互关系，等等。而动作间协调的不断重复，便形成了行动的逻辑（logic of actions，也译为"动作逻辑"）。"凡能在动作中可以重复和概括的东西，我们称之为格式（scheme）……格式之间是可以互相协调起来的，因此就蕴涵着有一个总的动作的协调。这种协调便形成了一种动作逻辑。"④ 例如，一个动作的总格式与其子格式之间构成一种包含关系；在达到目标的过程中，动作的不同步骤之间又存在一种次序关系；而当儿童模仿某一对象时，模仿与对象之间就形成了一种对应关系，等等。在皮亚杰看来，思维的逻辑正是起源于这种行动的逻辑。在活动中，"有一定的包含逻辑，一定的序列逻辑和一定的对应逻辑……这些逻辑就是逻辑数理结构的基础。"⑤ 从动作的协调到逻辑数理结构的形成，经历了一个漫长的过程，具体包括感知运动、前运演、具体运演、形式运演等阶段。最后，当实物性的动作结构借助符号而沉淀为逻辑运演的形式时，行动的逻辑便内化为思维的

---

　　① 参见黑格尔，1991，《逻辑学》，杨一之译，商务印书馆，下卷，第526页。"行动的推理"，杨译作"行动的推论"。另，"syllogism"系德文"Schluss"的英译，可泛指推理、推论，亦可具体指三段论这种推理。

　　② 列宁，1990，《列宁全集》，人民出版社，第55卷，第186页。"逻辑的式"，旧译为"逻辑的格"。

　　③ 皮亚杰、海尔德，1981，《儿童心理学》，吴福元译，商务印书馆，第69页。

　　④ 左任侠、李其维主编，1991，《皮亚杰发生认识论文选》，华东师范大学出版社，第78页。

　　⑤ 左任侠、李其维主编，《皮亚杰发生认识论文选》，第79页。

逻辑。

有见于列宁"逻辑起源于社会实践"和皮亚杰"行动逻辑内化为思维逻辑"的思想在论证思维逻辑的经验起源方面的重要意义，冯契认为，"我们不一定赞同皮亚杰的结构主义学说，但他的逻辑思维是行动逻辑的内化，而行动的逻辑在语言出现以前就已出现了这个观点，我认为是基本正确的。这就是说，具有抽象概括性质的模式、结构、逻辑，是在行动、活动中开始的，而思维的逻辑是行动的逻辑的内化，这种行动的逻辑是先于语言出现的。"[1] 在他看来，先验论者的错误之处就在于把人类的逻辑思维能力看成是完全与人的实践经验没有关系的。归根结底，就"全人类来说，逻辑思维的范畴与运用范畴的思维能力都是从实践、行动中得来的"[2]。

不过，虽然思维的逻辑是行动的逻辑的内化，公理是人们亿万次实践重复才在人脑中固定下来的，冯契认为对思维逻辑的经验起源、后验性不能强调过分，否则就会倒向经验论。为此，他尝试援引恩格斯关于"数学公理的不言而喻源于获得性遗传"的猜想，来为个体的逻辑思维能力作为遗传下来的自然赋予的能力所具有的先验性进行辩护。在谈到"关于现实世界中数学的无限的原型"时，恩格斯指出，现代自然科学已经以某种方式扩展了一切思维内容都来源于经验这一命题。由于现代科学承认获得性状的遗传，便把经验的主体从个体扩大到类；每一个体都必须亲自去经验变得不再必要；个体的个别经验在某种程度上可以由个体的一系列祖先的经验的结果来代替。例如，一些数学公理对每个八岁的小孩来说都好像是不言自明的，用不着从经验上来证明，这完全就是"累积的遗传"的结果。[3] 简言之，数学公理之所以具有独立于个体的特殊经验的性质，乃是"累积的遗传"的结果。

受此启发，冯契强调，"人的头脑中并没有天赋的观念，人的头脑在生下来时确如洛克所说的白板一样，但如恩格斯所说，有一种遗传下来的自然赋予的能力，这种能力经过经验的启发，就能把握一些自明的公理（如整体大于部分）。当然，究竟是如何遗传的，还需要研究再研究。恩格斯关于获得性遗传的说法，现代遗传学家不大会同意，但有一种自然赋予的能力是可以说的。"[4] 应该说，冯契在此问题上的态度是非常严谨的。一方面，他赞同恩格斯的猜想，主张个体的逻辑思维能力具有一种遗传下来的自然赋予的性质，当然就全人类来说，逻辑思维

---

① 冯契，《逻辑思维的辩证法》，第 56 页。

② 冯契，《认识世界和认识自己》，第 194 页。

③ 参见马克思、恩格斯，1995，《马克思恩格斯选集》，人民出版社，第 4 卷，第 365 页。

④ 冯契，《逻辑思维的辩证法》，第 246—247 页。

的范畴与运用范畴的思维能力都是从实践、行动中得来的。[①] 另一方面，冯契又对恩格斯以获得性遗传为论据的做法表示怀疑，因为获得性状是否能遗传一直是生物进化研究中争论的焦点，而且现代生物学也不认为获得性遗传是生物进化的主要动力。因此，"究竟是如何遗传的，还需要研究再研究"。进一步说，即便个体确实具有这种经由遗传而得的自然赋予的能力，它也仅仅是一种潜能，还需要经过"经验的启发"、系统的学习和长期的实践，才能转化为现实的逻辑思维能力。

四、逻辑原则：经验性与先验性的统一

从"逻辑"一词的多重含义看，蒯因论说的逻辑的经验特征及其可修正性主要展开于排中律、矛盾律等逻辑法则的层面，他既没有具体阐明逻辑原则与经验发生联系的途径和方式，也没有深入解释当逻辑面对经验挑战时所采取的最小伤害准则何以又使得逻辑原则具有了一种先验性。而冯契明确断言，"人的思维本性既遵守形式逻辑的同一原则，又遵守辩证逻辑'以得自现实之道还治现实'的原则。这些逻辑原则是知识经验的必要条件，对于人的知识经验来说具有先验性，不过，它归根到底来源于实践经验。"[②]

在对思维逻辑作认识论考察时，与思维逻辑的起源问题相关联的是逻辑形式与规律的本质问题。冯契指出，把逻辑原则从思维模式、知识经验中抽象出来加以研究，很容易只注意它独立于经验，超越于时空限制的性质，因此忽视了它与经验的联系，把它说成是心灵的固有原则，或者以为它有另一个来源，是出于约定。在他看来，"逻辑原则有其先验性，但按其来源说，仍是后验的，因为行动模式先于思维模式。"[③] 如前所述，皮亚杰认为，主体的活动可以通过协调而形成某种格式或结构，而这种结构又是思维逻辑之运演结构赖以发生的基础，于是进一步

---

① 在此问题上值得一提的是波普（Karl Popper）。他一方面认为"天赋观念论是荒唐的"，另一方面又主张"我们……生来就有'知识'，这些知识尽管不是先验地有效（*valid a priori*），在心理学上或遗传上却是先验的（*psychologically or genetically a priori*），即先于所有的观察经验"。援引从生物学角度对逻辑所作的研究，库珀（William S. Cooper）对波普的这一论点作了进一步的引申：逻辑知识（logical knowledge）对于个体而言可以看做是先验的，因为它在遗传上是继承而得的；但对个体而言是先验的东西，对一个观察形成知识之群体过程（population process）的人来说，却是后验的。参见 Karl Popper, 1963, *Conjectures and Refutations: The Growth of Scientific Knowledge*, London: Routledge & Kegan Paul, p. 47; William S. Cooper, 2001, *The Evolution of Reason: Logic as a Branch of Biology*, Cambridge: Cambridge University Press, p. 81。

② 冯契，《认识世界和认识自己》，第 186 页。

③ 冯契，《认识世界和认识自己》，第 211 页。

的问题就是：行动结构本身的根据是什么？为了解决这个问题，就不能不考察活动结构与客体的关系。客体本质上是受必然规律支配并具有内在秩序的客观对象。如果将主体的活动结构与客体的结构进行比较，不难发现前者实质上以某种特殊的形式映射了后者。例如，活动在时空上的协调性（不同动作的相继发生及其在空间上的展开），客观上折射了客观对象运动的次序性、顺序性；活动的重复性（以同一动作去获得同一结果），或多或少对应于客体的相对稳定的同一关系；至于比较复杂的活动格式与较简单的子格式的包含关系，则与整体与部分、类与个体之间的从属包含关系具有明显的一致性。可以说，人的活动的格式和结构，本质上是由对象的客观结构所规定的。因此思维的逻辑在内化行动的逻辑同时，实质上也反映了客体的最一般的联系。也正是在这个意义上，列宁一方面肯定逻辑是"人的实践经过亿万次的重复"的积淀，另一方面又强调"逻辑形式和逻辑规律不是空洞的外壳，而是客观世界的反映"①。

历史地看，亚里士多德已经多次强调，"同一个属性在同一时间不可能在同一方面既属于又不属于同一个对象"，"对任何人而言都不可能相信同一个东西既存在又不存在"，"一切信念中最无可争辩的就是矛盾的陈述不能同时为真。"② 又如莱布尼茨认为，"凭借这条原则（充足理由原则——引者注）我们认为，没有事实可以是真的或存在的，没有陈述可以是正确的，除非存在着为什么是这样而非那样的充足理由，尽管这些理由通常总是不能为我们所知。"③ 不难看出，亚里士多德、莱布尼茨在把矛盾律或充足理由律表述为认识、思维的规律的同时，又把它们表述为事物存在的规律，其实已经触及了"逻辑形式和逻辑规律的本质是对客观世界的反映"这一思想。

正是基于列宁有关唯物辩证法、认识论和逻辑三者一致的思想，以及概念和理论摹写现实与规范现实的统一，冯契认为形式逻辑和辩证逻辑的基本原则都有其客观的基础。就前者说，金岳霖已经提出三条基本思维规律是"最直接地反映客观事物的确实性只有一个这样一条相当根本的客观规律的"④，冯契对此表示赞同并作了进一步的发挥。最初在讲授逻辑思维的辩证法时，他认为事物处于相对稳定状态时各类事物所有的质的规定性是同一律的客观基础，而矛盾律和排中律在一定意义上乃是同一律的另一种表述，所以"它们是从不同角度反映了事物相对

① 列宁，《列宁全集》，第 55 卷，第 151 页。
② Aristotle, 1984, *The Complete Works of Aristotle*, Edited by Jonathan Barnes, Princeton, N. J.：Princeton University Press, Vol. 2, 1005b18 – 19, 1005b23 – 24, 1011b15.
③ R. S. Woolhouse and Richard Francks（ed.），1998, *G. W. Leibniz Philosophical Texts*, Oxford, New York：Oxford University Press, p. 272.
④ 金岳霖，1990，《金岳霖学术论文选》，中国社会科学出版社，第 636 页。

稳定状态时质的规定性。"① 后来在作"认识世界和认识自己"的系列讲座时，他的提法有了变化。冯契认为，现实并行不悖是事实界的基本秩序之一。从消极方面说，现实并行不悖是指现实世界没有不相融的事实，而所谓相融则是指空间上并存、时间上相继的现实事物之间不存在逻辑矛盾，我们可以用两个命题表示两件事实而不至于矛盾。就积极方面说，并行不悖是指一种自然的均衡或动态的平衡，这种均衡使事实界在运动变化过程中始终保持一种有序状态。而事实界并行不悖的秩序既为理性地把握世界提供了前提，也为形式逻辑提供了客观基础："形式逻辑规律以及归纳演绎的秩序，与现实的并行不悖、自然均衡的秩序是相一致的。"②

事实界的另一基本秩序是矛盾发展。自然的均衡总是相对的，事物间的并行也有一定的时空范围，事实界的对象、过程本身都包含着差异、矛盾，因而现实既并行不悖又矛盾发展。冯契一再指出，只有把现实并行不悖与现实矛盾发展结合起来，才能完整地表述现实原则。如果只讲并行不悖而不谈矛盾发展，便只是描述运动、变化，而无法揭示运动的根源。事实界既有以并行、均衡的形式表现出来的秩序，又有以矛盾运动的形式表现出来的秩序。正如前者构成了形式逻辑基本原则的客观基础一样，后者构成了辩证逻辑"以得自现实之道还治现实之身"的原则的客观基础。"现实不仅并行不悖而且是矛盾发展的，所以广义的逻辑，包括形式逻辑和辩证逻辑，都有其客观基础。"③

需要指出的是，逻辑原则有其客观基础，并不意味着逻辑原则就没有先验性。冯契强调，就像金岳霖讲的——孙悟空翻跟斗跳不出如来佛的手心一样，知识经验不可能违背逻辑的秩序。无论是形式逻辑还是辩证逻辑，其基本原则都超越于、独立于经验事实，所有的经验事实都受其规范。受到金岳霖曾论及的"同一是意义的条件，矛盾是逻辑之所舍，必然是逻辑之所取"这一观点的影响，④ 冯契认为，思维按其本性，遵守形式逻辑的同一原则，遵循辩证逻辑"以得自现实之道还治现实"的原则，二者构成了知识经验的必要条件，为科学知识的普遍有效性提供了理论上的担保。⑤ 知识经验领域，有时空秩序，有逻辑的联系。正因为遵循这种时空秩序和逻辑原则，所以科学知识是可证的，即可以证实或否证。时空秩序与逻辑范畴相结合为思维模式，内在于经验又超越于经验。正是由于这种内在而又超越的两重性，科学的普遍命题，既可以遵循逻辑联系进行论证（或驳斥），又因其与经验相联系而可以得到事实的验证（证实

---

① 冯契，《逻辑思维的辩证法》，第 240—242 页。
② 冯契，《认识世界和认识自己》，第 325 页。
③ 同上书，第 327 页。
④ 参见金岳霖，1982，《逻辑》，生活·读书·新知三联书店，第 258—259 页。
⑤ 参见冯契，《认识世界和认识自己》，第 215 页。

或否证），因此科学命题的普遍有效性在理论上是有担保的，在经验上是有现实根据的。

如前所述，虽然蒯因的逻辑观被认为是经验论的或自然主义的逻辑观的典范，但诚如麦迪所指出的，蒯因所强调的最小伤害原则又赋予了逻辑一种先验性。那么究竟该如何来理解这种先验性呢？站在冯契的角度，我们可以说，最小伤害准则所赋予逻辑的那种先验性，其实质就是冯契一再强调的逻辑原则是知识经验的必要条件；而蒯因希望通过对逻辑的最小化伤害来确保知识或信念整体的稳定，证明科学有关未来预见的正确性，也就是冯契所说的超越于经验、不受特殊时空限制的逻辑原则为科学知识的普遍有效性提供了理论上的担保。

当然，承认逻辑原则的先验性，并不意味着就赞成先验论。冯契一再指出实践是认识的基础，知识都来源实践经验。正因为概念、逻辑都来源于实践经验，根据概念和理论摹写现实与规范现实的统一，它才可以有效地还治经验。不过，经验中有飞跃。从感性直观到抽象概念是飞跃，行动的模式内化为逻辑结构，也是飞跃。飞跃即是超越，但认识的超越性并不和经验相隔绝，它必须和经验保持着联系。只有这样，既超越又内在于经验，人的认识才能由现象达到本质。所以，并没有超验的形而上学的逻辑原则，逻辑原则有其客观基础。

进一步的讨论

总结本文的讨论，我们可以看到，无论是冯契对"逻辑"一词所包含的多重含义的区分，还是在思维逻辑的层面上对其经验起源与自然赋予相统一的论证，抑或是在逻辑原则的层面上对形式逻辑和辩证逻辑之基本原则的经验性与先验性相统一的论证，都较之蒯因在相关论题上的论说要更为全面与深入。

尽管蒯因对多值逻辑（many-valued logic）、直觉主义逻辑（intuitionist logic）等具体的逻辑系统的可修正性进行过讨论，但这些逻辑系统的经验性与先验性并没有进入其理论视野。[①]与蒯因近似，冯契也没有对具体的逻辑理论的经验性与先验性展开明确的论述。按照冯契的用词法，理论的经验性与其客观基础有关，突出的是理论对现实的摹写方面；理论的先验性侧重的是理论独立于在其适用范围内的特殊事例、特殊时空关系，反映了理论对现实的规范作用。以概念和理论的摹写与规范现实的统一为前提，考察一个具体的逻辑理论是否体现经验性与先验性的统一，其实就是去考察一个逻辑理论的证成（the justification of a logical theory）问题，即判定一个逻辑理论是否合理、正当，是否体现了描述性与规范性的统一。

---

① 参见 W. V. Quine，*Philosophy of Logic*，pp. 80–94.

逻辑理论的证成问题在当代逻辑实践转向（the practical turn in logic）的背景下显得尤为重要。近几十年来，作为一种推理理论，标准逻辑或者说经典逻辑主要受到了来自两方面的质疑和批判，其一是计算机科学，包括人工智能的研究；其二是非形式逻辑（informal logic）和论辩理论（argumentation theory）。前者认为很难从命题演算和谓词演算中获得似真的人工智能模式，后者则着眼于逻辑理论的规范性，认为标准逻辑并没有为分析和评估真实生活中的推理提供足够的工具。正是不满于逻辑的数学转向以及由此造成的理论与实践的脱节，[①] 在推理理论的建构方面新近出现了一种新的学科配置，不同理论传统的学者开始对真实生活中的推理产生兴趣，并在实践推理（practical reasoning）这一主题上会聚起来，共同致力于去揭示那些存在于真实情境中的、旨在导致某种行动的真实推理的结构。鉴于逻辑理论的证成，既涉及一个逻辑理论是否有其客观基础，也关乎这个理论对真实推理的规范是否有效，盖贝（Dov M. Gabbay）和伍兹（John Woods）认为，要深刻把握实践转向的实质与意义，就必须对推理理论的描述的充分性（descriptive adequacy）与规范的合法性（normative legitimacy）之间的关系等进行深入的考察。[②]

笔者认为，虽然冯契没有对具体的逻辑理论的证成问题展开具体论述，但他提出的"概念的双重作用"这一理论，已经为科学地回答逻辑理论的描述性与规范性的统一如何可能指明了方向。简单地说，要证成一个逻辑理论的描述性与规范性的统一，逻辑学家应当遵循如下的工作程序：

（1）随着人们逻辑思维和认知实践的发展以及逻辑研究的深入，现有的逻辑理论或者不能有效描述、分析和评估人们的逻辑思维与认知实践，或者与其他的理论存在着不一致。

（2）为了解决上述问题，对逻辑思维与认知实践的相关方面、环节、过程或领域展开预备性的经验考察，并在此基础上进行理论的分析与提炼，以建构相应的假说。

（3）从逻辑技术、认识论证成与实际效果等方面对假说进行多方面的、反复的验证和修改，使其能够转化为逻辑理论。在此过程中，如果提出的假说是以演算系统为表现形态，那么技术方面的考量就是要为这些系统提供以可靠性与完全性为核心的元逻辑证成。由于可靠性和完全性仅仅是证成一个逻辑系统的必要条件，因此对于逻辑系统以及更多不以演算系统为表现形态的假说来说，还必须从认识论的角度检查它们是否与人们的逻辑思维与认知实践相吻合，

---

① 参见晋荣东，"'概念的双重作用'与逻辑理论的证成——对冯契理论的一点引申与应用"，《华东师范大学学报》（哲学社会科学版），2007 年第 2 期，第 9—14、19 页。

② Dov M. Gabbay and John Woods, 2005, "The Practical Turn in Logic", in D. M. Gabbay and F. Guenthner (ed.)：*Handbook of Philosophical Logic*, Second Edition, Dordrecht：Springer, Vol. 13, p. 15.

有无严重抵触甚至违背人们日常语言直观和常识的情形出现。当然，最为重要的是去看这些假说是否有效地解决了最初的问题，即是否有效地描述、分析和评估了相应的逻辑思维与认知实践，是否消除了与其他的理论之间的不一致，等等。

（4）正是在这种描述性研究和规范性研究的往复运动中，由最初的假说转化而来的逻辑理论将逐步拥有冯契所强调的"以得自现实之道还治现实之身"的本性，实现理论的摹写与规范、经验性与先验性、描述性与规范性的统一。

The Aposteriority and Apriority of Logic
——from Quine to Fengqi
Rongdong Jin

East China Normal University, Shanghai

Abstract: Quine's empiricist view on logic doesn't clarify the particular ways by which logic is related to experience and doesn't explain why the maxim of minimum mutilation makes logic to be a priori either. By applying the theory of dual function of concept in practice, Fengqi puts forward a more comprehensive and detailed investigation on those issues. First, he discriminates logic of thinking, logical laws and logical theories connoted by the term of logic. Second, he argues for the unity of the empirical origin and genetic inheritance of logic of thinking and the unity of aposteriority and apriority of logical laws. Finally, he opens the possibility of the justification of the unity of description and nomativity of logical theories.

Keywords: logic; aposteriority; apriority; Quine; Fengqi

心灵哲学

现象概念与物理主义 *

◎ 黄益民

　中国社会科学院

　　摘　要：现象概念策略是目前心灵哲学中支持和捍卫物理主义的最有影响的论证之一。它提倡一种现象特性与物理特性之间的本体一元论，并且以一种对现象概念的阐述来化解主要的反物理主义论证。国外对现象概念策略的最新批评试图展示即便现象特性与物理特性是同一的，现象概念策略也不能以此来成功地化解像可想象性论证以及解释空缺论证这样的主要的反物理主义论证。但是这些批评意见都没有抓住现象概念策略的真正弱点。现象概念策略所面临的实质问题在于它不能证明作为其基础的特性层面上的本体一元论，关于这个问题的争论目前已经达到探究心灵特性的现象层面是否具有隐藏的物理本质的深度。对现象概念策略的进一步研究要求我们思考一些涉及本体论、模态论，以及语义学方面的更深入的哲学问题。

　　关键词：物理主义；现象特性；现象概念；现象概念策略；特性二元论论证

一、　支持物理主义的现象概念策略

　　当前心灵哲学中关于意识的物理主义与反物理主义之争主要是围绕下列三大类型的反物理主义论证而展开的①：首先，根据可想象性论证，我们可以想象一种完全无意识的躯体（zombie），它与正常人的身体在物理结构和功能上完全一模一样，但是这种躯体内部却没有任何意识感受性。因为这种无意识躯体是可想象的，所以它是可能存在的。这就否定了物理主义的一个基本原则，即大脑的物理状态**必然地**决定相应的意识感受状态。这里无意识躯体和正常人身体的大脑的物理状态完全一样，但是它们相应的意识感受状态却大不相同。其次，知识论证指

---

　　* 本文的一个略为不同的版本发表于《学术月刊》2009 年第 4 期

　　① 关于心灵哲学中围绕物理主义的争论以及主要的反物理主义论证，比较详细的介绍请参见：黄益民，《当前心灵哲学中的核心课题》，《心灵哲学中反物理主义主要论证编译评注》，载《世界哲学》2006 年第 5 期。

出，即使一个人从出生起就一直在一个黑白的环境中学习并掌握了关于物理世界的所有物理知识，当她第一次接触到彩色的世界时，她仍然会获得关于"颜色的意识感受性究竟是怎样的"新知识。因为从物理知识不能先天地（a priori）推出相关意识感受性的现象知识，所以大脑的物理状态并不能必然地决定相应的意识感受状态。最后，解释空缺（explanatory gap）论证强调，即便物理主义在本体论层面上是对的，它在认识论层面上仍然是令人困惑的。当我们用关于水分子运动的物理理论解释水沸腾的现象时，我们可以先天地完全解释相关的现象。与这类成功的科学理论解释不同的是，当我们试图用关于大脑的物理状态的理论解释意识感受性时，我们却无法先天地解释相应的意识感受性为什么会是那种特定的样子，从而总是在认知上留下一个解释的空缺。

对于这些反物理主义论证，物理主义哲学家们给出了各种各样的回应。最近一种得到强烈关注和热烈讨论的物理主义回应被称为"现象概念策略"。①像疼痛或者红色视觉感受这样的意识感受性（qualia）也被称为现象状态（phenomenal state）或者现象特性（phenomenal property），而关于这些现象状态/特性的概念就叫做现象概念（phenomenal concept）。因此典型的现象概念就是关于疼痛这种意识现象的概念或者是关于红色视觉感受这种意识现象的概念。我们用现象概念思考、谈论和指称相应的意识现象特性，并获得和交流关于这些现象特性的现象知识。和这些意识现象状态/特性相关的大脑的物理状态也被称为物理特性，关于这些物理状态/特性的概念就叫做物理概念。

现象概念策略的核心思想就是要找到一种关于现象概念的分析和阐述，并使之既能符合物理主义的基本原则，又能把上述的反物理主义论证在合理的解释中消解掉（explain away）。具体来说，现存的各种版本的现象概念策略都包含了以下三个部分：

（P1）一种本体一元概念二元的理论（ontological monism and conceptual dualism）：这是典型的现象概念策略都认同的一点。所谓本体一元论就是指在本体论层面上只存在一种特性，即物理特性。而现象特性即便存在，也与相应的物理特性是**同一的**。例如，疼痛这个现象特性和相应的大脑 C – 纤维肿胀这个物理特性是同一的，本质上是一个物理的特性。本体一元论意在和物理主义基本原则保持相容。所谓概念二元论是指在本体论上同一的物理特性和现象特性却对应于两个不同的概念，比如关于疼痛的现象概念与关于大脑 C – 纤维肿胀的物理概念就是两

　　① 关于国外现象概念策略的前沿研究状况，请参见：Torin Alter and Sven Walter（eds.），2007，*Phenomenal Concepts and Phenomenal Knowledge*：*New Essays on Consciousness and Physicalism*，Oxford：Oxford University Press. 本文此后将把这本文集简记为：T. Alter and S. Walter（eds.），2007.

个不同的概念。概念二元论意在解释为什么我们会产生反物理主义的直觉或者说（在物理主义哲学家眼中的）幻觉。

（P2）对现象概念的一种分析和阐述：各种版本的现象概念策略都会提出它自己独特的关于现象概念的分析、阐述及理论。

（P3）各种版本的现象概念策略最后都要用自己关于现象概念的独特的分析、阐述和理论在合理的解释中消解掉反物理主义的直觉和论证。

下面是一些具有代表性的版本的现象概念策略所提供的对现象概念的分析和阐述[①]：（1）直接识别（direct recognitional）理论：现象概念策略是由罗耶（Brian Loar）在一篇题为《现象状态》的论文中首先提出的。在这篇现在已经被视为经典的论文中，罗耶认为现象概念都是直接识别的概念。这里面包含了两个思想，一是现象概念是直接地指称（refer directly）相应的现象特性的，二是现象概念的呈现模式（mode of presentation）中以某种方式包含了相应的现象特性本身。[②] 后来出现的关于现象概念的理论大致可以分为两类，一类发展了罗耶的第一个思想，即强调现象概念的直接指称性；另一类则着重于罗耶的第二个思想，即强调现象特性对于现象概念呈现模式的某种构成性。（2）因果识别（causal recognitional）理论：塔艾（Michael Tye）认为，现象概念是一种特殊的识别概念，它们是直接地指称相应的现象特性的，并且它们本身不带确定其指称的描述语，换句话说，它们的呈现模式是空的。塔艾进一步指出，现象概念是通过在正常条件下的内省中它们与相应现象特性的因果连结而进行指称的。[③]（3）指示词（demonstrative）理论：有些哲学家建议把现象概念视为像"这"、"那"一类的指示词。佩瑞（John Perry）认为现象概念就是指示词，等同于"这种样子的现象特征"，这样的指示词由相应的知觉状态引向作为它们指称的现象特性。莱文（Janet Levin）进一步指出，现象概念应该是类型（type）指示词，并且不具有任何呈现模式。[④]（4）高阶意识（higher-order consciousness）理论：凯鲁萨（Peter Carruthers）认为，现象概念是一种不具备任何描述性呈现模式的识别概念。但是他又指出，为了在我们的内省中将现象概念引导向作为它指称的现象特

① 有关现象概念的最新介绍和讨论，请参见：Katalin Balog, 2009, "Phenomenal Concepts", in B. McLaughlin, A. Beckermann, and S. Walter (eds.), *The Oxford Handbook of Philosophy of Mind*, Oxford: Oxford University Press.

② Brian Loar, 1997, "Phenomenal States", in N. Block, O. Flanagan, and G. Güzeldere (eds.), *The Nature of Consciousness*, Cambridge, MA: MIT Press, pp. 597-616.

③ Michael Tye, 2003, "A Theory of Phenomenal Concepts", *Philosophy* 53, pp. 91-106.

④ John Perry, 2001, *Knowledge, Possibility, and Consciousness*, Cambridge: MIT Press.
Janet Levin, 2007, "What is a Phenomenal Concept?", in T. Alter and S. Walter (eds.), pp. 87-110.

性，我们需要和我们的现象经验有一种亲知（acquaintance）关系，由此他提出了感知我们现象经验的一种高阶意识理论。① （5）概念角色（conceptual role）理论：希尔（Christopher Hill）和麦克劳林（Brian McLaughlin）认为现象概念是由它们所扮演的独特的概念角色所决定的。当我们用现象概念来区分和归类我们的现象经验时，引导和保证现象概念的运用的现象经验总是和作为现象概念指称的现象特性相符合。② （6）引用（quotational）理论：帕帕纽（David Papineau）提出现象概念可以用具体引用相应的现象经验的方式来表述。例如：疼痛这个现象概念就可以被表述为"经验：疼痛（这是指疼痛这个现象特性本身）"。一般地，一个现象概念 PC 可以被表述为"经验：__"，其中的"__"所表示的空白处由相应的现象特性本身所填入。③ （7）条件分析（conditional analysis）理论：现象概念的条件分析是指我们的现象概念究竟是指称非物理的现象特性还是指称物理特性，这完全取决于我们的现实世界究竟是怎样的。如果我们的现实世界如物理主义者所断言的那样是完全物理的，那么现象概念就指称物理特性。如果现实世界含有非物理的现象特性，那么现象概念的指称就是这些非物理的特性。有哲学家争辩说，这种现象概念的条件分析可以被用来反驳可想象性论证，从而支持物理主义。④

在众多版本的现象概念策略中，帕帕纽的理论非常有影响。这一方面是因为帕帕纽已经把他自己的理论发展得相当细致和完备；另一方面更重要的是，帕帕纽的理论给了现象特性（即我们的意识感受性中"那究竟是像什么样"的现象特征）足够的重视和本体论地位。而对体现了"那究竟像什么样"的现象特性的看重恰恰是产生反物理主义直觉及论证的根源。帕帕纽的立场是：即使给了现象特性充分的本体论地位，他的现象概念策略仍然能证明物理主义是对的，并且能解释为什么会产生反物理主义的幻觉（直觉）以及反物理主义论证为什么是错的。本文将以帕帕纽的理论为范例展开对现象概念策略的批评和探讨，但是我最终提出的批评意见并不受帕帕纽特定版本的限制。

我们上面介绍过，一个完整的现象概念策略由三个部分组成。下面是帕帕纽版的现象概念策略的三个组成部分以及每个部分所包含的主要观点和重要思想。

---

① Peter Carruthers, 2004, "Phenomenal Concepts and Higher-Order Experiences", *Philosophy and Phenomenological Research* 68, pp. 316 – 336.

② Christopher Hill and Brian McLaughlin, 1999, "There are Fewer Things in than are Dreamt of in Chalmers's Philosophy", *Philosophy and Phenomenological Research* 59, pp. 445 – 454.

③ David Papineau, 2002, *Thinking about Consciousness*, Oxford：Oxford University Press.

④ Jussi Haukioja, 2008, "A Defence of the Conditional Analysis of Phenomenal Concepts", *Philosophical Studies* 139, pp. 145 – 151.

第一个部分，一种本体一元概念二元的理论：以疼痛为例，帕帕纽断言疼痛这个现象特性与 C - 纤维肿胀这个物理特性在本体论上是同一个特性，而且这实质上就是一个物理特性。我们之所以很难接受这样的同一性事实，主要是因为关于疼痛的现象概念和关于 C - 纤维肿胀的物理概念是两类完全不同的概念。对于这个基础性的核心断言，帕帕纽提供了两个关键的理由：（1）20 世纪前半叶，分子生物水平上的神经生物学研究迅速发展。但是在近 50 年的研究中，神经生物学家始终没有在生物体中发现可以被还原为基础物理力之外的其他特殊的力。换句话说，人们一直没有发现来自物理世界之外的因果作用。而通常我们认为像疼痛这样的意识感受特性对我们的身体是会产生因果作用的。这样的话，我们就可以推出疼痛这个现象特性同一于相应的大脑物理特性。[1]（2）假设我们通过科学研究发现疼痛就是 C - 纤维肿胀，那么我们就不需要再解释为什么它们是同一个特性了。因为真正的同一性（即一个对象同一于它自己）是一个逻辑事实，一个无须解释的"野蛮事实"（brute fact），所以说真正的同一性都是无须解释的"野蛮同一性"（brute identities）。[2]

第二个部分，对现象概念的一种分析和阐述：帕帕纽近期改进后的现象概念理论包含了以下三个要点：（1）现象概念具有一种引用式的结构，这个结构可以被表述为"经验：__"，其中"__"所表示的空白位置必须由一个实际的知觉经验或者由对这个知觉经验在想象中的一个实际再创造所填入。（2）现象概念不是指示词，而是一类特殊的知觉概念。我们用知觉概念思考知觉经验中的物体和对象，类似地我们用现象概念思考知觉经验本身。（3）当我们用现象概念现象地指称相应的现象特性时，我们需要启用这一现象特性自身。换句话说，现象概念需要启用（use）现象特性本身才能提及（mention）这个现象特性。这里"提及"意味着思考、谈论这个现象特性。[3]

第三个部分，对三大反物理主义论证的解释：（1）关于可想象性论证，帕帕纽认为，当科学研究的最新结果在因果层面上支持我们推出疼痛和 C - 纤维肿胀是同一个物理的特性之后，这一同一性就成为了无须任何解释的逻辑事实。一个特性与它自身同一这一逻辑事实当然是必然真的。因此像无意识躯体那样大脑呈现 C - 纤维肿胀特性而没有疼痛的现象感受特性在本体论上是根本不可能存在的，尽管因为同一个特性由两种不同的概念表述，从而导致我们在认知

---

① David Papineau, 2002, *Thinking about Consciousness*, Oxford: Oxford University Press, pp. 17 - 18, pp. 253 - 254.

② David Papineau, 2002, *Thinking about Consciousness*, Oxford: Oxford University Press, p. 144.

③ David Papineau, 2007, "Phenomenal and Perceptual Concepts", in T. Alter and S. Walter (eds.), pp. 120 - 124.

上产生无意识躯体是可能的这样的错觉和幻觉。① （2）关于知识论证，如果红色视觉现象特性 Q_R 与相应的大脑物理特性 P_R 在本体论上是同一个物理特性，那么那个一直在黑白环境中学会和掌握了所有物理知识的科学家所欠缺的只是启用现象概念在认知层面上换一种方式把握她原来就已经掌握的知识。因为世界上只有物理特性，所以世界上只有物理知识。而科学家在接触彩色世界前就已经掌握了所有的物理知识，因此她走出黑白环境后也不可能再获得任何新的（物理）知识。② （3）关于解释空缺论证：给定疼痛这个现象特性和大脑 C – 纤维肿胀这个物理特性在本体论上实际是同一个物理特性 P。当我们用现象概念疼痛把握 P 时，我们需要启用疼痛这个知觉经验本身；而当我们用物理概念 C – 纤维肿胀把握 P 时，我们完全不需要启用疼痛这个知觉经验本身。这就是解释了为什么当我们试图用关于大脑的物理理论/概念来解释意识感受特性时，我们总感觉遗漏（leave out）了什么，因此总在认知上留下了一个解释的空缺。那么为什么我们在用水分子运动的物理理论解释水沸腾现象时却没有这样的空缺呢？帕帕纽的回答是，因为那儿不涉及现象概念这种非常特殊的概念。因此他运用现象概念的"启用（use）– 提及（mention）"这个特殊性来化解解释空缺论证对物理主义的挑战。③

二、 对现象概念策略的几种批评意见

在本节中，我们首先介绍和分析最近出现的对现象概念策略的三种批评意见。查尔默斯（David Chalmers）2007 年发表了一篇题为《现象概念与解释空缺》的论文。在这篇文章中，查尔默斯提出了一个他认为可以驳倒一切版本的现象概念策略的"万能"论证（master argument）。这个万能论证的主要框架由以下三个步骤构成。

第一步，查尔默斯指出，所有版本的现象概念策略都会提出它们各自独特的有关人类心理的关键特征的命题 C，然后它们都宣称它们自己提出的 C 同时满足下列三个条件：（i）C 是真的，即人类确实具有如 C 所描述的那些心理特征；（ii）C 能够解释我们关于意识的认知形势，以及为什么对于意识的物理主义化我们会在认知上遇到一个解释的空缺；（iii）C 自身也能得到

① David Papineau, 2007, "Phenomenal and Perceptual Concepts", in T. Alter and S. Walter (eds.), p. 141.

② David Papineau, 2007, "Phenomenal and Perceptual Concepts", in T. Alter and S. Walter (eds.), pp. 126 – 127.

③ David Papineau, 2007, "Phenomenal and Perceptual Concepts", in T. Alter and S. Walter (eds.), pp. 135 – 136.

一个物理主义的解释。

第二步，查尔默斯争辩说，没有关于人类心理的命题 C 能够同时满足第一步中的条件（ii）和条件（iii）。换句话说，对于任何 C，或者 C 自身不能得到物理主义的解释或者 C 不能解释我们关于意识的认知形势。问题的关键是：P& ~ C 是否是可想象的？这里 P 是指我们现实世界中的所有的物理真理，P& ~ C 是指"P 且非 C"。展开了说，问题的关键就是：我们现实世界中所有的物理状态都不变但是 C 所描述的我们的心理特征却消失了，这样的情形是可想象的吗？我们可以将查尔默斯的意思解读如下：如果这种情形是可想象的，那么这种 C 就是由意识感受性或者说意识现象特性所构成的。这种 C 自己不能得到一个物理主义的解释，尽管它能解释我们关于意识的认知形势。而如果"P& ~ C"这种情形是不可想象的，那么这种 C 就不是由意识现象特性所构成的，而是由某种物理特性所构成的。这种 C 不能解释我们关于意识的认知形势（因为它不能解释我们意识感受性中"那究竟像什么"的特征），尽管它自身能得到一种物理主义的解释。

第三步，由此所有的现象概念策略都面临这样一个两难的困境：或者它提出的 C 自身得不到一种物理主义的解释，或者它提出的 C 不能解释我们关于意识的认知形势。因为没有一个版本的有关人类心理特征的命题 C 能够同时满足第一步中的条件（ii）和条件（iii），所以所有版本的现象概念策略就都失败了。①

对于查尔默斯的批评意见，帕帕纽是这样回应的：帕帕纽说对于"P& ~ C"这种情形是不是可想象的这个关键的问题，他的回答是：这种情形既是可想象的又是不可想象的。为什么会这样回答呢？因为对帕帕纽的理论来说，关于我们心理特征的命题 C 所涉及的特性在本体论上是一元的，都是物理特性。而在认知的概念层面上 C 又是二元的，这些同一的物理特性既可被物理概念所描述又可被相应的现象概念所描述。对于查尔默斯的关键问题：P& ~ C 是否（在认知上）是可想象的呢？帕帕纽的回答是：我们可以在认知上以现象概念把握 C，那样的话，P& ~ C 就是在认知上可想象的；但我们同时又可以在认知上以物理概念把握这同一个 C，那样的话，P& ~ C 在认知上就是不可想象的。尽管在认知上 P& ~ C 既是可想象的又是不可想象的，但是由于 C 所涉及的特性在本体论上既是现象特性又是同一的物理特性，因此，从涉及现象特性的方面看，C 能解释我们关于意识的认知形势，而从同时又涉及同一的物理特性的方面

① David Chalmers, 2007, "Phenomenal Concepts and the Explanatory Gap", in T. Alter and S. Walter (eds.), pp. 172 – 179.

看，C 又同时能自己得到一个物理主义的解释。① 这样的话，查尔默斯所构建的两难困境对帕帕纽的理论来说就是不存在的。

我认为帕帕纽的上述回应是成立的。我们回忆一下，现象概念策略都有三个组成部分：（P1）关于意识感受性的本体一元概念二元的理论，（P2）一种关于现象概念的理论，（P3）运用（P1）和（P2）化解反物理主义论证。查尔默斯在他的批评意见中从未明确清晰地挑战和攻击（P1），他似乎是默认了（P1），然后试图证明：即便给他们（P1），现象概念策略的倡导者们仍然不能同时得到（P2）和（P3）。但是我们从帕帕纽的回应中可以看到，让出（P1）让得实在是太多了，从（P1）可以得出在本体论上现象特性和相应的物理特性是同一个特性，且实质上是一个物理特性。这样一个既有"现象面"又有"物理面"的"双面"的实质上物理的特性可以推出令人吃惊的结果，包括对于上述关于人类心理特性的命题 C 来说，在认知层面上使得 P& ~C 既可想象又不可想象，同时在本体论层面上使得 C 既能解释我们关于意识的认知形势又同时能自己得到一个物理主义的解释。

对于现象概念策略的第二个批评意见来自列文（Joseph Levine）2007 年发表的一篇题为《现象概念与物理主义约束》的文章，列文的批评意见包含下面三个要点：（1）现象概念策略必须受到物理主义约束，即在化解初始的解释空缺现象的过程中不能求助于任何基本的（basic）心灵的（mental）特性和关系。（2）假设我们在化解解释空缺现象的过程中运用了相应的现象概念 PC，再假设我们对现象概念 PC 进行现象方面的把握时的意识感受特性为 Q_{PC}，而与 Q_{PC} 相对应的大脑物理特性为 P_{PC}。列文称在现象特性 Q_{PC} 和相应的物理特性 P_{PC} 之间产生了一个新的解释空缺，我们可以把这个新的来自于现象概念的解释空缺称为二阶解释空缺。（3）列文猜测我们在认知上对现象概念的把握需要一种基本的、心灵的亲知关系，而这种亲知关系无法以满足（1）中提到的物理主义约束的方式得到一种物理主义的解释。②

在其 2007 年的论文中，帕帕纽自己并没有对列文的批评作出回答。我觉得帕帕纽似乎可以这样回应：按照本体一元论，对于**任意的**一个意识感受现象特性 Q 及其对应的大脑物理特性 P 来说，Q 和 P 在本体论上是同一个特性，一个物理的特性。Q 和 P 之间的解释空缺现象可以被解释为 Q 和 P 的概念不同。这其中 Q 的现象概念可以被表述成"经验：Q"，这里 Q 实质上是一个物理特性，所以 Q 的现象概念按帕帕纽的理论实际上是完全被物理主义地表述的。至于我

① David Papineau, 2007, "Phenomenal and Perceptual Concepts", in T. Alter and S. Walter (eds.), pp. 136 – 143.

② Joseph Levine, 2007, "Phenomenal Concepts and the Materialist Constraint", in T. Alter and S. Walter (eds.), p. 150, pp. 164 – 165.

们对 Q 的现象概念的亲知把握，不管它在现象层面上显得有多么基本和心灵，它在本体论上永远同一于相应的大脑物理特性或者物理过程。这样帕帕纽的理论可以为**任意一对**现象特性 Q 和相关物理特性 P 所产生的解释空缺现象提供完全物理主义的解释，而列文上述（2）中产生二阶解释空缺的现象特性 Q_{PC} 和物理特性 P_{PC} 只是全体"任意一对"现象特性和相关物理特性中的一对而已，所以它们所产生的解释空缺现象当然也可以以完全物理主义的方式来得到解释。我们看到列文也是在默认现象概念策略的第一部分（P1）的前提下，想证明即使让出（P1），对方也不能从（P2）得到（P3）。但是这样做即使不是不可能的，也是非常困难的，因为让出（P1）实在是让出得太多了。①

桑德斯特努（Pär Sundström）2008 年发表了一篇题为《神秘之物是幻觉吗？帕帕纽论意识问题》的论文，在其中特别针对帕帕纽版的现象概念策略提出了第三种批评意见。我们前面提到过，帕帕纽是这样来化解解释空缺现象的：首先，现象概念具有一种"启用（use）–提及（mention）"的特殊性，也就是说，我们需要启用现象特性本身才能提及这个现象特性。其次，虽然现象特性 Q 和相应的物理特性 P 在本体论上是同一的，但是因为 P 的物理概念中完全缺乏 Q 的现象概念中由被启用的现象特性所呈现的那种特定的现象，所以我们在认知上对 P 和 Q 的同一性会感到困惑，并且产生一个解释的空缺。桑德斯特努对帕帕纽的上述阐释提出了质疑，他考虑了下列这些案例：（a）我兄弟此刻最明显的意识感受性＝我此刻的白色视觉意识感受性，（b）一堆 H_2O 分子＝水；（c）克拉克·肯特＝超人。桑德斯特努指出，在上面的三个例子中，等式左边的概念中均缺乏等式右边概念所呈现的那种特定的现象，然而和"P＝Q"同一性不同的是，我们对上述三个等式所表述的同一性均不感到任何困惑。②

和查尔默斯及列文不同的是，桑德斯特努的批评意见转向了现象概念策略的第一部分（P1），即所有版本的现象概念都认同的一种本体一元概念二元的理论。帕帕纽想运用他自己的现象概念理论中关于现象概念的"启用（use）–提及（mention）"的特殊性来解释为什么我们会产生现象特性 Q 及其相应的物理特性 P 是不同的特性的直觉。然而桑德斯特努的批评意见正确地指出：我们有关于 Q 和 P 是不同的特性的直觉。但更要紧的是，当我们被物理主义同一论者告之 Q＝P 时，我们对这个同一性感到神秘难解和困惑（mystified）。而在（a）（b）（c）这

① 查尔默斯和列文这样做不但没有说服现象概念策略的倡导者，反而被指责为没有"认真对待"这种物理主义理论，请参见：Janet Levin, "Taking Type-B Materialism Seriously", *Mind & Language* Vol. 23 No. 4 September 2008, pp. 402–425.

② Pär Sundström, 2008, "Is the Mystery an Illusion? Papineau on the Problem of Consciousness", *Synthese* 163, pp. 133–143.

些案例中，虽然等式左边的概念中均缺乏等式右边概念所呈现的那种特定的现象，但是我们对这些同一性都不会感到神秘难解和困惑。因此帕帕纽上述建立在现象概念特殊性上的解释是错误的。

桑德斯特努并没有讨论为什么在上述的四个同一性中只有 Q = P 让我们感到神秘难解和困惑，从而也没有讨论帕帕纽的解释究竟错在哪儿。我想我们至少可以分析指出：在上述的四个同一性中，只有对于 Q = P 这个等式来说左边的现象特性 Q 是私人的且没有空间性的（至少是空间性非常不明确的），而右边的物理特性 P 却是公共且占有明确空间位置的。在涉及两个物理特性的同一性时，下面的（L）似乎应该是一个相当普遍的法则：（L）如果两个物理特性是同一的，那么不可能其中的一个是私人的且没有空间性（或者是空间性非常不明确），而另一个却是公共的且占有明确的空间位置。因为在上述的四个同一性中，只有 Q = P 违反了（L）这个普遍法则，这也就解释了为什么只有 Q = P 使我们感到神秘难解和困惑。由于帕帕纽的解释完全忽略了这一点，所以说他的解释存在严重的缺陷和不足。

在分析讨论了对现象概念策略的三种批评意见之后，在本节的最后，我将提出第四种批评意见。这种批评意见将集中质疑帕帕纽在其现象概念策略的第一部分（P1）中为本体一元论所作的辩护。帕帕纽声称意识现象特性 Q 和其相应的大脑物理特性 P 在本体论上是同一的特性，且实质上是一个物理的特性。我将在两个层面上对他的这个基础性的核心断言来进行质疑。首先，在现实世界的层面上，帕帕纽为"Q 和 P 在现实世界中是同一的"这一论断所提供的唯一确凿的证据是下列的心灵因果性论证：

前提1：意识心灵感受具有物理后果。

前提2：所有的物理后果都完全由先前的物理历史所引起。

前提3：由意识感受原因所引起的物理后果不是由不同的原因所过度决定的。

结论：关于意识的本体一元论是正确的。

具体来说，根据前提1，意识现象特性 Q 具有物理后果 R。根据前提2，物理后果 R 必须有一个物理特性 P 作为它的物理原因。根据前提3，物理后果 R 只能有一个原因，而且再根据前提2，这个原因只能是物理特性 P。最后的结论是：在现实世界中，为了现象特性 Q 和物理特性 P 能产生同一个物理后果 R，Q 和 P 在本体论上必须是同一的特性，并且这是一个物理的特性。

我们看到，上述的心灵因果性论证并不是一个逻辑上的证明，而是一个建立在特定的价值取向上的实用的证明。因为20世纪分子生物水平上的神经生理学的研究发展为前提2这样的物理世界的因果封闭性和完备性提供了比较强的证据，再加上看重前提3这样的因果非过度决定的原则，上述的心灵因果性论证才能得以成立。但是即便是这样，它仍然是以违反像（L）这样的同一性普遍法则为代价的。为什么我们要如此看重前提 2 和前提 3 而看轻（L）这样的普遍法则？对此帕帕纽没有给出解释。换句话说，他并没有为自己特定的价值取向提供充分的说明和论证。因此，即使在现实世界的层面上，帕帕纽为 Q 和 P 在现实世界的同一性所作的辩护也是可以被质疑的。

我对帕帕纽本体一元论的质疑主要是在可能世界的层面上。为了论证上的缘由，让我们暂且认同帕帕纽在心灵因果性论证中特定的价值取向和实用考量，从而暂且认同在现实世界中，意识现象特性 Q 和相应的大脑物理特性 P 是同一的特性，并且这实质上是一个物理的特性。我们知道心灵物理主义的底线原则是：P 必然地决定 Q，即在每个可能世界中，只要有 P，就一定有 Q。帕帕纽认为从 P 和 Q 在现实世界中的同一性就能推出上述的物理主义底线原则。他的论证是这样的：如果 P 和 Q 在现实世界中是同一的，那么一个东西和它自己同一就是一个逻辑事实，一个逻辑事实当然在任何可能世界都是真的，因此，在任何 P 存在的可能世界中，P 一定同一于 Q，所以 Q 一定存在于那个可能世界中。但是这样的论证存在着严重的问题：首先，P 和 Q 在现实世界中的同一性不是一个逻辑事实，而是我们在特定的价值取向下，以现实世界的科学证据为支持，以牺牲像（L）这样的同一性普遍法则为代价，在实用的综合考量下，才把 P 和 Q 在现实世界中当做（认同为）同一的物理特性。如果因为环境的剧变和科学的发展，我们发现科学的证据反过来支持物理世界不是因果封闭的和完备的了，在那样的可能世界中，我们将会有足够的理由把 P 和 Q 认定为两个不同的特性。因此从 P 和 Q 在现实世界的同一性推不出它们在可能世界的同一性。其次，让我们用 Q 代表疼痛这个现象特性并且用 P 代表 C–纤维肿胀这个物理特性，在现实世界中它们是同一的物理特性，记为 A。在现实世界中 A 有两种呈现方式，P 的呈现方式和 Q 的呈现方式。假设在一个自然法则和我们现实世界非常不同的可能世界中，A 只保留了 P 的呈现方式而完全失去了 Q 的呈现方式，即我们仍然以 C–纤维肿胀的方式感受到 A，但同时我们完全不能以疼痛的方式感受到 A 了。那么这时 A 还是疼痛吗？根据我们现阶段对"疼痛"这个词的社区用法，在这种时候，A 已不再是疼痛了。在这样的可能世界中，A 这个物理特性还是同一于它自身，但是这是一个大脑 C–纤维肿胀存在而疼痛却不存在的可能世界。因此从 P 和 Q 在现实世界的同一性根本就推不出物理主义的底线原则。① 如果现象概念策略中的本体一元论不能确保物理主义的底线原则，那么它为物理主义所提供的支持和

① 关于我与此相关的论述，请参见黄益民：《从野蛮必然性到野蛮同一性——对大卫·帕帕纽〈思考意识〉一书的质疑》，载《哲学动态》2007 年第 9 期。

辩护从根本上就是不成功的。

三、 关于现象概念策略的更深一步探讨

2007 年布劳克（Ned Block）发表了一篇分量很重的长篇论文，这篇论文的题目是《麦克斯·布莱克（Max Black）对身心同一性的反对意见》。这篇论文的焦点是分析和批判特性二元论论证（property dualism argument），这个据说是由麦克斯·布莱克首先提出的论证的中心思想可以这样来被描述：在晨星 = 暮星这个同一性中，虽然在个体对象层面上只有一个星球，但是在特性层面上这同一个星球却有"晨星式的"与"暮星式的"这样两种不同的呈现方式，从而对应于两个不同的特性。因此从这个同一性中，我们仍然可以得到一种特性二元论。类似地，在疼痛 = 大脑 C - 纤维肿胀这个身心同一性中，虽然在个体特性层面上只有一个物理特性，但是在更深一层的特性层面上，这同一个物理特性却有"疼痛的感受的"与"大脑 C - 纤维肿胀式的"这样两种不同的呈现方式，从而对应于两个更深层面的不同的特性。有反物理主义哲学家认为，那个由"疼痛的感受式的"呈现方式所决定的更深层面的特性就是一个非物理的心灵特性。因此即便从物理主义的特性同一性出发，我们仍然可以得出反物理主义的特性二元论。

布劳克对上述的反物理主义特性二元论论证进行了非常精细的分析和批判，他的批判的核心是：反物理主义特性二元论者没有证明那个由"疼痛的感受式的"呈现方式或者说呈现方面所决定的更深层面的特性（记为特性 DM）本身就一定没有隐藏的物理本质（hidden physical essence）。如果特性 DM 本身有隐藏的物理本质，那么这个更深层面的特性也不是一个非物理的心灵特性。①

布劳克的文章的重点是检验反物理主义哲学家是否能通过特性二元论论证证明存在非物理的心灵特性，从而成功地捍卫反物理主义。与此不同的是，我们这篇文章的重点是检验物理主义哲学家是否能通过现象概念策略证明物理主义的底线原则（即大脑物理特性 P 必然地决定相应的意识感受特性 Q），从而成功地捍卫物理主义。我在上一节中争辩说现象概念策略的倡导者

---

① Ned Block, 2007, "Max Black's Objection to Mind-Body Identity", in T. Alter and S. Walter (eds.), pp. 289 – 297. 最近对反物理主义特性二元论的辩护还没有充分考虑和回应布劳克的这个反对意见，请参见：Stephen White, 2007, "Property Dualism, Phenomenal Concepts, and the Semantic Premise", in T. Alter and S. Walter (eds.), pp. 210 – 248. Martine Nida-Rümelin, "Grasping Phenomenal Properties", in T. Alter and S. Walter (eds.), 2007, pp. 307 – 338.

没有完成他们所需要完成的证明。我的批评意见主要是在可能世界层面上，也就是说，即使我们暂且认可在现实世界中疼痛感受的现象特性 Q 和大脑 C－纤维肿胀的物理特性 P 是同一个物理特性，记为 A，在一个可能世界中特性 A 仍可能失去由 Q 决定的呈现方面而同时却继续保持由 P 决定的呈现方面。这样的话，大脑 C－纤维肿胀就不是必然地决定疼痛，物理主义的底线原则就没有被证明。这里"由 Q 决定的呈现方面"可以被认为是等同于前面提到的"由'疼痛的感受式的'呈现方式所决定的更深层面的特性 DM"。那么，布劳克涉及特性 DM 的对特性二元论论证的批判是否也适用于我的论证呢？如果像布劳克所说的特性 DM 具有隐藏的物理的本质，那么这是否意味着在任何一个可能世界中，DM 都不可能脱离它的深层物理本质而单独消失呢？我认为布劳克的批判不会影响到我的论证，理由如下：首先，布劳克只是指控反物理主义特性二元论者没有证明特性 DM 一定没有隐藏的物理的本质。可是他自己也并没有为物理主义一元论者证明 DM 就一定有隐藏的物理本质。更关键和重要的是，即便我们暂且承认 DM 有隐藏的物理的本质 HPE，布劳克也没有讨论 DM 与其隐藏的物理本质 HPE 的模态关系，特别是，有 HPE 是否必然地有 DM？我认为对这个模态问题的答案应该否定的，因为水的现象特性（无色、无味、无臭等等）就有隐藏的物理本质 H_2O，但是我们可以想象一个可能世界，这其中一堆 H_2O 分子却呈现和牛肉一模一样的现象特性。因此即使 DM 真有隐藏的物理本质 HPE，在一个可能世界中，DM（即疼痛的感受性）也可能脱离其物理的本质 HPE 而独自消失。

我在本文的论证中反复用到下面这个模态原理：（M）凡是在认知上可想象的都是在本体论上可能的。现象概念策略的倡导者们可以通过否定模态原理（M）来否定我的批评论证。但是他们这样做就会使自己面临一个老问题：在物理主义与反物理主义之争的初级阶段，就有物理主义者试图通过否定（M）来捍卫物理主义的底线原则，即"有 P 而没有 Q"虽然是先天可想象的，却是不可能的，因为"P 必然地决定 Q"是一种后天的必然性。但是否定（M）这样的普遍原理是要在哲学上给出理由的，当初物理主义哲学家给出的理由就是克里普克提供的后天必然真的例子。后来查尔默斯等哲学家通过二维语义学的工具展示了克里普克的例子都是不成立的，这样否定普遍模态原理（M）的所谓后天必然性就成了没有论证和道理支持的"野蛮的必然性"（brute necessity）。物理主义哲学家都不愿意依靠"野蛮必然性"来支持和证明他们的底线原则。于是帕帕纽等哲学家试图通过现象概念策略来绕过（M）（即避免对（M）的无论证和理由的野蛮否定）而达到目的。我在本文的主要目的之一就是想阐明：现象概念策略并不能帮助物理主义者绕过和避开（M）。或许他们应该做的是直面（M），重新寻找否定（M）的道理上令人信服的论证。

我的论证还会面临一个语义学方面的挑战：如果存在一个可能世界，在其中疼痛的感觉消失了，而大脑 C-纤维肿胀还存在，我以我们的语言社区现阶段关于"疼痛"这个词的用法为根据，宣称这时候那同一个物理特性 A 就不是疼痛了。有些物理主义哲学家会否认这个语义学上的论断。他们会坚持疼痛的指称就是大脑 C-纤维肿胀这个物理特性，而疼痛的感觉只是这个物理指称的一个偶然特性罢了。但是他们这样武断地否定我们语言社区现阶段的语义用法以及由此而产生的强烈的语义直觉的做法似乎并不能令人信服。然而这种比较强硬的物理主义立场却向我们提出了下列这些更深一步的哲学问题：像"疼痛"这样的关于意识感受性的词语的语义内容究竟是什么？它们的语义内容究竟应该由什么因素所决定？意识感受特性可能具有的隐藏的物理本质以及它们与这种深层物理本质之间的可能的模态关系究竟会对关于意识感受性的词语的语义内容产生怎样的影响？① 通过本文的讨论和分析我们可以看到，有关现象概念策略的研究会自然而然地引导和要求我们去关注和思考本节所提到这些涉及本体论、模态论，以及语义学方面的更进一步的哲学问题。

---

① 我在最近的一篇论文中对这方面的相关问题进行了一些初步的探讨，请参见黄益民，《公共疼痛及孪生地球疼痛：对心灵哲学中渐逝型取消主义的一种阐述》，载《哲学研究》2008 年第 7 期。

Phenomenal Concepts and Physicalism
Yimin Kui

Chinese Academy of Social Sciences

Abstract：Phenomenal concept strategy is presently one of the most influential arguments that support and defend physicalism in the philosophy of mind. It advocates a version of ontological monism concerning phenomenal properties and physical properties, and it provides an account of phenomenal concepts and uses that to explain away the major anti-physicalist arguments. The most recent overseas criticisms of phenomenal concept strategy attempt to show that even if phenomenal properties are identical with physical properties, phenomenal concept strategy cannot use this to successfully explain away major anti-physicalist arguments such as the conceivability argument and the explanatory gap argument. But all these criticisms miss the real weakness of phenomenal concept strategy. The real problem faced by phenomenal concept strategy is that the strategy itself cannot prove the ontological monism with regard to properties, which is a fundamental thesis of the strategy. The debate concerning this problem has currently reached the depth of investigating whether there exists hidden physical essence of the phenomenal aspect of a mental property. Further studies of phenomenal concept strategy will demand us to think about certain deeper philosophical issues concerning ontology, modality, and semantics.

Keywords：physicalism; phenomenal; property; phenomenal concept; phenomenal concept strategy; property dualism argument

经验的现象特征与表征主义

◎ 王华平　黄华新
浙江大学

　　摘　要：经验同时具有意向性和现象性。表征主义认为现象性完全可以用意向性来说明。这样认为的一个重要理由是经验的透明性。然而，模糊视觉表明，经验并不完全是透明的，从而经验的现象特征并不能被表征内容穷尽。更为重要的是，经验的意向性和现象性是形而上学上不同的两个方面。前者是整存的，后者则是分存的。这表明，无论是根据意向性来理解现象性，还是根据现象性来理解意向性，都是不充分的。不过，经验的两个方面的确是有联系的。可以认为，意向性对现象性来说是必要的。

　　关键词：表征主义；现象特征；经验的透明性；经验的形而上学

　　当代心灵哲学的一个争论焦点便是经验的性质。一般认为，经验具有两种性质：意向性（intentionality）和现象性（phenomenality）。意向性是心灵指向或表征世界中的事物或性质的能力。[①] 经验能给予我们以环境的信息，这表明它是负载信息功能的状态，即表征（representation）。经验所表征的东西也就是它所指向的东西，即意向对象。按照这样的理解，经验具有意向性。另一方面，经验还能让处在它之中的感知者产生一种质的感受（qualitative feel）。例如，我看到一棵四季青树，我会对树叶的醅绿有一种独特的感受。这种感受标示了主体经历某种经验时对他来说"像是什么"的方面[②]，称其为经验的现象特性（phenomenal property）。一种经验，例如看到一棵树，往往有多方面的现象特性，例如树叶那般的醅绿，树芽那般的嫩黄，等等。这些现象特性的总体就是经验的现象特征（phenomenal character）。经验的现象特征反映了经验现象性的一面。由于经验的意向性牵涉到知识的来源和性质，经验的现象性构成了心灵哲学的

---

　　① 在当代心灵哲学中，"意向的"和"表征的"是两个可换用的词。绝大多数当代心灵哲学家都同意知觉状态是表征状态的观点。但也有少数人持反对立场，如 Travis（2004），Clark（1994）和 Alston（1999）。

　　② "像是什么"（what is it like）是自 Nagel（1974）后流行的一种说法，人们喜欢用它来标识心理状态的主观方面。

"难问题"①，因此，经验的性质便成了哲学争论的渊薮。在这场争论中，处于风口浪尖的理论有表征主义（representationalism）、析取论（disjunctivism）和概念论（conceptualism）。② 这里，笔者打算对表征主义进行讨论。表征主义试图挑战经验双面性的传统区分，认为现象性的方面完全可用意向性的方面来刻画。笔者将表明，意向性和现象性的关系远比表征主义所认为的要复杂。

一、表 征 主 义

笔者要讨论的表征主义是新表征主义（NR），它不同于传统的表征主义（CR）。CR 试图回答这样的问题：我们在知觉中直接觉知（aware）到的是什么？或者说，知觉的直接对象是什么？常识告诉我们，是世界中的事物。例如，我看到你走过来，那么我直接看到就是那个实实在在的你。但是，你不在时我也有可能幻觉到你。那么我的幻觉对象是什么呢？CR 认为它是一类特殊的心理实体。这类实体至少部分地由心灵产生，并且依赖于某个心理状态而存在。历史上不同的时期它有着不同的称呼，例如"观念"、"印象"、"心像"（mental images）、"显相"（appearances）、"觉象"（percepts）或"感觉材料"（sense data）。下面笔者将统一使用"感觉材料"的称呼。CR 认为，感觉材料具有经验所呈现出来的那些性质，即"感觉质"（qualia）。我们可以通过感觉质断定感觉材料的存在，就像可以通过事物的性质确认事物的存在一样。罗宾逊（H. Robinson）称此为"现象原则"（Phenomenal Principle）。（1994，p. 32）"现象原则"体现了经验的现象性。CR 还认为，感觉材料担当了外部世界的影像或记号，所以我们可以通过它们感知到外部世界中的事物。正是在此意义上，CR 被称为"表征主义"。感觉材料的表征功能体现了经验的意向性。在 CR 那里，经验的确具有双重属性。

但 CR 存在严重问题。它甚至不是个连贯的理论。原因就在于，感觉材料实际上被过度决定了：它们既由"现象原则"确定，又受表征功能支配。再就是，CR 难以自我维持。如果直接觉知到的始终只是感觉材料，那么我们又据何以断言它是外部事物的表征呢？情况就像休谟所意识到的，我们的确无法在感觉材料的基础上确定外部世界的存在。于是经验的意向性就沦

---

① "难问题"的提法源自 Chalmers（1997，pp. 10 – 11）。它指的是这样一个问题，具有现象特征的经验如何可能从物质身体的神经活动中产生出来？

② 析取论是这样一种观点，它认为真实经验以事物本身为组分，幻觉经验则不然。因此，经验是真实经验与幻觉经验的析取。概念论认为经验的内容完全是概念的。有关这两个理论的讨论，分别参见 Haddock & Macpherson（2008），Toribio（2007）。

为一种无法说明的形而上学假设。还有，CR 会带来极其不好的本体论后果。一个明显的困难是，CR 会导致形而上学的滥冗（metaphysical excesses）。例如我幻觉到喷火的龙，根据"现象原则"，那么就存在一条喷火的龙。更一般地，所有我们能觉知到的，都是存在的。这似乎让人难以置信。而且，承认感觉材料的存在，等于承认了非物理实体的存在，这在物理主义看来是无法忍受的。

NR 据认为可以避开 CR 的问题。NR 的第一个改进是抛弃了"现象原则"：并非经验呈现出了某种可感性质，就一定存在拥有那种性质的东西。NR 认为，我们应该根据表征或意向性来理解经验。"意向的心理状态是这样一种状态……它可以在不存在任何它要表征的或指涉的特例 F 的情况下，表征或指涉一个 F，而实际上根本就不存在任何 F。"（Tye 1995，p. 96）简单地说，意向对象可以是并不存在或不可能存在的东西。这避免了形而上学的滥冗。事实上，当初安斯康姆（G. Anscombe）和欣蒂卡（J. Hintikka）将"意向性"的概念引入到分析哲学，就是为了解决知觉对象的非存在性问题。

显然，仅仅说知觉对象可以是非实存的是不够的。我幻觉到喷火的龙与我幻觉到会飞的猪是不同的。在无法将不存在的东西进行比较的情况下，我何以断言它们是不同的呢？奥妙就在于意向内容。一个意向状态将对象表征成所是的样子就是那个状态的意向内容。如果两个经验状态具有不同的表征内容，那么它们很可能就有不同的表征对象。请注意，"内容"在这里是有特别含义的——它意指可由 that 从句给出的东西。举个例子来说，我希望北京奥运会成功举行，然则我所希望的东西就是内容。这样的内容概念显然不是传统意义上的。在传统意义上，我们可以说装满水的水桶具有内容。但当我们说报纸具有内容时，内容的意义已经发生了改变，而这个改变后的意义才是内容概念的当代用法。据说，"内容"的引入是发生在 20 世纪 70 年代更为广泛的心灵哲学运动的一部分。（Crane，p. 6）自那时起，心灵哲学家们越来越关注心理表征及其内容。

回到 NR。NR 认为，意向状态可以通过指涉或表征事物及其性质而获得意向内容。至于意向状态为何具有指涉或表征事物或性质的能力，这可以用功能主义或目的论的术语来解释。[①]总之，意向性的自然化被认为是接近于解决，或原则上可以解决的问题。[②] 因而意向状态具有指涉或表征事物或性质的能力，这是可理解的。当然，意向状态的指涉或表征也有可能出现失

---

① 例如 Dretske 认为，表征可以根据它所负载的信息功能得到理解：一个系统 S 表征一种性质 F，当且仅当 S 具有指示一定范围的物体的 F 的功能，或提供关于 F 的信息的功能。（2005，p. 2）Millikan 认为，意向性是在生物进化过程中形成的某种规范的和专有的表征与被表征者之间的自然关系。（1984，pp. 95 - 96）

② 自然化（naturalization）意指在自然中为某种东西找到位置。

败，例如在不利的条件下或出现功能性故障时，它指涉或表征一个根本不存在的东西。但不管怎样，总是存在特定的条件，即正确性条件（correctness conditions），使得某个状态可以指向那些事物或性质。当具有内容的状态所指向的事物确实存在时，或者说，当内容得到例示（instantiate）时，我们就说它是正确的。正确性条件对表征内容来说非常重要。塞尔说得好："理解表征的关键是满足的条件。具有适当指向的每个意向状态都是它的满足条件的表征。"（1983，p. 13）塞尔所说的"满足的条件"即正确性条件，它是判断一个状态是否具有意向内容的依据。

NR 不但宣称知觉具有内容，并且认为知觉内容是外部事物的性质而非内部的心理实体。举例来说，当我看到猫在草席上时，猫的性质就呈现在我的知觉内容中。这种内容是其他感知者也可以享有的。在我的头脑中，并不存在只为我个人所知的猫的感觉材料。这保证了表征内容可以用自然主义的词汇来说明。所以 NR 本身不会有反物理主义的问题。此外，由于内容是由外部事物的性质组成的，所以感知者在把握内容的同时也就直接感知到了外部事物。NR 认为这样就可以避开 CR 的认识论困境。

NR 的另一个改进是，否认经验双面性的传统区分。不过在这个问题上，NR 的支持者们发生了分歧。最引人注目的 NR 版本是泰伊（M. Tye）提出的。泰伊宣称："现象特征就是满足某些更进一步条件的表征内容。"（2003，p. 7）这是个很强的断言，它完全颠覆了双面性的区分。更多的人，例如哈曼（G. Harman）和伯恩（A. Byrne），只是宣称：经验的现象特征可被它的表征内容穷尽。称此为"穷尽论题"。"穷尽"的意思是说，现象特征完全可以根据表征内容来解释。这当然包括了它们之间的相同或不同。因此，"穷尽论题"蕴涵了如下"随附论"①：

（IP）意向内容随附于现象特征。

（PI）现象特征随附于意向内容。

还有一些人，例如莱肯（W. Lycan），只是坚持（PI），因为就现象特征的自然化而言这就够了。尽管存在这样或那样的分歧，共同地，上述版本的 NR 认为，经验的现象性可用表征内容来解释。称它们为"强的表征主义"（以下简称 SR）。如果 SR 成立的话，那么，在心理表征可被自然化的情况下，现象特征借助于表征内容也就获得了自然主义的解释。从而，有关心身关系的"难问题"也就迎刃而解。这足以让我们对 SR 刮目相看。

与 SR 不同，另一些版本的 NR 仅仅认为包括经验在内的所有心理状态都具有表征内容，但

---

① 随附（supervenience）是两类性质或事实之间的广义上的逻辑关系。简单地说，A 随附于 B 当且仅当 B 没有差异，A 就没有差异。A 随附于 B 意味着 A 的改变可以用 B 的改变来解释，所以 B 比 A 更基本。

不承诺"穷尽论题"。称此版本的 NR 为"弱的表征主义"（以下简称 WR）。WR 如今已不太有争议，但它在自然主义者看来是无趣的。人们关注的是像 SR 这样有抱负的理论。

二、经验的透明性与模糊视觉

SR 的抱负就在于，它试图通过将现象性纳入意向性的方式来实现自然化心灵的宏图伟业。其中关键的一步是"穷尽论题"。反对者也正是在这一点上施压。通常的策略有两种：一是构想出某些情形以表明经验的表征内容相同，但现象特征却不同。这样的例子有"倒置光谱"（inverted spectrum）、形相转换（aspect shift）。二是表明存在经验的现象特征相同而表征内容不同的情形，例如"倒置地球"（inverted earth）和"沼泽人"（swampman）。① 但正如尼克尔（B. Nickel）指出，这些假想的事例依赖于实质性的、有争议的经验内容以及经验现象学的理论。（p. 280）例如，"倒置地球"涉及到了经验的概念内容和非概念内容。退一步，即使承认这些事例是有效的，那也只是给 SR 出了一个难题，并未驳倒它的支撑性论证。鉴于双方都有理由，所以顶多只是打了个平手。正因如此，反驳一个理论最有效的方式通常是反驳它的支撑性论证。

那么，SR 的支撑性论证是什么呢？泰伊明确指出，是经验的透明性。（2003，p. 137）经验的透明性指的是这样一种常识现象：例如，当你注视一棵树，并且将注意力转向自己的视觉经验，你能发现的性质只是所呈现出来的树的性质。这表明，经验恰如眼镜的镜片一样，可以让我们透过它觉知到外部事物的性质。在此意义上，我们说经验是透明的。经验的透明性意味着，我们只能通过觉知到外部事物的性质的方式觉知到经验的现象特征。德雷斯克（F. Dretske）将这样的觉知方式称为"移位感知"（displaced perception）（2005，p. 40）。如果我们对现象特征的觉知只能是"移位感知"的话，那么，经验本身就不能成为觉知的对象，从而现象特征就不是经验本身的性质，因为否则它就会在经验中直接呈现出来了。相反，我们应该将现象特征归与外部事物，把它看做是知觉将外部事物表征得具有的性质。于是就有了泰伊的结论："现象特征就是满足某些更进一步条件的表征内容。"

但正如金德（A. Kind）所指出，只有承认强透明性论题，SR 的支持者才能得到他们想要的结论。强透明性论题是这样一个命题："我们不可能直接注意到自己的经验，也就是说，我们除了通过注意经验所表征的对象外别无它径注意到自己的经验。"（p. 230）与之对照的弱命

---

① 有关"倒置光谱"的讨论请见 Block（1996），后三个事例的讨论请见 Block（1998）。

题是：我们很难（但并非不可能）直接注意到自己的经验。弱命题几乎没有什么争议。但它非但不支持，而且不利于 SR。

然而，强透明性论题是值得怀疑的。怀疑来自两个层面。首先是概念层面。按照对表征的比喻性理解，我们可以认为相片表征了相片中的景物与人物。当我拿起一张我妈妈的相片观看时，我看到的是我妈妈而不是相片纸。在这个意义上，我们说相片是透明的，我们"透过它看到了世界"。但正如金德所指出，虽然我们可以透过相片看到对象，我们无疑也可以不这样而将注意力集中相片本身的性质上，例如相片的大小和色调。（p. 233）这告诉我们，表征的媒介（vehicle）不必是完全透明的。概念层面的可能性很容易就将我们引向事实本身。在事实层面，怀疑主要来自情绪和感觉，以及一些特殊的知觉现象，例如压眼闪光现象①。情绪，例如兴高采烈，可以改变我们对世界的看法。感觉，例如牙痛，似乎只有纯粹的现象性。不过 SR 的支持者认为这些都不是问题：经验者的情绪是他所经验到的他本人的性质，牙痛在经验者那里也的确呈现为牙齿的性质（Tye 2002，pp. 143 – 144），压眼闪光的经验虽然被表征得相当不确定，但仍然具有内容（Tye 2003，p. 24）。在这类情形中，经验仍然是透明的。不过笔者怀疑 SR 的支持者是否真能如愿以偿地维护强透明性论题。下面以模糊视觉为例来说明。

模糊视觉是这场争论中的著名例证。我们大多数人都有这样的经验：在眼睛没聚好焦时（比如刚摘下眼镜），看到物体是模糊的。显然，模糊不是物体本身的性质。那么，应该怎样归与（attribute）它呢？一种方式将它归与表征内容。另一种方式是将它归与表征而非表征内容。三是将它归与某个新的表征状态的要素。四是径直承认它是经验本身的性质。第四种方式等于直接承认强透明性论题的失败，是 SR 的支持者所无法接受的。那么，其他三种选择是否可行呢？笔者认为答案是否定的。

先看第一种选择。德雷斯克认为，在模糊视觉中，模糊并不是经验的性质（即表征的性质），而是经验将环境表征得具有一种它实际上并不具有的性质，即模糊。也就是说，模糊视觉只不过是误表征：主体错误地将模糊的性质归与被经验的物体。德雷斯克认为只有这样的归与才是合理的。他让我们对比一张边缘模糊的云雾的清晰照片和一张边缘清晰的冰块的模糊照片。设想两张照片看起来是一样的。这种情况下，如果我们认为模糊是表征的性质，从而认为冰块的照片是模糊的，那么我们也应该认为云雾的照片是模糊的。但后者实际上准确地表征了云雾的特征。这告诉我们，不应该将模糊看做是表征的性质，而应该将它看做是表征得所是的

---

① 压眼闪光现象是这样一种现象，当我们闭上眼睛用手指去压眼睑时，就会产生有光的感觉。在压光现象中，似乎只存在纯粹感觉的、非意向的视觉特征。

性质。（2003，p.77）前面说过，一个状态将某个对象表征得所是的东西就是内容。因此，按照德雷斯克的理解，模糊应该被归与给表征内容。笔者认为德雷斯克的理解是有问题的。如果我们赞同他的理解的话，我们将不得不承认，没有对好焦的照片本身不是模糊的，而是将环境表征得模糊。这显然不合常理。事实上，我们的确认为上述两张照片是不同的：云雾的照片是高质量的表征；冰块的照片是质量不好的表征。高质量的意思是，照片准确反映了物体的性质，即模糊；质量不好的意思是，照片的产生过程出了问题，以至于它本身模糊了。在后一种情形中，我们并未把模糊归与给对象（因而也就不是误表征），而是归与给了照片本身，即表征。因此，模糊不是表征内容中的性质，模糊视觉也不是误表征。

将模糊视觉视为误表征的另一个困难是，模糊视觉并没有错觉通常所具有的不可纠正性。即使我知道那根半浸在水里的棍子实际上是直的，但它在我看来仍然是弯的。这是因为知觉系统具有相对独立性，它不直接受诸如判断之类的高级认知能力的控制。但是，经历模糊视觉的人并不会禁不住去相信物体具有模糊的性质。顶多，模糊视觉只是让他在形成知觉判断时表现出迟疑。正如博格西安（P. Boghossian）和维尔门（D. Vellemen）所指出，近视者在摘下眼镜后并没有觉得刀片看来没那么锋利了。（p.96）很多时候，我们都不会认为物体本身是模糊的。这与我们看到边缘模糊的物体，例如一幅水彩画，是不同的。

泰伊注意到了第一种选择的困难。他承认，"在模糊地看物体的情形与将物体看成是模糊的情形之间确实存在**一种**（原文如此）区别。"（2002，p.147）前一种情况下，我们会说："视线有点模糊。"后一种情况下，我们会说："这个东西看起来有点模糊。"当然，有可能是物体边缘本身有点模糊，也有可能是我们将边缘清晰的物体，例如针尖，看成模糊的了。因此，共有三种经验到模糊的情形：模糊地看，将边缘模糊的物体看成是模糊的，将边缘清晰的物体看成是模糊的（后两种属于"看成模糊"）。泰伊认为，在第一种情形中，感知者并不能分辨出物体的轮廓和边界，他的视觉表征缺失了一些信息，特别是一些与表面深度和定位有关的信息。这意味着，视觉经验并未把物体边界表征成模糊的，从而也就没有"准确性"可言。（2002，p.148）也就是说，在这种情况下，"模糊"根本就不具有正确性条件，因而也就没有资格出现在内容中。在后两种情形中，视觉系统的确把物体的轮廓表征成模糊的，从而模糊也的确出现在了内容中。泰伊还认为，上述经验的不同会在现象层面上反映出来。首先是高阶意识。感知者通常能意识到模糊地看与看出物体是模糊的之间的不同。其次是边缘意识。模糊视觉会伴随着眼部身体感觉的不同。尽管有这些不同，但在所有三种情形中，"感知者直接觉知到的性质都被经验为他的经验所表征的表面和边缘的性质"。（2002，p.149）泰伊的结论是，模糊视觉既没有对强透明性论题，也没有对强表征主义构成威胁。

泰伊将模糊视觉归结为信息缺失，笔者认为是对的。尽管如此，他并不能利用这一点来维护强透明性论题。既然在"模糊地看"的情形中，模糊已经被认定是表征的性质（即信息的缺失引起的），它又怎么会是"经验所表征的表面和边缘的性质"呢？模糊视觉中的"模糊"要出现在表征内容中，只有两种可能：一是感知者错误地把它当成了外部事物的性质；二是作为表征的一个方面出现在表征内容中。如果是前一种情况，那么模糊视觉就是错觉。于是我们退回到了第一种方案。这是泰伊一开始就不同意的。如果是后一种情况，那么模糊就成了经验将物体表征得具有的性质。这与泰伊对模糊视觉的解释是矛盾的：模糊视觉并未把物体边界表征成模糊的，它根本就不具有正确性条件。无论如何，情况都不像泰伊所说的那样，在模糊视觉中，感知者直接觉知到的性质是他的经验所表征得具有的表面和边缘的性质。相反，将模糊视觉中的"模糊"归与视觉表征，这正好表明我们可以觉知到视觉经验的性质。因此，模糊视觉的确是强透明性论题的反例。

现在，我们反驳了 SR 的支撑性论证。但仍然不能排除这样的可能，或许，SR 所主张的"穷尽论题"事实上是对的，只是我们暂时没有找到合适的论证来证明它。很不幸，这样的愿望恐怕是不会实现的。按照泰伊对模糊视觉的解释，在"模糊地看"与"看成模糊"两种情形中，经验内容无论如何都是不会相同的，因为前一种情形中经验根本就未对物体边缘进行表征。但是，两种"模糊"的经验却有可能在现象上是相同的，就好比一张边缘模糊的云雾的清晰照片和一张边缘清晰的冰块的模糊照片看起来有可能相同一样。因此，有可能出现这样的情况：经验的现象特征相同，但表征内容却不同。显然，这违背了"穷尽论题"所蕴涵的（IP）。当然，泰伊会说，现象特征其实并不尽相同，因为对它们的高阶意识和边缘意识是不同的。所以在一阶范围内，"穷尽论题"仍然成立。但是，如果现象特征会发生"高阶溢出"的话，那么，"溢出"又会重新要求一个意向状态来"穷尽"它。这会导致无穷倒退。因此，模糊视觉不只是违反了强透明性论题，而且还会破坏"穷尽论题"。

当然，上述反驳并不能让 SR 的支持者死心，因为他们还有一根救命稻草，那就是（PI）。如果（PI）成立的话，然则 SR 自然化现象特征的宏图伟业仍然是可以实现的。但笔者会在下一节表明，即使（PI）也是不能成立的。这里，还是先看模糊视觉的第三种解释。

第三种解释实际上是对 SR 的否定，因为它断言充分解释现象特征需要援引内容以外的另一种状态要素，即"显现模式"（modes of presentation）。请注意，这里所说的显现模式不是弗雷格意义上的，因为它并不属于内涵，而是意向状态本身的要素。显现模式是意向状态表征事物的特定方式，它类似于塞尔所说的意向性的"侧面形态"（aspectual shapes）（1992，p. 161），查尔默斯将之称为"表征方式"（manner of representation）（2004，p. 155）。一个基本的想法是，不同模态的知觉经验，例如视觉和触觉，可以将某个物体表征得具有相同的内容，例如皮球是圆的。但是，两种经验的现象特征却有明显的不同。有人认为这样的不同是由显现模式带来的。显然，引入显现模式违背了 SR 所承诺的"穷尽论题"。不过，如果这样做能够帮助完成现象特征的自然化的任务，那也是异曲同工。可惜这依然是遥远的梦。且不说如何自然化显现模式的问题。一个明显的困难是，我们如何做到不循环地援引显现模式来解释经验的现象特征呢？就拿模糊视觉来说。模糊是有程度的。假设我现在正在经历模糊程度为 X 的视觉经验，如何解释我视觉经验的现象特征呢？一个显而易见的回答是，我的视觉经验以模糊程度 X 的显现模式表征外部事物。但这样的回答显然是循环的，并未对经验的现象特征给出真正的解释。

总结一下。这一节，笔者以模糊视觉为例说明了，强透明性论题是不成立的，因而并不能用来支持 SR。另外，笔者还说明了，事情并非像 SR 所设想的那样，经验现象性的方面可以完全被它意向性的方面穷尽，即使引入另外的状态要素也并非如此。

三、经验的形而上学

笔者说过，笔者会在这一节表明，即使是 SR 最低限度的承诺（PI），也是不成立的。这好像是笔者要专门地对（PI）进行反驳似的。实则不然。笔者的方法是一般性的。笔者认为，任何有关经验本性的断言都涉及到了经验的形而上学，所以，彻底的反驳应该有力度表明，某某断言在形而上学上是不可能的。这里，笔者将说明 SR 的"穷尽论题"是形而上学上不可能的。

首先应该知道，SR 对经验的形而上学作出了两个断言。第一个断言是经验具有罗素式内容。罗素式内容是由物体或性质本身组成的。罗素曾提出了这样的观点，单称词项只对它所在的句子所表达的命题贡献它的指称（Russell，p. 9）。按照这样的理解，命题是由单称词项的指称和谓词所表达的性质组成的。例如，"杭州很热"，这句话所表达的命题内容是由杭州和热这一性质组成的。这样的内容包含了单称词项的指称，而非视世界情况不同而挑选出不同物体的摹状词。因此之故，它们又被称为"单称内容"（singular contents）。与之相对是弗雷格式命题。弗雷格式命题并非由物体或性质，而是它们的显现模式组成，或者说，是由指称它们的概念组成。可以举一个熟知的例子来说明两者之间的区别。语句"晨星是行星"和"暮星是行星"具有不同的弗雷格内容，因为其中的"晨星"和"暮星"是两个不同的概念。但它们却有相同的罗素式内容，因为"晨星"和"暮星"指称的是相同的物体。

还应该知道，罗素式内容有强弱之分。强的罗素式内容既包含了物体，也包含了物体的性质。弱的罗素式内容包含了物体所显现出来的性质，但不包含物体本身。弱的罗素式内容又叫

"存在上限量的内容"（existentially quantified content）（Siegel，p. 364）。SR 认为知觉内容是由物体的性质组成的，这等于断言经验具有弱的罗素式内容。据说，认为经验具有弱的罗素式内容尊重了我们这样的直觉：对量上不同的物体，例如两个一模一样的物体，经验能将它们表征得一样。而按强的罗素式内容，两种经验由于包含了不同的物体，因而是不同的。另一个理由是，幻觉可以具有与真实知觉一样的内容，但由于幻觉经验的意向对象实际上并不存在，所以它的内容并不包含物体，从而真实知觉经验的内容也是如此。① 实际上，上述理由只能表明两种经验具有相同的现象学。能否从现象学的相同得出本体论的相同，这是很有争议的。析取论（disjunctivism）就明确认为不能。在真实知觉的情形中，经验以事物本身为组分，它具有强的罗素式内容。幻觉则不然。所以两者的确具有不同的本体论。

笔者认为，SR 的第一个形而上学断言会带来认识论问题。如果经验只具有弱的罗素式内容的话，那么如何确定内容的正确性条件呢？要知道，弱的罗素式内容不包含物体，因而物体是内容之外的，然则我们又如何能够超出内容之外去判定内容是否得到例示呢？如果物体本身始终不能和我们发生认知接触，那么它实际上就像康德的物自体一样不得而知了。如此看来，SR 在认识论上与 CR 一样地举步维艰。②

SR 对经验的形而上学作出的另一个断言是，经验的现象特征是外在的。请注意，说某样东西是外在的，意思是说那样东西至少不能由主体自身的要素充分决定。反之就是内在的。弗雷式内容如果被理解成完全由概念组成，那么它就是内在的。罗素式内容是外在的，因为它涉及到了外在于主体的物体或性质。SR 断言经验具有弱的罗素式内容，这相当于断言经验内容是外在的。内容外在论加上"穷尽论题"，就会导致 SR 的第二个断言，即现象外在论（phenomenal externalism）。按照现象外在论，即使是与主体的内部心理状态完全无关的东西，也会对现象特征作出贡献。例如，两个物理上相同的个体（比如说你孪生地球上的对应者），会由于各自所处环境的不同而享有不同的现象特征。这与我们的直觉相去甚远。一般认为，意向内容是外向的，而现象特征则是内向的，它反映的是主体内部心理状态的性状。所以内容外在论如今已没

---

① 有些哲学家，例如 John McDowell，认为只有真实的知觉经验（或错觉）才配得上是经验，因为只有它们才具有强的罗素式内容。幻觉则不然，它是"纯粹的显相"。因此，不存在幻觉经验。但日常语言确实允许"错觉经验"、"幻觉经验"的说法。我们认为，这样的分歧只是用词习惯的不同而已。只要厘清了它的内涵，我们仍然可以沿用那些可以给我们带来方便的日常用语。

② SR 认为真实的知觉经验与幻觉经验具有相同的罗素式内容，因而与 CR 一样都是关于经验的合取理论。与之相反的是析取论，它认为知觉经验与幻觉经验在本体论上并无"最大公因素"，详细的讨论请参见 Haddock & Macpherson（2008）。作者之一在其他地方详细说明了，所有合取理论都会遇到"知觉之幕"问题，见王华平（2008）。

有什么争议，但现象外在论多少有点匪夷所思。

尽管 SR 坚持认为现象外在论是可理解的（毕竟，哲学家乐于给出惊世骇俗的结论），但是，得出这一结论的核心主张（即"穷尽论题"），正如我们前面所看到的，并没有得到很好的辩护。我们认为，"穷尽论题"是不可能成立的。原因就在于，经验的现象性和意向性根本就是两个不同的形而上学范畴，所以无论哪一个都不能被另一个穷尽。经验的现象特征显然是历时的。我能感觉到我经验的流逝，你也一样。有感于此，孔子曾指着流淌的河水说："逝者如斯夫！"詹姆士特别强调经验的历时性，他说："意识并不是片断的连接，而是不断流动着的。用一条'河'或者一股'流水'的比喻来表达它是最自然的了。此后，我们再说起它的时候，就把它叫做思想流、意识流或者主观生活之流吧。"（p. 26）流动的经验就像是一幅不断展开的画卷，"同步地"将内心世界的动态报告给我们。我们不妨将心灵设想为一部摄像机，它连续不断地拍下经验的"快照"，只不过这些"快照"是不用"冲洗"的，因为它们在产生的同时就在心灵中一帧帧地呈现了出来（当然它们也可以在记忆的"暗房"中以"底片"的形式留存下来）。正因为经验表现为一个接一个的片段，所以塞拉斯（Sellars, p. 4, 33, 57, etc.）更喜欢用"片段"（episode）来称呼经验。但是，经验本身并不是其中的任何一个片段，也不是这些片段的连接，因为连接起来的东西是可以同时出现的，而流动的东西无法同时出现。譬如一场婚礼，你能说它是其中的任何一个场面吗？不能。它流动着，一个片段接一个片段地展开，但在任何一个时间点上都无法整个地出现。用形而上学的语言来说，这样的事物是分存的（perdurant）。经验流动的特性是我们内省时发现的，它属于经验的现象特征。因此，经验的现象特征是分存的。

但内容不同。内容是整存的（endurant）。说一个东西是整存的，意思是说那个东西在某一时间段的各时刻都整个地作为它自己而存在。例如一只水杯，在它被打破之前，它在每个时刻都是作为整体而存在的。表征内容就像物件一样，它总是整个地出现在某个时间段。为什么这样说呢？道理就在于，除非内容的所有组分同时结合在一起，否则就不可能确定内容的正确性条件是否得到了满足，从而内容也就不成其为内容。这一点，我们不妨依照吉奇（P. Geach）的说法来理解。吉奇在谈到思想的表达时说道："语词的言说在物理时间上会持续许久，一个语词接着一个语词被说出来……但除非整个复杂的内容被一起把握——除非观念（即意义，译注）全都同时呈现——否则思想或判断根本就不会存在。"（p. 104）吉奇的意思是，虽然思想的书写和言说是历时的，但思想在心灵中的呈现却不是历时的。例如，在我们作出"花很美"的判断时，如果我们只是先持有"花"的概念，接着再持有"美"的概念，我们是无法形成"花很美"的判断的。吉奇由是断言："判断是非接续的（non-successive）单位。"（p. 105）如果吉奇的论断是正确的，那么弗雷格式内容就一定是整存的。笔者认为，吉奇的论断同样适用于罗素式内容，因为我们可以仿照吉奇的口吻说：除非内容的组分同时呈现，否则内容的正确性条件根本就不会存在。这并不难理解。强的罗素式内容可表示为"o 是 P"，其中 o 指的是单称物体，P 指物体的性质。弱的罗素式内容可用如下形式的语句来表达："在位置 L 有一个为 P 的 O。"其中，O 是自然类。上述内容，缺少任何一个组分都不可能有正确性条件，从而也就不成其为内容。因此，内容是整存的。

如果上述理解是正确的，那么经验的现象特征和表征内容就有不同的形而上学。它们之间形而上学上的差别决定了，前者是不可能被后者穷尽的。反过来也是如此。这表明，在经验的现象性与意向性之间的确存在一道鸿沟，尽管它们有可能有着紧密的联系。由于它们之间的鸿沟是形而上学上的，所以任何现象上的或认识论上的论证都无法填平。这足以表明，即使 SR 最低限度的承诺，即（PI），也是不能成立的。

四、结　语

在如何理解经验的双面性这个问题上，一直存在两条不同的路线。一是坚持现象性是基本的，认为意向性只有在现象性的基础上才能得到真正的理解。塞尔是这条路线的坚定拥护者。塞尔认为，原生的意向性肯定是有现象意识的，至少也是潜在地有意识的。（1992，p. 132）因而现象性对意向性来说是基本的。另一条路线则认为意向性是基本的。一个重要的理由是，非意识或无意识的状态也可以具有意向性。例如，速度计的某个状态或主体发生盲视时的知觉状态也可以是表征的。① 越来越多的科学证据表明，意向性的发生的确早于现象意识。② 所以有理由认为，NR（包括 SR 和 WR）认为所有心理状态都具有表征内容的观点是对的。在这个意义上，我们可以认为意向性对现象性来说是必要的。但是，科学证据在表明意向性先于现象性的同时，也表明了它对现象特征来说是不充分的。速度计可以具有表征状态，但它的任何一个状态都不具有现象特征。一个心理状态究竟是如何获得现象特征的，这仍然是个有待解开的谜。可以肯定的是，主体的内部因素在决定经验现象特征的过程中起到了重要作用。所以，SR 所主张的现象外在主义是不能成立的。意向性和现象性的关系比 SR 所认为的要复杂。

---

① 盲视是这样的现象，一些脑部纹状皮层受损的病人看不到他正常视域内的物体，但却能辨认它，并对它的位置作出准确的判断。由于盲视病人的知觉经验是无意识的，所以不会具有现象特征。

② 例如心理学有充分的证据表明存在"隐知觉"（implicit perception），即感知者能接收环境信息但却意识不到所感知的东西。证据除了前面说到的盲视现象外，还有半侧忽视（hemineglect）现象。

参考文献

［1］王华平，2008，"错觉论证与析取论"，《哲学研究》第 9 期，第 93—99 页。

［2］Alston，William，1999，"Back to the Theory of Appearing". *Philosophical Perspectives*，13：181 – 203.

［3］Block，Ned，1996，"Mental Paint and Mental Latex". *Philosophical Issues*，7：19 – 49.

［4］Block，Ned，1998，"Is Experiencing Just Representing?". *Philosophy and Phenomenological Research*，58（3）：663 – 670.

［5］Boghossian，Paul and Vellemen，David，1989，"Colour as a Secondary Quality". *Mind*，98，（389）：81 – 103.

［6］Chalmers，David，1997，"Facing up to the Problem of Consciousness". In J. Shear（ed.），*Explaining Consciousness：The Hard Problem*. MIT Press，pp. 9 – 30.

［7］Chalmers，David，2004，"The Representational Character of Experience". In B. Leiter（ed.），*The Future for Philosophy*. Oxford：Oxford University Press，pp. 153 – 181.

［8］Clark，Andy and Toribio，Josefa，1994，"Doing Without Representing?" *Synthese*，101：401 – 431.

［9］Crane，Tim，1992，*The Contents of Experience*. Cambridge：Cambridge University Press.

［10］Dretske，Fred，1995，*Naturalizing the Mind*. Cambridge：MIT Press.

［11］Dretske，Fred，2003，"Experience as Representation"，*Philosophical Issues*，13：67 – 82.

［12］Geach，Peter，1957，*Mental Acts*. London：Routledge and Kegan Paul，pp. 16 – 17.

［13］Haddock，Adrian and Macpherson，Fiona，2008，In A. Haddock and F. Macpherson（eds.），*Disjunctivism：Perception，Action，Knowledge*. Oxford：Oxford University Press.

［14］James，William，2001，*Psychology：The Briefer Course*. New York：Courier Dover Publications.

［15］Kind，Amy，2003，"What's So Transparent about Transparency?". *Philosophical Studies*，115（3）：225 – 244.

［16］Millikan，Ruth，1984，*Language，Thought，and Other Biological Categories*. Cambridge：MIT Press.

［17］Nagel，Thomas，1974，"What Is It Like to Be a Bat?". *The Philosophical Review*，83：435 – 481.

［18］Nickel，Bernard，2007，"Against Intentionalism". *Philosophical Studies*，136：279 – 304.

［19］Robinson，Howard，1994，*Perception*. London：Routledge.

［20］Russell，Bertrand，1905，"On Denoting". *Mind*，14（56）：479 – 493.

［21］Searle，John，1983，*Intentionality：An Essay in the Philosophy of Mind*. Cambridge：Cambridge University Press.

[22] Searle, John, 1992, *The Rediscovery of Mind.* Cambridge: MIT Press.

[23] Sellars, Wilfrid, 1997, *Empiricism and the Philosophy of Mind.* Cambridge: Harvard University Press.

[24] Siegel, Susanna, 2006, "Subject and Object in the Contents of Visual Experience". *The Philosophical Review*, 115 (3): 355 – 388.

[25] Toribio, Josefa, 2007, "Nonconceptual Content". *Philosophy Compass*, 2 (3): 445 – 460.

[26] Travis, Charles, 2004, "The Silence of the Senses". *Mind*, 113 (449): 57 – 94.

[27] Tye, Michael, 1995, *Ten Problems of Consciousness.* Cambridge: MIT Press.

[28] Tye, Michael, 2002, "Representationalism and the Transparency of Experience". *Noûs*, 36 (1): 137 – 151.

[29] Tye, Michael, 2003, "Blurry Images, Double Vision, and Other Oddities: New Problems for Representationalism?". *Consciousness: New Philosophical Perspectives.* Oxford: Oxford University Press, pp. 7 – 32.

Phenomenal Character of Experience and Representationalism

Hua-ping Wang，Hua-xin Huang

Zhejiang University

Abstract：Experience has both intentionality and phenomenality. Representationalism claims that phenomenality can be fully explained by intentionality. The most important reason for this claim is the transparency of experience. Nevertheless，blur vision makes it clear that experience is not fully transparent. Thus the phenomenal character of experience cannot be exhausted by its representational content. And more importantly，the intentionality and the phenomenality of experience are two metaphysically different aspects. The first is endurant，while the latter is perdurant. This difference makes certain that it is insufficient whether to account intentionality in terms of phenomenality，or to account phenomenality in terms of intentionality. Nevertheless，there are some relations between these two aspects. It is almost certain that intentionality is necessary for phenomenality.

Keywords：representationalism；phenomenal character；the transparency of experience；metaphysics of experience

下向因果何以存在？ *

——兼评金在权对下向因果的消解

◎ 陈晓平

华南师范大学

摘　要： 下向因果关系的重要性在于，它表明包括心理功能在内的功能层面的性质具有实在性，尽管功能性质不能还原为物理性质。金在权通过对下向因果的消解来反驳包括主流功能主义在内的非还原的物理主义，并用还原论取而代之。笔者区分功能的两个层面即功能意义和功能结构，并主张，功能意义不能还原为物理层次，而功能结构则可以还原为物理层次。在此基础上，又区分了功能整体和功能实现的整体，强随附性、中随附性和弱随附性；进而指出，所谓下向因果关系实际上是功能实现的整体对其物理基础的关系，亦即整体对于部分的关系，而不是一般的层次之间的关系。对下向因果作这样的理解，加之对物理因果闭合原则的摈弃，可以使金在权的论证归于无效，从而为不可还原的功能主义做出辩护。

关键词： 下向因果；功能意义；功能结构；随附性；还原论

一、功能主义与下向因果

下向因果（downward causation）是相对于上向因果（upward causation）而言的，这一对概念对于非还原的物理主义（nonreductive physicalism）是至关重要的。非还原的物理主义是当代心灵哲学的主流，其中包括功能主义、突现主义、异态一元论等。相对而言，功能主义对于本文的讨论尤为重要。

功能主义得益于 20 世纪 50 或 60 年代计算机技术的发展。当我们考察一台计算机执行的计算程序时，我们实际上撇开了它的物质硬件。两台结构完全不同的计算机能够执行相同的软件

---

　* 本文最初发表于《哲学研究》2009 年第 1 期。这次重新发表时对全文作了必要的修改，并特别增加了"随附性与依赖性"一节。

程序，这种现象被叫做计算功能的"多重实现"（multiple realization）。多重实现表明：一方面，功能本身不同于实现它的物质基础，否则，功能和物质实现者之间只能是一一对应的关系，而不可能有功能的多重实现；另一方面，功能依赖于物质基础，即它必须由物质基础来实现。计算功能同实现它的物质基础分别属于不同的层次，一般把功能层次称为高层，把物质实现者称为低层。这也就是说，高层对象不能还原为低层对象，但是高层对象却依赖于低层对象。高层与低层之间的这种关系常常叫做高层对低层的"随附性"（supervenience）。**把世界现象看做具有随附性关系的层次结构**，这是所有非还原的物理主义的共同主张；功能主义进一步强调处于高层的**功能**对其物质实现者的随附性和不可还原性。关于心身问题，功能主义的主张是：心灵是一种功能，处于高层，身体是实现心灵功能的物质基础，处于低层。心灵状态不能还原为身体状态，但却依赖于身体状态。

功能主义的非还原论立场使他们不得不承认心灵具有某种实在性。功能主义的代表人物之一福多（Jerry Fodor）谈道："我并不真正认为精神是否物理的问题很重要，更不用说我们是否能够证明它。然而，我想得到**因果性地**导致我抻手，我痒**因果性地**导致我搔，我相信**因果性地**导致我说……如果这些都不是真的，那么，我对任何事情所相信的一切实际上都是假的，那将是世界的终结。"（Fodor，pp. 59 - 79）在这里，福多表达了他的一个信念，即：精神或心理对身体具有因果作用，因而精神或心理是实在的，而且这种实在性并不依赖于精神或心理性质是否可以还原为物理性质。用现象之间的因果作用来证明这些现象的实在性是被广泛接受的一种做法。这种做法的根据，金在权（Jaegwon kim）称之为"亚历山大格言"（Alexander's dictum），即："是实在的就是具有因果力"（to be real is to have causal powers）。（参阅 Alexander）

通常认为，精神或心理对身体的因果作用是一种下向因果关系，反之，身体对精神或心理的因果作用是一种上向因果关系。粗略地说，处于高层的功能或性质对于处于低层的物理结构所产生的因果作用是下向因果关系；反之，处于低层的物理结构对于处于高层的功能或性质所产生的因果作用是上向因果关系。对于功能主义来说，下向因果关系的重要性在于，它表明包括心理功能在内的功能层面的性质具有实在性，即使功能性质不能还原为物理性质。可以说，下向因果关系的存在是坚持非还原的物理主义的重要依据。

当然，在一定意义上，上向因果关系也能表明功能性质（如心理性质）的实在性，但是，这对于物理主义（无论是还原的还是非还原的）是没有说服力的，因为他们认为，上向因果关系恰恰表明物理层次决定心理层次，进而表明物理层次的实在性，而不是心理层次的实在性。正因为此，人们把争论的焦点仅仅放在下向因果关系是否存在的问题上。

在此，有必要提一下戴维森（Donald Davidson）的异态一元论（Anomalous Monism）。异态一元论也属于非还原的物理主义。戴维森说到："精神实体是物理实体，但是，精神概念却不可以通过定义或自然律还原为物理学概念。用更为一般和更为熟悉方式讲：它只承认本体论上的还原，而不承认概念上的还原。"（Davidson，p. 3）可以说，戴维森的异态一元论是**本体**一元论和**概念**二元论的结合。异态一元论与功能主义同属本体一元论，其区别仅仅在于，作为不可还原的第二元是功能还是概念或是其他什么？这个问题在笔者看来颇为重要，将在第三节详加讨论。

眼下更为迫切的问题是，下向因果关系是否存在？若不存在，非还原的物理主义将被还原的物理主义所代替。

二、金在权对下向因果关系的消解

金在权断然否定下向因果关系的存在。以心身关系为例，其论证简要陈述如下。（参阅 Kim，1993，pp. 353 – 357）

假设某一心理性质 M 因果性地导致某一物理性质（或生理性质）P^*，即存在 M 对 P^* 的下向因果关系。根据物理实现观点（the Physical Realization Thesis），心理性质 M 是被某一物理性质（或生理性质）P 实现的。既然 P 是实现 M 的基础，那么 P 是 M 的充分条件；又因 M 是 P^* 的充分条件，那么 P 也是 P^* 的充分条件。这样，我们便面临一个问题：为什么我们不能忽略 M 或者把 M 作为副现象，而把 P 作为 P^* 的原因？在金在权看来，我们没有理由不这样做。

假定我们正在寻找物理性质 P^* 得以出现的原因，我们发现在它之前 M 出现并且我们能用某一规则将 M 的出现同 P^* 的出现联系起来。然而，我们还发现，物理性质 P 与 M 同时出现，既然 P 是 M 的物理实现者；并且 P 和 P^* 之间也有某条规则相连接。这样一来，P 至少像 M 一样可以成为 P^* 的直接原因。既然如此，我们便不应继续把 M 作为 P^* 的原因。理由如下：

首先，根据**简单性原则**，对于物理性质 P^*，我们已经找到其物理原因 P，便没有必要再把心理性质 M 作为其原因了。也许有人说，M 是 P 与 P^* 之间的中间环节，在这个意义上，M 和 P 都是 P^* 的原因。然而，不要忘记，P 是 M 的物理实现者，它们是**同时**出现的，因此，M 不可能成为 P 与 P^* 的因果链条上的中间环节。

其次，如果坚持 P 同时具有两个充分的原因，那么便会遇到**因果解释的排他性问题**（the problem of causal-explanatory exclusion），这是一种对因果决定的过度诠释，几乎等于没有给出因果解释。也许有人说，M 和 P 各自都不是 P^* 的充分原因，而只是必要因素，仅当二者联合起来才构成 P^* 的唯一的充分原因，这样便没有因果解释的排他性问题了。然而，在金在权看来，P

和 M 的结合对还原论来说不成问题，但对反还原论来说则存在困难。在笔者看来，金在权的这一说法是欠妥的。一般而言，P 和 M 结合为一个原因，这对反还原论者也不成问题；相反，恰恰因为 P 和 M 是两种不同的性质，二者的结合才能构成一种既不同于 P 也不同于 M 的新的性质。与之不同，还原论所说的结合是把 M 归于 P，而不是一种真正意义上的结合。金在权之所以说 P 和 M 的结合对于反还原论不可行，他实际上还依据了一条原则，即**物质世界的因果闭合原则**（the principle of causal closure of the material world）。根据这条原则，导致物理性质 P* 的原因只能是物理性质，既然 M 不可还原为 P，那么 M 就不是物理性质，M 同 P 的结合也不是物理性质，因此，M 和 P 不能结合成为 P* 的物理原因。显然，在这一点上，金在权的论证只是对于接受了物质世界的因果闭合原则的人才是有效的。

事实上，金在权在其论证中把物理因果闭合原则作为另一个重要依据，由这条原则和因果解释的排他性原则导致的问题被看做非还原论所面临的难以解脱的困境。他说："此时此刻我们可以非常合情合理地说，对于排他性问题和物理因果闭合问题的唯一解决存在于某种形式的还原论，这种还原论将允许我们摈弃或者至少修改那种主张，即：心理性质不同于它们赖以存在的物理性质。"（Kim，1993，p. 356）本文最后一节正是针对这两个问题着手解构金在权的论证的。

三、功能结构与功能意义

以普特南（Hilary Putnam）、福多和布洛克（Ned Block）等人为代表的经典功能主义强调功能的实在性和不可还原性，与之相反，以金在权为代表的新功能主义却强调功能的非实在性和可还原性。金在权的还原的物理主义是以"功能还原模型"（the functional model of reduction）为其核心的。

功能还原模型的基本思想就是把被还原的性质 M 功能化，即把 M 与其他性质联系起来，形成一个因果链条或因果网络，显示其发挥作用的因果条件。如果发现另一低阶性质 P 也满足这一因果条件，那么由此可以确定：M = P；从而把高阶性质 M 还原为低阶性质 P。例如，对温度这种性质进行还原。首先从功能方面对它进行解释即：温度是物体的这样一种性质，当两个物体接触时，本来温度低的那个物体的温度就会升高，本来温度高的那个物体的温度就会降低。当温度足够高时会使某种材料燃烧起来，当温度足够低时会使某种材料变得易碎，等等。当我们发现物体分子的平均动能也满足这一因果条件，于是得出结论：温度 = 物体分子的平均动能，从而将温度还原为物体分子的平均动能。金在权把性质的功能化也叫做性质的关系化或外在化。

（Kim，1998. pp. 97 – 103）

功能还原模型受到许多批评，例如，作为反还原主义的突现论反对把高层性质功能化，其理由之一是高层性质对于低层性质来说是不可预测的。如水的流动性、透明性和无味性等不能仅从两个氢原子和一个氧原子的性质加以预测。对此，金在权不以为然。他说："我相信，此类解释或预测的关键是关于被解释现象或性质的功能解释。不妨考虑水的透明性：看来，一旦对这种性质给以功能的理解，即理解为某种实体完整无损地传播光线的能力，那么，对于 H_2O 分子为何具有这种力量的问题，在原则上便没有什么能够阻碍我们给出一种微观物理学的解释。"（Kim，1998，p. 100）这样，水的透明性或透明的功能便被还原为水的分子结构。总之，功能还原模型就是通过把所研究现象功能化，显示功能作用的因果条件，从而揭示这种因果条件的微观结构，据此将高层功能还原为低层结构。

前面提到，主流功能主义也是反还原的。针对主流功能主义，金在权谈到："我在这里所论证的恰恰相反，关于心理性质的功能主义观念对于心身还原来说是必要的。事实上，它对于可还原性既是必要的又是充分的。如果这是正确的，那么，关于心理现象的心身还原主义与功能主义方法便站在或滑入同一立场；他们分享相同的形而上学命运。"（Kim，1998，p. 101）这里出现一个有趣的问题：为什么同样强调功能的作用和地位，主流功能主义与金在权的新功能主义却得出截然相反的结论，前者主张功能性质是不可还原的而后者主张功能性质是可还原的？对于这一问题，我们可以从金在权的有关论述中找到答案的线索。

相对于最低层的性质即一阶性质，相邻的高层性质通常也被叫做二阶性质。金在权指出，这种叫法是令人误解的。在他看来，所谓二阶性质其实不是性质，而只是一阶性质的名称而已。因此，他建议称之为性质的"二阶摹状词"（second-order descriptions）或"二阶称谓"（second-order designators）或"二阶概念"（second-order concepts）。例如，第二层的某一功能现象 M 必须由第一层的性质 P_1 或 P_2 或 P_3 加以实现，说具有 M，不外乎说具有 P_1 或具有 P_2 或具有 P_3，M 本身不是一种独立的性质。正如某人谋杀了约翰斯，那个谋杀者是史密斯，或是约翰斯，或是王。我们不能把那个谋杀者看做这三人以外的某个人，此人叫做"史密斯 – 或 – 约翰斯 – 或 – 王"。"史密斯 – 或 – 约翰斯 – 或 – 王"只是关于人名的某种表述，而它本身并不是人名。类似地，所谓二阶性质只是关于性质的某种表述，而它本身不是性质。正因为此，在本体论上，只有一阶性质的位置而没有所谓高阶性质的位置，后者可以并且应该还原为前者。这是金在权对本体一元论的论证之一。（Kim，1998，pp. 103 – 104）

然而，另一方面，"二阶称谓也传达有价值的信息，也许在给定语境下这种信息是不可或缺的，即那些信息没有被一阶实现者的标准称谓所传达。"（Kim，1998，p. 104）例如，在普通语境下谈论**疼**这种心理状态（二阶概念或二阶称谓），如果我们通过对疼加以功能化而把它还原为一阶性质即神经系统的某种输入－输出性质，这并不能代替人们对疼的通常理解。因此，"从普通的认识和实践的观点看，对二阶性质称谓的使用或许是不可避免的，我们应该认识到，这些称谓引进了一组有用的和实践上不可避免的概念；对于描述和交流的目的而言，这些概念以一种实质性的方式将一阶性质组合起来。"（Kim，1998，pp. 104－105）这就是说，尽管关于性质的二阶称谓（如疼）没有本体论上的实在性因而是可还原的，但是，它们具有认识论或实践论上的意义，而且这种意义是实质性的和不可缺少的。

在笔者看来，金在权本应进而得出一个重要的结论即：关于性质的二阶称谓或二阶概念（如疼）虽然不具有本体论上的实在性，但却具有概念或意义上的实在性，因而在概念意义的范围内是不可还原的。这个结论属于概念二元论的主张，它同本体一元论是可以并行不悖的。令人遗憾的是，金在权并未这样做，而是试图把一元论的主张贯彻到底，这使他的理论留下一个致命的缺陷。他不得不承认，对于诸如疼这样的感受性质，他的功能还原模型是不适用的，这意味着他的还原论并不完全成功。与此对照，戴维森的异态一元论同时主张本体一元论和概念二元论，这是他高于金在权的方面。但是，由于他并未给出清晰的界定和论证，他的论点显得比较武断。这使异态一元论受到许多质疑，其中金在权的质疑和反驳尤为有力。

事实上，金在权有意无意地为功能主义暗示一条出路，即把经典功能主义同他的新功能主义结合起来。具体地说，把功能性质的实在性和不可还原性限制在功能意义上，而把功能还原模型的作用范围限制在功能结构上；也就是说，功能还原模型不是指功能意义的还原，而是指功能结构的还原。如疼这种心理功能在其意义上不能还原为某种神经活动，但在其结构上可以还原为某种神经活动。再如，红这种感觉功能在其意义上不可还原为某种光波对视网膜的刺激，但在其结构上可以做这种还原。由此可见，区分"**功能意义**"和"**功能结构**"这两个概念是至关重要的。我们可以同时主张**功能意义上的反还原论**和**功能结构上的还原论**，二者是并行不悖的。

需要强调，功能意义和功能结构是同一个对象即功能的两个侧面，而不是两个不同的对象。由于功能的这两个侧面对于低层结构即物质实现者有着相反的两种关系即：功能意义对于物质实现者的独立性和不可还原性，功能结构对于物质实现者的依附性和可还原性，功能作为整体对于其物质实现者的关系就是一种**随附性**。不仅如此，既然功能结构可以还原为物质结构，在这个意义上，功能同其物质实现者构成一个更大的整体，不妨称之为"**功能实现的整体**"，以区别于前一个较小的整体即**功能整体**。这个区分对于后面的讨论是重要的。

主流功能主义之所以在金在权等人的批评下显得有些无力招架，关键在于没有区分功能的两个方面即功能意义和功能结构，这使他们关于功能对物质同时具有依附性和不可还原性的主张显得有些自相矛盾，难以自圆其说。然而，当我们作了这种区分以后，主流功能主义所面临的那种困境便在原则上不存在了。在笔者看来，对功能意义和功能结构作出区分，这本是金在权的新功能主义和戴维森的异态一元论的应有之义，但是，他们二人都没有这样做，致使他们各执一端，针锋相对。

四、随附性与依赖性

我们知道，早在亚里士多德那里就提出**实体（substance）与偶性（accident）**的范畴，在康德那里继续保留这对范畴，尽管他对亚里士多德的其他一些范畴作了删除或替换。此外，康德强调了范畴的先验性和必然性。笔者也接受实体与偶性这对范畴及其先验性和必然性，并且把这对范畴放在更为凸显的位置上。（参阅陈晓平，2005）借助于这对范畴，我们可以以功能结构对其物理结构的还原——即金在权的功能还原模型——提供一定程度的辩护，尽管金在权本人没有这样做①。

实体与偶性这对先验范畴使人们不得不认为：属性随附于实体，相应地，功能随附于物质实现者即低层结构，因为功能是属性的组合，物质结构是实体的组合。正如属性依赖实体，功能也依赖物质结构；属性不能还原为实体，功能也不能还原为其物质结构。属性对于实体的这种既依赖又独立（不可还原）的关系就是最为基本的随附性关系，它是功能对其物质结构的随附性的形而上学基础，也是其他一切随附性关系的形而上学基础。

不过，我们说功能对其物质结构具有随附性，这只是一种较为粗略的说法，其确切的意思是，**功能结构**对其物质结构具有依赖性和可还原性，与此同时，**功能意义**对其物质结构具有独立性和不可还原性。因此，由功能意义和功能结构组成的**功能整体对其物质基础具有随附性**。金在权的功能还原模型的形而上学基础在于：功能结构对其物质结构具有依赖性和可还原性。在这里，功能还原模型的有效性限制于功能结构，而对功能意义是无效的。但是，金在权却没有意识到功能还原模型的这种局限性。

在此，必须区分两个看似相近的关系即**依赖性**和**随附性**。依赖性（dependence）是指属性

---

① 金在权在谈论功能结构还原的必然性时，并未提到康德的先验范畴，而是在很大程度上借助于科里普克（Saul Kripke）的"形而上学必然性"和"刚性"（rigid）概念。他认为，功能还原模型虽然没有达到形而上学必然性或刚性，但却具备律则的（nomological）必然性或准刚性（semi-rigid）。在笔者看来，科里普克和金在权的这些概念及其论证都是不够清晰的。

对于实体的关系，也是功能结构对于其物质实现者的关系；随附性是对依赖性和独立性的综合，即功能结构对物质结构的依赖性和功能意义对物质结构的独立性，这两种相反的关系构成功能整体对于物质结构的随附性关系。功能意义对物质结构的独立性可以看做一种突现性。不过，在有关文献中，"随附性"和"突现性"都是复杂的概念，其含义不只一种，在此仅对"随附性"的多种含义进行分析。

刚才所谈的随附性是弱于依赖性的，因此，我们不妨把依赖性叫做"强随附性"。强随附性是功能结构与其物理结构之间的关系。金在权最先把随附性区分为"强随附性"和"弱随附性"，他表明强随附性必然导致可还原性，而弱随附性虽然不导致可还原性，但它因缺少必然性而丧失哲学的重要性。（参阅金在权，1984 年）笔者同意其结论的前一半，而不同意其结论的后一半。笔者认为，弱随附性还可以分为两种：一种就是前边谈到的功能整体对于物质结构的随附性，它是功能结构对物质结构的依赖性（强随附性）和功能意义对物质结构的突现性的综合，不妨称之为"中随附性"，以同另一种更弱的随附性相区别；另一种更弱的随附性是整体对其元素或组成部分的随附性。① 下面就对这种弱随附性加以讨论，它涉及前面提到的"功能实现的整体"。

功能整体与其物质实现者即物质结构的关系是高层与低层之间的关系，与之不同，功能**实现的整体**与物质结构之间的关系是整体与部分的关系，因为功能实现的整体是由功能整体和其物质结构组成的一个更大的整体，它把物质结构包含于其中。显然，功能实现的整体不能还原为它的组成部分即物质结构，因为整体不能还原为它的某一部分，甚至不能还原为其部分之和，既然整体大于部分之和。整体与部分的关系不能简单地看作偶性与实体之间的关系，因为前者包含了更多的独立性，即部分是不同于整体的另一个实体—偶性的统一体。例如，一个水分子和构成它的氧原子、氢原子分别是不同的实体－偶性统一体。因此，就实体－偶性的统一体而言，一个整体同其部分或元素是平等的；正因为这样，整体和部分之间可以发生双向的因果关系，即上向因果和下向因果。

尽管如此，整体对其部分具有一种弱的随附性，即：如果一个整体的部分或元素不发生任何变化，这个整体也不会发生任何变化。请注意，这里没有另一种意思，即：如果部分或元素

① 这里所说的"强随附性"、"中随附性"和"弱随附性"分别相当于金在权所说的"强随附性"、"弱随附性"和"全总随附性"。金在权在《随附性概念》中把全总随附性等同于强随附性，后来在《"强"和"全总"随附性重审》中修改这一看法，认为强随附性强于全总随附性，弱随附性与全总随附性彼此独立。然而，笔者证明，弱随附性强于全总随附性，即全总随附性是三种随附性中最弱的。（参见陈晓平《"随附性"概念辨析》，载《哲学研究》2010 年第 4 期）

发生变化，那么这个整体也发生变化。这就是说，部分或元素的变化只是导致整体变化的必要条件，而不是充分条件。这种作为必要条件的随附性正是戴维森在提出"随附性"概念时所强调的。与之相比，功能结构与其物质基础之间具有一种必然的充分必要条件关系，即金在权给出的强随附性的共外延公式，从而成为可还原性的根据。由于整体与其部分之间不具有而且不包含作为充分必要条件的强随附性，因而比前面所说的"中随附性"还要弱，相当于前面所说的"弱随附性"。

至此，我们便得到三个随附性概念，即"强随附性""中随附性"和"弱随附性"。下面将表明，无论是中随附性还是弱随附性，都不会像金在权所说那样缺乏哲学的重要性。我们的这一论点的一个有力根据就是下向因果关系的存在。

五、下向因果是整体对其部分的关系

以上是从静态结构上揭示了整体对于其部分或元素的弱随附性（突现性）关系，如果这种关系被放入时间的进程中，则展现为从量变到质变再从质变到量变的动态过程。具体地说，从元素性渐变到整体性突变，然后又开始新的元素性渐变和新的整体性突变。用辩证哲学的术语说，这就是量质互变规律，也类似于内格尔所说的"进化突现"。举例来说，对冰块持续加温（元素性渐变），当温度超过0℃时，水的形态会由固体变为液体（整体性突变），从而开始新的元素性渐变即液体水的温度不断升高，和新的整体性突变，即水由液体变为气体。

在这一过程中，上向因果作用和下向因果作用随之出现了：元素性渐变对于整体性突变具有上向因果关系，整体性突变对于元素性渐变具有下向因果关系。对于心身关系而言，身体结构对精神意识具有上向因果作用，精神意识对于身体结构具有下向因果作用。例如，某根神经的细微变化不必导致疼痛的感觉，仅当这根神经的变化达到一定的程度才会引起疼痛；疼痛一旦产生便导致新的量变即生理上的某种渐变，当疼痛的生理变化达到一定的程度便产生新的质变如神志不清，神志不清又在时间进程中发生量的变化。

请注意，当某根神经发生细微变化的时候可以没有心理变化相伴随，但是，任何心理变化一定有相应的生理变化相伴随。可见，所谓心理变化实际上是整体变化，单纯的生理变化则是整体之要素的变化。这进一步表明：心理对生理的下向因果作用属于整体对其部分的作用，生理对心理的上向因果作用属于部分对其整体的作用。

需要强调，**功能整体**与物质实现者的结构之间不存在因果关系，因为二者之间是高层和低层的层次关系，不必包含因果关系的必要条件即**时间顺序**。下向因果关系和上向因果关系只存在于**功能实现的整体**与其物质结构的部分之间，而**功能实现的整体必须在时间的进程中才能实现自己**。这也就是说，功能整体与物质结构之间的中随附性关系是两个层次之间的关系，只能是共时性的，因而不伴随上向因果和下向因果的关系。与之不同，功能实现的整体与物质结构之间的弱随附性关系是整体与部分之间的关系，是两个不同的实体－偶性统一体之间的关系，因而既可以是共时性的，也可以是历时性的；从历时性的角度看，二者之间便具有了上向因果和下向因果的关系。

至此，我们便纠正了一个常见的错误，即把下向因果和上向因果看做平行的两个层次之间的关系。一般来说，层次关系是共时性的，不可能具备历时性的因果关系。层次关系的典型方式是由亨佩尔和内格尔等人揭示的两个理论之间的还原关系，如牛顿物理学从逻辑形式上可以还原为爱因斯坦物理学，但这两个理论层次之间不具有因果关系。具体地说，牛顿物理学对于爱因斯坦物理学只具有中随附性，即物理意义上的突现性和数学结构上的可还原性的结合，而不具有整体对其部分的弱随附性，因而不具有上向因果或下向因果的关系。

总之，上向因果和下向因果是整体与部分之间的一种关系，并且是在时间进程中展开的；二者在时间进程中交替起作用，呈现出从量变到质变，又从质变到量变的规律。这就是上向因果和下向因果得以存在的方式和根据。

六、对金在权论证的解构

第二节末尾指出，金在权消解下向因果的论证只对那些面临因果排他性问题和物理因果闭合问题的人才是有效的。对于笔者所理解的下向因果关系，这两个问题均不存在，具体说明如下。

金在权在论证中假设的境况是：某一心理性质 M 因果性地导致某一物理性质 P^*。心理性质 M 是被某一物理性质 P 实现的。既然 P 是实现 M 的基础，那么 P 是 M 的充分条件；又因 M 是 P^* 的充分条件，那么 P 也是 P^* 的充分条件。这样，P^* 便同时具有两个充分原因即 P 和 M，因而违反因果解释的排他性原则。

笔者在前一节表明，下向因果关系是整体对其部分的因果关系，这里的整体就是心理性质 M 和物理性质 P 的结合，它对其部分的因果作用体现为物理性质 P^*。请注意，这里的整体和部分是被放进时间进程中来考察的，M 和 P 的结合构成时刻 t 的功能实现的整体，P^* 是该整体在后续时刻 t' 的组成部分。因此，对于 P^* 不存在两个充分原因，而只有一个充分原因即 M 和 P 结合在一起的功能实现的整体。这样，便不存在违反因果解释的排他性的问题。

　　前面还指出，心理现象作为功能意义是实在的和不可还原的。于是，M 同 P 的结合并非纯粹的物理性质，这使它对 P* 的下向因果作用违反物理因果闭合原则。然而，笔者并不承认因果闭合原则的普遍性，也就是说，**世界上存在着超物理的因果作用**。

　　如果说这个命题对于物理学家有些意外，但对于哲学家却不应如此。因为自从休谟对因果推理提出质疑以来，因果关系的本质至今仍然是一个哲学之谜，更不用说因果关系一定是物理的了。在康德看来，因果关系不过是人的先验范畴，物理世界的因果关系说到底是人为自然立法。可见，所谓的物理因果闭合原则并没有哲学上的根据。我们从哲学上探讨下向果关系，笔者所持的观点确实违反所谓的物理因果闭合原则，但这没有什么了不得，也没有什么问题或困境可言。

　　事实上，笛卡尔所持的身心二元论早已违反物理因果闭合原则，在这点上笔者可以说是步笛卡尔之后尘。如果说有何不同的话，那就是笔者所持的不是笛卡尔的平行二元论，而是**有序二元论**，即承认心理性质对于物理性质的随附性。这一区别导致的一个后果是，笔者不认为心灵可以离开肉体而存在，因而不接受诸如"灵魂不死"这样的命题。另一方面，心理性质对物理性质的随附性也是大多数非还原的物理主义者所接受的，但我不愿意称自己为物理主义者，既然我坦然地承认，这个世界上存在着超物理的因果关系，如包含功能意义在内的功能实现的整体对于物质结构的下向因果作用。随附性这个概念对于不同的非还原论者有不同的理解，笔者的理解基于实体－偶性的先验范畴，与物理主义的理解相去甚远。正因为此，金在权关于消解下向因果关系的论证，尽管对于非还原的物理主义者构成严重的威胁，但是对于笔者，情况远非如此。

　　笔者之所以能够避免金在权论证的威胁，除了不承认物理因果闭合原则的普遍性以外，更重要的是对于下向因果和上向因果的作用给予新的解释，即把通常理解的上层和下层之间的因果关系理解为整体和部分之间的因果关系。具体地说，上向因果和下向因果所说的上下关系不是指功能性质与物质结构之间的高低关系，而是指功能实现的整体和物质结构之间的整体－部分关系，功能实现的整体是以物质结构为其组成部分的。

　　正如亚里山大格言所指出的，实体的根本标志是具有因果力。由于存在着上向因果和下向因果，这两种因果关系表明两种实体的存在；具体到心—身问题上，便是表明心灵和身体这两种实体的存在。正因为此，笔者的立场更接近笛卡尔的二元论，而不是物理主义的一元论。

参考文献

[1] Kim, Jaegwon, 1998, *Mind in a Physical World*, Cambridge：MIT Press.

1993. *Supervenience and Mind*, Cambridge：Cambridge University Press.

［2］Fodor, Jerry, 1989, 'Making Mind Matter More', *Philosophical Topics* 17.

［3］Alexander, Samuel, 1920, *Space, Time, and Deity*, vol. 2. London：MaCmillan.

［4］Davidson, Donald, 1993, "Thinking Causes", in J. Heil and A. Mele, eds., *Mental Causation.* Oxford：Clarendon.

［5］Kim, Jaegwon, 1984, 'Consepts of Supervenience', in Philosophy and Phenomenological Research, Vol. XLV, No. 2. （中译文见高新民、储绍华主编《心灵哲学》，商务印书馆，2002）

［6］陈晓平，2005，《关于可证实原则的形而上学基础》，《哲学研究》第 6 期。

［7］陈晓平，2010，《"随附性"概念辨析》，《哲学研究》第 4 期。

How does downward causation exist?
A comment on Kim's elimination of downward causation
Xiaoping Chen

South China Normal University

Abstract: The importance of downward causation lies in showing that functional properties including mental properties are real, although they can't be reduced to physical properties. Kim rejects nonreductive physicalism including leading functionalism by eliminating downward causation, and thereby returns to reductionism. In this paper, I make a distinction between the two aspects of function which are the functional meaning and the functional structure, and put forth that the functional meaning can't be reduced to the physical level while the functional structure can. On this basis, I make further distinctions between the integer of function, which includes the functional meaning and functional structure, and the whole of functional realization, and between the supervenience relations of the strong, the medial and the weak. the so-called downward causation is indeed the relation between the whole of functional realization and its physical realizer, which is a whole-part relation instead of the general relation between levels. As a result of understanding downward causation in this way and abandoning the principle of causal closure of the physical world, Kim's argument becomes invalid and nonreductive functionalism is justified.

Keywords: downward causation; functional meaning; functional structure; supervenience; reductionism

Defending Evidentialism[①]

◎ **Zhongwei Li**

Department of Philosophy, Peking University

Abstract: This paper presents and defends a version of evidentialism. The thesis I wish to develop and defend is the following: The epistemic justificatory status of one's belief is exclusively dependent upon one's evidence (EP). This thesis is then analyzed into or interpreted as three theses:

(ⅰ) Only evidence and nothing else can be *proper reason* for belief. (ExT)

(ⅱ) Equal evidence will justify a belief with equal epistemic force. (EqT)

(ⅲ) Evidentialism contains an *epistemic* normative dimension, i. e. belief is specifically regulated by epistemic norms. (PEN, for principle of epistemic normativity)

The core of my argument is to establish the relation between belief, truth and evidence. My strategy of argument for evidentialism actually boils down to this: Firstly, I have tried to establish the conceptual link between belief and ultimate truth-regulatedness of belief by using a revision of Moore's open question argument, which has the form like, e. g. , "p is true, but do I have to believe it?". And then, secondly, I find that since evidence is the only element that is conducive to truth, it becomes natural to infer that evidence is the only element that contributes to one's justificatory status when one holds any belief. During the process of defending the first two theses respectively, I will present counterarguments to both pragmatic conception of justification and variantism about evidence. According pragmatism, pragmatic factors can be considered as reasons for one's belief; while according to variantism about evidence, specifically contextualism, given the same evidence, if the contexts vary, then the justificatory status of one's belief can also change accordingly. The third thesis emphasizes the

① I am very grateful to two anonymous referees of my paper, whose criticisms and comments are really helpful for me when I revise this paper. This paper was first written for and presented at the 1ˢᵗ BeSeTo Conference of Philosophy for Young Scholars (Organized by Peking University, Seoul University, Tokyo University), Seoul, January 2007. I am a Ph. D student at Peking University. This paper was accepted when I was studying at Universität zu Köln, Germany, with a two-year scholarship from China Scholarship Council, to which I am greatly indebted.

epistemic normativity of the justification for beliefs.

Keywords: evidence; justification; evidentialism; pragmatism; contextualism; normativity

I

There are various interpretations of Evidentialism as it has been proposed and defended respectively and differently. I shall begin with some exemplary expressions of the idea of Evidentialism, I will present some preliminary remarks on this standpoint, and then I will propose a version of evidential principle I wish to develop and defend.

Earl Conee and Richard Feldman propose in *Evidentialism* that

[PEJ] Doxastic attitude D toward proposition p is *epistemically justified* for S at t if and only if having D toward p fits the evidence S has at t. ①

In *Ethics of Belief*, continuing the same thread, Feldman proposes the evidential principle as O2. For any person S, time t, and proposition p, if S has any Doxastic attitude at all toward p at t and S's evidence at t supports p, then S *epistemically ought* to have the attitude toward p supported by S's evidence at t. ②

In *A New Argument for Evidentialism*, following R. Moran, Nishi Shah writes that

[ET] The only *reason* I can have for the belief that *p* is evidence of *p*'s truth. I shall call this position, that only evidence can be a reason for belief, *evidentialism*. ③

Though the authors may have different concerns when these words were written, I have only made three observations as I am concerned. Firstly, from PEJ, it's clear that Conee and Feldman conceive evidence as a necessary and sufficient condition for one's epistemic justification of a belief. For a belief being justified in an epistemic sense, it is necessary to have evidence, and one does not need other non-evidential justifiers.

Secondly, nevertheless, PEJ alone is unclear about whether we can have non-evidential condition

---

① "Evidentialism", *Philosophical Studies*, 1985, p 15. (my own italics)
② "The Ethics of Belief", *Philosophy and Phenomenological Research*, Vol. 60, No. 3. May, 2000, pp. 667 – 695, p 679. (my own italics)
③ "A New Argument for Evidentialism" *The Philosophical Quarterly*, Vol. 56, No. 225, (October 2006) pp. 481 – 498, p. 482. (my own italics)

for the justification of a belief at all. The virtue of ET is that it is very explicit that *only evidence and nothing else can be proper reason for belief*. I shall refer to this as ExT [*Exclusiveness Thesis*] for it clearly excludes other condition for the epistemic justification of a belief. If we can successfully establish this thesis, as I will explain later, then we can also infer from this thesis that *equal evidence will justify a belief with equal epistemic force*. I will refer to this as EqT [*Equality Thesis*].

Thirdly, Feldman and Conee are using the terms such as "justification" and "ought" with the important qualification that they are *epistemic* rather than, say, moral. The important idea is that Evidentialism does have a normative dimension, for it does require normative constraint over one's belief, but the nature of the normativity is epistemic rather than moral[1].

I have finished my preliminary remarks about some evidentialist expressions; the Evidentialism I wish to propose and defend here is expressed by the following principle (though it's not entirely new at all)

Evidential Principle (EP): The epistemic justificatory status of one's belief is exclusively dependent upon one's evidence.

To establish EP on a solid basis, I will respectively argue that:

(i) Only evidence and nothing else can be *proper reason* for belief. (ExT)

(ii) Equal evidence will justify a belief with equal epistemic force. (EqT)

(iii) Evidentialism contains an *epistemic* normative dimension, i. e. belief is specifically regulated by epistemic norms. (PEN, for principle of epistemic normativity)

The theses do not respectively express unique ideas about Evidentialism. I formulate the theses in a somewhat overlapping way because I want to defend the idea of Evidentialism against various forms of criticisms. I will defend ExT against the pragmatist, who claims that evidence alone is not sufficient for the justification of belief, and that we have to identify a pragmatic condition for epistemic justification. [2]

---

[1] William. K. Clifford, who claims that "It is wrong, always, everywhere, and for anyone to believe anything upon insufficient evidence", embraces a moralistic view of Evidentialism. The normativity of Evidentialism he has in mind is extremely moral. In "The Ethics of Belief Reconsidered" Susan Haack argues that Clifford did not distinguish epistemic and moral sense of the key terms he is using.

[2] Evidence, Pragmatics, and Justification, Jeremy Fantl; Matthew McGrath *The Philosophical Review*, Vol. 111, No. 1 (Jan. , 2002), pp. 67 – 94.

Though EqT will be defended if we can establish ExT, I will defend EqT in service of the purpose of arguing against the contextualist, who holds that, with the evidence unchanged, the epistemic justification of a belief can become context-sensitive, that is to say, a belief which is justified in one context can be unjustified in different contexts, given the same amount of evidence. [1]

PEN is in view of the idea that Evidentialism is about the *justificatory status* of belief, and it's also about the *proper reason* for belief. The act of belief in the epistemic sense is categorially different from activities which are indeed regulated by moral norms, and therefore is not open to the constraining force of moral norms; it has its own norms which are proper to its epistemic essence. However, the idea of epistemic normativity will remain entirely obscure until we can give an intelligible account of the nature and source of this normativity.

The first thesis is the central one; the following two theses rely heavily upon it. But how is ExT logically connected with the kind of Evidential Principle we want to establish? In this way: to give reasons for a belief p is to justify it, and to give proper reasons for a belief p is to properly justify it. Therefore, if one is justified in believing p, we say that one is rational in believing p, and *vice versa*. We will need to establish that since belief is essentially aimed at truth, or *ultimately regulated* by truth, therefore, one can only cite something as reason if it *essentially* contributes to one's belief that p is true. What we want to establish is therefore that the only proper reason contributing to the belief that p is one's evidence. And that alone determines the justificatory status of one's belief. Other factors, such as one's pragmatic situation or confidence of the proposition one believes in different contexts, if they do not contribute essentially to the truth of one's belief, can count as reasons, but not epistemically relevant reasons. And therefore they should be not relevant to the justificatory status of one's belief. But we are ahead of ourselves.

I wish to establish the evidential principle and argue for the three theses; they are all propositions about our beliefs, though about different aspects. If we want to establish some general principle about a phenomenon, we have to examine the phenomenon first. In the following section, I will examine the phenomenon of belief and other relevant phenomena.

---

[1] Keith DeRose, Contextualism and Knowledge Attributions, *Philosophy and Phenomenological Research*, Vol. 52, No. 4 (Dec., 1992), pp. 913 – 929.

II

When one has a belief, then one has a propositional attitude toward a proposition. This propositional attitude is not like any other, such as "imagine" or "wish", because belief essentially involves believing such and such really being or not being the case, while the other two do not. This specific propositional attitude of belief is also called doxastic attitude. It is typical of this attitude that one accepts, or holds certain proposition to be true. However, when misconstrued, this distinction between doxastic attitude and the relevant content can be somewhat misleading, for it threatens to separate the proposition from the specific attitude it is colored with. As I can conceive it, though we can *distinguish* between the propositional attitude and the proposition itself, we can never *separate* an attitude from its content. ①

The phenomenon I wish to investigate is primarily belief as propositional attitude, for it's this attitude we need to give reasons and justify when we are asked the question "why do you believe p?" about the belief we have already held, and it's this attitude we sometime need to form in a process of deliberation (when we intend to answer the question whether to believe p?). But of course, we can also say that for a proposition p, there are some reasons to it. But it is not the reasons, or, if you prefer, justifications for a propositional content that I want to discuss, although the discussion of the justification of one's doxastic attitude necessarily involves the "reasons" for the proposition. Suppose I believe that q, now, we can say that the reason for my believing that q is "$p \wedge (p \rightarrow q)$", or better, my epistemically accessible justified true belief "$p \wedge (p \rightarrow q)$". One can also say that "$p \wedge (p \rightarrow q)$" justifies the proposition "q", and it justifies logically. But this is not the kind of justification I am talking about. I am talking about either the agent's justification of believing, or the doxastic justification, the justification for one's doxastic attitude.

So what I want to discuss is the doxastic attitude toward certain proposition p. To avoid the danger of separating the content of the attitude from the attitude, or to avoid the danger of hypostatizing the content as some kind of Platonic entities, I propose that you understand "attitude toward proposition

---

① Here we use a distinction between "distinction" and "separation". Or to use the terminology in formal ontology, the propositional attitude and the propositional content are dependent moments, not independent pieces. I will also use this distinction when it comes to the analysis of the phenomenon of belief.

p" in an adverbial way, i. e. , "a p – ly modified attitude". And it is so modified doxistic attitude I am trying to investigate, with regard to its justificatory status, and its relation to truth and evidence.

We need to investigate belief as a propositional attitude. This attitude is a psychologically complex phenomenon, and it can also mix with other very different psychological components. I will investigate this attitude from different perspectives, and this investigation will reveal to us what kind of complexities the phenomenon of belief involves.

As we have already pointed out, belief is different from other propositional attitudes. "Believe that p" and "imagine that p" or "assume that p" are essentially different. From a purely empirical point of view, the belief that p always goes with the evidence that we have of p's truth. But "imagine that p" and "assume that p" do not go with the evidence of p's truth whatsoever, we can imagine or assume any proposition at anytime without the proposition being true, though the proposition might be true. But the responsiveness of the belief that p to the evidence of p's truth cannot be interpreted as a purely empirical or psychological fact about us.

The responsiveness of belief to relevant evidence has a conceptual dimension. Belief as such is a *positing* act, that is, unlike imagination or assumption, it *posits* something as being true. The act of belief contains a dependent moment of "positing something", that is, a moment of the affirmation of something's truth. Although the belief may turn out to be false, however, for a belief to be a belief, we have to consider our belief as to "aim at truth"①, to express differently, a belief must be "truth regulated".

But how do we understand the claim that belief involves "truth regulation" or "aim at truth"? And how strong is the relation of "involvement" here? Let me consider two cases. In the process of forming beliefs: a) one can be influenced by factors which do not directly relate to truth, such as authority; or b) one can do some kind of Pascal's wager in forming one's belief. Given the fact one cannot have (sufficient) evidence for or against p, or one can only have equal evidence for and against p, if one believes in p is (infinitely more, in Pascal's case of believing that "God exists") more profitable than not believing in it, then one is more reasonable (justified) in believing p than denying it. Well, my answer comes in two parts. Firstly, I want to explain the concept of truth regulation of belief in terms of Moore's open question argument. Secondly, I will comment on the two cases mentioned above.

---

① "Aim at truth" is Bernard Williams's terminology, however, my special interest is to reveal the conceptual connection between belief and aim at truth.

The open question argument basically goes like this in Moore: suppose you know all the natural properties of an object, but it remains an open question concerning whether it is good or not, to argue otherwise one commits the so-called naturalistic fallacy. Putting the validity and soundness of Moore's argument aside, the form of the argument is the following. Suppose $(P \wedge Q \wedge R \wedge, \ldots, \wedge N) \ x$, where x is the variable for objects, and $(P \wedge Q \wedge R \wedge, \ldots, \wedge N)$ stand for the conjuncted property of x. But if for a property S, for every x, if it cannot be determined either Sx or (Sx, then we say, given $(P \wedge Q \wedge R \wedge, \ldots, \wedge N) \ x$, it remains an open question whether Sx. If it turns out that the truth of Sx can be determined, then we say, the question concerning whether Sx is a closed question.

Now, I use this kind of argument form to show the link between truth-regulation and belief. Suppose one says sincerely: "It is raining, but I do not believe it. " Now, according to the redundancy theory of truth, this is the same as to say "It is true that it is raining, but I do not believe it. " Or, to formulate it a little bit differently, with an evidential twist, "It is highly evident to me that it is raining, but I do not believe it. " Now, I think these sentences must strike you as very strange claims, while it is not the case in Moore's parallel formulation of naturalistic fallacy. But how can we formulate the intuition of the strangeness of the claims more explicitly and perhaps make a theory out of it? We seem to be compelled to say that either the person is not serious, or he misunderstands the concept of "believe" . Since by assumption, he is sincere in stating that it is raining, then he accepts it, but this is the same as to say that he believes it. Sincerely admitting the truth of a proposition seems to close the question whether one should believe it or not. Now sincerely stating and accepting p can be said to be the closure condition with regard to the question whether one should believe a certain proposition p. Now, in this sense, I say that a belief is truth-regulated.

But this is not so in the two cases we have mentioned. In the case of authority, it is always possible to ask: "He says so and so, but should I believe it?" It does not strike one as strange at all even if the person in question has huge amount of authority. Because by stating "He says so and so", one does not state a closure condition for one's belief. Nevertheless, this is not to deny that when we consider the question of belief, even if belief is aimed at truth or truth regulated, we do not consider authority as a source of regulation. Because although the authoritative statement of p does not offer the closure condition for one's belief of p, one can consider it seriously as an intermediary regulator, as authoritative statements, esp. for example, expert statements often tend to be true. And therefore to adopt expert statements often tend to make truth conveniently accessible. But one should notice, that the acceptance of the authoritative statement never states the closure condition for one's belief. And therefore, it can best be an intermediary regulator but never an ultimate one. Here, we can understand "truth regulatedness" as "ultimate truth-regulatedness".

Now, the case of Pascal's wager or similar cases can also be applied the same procedure. Shortly, what we will find that statements about the profits of believing something do not close the question of belief at all, and since statements about belief do not even relate to truth, it cannot be even an intermediary regulator.

Given our earlier analysis, we have linked truth regulation and belief very closely. Now I want to ask, how close they are connected. I can present a way to understand the relation between belief and "truth regulation". When we speak about physical object, we have to understand it as spatial-temporally extended. It's paradoxical to ask "it's physical, but is it spatial-temporal?" Being physical is being spatially-temporally extended; it's conceptual rather than factual. Even if there is no physical world at all, being physical is being spatially extended. It's just a conceptual truth that being physical implies being spatial. Belief is truth regulated; this also reflects a conceptual truth about belief. Properly understood, we can analyze a moment of truth-regulation out of the concept of belief, just as we can analyze the concept of spatially-extended out of the concept of physical object. Because this is such a conceptual truth, it explains that why if a person says "P is true, but should I believe p" we will be quite surprised, even if we do not know where the problem lies. According to one analysis, we can say he does not know the grammar of the word "believe" and commits what Ryle called "category mistake". The truth that belief is truth-regulated can be true without any belief actually existing. Even we are in a bad epistemic situation where we are not able to form any belief whatsoever, the conceptual truth about belief will remain true.

We have established the conceptual link between belief and truth-regulation. What about the relation between belief and evidence? We can consider the explicit cases where the visibility of evidence is high. In the process of explicit belief formation we have to form a belief p by finding out the truth of p[①]. But we try

---

① Of course, I am not saying all belief formation is explicit in a way that we somehow intentionally try to form belief about something. But in some cases, we do have explicit belief formation process, at least at the beginning. E. g. , if I want to form the belief about certain subject or simply the truth of $p \rightarrow q \leftrightarrow \neg (p \wedge \neg q)$, I will try to find out the evidence for the theories in the subject, and in the latter case, we will try to find the logical evidence for the formula (e. g. , by truth value analysis). And then, we need to go with the evidence, and it is really controversial whether we have control over the doxastic attitude in the face of evidence with or without manipulating the evidence beforehand.

to find out the truth or falsity of *p* by considering the evidence for it. Now, in the explicit cases, we try to only allow the truth-relevant factors, i. e. , evidences to function as proper reasons, i. e. , justifiers for one's belief. In not so explicit cases, which constitute a substantial body of our epistemic life, though we are influenced by a lot of factors, our standard of limiting the scope of proper reason for belief to relevant evidences can be applied after the implicit process of belief formation reflexively.

Now, since my target is to argue against contextualism and pragmatism about epistemic justification, I will take the conception of evidence to be neutral with regard to whether it is an internalist or an externalist conception. For what I have seen, evidence can well be internally accessible mental states, or to follow Alvin Goldman, it can well be "a reliable indicator of truth"[1], whether or not it is internally accessible. The only element that is connected to accepting *p*'s truth should be the evidence we have for it. We have informed that the act of belief is truth regulated, and the only element that is relevant to the truth is the evidence that we may have for it. Therefore, it's of normative force that we have to form our belief according to our evidence of p's truth. For a belief to be a belief, it must be conceived as evidence-sensitive. Since the only element that is relevant to one's enjoyment of a truth, belief must be also conceived as solely evidence-sensitive. There is also a conceptual truth about the connection between belief and its exclusive evidence-sensitivity.

However, as we have remarked earlier, belief is a psychologically complex phenomenon, and it also involves other psychological phenomenon. When I am in a status of having belief p, I may also have some other accompanying attitudes toward p. I can be more or less *confident* that p; I can be more or less *worried* that p; I can be more or less *afraid* that p; I can be very happy that p for some reasons. But none of these attitudes can be counted as proper reasons for a belief p. The psychological feeling of confidence about a proposition often goes with one's having evidence for a proposition, but it is not necessarily the case. For a certain proposition p, with the evidence unchanged, people may have different degree of confidence for the same belief at different time, on different occasion. But this does not affect the epistemic status of one's

---

[1] Although my sympathy lies on the side of internalists with regard to the conception of evidence, I do not prejudge the issue here. So my version of evidentialism presented here is different from Feldman and Conee's because I do not commit to internalism here. For a reliable account of evidence, see Alvin Goldman, "Toward a Synthesis of Reliabilism and Evidentialism" (to appear in T. Doughterty, ed. , *Evidentialism and Its Discontents*, Oxford University Press), also see, Juan Comesana, "Evidentialist Reliablism" (forthcoming in *Nous*). Both papers are now available on the author's website.

belief of p, just like one's worry concerning a proposition is not relevant to the epistemic status of a belief that p. The only relevant element that one may have for the truth of p is one's evidence.

However, to say that evidence is the only relevant element for one's justificatory status of proposition *p* is not to say that evidence is the only element that can influence one's belief. From a static point of view, one's belief can be accompanied by various kinds of psychological feelings. From a genetic point of view, one's belief can be influenced by various kinds of things other than evidence, and it can be the case that some of our beliefs are not due to an acceptable level of evidence. For instance, our belief-formation can be extensively influenced by wishful thinking in an undetectable way. Although one's wishful thinking can be said to be the *explanatory reason* of one's holding of particular belief, it cannot be cited as the *justifying reason* or *proper reason* for the belief. The only element we can recognize as justifying reason for one's belief is the evidence we may have for it, even if it's not the most significant element in one's formation of a belief.

It's widely held that a belief can be pragmatically consequential. And a belief of some proposition is often connected with certain concerns other than truth. If I believe the factual statement that "it's raining outside", combining with my personal concern that I don't want to get wet, I will take an umbrella with me when I decide to go out. If I believe the moral statement that "it's morally bad to lie", then it's probable that I will act according to my beliefs. In both cases, one's belief is connected to one's actions. The idea is that, one's belief is often connected with practical consequences. We can have various kinds of feelings and concerns for the practical consequences. But, these concerns and concerns cannot be cited as reasons for one's belief in certain propositions. I will defend this against the pragmatist.

We have learned from the analysis of the phenomenon of belief this much: The relationship between belief, truth-regulation, and evidence-responsiveness is conceptual rather than factual. Belief as an intentional act is distinguished from other kinds of act for it's governed by truth. Taking the relationship between evidence and truth into account, we also have to accept evidence as the exclusive relevant justificatory element for belief, and this is equal to our EP, which I wish to defend in this paper. Nevertheless, as I have promised, I will defend the principle as well as the other three theses against some initially appealing view about our belief.

III

In this section I will defend ExT against pragmatist, who claims that we have to identify a pragmatic condition for the epistemic justification of one's belief. As the pragmatist has argued: ①

(1) In case A, with the evidence (e1, e2), for a proposition p, S is obviously rational to believe p. However, (2) in case B, with the evidence (e1, e2), for a proposition p, S is not rational to believe p. (3) Therefore, evidence alone is not sufficient to decide the justificatory (or rational) status of one's belief. In order to explain the phenomenon in case A and Case B, one has to identify a pragmatic condition of justification for one's belief other than the condition of evidence.

The strategy of the pragmatist is this, they argue, in some cases, one is rational to believe p, but in some other cases, with the evidence unchanged, one is not rational to believe p. Evidence alone is not enough to determine the justificatory status of one's belief. It's noticed by pragmatist that a belief is connected with some practices. In one case, connected with the practice E, one is rational to act as if p. In another case, connected with practice F, with evidence unchanged, one can be no longer rational to act as if p. Therefore, the best way to deal with the indeterminacy of the justificatory status of proposition p is to identify certain pragmatic conditions. With some pragmatic condition for belief, it can determine the justificatory status of one's belief.

The whole argument depends upon the *indeterminacy* thesis; it's because of the indeterminacy of the justificatory status of belief with the same evidence that forces the pragmatist to identify an extra pragmatic condition for the justification of belief. Thus my strategy of arguing against the pragmatic condition for the determination of one's epistemic status will be to refute the *indeterminacy* thesis.

The refutation of the indeterminacy thesis involves an explanation of its initial plausibility. It happens very often that we act according to some beliefs, and we also use some information as important element in our practices. It can be the case that when our practices are unimportant for us, we can just adopt some propositions with initial plausibility without further inquiring. However, when our practices are tremendously important for us, we are not rational to adopt some propositions with just initial plausibility which is not proportionate to the importance of the practices, given the premise that we can inquire further with reasonable effort or cost.

However, the initial plausibility of indeterminacy thesis lies in its phenomenological and conceptual confusion. Phenomenologically, it does not distinguish between the epistemic status from its motivational

① Jeremy Fantl; Matthew McGrath, "Evidence, Pragmatics, and Justification", *The Philosophical Review*, Vol. 111, No. 1. (Jan. , 2002), pp. 67 – 94.

force for practice. As far as I can see, the belief's motivational force is relative to the actions one wish to perform or refrain from performing. Normally, for a belief p, with the evidence unchanged, the motivational force will remain unchanged. But in some scenarios, the motivational force of *p* may be able to motivate some actions but fail to motivate the same actions in different circumstances. This explains why we can feel comfortable to act as if p in one circumstances, while we can feel unjustified to act as if p in some other situations, and we will feel obliged to inquire further about p's truth. But the motivational force is phenomenologically different from the epistemic status of one's belief. One's epistemic status concerning a belief is exclusively dependent on the evidence, while the motivational force of a belief might well go with the evidence, it is not necessarily so, and it is indeterminate in different practical situations.

Conceptually, the indeterminacy thesis results from failing to distinguish various senses of justification and rationality. Justification and rationality are not unambiguous terms; they have different meanings in different contexts. In different practical cases, one can be said to act rationally according to a belief with certain evidence, while in other situations one can be said to act irrationally according to the same belief with the same evidence. The rationality of one's actions according to a belief with the same evidence may change, this does not mean the rationality of one's belief that p, with the same evidence, can be changed in different practical circumstances. The pragmatist uses the practical rationality to measure the theoretical rationality, thereby commits a category mistake.

Therefore, the pragmatist endeavor to identify a pragmatic condition for the epistemic justification of a belief fails.

IV

Contextualist does not accept the Equality Thesis, that *equal evidence will justify a belief with equal epistemic force*. The strategy they might have adopted is roughly as follows:[1]

(1) In context A, with the evidence (e1, e2), for a proposition p, S can be attributed the knowledge concerning p. However, (2) in context B, with the evidence (e1, e2), for a proposition p, S cannot be attributed the knowledge concerning p. (3) This phenomenon can be best explained by

[1] For a argument of this kind, see, Keith DeRose, Contextualism and Knowledge Attributions, *Philosophy and Phenomenological Research*, Vol. 52, No. 4. (Dec. , 1992), pp. 913 – 929.

the contextual principle that the standard of knowledge attribution is context-sensitive, and the justificatory status of one's belief with the same evidence can be contextually variable.

Like the pragmatic cases, the contextual principle also has some initial plausibility because it explains some puzzling phenomena. Let me illustrate its plausibility by presenting an example. When a stranger bumped into me and asked, "What time is it?" I will glimpse at my watch and tell her that it is 11 : 00. But she may continue to ask "are you sure about this? Is it 11 : 00 sharp, because I have to deliver the ransom at 11 : 15 to the kidnappers to get my son back, and, is your watch functioning properly, is it set in local Time?" Keith DeRose argues that in this case, it will be necessary to withdraw my former belief and inquire further. In the former context, I think I know with justification; however, in the latter context, when the person states her situation and asked again, I don't really know with the same amount of justification as the stake goes higher. With the context changed, the justifying force of one's evidence will vary accordingly.

As I have remarked earlier, a belief may be accompanied by various psychological feelings that are not really justifying elements for a belief. For instance, one's confidence may accompany a belief, and the confidence may change contextually. This explains why I can simply tell the stranger that the time is 11 : 00 in the former context, while I have to say "well, I am not sure, let me look at my watch again" in the latter context, when necessary, I will have inquire even further. But, this does not mean that I withdraw my former belief when the latter question is asked. As Jonathan E. Adler argues, it may be the case that my confidence about the proposition that "it's 11 : 00" has changed when the latter question was asked; however, this does not mean that I have withdrawn my former belief. The drop of confidence that p to a certain level does not imply withdrawing p. [1]

Now, an objection may go like this. Given the distinction between doxastic justification and propositional content justification, in the scenario we have just described, although the justification for the content remains the same, the justification for the doxastic attitude changes. Otherwise, how do we explain the change of confidence in both contexts? Well, I do not have anything extra to say about the justification or reasons for the content of belief. But I want to insist that doxastic justificatory status do not change in different contexts, if the evidences available in the contexts remain unchanged. Various contextual factors influence the confidence of one's belief in p, such as one's practical situation, one's

---

[1] Jonathan E. Adler, 2006, "Withdrawal and Contextualism", in *Analysis*, 66: pp 280 – 285.

emotional need, etc. But these contextual factors do not regulate and cannot ultimately regulate our belief in the sense that truth and the evidence conducive to truth do. This is not to deny the fact that our confidence do change across contexts. On the contrary, this is to explain it without accepting that it should count as factors contributing to the justificatory status of one's belief.

It's crucial to notice that, it's one's confidence about the belief has changed, and it can even be the case that the confidence of the justifying force of certain evidence can change contextually. But this does not mean that the justifying force of certain evidence has to change contextually.

Therefore, Contextualist has failed. Equal evidence will justify a belief with equal epistemic force.

V

I have proposed the third thesis that Evidentialism contains an *epistemic* normative dimension, i. e. belief is specifically regulated by epistemic norms. I think, by analyzing the phenomena of belief, we have made the nature of epistemic normativity much less obscure, because we have traced the normativity to the act of belief itself. We have observed that it's a conceptual truth that belief can only be conceived as belief if it is also conceived as truth-regulated and evidence-responsiveness. Belief as a truth-regulated intentional act has a *standard of correctness* of its own, to use Shah's language. It means that belief has an embedded conceptual moment of normativity. It is nonsensical to say: "I believe p, though p is not true" or, formulated in Moore's paradox: "although p is true, but I don't believe it. " There is a conceptual confusion in such paradoxes.

The deontological talk of "justification" and "ought" in the epistemic sense is misguided by a moral way of conceiving epistemic normativity. ①Clifford infamously claimed that to believe upon insufficient evidence is to violate some moral norms, and is therefore morally culpable. ②If we can be informed with the distinction between epistemic normativity which is proper to the act of belief, and moral normativity (or other forms of normativity), and if we can distinguish the epistemic use of these words from other uses at all, then some serious confusion in contemporary epistemology will be exten-

---

① It may also be misguided by other interpretations of these terms.

② W. K. Clifford, 1877, 'The Ethics of Belief', in his *Lectures and Essays*, Vol. II, London: Macmillan, pp. 339 – 363.

sively reduced. ①

VI

To conclude, basically, my strategy of argument for evidentialism actually boils down to this: Firstly, I have tried to establish the conceptual link between belief and ultimate truth-regulatedness of belief by using a revision of Moore's open question argument, which has the form like, e. g. , "p is true, but do I have to believe it?" And then, secondly, I find that since evidence is the only element that is conducive to truth, it becomes natural to infer that evidence is the only element that contributes to one's justificatory status when one holds any belief. I have taken contextualism and pragmatism about epistemic justification as my enemies in this paper. But I also realize that in Conee and Feldman's version of evidentialism, the most serious problem is to counter Goldman's externalist-reliabilist account of justification, as their conception of evidence is internalist, which states that evidence is the only justifying element, and this element must be internally accessible to the agent in question at the time of believing. But actually, although I am more sympathetic with the internalist version of evidentialism, I am not setting arguing for this version of evidentialism as my goal here. And I don't think I should argue for that much in one single paper. But, I want to suggest, if you want, you can understand the concept of evidence as neutral with regard to internalism or externalism-reliabilism. For example, if you are a reliabilist, you can follow Goldman by taking evidence as "reliable indicator of truth". Actually, some philosophers now try to offer a conception of evidence which combines the resources from both evidentialism and reliabilism②.

---

① See Note 5 in this paper.

② Alvin Goldman, "Toward a Synthesis of Reliabilism and Evidentialism" (to appear in T. Doughterty, ed. , *Evidentialism and Its Discontents*, Oxford University Press), also see, Juan Comesana, "Evidentialist Reliablism" (forthcoming in Nous). Both papers are now available on the author's website.

为证据主义辩护

李忠伟

北京大学哲学系

摘　要：本文提供一个认识论上证据主义的论题，并为这个论题辩护。这个论题是：某人信念的辩护状态完全取决于其所拥有的证据（EP）。这被我分解或者解释为三个论题：（1）除了证据，没有其它东西可以作为持有某个信念的恰当理由；（2）相同的证据所赋予信念的认知论上的辩护力量是一样的；（3）信念被认识论上的规范所制约。我的论证的核心是建立信念和真理，真理和证据之间的关系。通过对摩尔（Moore）的开放问题论证的一个运用，我们得出，由于信念是真理导向的，或者最终真理导向的，又由于只有证据才构成获得真理的本质相关要素，所以只有证据才构成信念辩护的合适的理由，而其它我们所考虑的因素，对于认知辩护来说，则无关紧要。在为证据主义辩护的过程中，本文还将会反驳关于认知辩护的实用主义和语境主义。

关键词：证据；辩护；证据主义；实用主义；语境主义；规范性

A Thought-Experimental Investigation into Replication[*]

◎ **Jun Luo**

Toronto University

Abstract: In making their arguments, contemporary analytical philosophers often rely on imagined replication scenarios. Some prominent examples include Putnam's "Twin Earth", Davidson's "swampman", Parfit's "fission cases", and Chalmers' "zombie copy". These arguments presuppose that the numerical identity and difference of the individuals involved in the replication are unproblematic, abstract away the concrete materiality implicated in replication, sometimes even explicitly claim that lossless replication of an individual is possible through copying at the molecular or atomic level alone, and thereby effectively but unwarrantedly deny that concrete materiality could be inexorably implicated in the issue at hand. Through a thought experiment conducted from the first-person perspective, this article details, phenomenologically, the "identity of indiscernibles" in the very eyes of the subject being replicated, and points towards concrete material differences as what crucially differentiate the individuals involved in replication. In contrast, because in the above-mentioned imagined replication scenarios, concrete materiality were ignored and numerical identity of and difference between the replica and the original were stipulated by fiat, unexamined assumptions about the constitution of individuality were thereby implicitly introduced. Consequently, these imagined replication scenarios cannot adequately support subsequent argumentation. Take the "qualia problem" as an example: if the concrete materiality of human beings actually cannot be reduced to combination of molecules or atoms, might not the ineffability of qualia be the signature of the concrete materiality of humans as the subject of consciousness? Might not the perplexity around the qualia problem symptomatic of a failure to understand materiality as much as consciousness?

---

* Acknowledgement: I thank Gwakhee Han and Alex Klein for pointing me to Black's 1952 article, Kevin Eldred and Sara Saab for encouragement, Jim Brink for topology, Brian Cantwell Smith for insights, Carolyn Richardson for writing, and Steve Hockema for disbelief.

Keywords: identity; materiality; replication; phenomenological point of view; first person; subjectivity; consciousness; qualia

Morning

Seven thirty, I got out of the bed. Walking to the washroom, the prospect of meeting him made my stomach tingle. The night before, I entered my room at eleven. According to the plan, after I fell asleep I would be replicated and the replica of me would be put in the other room in the dome. How exactly they were to make the replication I didn't know. But that should have already happened.

Although I was the "chief phenomenologist" there, engineers at the Vancouver Island Metaphysical Engineering Lab (a. k. a. VIMEL) never bothered to tell me much about how the dome was built. The main feat, according to what I gathered, was that it was built as a "D-system" —a system in which everything comes in qualitatively identical pairs and any change to one element in a pair comes with it a simultaneous and identical change to the other. The question concerning determinism, I was told, was thus evaded: if the dome starts out as a D-system, it will end up being a D-system, regardless of how the intervening changes come about—deterministically, emergently, freely, randomly, rationally, spontaneously, or voluntarily. "Hard to believe? Use your philosophical imagination!" I was advised.

The dome was built near the northern tip of Vancouver Island. It is about 50 meters across at the foot and 25 meters high at the center. Everything inside it is radially symmetric by 180 degrees with respect to the axis running from the "zenith" to the "nadir". At the "north pole" and the "south pole" of the dome were two studio apartments, one for me, the other for my replica. But I didn't know which was for whom.

Looking into the mirror while shaving, I started to relive the origin of the idea behind the dome:

Experimental thoughts

Still fresh in my pursuit of philosophy after leaving oceanology, I was often struck by the liberty professional philosophers took in their thought experiments with replication: a line or two will describe the setup, but before I could understand how this setup would make any sense, another line or two would have already reported the result, absent anything like the actual running of an experiment.

"What an intuition plug!" I often felt.

"Could a 'molecule-by-molecule replica' of me be dead?" I would ask myself. A frozen replica of me would have the same molecular composition, I suppose, but the freezing could kill him. Or, while retaining their molecular composition, the protein molecules that form the synaptic receptors in my replica could all misfold such that normal neural transmission, which requires correct folding, became paralyzingly disrupted.

But if a molecule-for-molecule replica of Davidson were dead, frozen or paralyzed, it certainly would not "move exactly" like him. [1]On what ground, then, can one claim, as Davidson does, that "moving like Davidson" is preserved across the physical replication while "cognizing like Davidson" is not? One might argue here that attribution to the replica of "moving like Davidson" requires that the replication honor a certain *extra-molecular* constraints. If that is the case, however, why can't we also attribute "cognizing like Davidson" to the replica on the ground that the *replication* honors these as yet unspecified constraints?

Apparent failure of molecular or micro determination of behavioral identity aside, a general worry concerns how one and one's replica are *situated* in and *enmeshed* with the world. Suppose, for example, I am in conversation with a friend in a coffee shop when the replication takes place. The glasses, the clothes, and the wristwatch I am wearing will presumably all be replicated. But how about the coffee mug in my hand? The table supporting my elbows? The chair I am sitting in? My half-finished utterance? The friend facing me? Will my friend be amused or troubled? Will our friendship be doubled or halved?

It won't help to dictate: "Only intrinsic properties get replicated!" Suppose the coffee shop is full and my replica is thus forced to stand by my chair. Difference in our body posture here means difference in muscle tension, proprioception, and metabolism. While I am looking at my friend's face in the shadow, my replica may be facing the street corner under bright sunlight and unwittingly register a traffic accident. I do not know whether the incessant photochemical transduction on our respective retina count as intrinsic to us or not. But I do know that its repercussions penetrate the very depth of our brains, and

---

① Davidson (1987, 443): "Suppose lightning strikes a dead tree in a swamp; I am standing nearby. My body is reduced to its elements, while entirely by coincidence (and out of different molecules) the tree is turned into my physical replica. My replica, The Swampman, moves exactly as I did; ⋯"

often also the depth of our personhood.

Such situational differences in our material enmeshing with the world, it seems to me, are the rule, not the exception, with their significance hard to ignore and their "cascading consequences" hard to underestimate. These we should know very well from our everyday life, without having to be reminded of the butterfly effect or Lewis' teaching. ①

The point is not that faithful replication is just impossible, but that it always comes with a certain discrepancy between the original and the replica in their material constitution and worldly enmeshing. And such discrepancy typically matters. When I fax my passport to a travel agency, for example, the facsimile must be both similar enough to the original and different from it. Only if there is enough similarity could the facsimile be used to stand in for the original. But only if there is enough difference could I still hang on to the original and use it as *the* original without concerns that an indistinguishable replica elsewhere may now vie for claim of authenticity. Likewise, one would want to have a computer file and its backup copy differently constituted and differently situated—implemented with different medium or stored at different enough places or both, such that one power outage, one inadvertent deletion, one system crash, or one household fire won't destroy both.

In the thought experiments, however, such material discrepancy as I would call it, if recognized at all, is typically presumed to be irrelevant.

But why can't such discrepancy between a person and their replica account for the difference in, for instance, their qualitative experience? A dead or comatose molecule-by-molecule replica of Dave certainly enjoys no qualitative experience and thus seems to fit the definition of a "philosophical zombie." ② Less extraordinarily—suppose I am driving when the replication takes place and my replica

---

① Lewis (1973, 420, original emphases): "We dream of considering a world where the antecedent [of a counterfactual] holds but everything else is just as it actually is, the truth of the antecedent being the one difference between that world and ours. No hope. Differences never come singly, but in infinite multitudes. Take, if you can, a world that differs from ours *only* in that Caesar did not cross the Rubicon. Are his predicament and ambitions there just as they actually are? The regularities of his character? The psychological laws exemplified by his decision? The orders of the day in his camp? The preparation of the boats? The sound of the splashing oars? Hold *everything* else fixed after making one change, and you will not have a possible world at all. "

② Tye (2007, original emphasis): "A philosophical zombie is a molecule by molecule duplicate of a sentient creature, a normal human-being, for example, but who differs from that creature in lacking *any* phenomenal consciousness. "

is thus forced to take the passenger seat. While I am still condemned to concentrating on the grayish pavement winding downhill, my replica may now savor a brilliant autumn scene, or rest in a dreamless sleep. The worry is that if being alive, being awake, or behaving normally does not in any simple way carry over molecular or physical replication, neither does "enjoying qualitative experience."

If one wants to disarm such worries and show that they are in the end no more than immaterial quibbles, one could "regiment" the material detail of the thought-experimental setup. One way to do that would be to perfect the replication so that no material discrepancy can be detected between the replica and the original or in their worldly enmeshing. ①This way, while the intuition behind the zombie thought experiment is preserved, no material discrepancy could be cited to explain the presence or absence of qualitative experience.

Philosophers certainly have thought carefully about perfect duplication: Black's world of two identical spheres comes to mind. I would be in good company in dealing with replication rigorously. ②One limitation with Black's setup, though, is that while we are thinking from outside this world, we are also supposed to think of it as an all-encompassing world, which has proved to be a very challenging task even for philosophers.

Wouldn't it be nice if we also had *subjects* replicated in a world of perfect duplication, so that they could report firsthand what things are like in such a world *for them*?③

To be sure, I wasn't the first to think about something like this. Klawonn inspired me. ④He imagined himself and his replica, identical in every detail, arriving from twin planets that are also identical in every detail, meeting at the Midway planet:

---

① An alternative is to distinguish, in a principled way, the sorts of material discrepancy that matter for what is in question from those that do not. But nobody seems to have addressed this issue in a noncircular way, i. e., motivating such a distinction independently of, rather than resting it on, the conceivability of the scenario in the thought experiment.

② Black 1952; see also Hacking 1975 and Adams 1979 for a discussion.

③ While Adams' (1979, 17f) counter argument against Hacking (1975) also exploits the presence of minds in the imagined world, he does not do his version of the thought experiment from the first-person perspective That allows plenty of room for my motivating intuition to diverge from his.

④ Klawonn (1987) sketched a series of thought experiments that are remarkably similar to those found in Parfit (1984)—both involving feasts of division, duplication, replication, and (faulty!) teleportation. Intriguingly, he used these experiments to motivate an intuition that is very much at odds with Parfit's.

Then I would have the strange experience of meeting a person who is not only (almost) exactly similar to me, but whose every movement corresponds exactly to mine. It would seem as though my will were moving his body. There would be no way of breaking out of this 'magic circle' until there is at least one experience that we do not share. And yet we are not the same person. I can see his eyes, but I cannot see my own. What is it that—for me—cause [sic] a '*me here*' and a '*he there*', in spite of the likeness? By contemplating this question one may perhaps once again become aware of the 'myself for myself' with no objective counterpart, i. e., the 'purely first personal dimension' —though it must be admitted that a thought-experiment where there is complete similarity between myself and my 'twin' does not make it quite as clear as it would have been if there were certain differences. I cannot for instance say: There are two persons, A and B: A is in pain, B is not in pain—the localization of the 'I-dimension' decides whether I or the other person is in pain. In the present situation I will not be in pain without my double being in pain too, and so a 'contrast argument' is excluded. But of course—if there is anything true in what has been said above—the 'myself for myself' is still 'in' one of the two persons, namely—by definition—me. It is pointless to object that this difference must be a subjective illusion, since the other person must view the matter in the same way. What I am talking about is precisely the subjective point of view which—*seen from my own point of view*—makes me identical with the one person and not the other. The fact that this subjectivity only exists from my own point of view '*defines*' it; it does not falsify or annul it. ①

While impressed by Klawonn's rigor about the setup, I was not as certain as Klawonn about the phenomenological transparency to himself of his ultimate distinctiveness from his replica, his "I-dimension." What is given in experience in such a world, I felt, could affirm an identity across difference as much as reveal a difference in identity. Trying to be a good phenomenologist, I did not want to jump to conclusions before seeing the things themselves.

"Can we actually construct a piece of 'augmented reality' that approximates Klawonn's thought experiment, following it in spirit, if not to the letter?" I wondered. Building a completely enclosed dome, it seemed to me, was a good way to shield off the flux in the rest of the world. That should make

---

① Klawonn (1987, 57).

it easier to contain the cascading consequences of material discrepancy at least. With some ordinary household items thrown into the dome, it could even allow extended stay and offer some "lived experience"!

That was how this whole thing started. It's been eight long years and finally I am here in the dome for real.

Soon I will experience it all. I will see for myself and, I suppose, for my fellow philosophers, what it is like to be with one's perfect replica. Klawonn assumed that his replica will experience pain as he does, for example. But what if his replica merely exhibits pain behavior? What will it be like to face a replica of me who is possibly a zombie? Will it be natural for me to address him in the second person? Ah, the second person, always absent from raging arguments about the first and the—

A first encounter

Pain! —In my absent-mindedness the razor cut into my chin. The cut wasn't too conspicuous, however. "I won't need to feel embarrassed about it when I face him," I thought.

I dressed and walked up to the door.

Across the dome at the other side was this figure walking towards me. It was instantly clear that he was mimicking me, with perfection and without hesitation. At one point, I raised my right hand and waved to him. I made sure this was abrupt enough. But he did the exact same thing, as if trying to trick me.

We were soon facing each other. Extending out my hand, I greeted him:

"Hi/Hi, my/my replica/replica, nice/nice to/to···" Startled by how I was addressed, I retracted my hand before touching his:

"You/You are/are my/my replica/replica, aren't/aren't you/you?" The clashing assertiveness was unsettling. And it wasn't funny. I hoped nobody was watching.

The engineers did say one of us was going to be the replica and I surely did not *feel like* a replica. Being a perfect replica, however, probably means that that fact is phenomenologically inaccessible. And anyhow whether I am the original or not wasn't part of the investigation. The point of the experiment was to see what it is like to be with somebody exactly like me. Having steadied myself with this thought, I smiled at him, only to see my smile on his face.

If a frame of reference could be established, I figured, if we could get some directions labeled, then we could get some leeway in personal differentiation. I decided that I would be the southerner and him the northerner:

"Let's/Let's call/call where/where your/your room/room is/is the/the north/north pole/pole."

"Hmmm/Hmmm, doesn't/doesn't work/work."

"Look/Look, let/let me/me toss/toss a/a coin/coin to/to decide/decide it/it," I thought of a way to challenge the VIMEL engineers.

Taking a dime out, I noticed him doing the same thing.

"What/what do/do you/you want/want?"

"Tail/tail."

"Look/Look, you/you don't/don't move/move. I'll/I'll toss/toss first/first to/to decide/decide who/who gets/gets to/to choose/choose."

Annoyed by the apparent deadlock, I resolved to throw the dime into the air. There were two glittering curves.

I opened up my left hand: "Tail! /Tail!"

I tried it again, and again and again: "Tail! /Tail!", "Heads! /Heads!", "Tail/Tail",

I wished I had brought with me a compass! I wondered whether that would work.

"Tail/Tail", "Heads/Heads", "Heads/Heads" …

During the whole time, I noticed nothing incongruent in the movement of the two coins.

Eventually, I stopped. He also stopped, looking pale. The cut on his chin stood out like a tiny blood-shot eye peering at me.

It seems that the VIMEL engineers had done their homework really well, whereas I had been too unprepared for an *actual* encounter with my perfect replica—naively expecting much more play, maybe out of a blind faith in the messiness of the world.

Challenged but defenseless, I turned around without a word and walked back to my room.

The rest of the day I occupied myself with replaying chess game records. I was really grateful to whoever introduced the walled studio apartment in the dome. Had everything he was doing now been in total view, had he been right in front of me, I would not be able to enjoy this moment of peace.

The next morning, feeling refreshed, I was determined to match up the perfection of replication in the dome with rigor in my philosophical reflection. I secluded myself in the room and opened my notebook:

January 7, 2008
Mirrored stage

The identity—that everything is exactly like its counterpart—and synchrony—that every change coincides with its counterpart—were apparently perfect and absolutely impressive. Kudos to the VIMEL engineers!

The impressiveness, however, depends on there being *two* copies of everything: him over there and me around here, his coin over there and my coin over here, and so on. Moreover, in spite of the perfection in identity, whatever I see, I see from *my* perspective and whatever he sees, he sees from *his* perspective. Each of us retains his "I-dimension", Klawonn would say. The psychic distress I suffered comes precisely from an ultra qualitative identity across a clear numerical difference. The qualitative identity is ever more striking because it is easily confirmed by my, so to speak, putting myself into his shoes through explicitly or implicitly imagining a rotation into his position. My sense of such a rotation, however, precisely serves to disclose, experientially, the quantitative difference in number.

The situation is analogous to our everyday dealings with mirrors. When I raise the razor with my *right* hand in front of a mirror, I see my mirror image puts up his *left* hand. This impression comes from my projecting myself onto him via an implicitly imagined rotation across the plane of the mirror. The only difference in the dome is that when I raised my *right* hand, he also raised his *right* hand, making the identification through rotation even easier and more complete.

Therefore, one way for me to understand the dome would be to treat the other as akin to my mirror image. Only that the whole "stage" —our dome with everything on it—is *mirrored*.

A game of chess

"But might the engineers have simply put in some special mirror-like device that reflects sound as well as light in an unconventional way?" My thoughts started to ramble. After all, mirroring seems less technologically challenging than material duplication and its virtual instantaneousness would provide close to perfect synchrony. After all, I haven't even touched him or anything on his side of the dome. Maybe if I had extended my hand further when I greeted him, I would have touched such an invisible device before reaching him?

"How about a game of chess with him?" I became excited. "That should give me plenty of chance to reach to his side!" Moreover, since my move is often the result of lengthy covert deliberation, maybe such autonomous mental process can give rise to some noticeable behavioral difference? Thus, if there is a mirror-like device at work, I could possibly touch it when moving pieces around during the game; and even if there are indeed two material copies of everything, my deep thought in the game could still be a potential source of perceivable discrepancy. Either way, a chess game would be something good to try out.

With my chess set under my arm, I walked out towards his room. He was also coming to me with something under his arm.

"Let's/Let's go/go play/play chess/chess in/in your/your room/room."

"Well/Well, well/well, let's/let's play/play here/here," we were quick to agree this time.

But we could place neither of the two boards exactly between us: they always ended up bumping into each other when I tried to push mine forward, and as I hesitantly retracted mine to allow the room for his, he also took his away.

"Is there indeed some sort of mirror here?" I wondered. To make sure that's not the case, I—we—walked around each other, or rather around the center, several times.

Finally, we sat down and put our boards side by side, mine to my right and his to his right. Very soon, we placed all the pieces on the boards, our hands and fingers moving in perfect synchrony.

Without a word, I went ahead with my first move on my board to my right, as he made the same move on his board to my left. I quickly responded, on his board, to his move there, only to see him responding in the same way to my move on my board. I felt quite amused with my playing two games at the same time. I even called the game on my board "this game" and the one on his board "that game."

Several moves later, however, these no longer felt like two games between two players. It became much more like one game in which I both made and responded to every move, a game between me and myself. In spite of the apparent twoness of the boards— "this" one on my right and "that" one on my left—I was experiencing only one *game process* unfolding on these two boards.

This revelation did not bother me too much, however, because I was used to playing games against myself. The trick is that when one considers a move for white, one shall always start with what's now on the board and rely exclusively on one's own early deliberation for white while ignoring that for black; and vice versa. This is kind of hard, especially if the two streams of game thoughts are to be separated enough to allow a sense of fooling and being fooled. But surprisingly interesting situations do emerge on the board and thinking through individual moves is as engaging as in an ordinary game.

What I normally do when playing against myself, but I didn't do here, was walking around the board to the other side to move the black pieces. I like doing that because the change of perspective on the board makes it easier to keep the two streams of game thoughts separate. Here, however, I merely turned my head to look at the right or left board as I alternately thought for white or black. "How convenient!" I felt.

Motivated to test how well the duplication of mental processes fare in the dome, I thought especially hard and made quite a few uncommon moves. The game engrossed me. Until about two hours later, I heard:

"Checkmate!/Checkmate!"

Startled by the sudden appearance of two voices, I was brought back into the recognition that there is another person sitting there right in front of me. Feeling inexcusable about having ignored him for so long, I quickly gathered up my chess set, said "thank/thank you/you", and left.

That night, lying in bed, the two boards would appear vividly in front of me whenever I closed my eyes. I could not keep myself from reliving the game:

At the very beginning, I certainly felt that I was playing *two* games on *two* boards against *another* person. But it quickly became clear there was only one game, played out in synchrony on two boards. Moreover, a simple turn of head was enough for alternating between seeing the game from the white and black sides. I first attributed this newly found convenience to the fact that one single game was presented on *two* boards. But when I was completely engrossed in the game, that difference of the boards dissolved, making me feel that my head turning merely changes perspective on *one and the same* board.

All such developments transpired quite unthinkingly as I was drawn into the game. What in retrospection was by far most striking, if at the time unnoticed, was that as I became no longer mindful of there being two boards, the other player also started to lose his presence as another person. The sense that a rotation was needed to identify with him gradually eroded away. I even started using "his" hands as if they were mine: when the pieces cluttered to occlude a target square on "my" board, for example, I often found myself looking at "his" board, relying on the better view it offers of the square to visually guide "his" hand over "his" board as I made the move on "my" board.

"Did I control 'his' hand remotely? Could neuronal spikes jump across the gap between us? Maybe through quantum tunneling?" That I didn't know. But this seemed clear: not only the games became phenomenologically one, in which I was lost; the boards, if not also the players, were also on the verge of collapsing into one. There was, however, also a "phenomenological gain" coordinated with such an "ontological deficit": I came to enjoy *two* perspectives on the same set of things.

"But if this phenomenological reconstruction of the chess game is accurate, my earlier mirror-inspired analysis must be wrong!" I quickly got up and turned to my notebook:

January 7, 2008

Precarious duality, precarious otherness

I was wrong about our everyday dealings with the mirror, and accordingly wrong about the way in which the dome may be considered a "mirrored stage".

A mirror does *not* replicate. It offers an extra view without generating material replicas.

As a competent mirror user, when I raise the razor to my right face, I see—through the mirror—*myself* raising the razor to *my* right face, rather than my replica raising a replicated razor to *his* left face. ①In learning to use mirrors, we learn to suppress involuntary reification of what appears in the mirror. This is why a competent driver looking into the rearview mirror sees the same road being left behind, rather than a different road extending ahead. The cat I had as a boy, in contrast, seemed to have never mastered the mirror: after grinning at its own mirror image and being bounced back by the mirror enough number of times, it opted to avoid the mirror rather than incorporating it into its daily grooming.

A mirror is useful to the extent that the "mirror image", rather than constitutes a replica of its

---

① Incidentally, it is because we are left-right symmetric (enough) and we can rotate ourselves actually or imaginarily with ease along the vertical axis that we tend to assume, mistakenly, that mirrors flip left and right. Mirrors flip front and back. Competent mirror use requires an implicit grasp of this fact.

source, remains an *image* that provides an alternative perspective on the source.

If mirrors do not replicate, is the idea of the dome being a "mirrored stage" simply unhelpful for our understanding the duality of things in the dome? This duality, after all, seems to run much deeper than in the case with ordinary mirrors. For one thing, it permeates the whole dome, without being constrained by anything like the limited size of a mirror. Neither does there seem to be any visible or tangible mirror-like device in the dome. Moreover, the fact that everything comes in radially symmetric pairs—if the VIMEL engineers were to be believed here—shall be immediately evident from the *third-person* point of view: just imagine somebody watching closed-circuit television taken from the zenith! Wouldn't such a take on the dome exhaust all that there is to say about the duality of the dome?

My chess game experience, however, points in a different direction. It suggest that from the first-person point of view one is liable to treat the appearance of two boards as two views on one and the same board and, accordingly, the appearance of one's replica as an alternative view on oneself. In that sense, from the first-person point of view, the dome essentially offers nothing more than what a mirror does. Quite ironically, once how mirrors work is correctly understood, the "mirrored stage" seems to remain an apt analogy for what things are like in the dome *from the first-person point of view.*

Therefore, if my experience in the chess game is to be trusted, Klawonn's interpretation of his own thought experiment seems phenomenologically misguided. It may only take an actual chess game on the Midway planet for him to find out that his "I-dimension" and that of his replica are not all that absolutely distinct. What is apparently his replica may turn out to provide no more than an alternative view on himself. Pointing out that he can see his replica's eyes but not his own won't help, because aided by an alternative view—through one's facing a mirror, visiting the Midway planet, or being in the dome—there may be no difficulty for one to see one's own eyes.

Admittedly, a certain duality incontestably remained from my first-person point of view even when I was completely lost in the game: there still *appeared* to be two boards, two players and two copies of everything else; when thinking about a move, I sometimes looked at "his board" and sometimes at "my board"; and when moving a piece, I sometimes guided "my hand" and sometimes "his hand".

Could such an undeniable duality ground a certain inexorable, if rarified, alterity? There is apparently a spatial gap between the two right hands. Couldn't such *spatial separation* ground a distinction between "here" and "there"? Even if the two right hands were to be identified as a single right hand of mine presented both "here" and "there", could my *self* as the site of *agency* remains only "here"? After all, while I certainly felt that I could move "his hand", I did not clearly feel that I was thinking his thoughts. And the two boards bumped into each other! They refused to be materially fused into one! Could such *physical resistance* ultimately secure an ontological duality?

When I was engrossed...

A glass

As I was writing down these last few words, it flashed across my mind that I wasn't carefully tracking how many rounds I went as we circled around the center—we were looking attentively at each other like wrestlers sizing up their opponent at the beginning of a match. "Did I actually walk two rounds, two and a half, or three? Could I have gone into his room rather than returning to my own?"

Startled by this thought, I jumped to my feet. My right elbow knocked a glass off the desktop. It shattered into pieces with a crashing sound.

After staring at the pieces on the floor for a few seconds, I realized this was an opportunity. I very quickly picked up a large piece of glass and ran out of the room. Seeing him coming out of his room, I hid the piece behind my back and passed him on his left without saying a word.

On his floor were also pieces of glass. It didn't take me long to fit the piece I brought to those on the floor. Dazzled by the perfection of the fit, I slowly rose to my feet, only to see this notebook on the desktop opened to a half-full page, where it read in my own handwriting: "When I was engrossed..."

I couldn't but feel that I was actually in my own room. Maybe the person whom I just ran past was, in reality, myself? Maybe the VIMEL engineers never really copied me? Maybe they just somehow warped space?

On my way back, I carefully maintained my distance from him, who appeared like a ghost image of myself returning from my own room to my own room.

The next day, I did not step out of my room, resolved to think through the whole thing and have all questions answered: duality, space, physical interaction, locus of agency, personal identity⋯I started with duality.

January 8, 2008
Presence in multiplicity

We have *two* eyes. When we look at a pencil in our hand, however, we normally do not see doubles but rather a single pencil at a specific distance, with the binocular disparity informing us of the distance.

As we walk around a barn, it presents itself to us in continuously varying profiles from continuously varying viewing angles. But again we perceive a single stationary barn, not a flux of profiles, because accompanying kinesthetic feedback allows us to separate out the coordinated profile change and perspective shift as due to our own locomotion rather than a change of the barn.

In the dome world, this sort of presence of unity and stability amid multiplicity and dynamics is still in operation. But there is clearly a new kind of multiplicity and dynamics rooted in having to do with the dome's being a D-system. The question, then, is whether this new kind also serves to present unity and stability.

If "he" is actually me, for example, how could "he" sometimes be so far away and appear so small?

This certainly does not seem to happen very often in our normal world. But something like it does happen. When I back away from a mirror, for example, the size of my mirror image tells me how far I am from the mirror. Since the center of the dome, like the mirror, is the axis of symmetry, might not the apparent size of "him" tell me how far I am from the center? If this is right, seeing "him" getting smaller would mean *I* am moving away from the center; seeing "him" getting larger would mean *I* am moving towards the center; and seeing "him" going out of view at the corner of my eyes would mean *I* am turning away from the center.

What about my head-turning between the two chess boards? If there were indeed only one board, why is it possible for me to see it in its two profiles by turning my head? How could turning my head from the "left board" to the "right board" be turning from the same board to the same board? But, again, isn't this like shifting my gaze back and forth between my hand and its mirror image when shaving? The game, after all, was played right around the center of the dome. We were, as it were, near the "mirror"!

Moreover, as the dome *somehow* allows a single board to be presented in two perspectives, the kinesthesis coordinated with my head-turning may in turn help to maintain my sense of the unity of the board, both *across* my two different perspective on it and *during* my shifting between these two perspectives.

To sum up, the presence of unity and stability amid multiplicity and dynamics does seem to generalize to the dome-specific duality. There remains, however, the more fundamental question: if there were only one copy of everything as my phenomenology suggests, where would that dome-specific duality come from?

It's about time to chart our dialectic here.

> **M:** Everything comes in two copies that are qualitatively identical but numerically different arranged in a radially symmetrical fashion.

Trusting the VIMEL engineers, I have always assumed that in the dome:

> **O:** Everything has only one copy; nothing, including the dome-specific duality, transcends the presence of unity in multiplicity; but space is weird: it is not isotropic and the center is special.

Now a competing hypothesis also seems to make sense of what's going on in the dome:

> **Challenge to M:** Identify a ground of difference that is both accessible from the first-person point of view and capable of securing the duality of things against its phenomenological precariousness.
>
> **Challenge to O:** Explain the source of the incontestably present dome-specific duality.

These two views, or *hypotheses*, also face different challenges:

To meet the challenges, we cannot reply simply that the VIMEL engineers did it, that they duplicated everything and fashioned the radial symmetry et cetera.

Such a reply, offered to meet the Challenge to O, amounts to giving up on Hypothesis O by admitting that after all there are two copies of everything. Put bluntly, the force of O lies in its defiance to the VIMEL engineers: "You may have never replicated anything. You may have merely pulled tricks with space. And I can see how that might go from being down here!"

On the other hand, if such a reply is offered to meet the Challenge to M, it risks unduly privileging the third-person point of view while sacrificing the rigor of phenomenology. To wit, if, while in the dome, I were to constantly remind myself of the historical origin of the dome in the hands of the VIMEL engineers, I would be appealing to my third-person knowledge acquired outside of the dome, rather than relying on my first-person experience from within the dome. The question is not what the VIMEL engineers know or how they may tell the paired things in the dome apart. How is it, for me, being in the dome, to keep a phenomenologically precarious pair as numerically distinct? That is the question.

In short, the contention between M and O hinges on how the dome-specific duality is to be understood from within the dome, by a dome dweller, and for a dome dweller.

More experimentation, not more speculation, seems called for. Now that we have two competing hypotheses, more data may help us evaluate them against each other.

Two moments

"While physical effects dissipate over space, dissipation of physical effects may in turn point to spatial separation. Maybe spatial separation, with the corresponding physical dissipation, could secure the duality?" I wondered.

Remembering the twoness in the voice when we spoke, I called out:

"How—How was—was your—your day—day?"

"Good—Good. "

His voice came to me damped. With the added delay, it sounded reassuringly like another person calling out to me. "That's what's so great about being in the dome!" I thought. "I can try things out and hear for myself!"

"What—what did—did you—you have—have for—for sup—sup—per—per?"

"Egg—egg and—and an—an—cho—cho—vy—vy sa—sa—lad—lad with—with toast—toast. "

. . .

I enjoyed this chat, which somehow made me feel vindicated.

Eventually, just as it began to suggest echoing, I ended the conversation:

"Good night! —"

"Good night!" The reply came back, more appeasing than ever.

For the first time, I felt there was an empathizing partner in the dome rather than just me myself or me with a badgering dupe.

The next morning, relaxed, I decided to go visit him. At the center we met. I reach out with an open hand. The moment our hands clenched together, I felt beyond any doubt that there is another person in front of me. It was *his* hand that pressed into mine. It was clearly an alien source of pressure.

That's even better than the "good night"! Thank God, our bodies are still distinct.

During the day, we played several quick chess games. At the end of each game, we shook hands and said "thank you". The handshaking helped to restore my sense of our numerical difference that had worn down during the game.

Going to bed that night, I thought I had had the best day since I came into the dome.

The morning after, however, this newly acquired assurance quickly gave way upon further reflection on space and physical interaction in the dome.

January 10, 2008

Space

Along the line of Hypothesis M, handshaking in the dome *might* be understood as follows: when we shake hands, I felt three things: (a) I was holding a hand; (b) my act of holding was resisted by the hand I held; and (c) my holding hand is also being held. Crucially, however, for the hand that I held, I did not feel the counterpart of (c). That is, I did not feel, from the receiving end as it were, that it was being held: my hand was being grasped by something from which I received no haptic feedback. This is in clear contrast with my left hand holding my right hand, in which case I will feel both hands holding and being held. Furthermore, the absence of haptic feedback from the hand I held matched what I saw with my eyes: the hand I held was connected to another person who was spatially separate from me.

This analysis, however, rests on the critical presumption that there were two hands holding each other. If to begin with there had actually been only one hand, as suggested by Hypothesis O, there would have been no other hand for me to receive haptic feedback from. And that would have explained why I felt no counterpart of (c)! The challenge to O, of course, would be to explain how one hand could, admittedly quite extraordinarily, prop up the appearance of two hands shaking each other. However, given that the handshaking took place at the center of the dome, which has already been identified as special under O, explaining why one hand may apparently "shake" with itself may not add any extra challenge to O.

Could the case of chatting across the dome make a difference? First, there was the delay between my hearing my own utterance and my hearing his, a difference suggesting that the other speaker was at a distance. Second, the decay of sound further enhanced the sense that another person was speaking at a distance.

From the perspective of Hypothesis O, however, this so-called chatting may indeed be a fancy sort of echoing. The delay and decay could be simply due to the extra distance the sound wave covers in traveling *back* to the source, without a second speaker being implicated. What explains the "visible duality" in the dome might also explain the "audible duality." Echoing, after all, is just "acoustic mirroring." Along this line of reasoning, the delay and decay of a "reply" tells me how far I am from the center, just like the apparent size of "him" tells me how far I am from the center: the longer the delay and the more the decay, the further away I am from the center. Delay and decay in the chat will then become a mode of my self-presence in the dome, posing no extra difficulty.

Back to the case of "handshaking". Suppose space in the dome somehow curves. Suppose the closer to the center, the more it curves. It will be possible for my hand reaching to the center to bend back and fold onto itself. This may allow my hand to "hold" itself. And it may feel like handshaking because my fingers may fold enough to press against both the back of the palm and themselves. This may also look like handshaking, if light is also bent such that, depending on the angle of reflection, some light beams travel more directly to my eyes and others travel around the center to form a complete image of two hands holding each other.

While this scenario might seem mind-boggling, it is actually not qualitatively different from the two chessboards apparently bumping into each other at the center. As the (one and only) board is pushed from behind towards the center, it will have bent so much that the right and left halves of its far edge will touch and push against each other, preventing the board from going further. Moreover, because light also bends around the center, it will appear visually as if two boards have bumped into each other.

If this story of bent space sounds incredible, my earlier analyses of "handshaking" and "chatting" from the perspective of M is not more convincing. The problem, again, is with the dearth of phenomenologically accessible alterity.

Normally when I shake hand with somebody else, some sort of mismatch is expected between how my hand holds and how my own hand is held (let alone mismatch in temperature, moisture, and skin texture etc）： while I may be clasping firmly， the other may return only a gentle touch. But there is no such mismatch when I "shake hands" with "him". Whenever I grasp the other hand harder or release it quicker， I also receive the effect of such an action. Nothing in the quality and dynamics of the experienced handholding differentiates one handholding action from a potential other， or me as the agent of one action from me as the patient of another. No variation in my action on "his" hand fails to reach back to mine. Thus， initial impression notwithstanding， "handshaking" with one's replica could serve to undermine， rather than secure an experiential differentiation of oneself from the other. ①

As time goes by

These revelations were simultaneously elating and disappointing. On the one hand， I felt that I genuinely understood something about the dome and I expected that an appropriate topology of the space， if it can be given， will turn Hypothesis O into a theory both complete and compelling. On the other hand， I wished that Hypothesis M had come out stronger， because while I definitely appreciated the appeal of Hypothesis O， I was still not convinced that it was simply *the* story about the dome and that Hypothesis M was simply wrong. Trying to be a good phenomenologist， I was still open-minded about the failure of Hypothesis O to do justice to my own experience in the dome.

I played along.

For a while， "he" and I enjoyed going to the center to shave each other's face. It was fun. And it made me feel good to have somebody else to care for. As my initially cautious maneuvers of the razor over "his" face began to resemble self-directed routine movements， however， this morning ritual soon lost its altruistic glamor.

Even the call of "Good night！"， which had given me great comfort， began to sound clearly like myself being echoed.

We would still play chess from time to time， but we only shook hands occasionally and， when we

---

① Discussion here is inspired by Stern （1985） on the Siamese twins （cited in Zahavi， 2000）. As Husserl （1960， 109; cited in Zahavi， 2000） once said： "if what belongs to the Other's own essence were directly accessible， it would be merely a moment of my own essence， and ultimately he himself and I myself would be the same."

did, only briefly.

The room, in spite of its walls, was no more refuge. After a few more visits to the other room, the difference between the rooms—one being here, closer to me, and with myself in it now, and the other being there, away from me, and with him in it now—gradually evaporated. I began to find myself inadvertently ending up sleeping in "his" room and continuing "his" notes.

To be sure, the duality persisted. But it came out ever more clearly as a duality of perspective. I often had to remind myself that, so long as the VIMEL engineers were to be trusted, there was a replica of me, which was numerically different from myself, no matter how perfect the replication had been, and so on and so forth. This was not a pleasant exercise at all, in particular because I found it poignantly ironic that to maintain a sense of first-person uniqueness, I had come to rely exclusively on a piece of third-person knowledge.

Gradually, I stopped fighting back. I stopped caring about who is who as I also stopped caring about who's is who's: socks, glasses, toothbrush, dishes, and, of course, the notebook. My way with the apparent duality of such household items turned completely utilitarian: I just used whichever was close and handy, like what I did in my first chess game. It became virtually impossible for me not to feel that I was the only lonely person in the dome.

By now I had lost track of which room I was in. But I did finally figure out the topology of space required by Hypothesis O, after a lot of sketching and scribbling on one or the other—or rather *my*—notebook:

January 15, 2008

Ontology and phenomenology

Consider making a cone from a piece of round waffle. You cut it into two semicircles; leaving one half aside, you roll up the other into a cone that has the center of the original circle at its apex. [1]The two radiuses of the circle along the cut will merge into a meridian of the cone. Nothing gets stretched during the process (under the idealization that the waffle is completely thin): any straight line on the original flat waffle still corresponds to a locally shortest path with the same length on the surface of the

---

[1] To make a real one in the kitchen, you do not cut, but simply roll the round waffle up into a cone!

cone;① right angles in the original waffle will still be right angles; and a square will retain its area.

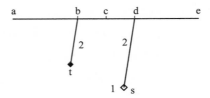

Figure 1: Radii *cba* and *cde* will merge into a meridian. Points *b* and *d* will merge into one point. Paths *sd* and *bt* will merge into the single shortest path 2 in Figure 2.

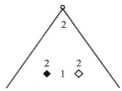

Figure 2: There are two shortest paths from one point to another. Path 2 goes around the cone surface

Our waffle cone *models* how a horizontal cross-section of the dome curves under Hypothesis O. It captures the gradual increase of curvature as one gets closer to the center of the dome, which corresponds to the apex of the cone model. ②It captures the fact that the center is a singularity, where curvature goes up to infinity. It also explains the presence of duality in the dome: between any pair of points on the waffle cone, there are *two* shortest paths, one that goes around the apex and the other that doesn't. Depending on the angle of reflection or emission, light traveling along the surface of the cone from one point to the other may take either of these two paths. This, as it turns out, could be the mother of all duality in the dome. ③

Crucially, however, because we started with only *half* of the original circular waffle, which cor-

---

① "Locally shortest" means that any change to the path, so long as it is small enough and is confined to the surface of the cone, will make the path longer. Such a path is called a "geodesic", the generalization to manifolds of the notion of a straight line in Euclidean space.

② Curvature increases as one goes from the base of a cone to the apex along a meridian.

③ To get a curvature model for the whole dome one can imagine a series of waffle cones with appropriately decreasing base and height, each of which corresponds to a horizontal cross-section of the dome. Then with the cone for the dome floor at the bottom—the largest one in the series—and the apices of the cones pointing downward, one keeps on dropping a smaller one into its bigger predecessor. At the end, one would get a cone "filled" up to roughly the "one-scoop" level. And that would be the model.

responds to half of a complete cross-section of the dome, we need only one copy of everything for the appearance of two to arise.

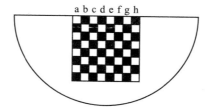

Figure 3: Squares a8, b8, c8, and d8 will bump against, respectively, h8, g8, f8, and e8

It is now easy to see how one chessboard could indeed "bump" into itself: when it is pushed to the center of the dome, it is as if it is pushed up towards the apex of the cone; and as it reaches the center, the left and right halves of its far edge will indeed wrap around the apex to contact each other at a meridian of the cone! As to the visual impression that one board is bumping into another board, this is indeed due to light traveling along two paths: one that goes around the cone surface (i. e., to the far side of the cone first) and gives rise to the impression of the far board and the other that does not and gives rise to the impression of the near board.

Along the same line, we can explain the "appearance of handshaking". And, importantly, because metrics are preserved as the cone is rolled up—there is no stretch—I won't feel any distortion as my hand bends back to itself around the center of the dome.

The story of curved space shall *allow ontology and phenomenology to cohere* under Hypothesis O: ontologically there is only one copy of every material thing, but thanks to the two shortest paths under the specific way in which space curves, one simultaneously has two perspectives on it. The apparent duality that arises, however, is strictly a duality of *perspective*. It does not warrant the distinctness of material things, but rather constitutes the presence of unity in multiplicity of a dome-specific sort: a difference between the dual perspectives serves to disclose how a *single* thing is positioned relative to the center.

This explains why the apparent duality of *things* turned out to be precarious. As I started to use "his" hand and "that" board in my first chess game, I was learning to coordinate these dual perspectives so that they triangulate on one and the same thing. When such coordination becomes adequate, *the* chessboard presents itself to me, phenomenologically, as a single thing seen from a duality of perspectives. As I learned to exploit this dome-specific duality of *perspectives* generally, the initial impression of two copies of everything was washed away.

If it is unclear what the outcome of such a learning process will be in general, let us imagine some hypothetical "natives". These natives would be born and grow up in the dome. Their whole actual world and world history would be confined to the dome. This shall help us appreciate *what it is like to be dome dwellers* under Hypothesis O.

They would not find a dual ontology either necessary or compelling. They might not have developed a *theoretical* account of curved space, but that should not prevent them from *practically* dealing with the presence of unity in duality. (After all, we had been competent mirror users for eons before the laws of optic reflection was first formulated.) If one denizen were to, knowingly, gun down their counterpart, for example, the native dome police would reasonably rule it as a suicide rather than a mutual murder or a simultaneous murder-suicide.

At some point, some of these natives might figure out that a "dual ontology" —our Hypothesis M—could also make sense of their world. But it would likely be regarded as a mere theoretical possibility that makes no dent on the community's actual ontological commitments. Advocates of a "Copernican revolution" in light of this dual ontology might meet strong resistance or even suffer the fate of Giordano Bruno. For their dual ontology to be taken seriously, they presumably would have to show that material difference can be actually detected between the apparently identical pairs, or that the dome is differentially embedded in a larger whole, such as a polarized geomagnetic field, and that such a differential embedding can be registered, with a compass for example, from within the dome.

A tile

The excitement from having figured out how space curves under Hypothesis O lasted for a few days. I entertained myself with thinking up oddities of the curved space and then tested them out: Can one make an iron ring that nobody can move without breaking it? [Yes.] Can one use a nutcracker without a bottom? [Yes.] Can one create a chessboard that is placed exactly at the center? [Yes.] Can one play a game of chess on this board? [No.] And so on.

As the excitement petered out, a sense of utter boredom crept in. Nostalgia about the days before I figured out the space did not help. Only reflections on the philosophical implications surrounding Hypothesis O made living in the dome bearable.

First of all, Klawonn created his thought experiment to illustrate how personal identity may be grounded in a phenomenological grasp of the "I-dimension": "What I am talking about is precisely the subjective point of view which—*seen from my own point of view*—makes me identical with the one person and not the other."① Unfortunately, he seems to have got the phenomenology wrong. Living in the dome, the "two of us" ended up collapsing into one person *from my own point of view*. Ironically, it is only by actively recalling the history of the dome and imagining its arrangement, from a *third-person* point of view, as it were, that I was able to hang on to a bare sense of my difference from "him".

As to thought experimenters attracted to the idea of a zombie, the irony lies in their *thinking immaterially about replication while thinking materially about experience*. By failing to give the inevitable material discrepancy in actual replication its due, they fail to recognize that if enjoying qualitative experience were to slip through the cracks of functionally or physically typed, as versus materially pregnant, replication, so could being alive, being asleep, being cognitive, being a person, or being an actual replica. In other words, the zombie thought experiment is caught in a double bind. On the one hand, if the replication is not regimented, the possibility is open for us to trace the source of alleged discrepancy in experience to the accommodated material discrepancy. On the other hand, if the replication is regimented such that no material discrepancy is accommodated, as is apparently the case with the dome, the replica and the original may fail to, from the first-person perspective, make up two distinct subjects that are needed to getting the "experimentation" going. ②The challenge to the zombie thought experiment, it seems, is how to strike the right balance between not getting a replica and thus not having a thought experiment at all, and having the alleged difference explained away too easily.

For days I killed time with such reflections. Until one night, while I was thinking about Parfit's thought experiments, about how they were not metaphysically innocent and thus already ethically lad-

---

① From Klawonn 1987, quoted above.

② Because the entitlement of the original to qualitative experience rests on the identity of the original with the thought experimenter, whose enjoying qualitative experience is not at issue, the failure in the dome of numerical differentiation between the replica and the original, *from the first-person perspective*, seems particularly suggestive: In a regimented version of the zombie thought experiment, is the *thought experimenter* really in a position to report from the first-person perspective *of the original alone* on an alleged phenomenological difference between the original and the replica, when their numerical distinction seems to be in doubt from the first-person perspective of the original?

en, I was startled by a sudden tremor in the ground.

"Earthquake! /Earthquake!" I shouted, rushing towards "his" room.

"Oh my God!" hearing my yelling perfectly echoed from "his" direction, I thought, "the dome works as a D-system even in an earthquake!"

When we were about twenty feet away from each other, the ground shook again violently. A crack was heard from the "zenith" of the dome.

Coming down towards us was a tile. But just as it was about to hit right at the center of the floor, the ground shook one more time. Landing about fifteen feet to my left, the tile broke into three pieces.

Silence for God knows how long.

"Let's call that the east," pointing in the direction of the broken tile, he finally said.

"That? OK," pointing at the broken tile, I agreed.

Since then, we played a chess game and used it to determine our future. We asked an old man on the square to toss a coin to decide who takes white. I lost the game, so I continue to study philosophy whereas he moved to his ancestral village on the Shandong peninsula of China to work as a fisherman.

When preparing this paper for publication, I emailed him to ask for permission to incorporate the journal entries from the dome. I felt he deserves as much credit, or blame, as I do. And he replied:

How curious you should ask! Isn't it clear both of us live only in the imagination of the real author? Hasn't he already spoken for himself through our voices in his narrative? Shouldn't it be clear that whatever we claimed and did not disown in his narrative represents his actual view? You must have lost your good metaphysical sense in thinking that you and I could, in our imagined existence, shoulder a true authorship or, for that matter, think a real thought, or truly enjoy qualia. Let me wish you some fictitious good luck with your fictitious paper!

P. S. Please do not assume just because you get to be the narrator in the fiction, you must thus be the true original whereas I the dupe.

References

[1] Adams, Robert M, 1979, Primitive Thisness and Primitive Identity. *Journal of Philosophy*, 76: 5 – 26.

[2] Black, Max, 1952, The Identity of Indiscernibles. *Mind*, 61: 153 – 164.

[3] Davidson, Donald, 1987, Knowing One's Own Mind. *Proceedings and Addresses of the American Philo-*

sophical Association, 60: 441 –458.

[4] Hacking, Ian, 1975, The Identity of Indiscernibles. *Journal of Philosophy*, 72: 249 –256.

[5] Husserl, Edmund, 1960, *Cartesian Meditations*. Trans. D. Cairns. The Hague: Martinus Nijhoff.

[6] Klawonn, Erich, 1987, The 'I': On the Ontology of First Personal Identity. *Danish Yearbook of Philosophy*, 24: 43 –76.

[7] Lewis, David, 1973, Counterfactuals and Comparative Possibility. *Journal of Philosophical Logic* 2: 418 –446.

[8] Parfit, Derek, 1984, *Reasons and Persons*. Oxford University Press.

[9] Stern, Daniel, 1985, *The Interpersonal World of the Infant: A View from Psychoanalysis and Developmental Psychology*. Basic Books.

[10] Tye, Michael, 2007, "Qualia". *Stanford Encyclopedia of Philosophy*.

[11] Zahavi, Dan, 2000, *Self Awareness and Alterity*. Northwestern University Press.

一个关于复制的思想实验

罗　军

加拿大多伦多大学

摘　要： 当代分析哲学家们经常利用假想的复制来进行论证，比如普特南（Putnam）的孪生地球（twin earth）、戴维森（Davidson）的沼泽人（Swampman）、帕菲特（Parfit）的分裂情形（fission cases）、查尔默斯（Chalmers）的行尸拷贝（zombie copy）等等。这些论证假定了复制前后个体各自的数量同一性（numerical identity）不成问题，相应简化甚至抽象掉复制所涉的具体物质性，断言复制可以在分子或原子层次上不失真地进行，从而在实质上否认具体物质性与所论证问题有本质关联。本文以第一人称思想实验的形式，从现象学视角详述复制之下主体眼里的"不可辨者之同一"（identity of indiscernibles），指出物质性差异实为复制前后个体之区分的关键。如此，前述各种复制假想由于忽略物质性并预设数量同一性而引入了未经审视的假定，因此不足以支持后续论证。以"感受质"问题为例，如果我们看到人的物质性并不能还原为分子或原子的组合，那无以名状的感受质（ineffability of qualia）或许正是人之作为意识主体的物质性之征？

关键词： 同一性；物质性；复制；现象学视角；第一人称；主体性；意识；感受质（qualia）

知识论证和 Frank Jackson 的表征主义回应策略

◎ 刘　玲

中国社会科学院

摘　要：Jackson 对知识论证的表征主义回应策略认为表征主义能满足回应知识论证所要求的约束问题，但是由于 Jackson 没有阐明如何对表征特征（感觉）进行物理主义说明，导致其表征主义论证对学习命题的否定以及对玛丽走出房间之后状态的正面说明缺乏牢靠的论证基础，故而达不到辩护物理主义的目的。

关键词：表征主义；知识论证；表征特征；现象特征

当今心灵哲学的一个核心议题就是感受性问题，它是物理主义和反物理主义争论的焦点。反物理主义者围绕感受性问题提出了许多思想实验和论证，来证明感受性是被物理主义所遗漏和不能解释的问题，其中知识论证是当前心灵哲学中少数几个最著名、最有影响的反物理主义论证之一，同时该论证也具有其他几个论证不具有的特点：Jackson 由 1982 年提出该论证，但是又于 20 世纪 90 年代转而反对这个论证。文章主要对 Jackson 在知识论证问题上的观点变化进行说明和研究，探讨他为什么由反对物理主义转向一种表征主义的、对物理主义进行强硬辩护的立场，以及他的这种辩护是否成功。

一、知　识　论　证

知识论证所描述的故事是这样的：玛丽是一位杰出的科学家，她从小在一间黑白屋子中长大，她所看到和接触到的东西都是黑白颜色的。假设她通过黑白书本、黑白电视等学习关于世界的知识，最后成为了出色的科学家，知道了所有关于世界的物理知识，那么，当她第一次走出黑白房间看到红色西红柿的时候，她是否学到了新的东西，她能否从所有这些物理信息中推出看见红色的感受性是什么样的？

在这里，我们会有这样的强烈直觉：尽管她已经拥有了关于颜色以及它们与我们相互作用的所有的物理知识，但是在玛丽走出房间之前，玛丽不知道当她第一次看见红色时究竟会有什么样的感受经验；然而如果她走出房间，看见红色，情况就会不一样了，她就会知道看到红色的感受经验究竟是什么样的。如果是这样，那么关于看见红色是什么样的感受性就是非物理的，因为如果是物理的，玛丽在房间之中就会知道，因为她知道所有的物理事实。反物理主义者用这个思想实验来说明，如果物理主义是正确的，玛丽在走出房间之后不会学到任何东西，而现在她学到了，因而是非物理的，所以物理主义是错误的。

Jackson 指出该论证主要有两个部分[1]：

（1）完全物理知识是不完全的——玛丽在房间中的物理知识是不完全的。玛丽走出房间之后学到了关于这个世界的某些东西，它扩大了玛丽关于这个世界共同性维度（dimensions of similarity）的认识。当玛丽还在房间的时候，她知道不同的人在看到西红柿时所共同具有的特征，包括他们自身以及他们与西红柿的关系等方面的特征。但是在她走出房间之后，她对这些共同性维度的认识被扩大了：不同的人在看到红色时还有另外一个共同的东西，即看到红色时的特殊感觉。

（2）既然玛丽知道所有的物理知识，那么，如果物理主义是正确的，玛丽走出房间之后所知道的关于世界的共同性维度就不应该被扩大，就应该在走出房间之前就知道了。所以，物理主义是错误的。

逻辑地说，该论证的结构是：

首先，如果物理主义是正确的，那么我们关于感受性的现象知识都可以从我们对世界的物理描述中先天地推演出来——先天演绎性命题。又，玛丽在房间之内已经知道了所有关于世界的物理知识——完全知识命题，那么，玛丽在走出房间之后就什么也没有学到。

但是，知识论证呈现出的强烈的直觉：玛丽不能从其所有的物理知识中推出看见红色是什么样的感受（知识直觉）。她在走出房间之后，其前后的知识状态发生了变化，她获得了看到红色是什么样的知识，学到了关于感受性的现象知识——学习命题。

最后，根据否定后件的假言推理，所以物理主义是错误的。

其中，学习命题是依附于知识直觉之上的，而完全知识命题是依附于先天演绎性命题之上的。实际上，知识论证问题就是研究知识直觉和先天演绎性命题之间的关系。而它们其实又是一个问题的两个方面：赞成前者就是反对后者，反之亦然。

二、Jackson 为什么转而反对知识论证？

　　Jackson 虽然对知识论证的看法发生了根本的改变，但是分析他后来几篇文章（Jackson，1998b，2003，2004）的论述，其中有一点是不变的——论证的出发点没有变。Jackson 始终认为物理主义包含一种先天演绎性命题（a prior deducibility claim）：如果物理主义是正确的，那么关于现象经验性质的认识就能从我们对世界的物理描述中先天地推演出来。* 这是当初 Jackson 之所以提出知识论证的出发点也是现今他批判知识论证的出发点：之前他认为这个演绎性命题是不可能的，因而提出知识论证挑战物理主义；现如今，他接受这个命题，并以此指出知识论证错在何处，为物理主义作辩护。知识直觉和先天演绎性命题是一个问题的两个方面，这"一个问题"就是先天演绎性命题，它是 Jackson 之前论证、之后辩护的出发点，可以说是知识论证的核心问题。Jackson 对先天演绎性命题非常重视，专门对它在知识论证问题中的地位进行了界定：它是任何一个满意的物理主义回应策略所应该满足的约束条件（constraint）。[2] 知识论证对此约束问题提供的就是一种否定的回答。

　　Jackson 之后反对知识论证和他提出的约束问题也直接相关。知识直觉是说我们不可能从对世界的物理描述而知道看到红色是什么样的感受。为了解释掉这个直觉，说清这个"假象"（illusion），Jackson 接受了表征主义，认为对感受性的表征主义说明可以很好地满足这个约束。也许事物并不是我们表征的那样，但是可以肯定的是，每一个感官经验都是将事物表征为这样或那样。经验的性质就是被表征的意向性对象所具有的性质。如果经验的性质源于感觉的意向对象的性质，是表征性的，那么就不存在经验的性质本身，不存在"红"这样的属性（property），而只有表征特征（representational character），而这个表征特征他认为是可以得到物理说明的。既然它们可以得到物理说明，既然玛丽在走出房间之前就知道了所有关于我们世界的物理知识，那么玛丽走出房间之后所看到、听到、感受到的所有原则上都可以从之前的物理知识先天地推出，都可以用物理的方式进行说明，所以她之前的物理知识不是不完全的。这在 Jackson 看来，就既说清了知识直觉问题，很好地辩护了完全知识断言，同时约束问题也得到了正面的回答。

　　Jackson 指出，批评知识论证的人往往更多地关注他分析的知识论证结构的第二个部分（他们认为承认玛丽知识的不完全性并不与物理主义相冲突），但是他认为更应该注意第一部分即

---

　　*　本文只是讨论假设在接受这个命题的前提下，Jackson 的论证是否融贯有力。

否定完全知识命题，承认学习命题的部分。Jackson 认为知识论证就错在了认为玛丽的知识是不完备的，他指出实际上这是一种认知假象（cognitive illusion），源于我们对感官经验的错误认识：感官经验似乎以不同寻常的"快和简单"来获取信息，并且还带有整体性的特点，这就使人觉得它们获取的是某种内在的性质，同时这种性质直觉上又不是物理的，因此呈现给我们的状况就好像是，玛丽获得的信息是某种非物理的、内在的属性。[3]实际上并不存在所谓的我们看到红色时所亲知到的属性，我们经验的性质实质上是意向性对象的性质，它的性质源于我们将事物表征成那样，因此感官经验性质本质上是表征性的。

三、Jackson 的表征主义论证

我们可以将 Jackson 的表征主义论证归纳如下[4]：

前提1：所有关于颜色经验的现象特征都在于这些经验的表征特征。

前提2：玛丽在房间中能从关于世界的物理事实中推出所有关于颜色经验的表征特征。

结论：因此，玛丽没有学到任何东西，不存在物理主义所遗漏的东西。

这个论证首先必须要回答两个问题：（1）经验的表征特征和现象特征的关系；（2）经验的表征特征、表征内容在 Jackson 那里指的是什么。

Jackson 偏爱表征主义的原因之一就在于他对表征特征和现象特征之间关系的判定。在 Jackson 看来，经验的现象特征依附于表征的特性，表征特征在决定经验性质方面起着决定作用。[5]作为一个曾经接受感觉材料理论的人来说，经验的透明性（transparency of experience or diaphanousness）特点对 Jackson 有着极大的吸引力。* 透明性命题是说，认识经验的性质就是认识它的对象的属性。虽然透明性命题与感觉材料理论和表征主义都相关，但是 Jackson 现在抛弃了感觉材料理论而接受表征主义，认为感觉材料的经验"对象"是现实的、时空的对象（an object in space-time），有很大的局限性，而表征主义因为其对象是意向性的对象（an intentional object）而更有说服力。

此外，视觉和感官经验自身的表征特点也让 Jackson 认识到现象特征依附于表征特征，而选择表征主义。（［5］，p. 6）当我们将其他表征装置如地图、句子等的表征与感官表征相比时

---

* 有必要提及的是，表征主义与经验透明性命题有密切关联，而且后者本身也充满争议，很多人正是通过批判这个命题来批判表征主义，但是对表征主义自身对错的讨论不是本文所要关注的，本文要关注的是表征主义和知识论证之间的关系：探讨表征主义论证的回应是否成功。

会发现，在前些种类的表征装置中，它们自身和所要表征的东西之间存在某种间隔，而在后者的表征中却不存在。我们可以用气象地图上的等压线之间的间隔来表征压强的变化程度，用 c、a、t 字母的排列方式表征某种动物，用地图上的绿色来表征雨林地带，但是我们在描述这些装置的时候也可以毫不提及它们所要表征的。而在视觉表征中却不可能这样做：当我们有一个关于红色圆的形状的表征时，这就是这个经验所表征的。我可能接受或不接受事物就是我们所表征的这样，但是事物都是被表征的，而这正是经验的本质特征。所以，想要了解一个经验现象特征，不可能不考虑这个经验表征的是什么；当我们注意我们的经验特性时，就会发现我们自己实际上是在进行着经验将事物表征成某样的过程，这实际上就是经验的表征内容，因此也可以说现象特征依附于这种表征内容。

那么，Jackson 所说的经验的"表征特征"是指什么？这和经验的表征内容密切相关，特征是由内容呈现出来的。Jackson 的表征主义是一种强表征主义（strong representionalism），主张经验如何将事物表征成那样已经穷尽了经验的性质——经验完全就是表征性的（exhaustively representational），不需要求助于任何其他本体上新的属性，认为一种经验部分地由表征部分和非表征部分组成是错误的，因为表征已经做了全部的工作。[6] 经验的性质只需诉诸于经验的表征内容就行了。正是因为经验完全就是表征的，所以表征理论才能回答约束问题，回应知识论证。那么经验的表征内容又是什么？

Jackson 说我们讨论表征主义、不同表征状态时，对"内容"应该有共同的理解——事物如何被表征成那样。（［2］，p. 434）但问题是，如果信念和知觉经验表征内容都是事物如何被表征成那样，我们为什么还是感觉知觉经验的表征有不同之处？用 Jackson 自己的话说就是，有的表征有"感觉（feel）"（指知觉经验），而有的却没有。我们可以解释为，虽然内容都是将事物如何表征成那样，但是具体到各个表征的具体内容，还是有不同之处。具体内容的不同造成了状态的不同，也使有的表征有感觉，有的却没有。Jackson 在其 2003 年的文章中集中对现象经验表征所具有的特别"感觉"进行了说明。这种特别感觉实际上就是 Jackson 所认为的经验的表征特征或内容。具体来说，当我们感官经验表征事物成这样和那样时，它具有五个方面的不同特征（［2］，p. 437）：

（1）这种表征是非常丰富的（rich）。视觉经验从颜色、形状、位置、广延、方向等方面来表征事物是如何的，触觉经验从形状、运动、质地、广延、方向以及温度等方面来表征事物是如何的。

（2）表征所具有的丰富性又是不可分割的（inextricably）。一个句子可以对 X 的红色和圆的形状分别进行描述，可以在对其红色进行说明的同时对其运动或位置却没有任何言说。但是在一个视觉经验中，我们不能将颜色部分和形状部分截然分开；在触觉形式的表征中，我们不可能仅仅单独对形状有所感觉，而对其质地或温度没有感觉。表征主义强调经验的整体性。

（3）这种表征是直接的（immediate）。通过我们的手（即使手又通过一根筷子）来感觉洞中物体的形状，与通过阅读一张纸上的说明来领会有一个如此颜色、形状的物体来感觉它，这两种感觉是完全不同的。

（4）我们与环境之间的因果关系是表征内容的一部分，表征内容中有一个起原因作用的因素。知觉经验的表征中，世界是与我们相互作用的。视觉经验就是表征某物通过视觉感官来影响我们。

最后，感官经验在两种信念状态的传递或转换之间起着特殊的功能性作用。

在介绍完五个方面之后，Jackson 认为如果一个表征状态的内容具有不可分割的、直接的丰富性，内容中有起原因作用的因素，发挥着正确的功能作用，那么我们就将经验的现象本质说清楚了。（［2］，p. 438）之前回答约束问题，批判非完全知识命题，否定知识直觉只是否定性的工作，Jackson 认为还需要有一个正面性的工作，即对玛丽走出房间之后发生了什么进行正面的述说。Jackson 指出玛丽在走出房间之后处在一种新的状态——具有以上五个方面特征的状态。在 Jackson 看来，表征内容的这五个方面都可以得到物理的说明。但是，这五个方面如何得到物理说明，它们如何从玛丽现有的关于世界的物理事实中推演出来？这是问题的关键，它实际上是除了以上所提及的表征主义论证需要首先回答的两个问题以外的、关系 Jackson 的表征主义论证是否有力更根本的问题。

Jackson 较重视第四个方面。他对自己为什么相信感官经验原则上可以从对世界的物理描述中推演出来的解释首先就是诉诸于我们对感官的知识有一个原因来源（causal source/origin）。（［3］，p. 418）比如，当我们表征有一种圆珠笔在面前的时候，我们的经验不仅仅是说这里有一个这样颜色的、形状的圆珠笔在我们面前，它同时也说明这个物体正以某种方式和我们相互作用，据此我们才能知道它的颜色和形状等特征。又比如，在面前多种圆珠笔中，我们只注意到其中这一种而不是其他，这更说明它是引起我们感觉的原因来源。据此，Jackson 认为我们关于看见红色和感到疼痛是什么样的知识有着纯物理上的原因。玛丽从不知道看见红色是什么样到知道的转变就可以用完全物理的术语给出因果的解释。但问题是，这个因果解释具体涉及哪些方面，又是如何进行的，这需要进行说明。即使是如此，我们还是会有强烈的直觉：玛丽走出房间之后似乎有某种特别的感受。

对于第五个方面，Jackson 只是提到了感官经验的功能作用，但是他对功能作用的分析并不在于指出这些功能性的作用如何让人产生了这样或那样一些感官感觉（如何是这样，至少可以设想怎样将感官感觉还原为这些物理的、功能性的因素），而是说明感官经验对于两种不同的信念状态的传递或变换的功能性作用。这似乎无助于我们理解感官经验自身的物理功能本质。即使是后者，Jackson 也没有对这个功能作用是怎样的进行说明。

至于其他三个方面即丰富性、整体性和直接性如何与物理状态相关联就更需要进行说明了，因为很多感受性实在主义者（qualia realists）、二元论者也肯定感受性的这些现象性特征。所以，Jackson 实际上对以上五个方面如何被物理地说明并没有进一步分析，他只是作出一个论断：如果表征状态的内容是不可分割的、直接的，如果该状态起着正确的功能的作用，我们就能说清现象经验了（get the phenomenology for free）。但 Jackson 对此却没有解释，这就有独断的倾向。很明显，Jackson 对知识论证的表征主义回答实际上存在着解释的断层，论证到关键部分就戛然而止了。虽然 Jackson 为感觉即现象特征或感受性在表征主义框架下找到了位置，但是却没有进一步地为它在物理主义框架下找到位置，而这正是回应知识论证所必须的。有人或许会认为这个问题对一个表征主义者来说根本不是一个问题：因为在表征主义者看来，如何将经验归于表征内容，比如何对这些内容进行物理的说明更重要，因为对他们而言，对意向内容或表征内容的自然化或物理的说明已经不是问题，所以 Jackson 在文中不需要对此问题进行过多的论述。但这并不能成为我们不继续追问以上五个方面具体如何得到物理主义说明的理由。毕竟，这个部分恰恰是反物理主义者最关心的，它正是物理主义回应反物理主义挑战的最关键的部分，必须给出说明甚至论证。此外，表征内容是否已成功地得到物理主义说明本身就还是一个有很大争议的问题，而问题本身就显示出进一步解释的必要性。

正如 Torin Alter 所批判的，Jackson 对知识论证问题的表征主义回答似乎仅仅是一种遮眼法（red herring）、一种转移注意力的策略。（［4］，p. 74）Jackson 的表征主义论证已将感受性问题转变为表征内容或特征的分析。知识论证的问题在 Jackson 那里，就由说明感受性能否得到物理的说明变为感觉能否得到物理主义的说明。这样到最后，我们还是要思考，他的感觉或表征内容究竟是物理的还是非物理的——原先围绕知识论证争论的问题仍然存在。这样，Jackson 的表征主义就仅仅是将原先的问题换一种方式提出来了。实际上，Jackson 说的否定方面和对感觉进行正面说明是一个问题的两个方面。Jackson 对后者没有很好地解释，对前者的否定效力也自然会受到影响。他没有对感觉作物理主义的说明，那么玛丽走出房间之后学到新东西的直觉就仍然存在，就并没有受到实质性的否定，约束问题也没有得到很好的解决和满足。

此外，Torin Alter 也批评 Jackson 在其分析中没有区分开表征内容和表征方式，指出表征方式不是意向对象的特性本身所具有的，而是现象经验自己所有的，这样就不能将表征内容完全的还原为对象的性质，其自然化就会有问题，对物理主义的辩护也就不成功。（［4］，p. 73）但是，Jackson 的分析中是否区分了表征内容和表征方式，是一个有待思考的问题。Jackson 曾经否认知觉经验是由于表征方式的不同，才有特别的感觉，他反对用方式的不同来解释现象特征，认为如果是这样，那么对同一种事态就会有两种不同的表征，而如果只有其中一种方式能引起现象感觉，这就会和表征主义关于现象特征的一个基本认识相左：现象特征依附于表征特征。（［5］，p. 26）但是，在其 2007 年文章中，在其对强表征主义的两个说明中，又确实强调了知觉经验的特殊的表征方式，认为强表征主义的理论就是主张现象经验的内容加上经验表征内容的特殊方式可以穷尽现象经验的性质。（［6］，p. 58）如果现象经验真的涉及独特的表征方式，那么这个方式本身也确实会如 Alter 所说，会给 Jackson 的物理主义说明带来问题。

四、Jackson 在知识论证问题上的观点总结

现今有影响的物理主义对知识论证的回应策略主要有取消论（Daniel Dennett）、能力说（David Lewis，Laurence Nemirow）、亲知说（Paul Churchland，Earl Conee）、新形式旧知识说（Brain Loar），以及两种物理概念说（Daniel Stoljar）等。Jackson 并没有集中对以上几种策略进行回应，但是在他的相关论述中，也有零星的评论（如对第四种策略的评价）。在知识论证问题上，Jackson 的总的观点包括：（1）不赞成对感受性的取消主义解释。也许有人会因为 Jackson 直接否定现象的红的属性而将其观点看成是取消主义的，但是 Jackson 自己明确地说过，他无意接受一种取消主义的立场，并认为在我们这个复杂的物理世界中，是存在现象意识的，问题就在于对这种现象意识如何说明（表征主义正是这样的说明）。（［1］，Forword）虽然 Jackson 和 Dennett 一样都关注知识论证中的完全知识命题，但是后者是一种取消主义的立场。（2）也不赞成亲知说。Jackson 虽然没有明确地评论过第三种策略，但是他指出，认为人们没有事实上经验过一种经验就不可能知道看见红色或感受疼痛是什么样的观点是错误的。（［5］，p. 7）（3）也不赞成新形式旧知识说和两种物理概念说。Jackson 指出如果坚持物理主义的话，那么所有有那些模式、方面和概念等就都是可以得到物理说明的，那么它们原则上在玛丽走出房间之前就应该已经知道了。（［1］，Foreword）（4）最后，Jackson 接受了能力假说。如前所述，Jackson 认为玛丽走出房间之后的情形就是：她处在一种拥有所有五个方面的新状态。进而，Jackson 说玛丽没有学到任何新的关于事物是如何的知识，而是有了一种新的、不同于她以前的表征状态。这种观点似乎也是一种新形式旧知识的看法：新状态意味有新旧状态的不同，而它们又都是物理的状态。然而问题是，他在 2004 年文章中明确批评了新形式旧知识说的观点。进一步，Jackson 又认为，玛丽走出房间之后获得的就是关于这种状态的某些东西——能识别、想象和记忆的能

力。（［2］，p. 439）这样，Jackson 最后站到了 Laurence Nemirow 和 David Lewis 能力假说的一边，而且他还断言能力假说只有通过表征主义才是正确的。然而，Jackson 目前的最终立场却是让人困扰、琢磨不透的。Jackson 对能力假说和表征主义关系没有更多地论述。我们可以猜想，也许在 Jackson 看来，能力假说所提及的识别、想象、记忆等活动都是针对意向对象的，因而都只有建立在表征的基础上才能进行，所以他才说能力假说离不开表征主义，只有在表征主义的前提下才是正确的。但是，如果最后持一种能力假说的立场，那么就正如 Torin Alter 所评论的，最后就是能力假说对知识论证而不是表征主义对知识论证的有效回应。（［4］，p. 72）此外，能力假说自身能否澄清知识直觉、捍卫物理主义也需进一步研究。

参考文献

［1］Jackson, F., 2004, Foreword, Looking Back on the Knowledge Argument, P. Ludlow, Y. Stoljar, and D. Nagas Jackson, aw（ed.），*There's Something about Mary：Essays on Phenomenal Consciousness and Frank Jackson's Knowledge Argument*, Cambridge：MIT Press.

［2］Jackson, F., 2004, Mind and Illusion, P. Ludlow, Y. Stoljar, and D. Nagasaw（ed.），*There's Something about Mary：Essays on Phenomenal Consciousness and Frank Jackson's Knowledge Argument*, Cambridge：MIT Press, p. 432.

［3］Jackson, F., 2004, Postscript on Qualia, P. Ludlow, Y. Stoljar, and D. Nagasaw（ed.），*There's Something about Mary：Essays on Phenomenal Consciousness and Frank Jackson's Knowledge Argument*, Cambridge：MIT Press, p. 419.

［4］Alter, T., 2007, Does Representationalism Undermine the Knowledge Argument, T. Alter and S. Walter（ed.），*Phenomenal Concepts and Phenomenal Knowledge：New Essays on Consciousness and Physicalism*, New York：Oxford University Press, p. 66.

［5］Jackson, F., 2000, *Some Reflections on Representationalim*, http：//www. nyu. edu/gsas/dept/philo/courses/consciousness/papers/RepresentationalismNYU5April00. PDF, p. 4.

［6］Jackson, F., 2007, The Knowledge Argument, Diaphanousness, Representationalism, T. Alter and S. Walter（ed.），*Phenomenal Concepts and Phenomenal Knowledge：New Essays on Consciousness and Physicalism*, New York：Oxford University Press, p. 57.

Knowledge Argument and Frank Jackson's
Representationalism Response
Ling Liu

Chinese Academy of Social Science

Abstract: Frank Jackson's newly reply to the Knowledge Argument (KA) argued that representationalism could meet the constraint problem required by the KA. However, because Jackson didn't explain how to give a physical description to his representional characteristics (feel), his denial to the learning proposition and his positive demonstration of the state after Mary out of the house lacked a solid argument foundation, and finally leaded to fail the purpose of defending physicalism.

Keywords: representationalism; knowledge argument; representational characteristics; phenomenal characteristics

语言哲学

Semantics without Metaphysics

◎ **Chienkuo Mi**
   Soochow University

Abstract: Semantics and metaphysics are different. However, many philosophers maintain that the two are very closely related. Semantics is usually considered as a linguistic subject that deals with the meanings of linguistic expressions. Metaphysics, on the other hand, is a philosophical enterprise that purports to explore the nature of the world and to describe the structures and constituents of it. We may also say that semantics has its eyes primarily on language, while metaphysics is focused on the world. It is not difficult to see why the two distinct areas can merge so intimately together. After all, we all agree that human languages and the world we know are closely connected. Because of this, some philosophers approach linguistic issues from the metaphysical perspectives and construct the theses of philosophical semantics based on their metaphysical positions. The problem is that this procedure results in various confusions of semantic and metaphysical issues. This paper aims to explore the confusions that lie between semantics and metaphysics and to suggest that we can execute the semantic project successfully without taking up any metaphysical dispute.

Keywords: Semantics; Matephysics; theories of truth

Truth is a semantic concept. Semantics is a linguistic discipline that deals with relations between expressions of a language and the objects or states of affairs represented by those expressions. According to this characterization, it is natural to think that truth is a focal point where our language and the world meet. By acquiring true expressions in our language, we seem to gain access to the world, or more specifically, to have access to the objects or states of affairs in the world. By virtue of true expressions, the world seems to find its way to be mirrored or to be represented by our language. So, if one is attempting to construct a semantic theory for the concept of truth, one would feel obligated to provide some metaphysical perspective with respect to what the world is like. However, it is my project to construct a pure semantic theory of truth without taking up any metaphysical position. A new model *cum* schema is suggested to show how our languages are confronted with the world.

Over last three or four decades, the discussions of what the concept of truth is, and of what a theory of truth can do or ought to be, have always been very important and popular issues in philosophy, but there seems to be no agreement reached among philosophers with respect to how we should understand the concept of truth and why we need a theory of truth.

When we study the concept of truth or try to find a definition for the concept, it does not necessarily lead us to the construction of a theory of truth. Correspondingly, when we endeavor to form a theory of truth, we are not required to focus on the concept of truth itself, nor are we forced to provide any definition for the concept. This situation is very similar to that we find in discussions of the concept of meaning and the theories of meaning. The conceptual analysis of certain concept does not necessarily connect with a theoretical construction bearing on the very concept at issue. A lot of philosophical discussions concerning the nature or the definition of the concept of meaning need not be regarded as constructing a theory of meaning. Some philosophical projects aiming at producing a theory of meaning may not be concerned with the nature of the concept of meaning, and one could do the theory of meaning without even taking up the concept of meaning. ①However, it is worth noting that there is an important difference between the cases of truth and meaning. The point that needs to be made is this: while we might have a theory of meaning without using or involving the concept of meaning, the construction of a theory of truth, if not directed to define the concept of truth, still presupposes or relies on the very concept of truth. Why is the concept of truth so fundamental for constructing a theory of truth, or indeed any theory? Why do we need such a theory of truth?

Michael Lynch, in the "Introduction" to his book *The Nature of Truth*, distinguishes all kinds of "Robust theories of truth" from the "Deflationary theories of truth" @ @ based on the starting point (or question): "Does truth have a nature?" So, it is immediately obvious for him to sort out various theories just depending on whether the attitudes toward the starting question are positive or negative. However, Lynch also notices that "there is a growing consensus among some philosophers that

---

① Consider a theory of meaning in the Davidsonian style in which "the one thing meanings do not seem to do is oil the wheels of a theory of meaning——at least as long as we require of such a theory that it non-trivially give the meaning of every sentence in the language." (Davidson, 1967: 20)

neither traditional robust theories nor deflationary theories are right. " If it is so, then he claims that "we must find new ways to think about this old concept. " (Lynch, 2001: 5) It is my belief that we could find a new way to think about the old concept of truth in this project—that is, viewing the concept from a theory of truth based on the linguistic perspective or language-involving phenomena.

1. Metaphysical Theory of Truth vs. Linguistic Theory of Truth

Dealing with the concept of truth can be a quite different philosophical concern from constructing a theory of truth, although the two different concerns may be closely related. A distinction Michael Devitt has introduced can help us here. In order to tell what exactly the difference is between the deflationary theory of truth and the correspondence theory of truth, Devitt attempts to make a distinction between the metaphysical and linguistic issues (or foci) with respect to these discussions of truth. He claims that " [w] hereas the focus of the correspondence theory is on the nature and role of *truth*, the focus of the deflationary theory is on the nature and role of *the truth term*, for example, of 'true'. The former focus is metaphysical; the latter, linguistic. " (Devitt, 2001: 580) According to the distinction made by Devitt, it seems that if the focus of our theory is *the concept of truth*, then the theory should be regarded as a kind of metaphysical theory; while if the focus of the theory is on *the truth term*, then the theory should be linguistic in kind. Devitt's distinction, it seems to me, is not only misleading (because the distinction might miss or obscure what the truly significant difference is between the correspondence theory and the deflationary theory), but also too trivial (because it is so obvious to treat the nature of truth as an metaphysical issue and the meaning of truth term as a linguistic issue), and too narrow at best (because it cannot capture the whole picture of the debates among so many different theories of truth existing in contemporary philosophy).

Contrast to what Devitt has suggested, I propose to draw a distinction between the metaphysical level and the linguistic level when we discuss the issues concerning *the theory of truth* (rather than concerning *the concept of truth*). Different from Devitt's proposal, my distinction of the different levels is based on *what we try to ask the theory of truth for* or *why we need to construct such a theory* (rather than being based on *what the object the theory focuses*). A theory of truth on the metaphysical level (I will call this MT) is a theory concerning with the nature and the role of the concept of truth, aiming at providing a definition or an explication for the concept. A theory of truth on the linguistic (or language-involving) level (LT for short) is a theory purporting to explain how various linguistic phenomena, such as communication, understanding, and interpretation, are possible by relating the concept of truth with other semantic concepts such as that of meaning and that of belief. We may also say that MT is a theory focusing on the concept of truth, whereas LT is a theory of truth focusing on ordinary linguistic phenomena.

I think that most contemporary discussions regarding the concept of truth have been loaded with traditional metaphysical burdens, and that many varieties of theories of truth are metaphysical in nature. Most contemporary theories of truth are concerned with the nature of truth, and hope to find the definition and philosophical significances of the concept. ①This situation should remind us of the controversy over the concept of "universal" begun in medieval times. Just like the three different kinds of metaphysical theories of universals (i. e., realism, conceptualism, and nominalism respectively), I suggest that there are three matching metaphysical theories with respect to the concept of truth too. Comparable to realism about "universals", we have the correspondence theory of truth; to conceptualism about "universals", we have the coherence theory of truth and the pragmatic theory of truth; and to nominalism about "universals", the deflationary theory of truth. The last two groups of theories of truth, just like their counter parts in the theories of universals, are anti-realist in nature.

The debates between realism and anti-realism can be characterized as the controversies as to whether there is at least something real that is independent of the representations of minds for its being. However, the controversies are not as simple as they look, because the domains or the objects in question vary with different contexts and discussions. For example, common-sense realists would assert that there is at least something existing in the physical world (the world in which we live) that is independent of the human minds, while common-sense anti-realists deny this. Scientific realists assert that there are at least some theoretical entities dealt in scientific theories that are independent of scientific representations of scientist minds for their beings, while scientific anti-realists deny that there are any of these independent entities. Realism about "universals" is a theory asserting that universals exist independent of human minds, while anti-realism about "universals" denies any such realistic univer-

---

① See Michael Lynch's "Introduction" in his book *The Nature of Truth.*

sal. Realism about "truth" or alethic realism①is a theory asserting that what makes a sentence or belief true is not merely dependent on the human minds, while anti-realism about truth denies that there is any mind-independent truth-maker. It is therefore important to notice the multi-domains (or different objects) involved in the realism-antirealism debates, if we want to make the best of this controversy.

Scott Soames has nicely generalized three main things that we may generally expect a theory of truth to do (Soames, 1984: 411). According to Soames's proposal, a theory of truth is generally expected:

(i) to give the meaning of natural-language truth predicates;

(ii) to replace such predicates with substitutes, often formally defined, designed to further some reductionist program; or

(iii) to use some antecedently understood notion of truth for broader philosophical purposes, such as explicating the notion of meaning or defending one or another metaphysical view.

With respect to Soames's classification, we may expect that there are at least three different kinds of theories of truth. Let's call them T1 (corresponding to (i)), T2 (to (ii)) and T3 (to (iii)) respectively.

The reason why Soames classifies these three different expectations for a theory of truth is to clarify what Tarski's theory of truth is meant to do. He claims that Tarski's definition of truth is neither an attempt to analyze the meaning of natural-language truth predicates (not a theory in the sense of T1), nor an attempt to use the notion of truth for broad philosophical purposes (not a theory in the sense of T3 either). Tarski's theory of truth is not a theory in the sense of T1 (not an attempt to give the meaning of natural-language truth predicates) because he restricts his definition to cases in which truth is predicated of sentences of certain formalized languages only. Nor is his theory of truth a theory in the sense of T3 (not an attempt to use the notion of truth for broad philosophical purposes) because for Tarski the concept of truth itself is just what has to be explicated and legitimated. Tarski's goal, according to Soames's understanding, is to replace truth predicates used in our natural languages with certain

---

① The term "alethic realism" (or Realism with a capital "R") comes from William Alston's book, *A Realist Conception of Truth*, in which the term is meant to stand for "realism concerning truth".

restricted but formally defined substitutes. Tarski's reductionist program of replacing natural-language truth predicates by the formally designed substitutes has two motivations: first, to remove the doubts of certain scientifically minded truth skeptics; second, to eliminate what he takes to be the inconsistency in our ordinary notion of truth brought out by the liar paradox. Therefore, Tarski's theory of truth should be understood as a theory in the sense of T2.

It is not my concern here to evaluate whether or not Soames's interpretation of Tarski's theory of truth is correct. I have to admit that Soames's classification of different kinds of theories of truth with respect to what those theories try to do may help us clarify some potential confusion and misunderstandings. However, I also have to point out that Soames's classification is *ad hoc* at best. As I mentioned above, his distinction of what one can expect from a theory of truth is meant to locate Tarski's theory in the right place in order to clarify and justify Tarski's reductionist program for the concept of truth. Besides, the distinction between T1 and T2 is not needed. The only reason Soames separates the expectation for a theory of truth involved in T1 from that in T2 seems to be that he wants to emphasize what Tarski has done for the concept of truth must be viewed in the context of a formalized language rather than any natural language. And the reason why Tarski restricts his explications of truth within the context of a formalized language is to avoid some truth skepticism and the well-known liar paradox. However, if our concern here is with what we may expect a theory of truth to do or what a theory of truth ought to be, T1 (giving the meaning of natural-language truth predicates) and T2 (replacing natural-language truth predicates with formally defined substitutes) are both fundamentally metaphysical in nature. The differences between T1 and T2 will depend on what the theory takes to be its metaphysical standpoint (i. e., whether we could reductively define the concept of truth or find the nature for it, or we could only minimally interpret or understand the truth predicate (or the truth term) in natural languages). The concerns about the truth skeptics or the liar paradox, and about its possible scope applied to formalized or natural languages are beside the point, or at least are not directly related to the issue. T1 and T2 are, according to my distinction drawn above, both theories of truth based on the sense of MT. T3 can be regarded as a kind of LT, because the purpose of that theory is not to define the concept of truth or to find the nature of it, but rather to use some antecedently understood notion of truth for broader philosophical purposes (for shedding light on various linguistic phenomena as I see it). Therefore, I generalize two main things that we may generally expect a theory of truth to do (corresponding to the distinction between MT and LT): either (i) to find the nature of the truth and to define the concept, or (ii) to explain how various kinds of language-based phenomena, such as communication, understanding, and interpretation, are possible.

I want to claim that (1) we don't need a theory of truth in the sense of MT: any attempt to find the nature of truth or to define the concept would either be circular or fail to have the explanatory power; (2) we do need a theory of truth in the sense of LT: the general concept of truth is relatively clear and fundamental on which a satisfactory theory of meaning and predication can be built. In order to argue for these two claims, I will focus mainly on the correspondence theory of truth, an oldest perspective and the most commonsensical view about truth, and show why this theory is troublesome; I will also rely on a Davidsonian point of view and explain why truth is not definable while at same time is essential for constructing a theory of truth that aims to explain various linguistic phenomena.

2. Why We Don't Need a Metaphysical Theory of Truth

As we shall see, following Davidson's claims regarding MT we will get all the negative points of views, while following his claims concerning LT we will see more positive perspectives and gain more interesting insights about the concept of truth and approach toward the theory of truth.

[Metaphysical Claims about the Theories of Truth]

(M1) Correspondence theories of truth are empty as definitions, and the concept of truth is not "radically non-epistemic"; but these theories do capture the general intuition that truth depends on how the world is.

(M2) Coherence and pragmatic theories of truth are mistaken in concluding that reality and truth are merely constructs of thought, and the concepts of truth is not "radically epistemic"; but these theories have the merits of relating the concept of truth to human concerns, like language, belief, thought and intentional action, and it is these connections which make truth the key to how mind apprehends the world.

(M3) A deflationary attitude to, or a disquotational view of, the concept of truth is not encouraged by reflection on Tarski's work, and the prospects for a deflationary or a minimalist theory of truth are dim. But Davidson is sympathetic with the deflationists because the attempts to pump more content into the concept of truth are not appealing for the most part their views can only serve negatively as avoiding well-marked dead ends and recognizable pitfalls.

(M4) The concept of truth is not definable, for it cannot be reduced to other concepts that are simpler, clearer, and more basic. The concept of truth may not be a goal of inquiry if it is to find substantiating evidence for our beliefs or to identify some entities for the concept to represent for or correspond to.

Claims (M1), (M2) and (M3) have appeared in several of Davidson's articles and strongly suggest that Davidson does not side with any contemporary philosophical attempts to define the concept of truth. Those attempts include correspondence theories of truth (or the "objective" theories so called by Davidson①), coherence theories and pragmatic theories of truth that in one way or another make truth an epistemic concept (or the "subjective" theories), and minimalist or deflationary theories of truth—or as I prefer to call them, realist theories (the objective views), conceptualist theories (the subjective views) and nominalist theories (the deflationary views) about truth.

Realism about truth has its focus on ontology, because it tries to define truth in terms of some objective entities to which the truth bearers can correspond. However the focus turns out to be the fatal wound for the theory itself. It has always been challenged that the realists fail to individuate, identify, or locate the fact of the world or the part of reality to which a true sentence corresponds. Conceptualism about truth has its worries focused on epistemology, and concentrates on connecting truth to human thoughts, beliefs, desires, and intentions. While conceptualism tries to reduce truth to various epistemic concepts—justification, warranted assertability and idealized justified assertability, it cannot avoid the problem that even a set of coherent beliefs or ideally justified beliefs could end up being a massive error. We seem to have the obvious reason to believe that a theory of truth is not a theory of justification. Indeed the concept of truth may not be epistemic at all. ②Realists about truth hold on to their ontological commitment, and tie the concept of truth directly to the entities located in the objective reality. Conceptualists about truth busy themselves weaving their epistemological web, and tie the concept of truth directly to the conceptual roles played in the web.

---

① For the discussions of, and the distinction between, objective and subjective views on truth, see Davidson's "Epistemology and Truth".

② Davidson has also said, "coherence definitions or 'theories' have their attractions, but only as epistemic theories, and not as accounting for truth" (Davidson, 2000: 67).

Nominalism about truth is mainly concerned with linguistic usage and logical notions. It wishes to explain the role of truth in linguistic acts like assenting to a proposition and in logical functions like a device of generalization. Nominalists, however, deny that there is anything more to truth than what is involved in the linguistic use or the logical function of the predicate "true". Nominalism about truth seems to be a natural result of, first, dissatisfaction with realistic views and conceptualistic views of truth, and second, the inspiration provided by the formal correctness of Tarski's theory of truth. The proponents of nominalism draw back from the unfruitful discussions of truth common to objective/subjective, realist/antirealist, and ontological/epistemic debates, and made the concept of truth a relatively trivial concept with no important connections with reality or any epistemic concept. In the meantime, they argue that the notion of truth in a given language seems to be completely captured by the so-called trivial truth definition or the "schema" involved in a Tarski-style theory:

(T) "p" is true if and only if p

for each sentence p expressible in the language. With this recognition, nominalists make their first move to the redundant theory, and claim that the concept of truth is redundant because the occurrence of "true" in any instance of the schema (T) (or just a T-sentence)—say, "snow is white" is true if and only if snow is white—plays only a redundant role as part of a truth-functional connective. But soon they realize that the concept of "true" can and does play a small role in our language; it has function in our ordinary talk. At least, to say of "snow is white" that it is true amounts to assenting to the sentence itself (that is, to the sentence "snow is white"). The function "true" plays in the T-sentence is disquotational because "true" can be attributed to a sentence "p" and this cancels the quotation out and brings us back to p itself. This is the nominalists' second move on the way to the disquotational theory. But this move still doesn't carry nominalism very far, for as some defenders of this view also know, it cannot be the whole story about how the word "true" is employed in our language. Paul Horwich, for example, presses the utility of the truth-predicate a step further, and sees the role of the truth-predicate as a device of generalization. But he still minimizes the meaning of the word "true" as merely consisting in the fact that "our overall use of it stems from our inclination to accept instances of the 'equivalence schema': the proposition u (that p) is true if and only if p" ([26], p. 20).

The whole nominalistic move regarding truth is at best negative and partial. It is negative because while it limits the content of the concept of truth within the linguistic uses and avoids well-marked ontological and epistemological dead ends, it also disconnects, and isolates, the concept of truth from other close related concepts like beliefs, meaning, reality, and objectivity, thereby depriving truth of its vital and essential role in our intuition about the concept of truth and our understanding of ordinary language. It is partial because (as we will see) it cannot comprehend the complete crux of the T-sentence or the equivalence schema mostly mentioned and approved by itself, and so cannot grasp the full-blooded content of the concept of truth. But what is the main crux of T-sentences? How can we completely grasp the general concept of truth? Or can we really grasp it after all? Are all prospects for pursuing the concept of truth negative? If not, what are some positive prospects for truth?

Claims (M1), (M2) and (M3) seem to naturally lead us to the negative conclusion made in claim (M4) that the concept of truth is indefinable. Davidson asks: "If all definitions of the general concept [of truth] fail, and none of the short paraphrases seem come close to capturing what is important or interesting about the concept, why do some of us persist in thinking it is interesting and important?" (Davidson, 2000: 70) And we have seen that what distinguishes much of the contemporary philosophical discussion of truth is that though there are many such formulas offered by realists, conceptualists and nominalists,[1] none of them seem satisfying. Many philosophers have also maintained or tried to prove that truth is an indefinable concept.[2] This idea that truth is indefinable has its root more firmly in the view that truth is a simple and basic concept. Sometimes, it is held that complex concepts are definable in terms of simple concepts, which are indefinable. We can use basic concepts to analyze other concepts, but they are too fundamental to be analyzed themselves. We cannot hope to underpin clear concepts with something more transparent or easier to grasp. If we have this kind of reductive definition in mind, and if we observe that the concept of truth has always been taken for granted as our starting point in the understanding of other concepts, then we should accept the fact that whatever it is that makes this concept of truth so fundamental must also foreclose on the possibility of defining it. And if the goal of pursuing the concept of truth is to reach deeper into the bedrock of our conceptual systems or knowledge, then this goal will be unattainable and the pursuit a hopeless enterprise.

The main purpose of this section is to testify against the correspondence theory of truth, based on the problem of predication, and the slingshot argument. I will first present two distinct versions of the

---

[1] Davidson sees all of them as, if not attempts at definitions in the strict sense, attempts at substitutes for definitions. And in the case of truth, Davidson maintains that there is no short substitute. See this claim in Davidson, 1996: 276.

[2] For example, G. E. Moore, Bertrand Russell, Gottlob Frege, and maybe Alfred Tarski, too.

correspondence theory, and then argue that neither one can escape the both horns of a dilemma.

I. Two Versions of the Correspondence Theory of Truth

The correspondence theory of truth is usually characterized as the view that truth is correspondent to a fact—a view that was advocated by B. Russell, J. L. Austin and the early Wittgenstein in the 20th century. However the label has also been applied much more broadly to any view explicitly embracing the idea that truth consists in a relation to reality, i. e. , that truth is a relational property involving a characteristic relation (to be specified) to some portion of reality (to be specified). The members of this family employ various concepts for the relevant relation (correspondence, conformity, correlation, congruence, agreement, accordance, copying, picturing, representation, reference) and/or various concepts for the relevant portion of reality (facts, states of affairs, situations, events, individuals, sets, properties, tropes). It is important to notice that there are two essentially distinct versions which differ in the way the truth-bearer corresponds to the truth-maker. There is a direct correspondence version, in the Austinean or the Wittgensteinian sense, where the truth-bearer as an unanalyzable self-contained unit directly corresponds to the whole fact. There is also a structural correspondence version, in the Russellian sense, in which parts of the truth-bearer structurally correspond to the matching parts of the corresponding fact. The former is sometimes called correspondence as correlation or picturing relation, and the latter correspondence as congruence①.

The direct version of correspondence, or the correspondence-as-correlation (or correspondence-as-picturing) theory, can trace its roots to Aristotle's remark that "To say of what is that it is not, or of what is not that it is, is false, while to say of what is that it is, or of what is not that it is not, is true. " This remark implicitly invokes a direct relation between *what is said* and *what is or is not*, but it is unclear what the relation exactly is and what the relata really are. It is not until Austin and Wittgenstein that we have a clearer sense in which how the relata are directly connected. For Austin②, a statement is said to be true when the fact to which it is correlated by the demonstrative conventions is of a

---

① See Richard Kirkham's discussions about the correspondence theory of truth in his *Theories of Truth: A Critical Introduction*, where he makes the distinction between two types of correspondence: correspondence as correlation and correspondence as congruence (1992: 119 – 140).

② The brief characterization of Austin's view presented here is based on his article, "Truth" (Austin, 1950).

type with which the sentence used in making it is correlated by the descriptive conventions. So, the sentence "Snow is white" is true when it is correlated to a certain type of situation; namely, the state of affairs that snow is white. If I use the sentence to make the statement that snow is white, the statement is true because it is correlated to a particular fact—the fact that snow is white. For Wittgenstein①, propositions can be true or false only by being pictures of reality. If an elementary proposition is true, the atomic fact exists; if it is false the atomic fact does not exist. So, if the proposition "Snow is white" is elementary and true, then it will picture an existing atomic fact that snow is white. Despite the complicating issues regarding statements/sentences and propositions as the truth bearers and taking states of affairs and (existing or non-existing) facts as truth makers, both Austin and Wittgenstein characterize the direct correspondence relation as the kind of correlation or picturing between the truth-bearer as an unalanyzable self-contained unit and the truth maker (or fact) as a whole.

The structural version of correspondence, on the other hand, still holds some kind of correspondence relation between truth bearers and truth makers, but the relation held between the relata is not direct. This version claims that there is a structural isomorphism between the components of truth bearer and the constituents of truth maker. The truth bearer in question, if it is true, has its components involving a relation of congruence with the parts of the corresponding fact. We might find the original idea of the structural correspondence theory in Plato's copy (or participating) theory of Idea. However the modern version of the correspondence as a congruence theory originates with Russell. Russell②advocates a structural version of correspondence in which a belief is true when the components of the belief are congruent with objects composing a complex unity related in the same way as the matching components in the belief. For example, suppose that Michael believes that Ernest fathers David. Michael's belief that Ernest fathers David is true when there is a complex unity, "Ernest's fathering David", which is composed exclusively of the objects related in the same order as those in Michael's belief. The relation "fathering" is one of the objects occurring now as the cement that binds together the other objects (Ernest and David in this exact order) of the corresponding fact. The point of Russell's idea lies in the structural correspondence relation (or correlation) that holds between truth bearers (beliefs) and

---

① For Wittgenstein's view about the picturing relation between propositions and facts, see his *Tractatus Logico-Philosophicus*.

② Russell's multiple-relation view presented here can be found in his book, *The Problems of Philosophy*, Chapter 12: "Truth and Falsehood".

truth makers (facts as the complex unities).

There are many philosophers who criticize and provide various arguments against the correspondence theory. Davidson is the philosopher who usually uses the slingshot argument to argue against the correspondence theory, and who also believes that the slingshot is sound. It is well known that Davidson's early project was to construct a semantic theory (or the theory of meaning) for natural languages, a project based on the formal structure of Tarski's theory of truth. As early as his famous article "Truth and Meaning" published in 1967, Davidson argued that the correspondence theory of truth will neither be able to provide an account that has explanatory power for the concept of truth, nor provide a satisfactory theory of how ordinary communication works. The reason is simple. The notion of correspondence plays a role only if we are able to say, in an instructive way, which fact or slice of reality it is that makes a particular sentence true. No one has yet succeeded in doing this. Worse still, if we try to provide a serious semantics for reference to facts, we discover that *they melt into one*; *the Great Fact.* The argument for this claim is so-called "the slingshot argument". Davidson (Davidson, 1967: 17 – 36; 1969: 37 – 54) rejected the attempts to make sense of truth as correspondence to facts by putting forth the argument as the most serious (and maybe fatal) objection to the correspondence theory of truth. We can read the result of Davidson's argument to be showing that there is exactly one fact (or "The Great Fact") described, represented or corresponded to by all true statements. In Davidson's works, the slingshot argument is used as an effective way of rejecting the significance of the correspondence theory of truth. It is worth mentioning that the conclusion of the slingshot argument is not that "there is nothing for true sentences to correspond to", but rather that "if true sentences correspond to anything at all, they all correspond to the same thing". The concept of correspondence is thus trivialized completely. The relation of correspondence is useless if there is only one thing to correspond to. To be a satisfactory semantic theory, the correspondence theory must explain the obvious semantic differences among distinct true sentences.

Frege's idea that the reference of a sentence is its truth value is customarily considered as the origin of the slingshot argument, but he has never employed this idea to argue against the correspondence theory. However, it is also interesting to note that Frege mentions two difficulties involved in the theory. [1]He

---

[1] Frege argues why the attempt to explain truth as correspondence will collapse by the following two reasons: first, no perfect correspondence can be made between two distinct things (e. g. , sentence and fact); second, there will be an infinite regress problem for the correspondence theory because we should have to inquire whether it is true that a sentence and a fact correspond in some specified respect. (Frege, 1918: 326 – 7)

argues that the attempt to explain truth as correspondence will collapse in any case. If the objections to the correspondence theory of truth are appealing, as both Davidson and Frege seem to be convinced, we ought to start actually evaluating the slingshot argument.

II. The Slingshot Argument

The slingshot argument is an important piece of reasoning which, if sound, would be disastrous for (1) the theory that true sentences correspond to facts, propositions, states-of-affairs, or situations; (2) the claim that there are non-truth-functional sentence connectives such as "necessarily", "possibly", and "because"; and (3) the general proposal that linguistic or mental entities represent some kind of reality. This technical-sounding argument which was originally attributed to Frege, has further been developed by Church and Gödel into two logically different precise forms, and finally has come to be called "the slingshot argument" by Barwise and Perry or "the collapsing argument" by Stephen Neale. [1]

"The slingshot argument" has been formulated in various forms for very different philosophical purposes, and even the conclusions of the variants will look not quite the same. The argument was first put forward by Church (Church, 1943: 298 – 304) in support of Frege's claim that sentences refer to truth-values and against Carnap's proposal that the designata of sentences are propositions. Church's argument (or the so-called Frege's argument) was directed to the effect that all true sentences designate the same proposition. Gödel (Gödel, 1944: 125 – 53) also employed this argument to illuminate the important connection between the concept of fact and Russell's theory of descriptions. Gödel's argument led inevitably to the conclusion that all true sentences have the same signification (as well as all the false ones), and it is Frege again who was accredited with having drawn this conclusion. Quine (Quine, 1953: 158 – 76) used the argument to show that quantified modal logic is committed to the

---

[1] For Frege's original idea, see his famous and important article "On *Sinn* and *Bedeutung*". The so-called Frege's argument developed by Church is first formulated in his "Review of Carnap's *Introduction to Semantics*", and developed by Gödel in his "Russell's Mathematical Logic". The label "slingshot" is introduced by Jon Barwise and John Perry in their article "Semantic Innocence and Uncompromising Situations", the name is dubbed this way because of the minimal machinery and presuppositions of the type of argument, and its giant-slaying potential. Finally, Stephen Neale in his recent book, *Facing Facts*, gives a very useful and comprehensive examination of the slingshot argument, and he also names it "the collapsing argument" because it is a kind of argument purporting to show that there are fewer items of a given kind than might be supposed previously.

view that the modal operators are truth-functional. And the conclusion of Quine's argument was that modal and non-modal distinction will collapse. "The slingshot argument" has also been developed in different ways. Church and Quine formulate it in terms of the class abstraction term ' (ŷ) ', such that (ŷ) Ay means "the class of all y such that y is an A". Gödel formulates it in terms of a definite description ' (ιx) ', such that " (ιx) Ax" means "the x such that x is an A". ①

I will examine presently how Davidson's slingshot argument can be employed to argue against the correspondence theory of truth, and then modify it into an argument form that can deal better with problems or challenges posted for Davidson's accounts of the slingshot argument.

There are two formulations of the slingshot which are involved in Davidson's works. The one is formulated in "True to the Facts" (the **TF** version), and the other in "Truth and Meaning" (the **TM** version).

[**The TF formulation**]

In the article "True to the Facts", Davidson tries to prove that the correspondence theory fails to be a satisfactory theory for defining the concept of truth. He provides his confirming argument as this:

"Let ' s ' abbreviate some true sentence. Then surely the statement that s corresponds to the fact that s. But we may substitute for the second ' s ' the logically equivalent ' (the x such that x is identical with Diogenes and s) is identical with (the x such that x is identical with Diogenes) '. Applying the principle that we may substitute coextensive singular terms, we can substitute ' t ' for ' s ' in the last quoted sentence, provided ' t ' is true. Finally, reversing the first step we conclude that the statement that s corresponds to the fact that t, where ' s ' and ' t ' are any true sentences. " (Davidson, 1969: 42)

We can analyze this argument and formulate it as the following formalization:

(1) Let S be any true sentence.

---

① In addition to the logical structures and formulations, it is important to note that the assumptions involved in Church's argument seems to be stronger than the ones in Gödel's. The conclusion of Church's slingshot can be validly derived only if the principle of substitutivity for logical equivalents (PSLE) and the principle of substitutivity for singular terms are assumed. However the key principle PSLE on which Church's argument relies appears not to be required in Gödel's slingshot.

(2) The statement that S corresponds to the fact that S. (Following the correspondence theory of truth.)

(3) The statement that S corresponds to the fact that $(\iota x)(x = a \,\&\, S) = (\iota x)(x = a)$ where a stands for any genuine proper name. ('S' and ' $(\iota x)(x = a \,\&\, S) = (\iota x)(x = a)$' are logically equivalent.)

(4) Let T be any true sentence too.

(5) The statement that S corresponds to the fact that $(\iota x)\ (x = a \,\&\, T) = (\iota x)(x = a)$. ('$S$' and '$T$' are co-referential singular terms.)

(6) The statement that S corresponds to the fact that T. ('T' and ' $(\iota x)(x = a \,\&\, T) = (\iota x)(x = a)$' are logically equivalent.)

(7) Any true statement can correspond to any fact.

Indeed, the principles assumed in the above argument are these: if a statement corresponds to the fact described by an expression of the form 'the fact that p', then it corresponds to the fact described by 'the fact that q' provided either (1) the statements that replace 'p' and 'q' are logically equivalent, or (2) 'p' differs from 'q' only in that a singular term has been replaced by a coextensive singular term. We can call the first principle PSLE (the principle of substitutivity for logical equivalents; logically equivalent statements are co-referential or correspond to the same fact) and the second PSST (the principle of substitutivity for co-referential singular terms; the reference or the corresponded fact of a statement remains the same if an expression or singular term in the sentence is substituted by a co-referential expression or term).

This formulation of the slingshot argument **TF** is clearly directed to trivialize the correspondence theory of truth; since aside from matters of correspondence no way of distinguishing facts has been proposed, and this argument shows further that even if a true sentence does correspond to a fact, there is exactly one fact to be corresponded to. Davidson insists that no point remains in distinguishing among various names of "The Great Fact", and we may use the single phrase "corresponds to The Great Fact" to attribute to every true sentence. Therefore any statement S (if true), according to the attribution above, will correspond to The Great Fact, and there will be apparently no telling this result apart from simply saying that S is true. The correspondence theory of truth as an attempt to be a semantic theory will be seriously damaged by this result.

[**The TM formulation**]

In the context of Davidson's "Truth and Meaning", the slingshot argument is designed to show the difficulty of identifying the meaning of a singular term with its reference, and further to prove that if the meaning of a sentence is what it refers to, then all sentences alike in truth value must be synonymous. The argument proceeds as follows:

"Suppose that 'R' and 'S' abbreviate any two sentences alike in truth value. Then the following four sentences have the same reference:

(1) R

(2) $(\hat{y})(y = y \ \& \ R) = (\hat{y})(y = y)$

(3) $(\hat{y})(y = y \ \& \ S) = (\hat{y})(y = y)$

(4) S

For (1) and (2) are logically equivalent, as are (3) and (4), while (3) differs from (2) only in containing the singular term ' $(\hat{y})$ $(y = y \ \& \ S)$' where (2) contains ' $(\hat{y})$ $(y = y \ \& \ R)$' and these refer to the same thing if S and R are alike in truth value. Hence any two sentences have the same reference if they have the same truth value." (Davidson, 1967: 19)

There are also two assumptions involved in the **TM** formulation, they are: the assumption that logically equivalent singular terms have the same reference (ALE), and the assumption that singular term does not change its reference if a contained singular term is replaced by another with the same reference (AST). This argument can also be formalized as follows:

(1) Let R and S abbreviate any two sentences alike in truth-value.

(2) 'R' and ' $(\hat{y})(y = y \ \& \ R) = (\hat{y})(y = y)$' have the same reference. (ALE)

(3) 'S' and ' $(\hat{y})(y = y \ \& \ S) = (\hat{y})(y = y)$' have the same reference. (ALE)

(4) ' $(\hat{y})(y = y \ \& \ R) = (\hat{y})(y = y)$' and ' $(\hat{y})(y = y \ \& \ S) = (\hat{y})(y = y)$' have the same reference. (AST)

(5) 'R' and 'S' have the same reference. ((2), (3), and (4))

(6) If any two sentences R and S are alike in truth-value, they will have same reference. ((1) through (5))

The moral of this argument will depend on what we take the reference of a sentence to be. As Davidson has noted, "it is perhaps worth mentioning that the argument does not depend on any particular identification of the entities to which sentences are supposed to refer." (Davidson, 1967: 19) If "a fact" is what a sentence refers to, then all true sentences will refer to the same fact (as well as all false ones).

The reason that I coordinate Davidson's two formulations of the slingshot argument here is to present precisely how various formulations, structures, and assumptions (or principles) may be used and applied in the argument. At least we can get some straightforward points in mind at the outset. First, the soundness of the slingshot argument will not be affected by whether or not we want to view sentences as singular terms. Second, the correctness of the argument will not be changed by whether we adopt the class abstraction operator " $(\hat{y})$ " or the definite description operator " (ιx) ". Third, the credibility of the argument will not be affected by whether or not we accept that a sentence has a reference (or nominatum) or by whatever we take the reference of a sentence to be. Finally, the logical consequence of both versions seems to be paradoxical, that is, any two sentences alike in truth value will have same meaning (if the reference of a sentence is what the sentence means or represents).

However there are two problems, raised by most opponents of Davidson's arguments, with respect to the accounts of the slingshot set up above:

Problem 1:

Some might question the assumptions of **TF** that permit substitution of logically equivalent sentences and substitution of coreferential singular terms occurred in the non-transparent context like "the fact that..." . If PSLE and PSST cannot be applied to those opaque contexts, the argument will not go through.

Problem 2:

Some might also object to the **TM** formulation that 'R' and '$(\hat{y})(y=y \ \& \ R) = (\hat{y})(y=y)$' are not logically equivalent, or that 'R' and '$(\hat{y})(y=y \ \& \ R) = (\hat{y})(y=y)$' do not correspond to the same fact. Similarly, one might also object to the **TF** formation that 'S' and '$(\iota x)(x=a. S) = (\iota x)(x=a)$' are not logically equivalent, or that 'S' and '$(\iota x)(x=a. S) = (\iota x)(x=a)$' do not correspond to the same fact. If the logical equivalence is not obtained in either the **TM** formulation or the **TF** formation, the argument will not go through.

In order to avoid these two problems, we might modify, using Gödel's approach, Davidson's versions of the slingshot as follows:

(1) If $\Phi \ (a)$ and $a = (\hat{y})(y=a \ \&\Phi(y))$ are both true sentences, then they correspond to the same fact.

(2) Assume Fa is true, and corresponds to the fact $f1$.

(3) Assume $a \neq b$ is true, and corresponds to the fact $f2$.

(4) Assume Gb is true, and corresponds to the fact $f3$.

(5) $a = (\hat{y})(y = a \ \& \ Fy)$ is true, and corresponds to the fact $f1$. By 1.

(6) $a = (\hat{y})(y = a \ \& \ y \neq b)$ is true, and corresponds to the fact $f2$. By 1.

(7) $(\hat{y})(y = a \ \& \ Fy) = (\hat{y})(y = a \ \& \ y \neq b)$

(8) $a = (\hat{y})(y = a \ \& \ Fy)$ and $a = (\hat{y})(y = a \ \& \ y \neq b)$ correspond to the same fact.

(9) $f1 = f2$.

(10) $b = (\hat{y})(y = b \ \& \ Gy)$ is true, and corresponds to the fact $f3$. By 1.

(11) $b = (\hat{y})(y = b \ \& \ a \neq y)$ is true, and corresponds to the fact $f2$. By 1.

(12) $(\hat{y})(y = b \ \& \ Gy) = (\hat{y})(y = b \ \& \ a \neq y)$

(13) $b = (\hat{y})(y = b \ \& \ Gy)$ and $b = (\hat{y})(y = b \ \& \ a \neq y)$ correspond to the same fact.

(14) $f2 = f3$.

(15) $f1 = f3$. By 9 and 14.

(16) Fa and Gb correspond to the same fact.

(17) Conclusion: Any two true sentences correspond to the same fact.

In this modified form of the slingshot argument, PSLE and ALE are no longer presupposed. However, the crucial steps involved in the argument are the steps 1, 8 and 13. One might at the very beginning object to the step 1 and deny that $\Phi(a)$ and $a = (\hat{y})(y = a \ \& \Phi(y))$ correspond to the same fact. But as the direct version of correspondence theory must concede, if $\Phi(a)$ and $a = (\hat{y})(y = a \ \& \Phi(y))$ are both true, it is the fact "$\Phi(a)$" that makes both of them true. And if "$\Phi(a)$" is the truth maker for $\Phi(a)$ and $a = (\hat{y})(y = a \ \& \Phi(y))$, then they are supposed to correspond to the same fact. If step 1 can go through, then steps 8 and 13 would not be difficult to accept. The reason that $a = (\hat{y})(y = a \ \& \ Fy)$ and $a = (\hat{y})(y = a \ \& \ y \neq b)$ correspond to the same fact and make "$f1 = f2$" is the identity between $a = (\hat{y})(y = a \ \& \ Fy)$ and $a = (\hat{y})(y = a \ \& \ y \neq b)$. Both of them, if true, express the same thing, that is '$a = a$'. The same goes for step 13, because if $b = (\hat{y})(y = b \ \& \ Gy)$ and $b = (\hat{y})(y = b \ \& \ a \neq y)$ are both true, they will express the same thing, '$b = b$'. So, we see no escape for the direct version of correspondence theory under the attack based on this form of argument. That is, if any true sentence corresponds to any fact at all, according to the characterization of the direct version, then all true sentences will correspond to the same fact.

However, this modified version, based on Gödel's approach, has its shortage too. Some friends of facts (Wittgenstein, for example) may not like the kind of "non-identical fact" such as "$a \neq b$", and "a $\neq$ b" is a crucial design and important step in the modified form of the slingshot argument. Without this step (step 3 in the above argument form), the slingshot argument will not go through. So, we might like to modify our argument form a step further to avoid this embarrassing situation. I suggest that we might do better to accommodate Davidson's original strategy with Gödel's approach and get the following results:

(1) If 'R' and '$(\hat{y})(y = y \,\&\, R) = (\hat{y})(y = y)$' are both true sentences, then they correspond to the same fact—that is the fact that R.

(2) Assume 'Fa' is a true sentence, and corresponds to the fact that Fa.

(3) Assume 'Gb' is a true sentence, and corresponds to the fact that Gb.

(4) Assume '$(\hat{y})(y = y \,\&\, Fa) = (\hat{y})(y = y)$' is true, then it will correspond to the fact that Fa. (By 1.)

(5) Assume '$(\hat{y})(y = y \,\&\, Gb) = (\hat{y})(y = y)$' is true, then it will correspond to the fact that Gb. (By 1.)

(6) If '$(\hat{y})(y = y \,\&\, Fa) = (\hat{y})(y = y)$' and '$(\hat{y})(y = y \,\&\, Gb) = (\hat{y})(y = y)$' are both true, then they are saying the same thing and therefore correspond to the same fact.

(7) The fact that Fa and the fact that Gb are the same fact. (By 4, 5 and 6.)

(8) The true sentences 'Fa' and 'Gb' correspond to the same fact. (By 7.)

(9) Conclusion: Any two true sentences correspond to the same fact.

Again, like our first modification, the crucial step involved in the new modified argument is the step 1. But as we have also discussed above, the direct version of correspondence theory must concede that if 'R' and '$(\hat{y})(y = y \,\&\, R) = (\hat{y})(y = y)$' are both true, it is the fact that R that makes both of them true. And if the fact that R is the truth maker for 'R' and '$(\hat{y})(y = y \,\&\, R) = (\hat{y})(y = y)$', then they are supposed to correspond to the same fact. Although the direct version is unable to escape the challenge of the slingshot argument, the structural version of correspondence theory can still resist the argument simply by rejecting the step 1. In the structural version, 'R' and '$(\hat{y})(y = y \,\&\, R) = (\hat{y})(y = y)$' (or '$\Phi(a)$' and '$a = (\hat{y})(y = a \,\&\, \Phi(y))$') do not appear to represent the same fact. This is because these two formulae contain quite different components, which in turn compose different structural facts. If the step 1 is blocked, the whole argument will not go through. However, this reply from the structural version of the correspondence theory can lead to some metaphysical problems. An immediate difficulty is that if we accept that it is two different facts which make the above two formulae true, then we must accept some unusual facts. If, as characterized by the structural version, the fact which makes 'R' true is different from the fact which makes ' $(\hat{y})(y=y \ \& \ R)=(\hat{y})(y=y)$ ' true, then it would appear that what makes 'R' true is, on the face of it, the fact that R; and what makes ' $(\hat{y})(y=y \ \& \ R)=(\hat{y})(y=y)$' true is just the fact that $(\hat{y})(y=y \ \& \ R)=(\hat{y})(y=y)$. But what kind of fact is " $(\hat{y})(y=y \ \& \ R)=(\hat{y})(y=y)$"? If we believe that ' $(\hat{y})(y=y \ \& \ R)=(\hat{y})$ $(y=y)$ ' can stand for a complex structural fact (or a complex unity as Russell would have called it), it would be an unusual fact distinct from the more ordinarily recognizable fact that R. We have to concede that the complex structural fact that $(\hat{y})(y=y \ \& \ R)=(\hat{y})(y=y)$" is composed not only of ordinary empirical objects, but also of logical and linguistic entities. I don't know whether correspondence theorists really want to accept these kinds of facts. But a more serious problem which we must face is this: having "dissected" propositions or facts in this way, how can we restore these separate parts back to their original unified form again? That is to say, any such structural version of the correspondence theory must face the problem of predication—the problem of the unification of a sentence and the problem of the unification of a proposition (or a fact).

III. The Problem of Predication

The problem of predication can be characterized as the problem that once plausible assignments of semantic roles have been made to the parts of sentences, the parts do not seem to compose a united whole. This problem has to do with the unification of a sentence and the unification of a proposition (or a fact). It is not only a problem at the semantic level that deals with how predicates are related to names or other singular terms and contribute to the unity of a sentence, it can also be a problem at the metaphysical level that concerns how universals are related to particulars to constitute a complex structural fact. This problem has its modern versions based on Bradley's problem, but it can also trace its traditional roots back to the so-called "third man problem" involved in Plato's theory of ideas or forms. It is strongly felt that without solving this problem any theory of language, mind, and reality will always have a hidden riddle and lack a satisfactory explanation.

A theory of predication should not be confused with a theory of predicates. A theory of predicates aims to provide semantics for all predicates—to explain the meaning and nature of predicates. But a theory of predication does more than that, the theory needs not only to explain the semantic role of predicates, but also to give a satisfactory account of how predicates can maintain their proper functions as parts of sentences while at the same time contribute to the unity of sentences in which they occur, the unity demanded by the fact that sentences can be true or false and can be used to express our judgments and thoughts.

The problem of predication should not be confused with the problem of universals either, although the two problems are closely related. It will help us differentiate the two problems more distinctly if we make a clear distinction between the metaphysical question of how particulars are related to properties and the semantic question of how subjects and predicates are related. The problem of universals is a problem at the metaphysical level. It is concerned with whether there is any real entity which can be called property. Strictly speaking, this problem is not about universals, because universals are part of a solution to the problem rather than part of the problem itself[1]. The problem can be characterized as the problem of showing how various different individuals or particulars can have the same properties. In recent decades there have been three competitive solutions to the so-called problem of universals. They are Universalism, Trope Theory, and Nominalism respectively. Universalism identifies the properties with universals and postulates universals as real entities that can be located in different places at the same time. For Universalism particulars and universals are two different types of entities. Trope Theory identifies the properties with tropes and postulates tropes to be real entities that, like individuals or particulars, cannot be located in more than one place at the same time. Thus for Trope Theory, tropes may be viewed as being the same type of entities as particulars, but they should be regarded as two different kinds of particulars. Nominalism does not use the word "properties" to refer to any entity over and above the particulars that are said to have the properties. For Nominalism proper, there are general words, general concepts, classes, or genuine resemblance relations, but there are no universals and no tropes. So, universals are only part of the solution (i. e. , universalism) to the so-called problem of universals. The concept of "universal" is not necessarily involved or linked to part of the problem itself.

The problem of predication, on the other hand, is primarily a problem at the linguistic level. It is a problem concerned with how predicates, occurring in any sentence, are related to names or other singular terms and contribute to the unity of the sentence in which they occur. It is only when the solution to the problem adopts some kind of metaphysical approach that the problem of universals will emerge

---

[1] A very nice discussion of this issue can be found in Rodriguez-Pereyra's *Resemblance Nominalism*.

and the problem of predication will become more complicated and get mixed up with the metaphysical issues. Historically, philosophers have always felt the need to introduce some kind of entity to explain the function of verbs or predicates. They argue for the reality of the entity committed or postulated in order to sustain the structure of sentences and judgments or the thoughts that sentences can be used to express. Once the idea of dealing with linguistic issues approached from the ontological considerations is formed, the problem of universals arises. Without solving the metaphysical puzzles in advance, this ontological approach toward the linguistic issues is doomed to failure. Even if we ignore the metaphysical problem and face the linguistic issues alone, we still need to discover a solution to the problem of predication.

So, what exactly are the problems? The problem of universals at the metaphysical level can find its original sin in Plato's theory of ideas or forms. It is also called the third man problem. Why third man? We all agree that an individual thing like man or flower can have many different properties and relations to other things, such as "being rational", "being red", "being a son of", or "being next to". But how can one thing have many different properties at the same time? Let's call this question the puzzle of "many over one"① . We all usually agree that many different individual things can have the same property, for example, many different individual men can all have the property of rationality. But how can many individual things have the same property? It is an old philosophical question and is commonly named the puzzle of "one over many". It is less controversial to admit that an individual thing is a real entity, a particular. But if we want to posit properties or relations as another kind of entity, we will get ourselves into trouble immediately. Plato should be held responsible for introducing new entities, such as ideas or forms, to explain our "platitudes" about the world and to answer the questions and puzzles following them. He seems to hold that the many different properties owned by a particular or the same property shared by many different particulars are ideas, and ideas are real entities. If both particulars and properties are real entities, then we need to explain how the two kinds of entities can be connected or glued together. Based on some of Plato's dialogues, we may interpret his view as saying that material particulars participate in, resemble, copy, or are modeled by the ideas or forms. If particulars really participate in, resemble, copy, or are modeled by the ideas, then there must be some

---

① It is called this way by Rodriguez-Pereyra, and presented in his *Resemblance Nominalism*, Section 3 "The Many over One".

genuine relation held between particulars and ideas or there must be another property shared by particulars and ideas. So, the "third man" comes in. We would need to posit another idea or form for the genuine relation held between, or the property shared by, particulars and ideas. This will lead to an infinite regress. Some might continue to ask why an infinite regress is a problem at all. Why is the infinite regress a problem for the theory of universals? The reason is simple. In order to explain our ordinary phenomena such as "Socrates is rational", philosophers committed to universals not only appeal to particulars like Socrates, but also introduce universals like being rational into their ontology. Now when one phenomenon is analyzed and separated into two entities, there is a question of what it is that makes them cooperate to make the unity of original phenomenon. And what the regress argument says is that, if you've got this congruence of entities, it's no good inventing other entities-the copula, the form, or any idea-and then just adding that in to the congruence, because then you've just got a bigger bunch of entities, and the same problem recurs again. So what the problem of infinite regress shows is that the metaphysics of universals does not provide any useful explanation at all.

It is worth noticing that the problem of predication itself should cast no doubt on the existence of ideas, forms, universals, or tropes. The question of whether ideas, forms, universals, or tropes exist is not a central issue involved in explaining linguistic phenomena or constructing any semantic theory. The more fundamental question is whether positing properties or relations as any kind of entity can really help us explain the linguistic phenomena and the semantic role of predicates better. In order to understand the problem of predication more clearly, let's focus on the structure and nature of judgments like the judgment that Socrates is wise and that Socrates walks. We want to know what makes the judgments true or false, and what the role the predicates play and contribute to the truth or falsity of the judgments. Now, we all agree that Socrates is an entity, a person, or a particular. He is wise and walks. If we decide to posit properties as entities, the properties of "being wise" and "walking" would be another kind of entity—ideas, forms, universals, or tropes that can be copied, participated, instantiated or realized by many different particulars. In our case here, Socrates is one of many particulars that copy, participate, instantiate, or realize the properties (or entities) of "being wise" and "walking". So, we are actually explaining what make the judgments that Socrates is wise and that Socrates walks true or false by saying whether or not Socrates copies, participates, instantiates, or realizes the properties of "being wise" and "walking". From what we have been describing, it is obvious that what make the judgments true—the facts themselves—don't just consist of two entities: Socrates and the property of "being wise" or Socrates and the property of "walking". What makes the judgments true is that Socrates and the property of "being wise", and Socrates and the property of "walking" stand in a certain relation of copying, participating, instantiating, or realizing to each other. If we think that properties should be regarded as real entities, we don't see why we should not view relations as real entities. If we are serious about taking properties and relations as entities, then the relation of copying, participating, instantiating and realizing should all be entities too. So, the simple facts expressed by our judgment in two parts (subject and predicate) or in just two words ("Socrates" and "walk") actually involve three entities rather than two. But if the third entity is involved, it is easy to reason that there surely are more than three entities involved in both judgments that Socrates is wise and that Socrates walks. We are confronted with an infinite regress again.

It is not my concern here to solve the problem of universals, neither is it my focus the question of whether there is any hope that we can solve the problem of predication. However, my point is to show that the correspondence theory of truth, viewed as a structural version, cannot provide a satisfactory semantic theory for dealing with the problem of predication. If this is the case, then the structural version of the correspondence theory cannot offer a satisfactory theory of truth either.

I have argued that the correspondence theory of truth is confronted with a dilemma. The direct correspondence version cannot escape from the challenge of the slingshot argument, and the structural correspondence version may be able to answer the slingshot but still has to face the problem of predication. Neither version of the correspondence theory can explain the general concept of truth satisfactorily.

3. Why We Do Need a Linguistic Theory of Truth

In order to see why the general concept of truth is so basic and indispensable, and to answer why we still need a theory of truth in the sense of LT, I would like to begin this section by generalizing four more positive claims from Davidson's works as follows:

[Linguistic Claims about the Theories of Truth]

(L1) Truth, if it operates as a truth-functional connective, has its rhetoric function in conversation but is cognitively redundant.

(L2) The concept of truth is essential and central in the understanding of language. Without a grasp of the concept of truth, not only language, but thought itself, is impossible.

(L3) The concept of truth has a close connection with meaning. To some extent, meaning is dependent on truth.

(L4) The concept of truth is important for determining the contents of our beliefs and utterances. The content of truth can be brought out only by relating the concept to our speech, belief and the evaluative attitudes.

With all these negative trains of thought about truth in last section, does it mean that truth just isn't a goal we should pursue? In an article titled "The Folly of Trying to Define Truth", Davidson claims, as is suggested by the title, that truth is an indefinable concept. But then he continues to express his attitude toward the pursuit of truth as follows: "This [claim] does not mean we can say nothing revealing about it... Nor does the indefinability of truth imply that the concept is mysterious, ambiguous, or untrustworthy." (Davidson, 1996: 265) And in a more recent paper titled "Truth Rehabilitated", Davidson even attempts to explain, as is again suggested by his title, why the concept of truth should be restored to its key role in our understanding of the world and of the minds of agents. What is the key role the concept of truth plays in the whole business here? What are some positive themes Davidson can contribute to the issues regarding truth? In the reminder of this paper, I will discuss what we can learn about truth from the kind of truth theory Tarski provided.

What is the main crux of T-sentences? This is a question we raised earlier and it still remains unanswered. Almost everyone would agree that it is trivial to say " 'snow is white' is true if and only if snow is white" and many other T-sentences as well. But what does the triviality of T-sentences convey or suggest to us? Nominalists about truth get their deflationary views by transforming the triviality of T-sentences into the triviality of the predication of "being true", and so truth as a concept becomes totally trivial for them. This way of looking at T-sentences is, as I claimed early, only partial and one-sided. Nominalists only see that the left-hand side ("snow is white" is true) of the equivalence in the T-sentence can be reduced to the right-hand side (snow is white) of it, and so focus on the fact that the role the concept of truth plays in this direction is either disquotational or redundant, because whatever the concept of truth can do (in the case that "snow is white" is true) can be substituted by the simple assent to the sentence itself (that is, snow is white). But they fail to see the other direction, and in particular the fact that the triviality of T-sentences also reveals the indispensability of the predication of "being true". The reason is simple. If the left-hand side of equivalence can be reduced to the right-hand side, then the right-hand side of equivalence can be reduced to the left-hand side too. The reduction in this direction shows that to assent to a sentence (that is, snow is white), we must be equipped with the concept of truth to attribute to the sentence itself (just in the case that "snow is white" is true). To make this point explicit, I would like to introduce a passage, in two parts, from Frege's work (Frege, 1918: 328):

[Part 1]:

It may nevertheless be thought that we cannot recognize a property of a thing without at the same time realizing the thought that this thing has this property to be true. So with every property of a thing is joined a property of a thought, namely, that of truth.

[Part 2]:

It is also worthy of notice that the sentence "I smell the scent of violets" has just the same content as the sentence "it is true that I smell the scent of violets". So it seems, then, that nothing is added to the thought by my ascribing to it the property of truth.

The passage [Part 2] tells a similar story to that of every nominalist. Seeing T-sentences from one direction, the concept of truth adds nothing more to our thought at all. But the formulation "it is true that I smell the scent of violets" seems to regard the concept of truth as something more like a logical operator rather than a genuine property. With respect to this way of reading T-sentences, I don't think Davidson has any objection to it. If we look back to the positive themes I summarize above, the theme (L1) just is a claim that truth as a truth-functional connective is cognitively redundant. But Davidson is also willing to accept the concept of truth as a genuine property—a property that can be predicated of some beliefs or utterances.

Is the concept of truth as a genuine property really redundant? The passage [Part 1] denies that. [Part 1] shows the other direction of reading the T-sentence and expresses the idea that the concept of truth is somehow presupposed and essential whenever we say or think that anything has any property whatsoever. Frege believes that whenever we say or think that something has a certain property, for example, snow has the property of whiteness, we are, in effect, saying or thinking that a certain thought is true—namely, the thought that snow does have the property of whiteness. So, whenever we say or think anything, we must have already been equipped with or implicitly invoked the concept of truth. This passage vindicates what I mean by saying the indispensability of the concept of truth. It is indispensable because if we are able to assent to a sentence (namely predicate some property of something), we have to previously grasp the concept of truth in accepting that sentence as true. Davidson's positive view about truth in the theme (L2) is another vindication for seeing the triviality of T-sentences as serving to reveal the indispensability of truth. Davidson's themes (L1) and (L2) perfectly represent both ways of focusing on the left-hand side and right-hand side of the equivalence in the T-sentences.

There is another interesting observation made by Davidson himself about the triviality of T-sentences. This observation is about the truth of T-sentences themselves rather than the concept of truth occurring within the formulations of T-sentence, and it will lead us again to the indispensability of truth. Davidson points out:

> The triviality of T-sentences is a guarantee of their truth, and this guarantee is passed on by Tarski's work to the 'partial definitions' of truth he provides. T-sentences are trivially true only if we know that the sentence described is identical with, or a translation of, the sentence that gives its truth conditions; but this is enough to display the sense in which we have a firm grasp of the general concept of truth. (Davidson, 1988: 179)

As most of people have realized, no definition in Tarski's style is a complete definition of the general concept of truth; each such definition involved in a T-sentence is a partial definition of truth for a particular language. This is why Davidson prefers to formulate T-schema as

> "p" is true-in-L if and only if p (where L stands for any particular language for which the truth theory is given).

rather than present it in the original way. Tarski's condition on satisfactory definitions of truth in L rests on the recognition that T-sentences are obviously true, and this recognition depends on our prior understanding of the more general concept of truth. Now if we are asked what this more general concept of truth is or what theory we could have for giving the truth condition of those T-sentences themselves, the only formally correct truth theory or truth definition seems to be a theory or definition that can formulate another T^*-schema for all T-sentences, which says:

"*T-sentence*" is true-in-M if and only if *T-sentence* (where M is the meta-language in which the truth theory for L is given).

If we are asked the same question again regarding the truth of T^*-sentences, we know we are forced into an infinite regress. The same result can be applied to the earlier point that whenever we say or think that something has a certain property, we are, in effect, saying or thinking that a certain thought (T') is true. Whenever we say or think that T' is true, it is just like we are saying or thinking that (T') has a certain property (the property of being true), and therefore we are, in effect, saying or thinking another thought (T", that is, "T' has the property of being true") is true. And T" has the property of being true if and only if the thought "T" has the property of being true" is true, and so on. Again this will lead us into an infinite regress. Will this infinite regress cause any problem for the concept of truth? I see no harm in this infinite regress; in fact it adds more strength to the idea that the concept of truth is ultimately indispensable. Every time we go a step further in asking for the general truth about the truth itself, we get a firmer idea that we must have a grasp of the general concept of truth already in the pursuit of truth. We couldn't appeal to or arrive at any other concept which is more general or fundamental than the concept of truth itself. The result reinforces the indefinability of truth, on the one hand, and the indispensability of truth, on the other. We should remember what Davidson says at the end of his article, "Epistemology and Truth": "If we want to speak the truth about truth, we should say no more than need be." (Davidson, 1988: 191) Have we said everything that need be said about the concept of truth? If not, what more need be?

We may still hope that a theory of truth can tell us something about the concept of truth. But can a theory of truth really provide what we need? It depends on what we want to know from the theory. Do we want a theory of truth in the sense of MT or the sense of LT? Recall that the original project Davidson had in mind was to construct a theory of meaning that incorporated Tarski's theory of truth and modified it to fit our natural languages. But neither Tarski's theory of truth nor Davidson's modified theory of truth provided any strict definition for the substantial concept of truth itself. As noted above, Tarski was not trying to define the concept of truth, but was employing that concept to characterize the semantic structure of specific languages. The so-called truth definition in his theory, if it could be called a definition, is only a definition of a truth predicate for each of a number of well-behaved languages. The truth definition in a Tarskian theory presupposes that we have a prior grasp of the concept of truth, that is, a prior grasp of the triviality of T-sentences. Davidson's modified theory of truth, on the other hand, makes use of the formal structure that went into Tarski's definitions and tries to modify and implement this structure or pattern into our ordinary natural languages. Davidson's project is to seek a theory that would explain how we can grasp the meaning of the utterances on the occasion of communication, a theory that would provide an interpretation of all the utterances of a speaker, and that would show how knowledge of this theory will suffice to understand the utterances. The whole project was directed towards the construction of a satisfactory theory of meaning that would be able to do these jobs. And Davidson apparently thought that a theory of truth in Tarski's style is the most ideal form for building up to such a theory. However, what has been accomplished by Davidson's project has a great deal to do with the issue concerning what a theory of meaning can do, but not much to do with the concept of truth itself, because from the very beginning the concept of truth was taken to be primitive in order to shed light on the concept of meaning. Ironically, this turns out to be one of a few positive things we can know about the concept of truth, as the claim (L3) has revealed: the concept of truth has its connection with meaning, and to some extent, meaning is dependent on truth. This project gives little explanation, or no explanation at all, of "the general concept of truth".

Davidson more than once suggests that we should think of a theory of truth for a speaker in the same way we think of a theory of rational decision as developed by Ramsey's version of Bayesian decision theory. Does this suggestion give us another hope for looking at the theory of truth from a new perspective? Yes and no! The answer is "yes" because Davidson's intention here is to extend his original project (the project that constructs a satisfactory theory of meaning based on the formal structure modified from the theory of truth in Tarski's style) to a new plan that would embed a theory of truth in a larger theory that includes more propositional attitudes: belief, desire, intention, meaning. As affirmed by the claim (L4), the genuine significance of truth can only be brought out by relating it to speech, belief and the evaluative attitudes. For Davidson, we are interested in the concept of truth only because there are actual objects and states of the world to which to apply it: utterances, states of belief, inscriptions. If we did not understand what it was for such entities to be true, we would not be able to determine the contents of these states, objects, and events. So, the plan that connects truth with those linguistic phenomena and human actions seems to try to assign contents to all the attitudes based on a prior grasp of truth. Does the theory of truth introduced in this new plan tell us anything about the general concept of truth? The answer will be "no" in this respect! That is, the theory of truth dealt by Davidson here is not a theory of truth in the sense of ML.

So, do we need a theory of truth? What is a theory of truth really *a theory of*? Is it really a theory of the general concept of "truth" *per se*? If Davidson is right, the question concerning a theory of truth should not be asked in this way. The question should be oriented in another direction, as the question: what is a theory of truth really *a theory for*? If my understanding of Davidson's view is correct, maybe we just don't need a theory of truth at all—if what we ask for from a theory of truth is a definition or clear formulation of the general concept of truth. From a Davidsonion point of view, we don't need any theory of truth either in the sense of T1 or in the sense of T2. But why does Davidson constantly use the theory of truth as if it could really reveal something truth about the concept of truth? The answer lies in Davidson's own words:

(1) "One effect of these reflections is to focus on the centrality of the concept of truth in the understanding of language; it is our grasp of this concept that permits us to make sense of the question whether a theory of truth for a language is correct. There is no reason to look for a prior, or independent, account of some referential relation. " (Davidson, 1990: 300)

(2) "Truth is important, then, not because it is especially valuable or useful, though of course it may be on occasion, but because without the idea of truth we would not be thinking creatures, nor would we understand what it is for someone else to be a thinking creature. It is one thing to try to define the concept of truth, or capture its essence in a pithy summary phrase; it is another to trace its connections with other concepts. " (Davidson, 2000: 72 – 73)

(3) "A theory of truth for a speaker, or group of speakers, while not a definition of the general concept of truth, does give a firm sense of what the concept is good for; it allows us to say, in a compact and clear way, what someone who understands that speaker, or those speakers, knows. Such a theory also invites the question how an interpreter could confirm its truth—a question which without the theory could not be articulated. " (Davidson, 1983: 156)

Passages (1) and (2) tell us again how important and central the concept of truth is for the understanding of language and for being a thinking creature, but also that the concept of truth is fundamental and indefinable because whether a theory of truth is correct for a language already presupposes the pre-analytical concept of truth. It follows that a theory of truth in the sense of MT is either empty or trivial, and hence unacceptable. However, as (3) suggests, we may still want a theory of truth for a speaker or a group of speakers to see what the concept of truth is good for. At least, a theory of truth, as understood by Davidson on the basis of his modification of Tarski's theory into a workable theory— serves to explicate the concepts of meaning, interpretation, and understanding, and even has a central role a more inclusive theory accommodating various prepositional attitudes and revealing the close relationship between the concept of truth and such attitudes. Such a theory is clearly philosophically significant and well serves its philosophical purposes. So, from a Davidsonian point of view, we do need a theory of truth, at least in the sense of LT.

4. Are There Two Different Concepts of Truth?

Truth is a semantic concept. Semantics is a discipline which deals with certain relations between expressions of a language and the objects (whatever entities they might be) referred to or talked about by those expressions. Therefore, truth should not be confused with a metaphysical object of which some philosophers dream to pursue, but should be seen as a concept which is attributed to things like expressions, beliefs or propositions (linguistic or epistemic entities which have a propositional content). But what is it for a sentence, a proposition, a belief, or a thought to be true? In order for a linguistic or an epistemic entity to be true, it seems to require two conditions, one immanent and the other transcendent. On the one hand, it seeks fulfillment in a kind of (linguistic or epistemic) systematic coherence or consistency. On the other hand, it seeks fulfillment in its object. ①Recent debates on what truth is can be divided into two camps: alethic anti-realism and alethic realism. Alethic anti-realists hold on to the immanence of truth and define the concept as fulfillment of epistemic systematic coherence or linguistic systematic satisfaction; their proposals humanize truth by making it basically epistemic. Alethic realists, on the other hand, focus on the transcendence of truth and define the concept as

---

① This reminds us the "Janus-faced" figure Quine employed to describe the special status of "observation sentences" (Quine, 1993: 109). According to Quine, observation sentences are the link between our language and the objective world: on the one hand, they have to face the web of language and beliefs of which they are only part of (the immanent face); on the other hand, they have to face neural intakes imported from external objects in the world (the transcendent face).

fulfillment of conforming or matching its object; their proposals promote some robust form of correspondence theory and make truth radically non-epistemic. If the satisfaction of epistemic coherence or linguistic consistency is merely an elaborate self-indulgence that bring us no nearer to objectivity, or if the apprehension of object does not lie in the line of speaker's or believer's interest, then the pursuit of truth would be vain. As we face the choice between alethic anti-realism and alethic realism, we may feel as if we are trying to steer between Scylla and Charybdis. It makes us wonder whether both the Scylla of alethic anti-realism and the Charybdis of alethic realism can be free from truth skepticism.

The concept of truth has always been ambiguous in the philosophical jargon. The ancient problem of truth was leveled on the metaphysical platform, and both Plato and Aristotle tried to solve the problem by providing some robust conceptions of truth. The modern problem of truth has been lifted by semantic ascent, and philosophers like Frege, Russell, Tarski and Quine all want to find a logically precise and clear expression for explicating the semantic concept of truth. However, as we have also witnessed, most contemporary discussions regarding the concept of truth have been loaded with traditional metaphysical burdens, and many varieties of theories of truth are metaphysical in nature. Most philosophers now will agree that when we talk about the concept of truth we are talking about the truth predicate of a language, although some will treat it as a genuine semantic predicate which ascribes the property of truth to what instantiates it and some will deny it as a genuine predicate or refuse to admit of the predicate any substantive property.

Since Tarski showed how we can avail ourselves of the truth predicate by his theory of truth, the concept of truth has been understood and applied in many different ways. Most of them try to make use of Taraki's T-schema and develop some kind of theory of truth in which the concept of truth is hoped to be better accommodated. The idea of Tarski's T-schema is to provide a minimal condition of any theory of truth that it will entail all instances of the following form (we can call the form T):

(T) 's' is true if and only if p,

where 's' is replaced by a systematic description of any sentence s and p is replaced by a translation of s.

There were times when philosophers were mostly concerned with what Tarski really meant by his theory of truth and how this theory should be properly interpreted. So, they would argue and question about whether Tarski has successfully offered a definition for the general concept of truth or has only succeeded in giving some mathematical proofs for the semantic concept of truth relative to some formal language, whether Tarski's project did succeed in incorporating truth into a physicalist picture of the world, and whether Tarski's theory should be taken as a kind of correspondence theory of truth or as a type of deflationary theory of truth. As time moves on, philosophers are becoming more interested in asking what the philosophical significances of Tarski's theory are, whether Tarski has done all that could be done for the concept of truth, and how we can apply his project further and build a scientifically respectable semantics.

Whether it is only a matter of interpreting Tarski's theory or it is a step further to apply Tarski's idea, the concept of truth involved in the schema T can be interpreted and has been applied in two fundamentally distinct ways. On the one hand, the truth predicate involved in the T-sentences, say " 'snow is white' is true if and only if snow is white", can be interpreted as truth for (or relative to) a particular language. The concept of truth is indeed understood as "truth-in-L1" for some particular language L1, and "truth-in-L1" for the language L1 and "truth-in-L2" for the language L2 are two different concepts. Most philosophers who take sentences or propositions (in its metaphysical neutral sense) to be the truth bearers will agree that Tarski actually defined various predicates of the form " 's' is true-in-L1", each applicable to a single language, but he failed to define a predicate of the form " 's' is true in L" for the variable 'L'. So, the form T according to this interpretation should be more properly formulated as follows:

(T1) 's' is *true-in-L1* if and only if p,

where L1 is a constant and stands for some particular language, 's' is a name of any sentence s in L, and p is a sentence in a language in which truth is being defined and a translation of s.

On the other hand, the truth predicate involved in the T-sentences has also been interpreted and further applied as truth for all particular languages. That is to say, the concept of truth is understood as a general concept that can be applied to any particular language L1, L2 or L3. The philosophers who adopt this interpretation usually take "propositions" (that is, the "meaning" of sentences, where this "meaning" is some kind of metaphysical entity) to be the truth bearers. If the meaning of sentences or the propositions are the truth bearers, then it will hardly make sense to say that p on the right side of the form T is the translation of s (a proposition in this case) on the left. The reason is simple. If p were the translation of s, then the theory of truth based on this form would have claimed that the meaning of a sentence (that is, a proposition) is true if and only if it preserves the same meaning. It will be against our intuition to maintain that the meaning-preserving situation is something that makes our propositions true. Instead, those philosophers who prefer propositions usually have a strong taste for metaphysics. They not only view propositions as some kind of metaphysical entities, when it comes to defining the truth of propositions, they are also inclined to posit facts or states of affairs (which are another metaphysical flavor) to which true propositions correspond. So, if they are going to apply the form T as a model for building their theory of truth, they would understand p on the right side of the form as sentences that refer to facts or states of affairs. The form T according to this interpretation would be reformulated as:

(T2) s is true in L if and only if p,

where L is a variable and can be replaced by any particular language, s stands for the meaning of a sentence or a proposition, and p stands for a fact or a state of affairs to which the proposition s corresponds.

Does either one of the two forms above provide a satisfactory definition of the concept of truth or illuminate the concept in general? As characterized by the form (T1), the truth predicate involved is a predicate applied to the sentences of a particular L1, that is, the predicate of true-in-L1. Even if some theory based on the form (T1) did successfully provide a definition for the concept of truth, it would not be a general definition of "true" in any language, but a definition of the different concepts of truth, or more accurately speaking, different definitions of "true-in-L1", "true-in-L2", "true-in-L3", and so on. The question remains: do those different truth predicates have anything in common that would constitute the nature of the concept of truth in general? Moreover, as characterized by the form (T2), although the concept of truth involved in the schema can be applied to all languages and therefore we do have a general concept that is universally true of any particular language, the definition provided must face some metaphysical puzzles as well as some logical paradoxes. The problems it causes for us are much more serious than the problem it can solve. The definition provided by the form (T2) just cannot be satisfactory enough.

Quine's view of truth is always closely associated with the deflationary attitude about truth, and is sometimes called the redundancy or the disappearance theory, each with its own reasons. But when the name "the disquotational view of truth" is set before us, it is Quine of whom we must think of first. Quine has made use of Tarski's theory of truth and developed his own disquotational view regarding the concept of truth. He explicitly says that "I have been guided by Tarski's Wahrheitsbegriff ever since it first came out (in 1935, dated 1936)." (Quine, 1995: 353) According to Quine's view, the truth predicate is a device of disquotation. The truth predicate has the cancellatory force or disquotational function in Tarski's paradigm: " 'Snow is white' is true if and only if snow is white", which is to say that 'snow is white' is true is just to say that snow is white. Ascription of truth to a sentence just cancels the quotation marks attached to the sentence.

The disquotational view of truth seems to have persistently appeared in Quine's works spanning over 30 years from his early essays in *From a Logical Point of View* to his later book *Pursuit of Truth*, and on this matter, he seems to have never changed his mind. Let's review some passages from his works to illustrate and acquaint us with this view:

[1] "Attribution of truth in particular to "Snow is white"... is every bit as clear to us as attribution of whiteness to snow. " (Quine, 1953: 138)

[2] "To say that the statement 'Brutus killed Caesar' is true, or that 'The atomic weight of sodium is 23' is true, is in effect simply to say that Brutus killed Caesar, or that the atomic weight of sodium is 23. " (Quine, 1960: 24)

[3] "The sentence 'Snow is white' is true, as Tarski has taught us, if and only if real snow is really white. The same can be said of the sentence 'Der Schnee ist weiss'; language is not the point. In speaking of the truth of a given sentence there is only indirection; we do better simply to say the sentence and so speak not about language but about the world. So long as we are speaking only of the truth of singly given sentences, the perfect theory of truth is what Wilfrid Sellars has called the disappearance theory of truth. " (Quine, 1986: 10 – 11)

[4] "Yet there is surely no impugning the disquotation account; no disputing that 'Snow is white' is true if and only if snow is white. Moreover, it is a full account: it explicates clearly the truth or falsity of every clear sentence. " (Quine, 1992: 93)

Quine's view as presented in the passages [2] and [4] seems to express the disquotational function of truth in its *superficial* and *straightforward* sense, that is, all the concept of truth does is simply to cancel the quotation marks. So, to say that 'Brutus killed Caesar' is true, 'The atomic weight of sodium is 23' is true, or 'Snow is white' is true, is simply to say that Brutus killed Caesar, that the atomic weight of sodium is 23, or that snow is white. However, as passages [1] and [3] have shown, the disquotation account seems to involve more than just "canceling" the disquotation marks, the concept of truth can also work back and forth between talking about the sentences and talking about the world. The truth predicate seems to be a design that can help us mention the sentence in question and affirm its truth. This will later be noted as a special feature of semantic ascent. On the other hand, the concept of truth seems to play a role in helping us back to talking about the world again while it plays its disquotational role in canceling the disquotation marks, or as I will refer to it later, truth is actually engaged in "epistemological descent".

Truth thus understood appears *prima facie* to be redundant and ascription of truth to a given sentence does not seem to play any vital role as commonly conceived. But Quine clearly notices that the truth predicate is not always superfluous if we consider cases in which we want to speak of the truth of sentences without having the sentences at hand, a sentence such as "Everything Socrates said was true", or when we generalize over a potentially infinite number of sentences, like "All sentences of the form 'If p then p' are true". The second group of the situations is what Quine calls "semantic ascent": ascent to talk of sentences themselves rather than talk of what the sentences are about, or simply ascent to a meta-language. Quine thinks that the role of the truth predicate is logically and scientifically vital when we want to generalize along a dimension that cannot be swept out by a general term and its use is invaluable in these cases of semantic ascent.

Quine recognizes further that the disquotational feature of truth has to be immanent: to call a sentence true is just to affirm or include it in *our language*, in *our own theory of world*, or in *our science*. We understand what it is for the sentence 'Snow is white' to be true as clearly as we understand what it is for snow to be white in our language or with respect to our theory of world. Truth in its immanent sense is transparent. Quine also claims that he bases this immanent sense of truth on three counts: "sententiality, disquotation, and naturalism" (Quine, 1995: 353). In spelling out the details and the bases of the immanence of truth, we can find some confusions as well as difficulties involved in Quine's conceptions of truth. This is what I will discuss and argue about in what follows.

By sententiality, Quine means two things. First, what are true are sentences rather than propositions, that is, meanings of sentences. Second, because sentences are tied to languages, a string of marks is true only as a sentence of some specific language, say L1. So, when we discuss issues about the concept of truth, we are giving our explanation with respect to a sentence being true in L1. The proposal of sententiality obviously shows that Quine's interpretation or application of Tarski's T-schema represents the form T1 above, that is,

(T1) 's' is *true-in-L*1 if and only if p,

where L1 is a constant and stands for some particular language.

But there is a problem here with respect to how *p* should be interpreted. If the schematic letter *p* in Tarski's original T-schema stands for a translation of the sentence of which 's' is a name, then Quine's disquotational view of truth will fail to represent the model Quine prefers. Let's use a paradigm in which Quine thinks that it can better reveal his disquotational view:

(T1') '____' is true-in-L1 if and only if ____ .

The first blank in quotation works the same as s in (T1), and the second blank should fit the letter *p*. Now, (T1') can hold only when any one sentence of L1 is written in both of the two blanks. If L1 is English, then " 'Snow is white' is true-in-English if and only if snow is white" and " 'Grass is green' is true-in-English if and only if grass is green" will both be good instances of (T1'), and the disquotation account can be fully explained here. But if what is written in the second blank is a translation of the sentence written in the first blank, then we might get a resulting T1'-sentence such as " 'Snow is white' is true-in-English if and only if der Schnee ist weiss". The T1'-sentence probably makes no sense at all for people who don't understand German, and the function of the truth predicate involved in it is far more than being disquotational in its superficial sense. It becomes necessary that L1 and the language in which (T1') is couched (namely, English) be the same, or at least that they overlap to the extent of any notations to which Quine proposes to apply the form (T1'). It follows that the T-schema used by Quine should be completed as the following:

The disquotational theory of truth will entail all instances of the form

(T1") 's' is *true-in-L*1 if and only if *p*,

where L1 is a constant and stands for some particular language, s is any sentence in L1, and *p* is replaced by the same sentence s in L1 or any language that contains L1 as a part. This theory will not be able to allow us to speak sensibly of the truth of sentences in one language using another language, if the latter does not contain the former. But we do speak sensibly of the truth of sentences in German sing our English. This will lead us to revisit and think over again the disquotational feature of truth that Quine prefers.

By disquotation, as we have discussed above, Quine means that ascribing truth to the sentence "Snow is white" has the same effect as asserting that snow is white. Literally speaking, when we read this disquotational feature of truth into Quine's paradigm (T1"), we understand what it is for the sentence "Snow is white" to be true as clearly as we understand what it is for snow to be white relative to *our own language*. But, surprisingly, Quine also explains his idea of "disquotation" by saying that

"To call a sentence true is just to include it in *our own theory of the world*" (Quine, 1995: 353). On the face of it, what Quine says here is nothing like "disquotation", but is more like "relativity". There seems to be a confusion regarding the question as to what truth is. The question can be expressed as saying *what it is for a sentence to be true* and saying *which sentences are true*. The disquotational feature of truth (the immanent sense in which truth is relative to our language) can be used to answer what it is for a sentence to be true and it answers this question by saying what the truth conditions of the sentences of a language L1 are; the relativistic feature of truth (the immanent sense in which truth is relative to our theory of the world) can answer what truth is by saying which of those sentences are true in our own theory of truth. We face a problem here in how to understand or interpret the immanent sense of truth. Is truth immanent to a language, a theory of the world, or both? This is a problem because we know perfectly well that a language is different from a theory of the world. Although we also learn from Quine that we cannot make a clear distinction between our language and our theory of the world, it doesn't entail that a language is exactly the same as a theory of the world. At least, if a language is the subject matter under our study, it is usually classified as the field of linguistics—whether it is syntax, semantics or pragmatics in question. If a theory of the world is the subject matter under our investigation, it is usually an epistemological project to seek justification or evidence for the theory or a metaphysical program to vindicate our world views. Now, if we understand the immanent sense of truth as being relative to a language, we are concerned with a semantic concept of truth. But if we interpret the immanent sense of truth as being relative to a theory of the world, we are actually dealing with an epistemic notion of truth or a concept of truth in the metaphysical sense. We have strong evidence for thinking that Quine does actually hold on to both semantic and epistemic senses of truth. If that is the case, the next thing we need to explain is why the confusion arises and how the problem can be solved. But before we proceed to explain these two questions, the third count on which Quine's immanent sense of truth is based, that is, Quine's naturalism, needs to be brought into the picture in order to make the whole situation clearer.

By naturalism, Quine's intention is to disavow any higher tribunal than our best scientific theory of the time. It immediately reminds us an old epistemological quest involved in Quine's naturalized epistemology: what are the foundations of our theory of the world? Quine's answer to this quest lies in his naturalistic approach: "It is rational reconstruction of the individual's and/or the race's actual acquisition of a responsible theory of the external world. It would address the question how we, physical denizens of the physical world, can have projected our scientific theory of that whole world from our meager contacts with it. " (Quine, 1995a: 16) Unlike Descartes, Quine holds that we own and use our beliefs of the moment until, through what is vaguely called scientific method, we change them here and there for the better. "Within our own total evolving doctrine, we can judge truth as earnestly and absolutely as can be; subject to correction, but that goes without saying. " (Quine, 1960: 25) It becomes obvious that when Quine bases his immanence of truth on naturalism, he does indeed have the epistemological quest in mind, and the immanent concept of truth (as relative to our theory of the world) is an epistemic concept at best. Quine's naturalism can be directed to the question "how do we know what is true?", "how do we know which of our ascriptions of truth are warranted?" or "how can we tell whether we can legitimately affirm a sentence?", and the answer lies in his immanence of truth. The ascription of truth to a sentence is simply to include the sentence in our theory of the world: in the case of "Snow is white" we just look at snow and check the color and we disavow of any higher tribunal than our best scientific methods in our time. Clearly, when Quine says truth is relative to our theory of the world, he must mean that what is true is relative to a theory, and that which sentences are true is relative to a theory. The concept of truth involved here is clearly an epistemic one rather than the semantic concept of truth.

Now, when we consider all three counts together on which Quine bases his immanence of truth, we can see more clearly the confusion involved in the disquotational feature of truth discussed above: the confusion between "to call a sentence true is just to affirm it in *our language*", and "to call a sentence true is just to include it in *our own theory of world*, or in *our science*". It is indeed "disquotation" plus "sententiality" that gives the immanence of truth a semantic dimension and is set up to answer the question as to what it is for a sentence to be true. It answers this question by making the truth predicate relative to our language and by saying what the truth conditions of the sentences of our language are. The result is purely disquotational, that is, ascribing the truth predicate to the sentence "Snow is white" has the same linguistic effect as asserting that snow is white in our language. On the other hand, "disquotation" and "naturalism" will give the immanence of truth an epistemic dimension and are set up to answer the question regarding which of those sentences are true. The answer to this question is to make the concept of truth relative to our theory of the world and to appeal to naturalism. Thus, the ascription of truth to a sentence is simply to include the sentence in our theory of the world—there is no higher tribunal than our best scientific theory of the time that will help us judge which of the sentences are true. Whether a sentence is true or not will depend on what our theory says about what there really are and how our scientific methods help us justify our claims. The result is not, strictly speaking, "disquotational", but more like "relativistic".

How would Quine solve this problem? How would he reconcile these two different dimensions involved in his immanent concept of truth? Would he prefer one to the other? If he would do, then which one would he prefer? Or would he be willing to accept this confusion and make the concept of truth both semantic and epistemic?

There are many places in Quine's early works in which Quine shows his interest more in the epistemic dimension of the immanent concept of truth, and the semantic dimension is therefore treated as being relatively trivial except in those places where we are "impelled by certain technical complications to mention sentences". But even in these cases in which the truth predicate has to be used, the purpose is still "to restore the effect of objective reference". This can be seen most clearly in the following quotes from his *Philosophy of Logic*.

"In speaking of the truth of a given sentence there is only indirection; we do better simply to say the sentence and so speak not about language but about the world. So long as we are speaking only of the truth of singly given sentences, the perfect theory of truth is what Wilfred Sellars has called the disappearance theory of truth. " (Quine, 1986: 11)

"Where the truth predicate has its utility is in just those places where, though still concerned with reality, we are impelled by certain technical complications to mention sentences. Here the truth predicate serves, as it were, to point through the sentences to the reality. " (ibid.)

"This ascent to a linguistic plane of reference is only a momentary retreat from the world, for the utility of the truth predicate is precisely the cancellation of linguistic reference. The truth predicate is a reminder that, despite a technical ascent to talk of sentences, our eye is on the world. This cancellatory force of the truth predicate is explicit in Tarski's paradigm: 'Snow is white' is true if and only if snow is white. " (ibid. : 12)

"Quotation marks make all the difference between talking about words and talking about snow. The quotation is a name of a sentence that contains a name, namely 'snow', of snow. By calling the sentence true, we call snow white. The truth predicate is a device of disquotation. We may affirm the single sentence by just uttering it, unaided by quotation or by the truth predicate; but if we want to affirm some infinite lot of sentences that we can demarcate only talking about sentences, then the truth predicate has its use. We need it to restore the effect of objective reference when for the sake of some generalization we have resorted to semantic ascent. " (ibid.)

Quite obviously Quine's attitude toward the semantic dimension of the immanent concept of truth, based on the passages above, is comparatively negative. The role the semantic concept (the truth predicate) plays is to cancel "a momentary retreat from the world" or serve as "a reminder of facing the world". The concept of truth, whether having its disquotational feature or its utility of resorting to semantic ascent, will ultimately give its way to the epistemic dimension and hinge on reality. After all, "no sentence is true but reality makes it so" (ibid. 10). If what Quine says here is correct, then the concept of truth should be endowed with a more positive feature which Quine failed to name: that is, truth is engaged in "epistemological descent". But as I will indicate later, when the concept of truth is engaged in "epistemological descent", it will go "transcendent".

Later in his works, Quine seems to notice more clearly this confusion and start giving the semantic dimension of the immanent concept of truth its due.

"In a looser sense the disquotational account does define truth. It tells us what it is for any sentence to be true, and it tells us this in terms just as clear to us as the sentence in question itself. We understand what it is for the sentence "Snow is white" to be true as clearly as we understand what it is for snow to be white. Evidently one who puzzles over the adjective "true" should puzzle rather over the sentences to which he ascribes it. "True" is transparent. " (Pursuit of Truth: 82)

This passage shows that the immanent sense of truth (in its semantic dimension), with its disquotational feature, is transparent. The puzzling questions regarding what sentences are true, what justification we have for including a sentence in our theory, and what evidence we have for ascribing truth to a sentence are epistemic questions of the sentences to which we ascribe truth (the sentences we believe that they are true) rather than of truth itself.

A most recent passage clearly shows that Quine has changed his mind and stressed our language rather than our theory of the world as being the place to which the immanence of truth should be relativized.

"When he [Gibson] has me relativizing truth "to a theory (or language)", however, I grant language but balk at theory. A theory that I hold true may turn out false; such is usage, and I accept it. Insofar, truth indeed goes transcendental; but I acquiesce in this as a linguistic effect. " (Quine,

1998: 685) ①

This last passage gives us a clear answer to the question: "Is truth immanent to a language or to a theory of the world?" Quine's solution to the problem that involves both a semantic dimension and an epistemic dimension in his immanent sense of truth is to give up the epistemic dimension of immanent truth—" truth" that is engaged in "epistemological descent", and let "truth" go "transcendental". The immanent sense of truth in its semantic dimension remains its unique feature of "disquotation" and its special utility of resorting to "semantic ascent".

The disquotational feature of truth gives the extension of a truth predicate only for a particular language. The concept of truth defined here should be understood as "truth-in-L1" for a particular language L1, and "truth-in-L1" for the language L1 and "truth-in-L2" for the language L2 are two different concepts. If we ask what all such truth predicates have in common, it is something that the disquotation account cannot answer. But the concept of truth we ordinarily understand and use is not relative to any specific language or theory, nor is it regulated and determined by them. Neither our language nor our science can fix truth. Quine knows pretty well that truth should hinge on reality but not language, and that our theory of the world can be proved wrong. It seems to be this concern that leads Quine to puzzle over a transcendent sense of truth, and allows the kind of truth to be something that scientists are always in quest of, or something that "looms as a heaven that we keep steering for and correcting to". The following words from Quine's works show not only that for Quine when truth is engaged in "epistemological descent" it will go "transcendent", but also that when truth goes "transcendent" it will become "metaphysical" and "mystical".

"We should and do currently accept the firmest scientific conclusions as true, but when one of these is dislodged by further research we do not say that it had been true but became false. We say that to our surprise it was not true after all. Science is seen as pursuing and discovering truth rather that as decreeing it. Such is the idiom of realism, and it is integral to the semantics of the predicate "true"." (Quine, 1995a: 67)

"To call a sentence true, I said, is to include it in our science, but this is not to say that science fixes truth. It can prove wrong. We go on testing our scientific theory by prediction and experiment, and

---

① Hahn, L. E. and Schilpp P. A. (eds), 1998, *The Philosophy of W. V. Quine* (expanded edition). Open Court.

modifying it as needed, in quest of the truth. Truth thus looms as a haven that we keep steering for and correcting to. It is an ideal of pure reason, in Kant's phrase. Very well: immanent in those other respects, transcendent in this. " (Quine 1995: 353)

Quine's immanent concept of truth, as it has be shown, should be understood as "truth-in-L1" in Tarski's theory (or at least the form T1 involved in the T-paradigm), and the transcendent concept of truth can be identified as the general concept of truth which is supposed to be applied to all and any particular language. But the question is: are the two concepts of truth different in kind or just different in degree? If the immanent concept of truth and the transcendent concept of truth are two different kinds of truth, then, we may wonder, what will be the relationship between the two? Does the understanding of the one help to explain the other? Or are they totally different and unrelated? Worse still, we may feel, will there be a tension between two of them—one is transparent and the other is relatively mysterious in nature? If the two concepts of truth are only different in degree, then with respect to what aspect or based on what criterion are the two concepts closely connected and then measured or evaluated? I want to argue that both of Quine's immanent and transcendent senses of truth should be accommodated at a linguistic level or should be included in some semantic project, rather than viewing them from a metaphysical point of view. Let's go over one passage, which seems to be underestimated by Quine himself and totally ignored by most philosophers, that it will give us a direction as to how we can adopt such an approach.

"Of course the truth predicate carries over to other language by translation. If this is transcendence, truth is indeed transcendent. But that much can be said even of reference, despite ontological relativity. It likewise carries over by translation. " (Quine, 1995: 353)

Even if "truth" goes "transcendent", we don't have to go down the metaphysical route—a dangerous route that will lead us into an embarrassing choice between "Scylla" and "Charybdis". We can still stay at the semantic level and design a project that will combine both the immanent sense and the transcendent sense of truth nicely. The key idea of designing such a semantic project lies in what can be "carried over to other languages" by translation or whatever procedures. We should first notice that Quine's original distinction between "immanent" and "transcendent" is based on the linguistic consideration (Quine, 1986: 19). An immanent notion is explained only for one particular language, while a transcendent notion is explained for all languages. Quine gives the example of *der* words in German as an immanent notion, defined only for words in German. The notion of "a word" would seem to be a transcendent notion because it would seem to make sense to ask for any language what the words of that language are. When we apply this distinction to the concept of truth, we can and should also restrict ourselves to the linguistic concerns and focus on the semantic project. As a matter of fact, Tarski's definition of truth yields an immanent notion that applies only to the particular language L1 for which the definition is given; it does not provide a transcendent definition of truth in L for variable L. Our job now is to figure out how we can construct a theory of truth (as a semantic project) which will give us a transcendent notion of truth that can be applied to all particular languages.

In order to accomplish this, I suggest that we can still use Tarski's Schema T and employ most of his apparatus for accommodating the concept of truth (however, only in its immanent sense). In addition, we will need to allow the truth predicate carries over to other languages by translation, and the truth predicate involved here is in its transcendent sense. A new schema is needed to combine both of immanent truth and transcendent truth here, and it will be called the Schema TT:

The new Semantic Theory of Truth will entail all instances of the following form:

(TT) $\ulcorner$'s' is *true-in-L1* if and only if $s \urcorner$ is *true* if and only if ('p' is *true-in-L2* if and only if p),

where L1 and L2 are constants and stand for some particular languages, s is any sentence in L1, p is any sentence in L2, and p is a translation of s. As a matter of fact, Davidson has made ingenious use of Tarski's theory of truth as the very structure of constructing a theory of meaning. A theory of truth in the Davidsonian sense is not to propose a better stipulative definition of truth or an alternative short summary for the concept of truth at the metaphysical level, but to suggest an empirical theory about the truth conditions of every sentence in some particular language. The theory in question (the truth-theoretic semantics, as one might suggest[1]) makes the concept of truth an essential part of the scheme we all employ for interpreting, understanding, translating and explaining the thought and action of others. The new Schema TT suggested here is intended to accommodate both Quine's two conceptions of truth and the Davidsonian theory of truth. If this new project in semantics can really be carried out successfully, then we will have a paradigmatic case in which the immanent notion and the transcendent notion of truth can both be dealt with at the linguistic level without involving any metaphysics.

---

[1]   A more detailed development and explication of Davidson's theory of meaning can be found in a recently published work by Ernest Lepore and Kirk Ludwig, entitled *Donald Davidson's Truth-Theoretic Semantics*. Clarendon Press, Oxford, 2007.

5. Semantics without Metaphysics

Semantics and metaphysics are different. However, many philosophers maintain that the two are very closely related. Semantics is usually considered as a linguistic subject that deals with the meanings of linguistic expressions. Metaphysics, on the other hand, is a philosophical enterprise that purports to explore the nature of the world and to describe the structures and constituents of it. It is not difficult to see why the two distinct areas can merge so intimately together. After all, we all agree that the language we use and the world we know are closely connected. Because of this, some philosophers approach linguistic issues from the metaphysical perspectives and construct their theses of philosophical semantics based on their metaphysical positions. It naturally results in various confusions of the semantic debates and projects with the metaphysical ones. This paper aims to explore the confusions that lie between semantics and metaphysics and to suggest that we can manage the semantic project successfully without taking up any metaphysical disputes.

One of the central themes in the tradition of metaphysics is the realism/anti-realism debate. Metaphysical realism claims that the entities (objects, properties, relations, or facts) the world contains exist independently of human thoughts about or perceptions of them. Antirealism denies either the existence of the entities the realists believe in or their independence from our conceptions of them. Unfortunately, the disputes between realists and antirealists have not been very fruitful, since they are full of ambiguities and confusions. One can generally characterize the debates between realism and anti-realism as the controversies as to whether there is at least something real that is independent of conceptions or representations of human minds. However, the controversies are not as simple as they look, because the domains or the objects in question vary with different contexts and discussions. For example, common-sense realists would assert that there is at least something (objects, things, facts, or states of affairs) existing in the physical world (the world in which we live) that is independent of human minds, while radical anti-realists deny this. Scientific realists assert that there are at least some theoretical entities (atoms, quanta or quarks) dealt with in scientific theories that are independent of scientific representations for their reality, while scientific anti-realists deny that there are any of these independent entities. Realism about "universals" is a theory asserting that properties exist independent of human minds, while anti-realism about "universals" denies this. It is therefore important to notice that one can be a realist about one subject-matter, and not about another. If we happen to call someone a realist or an antirealist without specifying what subject-matter is in question, we can be accused of using the label equivocally.

Because the subject-matter of the debates can be extended to various areas (common sense, natural science, linguistics, and so on), misunderstandings and confusions can easily arise. It has been a long tradition that metaphysical debates have always had great impact on epistemology and semantics. It should be called a scandal in philosophy that various controversies in epistemology and semantics all suffer from the infection of metaphysical virus, for example, the controversial issues of subjective vs. objective, internal vs. external, intension vs. extension, meaning vs. reference, immanent vs. transcendent, and so on. The current realism-antirealism debate on the concept of truth is also a good example. Issues concerning what the nature of truth is and what role the concept of truth can play in our understanding of the world have seemed to draw one's attention from both fields of metaphysics and semantics. The construction of a theory of truth is often viewed as a metaphysical project as well as a semantic project.

Truth is a semantic concept. Semantics is a linguistic discipline which, characterized broadly, deals with certain relations between expressions of a language and the objects or states of affairs represented by those expressions. According to this characterization, it is natural to think that truth is a main focal point where our language and the world meet. By acquiring true expressions in our language, we seem to gain access to the world, or more specifically, to have access to the objects or states of affairs in the world. In virtues of true expressions, the world seems to find its way to be mirrored or to be represented by our language. So, if one is attempting to construct a semantic theory for the concept of truth, one would feel obligated to provide some metaphysical perspective with respect to what the world is like. When one introduces entities such as objects, facts or states of affairs to define the concept of truth or to explain why expressions of a language are true, the debate between realism and antirealism can easily arise and the battles can be moved onto the stage of semantics. In fact, one of the hottest issues in recent philosophical studies of semantics is the realism-antirealism dispute with respect to the concept of truth, or the so-called "alethic" realism-antirealism debate[1].

I have been proposing that most contemporary discussions regarding the concept of truth have been

---

[1] The term "alethic realism" (or Realism with a capital "R") comes from William Alston's book, *A Realist Conception of Truth*, in which the term is meant to stand for "realism concerning truth".

loaded with traditional metaphysical burdens, and that many varieties of theories of truth are metaphysical in nature. Most contemporary theories of truth are concerned with the nature of truth, and hope to find the definition and philosophical significances of the concept. This situation should remind us of the controversy over the concept of "universal" begun in medieval times. Just like the three different kinds of metaphysical theories of universals (i. e. , realism, conceptualism, and nominalism respectively), there are also three matching metaphysical theories with respect to the concept of truth. Comparable to realism about "universals", we have the correspondence theory of truth; to conceptualism about "universals", we have the coherence theory of truth and the pragmatic theory of truth; and to nominalism about "universals", the deflationary theory of truth. The last two groups of theories of truth, just like their counter-parts in the theories of universals, are anti-realist theses in nature. Realism about truth has its focus on metaphysics, because not only does it try to define the concept of truth in terms of some objective entities which are thought to make our sentences true, but also emphasize that these entities (objects or facts) are independent of our representations and conceptions. The fundamental ideas of antirealism about truth are also metaphysical, because they deny either that what make our sentences true are something independent of human concerns, or that there is any substantial essence of truth which is worth being defined or pursued.

In a book, entitled *Naturalistic Realism and the Antirealist Challenge*, Drew Khlentzos nicely clarifies the claim and the position of realism, and presents forcefully the antirealist challenges to realism. He characterizes realism as a metaphysical thesis about what the world is like and what it contains. So, he formulates his working characterization of metaphysical realism as: "The objects and structures that comprise the furniture of the universe exist mind-independently. " (Khlentzos, 2004: 25) Although the common opposition of antirealists to metaphysical realism springs from very different metaphysical commitments, the major antirealist challenge occurs at the semantic level—*the problem of representation*, so called by Khlentzos. The questions antirealists urge in their various semantic challenges to realism can be simply put as: if the world is as resolutely mind-independently as the realist makes out, there is a problem about how our mental symbols and linguistic expressions get "hooked up" to mind-independent objects and facts, and how our thoughts and sentences target mind-independent states of affairs. Khlentzos's main contention in his book is that realism is vulnerable to antirealist attack precisely because the representation problem (antirealist semantic challenges) remains unsolved.

It is admirable that Khlentzos can clearly differentiate the semantic issues from the metaphysical ones when he faces the realism/antirealism debates. However, there are some clues showing that Khlentzos does not really make the distinction thorough enough when he criticizes Davidson's project on transcending the realist-antirealist debate. Khlentzos believes that "there has been no 'going beyond' the realist-antirealist debate, only a failure to appreciate which side of the fence they are really on." (Khlentzos, 2004: 43) So, he argues that even if we granted Davidson's rejection of a scheme-content division on both sides of realist and antirealist, Davidson's position is still an antirealist at best. I agree with Khlentzos that there has been no 'going beyond' the realist-antirealist debate, but it is only when we restrict ourselves at the metaphysical level. I want to argue that we are able to go beyond the realist-antirealist debate when we extend our perspectives and reach the semantic level. Khlentzos misunderstands what Davidson's project is really intended to accomplish because he has confused projects at a metaphysical level with those at a semantic level. Davidson is interested in providing a semantic theory of truth rather than defending any kind of metaphysical theory of truth. A distinction can be drawn between the metaphysical level and the linguistic level when we discuss the issues concerning what *a theory of truth* is. The distinction of the different levels is based on *what we try to ask the theory of truth to do* or *why we need to construct such a theory*. A theory of truth at the metaphysical level is a theory concerning with the nature and the role of truth, aiming at providing a definition or an explication for it. A theory of truth at the semantic (or language-involving) level is a theory purporting to explain how various linguistic phenomena, such as communication, understanding, and interpretation, are possible by relating the concept of truth with other semantic concepts such as that of meaning and that of belief. We can say that a theory of truth at the metaphysical level has its focus on *truth* itself, while a theory of truth at the semantic level emphasizes what *the theory* (as a semantic theory) can do to our semantic phenomena. Davidson's theory of truth should be understood as a theory at the semantic level, and he is trying to go beyond the realism/antirealism debate without importing any of his metaphysical commitment into his semantic project.

    Projects in metaphysics attempt to answer the question as to what the world is really like by exploring the structures underlying the world and by classifying the constituents contained in it. The realism/antirealism debate is, by its nature, a metaphysical issue which tries to argue further whether the structures and the constituents in question really exist independently of our perceptions or conceptions. The debate can be applied to different fields in linguistics, ethics, art, mathematics and natural science. But when it is applied to another field, say semantics, the realism/antirealism debate is still a metaphysical issue, or an issue at the metaphysical level. Projects in semantics usually aim to answer the questions as to why expressions of our language are true and what the meanings of expressions of our language are. When philosophers attempt to construct such a semantic theory, they always search for a metaphysical rescue. They hope that philosophical semantics can give an answer to the question of why linguistic expressions are true by appealing to some kind of truth-makers in the world; and an explanation to what the meanings of linguistic expressions are by referring to some kind of entities in reality. It then follows with the question as to whether the so-called truth-makers or entities referred really exist independently of human perceptions or conceptions. So, the realism/antirealism debate revives in the field of semantics.

It should be noticed that although the realism/antirealism debate is taking place in the field of semantics, the debate itself is still a metaphysical issue. However, according to my observations, the "alethic" realism-antirealism debate, just like its counterpart in metaphysics, has not been very fruitful either. I then wonder why we need to care so much about the metaphysical debate when we are executing the semantic project. Michael Lynch, in the "Introduction" to his anthology *The Nature of Truth*, distinguishes various kinds of "Robust theories of truth" from the "Deflationary theories of truth" based on the starting point (or question): "Does truth have a nature?" So, it is immediately obvious for him that we should sort out various theories just depending on whether the attitudes toward the starting question are positive or negative. However, Lynch also notices that "there is a growing consensus among some philosophers that neither traditional robust theories nor deflationary theories are right." If it is so, then he claims that "we must find new ways to think about this old concept." (Lynch, 2001: 5) It is not difficult to see that the distinction made by Lynch between "robust theories" and "deflationary theories" is based on a metaphysically oriented question or starting point. The central concern of all these different sorts of theories of truth is still the concept of truth, or more specifically speaking, the nature of truth (if any). A theory of truth built on this concern should be a theory at the metaphysical level. It is my belief that we do have "a new way to think about the old concept of truth". Instead of asking "whether truth has a nature", we can ask "what the concept of truth can contribute to a semantic theory", or "what we need a theory of truth for". I suggest that we can view the concept of truth from a theory of truth based on the semantic perspective or language-involving phenomena, and use truth to help us explain how various semantic phenomena work in our ordinary language.

Consider a theory of meaning in Davidsonian style in which the semantic project can be pursued even without taking up the concept of meaning, not to mention any kind of metaphysical entities connected with meanings①. The semantic theory of truth, as previously explicated, is another example that shows how we can deal with a semantic theory without involving ourselves in the muddle of metaphysical disputes. As a matter of fact, Davidson has made ingenious use of Tarski's theory of truth as the very structure of constructing a theory of meaning. A theory of truth in the Davidsonian sense is not to propose a better stipulative definition of truth or an alternative short summary for the concept of truth at the metaphysical level, but to suggest an empirical theory about the truth conditions of every sentence in some particular language. The theory in question (the truth-theoretic semantics, as one might suggest②) makes the concept of truth an essential part of the scheme we all employ for interpreting, understanding, translating and explaining the thought and action of others. If the Davidsonian projects in semantics can really be carried out successfully, then we will have a paradigmatic case in which we can do semantics without metaphysics.

References

[1] Alston, William, 1996, *A Realist Conception of Truth*. Cornell University Press.

[2] Austin, J. L., 1950, "Truth", *Proceedings of the Aristotelian Society*, vol. 24, pp. 111 – 128

[3] Barwise, J. and Perry J., 1981, "Semantic Innocence and Uncompromising Situations", *Midwest Studies in Philosophy*, vol. 6: *The Foundations of Analytic Philosophy*, pp. 387 – 403

[4] Blackburn, S. and Simmons, K., 1999, *Truth*. Oxford: Oxford University Press.

[5] Church, A., 1943, "Review of Carnap's *Introduction to Semantics*", *Philosophical Review*, 52, pp. 298 – 304

[7] Davidson, Donald, 1967, "Truth and Meaning." In Davidson (1984), pp. 17 – 36.

[8] Davidson, Donald, 1969, "True to the Facts", In Davidson (1984), pp. 37 – 54.

[9] Davidson, Donald, 1983, "A Coherence Theory of Truth and Knowledge." In Davidson (2001), pp. 137 – 153.

---

① Consider a theory of meaning in the Davidsonian style in which "the one thing meanings do not seem to do is oil the wheels of a theory of meaning——at least as long as we require of such a theory that it non-trivially give the meaning of every sentence in the language." (Davidson, 1967: 20)

② A more detailed development and explication of Davidson's theory of meaning can be found in a recently published work by Ernest Lepore and Kirk Ludwig, entitled *Donald Davidson's Truth-Theoretic Semantics*.

[10] Davidson, Donald, 1984, *Inquiries Into Truth and Interpretation*. Clarendon Press, Oxford.

[11] Davidson, Donald, 1987, "Afterthoughts." In Davidson (2001), pp. 154 – 157.

Davidson, Donald, 1988, "Epistemology and Truth." In Davidson (2001), pp. 177 – 192.

[12] Davidson, Donald, 1990, "The Structure and Content of Truth." In *Journal of Philosophy*, 87, pp. 279 – 328.

[13] Davidson, Donald, 1996, "The Folly of Trying to Define Truth." *Journal of Philosophy*, 93, pp. 263 – 278.

[14] Davidson, Donald, 1999a, "The Centrality of Truth." In Peregrin (1999), pp. 105 – 115.

[15] Davidson, Donald, 1999b, "Intellectual Autobiography." In Hahn (1999), pp. 1 – 70.

[16] Davidson, Donald, 2000, "Truth Rehabilitated." In *Rorty and His Critics*, Brandom, Robert B. (ed.), Cambridge: Blackwell, pp. 65 – 74.

[17] Davidson, Donald, 2001, *Subjective, Intersubjective and Objective*. Clarendon Press, Oxford.

[18] Davidson, Donald, 2005, *Truth and Predication*, Harvard University Press, Cambridge, Mass.

[19] Devitt, Michael, 2001, "The Metaphysics of Truth." in Lynch (2001), pp. 579 – 612.

[20] Etchemendy, J., 1988, "Tarski on Truth and Logical Consequence." in *Journal of Symbolic Logic*, 53.

[21] Field, Hartry, 1972, "Tarski's Theory of Truth." *Journal of Philosophy*, 69, 13: 347 – 375.

[22] Frege, G., 1892, "On *Sinn* and *Beduetung*", translated by M. Black, in M. Beaney (ed.), *The Frege Reader*, Blackwell, Oxford, 1997, pp. 151 – 171

[23] Frege, G., 1918 – 1919, "Thought." In *The Frege Reader*, pp. 325 – 4, ed. by Michael Beaney, Blackwell.

[24] Gödel, K., 1944, "Russell's Mathematical Logic", in P. A. Schilpp (ed.), *The Philosophy of Bertrand Russell*, Northwestern University Press, pp. 125 – 153.

[25] Grover, D., Campand, Jr. J. and Belnap, Jr. N., 1975, "A Prosentential Theory of Truth." In *Philosophical Studies* 27.

[26] Hahn, Lewis, 1999, *The Philosophy of Donald Davidson*. Open Court Publishing Co.

[27] Horwich, Paul, 1994, *Theories of Truth*. Dartmouth Publishing Company.

[28] Horwich, Paul, 1998, *Truth*. Oxford: Oxford University Press.

[29] Kirkham, R., 1992, *Theories of Truth: A Critical Introduction*. Cambridge: MIT.

[30] Khlentzos, D., 2004, *Naturalistic Realism and the Antirealist Challenge*, MIT Press.

[31] Leeds, S., 1978, "Theories of Reference and Truth." in *Erkenntnis* 13, pp. 111 – 129.

[32] Lepore, E. & Ludwig, K., 2007, *Donald Davidson's Truth-theoretic Semantics*, Clarendon Press, Oxford.

[33] Lynch, Michael, 2001, *The Nature of Truth: Classic and Contemporary Perspectives*. Cambridge: MIT.

[34] Neale, S., 2001, *Facing Facts*, Clarendon Press, Oxford

[35] Newman, A., 2002, *The Correspondence Theory of Truth: An Essay on the Metaphysics of Predication*, Cambridge University Press

[36] Peregrin, J., 1999, *Truth and its Nature (If Any)*. Kluwer Academic Publishers.

[37] Popper, Karl, 1968, *Logic of Scientific Discovery*. New York: Basic Books.

[38] Quine, W. V., 1953, *From a Logical Point of View*, Harvard University Press.

[39] Quine, W. V., 1953a, "Three Grades of Modal Involvement", in W. V. Quine, *The Ways of Paradox*, Harvard University Press, Cambridge, Mass., pp. 158 – 176.

[40] Quine, W. V., 1960, *Word and Object*. Cambridge: MIT.

[41] Quine, W. V., 1986, *Philosophy of Logic*, 2nd edition, Harvard University Press.

[42] Quine, W. V., 1992, *Pursuit of Truth*, revised edition, Harvard University Press.

[43] Quine, W. V., 1993, "In Praise of Observation Sentences", in *The Journal of Philosophy*, 90, pp. 107 – 116.

[44] Quine, W. V., 1995, "Reactions", in *On Quine*, pp. 347 – 361, edited by P. Leonardi and M. Santambrogio, Cambridge University Press, 1995.

[45] Quine, W. V., 1995a, *From Stimulus to Science*, Harvard University Press.

[46] Ramsey, Frank, 1990, "The Nature of Truth." *Episteme*, 16, pp. 6 – 16.

[47] Rodriguez-Pereyra, G., 2002, *Resemblance Nominalism*, Clarendon Press, Oxford

[48] Russell, B., 1912, *The Problems of Philosophy*, Oxford University Press

[49] Soames, Scott, 1984, "What Is a Theory of Truth?" *Journal of Philosophy*, 81, 8: 411 – 429.

[50] Tarski, Alfred, 1933, "The Concept of Truth in Formalized Language." in *Logic, Semantics, Metamathematics*, tr. J. H. Woodger; 2nd edition, ed. J Corcoran, Hackett, 1983.

[51] Tarski, Alfred, 1944, "The Semantic Conception of Truth." In *Philosophy and Phenomenological Research*, 1944, IV, pp. 342 – 360.

[52] Williams, Michael, 1986, "Do We (Epistemologists) Need a Theory of Truth?" *Philosophical Topics*, 14, pp. 223 – 242.

[53] Wittgenstein, L., 1922, *Tractatus Logico-Philosophicus*, German text with an English translation by C. K. Ogden, Routledge and Kegan Paul.

不具形上意涵的语意学
米建国

台北东吴大学

　　摘　要：语意学和形上学是两个不同的学科，但很多哲学家却主张这两者之间有着紧密的关联性。语意学一般被视为是个语言学的科目，用来探讨语言文字的意义；形上学则是个哲学的传统学科，主要的工作在于揭露世界的本质，并描述其结构与基本元素。我们也许可以说语意学的主要标的在语言，而形上学的焦点则在这个世界。我们不难看出为什么这两个学科会如此紧密结合，毕竟，人类的语言和我们所认知的这个世界有着密不可分的关系。正因为如此，有些哲学家在面对语意学相关的主题时，总喜欢采取形上学的进路来讨论；而且当他们在建构一套哲学的语意理论时，也总是站在形上学的立场来铺陈。问题在于，这种处理方式经常会导致许多语意论与本体论之间的主题混淆与范围模糊。本文的目的，就是要揭发存在于语意学和形上学彼此之间的诸多混淆与模糊之处，并积极建议：我们其实可以成功地主张一种纯粹的语意理论，而不需要借助任何来自于形上学的观点，也不需要涉入任何形上学的争辩之中。我的主要计划是：建构一套纯粹语意学上的真理理论，而不需要立基于任何特定形上学的观点之上，同时我也将建议我们的语言如何重新面对这个世界的一种新模式。

　　关键词：语意学；形上学；真理理论

限定摹状词的指称性使用与语义学的边界[*]

◎ 任 远

中山大学

摘 要：限定摹状词的指称性使用和归属性使用的区分奠定了新指称理论的基础。对该区分是语义性质还是语用性质的区分之争论至今仍在持续。论文从考察限定摹状词的指称/归属区分的划界入手，比较了摹状词的指称性使用与说话者指称的概念，通过考察回指现象以及分析萨尔蒙和怀斯坦对于区分性质的争论，我们提出用彻底的索引词解释来分析摹状词的指称性使用中的语义行为，以消除描述论者和指称论者各自可能面临的理论困难。

关键词：限定摹状词；指称性使用；语义学；索引词

当唐纳兰（K. Donnellan）1966 年发表《指称与限定摹状词》时，许多论者最初不过把该文看做是罗素与斯特劳森之间有名论战的一个延伸，或至多看做是对指称理论的语用学转向的一次修正。不少著名哲学家尽管明确承认唐纳兰的这一区分给他们带来重要启示，同时亦指出这一区分并不像表面看上去的那样清晰，特别是在它与内涵语义学的联系上。卡普兰（D. Kaplan）曾经转引欣迪卡（J. Hintikka）的评论说："在唐纳兰的出色的文章中，我唯一能找到的东西是清楚地意识到下述事实：他谈论的区分仅仅在受命题态度词或其他的模态词项的约束的语境下才起作用。"卡普兰本人也同样抱怨："在初读和再读唐纳兰的文章时，我总发现它引人入胜又令人烦恼。它之所以引人入胜是因为这个基本的区分非常清楚地反映出对语言用法的一个准确的见识；之所以令人烦恼是因为……它对与正在发展的内涵逻辑的知识系统没有给出清楚的说明，因而我们不能立即看出唐纳兰和内涵逻辑能彼此提供给对方一些什么东西。"（[5]，p. 223）。

直到新指称理论的影响日益深入并最终成为晚期分析哲学运动的最重要思潮，唐纳兰这一工作的经典性才能得到完整的评价。《指称与限定摹状词》可以算作是整个新指称理论运动的

---

* 本文的初稿在第 5 届全国分析哲学会议（杭州）报告并发表于《自然辩证法研究》杂志 2009 年第 6 期，此处对初稿作出了一些补充和修改。感谢文集的匿名评审人的意见。

第一篇文献。限定摹状词的指称性使用和归属性使用的区分（以下简称"指称/归属区分"）的意义在于首先将摹状词通过描述性识别用以确定指称的功能和摹状词对于句子语义值的贡献区分开来。以后，克里普克在《命名与必然性》（1972）中的对于名称的分析、卡普兰在《论指示词》（1977）中对指示词和索引词的分析，几乎是分别在不同种类的指称表达式上重复了这一发现。

多年来英美哲学界对摹状词的指称/归属区分的究竟是语义区分还是语用区分的争论持续进行着。限定摹状词的指称归属区分之所以在后期分析哲学文献中引人注目，一方面是由于该区分讨论的是含有描述性内容的短语能在多大程度上像真正的单称词项那样贡献于句子的语义内容，因而在主题上成为指称理论的两个主要阵营，即描述理论和直接指称理论论战的中间地带；另一方面，它又与另一组争议更大的区分，即语义学和语用学区分的划界问题密切相关，后者的厘定对于澄清意义理论的限度至关重要。本文从考察限定摹状词的指称/归属区分的划界入手，比较了摹状词的指称性使用与说话者指称的概念，通过考察回指现象以及分析萨尔蒙（N. Salmon）和怀斯坦（H. Weetstein）对于区分性质的争论，我们尝试消除对摹状词的不同使用下的语义行为分析中的困难。

1. 摹状词两种使用的区分的划界

限定摹状词的指称/归属区分是通过对某些语言现象的观察提出的，典型的例子如在法庭上某旁观者感叹"杀害史密斯的凶手是疯狂的"，或在酒会上聊天者对同伴说出"那个喝马爹利酒的人看上去很高兴"。一般认为这类句子在特定语境下的陈说有两种不同的读法，即如唐纳兰所言："在某断言中归属性地使用限定摹状词的说话者，陈述具有如此这般特征的人或物的某些事情；另一方面，在某断言中指称性地使用限定摹状词的说话者，使用摹状词以使得听者能够挑选出他正在谈论的人或物，并且陈述有关该人或物的某些事情。"（〔2〕，p. 285）

直觉上，这一区分似乎是明显的。进一步，我们可以据此初步将限定摹状词的归属性使用的特点表述为：说话者心目中没有特定的独一无二的对象，而只有描述条件，句子中所讨论的对象就是满足摹状词的描述条件的对象，由此意味着，可以为包含摹状词的句子添加表达式"无论作为'the F'的 x 是什么"而不改变句子意义。另一方面，限定摹状词的指称性使用的特点似乎是：说话者心目中事先已有打算被指称的对象，而摹状词只是去完成这一指称对象功能的一件顺手的工具，这也意味着，摹状词含有的描述条件不一定需要适合被用来指称的对象。

但是，正如我们将要看到的，这样的概括虽然粗略刻画了这一区分的特征，但是并没有给我们提供一个有关指称/归属区分的明确标准，没有指明限定摹状词的处于指称性使用状况的边界条件。如果缺乏这一标准，我们就不能对下述关键问题作出回答，也即，在何种条件下，说话者即使没有将摹状词正确地应用于他所谈论的对象上，但他仍然就他所谈论的对象说出了某些真实的情况；换言之，在何种条件下，进入句子之成真条件的成分不是摹状词的内容或满足摹状词的对象。对这一问题的回答不但关乎唐纳兰对罗素和斯特劳森提出批评的初衷，更是后来三十余年围绕这一区分的性质的论争的肯綮所在。

限定摹状词的指称性使用和归属性使用之区分的提出，首先是由于某些语义或语用的现象分别出现在摹状词的不同场合的使用中，粗看上去，这些现象似乎可以成为指称/归属区分的标志，但对这些现象的进一步分析又往往模糊了这一区分的界限。例如，我们可以整理出与该区分有关的几个典型特征：

特征 1：是否存在着满足限定摹状词的对象，以及所谈论的对象是否要满足摹状词。

特征 2：限定摹状词的使用与说话者关于摹状词的信念的关系。

特征 3：包含限定摹状词的句子的成真条件是独立于还是依赖于摹状词中包含的描述性内容。

事实上，特征 1 和特征 2 虽然常常伴随着摹状词的指称/归属区分的现象，却不能构成检验摹状词处于哪种使用之中的判决性条件。唐纳兰在最初的论文中对这两个特征反复进行了考察。特征 3 似乎构成了指称/归属区分的本质性刻画。因为按照唐纳兰的说法，在归属性用法中，限定摹状词是"必不可少的"，而在指称性用法中，摹状词只是"工具"或"标签"。这意味着，在归属性用法中，摹状词的描述性内容构成了所在句子的成真条件的一部分；而在指称性用法中，摹状词的描述性内容对于所在句子的成真条件是无关的。我们在后文中将看到，正是这一观察，成为对指称/归属区分的性质的争论的焦点。

另一方面，上述特征亦为我们细致分析限定摹状词的指称/归属区分提供了参考。对摹状词的不同使用情况稍作分类，便可发现这一区分涉及的相关因素包括：1. 限定摹状词作为语言表达式的描述性内容；2. 限定摹状词的指谓或语义指称；3. 说话者头脑中所意图谈论的对象；4. 说话者意图使听者识别的对象；5. 说话者关于意图谈论的对象的知识和信念；6. 说话者和听者的公共知识，包括语言学知识和背景知识；7. 说话者说出的句子的命题内容或成真条件。唐纳兰提出的摹状词的指称/归属区分首先明确地将上述因素 2 和 3 或 2 和 4 区分开，但是因素 3 和 4 之间的区别在唐纳兰最初的表述那里却似乎是模糊的。另一方面，即使因素 2 和 4 一致，只要因素 3 存在，直觉上就会认为摹状词处于指称性使用之中。无论如何，是否指称/归属区分就可以归结为因素 2 和 3 或因素 2 和 4 的区分呢？对此问题的一个肯定回答正是克里普克的观点。

2. 说话者指称与摹状词的指称性使用

由于唐纳兰并未提供一个判定指称/归属区分的明确标准，因此该区分的提出尽管引起了广泛的重视，同时也有不少评论对它的实质提出质疑。这种情况下，克里普克在 1977 年的论文中声称，尽管唐纳兰发现的区分真实而重要，但这一语言现象却对罗素的摹状词理论并没有造成丝毫损害；进一步，克里普克提出语义指称和说话者指称的区分，试图代替指称/归属区分并突出该区分中的语用学意味。说话者指称和语义指称的区分是根据格赖斯的说话者意义和句子意义的区分进行推广而得到的。克里普克把语义指称定义为是由说话者在某个场合指称某个对象的一般意向所给出的、由言语里的某些约定或习规就可以确定的对象；而一个指示性词组的说话者指称，克里普克则定义为"说话者想要谈论，并且自以为它满足成为该指示词的语义指称而应具备的条件的那个对象"（［6］，p. 18），即说话者指称是说话者的特殊意向给出的。如果说话者相信他在某一场合下想谈论的对象满足成为语义指称的条件，就是相信其特殊意向和一般语义学意向之间没有矛盾。克里普克认为，说话者对于其特殊意向和一般语义学意向相一致的信念有两种产生方式。在简单情形下：说话者的特殊意向就是其一般语义学意向，因此说话者指称和语义指称是一致的；在复杂情形下，说话者的特殊意向可能不同于其一般语义学意向，即说话者指称和语义指称可能不一致，但是说话者自认为两者是一致的。克里普克于是断言，唐纳兰所说的归属性用法就是上述简单情形，而指称性用法就是上述复杂情形。克里普克进一步认为，这种区分不但适合摹状词也适合专名，因此唐纳兰是错误的，因为唐纳兰把指称性使用仅仅当做是摹状词的使用，认为在指称性使用下摹状词看上去就像逻辑专名。

说话者指称这一概念似乎比指称性使用有着更强的直观含义，但唐纳兰并不认可克里普克的批评。尽管唐纳兰肯定说话者指称的现象总是存在的，但他质疑指称/归属区分能否通过说话者指称和语义指称的区分来解释。唐纳兰认为，不能通过说话者在使用摹状词时是否伴随着关于满足摹状词的对象的信念来判断摹状词处于那种使用之中，因为如果是这样的话，"这种区分就没有语义方面的意义，以及极少言语行为理论方面的意义。因为特定言语行为总是伴随大量因素，包括信念、欲求和各种环境因素等。这样此区分在语言哲学中就没有任何位置"。（［4］，p. 48）进一步，说话者指称也不能等同于说话者头脑中的对象，这样的话就忽略了说话者唤起听者识别对象的意图，其后果就会导致麦凯（J. Makay）在 1968 年对唐纳兰的批评，即在指称表达式的使用中抬高说话者自己的意图而贬低所使用的实指表达式的重要性。说话者指称应当被理解成说话者意图使听者识别出的那个对象，即使说话者头脑中已经有了某个对象，但是如果他没有打算使听者识别出该对象，就不能认为说话者在指涉该对象。

克里普克的这一区分是否比唐纳兰的区分更为基本和有效？不少论者同意说话者指称是一个非常基本的概念，但是就限定摹状词而言，讨论其语义指称并不总是可行。例如，巴赫（K. Bach）指出，对于像"当今法国国王"这样的空摹状词，正如罗素的分析，它实质上被用作量化短语，因而并不存在着对包含该摹状词的句子所表达的命题作出语义贡献的语义指称。当罗素说摹状词的指谓时，他事实上并没有在语义的意义上用这个词，因为摹状词的指谓并未进入包含摹状词的命题。（［1］，p. 218）另一方面，正如里卡那提（F. Recanati）所指出的，唐纳兰的指称/归属区分中实际包含了两对相互独立之区分：（1）摹状词使用的识别性和非识别性区分，这一区分在于摹状词的使用在于提供信息还是确定指称；（2）说话者指称和语义指称的区分，这一区分的关键在于摹状词的指谓和说话者的使用之间是否存在分歧。（［9］，pp. 281－283）如此看来，说话者指称和语义指称的区分事实上只是指称归属区分的一部分，而且唐纳兰使用指称归属区分主要刻画的是识别/非识别的区分而不是说话者指称/语义指称的区分。

本文认为，事实上，唐纳兰提出的摹状词的指称性用法的确不能还原成克里普克的说话者指称。即使我们暂不区分说话者头脑中所意图谈论的对象（前述因素3）和说话者意图使听者识别的对象（前述因素4），而笼统地按照克里普克的说法，认为说话者指称就是为"说话者想要谈论，并且自以为它满足成为该指示词的语义指称而应具备的条件的那个对象"，我们也不能说摹状词的归属性使用就是语义指称和说话者指称总是一致的情形，而指称性使用就是语义指称和说话者指称有可能不一致的情形。这是由于，固然当（1）语义指称不存在（从而说话者指称肯定不同于语义指称）以及（2）说话者指称与语义指称都存在而不相同的情形，都可以典型地算作指称性使用；但是在某些情形下有可能说话者指称也不存在，例如在"杀害史密斯的凶手是疯狂的"这个例子中，假定说话者并不知道具体是谁杀害的史密斯，这时语义指称也不同于说话者指称，但此处明显是归属性使用。唐纳兰在后来的文章中认为，当有说话者指称在场时，限定摹状词出现的语境可称为"指称性语境"；否则，当说话者指称不在场时，称此时的语境为"归属性语境"（［4］，p. 52）。也即，说话者指称与语义指称的区分并不能涵盖指称/归属的区分，相反前者却能被后者所解释，于是唐纳兰的区分而不是克里普克的区分才是更基本的。同时还要注意到两者还有一个细微的差别，即唐纳兰所使用的说话者指称是指说话者意图使听者识别的对象，而克里普克的说话者指称则是指说话者头脑中所意图谈论的对象。

3. 回指现象与指称/归属区分

指称/归属区分与说话者指称/语义指称区分除了上述差别，两者还有可能是不同性质的区分。克里普克提出的区分无疑是语用性的，而唐纳兰提出的区分的性质则始终处于争议之中。唐纳兰本人对指称/归属区分之性质的态度也并非前后一贯。在最初的论文中唐纳兰曾明确指出这一区分"不是句法或语义区分，而是语用区分"，因为"两者语法结构是相同的……从而不是句法模糊性"，也不是"语词意义的模糊性"，这种模糊"可能是语用上的模糊性……是说话者意图的功能"（［2］，p. 297）。需要注意的是，唐纳兰此处把语义模糊性看成是"语词意义的模糊性"，这与通常文献中的用法（成真条件的模糊性）不同。然而在 1978 年的文章中，唐纳兰更为明确地意识到他与克里普克之间的分歧。他在文章开头即提出下述问题，"限定摹状词的两种使用是否为两种语义功能，其中一种摹状词传达了说话者指称另一种则没有；还是限定摹状词被用于两种不同的环境，其中一种伴随着说话者指称的现象，虽然并未对语义指称产生影响?"（［4］，p. 28）

所谓表达式的语义指称的含义是指表达式的指称可以通过表达式的语言学构成与语义规则（包括句法规则及语义指派的组合性原则）相结合来得到的。例如，通常限定摹状词的语义指称就是满足摹状词的描述性条件而得到的指称。回指现象被唐纳兰认为是支持"语义说"的典型语言现象，因为它是可以根据语义规则系统解释的语言现象。我们对比考虑下述句子：

（a）一个人不慌不忙地走上发言台。他的脸上带着微笑。

（b）一个人不慌不忙地走上发言台。这个人的脸上带着微笑。

（c）一个人不慌不忙地走上发言台。不慌不忙地走上发言台的这个人脸上带着微笑。

这组句子中，后一句的主词是前一句的主词（先行词）的回指。前一个子句的作用在于引入某个个体，而不仅仅是存在概括。第三句后一子句句首的摹状词的语义指称就是前面子句中引入的个体。在该例子中，即使走上发言台的那个人并非真的不慌不忙，后一句断定此人面带微笑仍然可以是真的。因此此回指摹状词所指涉的个体并不必须满足摹状词中包含的描述性信息。即使前面的子句是错误的，说话者也能够成功通过它来引入一个后面所要谈论的个体，并且后一子句关于该个体的断言仍然可以是真的。可以看出，唐纳兰试图据此说明两点：首先，回指现象类似于摹状词的指称性使用；其次，后一子句中的回指摹状词的指称是由前一个句子中说话者所谈论的个体语义性地决定的。这样，某个个体可以成为复指摹状词的语义指称，即使该个体并不满足摹状词的描述性条件。因此，说话者指称不能从语义指称中分离出来。

　　我们甚至可以把回指现象看做是摹状词指称性使用的推广情形，也即，摹状词的指称性使用是回指先行词缺省的回指现象。这样说的时候意味着在摹状词的指称性使用中一定有某个说话者意图使听者识别的对象在场（或潜在地在场）。回指先行词的作用就在于肯定这一点。对于其所包含的摹状词处于指称性使用情况中的句子"the F is G"而言，它实际上等价于说下述回指句"有个 F 在那里。这个 F 是 G"。其中前一个句子作用在于引入个体或确定指称，后一个句子在于对前面所引入的个体加以述谓或进行断定。直接引入的限定摹状词和通过回指引入的摹状词的差别在于：说话者是否期待和意欲听者识别出说话者头脑中的对象。如果说话者带有这样的意图，他就会使用直接引入的摹状词；如果说话者没有这样的意图，他就会选择通过非限定摹状词引入和回指连接引入的摹状词。但是，尽管有这种说话者意图上的差异，唐纳兰认为，直接引入和回指引入这"两种结构的限定摹状词在成真条件和语义指称方面没有实质差异。"（［4］，p. 40）

　　根据将直接引入的摹状词改写成回指引入，限定摹状词的两种功能，通过描述性识别以确定指称的功能和对所在句子贡献语义值的功能，就被分开了。如果这一改写是合理的，那么唐纳兰也就不但成功地将指称/归属区分的划界问题和性质问题区别开来，而且分别给予了回答。所谓指称/归属区分的划界问题，是明确给出判定限定摹状词处于何种使用之中的充要条件，或者给出类似于充要条件的刻画，此处的关键是需要指出两种不同的使用之中涉及不同的交流机制。所谓指称/归属区分的性质问题，是说明这一区分具有语义意义还是只是在语用层面上才有意义。也即，如果是这一区分是语义上的，则包含摹状词的句子在处于两种不同的用法时语义上表达了具有不同成真条件的两个不同命题；如果这一区分是语用层面上的，则包含摹状词的句子在两种不同用法时语义上仍然只表达了同一个命题，但在指称性使用时语用上蕴涵了另一个具有不同成真条件的命题。

　　一方面，唐纳兰显然注意摹状词指称/归属区分的要害是由于说话者意图造成的，并且认为说话者意图的差异被带入了句子的成真条件中（所谓"主观指称"的观点）；另一方面，唐纳兰又要表明的是，包含回指成分的句子语义表达了单称命题（所谓"语义区分"的观点）。正如有些论者所认为的，这给唐纳兰的理论带来了紧张因素：包含主观指称的命题是如何被语义表达的？我们将在第 5 节回答这一问题，在此之前先考察指称/归属区分的性质问题的一场争论。

4. 萨尔蒙与怀斯坦的论争

　　1970 年代末期到 1990 年代初期，由于卡普兰和佩里（J. Perry）等人的工作，语言哲学界对于指示词和索引词的理论重要性有了更多认识。不完全限定摹状词（如"这张桌子"）和指示词（如第一人称词项"我"）之间的对应关系也被发掘出来。正如泰勒（K. Taylor）后来的总结，两者至少在三个方面有明显的平行：（1）独立于语境、单凭语法指派的语义内容不足以决定表达式的唯一指称；（2）只有补充说话者的意图才能使得它们成功实现指称；（3）在指涉由语境确定的对象上，"这张桌子"具有与"我"类似的基于语法的可预期性。（［14］，p. 86）

由于指示词的语义行为是可以系统解释的，而限定摹状词的指称性使用与指示词的情况类似，这就为指称/归属区分的"语义说"提供了支持。语言哲学家怀斯坦正是用这样的思路来为唐纳兰的观点作辩护。他提出的核心论证我们在此可归纳为：（［15］，pp. 50 – 58）

（1）不完全限定摹状词的语义行为类似于指示词的语义行为。

（2）不完全限定摹状词是唐纳兰的限定摹状词的指称性使用的典型情形。并且，在日常使用中，不完全限定摹状词的情形比严格限定摹状词的情形要更为普遍。

（3）限定摹状词的归属性使用可以通过罗素式摹状词理论来分析其语义行为。

基于上述三点，于是得出：

（4）限定摹状词有双重语义功能：描述（或性质归属）功能和指称功能；分别对应两种语义行为：罗素式的（对应归属性使用）和指示词式的（对应指称性使用）。

（5）限定摹状词的指称/归属用法的区分正是两种语义功能的区分。

其中对上述（1）的论证又可以展开为下述三步：

（1a）存在着不完全限定摹状词的语言现象需要进行语义解释。

（1b）罗素式的对摹状词的归属性解释不能解释这一现象。特别的，罗素的摹状词理论不能解释不完全限定摹状词：如果把不完全限定摹状词解释成省略语境的限定摹状词，就会导致解释的不确定性，因为省略语境的方式可以是无穷的，但带有不定摹状词句子在相关语境下表达的命题却是确定的。

（1c）假定这类摹状词的语义行为具有指示性指称的功能就能解释这个现象。

怀斯坦的这一论证，特别是第一点，看上去没有什么问题。我们不妨用它来分析包含不完全限定摹状词的句子所表达的命题。假定布朗怀疑琼斯是凶手，并在语境 C 中说出了如下句子 S：这个凶手是疯狂的。那么布朗在语境 C 中表达的是某个单称命题"他（琼斯）是疯狂的"，还是一组具有意义"如此这般的凶手是疯狂的"的一般命题呢？按照怀斯坦的观点，限定摹状词在语义上类似于指示词，指示词是典型的直接指称词项，因此上述句子 S 表达的当然是前者。然而萨尔蒙却认为，布朗使用句子 S 在语境 C 中实际上是断言（assert）了一组松散的命题，既有上述单称命题，也有上述一般命题，但是并没有明确地因为断言了其中一个而排除其他；另一方面，句子 S 在语境 C 中并没有语义上表达（express）一个关于琼斯的单称命题"他是疯狂的"。在萨尔蒙看来，怀斯坦的错误就在于从在语境 C 中布朗断言一个单称命题，推出在语境 C 中布朗表达了该单称命题。这即是说，怀斯坦把说话者断言的内容（言语行为的内容）和语义内容混为一谈。说话者断言的内容和语义内容的真实关系应该是：某人在一个适当的语境下说出某个句子，从这个句子的语义内容为 p 可以典型地衍推出说话者断言了 p，但反之不然。

在重构怀斯坦的论证后，萨尔蒙一般性地总结了怀斯坦在使用下述语义内容推理模式时所面临的方法论问题：说话者 A 在语境 C 中使用表达式 E 表达了概念 K，因此，E 将 K 作为其语义内容在语境 C 中表达出来。这种推理模式正是萨尔蒙所批评的"语用谬误"："语用谬误体现了下述观念，如果特定表达式的使用实现了某种说话者以言行事的目的，那么这一目的必定刻画了相对于说话者语境的表达式的语义功能"。（［12］，p. 91）所谓表达式的语义功能，包括语句的语义内容，语句的真假、指称表达式的语义指谓等。例如，如果我们根据某说话者 A 在语境 C 中使用句子 S 正确说出了某事，就断定 S 在语境 C 中是语义真的，在萨尔蒙看来，那就是犯了"语用谬误"。

萨尔蒙对怀斯坦的批评再一次把问题凸显出来，限定摹状词的指称性使用到底是摹状词的语义功能还是一种言语行为？相应地，摹状词使用的指称/归属区分到底是语义区分还是语用区分？对这些问题的回答必定要求我们进一步回答：包含有限定摹状词的句子在不同语境中究竟表达了何种命题？

5. 不同使用下的限定摹状词的语义行为

我们可以采用尼尔（S. Neale）的表述，把那些认为指称/归属区分看做是语用区分的论者（如罗素和格赖斯理论的支持者）称为描述论者，而把这一区分看做是语义区分的论者（如唐纳兰及其支持者）称为指称论者（［8］，p. 85）。无论是描述论者还是指称论者，都认同下述论题：说话者 A 在某个"the F is G"的陈说 u 中指称性地使用限定摹状词"the F"当且仅当存在某个对象 a，使得说话者 A 通过陈说 u 意指 a 是 F 且 a 是 G；也即双方都承认如下两点：（1）存在着对象 a 是说话者用摹状词所意图指称的对象；（2）说话者认为该对象 a 满足摹状词 F。

但是描述论者除此之外，还认为罗素的摹状词理论适合分析任何含有限定摹状词"the F"的句子的语义结构，"the F"仍然（和在归属性使用中一样）用作量词，句子"the F is G"的语义结构可由［μx：Fx］（Gx）给出。也即，描述论者会认为，在限定摹状词的指称性使用中：

（D1）限定摹状词在句子中用作量化短语；

（D2）包含限定摹状词的句子语义表达的是一般性命题（或不依赖于对象的命题）。

事实上，尼尔本人就是描述论者，他认为不仅对于限定摹状词"F"，短语"some F"和"every F"也都可以有指称性使用。（［8］，p. 88）尼尔认为，包含限定摹状词的句子可以用于交流依赖于对象的命题不应导致我们对限定摹状词的语义分析的复杂化（始终应遵守奥卡姆剃刀原则），因此罗素的分析已经够了。

反之，根据指称论者的观点，如果说话者 S 在某个"the F is G"的陈说 u 中指称性地使用限定摹状词"the F"，那么"the F"并非用作量词，并且 u 所表达的命题不是描述性的。也即，指称论者会认为，在限定摹状词的指称性使用中：

（R1）限定摹状词在句子中用作真正的指称表达式；

（R2）包含限定摹状词的句子语义表达的是单称命题（或依赖于对象的命题）。

总之，指称论者认为依赖对象的那个命题是被说话者使用的句子语义表达的（论题 R2），而描述论者则认为该命题只是在特定情境中被语用蕴涵的，含有限定摹状词的句子语义表达的命题是一个独立于对象的命题（论题 D2）。此外，描述论者和指称论者对于限定摹状词的归属性使用的看法当然是一致的，即罗素的摹状词理论是适当的，摹状词此时被用作量化短语。由于描述论者并不在语义层面区分摹状词的两种使用，也即，描述论者认为无论哪种情况下摹状词的语义行为都是一致的，即使有不同情况也无须通过语义来解释。于是对限定摹状词的指称/归属区分之性质的断定的关键就在于，在限定摹状词的指称性使用中，（1）摹状词在句子中用作量化短语还是真正的指称表达式；（2）含有摹状词的句子语义表达的是独立于对象的命题还是依赖于对象的命题。并且，按照通常的看法，这两点实际上是一回事，肯定其中一个也就相应可推出另一个。

前已论及，按照唐纳兰后期坚持指称/归属区分是语义区分的观点，就必须回答下述问题：包含主观指称的命题是如何被语义表达的？而克里普克也曾指出，说话者的意图可能偏离我们的语言习规，从而使得句子的语言学意义不同于说话者意图传达的命题。唐纳兰提出区分的其中一个动机就在于认为，在说话者说出句子"the F is G"时，即使说话者意图所指的对象不满足 F 而唯一满足 F 的对象亦不是 G 时，说话者也说出了某种为真的东西，根据唐纳兰，这恰恰就是句子所语义表达的单称命题。因此指称论者这里实际要说明的是，限定摹状词的语言学意义并没有进入其所在句子所语义表达的命题。

就这一点而言，索引词的语义行为与之类似。根据卡普兰式的二维语义学，含有索引词和指示词这类语境敏感的直接指称表达式的句子，其语言学意义和其所语义表达的命题是不同的。

语言学意义必须结合语境才得到句子所表达的命题，而包含索引词的句子语义表达的命题也是单称命题。按照指称论者的理解，在限定摹状词的指称性使用中，摹状词所指涉的对象也是通过语境确定的。但是，这种情况下，摹状词和索引词确定指称对象的方式仍然是迥然有异的：前者主要是借助说话者的主观意图，后者主要是通过语言学习规。只有当说话者的主观指称恰好满足所使用的摹状词时，才能说是通过摹状词的指称是通过语言学意义确定的。

因此关键就在于，如果按照对摹状词在指称性使用中的索引词解释，此时对于句子"the F is G"所语义表达的单称命题，进入命题成分的对象是主观指称还是由摹状词的语言学意义确定的对象。当两者一致时，这是容易处理的。例如雷默（M. Reimer）在 1990 年代末期的一篇论文中就提出，如果说话者所意图的指称对象满足所使用的限定摹状词时，那么形如 the F is G 的句子的陈说就表达了一个单称命题。但是雷默认为，当这个条件不满足时，尽管对话双方也可能交流了一个单称命题，但该句子并没有表达任何（单称的或一般的）命题。（［11］，p. 98）本文认为，这种看法将破坏我们对索引词解释的一致性，因为按照这种观点，存在着一些语法正确和用法清晰但没有明确语义的指称型语句。同样以索引词对比举出例子，假使某人在说"我在喝酒"时发生口误，说话者的意图本来是要指你在喝酒，此时我们认为这个句子仍然有意义地表达了某个单称命题，尽管它实际交流的可能是另一个命题。

因此，只要我们坚持摹状词在指称性使用时具有类似于索引词的语义行为，就必须承认即使在说话者误用摹状词的情况下，即主观指称并不满足摹状词的语言学意义时，相关句子也仍然语义表达了某个单称命题。当主观指称或说话者所意图的指称对象不满足所使用的限定摹状词时，显然不能认为句子语义表达的命题包含主观指称作为其成分，因为这将要求语义学与说话者在具体语境下的意图联系在一起，后者典型地属于语用学的范围。既然主观指称不能成为候选者，进入命题成分的只能是满足摹状词语言学意义的那个对象。

于是本文的解决方案可以小结如下，我们提出对指称性使用下的限定摹状词的语义行为作彻底的索引词解释，根据这种解释，在限定和非限定摹状词的指称性使用中，摹状词先是被说话者用于确定指称对象，但说话者使用的包含该摹状词的句子的成真条件却并不包含该摹状词的描述性内容，而是直接包含着满足摹状词的对象。一方面，不同于描述论者，我们认为包含摹状词的句子此时语义表达的是单称命题而不是可以分析成量化句的一般命题。另一方面，不同于传统的指称论者及温和的索引论者，我们认为进入该单称命题成分的对象不是主观指称而是满足摹状词的对象（因此这时摹状词的语义行为和索引词完全相同），而包含主观指称的命题此时是被语用交流而不是语义表达的命题（这一点上本文和描述论者的观点一致）。

这里可能存在的一个困难是，当情境中事实上没有对象满足摹状词时，相应的句子的成真条件似乎既不是一般命题（如描述论者的观点那样），也不是包含着主观指称的单称命题（如指称论者的观点那样）。这里面临的困难和直接指称论者在讨论空名时的困难是类似的。直接指称论者通常认为，包含空名的句子在语义上或者没有表达任何命题，或者表达的是间隙命题（gappy propositions）。我们在这里也可以采取类似的策略：当语境中没有满足摹状词的对象，从而使得摹状词缺乏语义指称时，相关的句子语义上没有表达任何命题（或表达了一个间隙命题），但在语用上蕴涵了一个单称命题。这里和雷默的立场是非常接近的，但雷默是用主观指称是否满足摹状词来作为相关的句子是否语义上表达了一个命题的衡量标准，而本文认为主观指称与一个句子语义表达的命题没有任何关系。

因此，我们的方案既保留了唐纳兰提出指称/归属区分时的直觉，即在指称性使用时，摹状词的描述内容是与所在句子的成真条件无关的；又对指称论者面临的难题给予了否定的回答，即包含主观指称的命题并不能够被语义表达。同时我们还希望维护关于语义/语用区分的一种直觉，即无论在摹状词的哪种使用中，一个句子语义所表达的命题总是由相对稳定的语言学习规决定的，而与说话者的意图无关。因此，根据彻底的索引词解释，限定摹状词的指称/归属区分仍然是一种语义区分，限定摹状词在指称性使用和归属性使用时分别具有两种不同的语义行为，这可以由索引词具有的二维语义特征获得解释。

参考文献

［1］Bezuidenhout, Anne and Reimer, Marga. (eds.), 2004, *Descriptions and Beyond*, Oxford：Oxford University Press.

［2］Donnellan, Keith, 1966, Reference and Definite Descriptions. *Philosophical Review* 75：pp. 281 – 304. (中译："指称与限定摹状词"，弁博译，载于《语言哲学》，［美］马蒂尼奇编，商务印书馆，1998 年 2 月出版，第447—474 页。)

［3］Donnellan, Keith, 1968, Putting Humpty Dumpty Together Again. *Philosophical Review* 77.2：pp. 203 –215.

［4］Donnellan, Keith, 1978, Speaker Reference, Descriptions and Anaphora. In *Syntax and Semantics*. Vol. 9. Ed. Peter Cole. NY：Academic, pp. 47 – 68.

［5］Kaplan, David. Dthat, 1978, In *Syntax and Semantics*. Vol. 9. Ed. Peter Cole. NY：Academic, pp. 221 – 243. (中译："论指示词的指示性用法"，韩林合译，载于《语言哲学》，［美］马蒂尼奇编，商务印书馆，1998 年 2 月出版，第608—635 页。)

［6］Kripke, Saul, 1977, Speaker's Reference and Semantic Reference. In *Midwest Studies in Philosophy* 2：pp. 255 –276. (中译："说话者指称与语义性指称"，弁博译，载于《语言哲学》，［美］马蒂尼奇编，商

务印书馆，1998 年 2 月出版，第 475—516 页）

[7] MacKay, A. F. , 1968, Mr Donnellan and Humpty Dumpty on Referring. *Philosophical Review*, 77: 197 – 202

[8] Neale, Stephen, 1990, *Description*. Cambridge MA: MIT Press.

[9] Recanati, François, 1993, *Direct Reference: From Language to Thought*, Oxford: Blackwell.

[10] Reimer, Marga, 1997, Wettstein/Salmon Debate. *Pacific Philosophical Quarterly*, 79: 130 – 151.

[11] Reimer, Marga, 1998, Donnellan's Distinction/Kripke's Test. *Analysis*, 58 (2): 89 – 100.

[12] Salmon, Nathan, 1991, The Pragmatic Fallacy. *Philosophical Studies*, 63 (1): pp. 83 – 97.

[13] Searle, John, 1969, *Speech Acts*. Cambridge: Cambridge University Press.

[14] Taylor, Kenneth, 1997, *Truth and Meaning*. Blackwell Publishers.

[15] Wettstein, Howard, 1991, *Has Semantics Rested on a Mistake*? Stanford University Press.

The Referential Use of Definite Descriptions and the Boundary of Semantics
Yuan Ren

Sun Yat-sen University

Abstract: The distinction between the referential use and attributive uses of definite descriptions lays the foundation for the new theory of reference. The debate on whether this distinction is semantic or pragmatic continues to the present day. This paper firstly compares the referential use of descriptions with the notion of speaker's reference. Then we examine the relation between anaphora and distinction. In order to understand the key point of the nature of the distinction, we discuss the debate between Salmon and Wettstein. Based on these analyses, we put forward a radical indexical account of the referential use of definite descriptions to avoid the shortcomings of available accounts.

Keywords: definite descriptions; referential use; semantics; indexical

概念的合用及合用度

——以维特根斯坦《哲学研究》为视角

◎ 陈常燊

中国社会科学院

摘　要：概念考察是分析哲学的重要任务。后期维特根斯坦结合"语言游戏"、"生活形式"、"样本与实指"等探讨了日常语言的概念问题，在《哲学研究》中不仅提出"家族相似"的思想，还对概念的合用性及合用度问题有过精彩的表述。概念的合用性与语言游戏、生活形式等相互纠缠、紧密相联；概念的模糊性与精确性一样，与合用性有着内在的联系；概念的合用性优先于其精确性，亦即真正合用的概念不是在绝对意义上多么清晰和精确的概念，而是相对于概念所生长于其中的语言游戏和生活形式而言足够精确、清晰的概念；一个概念的合用度是该概念处于合用状态时的最恰当的精确度，而非在绝对意义上的最高精确度；如果一个概念具有最高的合用度，我们就认为它的清晰度或精确度正处于一个相对的最佳点。

关键词：维特根斯坦；日常语言；概念分析；合用性；合用度

本文结合语言游戏、生活形式、家族相似、样本与实指、意义的使用论等维特根斯坦后期哲学的重要理论，阐释和引申《哲学研究》中关于概念的合用及合用度的思想。试图表明：概念的合用性与上述核心概念之间相互纠缠、紧密相联；概念的模糊性①与精确性一样，与合用性有着内在的联系；概念的合用性优先于其精确性：足够清晰和精确的概念不是在绝对意义上多么清晰和精确的概念，而是相对于概念所生长于其中的语言游戏和生活形式而言合用的概念；如果一个概念具有最高的合用度，我们就认为它的清晰度或精确度正处于一个相对的最佳点。

1. 概念的模糊性、家族相似与合用

自然语言中大量出现这样的情况：同一个语词所指代的概念在不同的语境或语言游戏

---

① "模糊性"一词可以在不同的层面上取得含义，比如通常的意义上、科学的意义上、逻辑的意义上，评判概念之模糊性也可以有经验的标准，抑或逻辑的标准。本文基于日常语言分析，在日常意义上、以经验标准界定"模糊性"概念。

（Sprachspiel，language-game）中，其含义可以相差很远，它或者被精确地使用着，或者被模糊地使用着。例如，"多"就是这样的一个语词：在几何学上，当我们说"这是一个多边形"时，这里的"多"确切地指平面图形的边数≥4①；在日常生活中，当我们说"她朋友很多"时，这里的"多"就无法用一个精确的数字表示出来。不难看出，在相对的意义上，"多"的日常语言用法比数学（科学）语言用法模糊了许多。维特根斯坦把清晰、精确的概念和模糊的概念分别比作一幅清晰的图画和另一幅模糊的图画，同时认为，"清晰的图画与模糊的图画在何种程度上**能够**相似取决于后者的模糊程度。"（PI，§77）这就是说，对于各领域使用同一个语词 W 的情况，语词 W 在 A 语言游戏里所代表的较清晰的概念与在 B 语言游戏里所代表的较模糊的概念之间，到底存在多大的相似性，这取决于后者的模糊程度。当后者模糊到一定程度后，我们就面临着这样一个困境：这两个概念之间的相似性到底何在？这种困境在人文领域最容易出现，"举例来说，在美学或伦理学里寻找与我们的概念对应的定义，你的处境就是这样的"（PI，§77）。

既然我们难以在语词 W 所代表的较为清晰的与较为模糊的概念之间找出明显的相似处——无法为后者划定一个清晰的边界，那我们又为何都使用同一个语词 W 来指代这两个概念呢？这归根结底是要问："我们究竟是如何**学会**这个词（如"好"）的含义的？通过什么例子？通过哪些语言游戏？"（PI，§77）这些问题让我们联想到，维特根斯坦从试图追问各式各样游戏的共同之处出发，引领我们走进了一个个由同一个语词 W（如"游戏"、"数"）的各种含义组成的家族，各个概念家族有一个共同之处：并不存在一个共同的性质贯穿于其中的所有概念之中，而是这些概念处于一种"两两相似"的家族相似（Familienähnlichkeiten，family resemblances）关系中。家族相似中的"家族"就是由相同或近似语词在各种语言游戏（我们在不同生活场景中玩不同的语言游戏）所代表的一群在各自语言游戏中合用的概念所组成的一个家族。在维特根斯坦看来，对于诸如"游戏"、"数"、"语言"这些重要概念来说，用"家族相似"来表达它们所包含的诸外延概念（如各种游戏）之间的各种相似性质来说，是最好的方式。具备家族相似性质的概念当然远不止这些。② 这些概念都有一个特点：其自身的界线是模糊的。这种模糊性既体现在内涵上，也体现在外延上，它至少有两层含义：1）内部的模糊性，即同一概念内部诸外延（包括下层概念和专名）之间的分界线是模糊的；2）外部的模糊性，即不同概念

---

① 也有认为多边形至少是五条边的，但无论最少四条边还是五条边，"多边形"在数学上都是一个相对清晰和精确的概念。

② 本文暂不讨论以下问题：维特根斯坦是认为只有诸如游戏、数、语词这类概念具备家族似性质呢，还是推而广之认为所有的概念都具备这种性质？甚至认为诸如"摩西"这样的专名也是家族相似的？

之间的界线也是模糊的。这里值得注意的是，"模糊"这个概念本身也是模糊的，说一个概念具有模糊性意味着一种相对性：既相对于其他（或者更清晰，或者更模糊，或者差不多模糊）概念，又相对于这个概念使用的语境——语言游戏。

在《哲学研究》第 71 节，维特根斯坦用反问的语气指出：1）并不是在任何情况下，用一张清晰的照片代替一张模糊的照片都会更好些；2）不清晰的照片经常正是我们所需要的照片。这表明，清晰的图画与模糊的图画都可以是合用的（或者是更好的，或者是更需要的，等等）。"合用的（brauchbar，usable）"一词在《哲学研究》里，指一个概念相对于它用于其中的语言游戏和生活形式（Lebensform，a form of life）而言的一种合适的用法。这里的"合用性（usability）"与通常所说的"有用性（usefulness）"区别至少在于，前者相对于概念的清晰、精确与模糊程度与作为其背景的语言游戏与生活形式是否匹配而言，后者则侧重强调概念的实用目的。按照维特根斯坦，一个概念之所以合用，不在于它有多么精确或清晰，而在于我们拿它做语言游戏时，用起来很合适，很顺手。① 各式概念处于不同的合用状态——试想想有时清晰的照片更合用些，有时模糊的照片更合用些——决定了处于同一家族的概念之间，只会相似，不会相同。同时也要提请注意，"照片"这个概念里虽然经常用来指称清晰的照片，但这个概念本身是模糊的。

从具有家族相似性质的概念并非单纯追求精确和清晰来看，它们是模糊的概念，但也是合用的概念。适当的模糊正如充分的清晰一样，它与合用似乎有一种天然的联系。在《哲学研究》第 79 节，维特根斯坦举例道：假设 N 是我的一个朋友，当你问到在"N"这个名下我所理解的是什么，我会列举这些描述：i）我曾经在某某地方见过；ii）看上去是某某样子（有照片为证）；iii）做过某某事情；iv）在社交圈子里用"N"这个名字。诸如此类。有一天我说"N死了"，意思是说符合以上描述的那个 N 死了。但问题是：如果上述描述中的一条或几条后来被证明不成立，那么是否就足以否证"N死了"这个陈述呢？或许你会说，其中的某些描述比别外一些描述对我定义 N 这个人更为重要或根本，只有这些最核心的陈述被证伪了，才足以反驳道：我所说的"N死了"是个假陈述。对此，维特根斯坦反驳道：你说某些描述比另一些描述重要，那"轻重"的界线又在哪里？或许我们并没有这样的界线：原则上，任何一个或几个陈述为假，都不足以证伪我这个"N死了"的陈述。当然，和我作出的其他陈述一样，"N死

---

① 显然，合用性与精确性，属于两个不同的标准，并且出于两个不同的目的；同时，不能用合用性否定概念的精确性。合用的概念并非必定不精确，因为在一定的语境中，精确的概念同样也可是合用的概念。合用性的标准恰恰在于概念取得了恰当的精确性。

了"也可能是假陈述。为了能使我对 N 的理解处于自洽状态，我会适时地修正某些陈述——修证我对 N 的理解。总之，"我不在固定含义上使用名称 N"。试设想，如果我在固定的（比如在其中第 i）条描述）意义上使用名称 N，会导致什么后果呢？1）如果该描述被证伪了，那我用 N 所指称的那个人是不存在的——实际上，我与 N 已经是多年的朋友了；这样，2）我不得不再为 N 找一个固定的描述，因而仍然避免不了类似于 1）的问题。这并不符合我生活中的实际情况：我对 N 的理解是建立在一系列的陈述上面的，尽管我随时可能修证这些陈述，但 N 对于我来说，始终是存在的。这个例子表明，在某个固定含义上使用 N 这个名称，精确倒是精确了，但其实并不合用；N 这个名称模糊如果不在固定含义上使用，模糊是模糊了点儿，但更加合用。进一步不难引申出，在某些情形中，相对模糊的概念，有可能是更为合用的概念。①

2. 概念的精确与合用

针对可能存在这样的反驳："模糊的概念竟是一个概念吗？"维特根斯坦回答道：模糊的概念不仅可以是一个概念——比如"游戏"就是这样一个概念——还可以是一个相当合用的概念。在《哲学研究》第 71 节，他举例道，诸如"这边"、"那边"这些表示方位的概念无疑是相当模糊的，但这并不意味着：我对站在广场上离我稍远处的另一个人说"你就停在那边"就毫无意义。尽管这时我不会划出任何界限，而只是随手作了一个指点的动作，这个动作所指的位置显然不是非常精确的——你可能会说，它大致是精确的，请你别忘了"大致"恰恰是一个提示模糊性的概念。在这种语言游戏中，"这边"、"那边"获得了适当的使用。假设我们精确地规定：所谓"这边"指的是离我 10 米之内的位置，"那边"指的是离我 10 米之外的位置，那会导致什么后果？这意味着：如果我们打算使用这两个方位词，必须随身携带一把皮尺和一支粉笔，在使用它们之前，做好仔细的测量和记号。这时，"这边"、"那边"已经变成两个很不合用，甚至没法用的概念——在许多情况下，精确的测量和记号都无法做到。这个例子进而表明，本该模糊的概念，一旦人为地精确化之后，反而成为一个不合用的概念。关于模糊的概念也可以是很合用的概念，维特根斯坦还举了一个例子：

但若游戏的概念是这样没有界限的，那你就不知道用"游戏"意谓的究竟是什

---

① 对于概念来说，只有它们被界定得充分清晰时，才是合用的。但这里的"充分清晰"并不意味着一味地越清晰越好，因为在某些情形中，单纯追求清晰、精确会使得概念变得不合用。

么。——我描述说：植物覆盖了这整片地面。——你会说我如果不能给"植物"下个定义，我就不知道自己在说什么吗？（PI，§70）

也许"植物"对我而言是一个模糊的界定，尽管不精确，但已经够用了，合用了。

其实怎么样才算"精确"，本身就是一个问题。就上面那个例子来说，如果对方不明白我说的"那边"的具体位置，我就可以走过去，指着脚下一小块地方，对他解释道："你差不多就站在这儿！"这种解释比在远方用手一指是精确多了，然而也谈不上有多么精确。对此，维特根斯坦在《哲学研究》第88节进行了分析：

"但难道这个解释不是不够精确的？"——是的，干吗不可以说它"不精确"？可我们先得明白"不精确"的含义是什么。因为在这里它的含义可不是"不合用"。让我们考虑一下，相对于这个解释，我们把什么称为"精确"的解释。也许是用粉笔线画出来的一个区域？这时我们立刻想到线是有宽度的。那么，粉笔线颜色的边界要更精确些。但这种精确在这里还有什么作用？岂非无的放矢？而且我们还没有确定什么才算越过了这条鲜明的界线，用什么方式什么仪器来确定。等等。

维特根斯坦的意思大概是，1）我们不可能制定出一个衡量概念精确性的理想标准，正如他自己所说："从来没有规定出精确性的唯一理想；我们不知应该怎样来想象这种理想——除非你自己设定应该把什么称作这个理想。"（PI，§88）也就是说，概念的精确性总是相对的。2）概念的精确与合用之间，并不存在必然的联系：比如在这个例子中，不精确的概念反倒合用。

说话为了让对方领会，我们经常不得不界定一些概念，使它们更为精确和清晰。上面那个例子就说明了这种情况。这种出于顺利交流的目的就是合用的目的。我们为了一个概念更加合用，经常要对概念做精确化和清晰化的工作——有时通过定义，有时通过行为，但无论通过什么方式，都发生在语言游戏之中。的确，过于模糊的概念有时会影响我们使用。例如，你对我说："请给你买一些苹果回来！"我立刻就会问你："你要买几斤？"从"一些"到"斤"的概念变换过程就是概念精确化、清晰化的过程。在某些情况下，我还要再问你："你要的是上好的苹果，还是普通价位的？"或者"你是要'红富士'吗？"这是对你使用的"苹果"这个概念进一步澄清或精确化。显然，我这样问出于生活上方便、合用的目的。

如果我们原来有这样的疑惑：概念必须越精确越好吗？现在就可以这样回答：由于过于精确的概念未必合用，因此对于一个概念来说，合用性要求优先于精确性要求。泛泛地说界定一个概念是为了追求清晰和精确，这没有问题。但同时不能忘记，之所以要追求清晰和精确，是要服务于合用这一宗旨。同样的道理，定义是使得概念的含义清晰化精确化的一项活动，但按照维特根斯坦，定义的目标根本不在于刻意地、理想化地追求清晰精确，而在于寻求概念的合用状态。定义本身就是合用的工具，"清晰"、"精确"这些定义的标准也是合用的工具，除却了这些语言游戏的合用性来谈定义的清晰和精确，还有什么意义呢？一方面，我们或许要说，脱离了概念由以生长的土壤——特定生活形式中的语言游戏，概念自身是无所谓清晰不清晰、精确不精确的，之所以要把某些概念清晰化、精确化，就在于我们想要把它们做得更为合用。另一方面，为了合用的目的，概念才需要被清晰化、精确化，但不能因为合用的需要而否认清晰化、精确化的需要，这两者根本上并不冲突。

3. 合用的概念：对特定语言游戏和生活形式而言足够精确、清晰的概念

经常会有类似这样的问题困惑我们：为什么我们可以清晰精确地定义矩形，而对于正义这个概念，我们却深感难以做到这一点呢？仔细想想不难发现，其实生活中的许多事情都容不得整齐划一的定义。这里借用一个《哲学研究》中的例子。我们发现"步"这个量词所指称的对象是非常不精确的：它究竟表示多少厘米呢？假定我们规定一步 =75 厘米，那么高个子一步迈出 100 厘米，矮个子一步迈出 50 厘米，我们会说：前者迈出了 $1\frac{1}{3}$ 步，后者迈出了 $\frac{2}{3}$ 步吗？维特根斯坦写道：

> 我们可以划出一个界限——为一个特殊的目的。但划出界线才使这个概念合用吗？根本不是。除非是对于那个特殊的目的。就像用不着给出"一步 =75 厘米"这个定义才使"一步"这个长度单位变得合用。你要愿意说："但在这之前它不是一个精确的长度单位"，我就会回答说：好吧，它是一个不精确的长度单位。——但你还欠我关于"精确"的定义。（PI，§69）

尽管我们很难为"清晰"、"精确"这些程度形容词或程度副词作出一个绝对清晰、精确的定义，但也许没人会否认一米比一步更精确，矩形的概念比正义的概念更为清晰。这就足够了。我们的确需要一个足够清晰和精确的概念。然而，什么叫做一个"足够地"清晰和精确的概念呢？用维特根斯坦的话来说就是：合用的概念。他认为，界定一个概念，其特殊目的就是为了合用。对他来说，足够清晰和精确的概念不是在绝对意义上多么清晰和精确的概念，而是相对

于概念所生长于其中的语言游戏和生活形式而言合用的概念。

这又是为何呢？可以这么说，在原则上，我们完全可以把"一步"与"一米"界定得同样精确，把"正义"和"矩形"定义得同样清晰。难道即便纯粹从理论上说，我们也做不到这点吗？你也许会说，一个数学家得出的对矩形的定义容易得到其他数学家一致认可，但一个哲学家对何谓"正义"的定义很难——甚至根本不可能——得到所有其他哲学家的普遍接受。对此我是这么看的：之所以会导致这种情况，就在于人们出于"合用"的标准去看待每一个定义，而不在于有一些概念原本就无法清晰地被定义。矩形被清晰地定义了，人们（包括数学家）觉得它合用；若以同样的标准为"正义"给出一个"清晰的"的定义，人们（至少是哲学家）会觉得它不合用，因此就无法有一个大家一致认可的关于"正义"的"清晰的"定义。或许你要问，我们为什么就不能清晰地定义"正义"呢？想想为什么我们无法精确地定义一步的距离吧。假设我们把一步精确地界定为 75 厘米，那么只要我们迈步一走，就可能出现以下情况：

第一步迈出 63/75 步，第二步迈出 73/75 步，第三步迈出 51/75 步……

这种情况意味着什么呢？不难看出，我们在说出"第一步"和"63/75 步"时，都用了"步"这个词，但实际上我们无法将它们看做同一个概念。只要概念无法维持其自身的同一性，势必会有另一个语词来承担这种分殊，只有这样，才会避免因概念歧义而导致的不便。在这个例子中，我们或者可以发明另一个类似于"米"这么精确的长度单位来取代"63/75 步"中的"步"，或者我们找出一个其功用类似于"第一步"中的"步"的词——比如古语中的"不积跬步，无以至千里"（《荀子·劝学》）中的"跬"——来代替这个"步"。"正义"的概念也是如此。假设第一个使用"正义"概念的哲学家规定，"正义"在我这里的用法是其唯一的定义——这还得保证这个概念在他那里就是那么精确、清晰地使用的，并且取得了类似法律那样的独家解释权，那只会导致一种后果：任何一位后来的哲学家，如果要表示一个其含义与前人的"正义"多少有些相似的概念，不得不再另找一个词——最好是发明一个从未有人用过的新词。这种新造生词或老词新用彻底泛滥的情况，并不符合概念或语词的经济化原则，也不利于思想的交流和学术的发展。

如果说概念往往需要一定程度的模糊性才合用的话，那么精确、清晰如"矩形"这样的概念，怎么就合用了呢？"矩形"原本就是一个理想的定义，一个纯理论的意义。想想：现实中没有一个完全符合定义的矩形物件。由同一套概念系统所理解的世界是连续的。"矩形"和"正义"的定义的清晰度和精确度之间，并没有绝对清晰的分界线。从理论上看，我们可以同时把"矩形"和"正义"清晰和精确到任何一个程度，但我们在现实中未必能找到严格符合我们定义的矩形和正义。显然，这样经过任意精确化之后的概念，是没法用的。高度精确的概念并非只为实用的目的，而是为研究的目的，为认识的目的，我们所说的"合用"并非只在实用层面上而言，更重要的是人们通过概念把握世界的目的。

我们经常对概念进行划分——或许你要说，概念的分叉是概念自身在生活土壤中自然生成而非人为划分的结果，确实不易回答穷人／富人是人为的划分还是自然长成的分别——自然长成的，肯定是合用的，因为"自然长成"和"合用"都以特定的生活形式为座基；人为划分也并不是任意的，而同样要结合实际需要，以合用性为原则。试想想：把人划分为男人女人，至少在大多数情况下，比把人划分为出生月份是奇数还是偶数更合用，更有意义。概念的二分、三分或 N 分，是概念精确化清晰化的努力，我们会有各式各样的划分依据，合用则是划分依据的依据：显然我们是以某种合用性为原则进行划分的。科学上的分类也许不是出于实用的目的，而是出于更好的认识和研究，但我们把合用性当做概念精确到或清晰到何种程度才更好地被认识和被研究的一个标准。

整个概念系统是镶嵌在语言游戏和生活形式中的，对一个具体的语言游戏来说，过于精确或过于模糊的概念，都不是在生活上合用的概念。假设有这样一个概念系统，其中的所有概念都无比地精确、清晰，可以想象，这个概念系统所能匹配的语言游戏和生活形式一定与现实世界中已有的语言游戏和生活形式相距甚远。

4. 合用度：概念处于合用状态时的最佳精确度

上面说过，对一个概念的精确性的追求，应该以达到它的合用状态为目标：我们要的不是无限精确的概念，而是相对精确的概念——相对于概念的合用状态而言。所谓"合用状态"，这里是指一个概念在特定的语言游戏中得到合适的使用时所处的那个状态。至于什么叫"合适的使用"，这本不是一个纯理论问题。我们不难明白：精确如"矩形"这样的概念在几何学中是合用的，模糊如"漂亮"这个概念在日常生活中也是合用的，在于我们在相关的语言游戏中都能合适地使用它们。我们把一个概念处于合用状态时的具备的某个清晰度或精确度称作这个概念的"合用度（limit of usability）"，当这个概念的清晰度或精确度达到某个最佳点时，它具备最高的合用度，这个点代表其合用度的极限（limit），未达到这个极限，或超过这个极限，这个概念都不是最合用的。这里要说明两点：1）这个合用的"度"不是一个可以通过数值表示的清晰精确的点，它只具有相对的——相对于合用度不同的概念；相对于概念用于其中的语言游戏——意义；2）这个合用的"度（limit）"与概念的"边界（Grenzen，boundary）"之间存在密切的联系，但不是一回事：概念的合用度相对于其处于合用状态下的清晰度或精确度而言，概念的边界相对于其内涵与外延而言。

《哲学研究》第 72 节到第 74 节专门讨论样本（Muster, sample）问题。维特根斯坦借蓝色、绿色和叶子的样本从另一个角度解释了家族相似概念的形成。当我们看过一些蓝色样本之后，会把所有这些色样的共同之处称为"蓝色"，我们以这些相对有限的色样作为样本，把它们当成一种"典型的"蓝色，但在实际指认时可能要面对深浅程度更为变化多样的具体的蓝色。各种蓝色的色样和更加多样的蓝色的实指，都在"蓝色"这一家族中处于大致相似的关系之中。我们之所以需要样本，一方面是由于"蓝色"是个模糊的概念，一方面方便我们实指。维特根斯坦进而指出，样本的意义在于样本的用法。你给我一小片绿叶，你是要把"绿色"的样本给我呢，还是要把"树叶"的样本给我，抑或把"绿叶"的样本给我？这个问题只能到样本的实际用法中去找寻答案。原则上，样本所处的那个位置，提示了该概念的合用度：所有与样本一致或相似的实指都处于该概念的合用状态之中。要提请注意的是，"样本"本身若要成为一个合用的概念，也必须落实到它的实际用法中。

概念的合用没有整齐划一的标准，不同的概念之间，同一语词所指代的不同概念之间，以及同一概念的不同用法之间，都不会有处于同一水平的合用标准。在《哲学研究》中，维特根斯坦告诉我们：一个概念只有界定到某个"度"才是合用的。（PI，§71）例如，矩形和正义的合用度就不一样。超过度就没法适当地用它了，就像我们把"步"定义为 75 厘米就没法再用"步"这个概念了一样。对概念清晰精确性的盲目的追求是徒劳的，也没有必要。我们要做的，是要找到概念的合用度在哪里。我们作概念分析，不是要把每个概念都绝对精确化、清晰化，而是要把它们精确清晰到一个合适使用的度，就可以了。从另一个角度我们也能说，这个度存在于一个概念与其他概念的关联之中，而不是对概念的实际使用之中。但概念之间的关联本身，也可以在实际使用中被呈现出来。

概念是否合用不是由这个概念本身来决定的，我们无法"先验"地证明矩形的概念必然比正义的概念更清晰。在概念的使用环境中，自然隐藏着这样一种适合这个概念在其中生长的环境和土壤。某些土壤和环境需要一个清晰度和精确度比较高的概念，这个概念就会往清晰和精确的方向"走"，比如数学中的概念。而在人文—社会学科领域，以及日常生活中，对概念的使用是很模糊的，人文和日常生活的土壤中无法生长出高度精确性的概念，尽管人文领域和日常生活中使用的概念，在很大程度上是与科学—数学概念混用的。我们说"她朋友很多"，和"这是一个多边形"，同样使用"多"这个语词，实际上在使用不同的概念。再比如，我们说某人长得好看，那人品德很好，这两个"好"尽管都是模糊的，但其模糊程度未必一样。也正是由于这种各个领域共用一个语词的现状，才使得我们意识到正确的区分一个概念的合用度是非常重要和迫切的。

然而，"矩形"与"正义"怎么就会有不同的合用度呢？这个度是由什么决定的？会不会出现这种情况：我不知道一个概念的合用度何在？不同的合用度，代表着不同的语言游戏。①语言游戏是否能够顺利进行，是检验参与其中的语词是否合用的标准。并且，在不同的语言游戏中，同一个概念的合用度是不同的；在不同的生活形式②中，这种情况仍然存在。由于生活形式不尽相同，在一门语言中存在的概念模糊性问题，在另一门语言中也许就不存在，或者以另一种形式出现。在刚才举过的例子中，"这是一个多边形"与"她朋友很多"这两句话中的"多"在英语中分别是两个语词：名词"polygon"和形容词"many"。提请注意的是，即便在英语中这两个词仍然是表示模糊概念。

概念不合用既表现为不准确地（程度上没有把握好——不在其合用度上）使用一个概念，也包括不正确地（含义就根本搞错了）使用一个概念。误解或误会他人，有时体现为不恰当地使用概念。例如，朋友向你迎面走来，但他似乎没看见你。这时你可能会说：他实际是装作没看见自己。你这么说自有你的理由，但假设真实情况是，他真的没有看见你。你错误地以为别人在假装，进而错误地使用了"假装"这个词。"假装"在这个语境中，显然是不合用的。这种不合用，准确地说是误用。

概念的生命力在于它有内在的张力，而开放性和包容性是这种内在张力的重要体现。这种开放性和包容性体现在：1）概念的家族相似性；2）概念的合用性。概念的合用性，提示了概念在使用上的一种弹性。合用的概念是最具有开放性的概念，因为它随时面向复杂多样的语言游戏和生活形式，随时准备调整自己的合用度；合用的概念是最具包容性的概念，因为它主动承担了来自"他者"——概念的不准确用法或误用——的挤压力；合用的概念是最具生命力的概念，因为它直接扎根于语言游戏与生活形式的土壤之中，并与它们保持同步的脉动，始终处于生生不息的状态。

---

① 可以对照维特根斯坦的一句话："确定性的种类是语言游戏的种类。"（PI，p. 224）

② 在维特根斯坦那里，是所有人共同拥有一种生活形式，还是不同文化模式下生活的人群有不同的生活形式？我以为"生活形式"就像"语言游戏"概念一样，也是一个家族相似式概念：处于不同文化背景下的人群拥有不同的生活形式，这里的"不同"是指不完全相同，即一种相似关系。说所有人共有一种生活形式，那是相对于狮子的生活形式而言："即使一头狮子会说话，我们也听不明白。"（PI，part II，p. 223）更多关于生活形式的论述参见江怡，《维特根斯坦——一种后哲学的文化》，第五、六章，社会科学文献出版社，2002 年第三版。

参考文献

［1］ Ludwig Wittgenstein，1958，*Philosophical Investigation*（PI），Basil Blackwell，Oxford.

［2］ 陈嘉映，2003，《语言哲学》，北京大学出版社。

［3］ 江怡，2002（第三版），《维特根斯坦——一种后哲学的文化》，社会科学文献出版社。

［4］ 维特根斯坦，2001，《哲学研究》，陈嘉映译，上海人民出版社。

［5］ 泽诺·万德勒，2002，《哲学中的语言学》，陈嘉映译，华夏出版社。

The Usability and Its Limit of a Concept
——From the perspective of Wietgenstein's
Philosophical investigation
Changshen Chen

Chinese Academy of Social Sciences

Abstract: Conceptual investigation is an important task of analytic philosophy. Later Wittgenstein combine with some famous theory such as "language games", "form of life", "sample and designation", investigated the problems of ordinary language. In his *Philosophycal Investigations*, he not only brought up "family resemblances", but also had splendid discribe on the theory of usability and its limit of a concept. According to him, the degree of vagueness of a concept, as well as it's degree of clearness, closely contact with it's usability; the usability of a concept, priori to it's clearness, means that an usable concept is not a clear one in absolute meaning, but an enough clear one related to certain language-game and form of life; the limit of usability of a concept is it's degree of clearness when it is usable, not it's highest degree of clearness in absolute meaning; if a concept has highest degree of usability, it shoud be considered as on the best point on the degree of clearness in relative meaning.

Keywords: Wittgenstein; ordinary language; conceptual analysis; usability; limit of usability

道德哲学

斯特劳森论道德责任 *

◎ 徐向东

北京大学外国哲学研究所

　　摘　要： 道德责任的问题被认为面临一个两难困境：一方面，如果决定论是真的，那么我们就没有道德责任，因为决定论排除了自由意志的可能性，而具有自由意志被认为是能够承担道德责任的一个先决条件；另一方面，如果非决定论是真的，那么我们也没有道德责任，因为道德责任至少要求我们要对自己的行为有所控制，但非决定论排除了我们对自己的行为实施控制的可能性。这样，如何理解道德责任的可能性就变成了一个很棘手的问题。本文主要考察彼特·斯特劳森对这个困境的诊断以及他提出的自然主义解决。我将表明，为了应对一些理论家对斯特劳森的理论的批评，斯特劳森必须进一步承诺一种道德实在论和道德普遍主义的观点；我也试图表明，即使斯特劳森有理论资源应对一些批评，但他能够辩护自己理论的尝试是有限的，我们仍然需要寻求解决这个困境的新方式。

　　关键词： 道德责任；反应态度；自然主义转向；因果历史

　　按照某种日常的理解，具有自由意志是一个人能够承担道德责任（moral responsibility）的一个先决条件。如果是这样，那么道德责任的问题就会面临一个困境：一方面，如果英瓦根后果论证（或者类似的论证）是可靠的，那就表明决定论与自由意志是不相容的，[①] 进一步，如果道德责任要求自由意志，那么决定论与道德责任也是不相容的，也就是说，在决定论的条件下，没有任何人能够对自己所采取的行为负责；另一方面，道德责任可以被认为与非决定论也是不相容的，因为在非决定论的条件下，任何一个事件都是以一种随机的方式发生，而这样发生的事件一般来说也不是我们人类行动者所能控制或支配的，但是，如果能够控制或者支配一个行动也是行动者能够承担道德责任的一个先决条件，那么非决定论与道德责任也是不相容

　　* 本文的写作得到教育部人文社会科学重点研究基地项目"自由意志与道德责任问题研究"的资助。
　　① 参见 Peter van Inwagen, *An Essay on Free Will* （Oxford：Clarendon Press，1983）。对英瓦根的论证的讨论，参见拙著《理解自由意志》（北京大学出版社，2008 年）有关部分。

的——在非决定论的条件下，我们也不可能对自己的行为承担道德责任。这样，不管我们所生活的世界是决定论的还是非决定论的，我们似乎都不能对自己的行为负责。如何理解道德责任的可能性于是就变成了一个很棘手的问题。在其开创性论文"自由与怨恨"中①，彼特·斯特劳森试图通过他的自然主义承诺，从一种先验论证的视角让我们摆脱这个形而上学困境，并由此揭示了对道德责任的一种独特理解。本文将考察斯特劳森的探讨及其所存在的一些问题。

一、道德责任与反应态度

在试图把道德责任赋予某个人并对其行为进行道德评价时，我们能够有意义地这样做，取决于我们把他看做是一个能够认识到道德理由，并能够按照那个认识来调节其行为和回应其他人的道德反应的行动者。斯特劳森注意到，在两种情形中，我们并不让一个行动者对其行为承担责任。第一种类型的行动者是这样的行动者：他们无法抑制自己做某件事情，在做那件事情上似乎别无选择。这种行动者要么是亚里士多德所说的"出于无知而行动"的行动者，要么是在某种心理强制下只能采取某个单一行为方式的行动者。第二种类型的行动者是那些心理变态或者反社会的人。这种行动者既不是出于无知而行动，也不是因为受到强制而行动。相反，他们的行动在某种意义上是志愿的：他们能够认识到自己的行为可能对别人造成伤害，甚至是有意伤害别人。这种行动者缺乏对道德情感和道德态度进行回应的能力。在斯特劳森看来，我们应该把这些人排除在道德责任赋予的实践外。对于这种行动者，我们将采取一种完全不同的态度：

> ［我们对他们的态度］可以包括厌恶或恐惧，也可以包括怜悯甚至爱，尽管不是所有类型的爱，但不能包括那些属于与他人一起介入或参与人际关系的反应态度或反应情感，不能包括怨恨、感激、宽恕、愤怒，或者两个成人之间有时候能够互相感受到的那种爱。如果［我们对待这样一个人］的态度是客观的，那么尽管我们可以与他争斗，但不能跟他争吵，尽管我们可以与他交谈，甚至可以与他谈判，但不能跟他讲道理。［我们］至多只能假装与他争吵或者与他讲道理。②

---

① Peter Strawson, 1962, "Freedom and Resentment", reprinted in Gary Watson (ed.), *Free Will* (Oxford: Oxford University Press, 1982), pp. 59–80.

② Peter Strawson, "Freedom and Resentment", p. 66.

斯特劳森把我们对待这些人的态度称为"客观的",是因为这些人并不接受正常人相互之间用来表示道德责任赋予的那些态度和情感,因此好像我们就必须在道德责任赋予的实践外来看待他们。为了理解我们为什么把这些人排除在道德责任赋予的实践外,我们就需要理解斯特劳森所谓的"参与性的或者主观的反应态度(reactive attitudes)"。

按照我们日常对道德责任的一种理解,在说某个人是道德上负责任的时,我们所说的是,他能够认识到道德理由,能够回应我们根据道德理由对他作出的道德评价和道德反应。如果一个人无论如何都不能回应我们对他的道德反应,那么用康德的话说,他在"道德上已经死去",所以就不可能参与我们的道德责任赋予实践。在参与和分享某种类型的人际关系时,我们往往对这种关系的本质有一个基本的认识和判断,因此就会对进入这种关系的人们的表现产生某些合理期望。如果对方满足了那些期望,我们就会对他们表示感激,赞扬他们;如果他们不能合理地满足那些期望,我们就会对他们表示愤怒,责备他们。斯特劳森把我们相互之间表示出来的那种态度称为"反应态度"。反应态度一方面反映了我们相互间的善意、感动和尊重,另一方面反映了我们相互间的轻视、冷漠和恶意。我们确实通过互相赋予反应态度来规范和调节我们相互之间的行为。实际上,从功利主义立场来探讨道德责任的理论家就是这样来看待反应态度的作用的①,不过,斯特劳森却对这种态度的本质提出了一个截然不同的理解。

斯特劳森把反应态度描述为"我们对其他人对待我们的善意、恶意或者冷漠的自然反应,[他们对待我们的那些方式]就表现在他们的态度和行动中"②。这种态度当然是在人际关系中显示出来的,实际上可以从第一人、第二人和第三人的观点来看待。例如,如果我是一个具有道德良知的人,那么当我的行为无意中对他人造成伤害时,我自己就会感到内疚或罪过。但是,第二人的回应是最常见的:对于有意伤害我们的某个人,我们感到愤怒,对于不计自己得失帮助我们的某个人,我们感到感激。在第三人的情形中,我们会因为 A 虐待 B 而对 A 感到愤慨,会因为 C 牺牲自己的利益来促进 D 的幸福而赞扬 C。这三种反应态度是逻辑上相联系的。首先,它们都反映了人们在社会生活中所抱有的一套相互期望和相互要求;一旦我们认识到这种期望和要求没有得到满足或者甚至受到蔑视,我们就会感到愤慨和怨恨,另一方面,要是我们自己没能满足这种期望和要求,我们自己就会感到内疚或罪过。其次,当我们把这种态度赋予某个人时,我们的赋予是否恰当取决于某些条件,尤其是取决于我们对那个人行动的本质和动机的理解。比如说,如果你偶然打破了我的花瓶,我对你的愤怒可能就是不合适的,因为你并不是

① 例如,参见 J. J. C. Smart, 1961, "Free-Will, Praise and Blame", *Mind* 70 (279): 291–306。
② Peter Strawson, "Freedom and Resentment", p. 67.

要有意打破我的花瓶。或者，如果 A 只是无意中伤害了 B，我们对 A 的愤慨可能也是不合适的。也就是说，为了判断我们对一个人表示出的反应态度是否恰当，我们就必须了解他行动的目的、动机和意图以及他在履行该行动时所处的实际处境。我们可以认为一个人对某个**特定的**行动不负有道德责任，但仍然可以继续把他看做一个能够承担道德责任的行动者。但是，在某些极端的情形中，道德责任的赋予也许是完全不合适的。斯特劳森鉴定出两种道德责任的免责条件。在第一种情形中，行动者的行为缺乏任何程度的恶意或轻视。虽然那个行为可以对他人造成伤害，但那种伤害在某个方面是偶然的或无意的。在第二种情形中，出于某些原因，行动者是"异常的或者不成熟的"，例如精神病患者和小孩子，因此，我们就不能合理地指望他们能够对他人表示出恰当的关心、关怀和尊重。这样，即使他们做了伤害我们的事情，对他们加以责备也是不合适的。

对斯特劳森来说，正是我们体验、抑制和取消反应态度的模式塑造了我们的道德责任概念，并对这个概念提供了具体内容。这些态度以及有关的实践（例如道德评价和法律制裁）以一种构成性的方式表示了我们的人际关系。为了具有反应态度和恰当地赋予这种态度，我们首先必须具有**行动**的能力，更具体地说，具有在行动中把善意、恶意、冷漠之类的情感和态度显示出来的能力。我们的行动并不仅仅是纯粹的身体运动，而是**表示了**我们的意图和动机、情感和态度。所以，如果我们能够按照这些情感和态度来行动，那就意味着我们对什么东西算作善意或恶意、什么东西算作对他人的有意冷漠有了一个基本的理解。按照斯特劳森的观点，这些情感和态度是相对于一套公认的期望和要求而论的。当我有意地轻视这些期望和要求时，我就显示出一种恶意。当然，如果我对这些期望和要求缺乏基本的理解和把握，我也不可能有意地在我的行为中对你表示出善意或恶意。因此，成为反应态度的恰当对象意味着已经有能力理解和把握这些期望和要求。但是，为了具有这种能力，我们就得亲自体验到这些反应态度，愿意接受和参与道德责任赋予的实践。此外，为了正确地体验到反应态度，我们也必须有能力在其他人的行动中辨别出他们行动的意图。因此我们可以说，成为一个道德上负责任的行动者就是有能力让他人和自己成为反应态度的恰当对象。一旦我们已经具有现实的能力成为这样的人，我们也就参与到反应态度的实践中来。

另一方面，如果我们发现某些行动者不能成为反应态度的恰当对象，既不能回应我们对他的道德反应，又不愿意接受我们对他的道德反应，那么我们就只能对他们采取一种客观的态度。我们可以对这种人表示怜悯和同情，但是，既然他们并不具有必要的道德回应能力，我们就无法把他们看做是道德上负责任的行动者。换句话说，他们丧失了参与正常的人际关系的能力，因此，用只具有这种能力的人才具有的反应态度来对待他们是不合适的。对这种人来说，我们需要把他们看做是"社会政策的对象；看做在一种广泛的意义上可能需要加以处理的主体；看做一种需要加以考虑……需要加以管理、处置、治疗或训练的对象"①。

于是，按照斯特劳森的观点，对正常的人类关系的参与至少要求参与者能够回应彼此的意图。这意味着，如果我们发现某个人无论如何都不具有这种回应能力，那么我们就倾向于把他从这种关系中排除出去。只是对于那些具有这种能力，能够认识到道德情感和道德要求的含义的个体，反应态度的彼此赋予才是合法的和恰当的。从他对反应态度的本质及其与道德责任的关系的分析中，斯特劳森引出了两个重要结论。首先，道德责任的赋予并不需要**外在的**辩护：在正常情形中，我们容易感受到反应态度和道德情感，这种倾向是我们的人性给予我们的；如果一个行动者没有这种倾向，那么我们就很难把他识别为一个完整意义上的人。反应态度，或者更精确地说，我们容易感受到它们的那种倾向，表达了关于人性和人类状况的深刻事实，构成了人类生活的一个核心领域。因此，这种态度以及我们对它们的严肃看待并不取决于任何超越于人类社会生活的条件。要是有人试图追问"究竟是什么东西辩护了人类生活的这个核心领域"这一问题，那就表明他完全误解了反应态度的本质，误解了道德责任赋予的实践。试图通过诉诸某些外在于这个实践的事实来辩护这个实践，就类似于试图按照这些事实去辩护人性。但是，我们显然不能合理地用任何与人性无关的事实来辩护人性。其次，有能力成为反应态度的恰当对象就是人之为人的一个标志，因此，尽管反应态度的彼此赋予可以具有规范和调节人们行为的作用，但这并不是它的本质功能。人们有理由对某些行为表示愤怒和愤慨，对某些行为表示赞扬和感激，乃是因为这些反应就是我们作为人而具有的自然反应，不管这样做是否有助于促进某个社会效用。正如斯特劳森所说：

> 不管道德谴责和法律惩罚是文明的还是野蛮的，我们都相信这些实践的效用。但这些实践的效用……并不是我们现在要加以考虑的问题。我们现在所要说的是……只是按照社会效用来谈论［道德责任赋予的实践］遗漏了在我们对这些实践的看法中某些至关重要的东西。要是我们注意到，我们所认识到的道德生活的一个本质部分就是由这些态度和情感编织而成的那个复杂网络形成的，那么我们就可以恢复这些至关重要的东西。只有通过注意到这一系列的态度，我们才能从我们所知道的那些事实中重新获得我们对道德语言的理解，对应得、责任、罪过、谴责和公正等概念的理解。但我们**确实**是从我们所知道的这些

① Peter Strawson, "Freedom and Resentment", p. 66.

事实中获得这种理解的，我们无须超越那些事实。①

这段话实际上是要表明，不管决定论论点是否为真，不管我们是否确实是生活在一个决定论的世界中，这些形而上学问题并不影响道德责任赋予的实践。斯特劳森试图在我们所讨论的这篇文章中实现一个"调和"计划，表明由决定论论点所引发的关于自由意志的争论，既没有影响又没有威胁到道德责任赋予的日常实践。那么，斯特劳森何以持有这种观点呢?

二、自然主义转向

在我们是否能够对自己的行为承担道德责任这个问题上，有两种对立的观点：乐观主义的观点和悲观主义的观点。斯特劳森试图调和这两种观点之间的对立。乐观主义者往往是相容论者，他们认为与道德责任相联系的那些态度和实践并没有受到决定论论点的否决。悲观主义者往往是不相容论者，他们认为，如果决定论论点是真的，那么它就会削弱我们对这些态度和实践的承诺。在试图调和这两派观点时，斯特劳森接受了悲观主义者的这一看法：乐观主义者对道德责任的说明遗漏了一个至关重要的东西——他们没有注意到，为了使行动者能够对其行动真正地承担责任，因此的确**值得**道德上的赞扬或责备，行动者就必须是自己行为的**终极创作者**。② 但是，斯特劳森并不认为，为了满足这个要求，我们就必须假设决定论是假的，并由此采取一个非决定论的或者反因果的自由概念。换句话说，斯特劳森认为，即使乐观主义者的论述确实遗漏了某些至关重要的东西，但这个空白不是要由"自由意志论的那种含糊其词、惊慌失措的形而上学"来填补。斯特劳森其实比较同情乐观主义者的立场，于是他就认为，为了发现从乐观主义和悲观主义的论述中都被遗漏掉的东西，我们就需要采取他所说的"自然主义的转向"。

大致说来，这个自然主义转向涉及不去追究与"自由"和"道德责任"这两个概念的概念分析有关的问题和争论，而是要去描述当我们让一个人承担道德责任时，究竟发生了什么事情。也就是说，斯特劳森的方法论并不那么取决于概念分析，而是取决于对人类实际的道德心理提出一个**描述性**的说明。此外，斯特劳森的自然主义转向不仅在方法论上偏离概念分析，转向道

---

① Peter Strawson, "Freedom and Resentment", p. 78.

② 这是不相容论者反复强调的一个论点，例如，参见 Robert Kane, 1996, *The Significance of Free Will*, New York：Oxford University Press。

德心理，而且也强调情感在道德生活中的重要性。斯特劳森采取这个策略，是因为他认为，乐观主义者和悲观主义者都把自由意志和道德责任的争论过分理智化，而正是这种做法使我们在这个问题上陷入困境。在他看来，正确的做法是，我们要去详细描述反应态度赋予的具体情景，看看在什么情况下我们可以恰当地把反应态度赋予他人，在什么情况下我们必须悬置或者收回我们的反应态度。这个描述性的分析导致他提出了两种类型的免责条件，进而认为那些没有能力参与正常的人际关系的行动者不是反应态度的恰当对象。最终他得到了这一结论：道德责任赋予的实践并不需要外在的辩护，因为这个实践就是我们的人性给予我们的，只有那些在正常情况下倾向于具有反应态度和道德情感的行动者才是完整意义上的人。

到此为止我们可以看到，为什么斯特劳森会认为决定论问题与道德责任赋予的日常实践无关。悲观主义者认为，道德责任要求真正可供取舍的可能性；然而，如果决定论是真的，我们就没有这样的可能性，因此也就无法对我们的行为承担责任。进一步，即使悲观主义者可以承认我们的行动在没有受到强制或者心理失常的条件下是自由的，但他会强调这个意义上的自由行动仍然是**形而上学**上被决定的，所以追根究底我们还是无法对自己的行动承担道德责任。因此，道德责任要求形而上学意义上的自由。乐观主义者之所以认为道德责任与决定论是相容的，是因为他们倾向于按照功利主义的观点来理解反应态度和法律制裁这样的实践。如果是否让一个人对其行为承担道德责任只是取决于这样做是否有助于促进社会效用，那么决定论是否为真的问题就不会影响这个实践——实际上，正如我们已经看到的，一些乐观主义者认为道德责任赋予的实践要求或者预设了决定论。悲观主义者当然无须否认赞扬和责备、惩罚和奖励的社会效益，但他认为我们应该把效用与合法性区分开来：在某些情况下，责备或惩罚一个人可以提高社会效用，但如果那个人本来就不应该受到责备或惩罚，那么责备或惩罚就是不公正的，而有关的社会效用也并没有消除这种不公正。

斯特劳森接受了悲观主义者的这个说法。但他认为，乐观主义者的问题并不在于他忽视了这个事实：如果一个行动者是形而上学上被决定的，那么因为他做了某件事情而惩罚他就是不公正的。确实，如果我们只能做我们被决定要做的事情，如果我们在做这些事情上别无选择，那么就不可能有道德责任这样的东西，因为在这种情况下，没有谁会因为他所做的事情而**值得**惩罚或**值得**奖励。但是，乐观主义者并不认为我们是形而上学上被决定的行动者，这就是他与悲观主义者的分歧所在。按照斯特劳森的诊断，乐观主义者所忽视的是我们的人性。在斯特劳森看来，我们并不是为了获得某些社会效益而假装相信其他人是道德上负责任的；相反，我们确实相信那些具有正常能力和正常心理的人是道德上负责任的。在正常条件下，这样来看待他们就是我们无法逃避的本性。斯特劳森由此断言，悲观主义的论调也是错误的。他从两个层面上来论证这个观点。首先，他论证说，就算决定论是真的，它也没有用任何系统的方式否决了我们的反应态度。反应态度的恰当赋予取决于我们的这一判断：一个具有正常能力和正常心理的人是否有意地对我们显示出恶意，或者缺乏对我们的恰当关注。但是，决定论并不意味着某个人对别人造成的伤害都总是无意地或者偶然地产生的。决定论也不意味着每一个行动者都是心理上异常的或不成熟的，或者以某种方式丧失了加入和参与正常人际关系的能力。因此，除非斯特劳森所提到的那两种免责条件对所有人都普遍使用，否则我们就不能认为决定论论点在理论上削弱了我们对反应态度的承诺。其次，斯特劳森论证说，即使我们有一些**理论上**的理由放弃或悬搁反应态度，但我们不可能在**心理上**这样做，因为这样做意味着我们对他人采纳一种**完全客观**的态度，但这恰恰是我们无法做到的。当然，我们确实对某些类型的行动者采纳这种态度，而且，有时候出于自我保护的目的，我们甚至也对一个"正常"人采取类似的态度。但在斯特劳森看来，我们这样做，并不是因为我们相信决定论论点在这种场合是真的，而是因为我们出于某些实际考虑在这种场合放弃了反应态度：

> 在异常的情形中，但不是在正常的情形中，我们之所以采纳客观的态度，是因为我们认为相关的行动者在某些方面或者所有方面丧失了建立日常的人际关系的能力。他之所以丧失这种能力，也许是因为他心目中的现实是纯粹的幻想，在某种意义上他并不生活在真实的世界中；或许是因为他的行为部分地来自于无意识的目的；或许是因为他是一个白痴，或者是一个道德上的白痴。①

所以，如果我们排除斯特劳森的两种免责条件的情形，那么道德责任赋予的日常实践似乎与决定论论点的真假毫无关系。我们确实可以选择在某些场合、对某些类型的行动者采取客观的态度，但是我们不可能在任何时候、对任何人都采取这种态度。此外，在道德责任问题上，即使我们可以把自己设想为上帝，站在人类共同体之外来为自己决定是否要保留我们对反应态度的自然承诺，但"只有按照［我们对］人类生活的得与失、丰富与贫乏的评价，我们才能合理地作出这样一个选择；决定论论点是真是假对**这个选择**的合理性没有影响。"② 如果我们没有理由选择一个情感上贫乏、丧失了人性的生活，那么，即使决定论论点是真的，它也不会影响我们的这种选择。

---

① Peter Strawson, "Freedom and Resentment", p. 69.
② Peter Strawson, "Freedom and Resentment", p. 70, emphasis in original.

因此，斯特劳森认为，一旦我们正确地理解了反应态度的本质和道德责任赋予的实践，那么我们就可以在乐观主义者和悲观主义者之间实现一种调和。一方面，我们要让乐观主义者认识到他的观点中确实遗漏了一些至关重要的东西，即对人类态度和情感的忽视；另一方面，我们必须要求悲观主义者交出他的那种"含糊其词、惊慌失措的形而上学"，① 因为道德责任赋予的实践无须得到这种形而上学的支持。这样，如果乐观主义者和悲观主义者都能够承认他们各自对道德责任的理解是有问题的，那么这种调和也就得到了实现。对这个调和计划的主要思想，斯特劳森自己提出了一个很好的总结：

> 乐观主义者和悲观主义者都用很不相同的方式误解了［我们从道德责任赋予的实践中了解到的］事实。但在一种深刻的意义上，他们的误解其实有一些共同之处。他们都用不同的方式把这些事实过分理智化。在我所谈论的人类态度和人类情感的一般结构的内部，对这种态度和情感加以修正、重新导向、批评和辩护的余地都是无穷无尽的。然而，辩护问题是内在于这一结构的，或者关系到这个结构的内部修正。反应态度的一般框架是随着人类社会一同存在的，因此在这个意义上是我们无法回避的。作为一个整体，它既不要求也不允许一个外在的'理性'辩护。悲观主义者和乐观主义者都用不同的方式同样表明他们无法接受这一点。乐观主义者把这些事实过分理智化，其做法就体现在一种很不完备的经验主义和一种片面的功利主义中。他试图在经过计算的后果中来为某些社会实践发现一个恰当基础，但却忽视（也许想要忽视）了把这些实践部分地表示出来的人类态度。悲观主义者并没有忽视这些态度，但却无法接受这一事实：正是这些态度本身填补了乐观主义说明中的疏漏。于是他就认为，只有当某个一般的形而上学命题反复得到证实，在所有适合于道德责任赋予的情形中都得到证实时，这个疏漏才能得到填补。②

当然，斯特劳森的目的并不仅仅是要在乐观主义者和悲观主义者之间实现一种调和，而且也是要通过他的自然主义转向来回答关于道德责任的怀疑论，尤其是针对他称为"悲观主义者"的那些理论家。我们很容易看出，斯特劳森的调和计划并非没有预设。在对道德责任的本质和条件的论述中，情感在人类生活中的重要地位扮演了一个关键角色。尽管斯特劳森并没有

① Peter Strawson, "Freedom and Resentment", p. 80. 这种形而上学是含糊其词的，大概是因为它并没有很明确地阐明对非决定论或者对行动者因果性的诉诸如何能够说明自由意志和道德责任的可能性；它是惊慌失措的，大概是因为它是不相容论者为了逃避他们眼中的"决定论威胁"而苍茫采取的举动。

② Peter Strawson, "Freedom and Resentment", p. 79.

明确提及这个观点的历史来源，但我们可以在休谟和亚当·斯密的道德感理论中发现这个来源。这两位理论家都认为，我们对其他人的道德反应就是人性给予我们的东西，涉及从我们对行为和性格的信念中产生出来的情感和态度。斯特劳森认为我们在心理上无法放弃我们对反应态度的承诺。在提出这个主张时，他是在把这种承诺看做是自然的：这种承诺以及有关实践构成了引导我们的思想和行动的无法避免的心理机制。因此，尽管我们可以出于某些**理论上**的考虑对道德责任的根据采取一种怀疑论态度，但我们无法在心理上放弃道德责任赋予的日常实践：

> 人类对参与日常的人际关系的承诺，在我看来，是如此彻底、如此根深蒂固，以至于我们无法严肃地接受如下思想：一个一般的理论信念有可能会这样改变我们的世界，使得其中不再有我们通常所理解的人际关系这样的东西；［但是］与我们通常所理解的人际关系发生牵连就是面对一系列这样的反应和情感。①

尽管我们无法**在理论上**辩护我们对外在世界的信念，但在现实生活中却有一种强烈的自然倾向相信外在世界存在。与此类似，斯特劳森认为，即便我们无法从理论上辩护道德责任赋予的实践，但在实际生活中我们却无法放弃这样的实践。斯特劳森对"道德责任"的理解是一种自然主义的理解，就是因为他是按照休谟处理归纳怀疑论的方式和托马斯·里德处理外在世界怀疑论的方式来处理道德责任。②

三、对斯特劳森理论的批评和改进

在两个意义上，我们可以说斯特劳森的探讨对有关自由意志和道德责任的争论做出了一个很重要的贡献。首先，如果他的论证是可靠的，那么他的调和计划就消解了在这个问题上的两种对立观点之间的张力。其次，通过把我们对冒犯者的法律（或者准法律）处理以及我们彼此间的反应态度包含在我们对道德责任的研究中，斯特劳森扩展了这一研究的范围。正是因为这样一种原创性，斯特劳森的文章激发了强烈的反响和批评。在这些反响和批评的基础上，一些对他的探讨表示同情的理论家进一步改进和发展了他的理论。在这里，我将简要地考察对他的

---

① Peter Strawson, "Freedom and Resentment", p. 68.

② 参见 Peter Strawson, 1985, *Skepticism and Naturalism*, New York: Columbia University Pres, especially p. 39. 对斯特劳森"自然化"道德责任的方式的进一步说明，参见 Paul Russell, 1992, "Strawson's Way of Naturalizing Responsibility", *Ethics* 102（2）: 287 – 302.

理论提出的三个（或者三组）主要批评，同时考察一些理论家对这些批评的回应。

第一个批评直接来自斯特劳森对道德责任的理解。按照他的观点，有能力回应反应态度就是有能力承担道德责任的一个本质标志（或者说一个必要条件）。当然，这并不意味着具有这种能力的人必定应该对他所履行的行动承担道德责任：即使我们具有这种能力，但我们可能是出于无知而行动，或者是因为受到了强制而行动。在这种情况下，即使我们的行动对他人造成伤害，责备我们确实是不恰当的，因为不论是无知还是受到强制可能都不是我们自己的过失。说一个人因为强制行动，就是说他被迫采取的行动的根源并不是来自他自己，或者至少不是完全来自他自己。另一方面，行动，作为一种事件，是可以产生一系列因果影响的。即使一个人充分理性，具有他所能得到一切相关信息，他大概也无法精确预知他的行动可能产生的全部因果结果。在这种情况下，因为他的行动的某个因果结果对他人造成了伤害而责备他就是不恰当的。斯特劳森的理论能够说明这个事实，因为他把这种情形划归在他的第一种免责条件下。此外，在某些特殊的情形中，如果我们对行动者的意图或者其他有关精神状态持有错误的信念，那么我们对他采取的反应态度可能就是不合适的。或者，即使我们对他的行为和性格有充分恰当的了解，我们可能出于某些原因对他没有任何道德反应。在这些特殊的情形中，道德责任与反应态度之间并没有可靠的联系。不过，这种现象也没有对斯特劳森的理论造成严重威胁，因为正如我们已经表明的，他的理论允许我们因为认知错误或介入的负担（strains of involvement）而收回我们已经作出的反应态度，或者决定不对某些人作出道德反应。不过，就反应态度与道德责任的关系而论，斯特劳森理论所面临的一个严重困难据说是这样出现的：

斯特劳森的理论可以被合理地认为对"行动者被认为负责"的概念提出了一个说明，但问题是，在"**被认为是**负责的"和"**实际上是**负责的"［这两个概念］之间是有差别的。确实，有可能的是，一个人能够被认为［要对某件事情］负责，即使他实际上不［对那件事情］负责，反过来说，一个人能够是负责任的，即使他实际上没有被处理为一个负责任的行动者。［斯特劳森］主要是按照对行动者采纳或者不采纳某些态度的实际实践来理解道德责任的，通过这样做，他的理论就冒险抹杀了这两个问题的差别。①

① John M. Fischer and Mark Raviza（eds.），1993，*Perspectives on Moral Responsibility*，Ithaca：Cornell University Press，p. 18，作者原来的强调。参见 John M. Fischer，1994，*The Metaphysics of Free Will*，Oxford：Blackwell，pp. 211 – 213.

这个批评的产生，是因为斯特劳森持有两个观点。首先，斯特劳森认为，让他人对其行为承担责任是关于人类生活的一个"自然"事实，这样一种实践并不需要任何"外在"辩护。其次，斯特劳森似乎也认为，让一个人对其行为承担道德责任就在于其他人认为他是道德上负责任的——也就是说，成为反应态度的接受者与成为道德上负责任的行动者似乎就是同一回事。现在，如果道德责任赋予的实践是内在地得到辩护的，并不取决于一个共同体之外的任何因素，进一步，如果"**实际上负责任**"就等同于"**被认为负责任**"，那么按照这些批评者的说法，斯特劳森的理论就是成问题的。

为了看到这个批评的实质，我们不妨设想这样一个社会，在这个社会中，有些精神迟钝的人因为不能遵守社会规范而遭到其他人的愤怒、愤恨和愤慨，乃至受到责备或处罚。然而，即使社会中的所有其他成员都具有这些情感，这个事实本身并不足以表明他们对那些人所采取的态度是道德上有辩护的。另一方面，如果道德责任赋予的实践只能内在地加以辩护，如果实际上能够承担道德责任就等于被认为能够承担道德责任，那么他们对待那些人的态度似乎就得到了辩护。但这似乎违背了日常的道德直观。类似地，设想这样一个社会，在这个社会中，有些年轻女性的行为方式在某些方面并不符合她们所生活的社会的标准，因此就遭到了其他人的愤恨、谴责和蔑视。她们被称为"女巫"，被认为要对其他人所遭受的不幸和灾难负责。但是，我们显然不应该把其他人所遭受的不幸和灾难归咎于她们。然而，如果我们认为实际上负责任就等于被认为负责任，那么我们似乎就得接受这个不合理的结论。① 因此，斯特劳森的理论是有问题的。

这个批评提出了一些复杂问题。第一个问题明显地关系到我们对待道德相对主义的态度。按照道德相对主义，一个社会的道德标准完全是内在于这个社会的，只有通过这个社会的文化、传统和实践才能得到辩护，并没有超越任何一个社会的普遍的道德标准。这样，道德相对主义就具有（或者被认为具有）这样一个含义：被一个社会接受为正确的东西就是正确的，被一个社会看做是错误的东西就是错误的。既然我们不可能从一个外在的观点来评价一个特定社会的道德规范，因此我们就不可能说，在前面所设想的那两个社会中，社会的其他成员对待其中某些人的态度得不到辩护。斯特劳森的理论似乎与道德相对主义有些联系，因为他一方面认为我们的反应态度和有关的实践是我们的社会生活的基本框架的一个**不可避免**的部分，另一方面又认为这样一个实践只能**内在地**加以辩护。如果每一个社会的反应态度框架都是这个社会所特有

---

① 关于这个例子，参见 Laura W. Ekstrom, 2000, *Free Will: A Philosophical Study*, Boulder: Westview Press, p. 148.

的，不可能从任何外在的观点来加以评价，甚至不可能按照其他社会的道德观念来加以评价，那么斯特劳森的理论确实就有点违背我们的道德直观。纳粹统治时期的德国在某种意义上构成了一个自足的共同体，希特勒的邪恶行径在那个社会中或许被认为是有辩护的，但对我们来说则是道德上可耻的和值得谴责的。如果我们只能从那个共同体内部的观点来看待希特勒的行为，我们大概就不能认为希特勒应该对他的邪恶行为承担道德责任。但大多数人都会认为希特勒应该对他的行为承担道德责任，并因此而值得接受惩罚（尽管他已经自杀身亡）。实际上，甚至在一个共同体中，我们发现人们对待某个人的态度是可以发生转变的。这个可能性表明：我们是否把一个人看做是一个道德上负责任的行动者，并不**仅仅**在于或取决于我们把他看做是反应态度的对象。我们确实是按照某些更加深层的东西来判断他是否是反应态度的**合适**对象。具体地说，我们认为，正是因为一个人具有了某些**道德**能力，他才能充分地参与一个共同体的道德实践。因此，我们必定是按照一个行动者是否具有所要求的那种道德能力来判断他是否能够成为反应态度的恰当对象。这样，当我们断言一个人是反应态度的恰当对象，进而断言他应该对其行为承担道德责任时，我们在这两者之间作出的推理并不是直接的，而是取决于我们对道德能力的解释和理解。

斯特劳森强调具有反应态度是人类生活的一个自然事实，或者说是人之为人的一个主要标志。这个说法似乎意味着，对于什么样的行动者是一个完整意义上的人，什么样的人际关系是一种正常的人际关系，他应该有一个一般的理解，尽管他并没有明确地提出这样一个理解。反应态度存在，是因为进入人际关系中的人们彼此持有一些期望和要求，这是人类生活的一个基本事实。按照这样一种关系的本质，这些期望和要求可以被判断为合理的还是不合理的。比如说，我们都知道在友谊这种关系中朋友之间**应该**满足什么期望和要求。既然斯特劳森认为反应态度的存在取决于这种期望和要求的存在，既然这种期望和要求来自于我们看做是"正常的"人际关系的那种东西，斯特劳森的理论其实就**应该**预设我们对人际关系的一种**规范**理解。当然，斯特劳森并没有明确指出什么样的期望和要求是合理的，因此我们也很难就这个问题来评价他的理论。不过，正如我已经指出的，他的理论原则上要求我们对人际关系持有一种规范的理解。因此，如果我们能够表明这种理解能够是普遍的，比如说，如果我们能够表明在一种人际关系（例如友谊）中所涉及的期望和要求在任何一个社会中都有一些核心要素，因而使得跨社会的道德评价在某种程度上变得可能，那么我们至少就可以缓和上面提到的那个批评对斯特劳森理论的冲击。实际上，我认为斯特劳森想要强调的是，反应态度以及相关的实践是内在于**人类**生活的，在**实践的**层面上并不受制于任何形而上学信念的影响。

然而，如果我们用这种方式来理解斯特劳森，我们就需要对他的理论作出某些改进。斯特劳森强调我们彼此持有的反应态度是通过某种情感表现出来的：我们用怨恨与责备、赞扬与确认之类的情感来对他人作出回应，有时候也用它们来对自己作出回应。然而，尽管这些态度是情感性的，但是，当我们用这些情感来回应他人时，我们显然并不仅仅是在对他人表达出我们的情感。我们用某种负面的态度和情感来回应他人，是因为我们**认识**到他们没有满足我们的合理期望和要求。我们原谅一些人，免除一些人的道德责任，或者并不认为他们能够承担道德责任，也是立足于我们对他们的行为和性格的判断。因此，我们的态度和情感不仅具有**认知的**根据，而且，我们对他人表现出来的态度和情感是否恰当，取决于我们在这种根据的基础上做出的判断是否恰当。反应态度与道德责任赋予的联系并不是无条件的。我们可以因为某个人作了一件事情而责备他，但我们的责备也许得不到理性辩护。比如说，我们可能弄错了关于他的行为的一些事实，我们可能不太了解他在履行那个行动时的实际处境，我们甚至可能是因为对他持有偏见而责备他，等等。因此，当我们准备用一个情感或态度来回应他人时，我们就必须充分理性，不仅要尽可能摆脱一切偏见和成见，尽可能了解那个人行动的意图和处境，而且也要确信我们已经正确地把握了有关的道德理由。只有在这些条件得到满足的情况下，我们才能在反应态度和道德责任的赋予之间建立起某种合理联系。

斯特劳森强调道德责任的概念是在反应态度的实践中塑造出来的，并认为在反应态度的一般结构中，对它们"加以修正、重新导向、批评和辩护的余地都是无穷尽的"①。但是，这无需意味着我们对道德责任的**原初**理解不是由某些**先于**反应态度的事实决定的。② 确实，也许正是人性和人类的生活状况使我们倾向于具有各种各样的反应态度，某些情感反应也有可能是先于我们的理性而形成的，并在我们的生存中扮演了一个重要角色。然而，否认我们的情感具有认知价值并且经常是以我们的信念和判断为中介的也是不恰当的。我们的情感反应是否恰当的确取决于有关的信念和判断是否正确，而这些信念和判断是否正确也取决于某些并非情感性的东西（尽管可以是一些**关于**我们的情感的东西）。因此，我们无须否认斯特劳森的一般论点，即：我们对道德责任的理解是在反应态度的实践中塑造出来的。但我们必须强调的是，反应态度与道德责任的关系取决于某些更深层的东西，例如我们对道德能力、应得、公正等概念的认

---

① Peter Strawson，"Freedom and Resentment"，p. 79.

② 不相容论者可以就此认为，在与道德责任的赋予有关的能力当中，一种重要的能力就是选择按照其他方式来行动的能力，或者说，具有自由意志论者所说的那种自由意志。因此，他们可以就此否认斯特劳森的观点：道德责任赋予的日常实践与决定论论点是否为真没有关系，或者与其他形而上学问题没有关系。我将在后面考虑这个批评。

识，而这些概念显然超越了纯粹情感的范围，或者毋宁说，恰当的情感反应取决于这些概念所指示的东西是否存在，取决于我们对那些东西的理解。我们对他人的情感反应是否恰当，其中的一个重要方面就在于他们是否能够理性地确认我们对他们的反应是公正的。斯特劳森已经允许我们按照一些事实来判断我们是否应该免除一个行动者的道德责任。这表明，我们是否应该让一个人对其行为承担责任要求我们回答一个预先的问题，即：他是否**事实上**对那个行为承担责任。我们用来判断道德责任的事实可以在两个层面上出现：一方面是与一个人的行为以及导致他履行该行为的环境因素和心理条件有关的事实，另一方面是与我们对道德正确性的认识有关的事实。换句话说，我们一方面需要按照某些道德上相关的事实来判断一个人是否确实做错了一件事情，另一方面也需要按照一个人的心理条件和环境因素来判断他是否值得被认为要对他的行为负责。这些判断所依赖的事实可以是内在于一个道德共同体的，但我们必须首先承认它们的存在。此外，尽管这些事实不一定是某种"不可更改"的硬事实（hard facts），例如某种类似于物理事实的东西，但我们对反应态度的"修正、重新导向、批评和辩护"必须立足于这些事实。

这样，一旦我们接受了这个观点，我们就无须认为，不管是在什么情况下，说一个人要对某件事情负责仅仅意味着我们（或者其他人）认为他要对那件事情负责。只有在两个条件得到满足的情况下，我们才能认为这两个说法之间是有联系的：首先，不仅我们（道德责任的赋予者）认为让行动者对他所做的事情承担责任是公正的，而且行动者自己也能够理性地承认我们把这样一个责任赋予他是公正的。① 当然，要做到这一点并不容易。作为道德责任的赋予者，我们不仅要有正确地把握道德理由和正确地作出道德判断的能力，而且也要充分明确地认识到行动者采取一个行动的动机和意图，认识到他在履行那个行动时的实际处境以及他的性格特征（甚至他的性格的形成历史）。对行动者自身来说，能够承担道德责任的要求甚至更强。比如说，我们可以列举出至少三个条件。首先，他需要具有刚才提到的那种能力，愿意按照道德要

---

① 华莱士基本上是沿着类似的思路来改进和发展斯特劳森的理论。不过，与我不同，他否认我们对道德责任的判断（关于是否应该让一个人对其行为承担道德责任的判断）是由先于这个实践的某些事实决定的，认为这样的判断仅仅取决于道德责任的赋予是否公正。当然，我并不否认我们对公正性的理解是内在于道德责任赋予的实践的，但我强调这样一个理解必须立足于另外的事实，尽管这些事实在一个道德实践的共同体中并不是不可修改的。这个问题涉及我们对道德事实和道德客观性的理解，一些相关的论述，参见拙著《道德哲学与实践理性》（商务印书馆，2006 年）。华莱士否认我上面提到的这一点，大概是为了表明道德责任并不要求意志的自由。但我并不认为对这种事实的承诺必定要求我们采纳一个不相容论的自由意志概念。关于华莱士的观点，参见 R. Jay Wallace, 1994, *Responsibility and the Moral Responsibility*, Cambridge, MA：Harvard University Press, especially chapter 4.

求和道德理由来回应其他人对他作出的反应。其次，他必须按照这种能力来有效控制他的行为，他所采取的行动也必须是他能够按照他的意志来有效支配的行动。最终，在回应其他人对他的道德反应时，他必须诚实开放，具有自我反思的意识和自我批评的精神。当然，满足最后这个要求并不是一件容易的事情，因为这涉及一些与自我知识和自我欺骗有关的复杂问题。① 不管怎样，道德责任的赋予要求我们承认和分享道德理由，要求我们不要人为地制造使人们不负责任或者无法负责任的社会条件。在这个意义上，道德责任是我们必须共同来承担和分享的事情。

以上对道德责任及其赋予的理解有助于我们认识到斯特劳森理论所面临的第二个主要困难。斯特劳森说，反应态度是人类社会生活的基本框架的一个部分，因此不可能受制于进一步的辩护性要求。然而，这个主张是含糊的，很容易引起批评。例如，有些批评者认为，**一般来说**，把一个人判断为道德上负责任是对这个人提出一个**事实**主张；大概是说，他是否要对他所做的事情承担道德责任，这样一个判断可以不涉及任何反应态度。有一些行动是道德上无关紧要的，或者，即便不是道德上无关紧要的，但却是我们普遍期望的，比如给自己的孩子食物和衣服。就这些行动而论，我们确实可以判断一个人是否是负责任的，但在我们的判断中并不需要出现任何可辨别的态度。此外，我们也可以设想一些具有理性但却没有情感的存在者，他们很关心道德上的对错这样的事情，也相信行动者是道德上负责任的；然而，他们可以相信做错事情的行动者要承担道德责任，但无须具有斯特劳森所提到的任何情感态度，例如义愤或者道德怨恨。② 这个批评的要点是：道德责任与反应态度可能没有本质上的联系。

为了回答这个批评，我们就需要澄清斯特劳森的含糊主张。我们至少可以用两种方式来解释这个主张。一方面，我们可以认为，当斯特劳森提出这个主张时，他是在阐述关于人性和人类生活状况的一个**经验**事实。这个解释符合他对所谓"描述的形而上学"的承诺，因为这种形而上学只是"满足于描述我们关于世界的思想的**实际**结构"。③ 按照这种解释，斯特劳森所说的

---

① 在这个问题上，特别针对斯特劳森的观点而进行的一些相关讨论，参见 Akeel Bilgrami, "Self-Knowledge and Resentment" (unpublished manuscript), Jonathan E. Adler, 1997, "Constrained Belief and the Reactive Attitudes", *Philosophy and Phenomenological Research* 57 (4): 891 – 905.

② 关于这个批评，参见 Derek Pereboom, 2001, *Living Without Free Will*, Cambridge: Cambridge University Press, xx – xxi.

③ Peter Strawson, 1959, *Individuals: An Essay in Descriptive Metaphysics*, London: Methuen, p. 9, 我的强调。

是，具有或者倾向于具有反应态度就是人性的一个基本特征。在这个意义上，这种态度是我们在心理上无法避免或摆脱的。所以，斯特劳森可以说，对我们人类来说，道德责任的赋予总是与这种态度相联系的，尽管这种联系可能很复杂，比如说，斯特劳森自己认识到，由于所谓"介入的负担"，有时候我们甚至可以对某些成年人悬搁这种态度，即使我们仍然可以把他们看做是道德上负责任的行动者。正是因为我们的人性就是用这种方式来构成的，在受到有意伤害时，我们确实倾向于对行动者产生情感性的反应。情感生活是我们人类生活的一个本质方面；即使有些电脑或机器人显示出高度的智能，但我们并不倾向于把它们看做是人，主要就是因为它们缺乏我们所具有的那种内在的情感生活。正如苏珊·沃尔夫所说的那样，我们无法完全用一种客观的态度来看待我们自己和他人："如果我们要客观地看待我们自己，那么我们就像机器人一样，必然会把我们自己的一部分遗留在［我们对人性的全面认识］之外。在对我们自己采取任何态度时，包括在采取'我们不是自由的或者能够负责任的存在者'这个态度时，我们是在断言我们自己**是**自由的和能够负责任的存在者"①。在这里，沃尔夫所说的是，不管我们对我们自己采取什么态度，我们是在对自己采取一种态度，而态度本身就是我们**因为具有了主观性**而对一个对象（包括我们自己）所采取的一种观点。因此，如果反应态度就是我们主观性的一种体现，那么这种态度确实是我们无法避免的东西——也就是说，是我们的人性的一个必然要素。所以，如果我们是在这个意义上来理解反应态度，那么，当斯特劳森宣称"反应态度是我们在心理上无法避免的"时，他确实是正确的。甚至当我们认为道德责任的赋予要求得到一些事实的辩护时，也正是因为我们的人性，因为我们想知道人们是否确实是自由的、能够承担责任的存在者，我们才有一种实际兴趣要按照那些事实来生活。换句话说，正是因为我们特殊的人性构成，我们才对真理这样的东西产生了兴趣。

四、道德责任与因果历史

另一方面，如果斯特劳森所说的是，作为我们心理构成的一部分，我们所具有的任何反应态度既是不可更改的又不受制于进一步的辩护要求，那么他的主张确实是有问题的。有些批评者认为，反应态度，不像我们所具有的某些更基本的情感，比如说恐惧或者爱，并不是人性的永恒不变、不可避免的特点。我们应该把它们看做是在特定的历史和社会条件中产生出来的人为的文化设施。当然，反应态度确实涉及我们在参与社会生活的时候所获得的一套倾向和期望，

---

① Susan Wolf, 1981, "The Importance of Free Will", *Mind* 90: 386–405, quoted on p. 399.

但它们并不像斯特劳森所设想的那样是固定不变的。相反，就像与道德责任相关联的那些基本概念和实践一样，反应态度也可以在我们的理论反思下发生根本的转变和改变。① 这个批评在我看来确实是正确的，而且提出了一些与我们对道德责任的思考有关的重要问题。正如我们已经看到的，斯特劳森的理论有一个严重的缺陷，那就是他似乎把道德情感或反应态度设想为一种没有命题内容的单纯感受。然而，这个想法实际上不太符合他对反应态度的本质的基本理解：反应态度存在，正是因为我们在进入人际关系时彼此产生了一些期望和要求；即使反应态度具有内在的情感根源，但根本上说，它们只是以一种**外在的**方式表示了我们对那些期望和要求是否得到满足的认识和判断。某个人对我们的伤害可能会激发我们对他的愤慨和怨恨，但是，一旦我们认识到（比如说）他并不是要**有意**伤害我们，我们就会收回我们对他的反应态度，或者至少原谅他对我们所造成的伤害。我们无须否认我们的生活的一部分是由这些态度构成的——我们部分地生活在这些态度之中。但是，我们对他人的情感反应是否恰当，取决于我们对有关的道德理由的认识和接受，取决于我们对行动者的动机、意图、性格和处境的认识，取决于我们对一种人际关系的接受和承诺。当然，不管是道德理由和道德要求，还是在人际关系中体现出来的期望和要求，都只有在人类生活的实践框架中才能存在。但这并不意味着与反应态度相联系的那些要求和标准只能随着**当地的**习俗和习惯而变化，此外就没有更深的事实决定反应态度的恰当性。换句话说，即使我们承认道德责任及其赋予与反应态度具有某些本质联系，但这并不意味着没有更深层的事实信念和价值观念，以便我们可以利用它们来评价和批评道德责任赋予的日常实践。

因此，只是在以上提到的第一个意义上，斯特劳森的主张——反应态度构成了人性的一部分，因此在心理上也是我们无法回避的——才是成立的。然而，如果只是在这个意义上来理解反应态度，那么这种态度与道德责任的联系就被削弱了，因为在这个意义上，斯特劳森就等于说情感是人性的一个本质要素，因此，我们容易感受到情感和情感反应的那种倾向也是我们无法避免的。当然，大概没有任何人会否认这个事实。然而，正如我们已经看到的，能够与道德责任发生重要联系的反应态度必须具有**理性的**辩护，也就是说，我们必须提出理由来表明为什么我们对某个人持有某个态度，为什么我们对他采取那个态度是正当的或恰当的。道德责任的赋予必须得到某些事实信念和价值观念的支持，但对这些事实信念和价值观念，斯特劳森缺乏

---

① 关于这个批评，参见 Gary Watson，1987，"Responsibility and the Limits of Evil: Variations on a Strawsonian Theme"，reprinted in John Fischer and Mark Ravizza (eds.)，1993，*Perspectives on Moral Responsibility*，Ithaca: Cornell University Press，pp. 119 – 150. 也见 Derek Pereboom，*Living Without Free Will*，and R. Jay Wallace，*Responsibility and the Moral Responsibility*，有关部分。

一个充分详细的说明。因此，他也就无法说明什么时候一个人可以被免除道德责任，以及为什么他可以被免除道德责任。不错，他确实描述了我们不让别人承担责任的两种情形。在第一种情形中，对于某些人的某些行动，我们把我们的反应态度悬搁起来，因为我们并不认为他们的行动反映了他们的意志的品质。例如，如果一个人在拥挤中偶然踩了我一脚，我会原谅他，不让他对他的行为承担责任。我原谅他，并不是因为在这种情况下他踩了我一脚这件事是被决定了的，而是因为他并非出于恶意这样做。原谅并不取决于决定论是否是真的。在第二种情形中，行动者并不是我们的反应态度和责任赋予实践的恰当目标，因为我们认为他们是心理上异常的，把他们排除在这个实践之外。按照斯特劳森的说法，在这种情形中，我们免除他们的道德责任，并不是因为他们的行为是被决定的，而是因为他们对道德实践缺乏正确的敏感性——他们要么尚未发展出有关的道德能力（例如小孩），要么由于某种原因而丧失了那种能力。但是，斯特劳森强调说，不论是原谅还是免责都没有受到关于决定论的抽象真理的影响，因为我们对原谅条件和免责条件的理解本身就是**内在于**我们的道德实践的，与决定论是否为真毫无关系。

然而，在作出这个结论时，斯特劳森似乎过于轻率。他确实认识到并强调说，为了参与正常的人际关系，一个人至少必须具有对他人的意图**进行回应**的能力，因此，没有这种能力的行动者就被排除在人际关系之外——对于这种人，我们只能采取所谓"客观的态度"。他也正确地指出，只有具有这种能力的行动者（即能够认识到道德主张和道德要求的含义的行动者）才能成为反应态度的合法对象。但他并没有充分认识到这个问题：为什么有些人会丧失了道德响应的能力？他好像也低估了这个问题的重要性。形而上学决定论也许与我们对道德责任的判断无关，但某种社会的或心理的决定论也许会影响我们的判断。一些人之所以成为斯特劳森所说的"心理上异常"的人，要么是因为受到了某种遗传因素的影响，要么是因为在道德发展的某些关键阶段，他们所生活的环境使他们变成了这样的人。即使这些人可以成为斯特劳森所说的"社会政策"的对象，并在一些社会实践中确实被处理为这样的对象，但是，一旦我们了解到与他们的成长和发展有关的事实，我们对他们的态度可能就会发生转变。在这一点上，沃森对斯特劳森的理论提出了一个值得关注的批评。[①] 很多批评者都注意到，对一个人在何时可以被免除责任、不可以被免除责任，斯特劳森缺乏一个充分详细的说明。沃森进一步指出，不论是对原谅条件还是免责条件，斯特劳森的说明都是严重不完备的。例如，斯特劳森认为我们应该免除那些心理异常的人的道德责任，但在日常生活中，我们还是可以发现，甚至对这些人来说，

---

① Gary Watson，"Responsibility and the Limits of Evil：Variations on a Strawsonian Theme"．

我们实际上是有反应态度的。如果反应态度与道德责任具有内在联系，正如斯特劳森所认为的那样，那么他就无法说明为什么我们允许这些人不对其行为承担责任。当然，斯特劳森对这个问题确实有一个回答：他说，我们免除这些人的道德责任，是因为他们是"错误类型的人"——他们并不具有正常的道德回应能力。但他并没有去进一步追究为什么这些人没有形成这种能力，或者为什么丧失了这种能力，而正是这个问题对他的理论产生了威胁，因为有可能的是，这些人正是**在决定论的条件下**没有形成这种能力，或者丧失了这种能力。实际上，当我们准备把反应态度赋予某个行动者时，我们假设他有能力认识到我们提出的道德理由并接受这些理由——他们把他看做道德共同体的潜在对话者，认为对他进行道德说教不仅是可以理解的，而且也是有效的。斯特劳森确实正确地认识到，对于没有道德回应能力的人，对他们进行道德说教大概没有什么意义。另一方面，在沃森的哈里斯的例子中，一旦我们理解到哈里斯的性格的某些方面是由他无法控制的某些因素因果地决定的，那么我们对他的义愤态度就会缓解，并逐渐让位于一种道德上的悲哀——不仅对他的过去感到悲哀，也对他的性格和他的恐怖行为感到悲哀。当然，出于某些实际目的，我们仍然可以把哈里斯以及与之类似的人处理为"社会政策"的对象，对他们采取所谓的"客观"态度。但问题是：一旦我们了解到哈里斯的成长经历，了解到他后来的邪恶行为来自他在道德发展的关键时期所遭受的不幸，进一步，如果我们反思一下自己，认为要是我们处于他那样的环境，我们也可能成为一个邪恶的人，那么对决定论的接受可能就会影响我们的反应态度。这样，按照斯特劳森的理论，哈里斯的情形似乎就暗示了一个悖论性的结论：如果极端的邪恶是本性和养育的共同结果，那么那种邪恶本身也可以成为使自己免受责备或惩罚的理由。①

因此，在了解到哈里斯的成长经历后，如果我们确实对他采取了一种态度上的转变，那么这种转变就促使我们去思考某种形式的决定论与我们对道德责任的判断的关联。即使另一个与哈里斯具有同样生活历史的人不一定成为哈里斯第二，但具有这样的历史显然限制了他能够得到的选择。因此，性格和行为的**历史**和**起源**问题似乎对斯特劳森的理论提出了一个挑战。上面我们已经看到，**理论信念**确实能够影响道德判断的实践。比如说，如果我们相信，在理论推理和实践推理的能力上，在取得创造性成就的能力上，在发展成熟的人类关系的能力上，不同种族和不同性别的人们实际上是没有差别的，那么种族歧视和性别歧视的态度就会受到削弱。这

---

① 有一些理论家仍然同情斯特劳森对道德责任的探讨，他们认为，一旦我们对日常的道德责任概念采取一种"修正主义"的理解，我们仍然可以避免沃森提出的批评。在这里我将不探讨这个可能性。关于这样一个"修正主义"观点，参见 Michael S. McKenna, 1998, "The Limits of Evil and the Role of Moral Address: A Defense of Strawsonian Compatibilism", *The Journal of Ethics* 2: 123 – 142.

种反思能够改变和应该改变我们的一些态度和实践，即使那些态度和实践在历史上已经很根深蒂固。类似地，如果我们相信我们的性格都是在我们无法控制的因素下形成的，我们的行为都是由我们无法支配的因素决定的，那么我们就会怀疑我们能够真正地承担责任，正如托马斯·内格尔所说：

> 当我们首次考虑"所有人类行动都是由遗传和环境所决定的"这样一种可能性时，那种可能性就威胁着要解除我们的反应态度，正如我们了解到一个特定的行动是由某种药物的效应引起的时，[我们就会取消我们对那个行动的反应态度]。……我们的行动所受到的一些被内在施加的限制对我们来说是明显的。当我们发现其他的、不太明显的内在限制时，我们对那个受到影响的行动的反应态度往往就会消失，因为我们似乎不能用所要求的那种方式把［那个行动］归因于必须成为那些态度的目标的那个人。①

所以，如果道德责任的概念确实有一个历史的方面，那么，即使我们并不确切地知道决定论是否是真的，但我们对因果决定论的**理论**信念本身就足以影响我们的反应态度。因为这个历史的方面意味着，如果一个行为是由行动者不能承担责任的原因必然化的，那么他就不能对这个行为负责。当然，意志自由论者可以承认，我们只需对我们接受和同意的事情负责，但他强调说，接受和同意这个活动本身必须不是由任何外在于或者内在于行动者的原因所必然化的。这等同于说，除非这个活动本身不是被决定的，否则我们就不可能成为我们的行为的真正创始者。斯特劳森曾经把意志自由论者的这种形而上学称为"含糊其词、惊慌失措"的形而上学。然而，如果道德责任的概念确实有一个历史的方面，那么我们就无法轻易地把这种形而上学打发掉。② 通过把具有正常道德回应能力的行动者与不具有这种能力的行动者区分开来，斯特劳森试图表明对这种形而上学的诉诸是不必要的。然而，即使我们承认在前一种行动者的情形中，道德责任判断的实践是一种规范的实践，不会受到形而上学决定论的影响，但是，在后一种行动者的情形中，尤其是在被他划分在"免责条件"下面的那种行动者的情形中，某种形式的决定论与我们对道德责任的判断并不是没有关系。如果是这样，如果可以表明我们**所有人**都是生

---

① Thomas Nagel，1986，*The View from Nowhere*，New York：Oxford University Press，p. 125. 类似的观点，参见 Gary Strawson，1994，"The Impossibility of Moral Responsibility"，*Philosophical Studies* 75：5-24.

② 或者，要不然我们就得修改我们日常的道德责任概念。对于从一个"修正主义"的观点来试图维护斯特劳森的观点的努力，参见 Manuel Vargas，2004，"Responsibility and the Aims of Theory：Strawson and Revisionism"，*Pacific Philosophical Quarterly* 85：218-241.

活在决定论的条件下，那么也许我们真的无法对我们的行为承担道德责任。相容论者是否能够回答这个挑战，性格或行为的因果历史是否确实与我们对道德责任的判断有关，这些问题以及其他相关问题都是我们需要进一步探究的。

Peter Strawson on Moral Responsibility
Xiangdong Xu

Peking University

Abstract: The issue of moral responsibility is held to face a dilemma: on the one hand, if determinism were true, we would have no moral responsibility since determinism rules out the possibility of free will, and possessing free is regarded as a precondition for being able to take moral responsibility; on the other hand, if indeterminism were true, we would also have no moral responsibility since moral responsibility at least requires that we have control over our actions, and yet indeterminism renders it impossible for us to control our behavior. Thus how to understand the possibility of moral responsibility becomes a quite hard problem. This essay is devoted to examining Peter Strawson's investigation of the dilemma in question. I will argue that Strawson would have to commit himself to some form of moral realism and moral universalism as well to deal with some criticisms some theorists put of his approach. I will also try to show that even though Strawson has conceptual resources to cope with some challenges, his attempt to justify his own approach is quite limited. Accordingly we still need to seek some new ways to dissolve the dilemma.

Keywords: moral responsibility; reactive attitudes; naturalist turn; causal histories

知识、道德和政治：欧克肖特的洞见和盲点[*]

◎ 郁振华

华东师范大学

摘 要：本文的主旨是要质疑欧克肖特的习惯性道德的观念。温奇敏锐地意识到，习惯性道德的观念是成问题的。笔者同意温奇的判断，并且进一步提出温奇尚未见及的六个方面，以期深化对习惯性道德的观念的批判。笔者认为，欧克肖特对道德和政治的处理是不平衡的，他在道德问题上的盲点有其知识论上的根源。在西方理性主义的背景下，欧克肖特对反思性道德的批判有助于形成一种厚实的道德观，但是，他没有看到这个厚实的道德观同时也是一个三分的道德观，包括习惯、能力和原则三个层次。欧克肖特混淆了习惯和能力，结果是习惯性道德和反思性道德的僵硬二分。

关键词：习惯性道德；反思性道德；说服式论证；证明式论证；默会认知

　　欧克肖特是 20 世纪重要的政治哲学家。自他 1990 年去世以来，在世界范围内，他的影响越来越大。欧克肖特被认为是一个带有保守主义倾向的自由主义者，他在对自由的辩护中强调了传统、惯例、习俗等因素的重要性。这个思路既有洞见也有盲点，他的核心观念之一，即习惯性道德的观念就突出地体现了这一点。欧克肖特对习惯性道德的讨论旨在批判西方近代的理性主义的道德，这有助于形成一个厚实的道德观（thick conception of morality），但他对习惯性道德的论证颇多漏洞，在论理上有不少粗疏之处。温奇（Peter Winch）敏锐地看到习惯性道德的观念的破绽，认为它是成问题的。笔者同意温奇的判断，但觉得温奇只是破了题，没有把文章做下去。本文从温奇止步处，继续前行，试图通过检讨欧克肖特在道德、政治和知识等问题上的有关思想，把对习惯性道德的观念的批判，引向深入。

---

　　* 本文的删节版已发表在《哲学研究》2009 年第 4 期。此次发表的是该文比较完整的版本。本文的写作得到了上海市重点学科建设项目资助，项目编号：B401

一、非反思的习惯性道德？

欧克肖特在其著名论文《巴别塔》中区分了两种道德。第一种是习惯性道德，在这种道德形式中，"应对日常生活的具体情景，不是通过有意识地将某种行为规则应用于我们自身，也不是作出被认为是表达了某种道德理想的行为，而是根据某种行为习惯来行动。"① 习惯性道德的基本特点是不依赖于反思。欧克肖特指出：

> 这种形式的道德生活并不源自对各种可能的行为方式的意识，以及由某种意见、某条规则或某种理想所决定的对这些可能性的选择；在没有反思的情况下，行为也是近乎可能的。因此，生活中的绝大多数情景，不需要作出判断，也不表现为需要解决的问题；这里没有对各种可能性的权衡或对各种后果的反思，没有不确定性，没有踌躇犹豫。有时候，需要的不过是对我们在其中成长起来的行为传统的非反思的遵循。②

与习惯性道德相不同，第二种形式的道德本质上是反思性的。"其中，活动不是由行为习惯所决定的，而是由对某种道德标准的反思性应用所决定的。它通常表现为两种形式：作为对道德理想的自觉追求，作为对道德规则的反思性的遵循。"③ 在欧克肖特看来，这两种道德形式实质上是两个理想性的极端（用韦伯的术语来说，两种理想类型），在实际生活中，它们总是结合着出现的。在这种结合中，有时是这种形式、有时是那种形式占主导地位。欧克肖特认为，西方社会的道德，从古希腊罗马时期以来，特别是近代以来，对道德理想的自觉追求，一直在这种结合中占主导地位。他哀叹道，这是一种不幸。

温奇在其《社会科学的观念》一书中，在讨论有意义的行为时，对欧克肖特的习惯性道德的观念提出了质疑，指出了它内在的不一致性。在欧克肖特看来，习惯性道德不依赖于反思。但温奇指出，欧克肖特赋予习惯性道德的一些特征，没有反思是不可能的。温奇的批评大致包括如下三个方面的论证。

首先，温奇聚焦于习惯性道德富有弹性和适应性的特征。欧克肖特认为，在习惯性道德中，

---

① Michael Oakeshott, 1991, *Rationalism in Politics and Other Essays*, new and expanded edition, Indianapolis: Liberty Press, p. 467.

② Oakeshott, *Rationalism in Politics and Other Essays*, p. 468.

③ Oakeshott, *Rationalism in Politics and Other Essays*, p. 472.

没有什么东西是绝对固定不变的。习惯性道德富有弹性，能够承受变化。习俗或习惯通常被认为是盲目的，但欧克肖特强调指出，在习惯性道德中，习俗不是盲目的，它"具有适应性，并且对具体情景的细微差别颇为敏感"，它"能变化并作局部变动"。① 问题是，如何阐明习惯性道德的弹性和适应性？欧克肖特的回答是："应该看到，由于这种形式的道德生活的内在律动不是源自对道德原则的反思，而只是反映了对道德行为传统的精神特质的无意识的开发，所以它不会导向道德的自我批判"。② 温奇断然否定了这个答案。他说：

> 欧克肖特认为，他在此所说的变化和适应性是独立于反思性原则的，我则认为，反思的可能性对于那种适应性是必要的。缺乏这种可能性，我们所处理的不是有意义的行为，而是仅仅对刺激的反应，或者确实是盲目的习惯的体现。③

在温奇看来，褫夺了反思的习惯性道德，不过是盲目的习惯，或者仅仅是对刺激的反应，不能算作有意义的行为。欧克肖特反对把习惯性道德等同于盲目的习惯和仅仅是对刺激的反应，他强调，在习惯性道德中，习惯或习俗不是盲目的，因为它对变化和适应性颇为敏感。温奇认为，欧克肖特赋予习惯性道德的那种变化和适应性，没有反思是不可能的。简言之，如果习惯性道德要容纳欧克肖特所说的那种变化和适应性，它必须是反思性的，而这与欧克肖特对习惯性道德的定义是相悖的。可见，在富于变化、善于适应的特性与习惯性道德的定义之间存在着明显的紧张，这是温奇所揭示的习惯性道德的观念的第一个困难。

其次，温奇通过强调两种形式的道德都必须面对永在变迁中的环境这一事实，来批判欧克肖特的习惯性道德的观念。他的批评是：

> 他（指欧克肖特）说，"在此，我该如何行动"这种形式的困境，只会对自觉地遵循被明确表述的规则的人才会出现，而不会对非反思地遵循习惯性行为模式的人出现。这很可能是对的，即如欧克肖特所言，这种内心反省的必要性对于试图遵循明确规则——其应用在日常经验中缺乏基础——的人来说，可能更为惯常和紧迫。但是，诠释和一致性的问题，也就是说，**反思**的问题会经常出现，这不只是因为传统的习俗性行为模式已经瓦解，

---

① Oakeshott, *Rationalism in Politics and Other Essays*, p. 471.
② 同上。
③ Peter Winch, *The Idea of a Social Science*, second edition, London: Routledge, p. 63.

而且还由于情景的新颖性，我们必须在这样的情景中延续那些行为模式。①（着重号为原文所有）

这一批评的要点是，在一个急剧变化的世界里，需要的反思的问题，不仅会对反思性道德出现，而且会对习惯性道德出现。"在此，我该如何行动"这样的问题，即使对于那些仅仅想坚持传统行为模式的人来说，也是不可避免的。温奇说，"在应对环境变化中能够获得有意义的发展的唯一生活模式，在其自身中包含了评价它所规定的意义的手段。"② 无疑，在这句话中，评价意义是一种反思形式，它对于某种生活模式的有意义的发展而言是构成性的。这一点适用于一切生活模式，不管是反思性道德还是习惯性道德。温奇坚信，反思是有意义行为的内在构成因素。习惯性道德若要区别于盲目的习惯或仅仅是对刺激的反应，必须在自身中包含一种反思形式，不然，它就不能在一个永在流变的新环境中获得一种有意义的发展。习惯性道德须面对的急剧变化的环境与习惯性道德的定义之间，存在着紧张。前者蕴含反思，后者则否认反思。这是温奇在欧克肖特的习惯性道德的观念中发现的第二个困难。

温奇的第三个批评指向了欧克肖特自己对道德生活的界说。欧克肖特认为，道德生活"是具有其他可选项的行为"③。紧接着这一界说，欧克肖特作了一个保留："这一其他可选项不必有意识地出现在心灵之前；道德行为不必包含对某特殊行动作反思性的选择。"④ 温奇接受欧克肖特对道德生活的界说，但是他对欧克肖特的保留提出了批评：

> 尽管这个"其他可选项"不必有意识地出现在行动者的心灵之前，但它必须是某种**能够**被置于他心灵之前的东西。要满足这一条件，行动者必须针对人们关于他应该做其他事情的主张，为自己的行为作辩护。或者他至少必须**理解**以不同的方式行动意味着什么。……理解某事也包含理解其对立面：我理解了诚实地行动意味着什么，正好等于我理解了不诚实地行动意味着什么。所以，作为理解的产物的行为，正是具有其他可选项的行为。⑤

具有其他可选项的道德生活是理解的产物，正是这种理解赋予了我们的行为以道德的品格。没

① Winch, *The Idea of a Social Science*, pp. 63 – 4.
② Winch, *The Idea of a Social Science*, p. 64.
③ Oakeshott, *Rationalism in Politics and Other Essays*, p. 466.
④ 同上。
⑤ Winch, *The Idea of a Social Science*, p. 65.

有理解，人的行为就没有道德的意义。温奇把这种理解看做是一种反思形式。他指出："欧克肖特对反思性的态度，事实上是与他在前面的讨论中提出的一个重要观点是相矛盾的。他说，道德生活是'具有其他可选项的行为'"。① 温奇认为，欧克肖特关于习惯性道德和反思绝缘的主张，是与他关于道德生活的定义相矛盾的。道德生活是具有其他可选项的行为这一界说，蕴涵了如下主张，即道德本身内在地包含了反思性的因素。习惯性道德，只要它是道德的一种形式，必然在本性上是反思性的。褫夺了反思的习惯性道德是自相矛盾的。这是温奇所看到的习惯性道德的观念所包含的第三个困难。

温奇对欧克肖特的习惯性道德的观念的上述困难的揭示，无疑是富有洞见的。但是，不能令人满意的是，他就此止步了。事实上，还有很多问题值得我们作进一步的探讨。以下，笔者将强调温奇尚为见及的其他六个方面，希望以此来深化对欧克肖特的习惯性道德的观念的批判。

首先，让我们从温奇的第三个论证开始。温奇敏锐地看到了欧克肖特对道德生活的界说和他的习惯性道德的观念之间的相悖之处。他接受欧克肖特对道德生活的界说，即道德生活是具有其他可选项的行为，并且同意欧克肖特的看法，认为这个其他的可选项不必有意识地呈现在行动者的心灵之前。我认为，后一点是误导的。如上所述，温奇认为，道德行为是理解的产物。令人难以理解的是，一个人怎么可能理解了其他可选项，同时却对之毫无意识。因此，笔者认为，我们可以十分明确地说，欧克肖特的"道德生活是具有其他可选项的行动"的主张，是与他的如下保留是相矛盾的："这个其他可选项不必有意识地呈现在心灵之前；道德行为不必包含对某特殊行动的反思的选择。"与盲目的习惯不同，道德行为对其他可选项是有意识的。面对一组可选项，对它们作反思的、有意识的选择，对于道德行动来说是不可或缺的。②

反思和自我意识总是相伴而行。一旦承认反思，自我意识也必须被承认。温奇似乎也没有充分地认识到这一点。如上所述，欧克肖特试图用"对道德行为传统的精神特质的不自觉（unselfconscious）的开发"来阐明习惯性道德富于变化和善于适应的特征。温奇已正确地指出，习惯性道德富于变化和善于适应的特征没有反思是不可能的，现在，我们可以进一步说，它也不可能是"对道德行为传统的精神特质的**不自觉**的开发"的结果。相反，习惯性道德的富于变化和善于适应的特征，只能用对道德行为传统的精神特质的反思的、**自觉的**开发来阐明。

其次，我想讨论一下习惯性道德的另一个特征，即它对怪异反常（eccentricity）的包容。

---

① Winch, *The Idea of a Social Science*, p. 65.
② 也许有人会为温奇辩护说，温奇虽然没有肯定其他可选项必须**现实地**呈现在意识之前，但他强调它必须能够（亦即**潜在地**）呈现在意识之前。对此，笔者的回答是，这种主张太弱了，在道德行为中，对其他可选项的意识必须是现实的。

欧克肖特的习惯性道德不仅容纳了变化和适应性，还容纳了怪异反常。"我们有时想，对于习俗性道德的偏离，必须总是在某个被表述的道德理想的指导下发生的。但事实并非如此。在每一个传统生活方式的核心处，存在着一种自由和独创性，偏离是对那种自由的表达，它源自对传统本身的敏感，同时又保持对传统形式的忠诚。"① 作为自由的表达，对习惯性道德的偏离不可能无意识地实现。同样，难以想象一个传统的自由和独创性不是试图延续该传统的人反思的结果。他们对传统的敏感，无疑是一种特殊形态的反思。在此，我们看到了欧克肖特习惯性道德的观念的又一个矛盾，即对怪异反常的包容与习惯性道德的定义之间的矛盾。笔者以为，一个人如果能看到富于变化和善于适应的特征与习惯性道德的定义之间的紧张，他就不难看清对怪异反常的包容与习惯性道德的定义之间的矛盾。吊诡的是，温奇看到了前者，却看不到后者。

　　第三，对于人在紧急情况下如何行动这个问题，欧克肖特的认识有明显的偏颇。在紧急情况下，人们既可以非反思地行动，也可以反思地行动，但是，欧克肖特只看到了前者，而忽略了后者。在阐述习惯性道德时，欧克肖特说，"我所描述的，是在所有生活的紧急情况下，当缺乏反思的时间和机会时，道德行动所采取的形式（因为它不能采取其他的形式），同时我认为，适用于生活的紧急情况的，也适用于人类行为摆脱了自然必然性的绝大多数情形。"② 在紧急情况下，人们也许会作出本能反应，即以非反思的方式行动。这时，反应不过是根据盲目的习惯来行动，或者不过是对刺激的反应，或者是一种反射。但是，这不是在紧急情况下人们作出反应的唯一方式。在各种形式的即兴活动中，还有另一种形式的反应。在富有才智的即兴活动中，人们是以一种反思的方式作出反应的。Donald A. Schön 对于优秀的爵士演奏家的即兴表演的描述，为我们提供了一个精彩的例证。Schön 写道：

　　　　即兴演奏就在于变更、结合以及重新组合某个模式中的一组音型，该模式是跳动的并且给予表演以某种连贯性。当音乐家们感受到从他们相互交织的贡献中发展出来的音乐的方向时，他们对它有了新的理解，并根据他们的理解来调整他们的表演，他们在行动中反思（reflecting-in-action）他们集体创作的音乐，反思他们每个人对于该音乐的贡献，思考他们当下的表演，在此过程中，改善他们的表演方式。③

---

① Oakeshott, *Rationalism in Politics and Other Essays*, p. 472.
② Oakeshott, *Rationalism in Politics and Other Essays*, p. 468.
③ Donald A. Schön, 1983, *The Reflective Practitioner*, New York: Basic Books, pp. 55–6.

显然，音乐家在演奏过程中的即时调整（the on-the-spot adjustments）是一种反思的形式。不幸的是，这似乎完全落在欧克肖特的视野之外。

第四，欧克肖特怀具的反思观念是很不完备的。他只看到了两种形式的反思。在阐述反思性道德时，欧克肖特指出，"不仅规则和理想是反思的产物，而且把规则或理想应用于具体情景也是一种反思的活动。"① 反思性道德的第一种反思形式，事关对道德理想和规则的语言表达。首先"要把道德渴望用语词表达出来——表达为生活的规则，或者表达为一个抽象理想的体系"②；其次，当这些被表达的渴望受到攻击时，那些拥护反思性道德的人应当起而为之辩护。可见，在这种情况下，反思主要表现为抽象思维。反思性道德的第二种形式事关把理想和规则应用于当下的生活情景。"把规则和理想应用于具体情景绝非易事；理想和情景通常都需要诠释，生活的规则总被发现有欠缺，除非我们用细致的决疑法或诠释学来作补充。"③ 在这种情况下，反思表现为对抽象的东西和具体的东西的联结。一个成功的联结需要在这两个极端之间达成反思的平衡。欧克肖特所思及的，基本上就是这两种形式的反思。

如果我们将欧克肖特的反思观念与 Schön 在谈论实践中的反思（reflecting-in-practice）时所思及的内容相比照，我们会惊讶地看到，欧克肖特的反思观念是何等的贫乏！Schön 说：

> 当一个实践者在实践中反思，以及对实践加以反思时，他反思的可能对象与呈现在他面前的现象种类一样多，与他赋予它们的实践中的认知系统（the systems of knowing-in-practice）一样多。他可以反思作为一个判断之基础的隐含的规范和评价，或者反思隐含于行为模式中的策略和理论。他可以反思对某情景的感觉，这种感觉引导他采取一种特殊的行动，也可以反思他表述问题的方式，这个问题是他想解决的，或者反思他为自己在一个更大的体制脉络中建构的角色。④

实践中的反思采取了各种各样的形式，其中的一些在这里被提及了。笔者相信，Schön 在此并不旨在给出一个关于实践中的反思的完备清单。Schön 的这段话蕴涵了一个开放、灵活的反思观念，它有助于我们克服欧克肖特狭隘的反思观念。

---

① Oakeshott, *Rationalism in Politics and Other Essays*, p. 473.
② 同上。
③ 同上。
④ Schön, *The Reflective Practitioner*, p. 62.

在此语境中，笔者想指出的是，欧克肖特实际上触及了一种重要的反思形式，但是其狭隘的反思观又遮蔽了它。上文曾提及，欧克肖特把习惯性道德之富有变化和善于适应归结为"对道德行为传统的精神特质的不自觉开发"，现在我们知道，这是错误的归因，应该改为"对道德行为传统的精神特质的自觉开发"。另外，在讨论习惯性道德中的怪异反常现象时，他提到了"对传统本身的敏感性"。我想指出的是，在对传统的精神特质的开发和对传统的敏感性中，包蕴着一种反思的形式。这是一种特殊种类的反思，它一方面区别于盲目的习惯，一方面又区别于反思性的道德。

因此，在我看来，欧克肖特和温奇都没有看到，这里事实上存在着三项内容：盲目的习惯、反思性道德和某种居间的东西。欧克肖特的盲点在于，他混淆了盲目的习惯和居间者。结果，他看到的不是三项，而是两项，即习惯性道德和反思性道德的二分法。

笔者认为，在这里，真正的挑战是要阐明这第三项内容。这是一个特殊种类的反思，但欧克肖特在讨论道德问题时却无视它的存在。但是，有意思的是，在道德领域中含混不清的东西，在政治领域中却显得清楚明白。在欧克肖特对政治的讨论中，这种类型的反思被勾画得轮廓分明。这就引向了笔者对欧克肖特的**第五点**批评，即在欧克肖特对道德和政治的处理中，存在着某种不对称性，显然，这是温奇未尝见及的。在下一节中，我们将在政治领域中阐明这种类型的反思。

二、政治论证：说服性的还是证明性的？

在欧克肖特看来，政治就是参加一个社会的各种安排的活动。有些人倾向于把政治理解为一种经验活动，即对暂时欲望的追求；有些人倾向于把政治理解为一种意识形态，即被独立地预先思考的抽象原则。欧克肖特认为，这两种倾向都是对政治本质的误解。在他看来，要充分地理解政治，我们需要探究的首先是传统的政治行为方式，而不是暂时的欲望和抽象的原则。"在政治中，唯一可觉察的具体活动方式，是这样一种情形，其中，经验主义和所要追求的目的——无论就其存在而言还是就其运作而言——都依赖于一种传统的行为方式。"[1] 政治的秘密驻扎在比经验主义和政治意识形态更深的东西即传统的政治行为方式之中。在对政治活动的阐述中，欧克肖特说，

---

[1]　Oakeshott, *Rationalism in Politics and Other Essays*, p. 56.

　　　　这种活动，既非源于即时的欲望，也非源于一般的原则，而是源于现存的行为传统自身。它所采取的形式——因为它不能采取其他形式——是通过探索和追求现有的安排所暗示的东西，来对它们加以修正改善。①

政治本质上就是追求现存的行为传统的暗示，这是欧克肖特关于政治的本质的核心主张。具体来说，在政治中追求传统的暗示到底是如何运作的呢？欧克肖特解释说：

　　　　构成一个能够作出政治活动的社会的各种安排，不管它们是习俗，或建制，或法律，或外交决定，都是既连贯又不连贯的；它们构成了一个模式，同时它们暗示了对于某种尚未充分出现的东西的同情。政治活动就是探索那种同情；相应地，**相关的政治推理**会令人信服地揭示已然呈现却尚未被跟进的同情，并且令人信服地证明，现在正是认可这种同情的时候。②（着重号为笔者所加）

正是一个社会现有的各种安排的不连贯性，令人信服地提出了修正补救的要求，并且指向了对将要在未来实现的某种东西的同情。所谓在政治中追求传统的暗示，就是以这样的方式展开的，我们基本上也就是以这样的方式来从事政治活动的。按照同样的思路，欧克肖特讨论了政治危机等问题。

　　显然，追求政治活动的某个传统的暗示，远不是根据盲目的习惯行动，或者只是对刺激的反应。这是一种有意识的、反思的行动。正如上述引文所表明的那样，它包含了某种政治推理。现在的问题是，这是一种什么样的政治推理？这种政治推理有什么特点？

　　欧克肖特认为，一套政治话语是由一组信念语汇和一个逻辑设计所构成的。他在讨论政治话语的过程中强调了两种类型的逻辑设计，它们分别对应于两种政治论证，即说服性论证和证明性论证。

　　欧克肖特所说的说服性论证的一个典型例子，是伯利克利于 432 B. C. 在雅典公民大会上的讲演，当时他试图说服他的同胞及时采取措施对抗斯巴达。同时，欧克肖特吸收了亚里斯多德《修辞学》的不少思想来阐发这种类型的逻辑设计的特征。这种类型的政治推理事关人类幸福，旨在说服却不能证明，它"被设计来在一个偶然的情景中建议做什么和不做什么，对这种情景

---

① 同上。
② Oakeshott, *Rationalism in Politics and Other Essays*, pp. 56 – 7

来说，存在着其他各种可选的行动的可能性"①。具体来说：

> 它的论证关注的是偶然性而非必然性；是或然性和期待而不是证明的确定性；是猜想而不是证明；是猜测而不是计算。这种推理是用来说服人们作出决定和行动的，这是建议中所包含的对命题的证明和反驳所不能提供的。②
>
> 这种论证必须采取的形式是对正反两方面的权衡，对行动的可能后果的猜想。③

欧克肖特认为，自古以来，说服性论证是政治话语中最常见的逻辑设计。然而，在西方政治思想史上，一直存在着一种倾向，它不满足于说服性论证，试图超越猜想和意见，向往能够证明和反驳政治主张的逻辑设计。换言之，它所追求的是不容置疑的政治话语，或者说是政治话语中的证明性论证。

欧克肖特指出，在西方政治思想史上，存在着两种进路可以通达证明性论证：

> （1）人们认为，如果存在着已知的具有绝对确定性和普遍应用性的原则或公理，任何政治主张须借以决定其优劣，那么，就会出现证明性政治话语。或者（2），如果我们对人类行为、人类的处境、事件的进程，以及人们有时称之为政治社会的条件，拥有绝对的知识，它能使我们不是猜测，而是在将不同决定付诸实施之前能够预测各种后果，能够使我们证明我们关于如下判断的正确性——即关于在任何情况下什么该做、什么不该做或者什么应当坚持的判断——这时，证明性论证就会出现。④

欧克肖特指出，无论是根据公理还是根据关于人类境况的绝对知识的证明性论证的最大问题在于，它与在具体、偶然的情景中需要作出的政治决定是不相干的。它只关注抽象观念之间的关系，所以不能直面具体的政治情景，不能为我们提供关于具体的政治活动的富有信息量的命题。欧克肖特认为，这两种进路都是注定要失败的。

现在我们可以回答上面提出的问题了，即欧克肖特对政治的理解中所包含的是一种什么样的政治推理？不难看出，政治作为对传统的暗示的追求，内含的政治推理不是证明性推理，而

---

① Oakeshott, *Rationalism in Politics and Other Essays*, p. 79.

② Oakeshott, *Rationalism in Politics and Other Essays*, p. 80.

③ 同上。

④ Oakeshott, *Rationalism in Politics and Other Essays*, p. 82.

是说服性推理。但是，对证明性论证的渴望阻碍了人们认清这一事实。欧克肖特提醒我们，对证明性论证的渴望会给政治造成各种破坏，其中之一与本文的主题相关：

> 这种对证明性政治论证的渴望，会使我们对日常的政治话语产生不满，因为日常的政治话语不是证明性的，我们会受诱惑把它看做是一种非理性的东西。这将是一种灾难性的错误。它是一个错误，因为处理猜想、可能性以及对情境性的正反两方面加以权衡的话语就是推理，且是唯一适用于实践事务一种推理。……它将是灾难性的，因为它会给政治话语带来坏名声，使得我们倾向于完全不理睬它——即放弃反思和论证，因为它们不可能是证明性的。①

在这段引文中，事实上存在着欧克肖特与那些在政治中倡导证明性论证的人之间的一番往复辩难。让我们对这一争论作一番重构。在那些支持政治中的明证性论证的人看来，以说服性论证为特征的日常政治话语完全放弃了反思和论证，因而是一种非理性的东西。欧克肖特则认为，这种看法是一个灾难性的错误。他的反驳意见大致可以概括为：1）证明性论证的支持者所怀具的反思和论证的观念太过狭隘。他们倾向于认为，不是证明性的就不是反思和论证。而在欧克肖特看来，证明只是反思和论证的一种形式，说服是另一种重要形式。2）唯一适合政治话语的推理形式是说服性论证。它通常采取的形式，是在一个偶然的、具体的政治情景中对正反各方面的情况加以权衡，给我们提供猜想和意见。在日常的政治话语中，这是我们最通常的行事方式。说服性论证是唯一适合于政治话语的推理形式这一主张，意味着在政治中对证明性论证的渴望根本上是一种不合法的企望。

有意思的是，尽管上述引文讨论的主要是政治，但是它并不限于政治。在提及说服性论证时，欧克肖特说它是"是唯一适用于实践事务一种推理。"如果我们在古典的意义，即亚里斯多德的意义上来理解"实践事务"这个术语，我们会得出结论说，这一主张不仅适用于政治，也适用于道德。但是，在欧克肖特对政治和道德的处理上，存在着某种不对称性。

我们已经看到，在欧克肖特对道德的处理中，只有对理想和规则的语言表述以及把理想和规则应用于具体的生活情景被认为是反思性的。根据这样一种对反思的看法，传统和反思之间的联系彻底失落了。一旦提及传统，欧克肖特谈论的是对道德行为传统的**不自觉的遵循**。在他那里，任何源自道德行为传统的东西，都被褫夺了反思的品格。因此，他讨论道德的结论是习

---

① Oakeshott, *Rationalism in Politics and Other Essays*, p. 95.

惯性道德和反思性道德的二分法。如上所述，习惯性道德按定义是非反思的，但欧克肖特赋予它的某些特征却蕴涵了反思的因素。习惯性道德的观念之所以含混，是因为它混淆了盲目的习惯和某种本质上是反思的东西。

相反，在欧克肖特对政治的讨论中，政治活动作为对传统的暗示的追求包含了一种特殊形态的推理，其特征是说服性的论证。它是一种特殊形态的反思，不同于证明性反思。说服性论证和证明性论证的区别，不是非反思的东西和反思的东西之间的区别，而是两种反思类型之间的区别。两者都不同于盲目的习惯或者仅仅是对刺激的反应。所以，在政治领域中，我们面对的是三个项目：盲目的习惯、说服性论证和证明性论证。

所以，我们有充分的理由说，在欧克肖特对道德和政治的处理中，存在着某种不对称性。如果我们把欧克肖特在讨论政治问题时所获得的识度推广到道德领域，欧克肖特思想中的内在紧张是可以克服的。这需要我们对成问题的习惯性道德的观念作一番批判的考察。通过对这个观念作仔细的分析，我们可以把其中的非反思成分归结为人类活动中的习惯这一层面，把其中的反思因素归属于一种源自道德行为传统的道德反思，它不同于欧克肖特所说的反思性道德。这样，在道德领域中，我们也得到了三个项目，正如在政治领域中一样。

三、默会认知之体现智力的、反思的和批判的品格

笔者的第六点批评，也是温奇并未意识到的，与如下事实相关，即欧克肖特对两种道德的区分对应于他关于两类知识的区分。在欧克肖特看来，任何人类活动都包含知识。这知识普遍地包含两种类型，一类是技术知识，一类是实践知识。技术知识的主要特点是能够精确地加以表述。它"能用规则、原则、指令和准则，总起来说，能够用命题来表述"[1]。实践知识"只存在于使用中，是**非反思的**，而且（不同于技术）不能用规则来表述"[2]。（着重号为笔者所加）"它通常表达为习俗性的或传统的行事方式，或者简单地说，表达为实践。"[3] 不难看出，能够作精确的语言表述的技术知识对应于反思性道德，而非反思的实践知识则对应于习惯性道德。或者，人们也许可以说，在欧克肖特那里，实践知识和技术知识的区分是习惯性道德和反思性道德的区分的认识论基础，而习惯性道德和反思性道德的区分则展示了实践知识和技术知识的

---

[1] Oakeshott, *Rationalism in Politics and Other Essays*, p. 14.
[2] Oakeshott, *Rationalism in Politics and Other Essays*, p. 12.
[3] Oakeshott, *Rationalism in Politics and Other Essays*, p. 15.

区分的道德意蕴。

在时下关于默会认知（tacit knowing）的讨论中，人们普遍认为，欧克肖特关于技术知识和实践认识的区分，相当于赖尔关于 knowing that 和 knowing how 的区分，也相当于波兰尼关于明述知识（explicit knowledge）和默会认知的区分。但是，笔者认为，在此，有一个重要的差异被人们普遍地忽视了，那就是，knowing how 和默会认知都是体现了智力的、反思的和批判的，而实践知识，按照欧克肖特的定义，是非反思的。下面我们将看到，赖尔和波兰尼都致力于界分 knowing how、默会认知和盲目的习惯。这将有助于我们认识到，欧克肖特关于实践知识的界定是成问题的。

众所周知，赖尔对于人们在日常生活中熟知的 knowing that 的 knowing how 的区别在哲学上给予了高度重视。在赖尔看来，knowing that 包含不同的内容，其共同特征是能够用各种类型的命题加以表述。相反，"knowing how" 则是非命题性的，是一种行动中的知识或实践中的知识。

赖尔考察了一系列智力概念，如"智慧的"、"合乎逻辑的"、"通情达理的"、"审慎的"、"狡猾的"、"灵巧的"、"谨慎的"、"有趣味的"、"机智的"等，及其相反情形，如"不聪明的"、"不讲逻辑的"、"愚蠢的"、"不谨慎的"，"毫无趣味的"，"缺乏幽默感的"等等。他的结论是，这些智力词汇是能用 knowing how 而非 knowing that 来加以界定的。赖尔认为，knowing how 体现了智力。"当一个人知道如何做某类事情时，我们称他为'敏锐的'、'精明的'、'谨慎的'、'智巧的'、'富有洞察力的'、'一个内行的厨师'、'一个出色的的将军'、'一个好的主考者'等等。当我们这么做的时候，我们是在描述他的品格的一个部分，或者说赋予他某种倾向性的卓越（dispositional excellence）。"① 我们有充分的理由把这种倾向性的卓越看做他的第二天性。在此，赖尔提醒我们，不要把体现了智力的 knowing how 混同于习惯。习惯当然也是第二天性，但只是一种类型的第二天性，而不是唯一的第二天性。认为所有第二天性都只是习惯，是错误的。赖尔认为，看清体现智力的能力（intelligent capacities）和习惯之间的差异，具有根本的重要性。

赖尔对于体现智力的能力和习惯之间的差异有一些精到的观察。

首先，习惯性行为是机械自动的，而体现智力的实践则是警觉用心的。赖尔说："当我们说某人按纯粹的或盲目的习惯做某事时，我们的意思是，他是在机械自动地做该事，不必留心自己在做什么。他不必在意，不必警觉，不必有所批评。……对于仅仅是习惯性的实践来说，

---

① Gilbert Ryle, 1946, "Knowing how and knowing that", *Proceedings of the Aristotelian Society*, Vol. 46, p. 14.

某个行动本质上只是原先行动的复本，而对于体现智力的实践来说，某个行动本质上会受到原先行动的影响而有所改变。行动者还在学习过程中。"① 只要想想一个成年人在正常情况下在人行道上漫步与一个登山者在风雪交加的黑夜里在寒冰覆盖的山岩上行走这两者之间的差异，我们就能体会出习惯性实践和体现智力的实践之间的差别来。

其次，我们通过训练（drill）而形成习惯，经过培养（training）而形成体现智力的能力。② "反复练习会产生机械自动的行为，即不需要智力就能很好完成的行动。这就是习惯化，即盲目习惯的形成过程。教育或培养产生的不是盲目的习惯，而是体现智力的能力。在传授一种技巧的过程中，我不是培养学生盲目地做某事，而是聪明地做某事。训练免除了智力，而培养则扩展了智力。"③ 赖尔严格区分了训练和培养。通过足够数量的重复，新兵能通过训练学会行军和扛枪，正如马戏团里的海豹通过训练，能学会表演一些复杂的把戏。但是，一个新兵不能通过训练就学会射击和阅读地图，他必须通过培养才能做到这一点。通过培养，他学会了正确地行动，即用"他的脑子"来射击和使用地图。他是他自己的行动的评判者，他学会如何去发现错误，如何去避免和纠正错误。他所获得的不是一个习惯，而是一项技巧。尽管技巧包含习惯在内，但是前者不能归结为后者。

第三，习惯是简单的、单轨的倾向，而体现智力的能力则是一种具有无限多样实现方式的倾向。如上所述，knowing how 被赖尔描述为一种倾向性的卓越。在赖尔看来，"拥有一种倾向性的属性，不是处于某个特殊状态，或者去经历某种特殊变化；而是当某个特殊条件得到满足时，它倾向于处于某个特殊状态，或者倾向于去经历某种特殊变化。"④ 重要的是要认识到，存在着不同的倾向。有些是简单的、单轨的倾向，其实现几乎是一致的，比如玻璃是脆的，我有抽烟的习惯，等等。但也有许多倾向，其实现会有无数途径，比如某物是硬的，某种动物是群居性的，等等。体现智力的能力属于后者。赖尔说，"Knowing how 是一种倾向，但不是像反射或习惯那样的单轨的倾向。"⑤ 体现智力的能力，作为一种倾向，其实现途径是无限多样的。

总之，赖尔认为，knowing how 体现了智力，不同于盲目的习惯或反射。当一个人知道如何做某事时，他的行动不是机械自动的，他警觉用心地行动着，他是自己行动的裁判者，他的体

① Gilbert Ryle, 1949, *The Concept of Mind*, University Paperbacks, New York：Barnes & Nobles, p. 42.
② 通常人们把 drill 和 training 看做是同义词，但赖尔在此特别强调了两者的区别。为此，我们分别用"训练"和"培养"来对译 drill 和 training。
③ Ryle, "Knowing how and knowing that", p. 15.
④ Ryle, *The Concept of Mind*, p. 43.
⑤ Ryle, *The Concept of Mind*, p. 46.

现智力的实践，是反思的和自我批判的。

在这方面，波兰尼很好地呼应了赖尔。我们将看到，他的默会认知也有一个反思的、批判的维度。他认为，默会认知是人的体现智力的努力的结果。

> 考察一下我们是如何学会使用一个工具或探棒的。作为视觉正常的人，如果我们被蒙住了双眼，那么，我们用手杖来探路，不如一个练习了很久的盲人那么熟练。我们不时地会感到手杖触及了什么东西，却不能把这些事情联系起来。只有通过一种**体现智力的努力**，对手杖所触及的东西形成一种连贯的知觉，我们才能学会做到这一点。……所以，把这仅仅描述为**重复**的结果是误导的；这是一种结构性的转变，是通过重复的心智努力而获得的，它为了实现某种目标而利用了某些事情和行动。① （着重号为笔者所加）

在波兰尼看来，为了认知一个对象（一个综合体、一个整体），我们需要把它的各种线索、细节和部分整合起来。认知者从对后者的辅助觉知（subsidiary awareness）转向对前者的焦点觉知（focal awareness），这是默会认知的基本结构。认知者的整合不只是重复的结果，而是体现智力的努力的成就，后者包含了前者但不能归结为前者。这令人回想起赖尔的主张，即技巧包含了习惯却不能还原为习惯。在此语境中，波兰尼强调了自己的默会认识论和格式塔心理学之间的差异：

> 格式塔心理学已经描述了将一个对象转化为一个工具的过程，以及伴随的感觉转换，比如从掌中感觉到棒端感觉的转换，把它们视为将部分纳入整体的实例。我用略为不同术语刻画了同样的内容，以期阐明一种逻辑结构，在这种结构中，一个人通过**刻意地**（deliberately）把他关于某些细节的觉知融合进对一个整体的焦点觉知来使得自己对某些信念和评价作出承诺。这种逻辑觉知在对视觉整体和听觉整体的**自动的**（automatic）知觉中是不明显的，而格式塔心理学正是从这种知觉中获得其各种流行的概括的。（着重号为笔者所加）②

与格式塔心理学之强调知觉整体形成过程的自动品格不同，波兰尼的默会认识论强调了整合的

---

① Michael Polanyi, *Personal Knowledge*, London: Routledge, pp. 61 – 2.
② Polanyi, *Personal Knowledge*, p. 57.

刻意性，换言之，整合不是不费气力就能获得的。

在赖尔的新兵例子中，我们看到，新兵在其体现智力的行动中，是自己行动的评判者。当波兰尼试图展示默会认知中的评价因素时，他触及了同样的内容。"因为任何一种个人认知的活动都会评价某些细节的连贯性，所以它也蕴涵了对某些连贯标准的接受。当运动员或舞者有最佳表现时，他们是自己的表现的批评者，鉴定专家被认为是物种的优良性状的批评者。所有个人认知都根据它自取的标准来评价它的认识对象。"①

在此语境中，笔者要指出，波兰尼的"无涉批判的"（a-critical）这个术语是误导的。为了阐明明述知识（explicit knowledge）和默会认知的差异，波兰尼引入了"无涉批判的"这个术语。他的基本想法是，我们可以对明述知识取批判的或非批判的态度，但把"批判的"和"非批判的"这样的术语引用于默会认知是不合法的，我们是用其他标准来对默会认知作出判断的，所以我们对默会认知的态度是无涉批判的。我已经在其他地方作过充分的讨论，指出波兰尼的这番论说是站不住脚的，这里只是简要地陈述一下我的结论。② 我的看法是，波兰尼并非要主张默会认知是免于反思、怀疑和批判的，他的真正意图是要指出，默会认知接受批判的方式是不同于明述知识的。在波兰尼的著述中有不少段落表明，默会认知也是可反思、怀疑和批判的。他对默会怀疑（tacit doubt）的讨论更是有力地支持了我的看法。默会怀疑是一种特殊形态的怀疑，是对默会认知的怀疑，体现为内在于各种启发性努力之中的内在的疑虑、非言述的犹豫，比如射手犹豫地扣动扳机。所以，我建议把"无涉批判的"这个术语从他的后批判的哲学中清除出去。一旦我们驱散了"无涉批判的"这个术语所产生的迷雾，我们就会更清楚地看到，在波兰尼那里，默会认知有一个固有的反思的、批判的维度。

现在，让我们回到欧克肖特的实践知识的观念。我们可以看到，褫夺了反思性，表达为习俗的或传统的行事方式的那种知识，是难以与盲目的习惯或仅仅是对刺激的反应区别开来的。但是，如果我们不只局限于欧克肖特对实践知识的定义性说明，如果我们能对欧克肖特关于实践知识的论说拥有一个全面的认识，我们就会发现，把非反思性赋予实践知识是与实践知识的本质特征是相悖的。为了避免空洞的思辨，让我们来看看实践知识的一些具体例子：

因此钢琴演奏者获得了技术也获得了**艺术才能**；棋手既获得了关于走棋的知识也获得

---

① Polanyi, *Personal Knowledge*, p. 63.

② 参见郁振华：《怀疑之批判》，《哲学研究》2008 年第 6 期。

了下国际象棋的**洞见和风格**；科学家获得了某种**判断力**，它会告诉他什么时候技术在将他引向歧途，还获得了一种**鉴别力**，它使他能区分值得探索的方向和不值得探索的方向。①（着重号为笔者所加）

欧克肖特在此描述的是人们获取两类知识即技术知识和实践知识的各种情形。钢琴演奏者的"艺术才能"，棋手的"风格和洞见"，科学家的"判断力和鉴别力"被视为实践知识的范例。不难看出，这正是赖尔和波兰尼在讨论 knowing how 和默会认知时所举的例子。因此，可以说，当欧克肖特谈论实践知识的时候，他所意指的东西在本质上类似于赖尔的 knowing how 和波兰尼的默会认知。赖尔和波兰尼已经令人信服地证明了，作为体现智力的能力，像"艺术才能"、"风格和洞见"、"判断力和鉴别力"这样的东西，没有反思是不可能的。

所以，把非反思性赋予实践知识是实在是欠思考的，它显然是与实践知识的上述特性相矛盾的。那么，是什么促使欧克肖特在关于实践知识的定义性说明中赋予它非反思性的特征呢？答案可以从他那十分狭隘的反思观那里去寻找。欧克肖特对实践知识的定义性说明所自出的语境表明，他之所以把实践知识界定为"非反思的"，是因为实践知识不能像技术知识那样作精确的表述。显然，这个反思观比起他在讨论道德问题所怀具的反思观更为狭隘。

总之，欧克肖特的实践知识的观念就其本身而言是有漏洞的。所以，我建议拒斥将非反思性赋予实践知识这一制造混乱的做法。一旦清除了非反思性这一规定性，欧克肖特的实践知识与赖尔的 knowing how 和波兰尼的默会认识就完全一致了，而且，实践知识这个观念也将能更好地完成欧克肖特所赋予它的批判近代理性主义的使命。

关于西方近代理性主义，除了论及它的各种一般特性，如强调思想的独立、理性的力量，对权威、传统和习俗的挑战等之外，欧克肖特还从认识论的角度对理性主义作了界说。他认为，西方近代理性主义的基本特征是主张"技术的至上性"（the sovereignty of technique），即它不承认实践知识是一种合法的知识形态，认为一切人类活动中唯一的知识要素是技术知识。欧克肖特对实践知识的强调，就旨在挑战西方近代的理性主义。欧克肖特对理性主义的这种理解有其独到之处，他所说的理性主义贯穿于一般所说的经验论和唯理论，在他看来，培根和笛卡尔都是理性主义的代表人物，其共同特点是强调技术的至上性。理性主义对西方近代的政治、道德、教育等都产生了深刻的影响。

---

① Oakeshott, *Rationalism in Politics and Other Essays*, p. 15.

四、结　论

总结本文的讨论，我们已经清楚地看到，欧克肖特的习惯性道德的观念是成问题的。然而，值得指出的是，这个观念背后的动机却是值得嘉许的。欧克肖特关于道德的论说的矛头所向，是理性主义的道德观。"理性主义者的道德是一种自觉追求道德理想的道德，道德教育的合宜形式是通过规条、通过对道德原则的陈述和阐明来进行的。"① 不难看出，理性主义道德就是上文所说的反思性道德。在一个弥漫着理性主义气质的社会中，反思性道德是一种主导性的道德形式。"当代欧洲道德的显著特征是，不但它的形式主要为对理想的自觉追求所支配，而且这种形式通常被认为比其他形式更好、更高。行为习惯的道德被斥为是原始的和过时的；对道德理想（不管对理想本身有什么不满）的追求，被认为是道德启蒙。而且，它被看做是弥足珍贵的东西（从 17 世纪以来就因此而被珍视），因为它似乎提供了一种最为人向往的完美状态，即一种'科学的'道德。"② 但欧克肖特认为，这是一个骗局，是一种错误的意识。道德理想和原则只是道德行为传统的抽象和缩写，它们无法自立：

> 道德理想是一种沉淀物；只有当它们悬浮于宗教或道德的传统中，只有当它们从属于一种宗教生活和一种社会的生活时，它们才具有意义。我们时代的困境在于，理性主义者已如此长久地致力于抽干我们的道德理想悬浮其间的液体（并且弃若敝屣），以至于我们只剩下干燥的、沙砾般的滤渣，吞下时会令人窒息。③

欧克肖特说，由理想和原则组成的道德意识形态本身，是过于吝啬了。换言之，相对于道德整体而言，道德意识形态是过于单薄，过于贫乏了。按笔者的理解，沉淀物—液体的隐喻提示我们，存在着厚厚一层道德行为的习惯和传统，支持着道德意识形态。如果我们把理性主义的反思性道德称为单薄的道德（thin morality），那么，我们有理由把沉淀物—液体的隐喻所暗示的那种道德称作厚实的道德（thick morality）。如上所述，欧克肖特所批判的近代西方道德是一种混合物，其中反思性道德占主导地位。这种道德的构成部分之间，存在着一种内在的紧张。对

---

① Oakeshott, *Rationalism in Politics and Other Essays*, p. 40.
② Oakeshott, *Rationalism in Politics and Other Essays*, p. 486.
③ Oakeshott, *Rationalism in Politics and Other Essays*, p. 41.

道德理想的追求，对于道德行为的传统和习惯有一种分化瓦解作用，会不可避免地削弱道德理想和原则的生命之根，其结果是一种单薄的道德。相反，欧克肖特所向往的道德是这样一种混合物，其中习惯性道德是占主导地位。在这种道德生活中，道德行为的传统和习惯保持着活力，对它们的信心构成了道德行为的源泉。在此基础上，它兼容了反思性道德的优点。这就是欧克肖特为我们勾画的厚实的道德的大致轮廓。

置于西方近代理性主义这一思想背景，欧克肖特所构想的厚实的道德观是一种非凡的洞见。但是，欧克肖特没有看到的是，这个厚实的道德观，同时也是一个三分的道德观。它包括三个层面，即习惯、能力和原则。我用这些术语来指称以下三个层面：1）对道德行为传统的不自觉的遵循，2）在不诉诸道德理想和规则的前提下，对道德行为传统的暗示的追求和探索，3）把道德行为传统抽象或缩写为道德理想和规则。在此，需要对术语的使用作一点说明。"习惯"和"原则"应该没有什么困难，"能力"则略显笨拙。由于缺乏合适的术语，在这里，笔者是在一个高度限制性的意义上使用"能力"这一术语的，它是指对传统中的智慧的一种富有才智的使用。这是一种特殊的能力，一种道德领域中的实践知识，以此人们知道如何在没有抽象原则和一般理论可以依靠的情况下，在具体的、偶然的情景中从事道德活动。① 由于这种能力独立于一般原则，我们可以说，这种对传统的暗示的追求，从逻辑上说是一种创造性的类比思维的能力。② 笔者认为，剥离出这个层面很重要，欧克肖特的盲点就在于把这个层面的内容和盲目的习惯混淆起来，以至于得出了习惯性道德这样一个含混的观念。

---

① 在其论文《政治教育》的附录的结尾处中，欧克肖特写道："J. S. Mill，在放弃了将一般原则作为政治活动的可靠指导和令人满意的说明方法后，代之以'人类进步的理论'和他所说的'历史哲学'。当没有'原则'（它只是具体行为一个标记），也没有关于社会变化的特征和方向的一般理论，似乎可以为说明或为政治行为提供一种合宜的参考时，我在本文中所阐述的观点，可以看作是这种理智的朝圣的一个新阶段。"（Oakeshott, *Rationalism in Politics and Other Essays*, p. 69.）

② 关于这种能力的比较充分的讨论，参见，Kjell S. Johannessen, 2006, "Knowledge and Reflective Practice", in *Dialogue and Tacit Knowledge*, eds. Bo Göranzon, Méaria Hammerén and Richard Ennals, John Wiley & Sons, pp. 229 – 242. 郁振华，2008，《范例、规则和默会认识》，《华东师范大学学报》，第 4 期。

Knowledge, Morality and Politics: A Critical Examination of Michael Oakeshott

Zhenhua Yu

East China Normal University, Shanghai

Abstract: The target of attack of this paper is Oakshott's notion of habitual morality. Winch is brilliant in bringing to light that Oakeshott's notion of habitual morality without reflection is problematic. I would join force with Winch by pointing out six points that he does not see so as to carry on the criticism further. My discovery is that there is an asymmetry in his treatment of morality and politics, and that his blind spot in morality has its counterpart in his conception of knowledge. In conclusion, I would argue that a thick conception of morality that Oakeshott envisions against the background of Rationalism is a remarkable insight. However, Oakeshott fails to see that this thick conception of morality is also a tripartite conception of morality. It contains three levels, namely, habit, competence and principle. He confounds habit and competence and ends up with a dichotomy of habitual morality and reflective morality.

Keywords: habitual morality; reflective morality; persuasive argument; demonstrative argument; tacit knowing

维特根斯坦研究

维特根斯坦的遗稿：道路或背景？

◎ 楼　巍

浙江大学

摘　要：对维特根斯坦的文稿，在读者和研究者中一直有大量理解上的分歧。为了改善这种状况，一些研究者把目光转向了从中汇编出那些以维特根斯坦之名出版的书的原始遗稿，希望通过查看遗稿的方式寻找文本在遗稿中的背景，准确地理解维特根斯坦，平息哲学中的争论。查看遗稿，或多或少会给研究者们带来一些新的信息和新的思路，但是对于"准确理解维特根斯坦"来说，重要的不仅仅是去查阅那些更加原始的文本，还要求人们放弃对建构性的、解释性的哲学理论的深刻依赖和追寻，学会把维特根斯坦的哲学当做是一个不断使思想变得清晰起来的过程。

关键词：维特根斯坦；遗稿；背景

一、维特根斯坦的遗稿和著作

以维特根斯坦之名出版的著作，都是编辑们从维特根斯坦的遗稿（Nachlass）中汇编出来的。

维特根斯坦去世于 1951 年 4 月 29 日。在此之前，他已经立下了遗嘱：我把我的那些没有出版的文字、手稿、打字稿的版权都交给剑桥大学三一学院的里斯先生、安斯康姆小姐和冯·赖特教授，他们可以自己来处理……我希望里斯先生、安斯康姆小姐和冯·赖特教授能够按照他们自己的意见来出版尽量多的文字，但是我不希望他们承担出版的费用，如果他们不期用版税或者其他的形式收回这些费用的话。[1]

维特根斯坦死后，他的遗嘱执行人迅速编辑并出版了《哲学研究》一书，后来陆续又出版了一系列的作品。他们的工作方式是：从维特根斯坦的大量遗稿中选取那些作者本人修改得最仔细的稿件——包括手稿和打字稿。编者更加青睐打字稿，他们认为打字稿是维特根斯坦对手稿的整理。此外他们还经常直接从原始手稿中选取材料，汇编成书，给这些"书"冠上编者自己拟定的名字。这里简要地介绍一下《论确定性》、《关于颜色的评论》、《关于心理学哲学的最后评论》第二卷这三本"书"和维特根斯坦遗稿之间的关系，从多本手稿选取材料的方式使得这三本书有了复杂的家族关系：手稿第 172 号的第 5 到 24 页为《论确定性》的 1 到 65 节，第 1 到 4 页发表于《关于颜色的评论》的第二部分，手稿第 174 号的第 15 页到最后为《论确定性》的 66 到 192 节，第 1 到 14 页则发表于《关于心理学哲学的最后评论》第二卷的第五节，手稿第 175 号发表于《论确定性》193 到 425 节，第 1 到 35 页构成了《论确定性》的 193 到 299 节，35 页到结尾构成了 300 到 425 节，手稿第 176 号的第 22 到 81 页为《论确定性》的 426 到 637 节，第 1 到 22 页发表于《关于颜色的评论》的第一部分，第 82 到 160 页发表于《关于心理学哲学的最后评论》第二卷的最后一节，手稿第 177 号为《论确定性》的 638 到 676 节。

有必要以时间为主线简要介绍一下这些"汇编出来"的书：

《1914—1916 年的笔记》（首版于 1961 年），该书节选自维特根斯坦的战时笔记。

1930 年到 1935 年：《哲学评论》（德语首版出现于 1964 年），这是 1929 年到 1930 年之间的写作成果；《哲学语法》（首版于 1974 年），这本书记录的是维特根斯坦对《大打字稿》前面部分的修改，包含了《大打字稿》末尾那些谈论数学哲学问题的章节（《大打字稿》是他在 1932 年到 1933 年之间整理起来的一个书的初稿）；还有《蓝皮书和棕皮书》，这是 1933—1934 和 1934—1935 学年用英语口述给学生的笔记。

1936 年到 1948 年：《哲学研究》，1936 年末，维特根斯坦草拟了一个《哲学研究》第一部分前 188 节的初期版本，该书的序言则写于 1945 年，过了 1948 年他就基本不再去弄这本书了；《关于数学基础的评论》，维特根斯坦有一个成稿于 1937 年到 1938 年的打字稿，这个打字稿中记录了他自己最满意，也是修改得最仔细的关于数学的评论，维特根斯坦本来打算把这个打字稿当做《哲学研究》第一部分的后续，不过后来它成为了《关于数学基础的评论》的第一部分，该书的第二、第三部分是从 20 世纪 30 年代末期到 40 年代初期的手稿中选取出来的；《关于心理学哲学的评论》的第一、第二卷和《关于心理学哲学的最后评论》的第一卷，这三本书基于 1945 年以后的手稿，据说这些手稿本来是用于《哲学研究》的第二部分的；《字条集》，这是对维特根斯坦的打字稿的采集，跨越了 1931 年到 1948 年，但是大部分集中于 1945 年到 1948 年。

维特根斯坦最后几年的手稿被整合成了三本书：《论确定性》、《关于颜色的评论》和《关于心理学哲学的最后评论》的第二卷。

此外还有两本跨越了维特根斯坦的一生的书：《文化和价值》是对他的遗稿中那些"非哲学"的简短评论的挑选汇集；《哲学的场合，1921—1951》则集结了维特根斯坦生前发表的文章和学生们做的记录。

前面遗嘱中提到的"没有出版的文字、手稿和打字稿"就是他的遗稿，总共有 12 000 页的手稿和 8 000 页的打字稿，他把这些遗产交给了安斯康姆、里斯和冯·赖特，后来他的手迹又时不时地出现。人们可以把能够找到的维特根斯坦的任何手稿、打字稿所组成的整体当做维特根斯坦的遗稿，不过研究者们总是倾向于扩大这个范围，挪威卑尔根（Bergen）大学维特根斯坦档案馆的比吉斯（Michael A. R. Biggs）和皮奇勒（Alois Pichler）认为"维特根斯坦的作品"除维特根斯坦自己的手迹和打字稿以外，还有维特根斯坦口述给别人的笔记，学生在听他的讲座时记下的笔记，以及别人对在与维特根斯坦的对话中获取的思想的回忆，维特根斯坦写给别人的信。[2] 按照冯·赖特的编目，遗稿中"手稿"的编目有 82 项，这 82 项是维特根斯坦的所有手迹，有的只有几页，有的多达几百页，打字稿则有 45 项，口述稿有 11 项。其中，有几项手稿和打字稿已经遗失了。

事实上，"遗稿"这个概念只能在和这些已出版的书的对比中才能获得意义：以各种形式出现的遗稿就像一堆原始材料，而上面所述的那些书，则是对原始材料的修剪、截取、节选、集合。

二、理解维特根斯坦文本的困难

这样一来，人们首先可以在这些书中分清那些"编辑痕迹"比较重的文本和那些维特根斯坦自己修订得臻于"完稿"的文本。一般来说，那些从几部手稿、打字稿中汇编出的书（尽管文字直接来自手稿、打字稿中，但是把材料组合在一起也是一种编辑），比如《关于心理学哲学的评论》和《关于数学基础的评论》，被认为是"编辑痕迹"比较重的，而从那些维特根斯坦本人修订得比较仔细，或者向学生们透露过完工迹象，或者曾经想要出版而最后没有出版的，换言之就是维特根斯坦自己做工作做得最多的打字稿及手稿中汇编出来的书，则是被认为"更接近维特根斯坦"的著作。不过研究者们很快就不得不沮丧地接受这样一个事实，那就是维特根斯坦似乎没有一个可以立即交给出版社，然后变成书的"完稿"。即使被维特根斯坦研究者们所公认的，维特根斯坦花心血最多，修订得也最仔细的《哲学研究》，也不是"完稿"，现在看到的《哲学研究》的第二部分写于 1945 年以后，而书的序言却写于 1945 年，谁也不知道他是不是把现在的第二部分当做他自己心目中的《哲学研究》的第二部分。有一个观点，认为现在出现在书中的第二部分是对第一部分的修订，正如《哲学研究》的"编者按"中写到的，"如果维特根斯坦自己来出版这本书的话，他会大量压缩本书第一部分最后三十页的内容，用更多的材料来修订现在的第二部分，放在那里。"[3] 在 1929 年继续哲学事业以后，维特根斯坦的写作从来没有出现过一个出版意义上的"完稿"，即使是重返哲学界以后，维特根斯坦最希望使之成为一本书的打字稿第 213 号（也就是所谓的《大打字稿》，维特根斯坦到底是不是在试图写一本书，关于这一点也是有争论的），也布满了维特根斯坦自己所作的修改，卑尔根大学维特根斯坦档案馆的网址上可以查看《大打字稿》原稿的照片[4]，一查看，人们就可以发现，他时不时地删去一些句子，甚至删去整个评论，或者改变一些评论的位置。还有一些评论前面标有特殊的标记，表示这个评论比较糟糕，但没有糟到删除的地步。有的地方，则并排竖着几个意义趋近的、供选择用的词，这是因为维特根斯坦难以从中筛选出一个他认为最恰当的词。另外，他还经常同时处理几个不同的主题，有的时候他会几个星期几个月甚至几年地放弃一个主题，后来才又重新转回来，他时不时地从手稿中挑选出一些东西，口述给打字员，用复写纸复写几份，然后修订和重排（也许打字稿并不比手稿完善）。

这就是维特根斯坦的工作方式吧，他是一个劳动着的完美主义者。

维特根斯坦从来没有可以付梓的"完稿"，而且他总是在不停地修改自己的文稿和打字稿。于是一些研究者开始琢磨这些出版的书和维特根斯坦本人的关系。首先，他们认为，既然书是以维特根斯坦的名义出版的，而除了《逻辑哲学论》外维特根斯坦自己没有出版过任何传统意义上的书，这样一来，书与读者隔了一层。其次，后来那些出版的书，都是编辑们从他的遗稿中汇编出来的，正如选编成书的时候摘录某人的这些或者那些文章，可以让读者对这个人的思想持不同看法，这"摘录"的过程是不是也会改变维特根斯坦本人的思想呢？这样一来，书和人之间又隔了一层。再者，如果维特根斯坦总是在修改自己的写作，那是不是意味着他总是在修改自己的思想呢？他的思想是不是就像火焰一样无定形呢？这些怀疑，在"理论上"当然是可以出现的，那些生活在这些自己设想出来的怀疑的恐惧中的研究者们，认为这种状态使他们不能准确地把握到维特根斯坦本人的思想，使得他们在很多时候不能就"维特根斯坦到底在说什么"达成一致。那些专门研究维特根斯坦的学者们也难以跟上维特根斯坦的思路，彻底弄清楚维特根斯坦的想法。

在这样的情况下，出现了很多维特根斯坦的文本的解释者，就《哲学研究》的解释者而言，最负盛名、最兢兢业业的，应该是牛津大学圣约翰学院的哈克（P. M. S. Hacker），他写了四卷大部头作品（其中有两部是他和贝克写的），逐段逐段地解释了《哲学研究》的第一部分，对浓缩在维特根斯坦的评论中的东西作了挖掘，同时也出版了他自己的一些与《哲学研究》的话题相关的文章，这种挖掘和解释的后果，就是把原本不到两百页的《哲学研究》的第一部分扩充到了两千多页[5]。哈克的"两千多页"，其实有点想要平息争吵的意思，但是却没有平息。在有关维特根斯坦的二手文献中，总有着大量的争论和所谓的"商榷"。维特根斯坦自己曾经说过他的工作是要给哲学带来安宁[6]，但是好像哲学变得愈加不安宁了。随便举几个例子，在《维特根斯坦后期哲学的可接近性》（*The Availability of Wittgenstein's Later Philosophy*）中，卡瓦利（Stanley Cavell）批评了坡尔（David Pole）的《维特根斯坦的后期哲学》（*Wittgenstein's Later Philosophy*），美国衣阿华大学的哲学教授斯特恩则在他的《维特根斯坦哲学的可接近性》（*The availability of Wittgenstein's philosophy*）批评卡瓦利对维特根斯坦的遗稿的肤浅看法。还有布鲁尔和林奇的"左派""右派"维特根斯坦之争（有一场争论的导火线就是《哲学研究》第一部分第 219 节的最后一句话"我盲目地遵从规则"），即便是维特根斯坦最亲密的两位学生，里斯和马尔康姆也有过"争论"，他们争论的话题是"本能行为是否可以用来解释语言游戏的确定性"[7]。

斯特恩蹙额疾首地谈到了这一情况，他说："维特根斯坦死后，有了数百本关于维特根斯坦的作品的书，数千篇的学术文章，但是读者们还是不能接近他的哲学。"[8]斯特恩指出，研究者们喜欢围绕维特根斯坦的著作中的少数几个貌似总结性的评论来写文章。有的时候，适当地动用一下"解释"，研究者们甚至可以用同一段话来支持截然不同的观点。

研究者们把哲学的不安宁和他们中间频频发生的争论（暂且不把这种争论当做身为哲学家的研究者们的一种倾向和习惯）归咎于编辑们（尤其是里斯）对遗稿的选择和汇编，他们认为之所以有争论是因为编辑们在某种意义上起着遮盖维特根斯坦原意的作用，而维特根斯坦的原意一定还"存在于"那些遗稿中。于是一些研究者热切地期望遗稿的出版，倡导维特根斯坦文本的阅读者把维特根斯坦的一个评论或者一段话放到更大的"背景"和"语境"中去。斯特恩继续说："哲学家们在寻找维特根斯坦的语言或者经验或者实践的理论，他们的目光局限于少数已经被讨论过多次的评论上，在这些评论中，维特根斯坦似乎在总结他接受（或者拒绝）一个具体观点的真实理由，寻找他的'基本承诺'的'证据'而不去认真地考虑这些引用的评论所处的背景。"[9]"维特根斯坦似乎在总结他接受（或者拒绝）一个具体观点的真实理由"到底是什么呢？回答这个问题不是那么简单，毋宁说这些"总结"也构成了家族相似。熟悉维特根斯坦写作的人应该知道，维特根斯坦偶尔会在评论中插入一些语气与前面的评论不太一样的段落，这样的段落在维特根斯坦自己编辑过的文本中出现的频率最高，它们一般都和前面的评论密切相关，有时是对哲学问题的"总结"，有时则是给出一些人们因为过于熟悉而看不到的事实，它给人的感觉就像维特根斯坦埋头劳动半天以后的片刻休憩。

人们把目光投向了维特根斯坦的全部遗稿。

三、作为"道路"和"背景"的遗稿

维特根斯坦的文本使得读者迷失在理解的困难中，也使得研究者的二手文献中充满了争论。维特根斯坦自己也曾经反思过这个问题，他对听了他的讲座后处于迷惑不解状态的德鲁利说：……最后一个困难，实际上和大多数冗长的哲学讲座紧密联系着，就是听众不能同时看到他正在被带领着走的路和这条路的目的地。也就是说：要么他会想"我理解他说的一切，但是他到底想要去哪里呢？"，要么他会想"我看到了他的目的地，但是他怎么能够到达那里呢？"。我能够做的，仅仅是请你耐心一些，希望最后你能够同时看清道路和目的地。[10]

这里的"道路"，如果我们以"进程"的图像来刻画维特根斯坦的思想的话，那就是维特根斯坦发展出自己思想的整个进程。人们相信这个进程只能在维特根斯坦各个阶段思想的相互关系中才能被找到，而这个各个阶段的思想的相互关系又只能在作为整体的遗稿中被找到。斯特恩说：人们把维特根斯坦所走过的路和达到的结果分了开来，这导致人们有了前期和后期维特根斯坦的争论，《逻辑哲学论》的作者和《哲学研究》的作者的争论，但是争论的双方都没有仔细地研究过一个既包含走过的路也包含取得的结果的遗稿本身。[11]曾经一度负责维特根斯坦遗稿的出版工作的耐杜（Michael Nedo）也曾经说过：理解维特根斯坦哲学的真正钥匙——基于他的表达方式的异质性（idiosyncratic）——是对评论之间的关系的研究：思想从一个评论走向另一个评论的复杂进程。[12]

研究者们认为这里所谓的"道路"是维特根斯坦发展出自己思想的进程。比如维特根斯坦对"唯我论"问题的处理，这个问题横贯了维特根斯坦的一生，他关于这个问题的处理和著述形成了一条有始有终的"道路"，而倘若研究者要在这个道路上躬行一趟，那么他们就不得不去查看做为整体的遗稿。而"背景"说的则是一个评论和其他评论之间错综复杂的血缘关系，维特根斯坦遗稿中的很多段落之间确实有着复杂的血缘关系，有的时候他的一个文本是对另外一个文本的修改，有的时候他干脆直接把此手稿中的文本抄写到彼手稿中去，有的时候一个文本中的句子和另外一个文本中的句子几乎完全一样。比如《论确定性》一书中的一些思想，早已经出现在1937年他写的一篇叫做《原因和结果：直觉的领悟》（Ursache unt Wirkung：Intuitives Erfassen）的文章中了。[13]

此外，还有一个情况使得人们对已经以维特根斯坦之名出版的书愈加不满。那是因为人们发现根据他的打字稿出版的书中没有给出维特根斯坦自己所作的文本与文本之间的间隔，也没有给出维特根斯坦本人的修改痕迹，而人们认为那些变体字、供选择的字词、改正、删除等痕迹，显示了一个正在行进中的维特根斯坦，是饱含信息量的。他们要求查阅和追踪这些修改的痕迹，要求查看更加原始的文献（遗稿被拍摄后制成微缩胶卷，放在康奈尔大学），但是，微缩胶卷的质量没有想像中的那么好，维特根斯坦又一向书写潦草，再加上他总是用一支秃秃的铅笔写字，手稿里的涂改又多，所以，以照片的形式出现的遗稿所起的作用是有限的。

照片、图片的形式不太合用，人们要求以纯文本的方式出版维特根斯坦的全部遗稿，尤其要求出版者把维特根斯坦自己的修改、变体字、供选择的字词等编辑痕迹也留在出版的遗稿中。挪威的卑尔根大学维特根斯坦档案馆一直在做这方面的工作，他们把手稿和打字稿转换成了文本文件，还以一张张图片的形式出版了所有原始遗稿。2000 年，牛津大学出版社出版了一套卑尔根大学版的维特根斯坦遗稿的 CD－ROM，把从照片中转换而来的文本文件和照片本身的图片文件一起刻录在 CD－ROM 上出版了，这些供计算机使用的 CD－ROM 为人们查看维特根斯坦的遗稿提供了便利。

此外还有一本出版于 2005 的英德对照的《大打字稿》，该书的主要特点就是全部保存了维特根斯坦自己所作的修改，老实地展现了最原始的素材。

其实在出版全部遗稿的工作开工之前，人们已经认识到了理解维特根斯坦的文本的困难之一，可能就是因为缺乏文本间的相互对照。于是另外一些加入到维特根斯坦书稿的编辑工作中来的学者对那些汇编自遗稿的文本来了一个"反汇编"，将它们重新放回源文本的大背景中，并找出它们在源文本中的具体位置，找出它们的写作时间，就是所谓的另一种"背景"。比如《文化与价值》，这本书的 1994 年版已经把维特根斯坦手稿中的变体字和供选择的字词全部放在了书中，做了很多脚注，并且在每一个评论后面附注着该评论出现于其中的手稿编目、页码和写作时间，这种改善应该归功于文本编辑者皮奇勒[14]。比吉斯和皮奇勒还写了一篇名为《维特根斯坦：两份源文本目录和一份目录》（*Wittgenstein：Two Source Catalogues and a Bibliography*）的文章，提供了维特根斯坦的书中的每一个图表在遗稿中的位置，提供了书中的一些评论在遗稿中的位置和写作时间。他们考证得最全面的是《关于数学基础的评论》和《哲学语法》。另外值得一提的是毛利（André Maury），他基本找到了《哲学研究》和《字条集》中的每一个评论出现于其中的遗稿的具体编目、页码和写作时间。[15]

这些人的工作和遗稿的出版，意味着人们对维特根斯坦遗稿的理解的加深，也寄托着人们想要平息哲学中的不安宁，准确地理解维特根斯坦的思想的良好心愿。不过，要打开维特根斯坦思想之门，遗稿所起的作用是有限的。正如长岛大学的撒维奇科（Beth Savickey）所言："遗稿，只有当其改变我们的文本解读和哲学分析的方式的时候，才能为我们提供洞见和理解。"[16]

四、看待遗稿的方式的转变

前面提到的出版遗稿和修订书籍的工作，其目的是为了找到所谓的"背景"，借此来准确地理解维特根斯坦的思想，平息关于维特根斯坦的争论，给哲学带来安宁。但是，正如游戏不是仅靠规则而被玩起来的一样，理解维特根斯坦仅靠遗稿的出版也是不够的，还需要转变看待维特根斯坦文本的方式，同时这也是看待维特根斯坦哲学的方式的转变。

很多研究者有一个错误的观念基础，那就是把不能准确地理解维特根斯坦原意的原因归为在维特根斯坦的书中缺乏"系统化的思想"。撒维奇科说："在二手文献中，人们用构建论点或系统化的思想，用连贯一致的文章的形式来重写他的评论，试图找到他的看法的哲学基础或目标。维特根斯坦的评论经常被节选出来，重新排列，整在一起，来形成一种更被人理解，或者更加完整的哲学思想。"[17] 是的，连贯一致的文章，正是维特根斯坦写不出来的东西。在《哲学研究》的前言中他自己幽默地说，如果他试图违背其自然倾向而强迫他的思想进入一个单一的方向，那么那些思想很快就会变成跛子。[18]

维特根斯坦的文本确实不合于人们概念中的"哲学文章和哲学书"，人们认为维特根斯坦的书是不系统的、片段的、异质的、不连贯的、没有严格逻辑的，反正，人们不能以自己所熟悉的方式来阅读它们。看来研究者们得在两条路之间选择一条，要么学会去熟悉另外一种文本，要么花点功夫来解释，让这些文本对他们变得熟悉起来。但是有一些研究者并不这么想，他们带着对业已出版的文本的不满，觉得遗稿会更像他们观念中的"哲学文章和哲学书"，而转向了遗稿。这其实是一种偏见，而偏见是一种严重的理智病。就拿词语的意义来说吧，他让我们去查看词的实际使用，而不要先入之见地浇筑好一个个意义的模型，固执地把意义当做图像（意象），当做词带给我们的感觉，当做某种实体，当做逻辑运算中的一个步骤，然后强迫词语的意义进入到这些模型，并且用一种例子来滋养自己的思想[19]。

维特根斯坦难道没有写过"像一本书"的书吗？他确实也尝试过想要写一本传统意义上的，有章节和目录的书，比如《大打字稿》；人们还发现《蓝皮书和棕皮书》（它们是两本书）好像是持续而完整的、连贯的，它们不以"片段"的形式出现，更像传统的书。但是这又怎么样呢？里斯认为这两本书是"对《哲学研究》的初步学习"，但是真的是这样吗？拿《蓝皮书》来说吧，这本书倒是不以片段的方式，而是以文章的方式出现的。但读蓝皮书也是困难的，困难就在于思想过于密集，简直让人无法休息（读《哲学研究》的人倒是可以在维特根斯坦自己喘气的时候喘一下气）。另外，这本书是维特根斯坦对学生的口述，在书中，这一次和那一次口述之间没有界限。维特根斯坦自己也体会到了这种困难，他在给罗素的信中写道：我觉得这些讲座是很难理解的，因为这里暗含着如此多的要点。它们只适用于那些听了这些讲座的人。正如我说的，你不读它的话也没有任何关系。[20]

"像一本书"的书反而更难懂，而那些试图在遗稿中找传统的文本，找哲学理论和哲学论点的研究者注定要失败了。维特根斯坦认为这种以文章和书的方式写作是毫无价值的，1933 年以后，他很快就放弃了这种哲学文章和哲学书的写作方式，转向了写评论的方式，并用空行将它们隔开。既然维特根斯坦已经放弃了传统的哲学文章和哲学书的写作，那么正如我们也可以看到的，在这一点上，他的遗稿也并没有什么变化。

很明显，遗稿对于那些试图在遗稿中寻找传统意义上的，以哲学文章形式写成的文本，找哲学理论的研究者是没有什么作用的。这也是为什么撒维奇科提醒我们要改变文本解读和哲学分析的方式的原因，因为正是这种方式，正是我们自身的期待，使我们难以理解维特根斯坦，难以从遗稿中找到理解的钥匙。

德语的"Bemerkung"，有着"评注、评语、意见、评论"的意思，而"评论"一定是"评论某物"，而不是自说自话。所以，如果不知道这些树好的哲学标靶，而把维特根斯坦的写作当做是一种自说自话式的，试图构建一个完整理论体系的写作活动，那肯定要与维特根斯坦背道而驰。维特根斯坦的靶子挺多的，有罗素、詹姆斯、弗雷格、逻辑实证主义者，以及他自己，不过维特根斯坦并不是特别关心具体的人，他更加关心的是那些滋养出混乱和很多无谓的"争论"的偏见，比如滋养出无数哲学问题的，同时也滋养出行为主义和内在主义的争论的，"感觉是私有、内在的"这样的一个"语法命题"，指明这些命题的无意义，是《哲学研究》的工作的一个重要组成部分。

维特根斯坦的文本的特殊性，首先来自这样的事实：维特根斯坦的评论是一次次地对胡说发起的进攻，带领人们"从遮遮掩掩的胡说过渡到明显的胡说"[21]。更重要的是，在指出胡说以后，维特根斯坦绝不会马上就奔向那晦暗的"没有胡说"的地方。当我们在搞哲学的时候，语言中总是充满了或明或暗的胡说，但人们以为借此可以走到一个没有胡说的地方，而那没有胡说的地方是很吸引人的。在维特根斯坦看来，那些试图构造一个关于数学、语言、人类行为的无所不包的理论的哲学家们，正是这些人的典型代表。

"从遮遮掩掩的胡说过渡到明显的胡说"以后，维特根斯坦干什么去了呢？他继续工作去了。所以，正如他对自己的评价一样，他的评论总是从一个话题跳到另外一个话题，有的时候甚至还要重新回到前一个话题，因为他发现那里还有一些东西没有说清楚，另外，即使是同一段话，甚至也可以包括很多的"话题"，这才是使他的文本显得十分"错综复杂"的真正原因。

维特根斯坦的遗稿，可能只有当人们对它的看法真正转换以后才能起到应有的作用吧。

参考文献

［1］转引自 Hans Sluga，David G. Stem，edited，1996，*The Cambridge companion to Wittgenstein*，Cambridge University Press，p. 454.

［2］Michael Biggs and Alois Pichler，1993，*Wittgenstein：Two Source Catalogues and a Bibliography*，Working papers from the Wittgenstein Archives at the University of Bergen，No. 7，p. 4.

［3］Ludwig Wittgenstein，1997，*Philosophical Investigations*，Oxford：Basil Blackwell，p. 6.

［4］http：//wab. aksis. uib. no/wab_hw. page.

［5］哈克出版的书见 http：//info. sjc. ox. ac. uk/scr/hacker/PublicationsBooks. html.

［6］原文是"真正的发现是这个使我能够在想要停止的时候就停止搞哲学的东西。——这个东西给哲学带来安宁，所以哲学不再为给哲学自身带来问题的问题所折磨。相反地，我现在用举例子来表明一种方法；这一系列的例子是可以被打断的。——很多问题得到了解决（困难消散了），而不是一个问题。" Ludwig Wittgenstein，1997，*Philosophical Investigations*，Oxford：Basil Blackwell，§ 133.

［7］Rush Rhees，2003，*Wittgenstein's On Certainty*，edited by D. Z. Phillips，Oxford：Basil Blackwell，pp. 162 – 164.

［8］Hans Sluga，David G. Stem edited，1996，*The Cambridge companion to Wittgenstein*，Cambndge University Press，p. 442.

［9］Ibid，pp. 442 – 443.

［10］Rush Rhees，edited，1984，*Recollection of Wittgenstein*，Oxford：Oxford University Press，pp. 79 – 80.

［11］Hans Sluga，David G. Stem edited，1996，*The Cambridge companion to Wittgenstein*，Cambndge University Press，p. 450.

［12］Michael Nedo，1993，*Ludwig Wittgenstein：Wiener Ausgabe Introduction*，New York：Springer-Verlag，p. 53.

［13］Ludwig Wittgenstein，1998，*On Certainty*，Oxford：Basil Blackwell，and Ludwig Wittgenstein，1993，*Philosophical Occasions*，*1912 – 1951*，edited by James C. Klagge and Alfred Nordmann，Hackett Publishing Company，p. 377.

［14］Ludwig Wittgenstein，1998，*Culture and Value.* Edited by Georg Henrik von Wright in Collaboration with Heikki Nyman，Revised Edition of the Text by Alois Pichler，Translated by Peter Winch，Blackwell.

［15］A. Maury，1981，*Sources of the Remarks in Wittgenstein's Zettel.* Philosophical Investigations 4，pp. 57 – 74 and，1994，*Sources of the Remarks in Wittgenstein's Philosophical Investigations.* Synthese 90，pp. 349 – 378.

［16］Beth Savickey，1998，*Wittgenstein's Nachlass.* Philosophical Investigations 21. 4，p. 357.

［17］Ibid，p. 347.

［18］Ludwig Wittgenstein，1997，*Philosophical Investigations*，Blackwell，p. 8.

［19］Ibid，§ 593

[20] Brian McGuinness, edited, 2008, *Wittgenstein in Cambridge*, *Letters and Documents 1911 – 1951*, Oxford: Basil Blackwell, p. 250

[21] Ludwig Wittgenstein, 1997, *Philosophical Investigations*, Oxford: Basil Blackwell, §464.

Wittgenstein's Nachlass：road or background

Wei Lou

Zhejiang University

Abstract：Researchers have disputed a lot concerning Wittgenstein's writing，but his philosophy still remains unavailable. While the works published under Wittgenstein's name were all complied from his whole Nachlass，people tried to get the published works' background through checking the Nachlass through which they wanted to understand Wittgenstein exactly and give philosophy peace finally. Checking the Nachlass of course can bring some new information and thinking，but this can not alone lead to the completely exact understanding of Wittgenstein，people should rather give up their hungry seeking of constructive and interpretive philosophical theories and try to treat Wittgenstein's philosophy as a praxis process through which thoughts can receive its clarification.

Keywords：Wittgenstein；Nachlass；Background

后期维特根斯坦哲学研究评析

◎ 徐 弢

南开大学

摘 要：本文试图通过分析后期维特根斯坦哲学研究视角的转换，从而阐明其后期哲学研究的本质是一种特殊的语法研究，同时分析其语法研究的主要方法与存在的困难，最后对其后期哲学研究进行简短地评论。

关键词：哲学研究；视角；语法研究；纵观；描述

一、哲学研究视角的转换

众所周知，后期维特根斯坦的哲学研究与他前期的哲学研究相比，两者之间存在着巨大的差异。这种差异首先就体现在前后期哲学中存在的两种不同的哲学研究视角。前期维特根斯坦由于受到弗雷格和罗素哲学思想以及逻辑分析研究方法的影响，主张我们需要对语言和命题进行充分地逻辑分析，从而发现传统的哲学问题产生的根源。他前期哲学研究的视角可以说是一种主张彻底充分的逻辑分析的研究视角。他在《逻辑哲学论》的序言里明确宣称"本书讨论哲学问题，而且我相信它指出了这些问题都是由于误解我们语言的逻辑而提出来的"[1] "有关哲学的东西所写的命题和问题并非谬误，而是无意义的。因此，我们根本不能回答这类问题，而只能明确指出其无意义性。哲学家的问题和命题大多是基于不了解我们的语言逻辑"[2]。 在他看来，传统的哲学问题就是由于误解了我们的语言的逻辑句法而产生的，很多是无意义的，因为它们超出了我们有意义言说的界限。所以前期维特根斯坦认为"全部哲学都是对于我们的'语言批判'"[3]。正因为前期维特根斯坦持有以上这种看法使得他坚信，我们需要坚持逻辑分析作

---

① 维特根斯坦，2003，《逻辑哲学论》序言，《维特根斯坦全集》第 1 卷，陈启伟译，河北教育出版社，第 187 页。

② 同上书，4.003，第 204 页。

③ 同上书，4.0031，第 204 页。

为基本的哲学研究视角，并对于我们的语言和命题中内在的逻辑进行分析和批判，阐明我们对于语言和逻辑的哲学误用，划分有意义与无意义的界限，从而达到澄清哲学问题的目的。

随着维特根斯坦对于哲学和日常语言之间关系理解的逐步加深，他开始认识到前期的逻辑分析方法作为哲学研究的视角所带来的很多不足与问题，进而主张对之进行有力的批判，而是主张从日常语言的实际使用角度出发，澄清和解决哲学问题。尽管他还强调语言的研究对于哲学研究的重要意义，但是他开始关注语言的实际使用，而不是纯粹的单一的逻辑分析。在后期他所践行的哲学研究其实从根本上来说是一种哲学语法的研究。一方面他否认前期所主张的存在一切命题都共有的逻辑形式和结构，抛弃了命题意义的图像论，以及语言与实在之间的同构关系的看法，否定逻辑形式，而是强调日常语言的语法结构和使用规则，认为语词的意义在于使用；另一方面，他放弃了前期所主张的对于哲学问题需要进行逻辑分析的研究视角，而是主张对于哲学问题进行治疗，找出哲学病的病因，从而彻底地消除哲学问题。哲学的治疗就是一种语法上的治疗，即运用日常的语言来描述语言的日常用法，将对于日常语言语法规则的研究视为哲学研究的任务。所以，他认为"当语言休假时，哲学问题就产生了"。"我们的混乱是当我们的语言机器在空转而不是在正常工作时产生的"。①

在《哲学研究》中，他对于逻辑分析的研究方法的批评更加激烈。他说我们"愈细致地考查实际语言，它同我们的要求之间的冲突就愈尖锐。（逻辑的水晶般的纯粹远不是我得出的结果，而是对我的要求。）这种冲突变得不可容忍；这个要求面临落空的危险。我们踏上了光滑的冰面，没有摩擦，因此在某种意义上条件是理想的，但我们也正因此无法前行。我们要前行，所以我们需要摩擦。回到粗糙的地面上来吧！"② 这也就是说，逻辑分析的研究方法虽然很纯粹、严格，但是却和实际的语言状况存在很大的差距与冲突；我们想通过逻辑分析的方法来研究语言的希望注定是危险的，要落空的。因此，维特根斯坦主张我们要关注语言的实际使用情况，即所谓的"回到粗糙的地面上来"，也就是将考察语言的逻辑的、理想的视角，转移到语言的实际使用的视角上来。在接下来的 108 节他继续强调我们必须抛弃逻辑分析的方法。他说："但现在逻辑成了怎样的？它的严格性在这里好像脱胶了……只有把我们的整个考察扭转过来才能消除这晶体般纯粹的先入之见。（可以说：必须把考察旋转过来，然后要以我们的真实需要为轴心。）"③ 在维特根斯坦看来，那些主张用纯粹的逻辑方法就能解决哲学问题的观点其实

---

① 维特根斯坦，2005，《哲学研究》，李步楼译，陈维杭校，商务印书馆，第 29，77 页。
② 维特根斯坦，2001，《哲学研究》，陈嘉映译，上海世纪出版集团 上海人民出版社，第 70 页。
③ 同上书，第 71 页。

只是一种先入之见，不符合我们的真实需要。因为我们所讨论的是时空中的语言现象而不是那种非时空的"非物"，而纯粹地用逻辑分析方法来考察语言的话，就是将语言看成是非时空中的东西，这在根本上就是弄错了方向。

后期维特根斯坦不仅明确地指出逻辑分析方法对于研究语言哲学问题不靠谱，而且分析了其产生的原因。为什么大家都喜欢用逻辑分析的方法去解决语言和哲学的问题呢？这在维特根斯坦看来，主要是由于我们对于我们的语言形式有着很多的误解。这些误解包括：我们总以为我们的语言形式可以通过逻辑分析的方法得到一种最终确定的分析，一个表达式也只有唯一的一种充分的解析形式。本质的东西隐藏在未经分析的语言之中，我们只要分析揭示隐藏的东西，我们就可以把握语言形式背后的本质，澄清语言的表达和相关的哲学问题。这也就是说，我们总想通过充分的逻辑分析来追问语言、句子以及思想的本质，探索语言的功能和结构，以此希望获得一个一劳永逸的、独立于任何未来经验的答案，以便彻底地解决所有的问题。这样一来，我们就将思想的本质完全看成是逻辑的东西，认为它表现着世界先验的秩序。这种观点还以为世界和思想必定存在种种逻辑上的可能的秩序。秩序是最简单的，同时也是最确定的。所以，维特根斯坦在《哲学研究》的 97 节的末尾里说："我们有一种幻觉，好像我们的探索中特殊的、深刻的、对我们而言具有本质性的东西，在于试图抓住语言的无可与之相比的本质。那也就是句子、语词、推理、真理、经验等等概念之间的秩序。这种秩序是——可以说——超级概念之间的超级秩序。其实，只要'语言'、'经验'、'世界'这些词有用处，它的用处一定像'桌子'、'灯'、'门'这些词一样卑微。"① 维特根斯坦后期对于这些所谓的"超级概念"不感兴趣，他关注的是语言语词的使用之间的精微的差别，考察的是语言的实际用法。所以他强调"我们把语词从形而上学的用法重新带回到日常的用法"②。

维特根斯坦正是通过对于逻辑分析方法的批评，即批评逻辑研究方法的单一性、纯粹性以及形式的统一性，来达到对于哲学的重新认识。哲学问题不可能通过严格的逻辑分析来彻底地获得解决。我们应该首先关注的是语言的具体用法，而不是语言的抽象的逻辑分析。我们所要做的是对于已经敞开在我们眼前的东西加以理解，而不是发掘隐藏的本质的东西。所以后期维特根斯坦强调哲学"不可用任何方式干涉语言的实际的用法；因而最终只能描述语言的用法。它让一切如其所是"③。

---

① 维特根斯坦，2001，《哲学研究》，陈嘉映译，上海世纪出版集团 上海人民出版社，第 67 页。
② 同上书，第 73 页。
③ 同上书，第 75 页。

二、哲学研究的重新定位

既然哲学问题已经不再是用逻辑分析方法就可以解决的，哲学只能描述语言的用法，那么哲学到底具有什么样的性质和特征呢？或者说他的所谓的"哲学研究"到底是指什么类型的研究呢？在后期维特根斯坦看来，真正的哲学研究是指对于我们语言的语法研究。他在《哲学研究》的第90节中说"我们的考察是语法性的考察。这种考察通过清除误解来澄清我们的问题；清除涉及话语用法的误解。导致误解的一个主要原因是，我们语言的不同区域的表达形式之间有某些类似之处。这里的某些误解可以通过表达形式的替换来消除。"① 因而在他看来，考察我们语言的实际用法，清除由于各种原因所造成的误解，才是哲学研究的真正主要任务。产生哲学问题的最大的根源也就在于此，即对于语言语法特征的误解。他分析我们误解语言语法的一个主要原因就是对于不同的语言表达形式之间的某种随意的类比，从而产生了混乱。例如，我们经常会像说"我想拥有一个房子"一样说"我想拥有一个心灵"。在这里，虽然这两个表达式表面上看去很相似，但其实内在的语法很不一样。因为"心灵"并不是像房子那样可以直接拥有的东西或对象。再例如"红是一种颜色"与"所有能够被叫做红的，也能被叫做颜色的"，这两个表达式表面上看语法不同，其实它们表达了相同的含义。所以有时，语法形式存在表面的相似性，但是却有着内在用法与含义的不同。另外，维特根斯坦还认为"本质在语法中道出自身"。"一大团哲学的云雾凝聚成一滴语法"。② 因而，研究语言的语法对于理解语言的实际意义十分重要，从而在他看来，语法研究是他后期哲学研究的主要内容。因而正如英国学者 M. 麦金所说："'一种语法研究'的观念在维特根斯坦后期哲学中居于中心地位，也是理解其作品的关键。《哲学研究》可以视作特殊语法研究的大汇总。"③

维特根斯坦的语法研究中的"语法"概念比较独特，与语言学家所讲的"语法"不一样。维特根斯坦的"语法"又可以叫做"哲学的语法"，实质是指"概念的分析"。这一点他在《哲学研究》的383节中曾明确地提出来。他说："我们不分析现象（例如思想），而分析概念（例如思想的概念），因而就是分析语词的应用。"④ 这也就是说，维特根斯坦不像语言学家们那样去研究"语法"的理论建构，而是把他的语法研究集中在分析语言的概念，以便消除哲学的

---

① 维特根斯坦，2001，《哲学研究》，陈嘉映译，上海世纪出版集团 上海人民出版社，第67页。
② 同上书，第178，348页。
③ M. 麦金，2007，《维特根斯坦和〈哲学研究〉》，李国山译，广西师范大学出版社，第15页。
④ 维特根斯坦，2001，《哲学研究》，陈嘉映译，上海世纪出版集团 上海人民出版社，第181页。

混乱。维特根斯坦的"语法"是"哲学的语法",是"广义的语法",这种语法研究其实就是对于语言现象中的概念进行分析,发现不同语言表达式用法的差异和相似之处,达到一种对于语言语词用法的整体把握,从而消解掉由于误解语言用法而产生的哲学问题。因而正如学者贾维尔(Newton. Garver)所说:"维特根斯坦的语法不仅与语言学对立,而且与 Austin、Searle 的言语行为理论相对;将哲学看成语法意味着哲学有时像教育学,有时像治疗,但它绝不像科学。"①

在后期维特根斯坦看来,哲学研究其实就是语法研究,因而在这个意义上,我们可以发现哲学的性质与其他的科学性质的不同。哲学不再像以往的传统哲学那样完全是理论的建构,它不提出任何理论,而只是描述语言的用法。维特根斯坦在《哲学研究》的 109 节里也明确提到这点:"说我们的考察不可能是科学的考察,这是对的……我们不提出任何一种理论,我们的思考中不可能有任何假设性的东西,必须丢开解释,而只用描述来取代之。"② 关于哲学的治疗的比喻,维特根斯坦在后期的著作中多次提到。他认为哲学不是一种体系或理论的建构,而是一种理智的澄清活动,这种活动就像医生给病人治病一样,哲学的研究工作也就是防止我们的理智生病。

维特根斯坦的语法研究或者说哲学研究的目的是对哲学概念进行澄清,让哲学问题"自动消失",使得"思想归于宁静"。他说:"我们所追求的当然是一种完全的清晰,而这只是说:哲学问题应当完全消失;真正的发现是这一发现——它使我们能够做到的只要我愿意我就可以打断哲学研究——这种发现给哲学以安定,从而它不再为那些使哲学自身的存在成为疑问的问题所折磨。""你的哲学的目标是什么?——给苍蝇指出飞出捕蝇瓶的出路"。③ 在维特根斯坦看来,我们被哲学问题所困扰就像苍蝇飞进了捕蝇瓶,我们深陷哲学问题的陷阱而不得出。哲学问题的陷阱其实也就是我们所用语言的语法的陷阱,我们被我们的语法幻象所迷惑,因而我们只有进行语法研究,对语法概念进行细致地分析,厘清我们语言的实际用法,才能让哲学问题自动消失,才能使得我们的"思想归于宁静"。

维特根斯坦还对"语法"这个概念进行了区分,即区分了"表层语法"和"深层语法"。他在《哲学研究》的 664 节里写道:"在一个词的用法里,我们可以区分'表层语法'和'深层语法',使用一个词时直接给予我们印象的是它的句子结构里的使用方式,其用法的这一部

---

① Garver, 2006, *Philosophy as Grammar*, *The Cambridge Companion to Philosophy*, Edited by Hans Sluga, David G. Stern, Cambridge University Press, p. 151.

② 维特根斯坦,《哲学研究》,陈嘉映译,上海世纪出版集团 上海人民出版社,第 181 页。

③ 同上书,第 132,158 页。

分——我们可以说——可以用耳朵摄取——再拿例如'意谓'一词的深层语法和我们会从其表层语法推向的东西比较一下。难怪我们会觉得很难找到出路。"① 在此，维特根斯坦不仅对于"表层语法"和"深层语法"之间作了明确的区分，而且还承认发现"深层语法"的确很难。维特根斯坦的"表层语法"是指语词结构的使用方式，很容易就能被我们鉴别出来。"可以说，他所说的表层语法就是指语言学中的语法规则，即人们为了正确使用表达式都必须遵守的那些规则，如词法规则、句法规则等等。"② 其实维特根斯坦所讲的"表层语法"就是我们通常所理解的语法规则。这个很好理解。我们只有通过遵守一定的句法和词法规则，才能够构造符合语法的句子，才能完成交流的目的。

但是，要想真正地理解什么才是维特根斯坦所谓的"深层语法"却不是一件易事。维特根斯坦所谓的"深层语法"到底是指什么？他自己似乎对此也没有清楚地给出一个关于"深层语法"的详细说明。我们只能按照维特根斯坦对于"表层语法"和"深层语法"区分的线索，来寻找"深层语法"的踪迹。其实，维特根斯坦关于"深层语法"暗示体现在诸多的例子之中。维特根斯坦在《哲学研究》中 665 节里举例说道"设想某个人面部带着疼痛的表情指着自己的面颊，同时说'阿玻拉卡达玻拉！'——我们问：'你什么意思？'他回答说：'我这话的意思是牙疼。'——你马上会想：怎么竟可以用这话来'意谓牙疼'呢？或，究竟什么叫做：用这话意谓牙疼？然而在另一种上下文里你却会主张，如此这般意谓的心灵活动在语言使用中恰恰是最为重要的东西。但怎么呢，——我就不可以说'我用'阿玻拉卡达玻拉！'意谓牙疼'吗？当然可以；但那是个定义，不是在描述我说这话时在我的心里发生的事情。"③ 在这里，维特根斯坦举了一个关于"意谓"一词的"深层语法"的例子。说话者可以随便用一句话来"意谓"他的牙疼，因为这一过程本身就体现了语法用法规则的任意性。但是一句话、一个词语都是一组符号，这组符号可以承载说话者所赋予的深层含义。即使像"阿玻拉卡达玻拉"这样的一个在正常人听来毫无意义的语词，它也可以被说话者用来表示特殊的深层的含义。

但是关键的问题是，这种任意的意谓到底具有或不具有那种公共性？也就是说，你用的那个符号表达特定的含义，别人是否认可你的做法？这是存在很大争议的。有的人可能认可你的说法，承认你可以将一符号赋予特定的内涵；但是也有人会质疑你的这种做法的合法性。他会说语言的用法应该是公共的，而不是私人的，不能私人地赋予任一符号以特定的含义，如果那

---

① 维特根斯坦，2001，《哲学研究》，陈嘉映译，上海世纪出版集团 上海人民出版社，第 262 页。
② 涂纪亮，2005，《维特根斯坦后期哲学思想研究》，江苏人民出版社，第 109 页。
③ 维特根斯坦，2001，《哲学研究》，陈嘉映译，上海世纪出版集团 上海人民出版社，第 262 页。

样的话，就等于毫无意义。维特根斯坦注意到，如果我们大家只要用一个语句或语词再加上"意谓"一词就可以表达所谓的"深层语法"的含义的话，那么这种做法也仅仅是一个形式的定义，其本身并不能描述说话者自身真实的想法和意图。所以，这也就是说，用"意谓"来定义"深层语法"是有局限性的。

像这样的例子还很多，维特根斯坦举出这些例子的目的就是想让我们注意到我们语言的实际使用中的用法的不同，注意到差别和冲突，消除哲学混乱，澄清哲学问题，从而达到"思想的宁静"的哲学目的。维特根斯坦的语法研究，就是要详细地考察我们语言的具体的、实际的使用情况；以前的哲学问题和混乱的产生就是因为没有细致地考察语言的实际用法，从而导致了很多的神话和虚构。所以，在我们看来，后期维特根斯坦的哲学研究主要就是语法研究，即对于我们语言的用法进行细致的描述和概念分析；哲学的性质就是语法研究。并且正如英国学者 M. 麦金所说"维特根斯坦的语法探究，旨在产生一种理解，这种理解就在于，于明摆在眼前的东西中看出先前我们所忽略的型式和形式。正是通过慢慢地意识到这种形式，我们才得以逐步地揭示并理解语言、意义、理解等的本质。"①

三、语法研究的主要方法

后期维特根斯坦的语法研究方法到底是指哪些研究方法？他的哲学研究方法有哪些？在维特根斯坦看来，哲学的研究方法是多元的，不是单一的；语法研究的方法也是多种多样的，不是唯一的。他在《哲学研究》的 133 节里也强调了这一点。他说："并没有单独一种哲学方法，但却有哲学方法，就像有各式各样的疗法。"② 这就是说，哲学的研究或者说哲学式的语法研究就如同医生给病人治病一样，应该对症选择疗法，根据不同的哲学"症状"或语法误解的"症状"选择不同的方法。维特根斯坦本人在其后期主要代表作《哲学研究》中大量地运用了不同的语法研究的方法，一般来说，主要有描述的方法和综观的方法。

第一，维特根斯坦语法研究的首要方法——描述的方法。描述的方法是维特根斯坦语法研究的十分重要的方法，因为他认为我们的语法研究根本上也就是一种对于语言实际用法的描述。这种描述的方法和那种理论建构或解释的方法相对。在他看来，那种理论的建构的方法或解释的方法其实是出于对哲学的一种误解，即误解了哲学问题和哲学性质本身。因为在他看来"语

---

① M. 麦金，2007，《维特根斯坦和〈哲学研究〉》，李国山译，广西师范大学出版社，第 30 页。

② 维特根斯坦，2001，《哲学研究》，陈嘉映译，上海世纪出版集团 上海人民出版社，第 78 页。

法不说明语言必须怎样构造才能达到其目的，才能如此这般地对人起作用。语法只描述符号的用法，而不以任何方式定义符号的用法"。他还说"我们必须丢开一切解释而只用描述来取代之。"① "哲学不以任何方式干涉语言的实际用法，因而最终只能描述语言的用法。"②

既然描述的方法很重要，那么我们如何运用描述的方法对于语言的使用情况和现象进行研究呢？在维特根斯坦看来，我们的描述的方法和技巧很多，根据不同的需要进行不同的描述。例如，我们可以设想同一个语句在不同的语境中的使用；我们可以通过描述一些语言游戏以便向某人解释什么是游戏这一概念；比较不同的形式的语句所表达的相同的涵义；追问在我们正确表达思想之际，到底发生了什么；通过训练学生遵守语言游戏中的规则并教会他们一些语词和概念；设想不同的模型和试验来构造我们的感觉表达式的语法以便检验其有效性；回忆不同种语言游戏之间的差异和相似，如此等等。维特根斯坦认为不同的描述的方法就是为了实现不同的目的。他说"我们称为'描述'的，是服务于某些特定用途的工具。"③ 不同的描述方法就如同摆在机械师面前的不同图纸，有机器图纸，有剖面图以及标有比例尺的正视图等。不同的描述方法就是勾画不同语言游戏中语法应用的不同的工具，就如不同的图纸对于机械师所起的重要作用那样。

因而，在后期维特根斯坦看来，哲学的方法或语法研究的方法首先是描述的，即描述语言的使用，也就是在语言言说的实践中标明语词如何被使用，用法建立了正确使用的标准。描述的方法是后期维特根斯坦进行语法研究的基础。我们通过对于语词用法的细致描述，以便为其他的语法研究方法做好准备。

第二，维特根斯坦语法研究的又一十分重要的方法就是综观的方法。那什么是"综观"④方法呢？维特根斯坦在《哲学研究》的第122节里明确提到"综观"的研究方法。他说："我们对某些事情不理解的一个主要根源是我们不能综观语词用法的全貌——我们的语法缺乏这种

---

① 同上书，第214，72页。

② 同上书，第75页。

③ 同上书，第152页。

④ "综观"一词是遵从陈嘉映先生的译法。"综观"一词的原德文词是"die Übersicht"，表示一种概括能力，概观力，观察力。其动词形式 Übersehen 表示鸟瞰，俯瞰，眺望，预料到，看出来。其形容词形式是 Übersichtlich，表示一览无余的，条理清楚的，层次分明的；与之派生的名词形式 die Übersichtlichkeit 表示概观。关于 Übersicht，Übersichtlichkeit，Übersehen 这三个词的英译，著名学者 P. M. S. Hacker 在《洞见和幻觉》一书中认为英译很不统一，比较混乱。他主张英译为"surview"，"to survery"，"surveryable"。（参见 P. M. S. Hacker，1986，*Insight and Illusion—Themes in the philosophy of Wittgenstein*，Revised edition，Clarendon Press，Oxford，P151.）

综观。综观式的表现方式居间促成理解，而理解恰恰在于：我们'看到联系'。从而，发现或发明中间环节是极为重要的。综观式的表现这个概念对我们有根本性的意义。它标志着我们的表现方式，标志着我们看待事物的方式。"①，虽然"综观"这个词在《哲学研究》里出现的次数不多，就几次，但是在维特根斯坦看来，"综观"的研究方法对于语法研究具有十分重要的意义。"综观"也叫"概观"，是指全面地观看、整体地看，综合地把握语言的实际使用情况。"综观"方法特别强调我们要全面地、概观式地看到我们日常语言游戏中的语言用法之间的联系和差别，以便促成真正的理解。这其实也就是指全面地把握语言现象的可能性，思索我们关于语法现象所作陈述的方式，全面考察语言语法中隐藏的结构，即看到语言表达式背后所谓的"深层语法"。简言之，"综观"的语法研究方法是指多视角地在不同的语言游戏中观看语词用法的可能性，审视语言用法的规则和使用的特定的语境，从而获得对于语言和语词意义的理解，最终消除哲学混乱，澄清哲学问题。

我们如何进行综观式的语法研究呢？著名的维特根斯坦研究专家 P. M. S. 哈克在《维特根斯坦：理解和意义》一书的第二版里曾经探讨过这个问题，并且就"综观"的方法的获得提出了精彩的看法。他说："当一个人有综观时，一个人所能做的就是考察一种有问题的表达法的近邻。一种综观的获得，如同正确的逻辑观点的获得一样，表示一组能力的获得。当一个人对于一个概念领域具有综观时，他知道自己的路在哪里，即能区别联系、不同、类比、非类比，从而消解或解决哲学的问题。"② 这也就是说，综观的方法要求考察语言表达法的周围情况；综观的方法的获得其实就是一组能力的获得，这些能力包括联系、区别、类比等。这就要求我们要细致地考察语言用法中的精细差别和相似，从而消除哲学问题。在对于语言的语法进行综观式的考察时，我们可以运用想像、回忆、概括，以及概念转换等多种辅助手段帮助我们进行概念分析，从而看到不同的语言表达法之间的相似性以及差异性。

例如，我们的语言中有"事情是如此这般的"这样的句子。我们现在试图分析一下这个句子。这个句子难道不是表达了与实在的一致或不一致么？如果不是这样的话，那么我们该怎样对这样的一个汉语语句进行综观式的考察和分析呢？首先，我们可以通过分析这个句子的结构，发现它有主语和谓语。这是一个合乎汉语句法的句子。这是很确定的。那么，人们是如何使用这个句子的呢？我们如何在我们的日常语言中使用这个句子？我们还可以通过我们的想像力，

---

① 维特根斯坦，2001，《哲学研究》，陈嘉映译，上海世纪出版集团 上海人民出版社，第75页。

② P. M. S. Hacker, 2005, *Wittgenstein：Understanding and Meaning*, Second, extensively revised edition, Blackwell Publishing, Oxford, p. 309.

设想在某一种情形下或者语境之中，人们使用这一语句，如"他向我说明了他的境况，如事情如此这般，因此他需要预支"。这样一来，我们就可以发现，"事情是如此这般"这个句子可以代表任何说法。因为，人们也可以不这么说，而换几种方法，说"事情如此如此"，"情形这样那样"，"事情那般这般"等等。更极端一点，人们还可以干脆就用一个字母或符号来表示这个句子。这样的话，我们就可以发现，这个句子就是一种格式，一种一般的形式。这个句子"事情如此这般"可以被用作一个句子变项，除此以外，没有更多的意义。而我们原先的理解即以为这个句子表达了这个句子与实在的一致或不一致，这种考虑其实就是很荒唐的。这个句子仅仅向我们表明了："我们的句子概念的一个特征是：听上去是一个句子。"①

　　这也就是说，我们在刚才对于"事情是如此这般"这一语句进行概念分析和考察时，运用了一种综观式的方法，我们寻求的是一种居间的理解，而不是由于语法的表面幻相所造成的误解。"事情是如此这般"并没有表达任何形而上学的意思，即没有说明它与实在的关系（一致或不一致），而只是让我们注意到我们的语言系统的语句，具有听上去是一个句子的这样一个特征。这样一来，我们就不会受到传统的哲学问题折磨了，因为它根本就不涉及哲学问题，如与现实的关系问题，而仅仅是一种语句形式，一个句子的变项。像这样的例子还有很多，维特根斯坦在《哲学研究》中运用"综观"的方法对于语言现象进行分析十分普遍，在此就不过多地列举这种方法的运用。总之，我们可以看到，通过"综观"或者说"概观"，我们可以清晰地分析语词和语句的用法，阐明不同用法之间的差别，因而它对于我们的语法研究和哲学研究，具有很重要的意义。

　　描述的方法和综观的方法之间的关系也是非常紧密的，不是相互分割开来的，而是相互联系的。描述的研究方法是语法研究的基础，是综观的方法的准备；综观的研究方法是描述的方法的更高级的目的，在一定程度上可以说，描述好各种语言游戏中不同语言表达式之间的不同使用就是为了更好地综观整个语言表达式用法区域背后的"深层语法"。另外，维特根斯坦除了提到描述的方法和综观的方法之外，他还提到了一些其他的方法如比较的方法、概念转换的方法以及思想实验的方法，但是这些方法不是最主要的，因而在此就不过多地展开详细论述。

四、哲学研究的主要困难：误解与诱惑

　　维特根斯坦一方面认为我们对于语言的实际用法进行周密细致的语法研究，有助于看到语

---

① 维特根斯坦，2001，《哲学研究》，陈嘉映译，上海世纪出版集团 上海人民出版社，第79页。

言用法之间的差别和近似，澄清语言的真正用法，从而消解哲学的问题。但是，他同时也看到，我们哲学上的语法研究存在着很大的困难，这些困难如此之大，有时让他对于哲学问题感到"找不到北"①。那么，维特根斯坦的语法研究的困难主要表现在哪些方面呢？这些困难又是如何产生的？笔者准备就这些问题从以下两个方面进行一些初步地探讨。概括地说，维特根斯坦的语法研究的困难主要体现在以下两个方面，即误解深，难消除；诱惑多，难抵制。这些方面其实也就是哲学研究为什么这么困难的原因所在。

首先，误解深，难消除。维特根斯坦认为我们对于哲学研究的误解既多且深，难以从根本上彻底消除。误解是多方面的，误解是经常发生的，并且很难彻底消除。误解主要有：既包括对于哲学性质的误解，也包括对于语言逻辑的误解；既包括我们对于语言语法研究特征的误解，也包括我们对于语言形式本身的误解。对于哲学性质的误解主要是指我们经常会认为哲学应该是一种理论、一种说明，哲学可以为某种问题提供充分的解释。但是在维特根斯坦看来，哲学却不是这样。他说"哲学只是把一切摆在那里，不解释也不推论。我们对于隐藏的东西不感兴趣"②。但在这种误解的影响之下，人们总是想对哲学问题作出整套的理论说明，即想通过合理的说明来达到解释哲学问题的目的。而且，在这种误解的影响之下，人们不断地追求理论的精致化和复杂化，以为这样就可以解决问题。但是在维特根斯坦看来这实际上却是徒劳的。他觉得这种做法就像"要我们用手指来修补一片撕破的蜘蛛网"③。

因为哲学性质本身就是不需要理论建构或说明的，而是描述，描述我们语言的实际用法，以此澄清哲学的概念，消解掉哲学问题。除此之外，我们还经常对于我们所用的语言的逻辑产生很深的误解。我们以为语句是非常了不起的东西，具有非同小可的、独一无二的功能。这种误解就是要把我们的语言的逻辑拔高到顶点的倾向。在这种误解之下，人们很容易说出一些耸人视听的话，如"'这个'才是唯一的真正的名称。"④ 在维特根斯坦看来，"这"这个词明显地不是名称，但是人们却偏偏把这个词弄成名称。不仅如此，我们还经常以为"语言（或思想）一定是某种与众不同的东西"。维特根斯坦认为，这其实也是由于语法的欺幻产生的一种迷信。所有这些混乱产生的原因都是由于我们对于语言的逻辑产生的误解。这种误解是很难消除的。

另外，维特根斯坦还认为我们对于我们的语言形式会产生很深的误解。他说："由于曲解

---

① 维特根斯坦，2001，《哲学研究》，陈嘉映译，上海世纪出版集团 上海人民出版社，第 75 页。
② 同上书，第 76 页。
③ 同上书，第 70 页。
④ 同上书，第 30 页。

我们的语言形式而产生的问题，有某种深度。它们在深处搅扰我们；它们的根像我们的语言形式本身的根一样，深深地扎在我们的身上；它们的意义重大，重如我们的语言本身。我们问问自己，为什么觉得语法笑话具有深度？（那的确是一种哲学的深度）。"①在这里，维特根斯坦明确地承认了我们对语言形式的误解很深。所以，正是由于我们对于我们的语言形式经常加以误解，从而也就导致我们对于语言的语法特征加以误解，只看到语法的表层，而没有看到表层语法之下所隐藏的深层语法，即很难真正地把握住语法的深层内涵。例如，我们经常说"我知道你疼"和"我知道我疼"。这两个表达式的表层语法是相似的，但是深层的结构却不一样。因为说"我知道你疼"这句话是符合"知道"一词的语法的，但我们却不能说"我知道我疼"。因为，我自己疼与不疼，只有我能"感觉"到，这是我的个人的感觉经验，而不是"知道"或"不知道"。因而，后一句话就是误解了我们的语言形式和语法特征，从而闹了语法笑话。但是，这种对于语言形式的误解是很深的，很难立刻就消除。这就增加了我们研究哲学和语法的困难。

其次，诱惑多，难抵制。维特根斯坦认为，我们在从事哲学研究或语法研究时，诱惑是非常多的，几乎是无处不在，而且很难加以抵制。概括地说，这些诱惑有来自我们自身本性的诱惑，也有来自文化和历史传统的诱惑。来自我们本性的诱惑包括：我们有强烈地渴求普遍性的倾向，试图提出具有很强解释能力的普遍的理论；我们还有追求统一性的欲望，以便将所有的多样化的语言现象纳入一个单一的模式或规则之下；我们喜欢将一种表达式和另外一种表达式或者将一种语言游戏与另外一种语言游戏进行类比，期望获得确定性的结论；我们具有很强地解释一切的冲动，总以为解释越多就越清楚；我们还有寻求定义和使用比喻的倾向，总以为给出了定义就可以获得事物的本质，运用了比喻就可以阐明复杂的语言现象，等等。来自历史和文化传统的诱惑有：我们总是想模仿科学家进行科学研究来进行我们的哲学研究，总喜欢借鉴和照搬科学研究的方法和模式来研究哲学问题；我们还喜欢应用数理逻辑或其他的新的逻辑方法来解决哲学问题；我们的历史习惯和所受的教育经常引诱我们把注意力集中在我们内部的感觉上，然后转移到我之外的客体上；我们总想作出非常精致的区别；在理解语词的意义时我们总想在心中构建一幅图画，以为只要抓住了图画，就理解了语词的意义，等等。

关于我们的本性的诱惑方面，例如，我们经常追问"什么是意义？""什么是思想？""理解的本质在于什么？"等等问题。我们总想对于这样的一些问题给予一劳永逸的、独立于任何经验的答案。这其实就是我们人性中的冲动和诱惑，即对于普遍性和统一性的追求的诱惑。我们总想在语言使用的知识中为了某一特定目的而建立统一的秩序，在维特根斯坦看来，我们建立

---

① 同上书，第72页。

的秩序其实只是我们许多可能秩序中的一种，而不是唯一的秩序。与之相关的是，我们总喜欢以改革我们的日常语言为己任，构造所谓的理想语言，以为这样就能解决哲学的问题。我们还喜欢对于不同的语言表达式进行所谓的分析，进行类比，其实这两个表达式是根本不同的。此外，我们天生就有解释的冲动，以为真理是可以通过解释获得的，对一个解释不断地进行另外一个解释，"仿佛一个解释若没有另外一个解释的支持就悬在半空中似的。"① 这其实在维特根斯坦看来，完全是没有必要的。因为他认为任何解释既然是解释，就不需要其他的解释，除非我们为了避免特定的误解。关于历史和文化方面，我们经常受到科学方法的诱惑，因为科学在不断地进步，新的科学方法不断取得成功，我们就以为哲学应该像科学一样，按照科学的研究方法，走上科学的道路。这样一来，就会产生无穷的混乱。维特根斯坦在《棕皮书》里说："哲学家们总是觉得科学的方法就在眼前，禁不住要以科学的方式提出问题，回答问题。这种倾向实际上造成了形而上学的根源，并引领哲学家们进入完全的黑暗。"② 总之，维特根斯坦强调我们在进行真正的哲学研究或语法研究时所遇见的困难是非常多的，这些困难有的是来自我们对于我们的语言形式或逻辑的误解，有的是来自我们对于我们自身中本性的诱惑和冲动，还有的是来自科学方法的诱惑，如此等等，不一而列。正因为我们的误解很深，诱惑很多，所以他强调哲学的研究具有疗法的性质，需要漫长的过程才能实现消除误解和诱惑的目的。所以，哲学研究和语法研究是非常困难的，是需要很多努力和训练才能逐渐达到的。

五、简短的评论

我们该如何评价后期维特根斯坦的哲学研究呢？后期维特根斯坦的哲学研究即语法研究其实是一种从语言实际使用的角度对于哲学所作的一种基础性的批判工作。这一批判研究的性质主要就是体现在对于语法概念的分析上面。维特根斯坦通过分析我们语言的用法中的概念，发现语言表达式的实际用法中存在的不少误解和幻相。为了消除我们日常语言中的诱惑和迷信，达到对于语言本身和哲学问题批判的目的。实际上，维特根斯坦的两种重要的语法研究的方法如描述的方法和综观的方法其实也正好高度体现了批判方法的性质。一方面，维特根斯坦的描述的方法不是我们通常所谓的"描述"，而是对于语言实际使用的情况的可能性的一种描述，这种描述的最大的好处就是能够全面地展现语言用法的不同层次和结构，不同的差异和类似，

---

① 维特根斯坦，《哲学研究》，2001，陈嘉映译，上海世纪出版集团 上海人民出版社，第 62 页。

② 转引自 M. 麦金，2007，《维特根斯坦和〈哲学研究〉》，李国山译，广西师范大学出版社，第 19 页。

从而为语言的意义和用法的批判的理解奠定了必要的基础；另一方面，维特根斯坦的综观的方法也是非常具有批判意义的方法，因为综观的本质其实就是消除偏见或成见，看到不同语法区域的联系和差异，立体地、概观地把握住语言背后的深层次的东西。

所以我们说维特根斯坦的"语法研究"本质上是批判的研究，其所谓的语法是作为批判工具的语法，其研究的目的是为了消解掉由于误解我们的语言的用法而产生哲学的问题，从而澄清思想。也正是在这个意义上，我们可以说他的研究不是如多数学者那样认为是消灭了哲学本身，而是恰恰相反，语法研究实质上是很好地定位了哲学研究的性质，最终起到的是拯救哲学的作用。因为维特根斯坦将哲学的研究定位为语法的考察是很高明的。这样可以避免哲学研究受到科学研究或其他方法的诱惑或干扰，避免被科学排挤和指责的命运。哲学研究就是研究我们的语言的实际使用的情况，清除语法的幻象和迷信，达到观念的清晰。最后关于维特根斯坦的后期的哲学研究，正如学者萨维基（Beth Savickey）所评价的那样"维特根斯坦的著作不仅是创造性的而且是极具生命力的……他的语法研究其实是一门艺术。他的作品充满了想像力的、富有幽默感的、迷人的和杰出的。它们是十分有趣、瞩目的和令人难忘的。最重要的是，它们是极具洞见的并且具有深深的阐明作用。"①

参考文献

［1］维特根斯坦，2005，《逻辑哲学论》，贺绍甲译，商务印书馆。

［2］维特根斯坦，2005，《哲学研究》，李步楼译，陈维杭校，商务印书馆。

［3］维特根斯坦，2001，《哲学研究》．陈嘉映译，上海世纪出版集团·上海人民出版社。

［4］涂纪亮，2005，《维特根斯坦后期哲学思想研究》，江苏人民出版社。

［5］M. 麦金，2007，《维特根斯坦和〈哲学研究〉》，李国山译，广西师范大学出版社。

［6］Newton. Garver，2006，*Philosophy as Grammar*，*The Cambridge Companion to Philosophy*，Edited by Hans Sluga，David G. Stern，Cambridge University Press.

［7］P. M. S. Hacker，1986，*Insight and Illusion—Themes in the philosophy of Wittgenstein*，Revised edition，Clarendon Press，Oxford.

［8］P. M. S. Hacker，2005，*Wittgenstein：Understanding and Meaning*，Second，extensively revised edition，Blackwell Publishing，Oxford.

［9］Beth Savickey，2002，*Wittgenstein's Art of Investigation*. London，Taylor & Francis e-Library.

---

① Beth Savickey，Wittgenstein's At of Investigation. London，Taylor & Francis e-Library，2002，P102

A Critical Analysis of Later Wittgenstein's *Philosophical Investigation*

Tao Xu

Nankai University

Abstract：The article argues that the essence of later Wittgenstein's philosophical Investigation is grammatical research. The article is to elucidate the main character and contents of later Wittgenstein's philosophy by reviewing his critiques to the logical methods. And then the article also is to point out the essence and intention of his grammatical research and analyze the different methods of his grammatical research as well as the existing difficulties in it, at last it is to give a short comment on his later philosophical investigation.

Keywords：logical analyzing；philosophical investigation；grammatical research

人物与事件

回忆洪谦教授[*]

◎ 洪汉鼎
北京市社会科学院

摘　要： 洪谦先生是引导我进入哲学殿堂的第一位老师。我的大学毕业论文指导教师就是洪谦先生，他讲的课程清楚简洁，逻辑性强，很有吸引力。在我担任贺麟先生助手期间，仍然从洪先生那里得到许多启发。由于各种现实的原因，洪先生的晚年生活比较凄凉，但他坚持自己的哲学研究，并取得了令人瞩目的成就。

关键词： 洪谦；维也纳学派；分析哲学；晚年生活

　　1956 年我从无锡辅仁中学考入北京大学不久，我就认识了洪谦教授。洪谦教授原本是维也纳学派成员，石里克的学生，卡尔纳普的朋友，20 世纪 30 年代末维也纳学派解体，洪谦教授回到了中国，以后就在清华大学、西南联大、武汉大学和北京大学任教。他的最早一部中文著作就是《维也纳学派哲学》，我是在中学读到这部书的，记得当时我有这样一种感觉，相对于黑格尔读物的艰深晦涩，洪先生这本书却清楚明了多了。因此 1956 年夏我到了北大后，除想认识贺麟教授外，就是想拜访洪谦教授。洪谦教授当时任北大哲学系西方哲学史教研室主任，该教研室聚集着全国最有名的一些哲学教授，如贺麟、黄子通、方书春、宗白华、熊伟、齐良骥、任华。当时他家和贺麟教授家一样，都是在北大东边成府街的燕东园，记得有一天晚上我到他家，第一个感觉是他有着洋人学者风度，他个子很高又清瘦，穿了一条吊带裤，他从冰箱里拿出一杯冰水给我。当时中国人很穷，冰箱乃稀有之物，我是第一次在他家才见到的。补充一下，我第一次看到电视机，也是在北京大学老图书馆上面的会议楼。一见面我就告诉他，我很喜欢维也纳学派哲学的语言分析，想请他指导我去选初步阅读的书，洪谦教授让我先读休谟，他说休谟的书是训练我们分析思维必不可少的著作。继后，他又告诉我，要学分析哲学，首先要学好数学和逻辑，我说我中学的数学都是高分，而且对数学，特别是几何学很感兴趣。洪谦教授

---

　　* 该文初稿曾于 2009 年 4 月在浙江省建德市举行的全国第五届分析哲学年会上宣读，经补充修订后发表于《世界哲学》2009 年第 6 期。

似乎很满意，他还告诉我，我们系的逻辑教授吴允曾先生很不错，头脑清晰，思维敏捷，是一位很好的逻辑教授。这次拜访对我启发很大，不仅使我明确了我读分析哲学应当从何下手，而且在第一学期我就选了吴允曾先生的数理逻辑课，给我今后研究分析哲学打下了一个有力的基础。我读分析哲学的第一本书，就是休谟的《人类理解研究》，这本书使我懂得什么叫思想清晰，概念明确。记得有次张世英教授告诉我，他原先本不是读哲学的，而是学经济的，只是因为读了休谟的《人类理解研究》后，对哲学论证的清晰确实性大感兴趣，因而转入哲学系。

当时北京大学哲学系，除一些必修课外，有许多哲学选修课，如贺麟先生的"黑格尔"，方书春先生的"古希腊哲学"，熊伟先生的"存在主义"，洪谦先生的"逻辑实证主义"，这些课我都选，当时系里要求每位老师必须写出批判性的讲稿，印发给学生，我现在还保存了当年洪先生的《逻辑实证主义讲稿》和熊伟先生的《存在主义讲稿》。当时我特别注重洪先生的课，原因是在那个时代，政治强奸学术，每上一课，除了马列外，老师都必须要加以批判，因此许多老师讲的课都是强烈的批判内容，得不到什么真正的哲学真诠。印象最深的是熊伟先生的存在主义讲课，似乎通篇都是什么"垂死挣扎的帝国主义哲学"，"最极端的主观唯心主义"等。和这些老师的讲课比较起来，洪先生的课很少大批判，他只讲逻辑实证主义家的理论内容和论证线索，因此我对他的讲课很重视，每上一堂课，我都记笔记，如有不懂，下节课一定要问。另外，洪先生的讲课本身的语言，也相当简洁、精练和清楚，逻辑性强，很有吸引力。从洪先生讲课中也可发现，他不仅德文好，而且英文似乎更好，但相比起来，他的中文反而见拙，至今我都记得，他有次讲到逻辑，想在黑板上用中文把逻辑两字写出来，结果写了好几次都不对，最后他笑了笑，还是写 logic 好了。

我的大学毕业论文是"维特根斯坦的《逻辑哲学论》"，导师是洪谦教授。这篇论文在当时中国可能是最早研究维特根斯坦的论文，对我来说，维特根斯坦那种论述方式，那种论述内容也同样是困难的，难以理解的。记得当时导师洪谦教授看到我的阅读困难，介绍我看安斯康姆（Anscombe，G. E. M.）对《逻辑哲学论》的解释，这本书在某种程度上的确帮了我很大的忙，所以在 20 年后我在德国洪堡年会上看到上年纪的安斯康姆时，还对她这本书表示了敬意，我曾经和她以及她的一位友人在德国作了短期旅游，我们一路上都是谈维特根斯坦。我的这篇论文当时虽然通过，但无法发表，直到 18 年后才出版在商务印书馆的《外国哲学》上。

1963 年，我带着灰色感伤的感情离开了北大，去到大西北的陕西，一待就是 15 年。我再次见到洪谦教授是在 1978 年冬，那时我刚从陕西回到中国社会科学院研究生院。此时可以说是洪谦教授在中国最风光的时期，他担任北京大学外国哲学所所长，而且直属于学校，与哲学系平行。当时他正主编《逻辑经验主义》一书，他立即让我参加此项工作，我翻译了两篇石里克的论文。其中有一篇"意义与证实"，我必须要说一下，这篇论文的英文本其实是在 1963 年我要离开北大时，从当时北大俄文楼外国期刊处借到的，当时没有复印技术，同时也不能外借，因此我只能好几天去那里用手抄英文，由于时间紧，手抄潦草，因而当我在陕西根据手抄本翻译时，产生很多错误，所幸后来洪先生交李步楼同学校改才好些。

此时洪谦教授经常邀请维也纳学派一些老同事来北大讲学，如 Feigl，H. Hampel，A. Nass 等。我与 Feigl 和 Hampel 只在北大见了一次面，听了他们的一次讲演，但与 Nass 却见了多次，因当时我在中国社会科学院哲学所，当 Nass 来我们所讲斯宾诺莎时，汝信同志让我去，并希望我提问。Nass 是挪威著名分析哲学杂志 Inquire 的主编，他本人也是分析哲学家，可是他对斯宾诺莎却发生很大兴趣，他曾经用数理逻辑符号整理斯宾诺莎的《伦理学》，试图用数学方法推出斯宾诺莎全部命题。Nass 把他的这本斯宾诺莎著作送给了洪谦教授，洪谦教授借给我看，我曾经把 Nass 的推演译成中文，结果发现 Nass 本人也未能全把斯宾诺莎的所有命题纳入他的数理系统中。

在此期间，我担任了贺麟教授的助手，我帮助贺麟教授校订他翻译的一些著作，如黑格尔的《小逻辑》，并整理他过去的一些论文，其中有他以前作为讲稿写的《当代西方哲学家》，由于其中也提到维也纳学派，所以我也常到洪谦先生家。这里我要特别讲到贺先生和洪先生两人的关系。从个人友谊方面来看，他们两人似乎还是不错的，每次在会上相互都很客气，彼此都尊重对方的学问，我的硕士论文答辩会上，贺先生还专门请了洪先生。但从学术观点看，他们差别相当大。大家知道，贺先生精通德国思辨哲学，尤其是黑格尔，而洪谦先生却精于分析哲学，本身是维也纳学派成员。显然，他们两人的哲学是水火不兼容的，有时我用当代西方哲学中分析哲学与思辨哲学之争，去说明他们之间的学术关系。这里我讲一些亲身的感受。有次去洪谦先生家，除了谈分析哲学的一些问题外，洪先生突然问我："汉鼎，你是懂分析哲学的，你看贺先生讲哲学的话是否清楚？"我知道他的意思，没有回答，他又说："甚至黑格尔本身也讲不清楚。"对于洪先生的学问，贺先生是怎样看的呢？有次贺先生和我谈到了洪先生："汉鼎，洪先生的学问的确很清楚，但那都是些鸡毛蒜皮的语言问题，对于人生价值有何意义呢？"这两位老师的观点使我看到了当代分析哲学与现象学的根本分歧。当时我深感处于他们两人之间的为难。

1985 年我从德国回来后，我和洪先生的接触更为频繁了。洪先生提议我们都用德文对话，虽然洪先生回国已经好几十年，但他的德语却非常好，我真非常佩服。我们的谈话大多是洪先生回忆自己一生的哲学经历，他曾讲到当时他年仅 19 岁在维也纳跟随石里克学习和研究的情景，他说石里克是他的老师，卡尔纳普是他的师叔，艾耶尔是他的同学，经常在星期四于维也纳一家咖啡馆谈哲学。洪先生讲到他和石里克的关系时说，"石里克当时是我心中的偶像，凡是他说的，我都照办。因此在一段相当长的时间里，我丧失了独立性，后来我在他的《箴言》里读到这样一句话：'追随别人的人，大多依赖别人'，这使我感到遗憾"。谈到卡尔纳普时他说："卡尔纳普是石里克之外我最难忘的师长。无论在学习上，还是在个人的事情上，他都会给我巨大的帮助"，并且还说："卡尔纳普后来移居美国后，我们还经常有书信来往，他甚至把他出版的每一本书都寄给我。他送我的最后一本书是《卡尔纳普的哲学》。接着我国发生了所谓'文化大革命'，我被禁止同国外通信。1978 年 Feigl 教授从明尼苏达写信告诉我，卡尔纳普时常同他谈起我。遗憾的是他于 1970 年与世长辞。"谈到艾耶尔时，他说："艾耶尔当时在维也纳其实并没有呆多久，大概是 1932 到 1933 这个学期，以后他就回牛津母校任助理教授和讲师了。斯特劳森说艾耶尔是一位反偶像论者，这种说法是很恰当的。艾耶尔对于任何一个学派的观点或论点都有其独特的见解，这些见解虽然不能说都具有高度的独创性，但很能表现他个人的哲学风格。"我想洪先生说这些是想把他自己与艾耶尔这两位石里克的最年轻学生作对比，以对自己偶像论的态度表示遗憾。

当然，洪先生也谈到他回国在北大和清大任教的情况，他说："石里克去世以后，1937 年初，我回到了北京，在北京大学和清华大学哲学系讲授维也纳学派的逻辑经验主义，重点是讲石里克的哲学观点。后来用这方面的论文编成《维也纳学派哲学》一书。"对于 20 世纪 50 年代末"反右"斗争后的我国的哲学境况，他表示遗憾，他特别告诉我，自那以后，他很少写文章，为什么呢？因为写文章必须要批判，这是违背学术的良心。他特别痛心的一件事，是写了一篇批判卡尔纳普的文章，他说这是他一生中的一个坏笔，因为当时上级一定要他写一篇批判文章，否则政治上过不去，最后他就硬着脑袋，简单地拼凑了一篇骂卡尔纳普的文章，发表在《哲学研究》上。洪先生还告诉我，他回国后做的最重要的事，就是组织、翻译和编辑出版了《西方古典哲学原著选辑》多卷本。从现在的情况来看，当时组织这套多卷本工作却是一项了不起的工作，一方面，它是一个利用当时不利环境发挥老教授特长的非常好的设计，我们上面讲过，当时北大哲学系集中了全国各大学知名的哲学教授，他们一般又不能授课，因此组织他们翻译一些哲学名著，这是一个非常好的想法；另一方面，相对于当时的哲学界情况，它又是对我国哲学事业的一大贡献，要知道在那个与外国学术隔绝的时代，我国年轻的哲学研究者不但外文不好，而且也没有外国的哲学书籍可看，因此在这时有这套翻译成中文的又是可信的多卷本哲学史读物，真可说一个伟大的贡献。

洪先生自己在他与哈勒教授的谈话中也是这样讲到他在解放后的主要工作的：

"您是问 1949 年中国解放后我在哲学方面做了些什么吧？当然，自那时起，直到前几年为止，我无法继续研究和讲授我长期以来喜爱的维也纳学派的科学哲学，不能继续从事被禁止宣扬的，被列宁称为'反动哲学'的马赫主义流派的研究工作。于是，我主要是做了些关于西方哲学史基本情况方面的工作。在中国，长期缺乏西方重要哲学著作的译本。我在担任北京大学哲学系西方哲学史教研室主任之后，为了给人们了解西方哲学史提供条件，主编了四卷《西方古典哲学原著选辑》。第一卷是《古希腊罗马哲学》，第二卷是《十六—十八世纪西欧各国哲学》，第三卷是《十八世纪法国哲学》，第四卷是《十八世纪末—十九世纪初德国哲学》。这一套《选辑》大量发行，成为我国各大学哲学系的基本教学参考数据。后来我又主编了《当代资产阶级哲学论著选辑》。近年来甚至还单独出版了逻辑经验主义的选辑。"

20 世纪 70 年代、80 年代，维特根斯坦在我国哲学界都被批判为主观唯心主义者、主观经验论者，对于这种状况，洪先生深表不满，认为这是在践踏维特根斯坦。即使后来研究深入一些，维特根斯坦也和逻辑经验主义的维也纳学派相联系，说维也纳学派的经验证实原则就是来自于维特根斯坦。对于这种情况，洪先生也不同意。1987 年，我写了一篇论文，论维特根斯坦与逻辑经验主义的差别，该文在北大学报发表后，我曾寄给洪谦老师，结果洪老师回了一信："接到你的信附有大作，非常高兴。你文中的看法，对于证实理论无论从 Wittgenstein 的 Tractatus 和 Vien Kreis 来说，都是不同的，即各有各的对 Verification Prinsip 的看法，不能同一而论。至于对 Wittgenstein 的（证实）意义理论的经验主义的解释，更是荒谬不过了，我同意你的解释和了解。"

当时中国出了一本维特根斯坦的专著，尽管作者花了不少心血写了这部著作，但由于当时的条件以及作者自然科学的视野，很多观点是不正确的，我曾为此写了一篇书评发表在 1983 年的《读书》杂志上。洪先生对那本书也很不满。我这里还保存了一封洪先生当年写给我的信，时间是 1987 年 10 月 16 日：

> 某一位中国 Wittgenstein 研究者，去年曾应一位华裔加拿大范克样先生之请（他们研究 Wittgenstein 的）去 Kirchberg，不过他的论文有些地方曾受到范的批评，有人对我这样（说）的。还有数月前，有一位当时参加会的教授对我说：他的（那位中国人）对 Wittgenstein 的了解和解释，从他来看，大多数当时与会的人都不懂其所以然。我没有见到他的论文，难于判断，不过，我从他的 Wittgenstein 一书来看，这是完全可能的，有人说：他还以中国 Wittgenstein 家自豪，实在可笑！
>
> 数年来，我国学风不好，不看书，不研究，即大发议论，夸夸其谈，实在不好。我们研究现代西方的东西还很幼稚，应当虚心方好，你的意见如何？顺问你好！　洪谦，1987，10，16

　　这封信指的人，我们可以不去管他，他也是我们哲学界一位很努力钻研西方当代哲学的学者，在那个时代能写出这样一部书，而且是我国第一部研究维特根斯坦的学术专著，应该说已很不错了。只是受到当时左倾思想和哲学观点的限制，对维特根斯坦未能全面把握。我想洪先生的批评也是指理解方面的缺陷而说的。不过在此信中，洪老师指出的当时学界情况，却值得我们大为重视。"数年来，我国学风不好，不看书，不研究，即大发议论，夸夸其谈，实在不好"。我相信洪先生持这种看法已不是一朝一昔的了，可能有好多年中国哲学研究的状况都使洪先生担忧。尽管洪先生是指当时的情况，但比较起来，现在的情况又何尝不是这样呢！

　　洪先生晚年最怕别人认为他思想落伍，有次我从德国回国去看望他，他对我说，"汉鼎，我思想没有落伍，我一直在看国外哲学杂志，关注分析哲学的最新发展。"他在 20 世纪 80 年代就经常参加国际分析哲学会议，并为会议准备了发表论文，1980 年国际维特根斯坦第五届讨论会，他发表了一篇题为"维特根斯坦与石里克"的文章，此文后来我翻译在洪先生的《逻辑经验主义论文集》里。他晚年有一篇论 Konstatierungen 的英文文章，发表在国外一家杂志上，后来他让我翻译成中文发表。此时洪谦先生似乎写作很勤，他有一新思想就立即写出来，发表后就寄给我一份。我这里有 1988 年 8 月 4 日洪谦教授写给我的一封信："洪汉鼎同志，寄去自然辩证法通信一本，内有我的一段东西，不知你收到没有？"

　　洪谦先生晚年生活似乎不好，在 20 世纪 80 年代后期，由于改革开放，中国面貌发生很大改变，年轻人的工资提升了，但老一辈的工资仍保持原样，因此相对于物价的飞速上涨，洪教授的生活水平似乎在下降。有一次我去他家，他不在，洪夫人在织毛衣，我问洪先生哪里去了，洪夫人说他刚出去转转，我问他是否又到中关村那家蛋糕店买布丁面包，洪夫人立即回复我一句："他现在哪里吃得起，他只能在外面看看！"洪夫人当时说这话的口气我至今还记得。还有一事，有一天，我同学张家桢打电话给我，说他在东四隆福寺的中国书店看到洪先生家的书，上面还有别人送给洪先生的签名，他怀疑是否洪先生家被偷。我立即打电话给洪先生问，洪先生只是简单地说他的书太多，卖了一部分，再未说别的，但我知道这同他家当时经济状况不好有关。我这里还有一封洪先生亲笔给我的信："有件事托你：如果你（有）办法，能否代我买一条牡丹的烟，我将照英镑还给你货款，谢谢你，顺问你好。"（写于 1988 年 8 月）

　　我曾将洪先生当时的窘况告诉了香港的周柏桥，希望他想办法请洪先生赴香港讲学，可以得到一些外汇。时巧当时香港中文大学有个学术研讨会，讨论他的思想，我们都鼓励他去，他自己也很兴奋要去，可是正在办理护照过程中他去世了。

　　洪先生仙逝的时间是 1992 年 2 月 27 日，死亡来得太突然，他本来想再到香港一游，可是老天不作愿，我们后学非常痛心，他没有任何交待就离开我们了。按照家属的意见，遗体告别是在医院里举行的。我手边还保留了一份当时北京大学外国哲学研究所写的讣告：

国际著名哲学家，北京大学外国哲学研究所前所长洪谦教授，因病医治无效，于1992年2月27日晨10时20分在北京逝世，终年82岁，遵照先生的遗嘱，丧事从简，不举行追悼会和遗体告别仪式。

洪谦先生生于1909年，安徽歙县人，早年曾从学于国学大师梁启超，并经梁公推荐，安徽同乡会资助，赴德国留学，后转赴奥地利，在维也纳大学学习数学，物理学和哲学。1934年以科学哲学为主科在维也纳学派创始人石里克教授指导下，完成了题为《现代物理学中的因果问题》的博士论文，获哲学博士学位，并成为维也纳学派的唯一的东方国家的成员。30年代末回国，先后在清华大学，西南联大，武汉大学任教。1945—1947年赴英国，在牛津大学新学院担任研究员，从事研究和教学工作。中华人民共和国建立后，历任武汉大学哲学系主任，燕京大学哲学系主任，北京大学哲学系外国哲学史教研室主任，北京大学外国哲学研究所所长，北京大学校务委员会委员，校学术委员会委员，校学位委员会委员，西方哲学专业博士生导师；社会兼职有：现代外国哲学学会名誉理事长，《中国大百科全书》哲学编辑委员会委员兼现代西方哲学部分主编，《世界哲学年鉴》名誉顾问，中国社会科学院哲学研究所兼任研究员和学术委员会委员，中英暑期哲学学院名誉院长；国外学术职衔和名誉学位有：牛津大学哲学会会员，牛津大学王后学院客座研究员，牛津大学三一学院客座研究员，日本东京大学客座教授，维也纳大学荣誉哲学博士。

洪谦先生毕生致力于西方哲学的教学和研究，无论对西方古典哲学还是对现代哲学都有精湛的研究和很高的造诣。他是休谟和康德哲学的专家，他主编的《西方古典哲学名著选辑》多卷本迄今仍是我国学者学习和研究西方哲学史必读的一套最完整的参考书。在现代西方哲学而特别是分析哲学的研究方面，洪先生在国内学术界享有崇高的声望，被中青年学者尊为一代宗师，在国际学术界负有盛誉，1984年维也纳大学马特尔院长在纪念洪谦博士学位50周年并授予他荣誉博士学位的庆祝会上盛赞他"在哲学上，尤其在维也纳学派哲学上，做出了卓越的贡献"。他在40年代发表的《维也纳学派哲学》一书无疑是我国最早系统而准确地介绍逻辑实证主义的一部权威著作。60年代以来，他陆续主编了《西方现代资产阶级哲学论著选辑，（近年经过重编扩大为两卷本《现代西方哲学论著选辑》），《逻辑经验主义》（上，下卷），并组织翻译了马赫的名著《感觉的分析》，均以选材精到和译文信实得到学术界很高的评价。他的一些论文发表在国外权威性的哲学刊物和丛书上，这是他的著作的极重要的部分，尚待译成中文。洪先生晚年曾多次出国，去英国，奥地利和日本讲学和参加学术会议，为国际文化交流做出了贡献。

洪谦先生治学极其严谨，极其勤奋，直至病重住院前犹殚精竭思，笔耕不已，留下了大量的手稿，他的逝世是我国哲学界的一大损失，他的未竟的学术工作将由我们来继承，他的杰出的学术业绩将永远为人们所怀念。

安息吧，洪谦先生。

一个月后，也就是 3 月 27 日，我去看望洪师母，洪师母对我讲了如下几点：1. 洪先生死前曾有遗嘱："我能遗留给你们的只是书籍，我很珍贵它们，请你们好好保存，虽然你们没有人会读"；2. 对夫人，他也说过："我对不起你"，洪夫人说，这是 50 年来第一次对我讲的，可见发自内心深处；3. 洪先生一生不问政治，专治学。洪先生回国如同"隐居"，基本上他没有写文章；4. 改革开放后，听说国外可出书，他很想再活几年，让他的书能出版；5. 不过遗憾的是，他没有手稿，只有构思，他写文章是一次写成，不打草稿。

如果有人问我，洪先生一生究竟应当怎样评价，那么我可以说："生不逢时"。按照洪先生当年在石里克身边的情况看来，他如果继续在奥地利或德国深造，他可能有更多更好的著作留给我们，有如他的国外同学和朋友 Carnap，Feigl，Hampel 以及他的英国小学弟 Ayer 那样，成为国际型的一流学者。尽管他回国组织编译了很多著作，也培养了不少后学，但真正说来，除了那本还属于介绍性的《维也纳学派哲学》外，就没有再出一本有分量的著作，这是他一生中的不幸，也应该说，是我们时代的不幸！

A Recollection for Professor Tscha Hung

Handing Hong

Beijing Academy of Social Sciences

Abstract: Professor Tscha Hung is my first teacher in philosophy. He was my tutor for my undergraduate theses. His lectures were always clear and concise, and they were appealed logically. During my assistance to Professor He Lin I also learnt much from Tscha Hung. Due to the difficult reality during the Cultural Revolution Professor Tscha Hung had a dreary life at his last time. However, he had insisted on his philosophical study and achieved much in high international reputation.

Keywords: Tscha Huang; Vienna Circle; analytic philosophy; the later time in his life

维也纳学派在中国的命运*

◎ 江 怡

北京师范大学

摘　要：洪谦先生是维也纳学派在中国的主要传人，但在历史上，第一个向国内学术界介绍维也纳学派的哲学家是张申府及其胞弟张岱年。洪谦对维也纳学派思想在中国的传播起到了关键作用。冯友兰也曾对维也纳学派做过介绍和分析，并试图利用逻辑分析的方法处理形而上学问题。金岳霖及其学生殷海光从逻辑学研究的角度对维也纳学派的哲学在中国的传播发挥了作用。洪谦与冯友兰之间在20世纪40年代发生的学术争论，反映了中西两种哲学思维方式的差异。虽然经历了政治上的磨难，但洪谦先生毕生坚持对维也纳学派思想的研究和发展，使其成为国际著名的哲学家。洪谦与冯友兰之间的思想交锋也反映了他们对哲学性质的不同理解。

关键词：维也纳学派；西方哲学在中国；逻辑分析方法；中西哲学的差异

2009 年是维也纳学派在中国的传人洪谦先生诞辰 100 周年，也是这个学派的宣言《科学的世界概念：维也纳学派》发表 80 周年。80 年前，奥地利的马赫学会和维也纳小组的成员为了挽留石里克不去德国波恩大学任教，起草了一份书信，表达了他们对石里克的感激之情。1929 年 8 月，该书信以《科学的世界概念：维也纳学派》为题发表在马赫学会的通讯上，由此，"维也纳学派"作为一种新的哲学思想的标志而闻名于世。据称，"维也纳学派"以及"科学的世界概念"的发明权属于纽拉特，而他之所以选择用"世界概念"（world conception）而不是用"世界观"（world view），是因为后一个词有太多形而上学的含义，在狄尔泰和文德尔班的"精神科学"中有特殊的作用。他希望，新的术语能够表明他们的哲学运动具有不同的哲学和科学倾向。[1] 虽然维也纳小组的讨论开始于 1924 年，而且在石里克的这个小组之前已经有了一

---

* 原文发表于《世界哲学》2009 年第 6 期，曾提交于 2009 年 10 月 24 日在北京大学举行的"纪念洪谦先生诞辰百年"学术研讨会。

① F. Stadler, *The Vienna Circle, Studies in the Origins, Development and Influence of Logical Empiricism*, Wein and New York：Springer, 2001, pp. 335 – 337.

个类似的讨论小组，但如今被看作是逻辑经验主义运动主要代表的维也纳小组，却是从 1929 年开始为世人所知的：当然，这不仅是由于他们发表了这个宣言，更重要是在这个宣言发表一个月之后在布拉格召开的第一届"精确科学认识论大会"。这次会议被称作确立了维也纳学派国际地位的主要标志。①

维也纳学派在中国是与洪谦的名字联系在一起的。维也纳学派的宣言发表之时，洪谦正在石里克身边学习，是一个年方 20 而生气好学的青年。虽然洪谦主要是作为石里克的学生和维也纳学派活动的直接参与者而为中国学人所知，但他在当代中国哲学中的意义已经不限于维也纳学派的中国代表，更重要的是作为西方哲学的科学精神在中国的象征，也是西方哲学在中国哲学语境中所受遭遇的一个典型缩影。时至今日，洪谦先生已诞辰百年、作古 16 载，维也纳学派的宣言也已发表 80 周年。在这个历史时刻，我想简要地回顾一下维也纳学派在中国的奇特经历，讲一讲在当代中国哲学中遭遇过维也纳学派的那些人、那些事，以及那些思想。

一、与维也纳学派有关的那些人

我们如今都知道，洪谦是维也纳学派在中国的第一人，但事实上，早在他之前，就有张申府、张岱年兄弟撰文向当时的哲学界推介过维也纳学派：1933 年 3 月 1 日，时年 24 岁的张岱年在《大陆》杂志第一卷第九期发表了《维也纳派的物理主义》一文，这被看做维也纳学派最早出现于中国的文章；1934 年，张申府又撰文《现代哲学的主潮》，把维也纳学派的哲学看做是当时世界哲学中的一个主要潮流。他们主要是通过阅读关于维也纳学派思想的著作来了解维也纳学派的哲学的，在当时的情况下，他们对维也纳学派思想的把握能够达到非常准确的程度，这完全依赖于他们在自然科学方面的深厚知识基础和方法论的训练。②

但我注意到这里有一个有趣的现象。我们知道，张岱年是张申府的胞弟，想当年他从河北献县来到北京师范学校附小读小学，就是由于其二哥张申府的帮助，后来考入清华大学和北京师范大学，也都与二哥有关，乃至后来的人生道路，都基本上是由张申府安排的。他发表在张申府主编的《大公报·世界思潮》副刊上的 30 多篇文章是他学术道路的开始，张申府还在其中一些文章中附加编者按，由此推进其弟文章在国内学术界的影响。1933 年，张岱年发表的《维也纳派的物理主义》一文主张把逻辑解析法与唯物辨证法结合起来，这个思想明显地与张

---

① 克拉夫特，1998，《维也纳学派》，李步楼、陈维杭译，商务印书馆，第 10 页。

② 胡军，2002，《分析哲学在中国》，首都师范大学出版社，第 182—183 页。

申府先前多次强调的观点完全一致。由此可以看出，张岱年对维也纳学派思想的介绍和分析应当是在张申府的直接影响之下，或者说就是对张申府思想的转述。张岱年 1933 年从北京师范大学教育系毕业后能够直接进入清华大学哲学系担任助教，一方面是由于他读书期间发表的大量文章（这当然与张申府有关）已经引起了当时国内哲学界的关注，另一方面（我认为毫无疑问地）是由于张申府的大力推荐。据称，早在 1934 年，张申府就曾在一篇文章中把钱钟书和张岱年并称为"国宝"，而时年两人不过是刚出大学校门的年轻人。所以，维也纳学派最早传入中国的文章虽然是由张岱年所写，但我们完全有理由把它看做是张申府努力的结果。[①]

张申府作为当代中国哲学研究的开创者之一，已经越来越多地为国内学术界所重视。他的哲学通常被看做是结合了逻辑分析方法和辩证唯物论思想的代表，但在我看来，他的最大贡献是向国人准确地介绍了罗素的哲学思想。他晚年回忆自己对罗素哲学的痴迷，非常人所能比及。他能够理解罗素的思想，有赖于他早年就读北京大学数学专业，虽然他很快转向了哲学，但他最重视的还是数理哲学，包括数学基础问题和数理逻辑，用他自己的话说，"我所学的是兼乎数学与哲学的，也是介乎数学与哲学，是数学与哲学之间的东西。"[②] 正是由于具备了数理逻辑的训练，张申府才能够真正理解罗素提出的逻辑分析方法，并很好地把这种方法运用到对日常事理和哲学问题的分析上。也正是由于对数理逻辑和逻辑分析方法的深刻理解和娴熟运用，张申府才能够对维也纳学派的哲学给予高度关注，认为它是现代哲学中"最活泼有生气，最有希望，最有贡献，最有成绩"的派别。[③] 他还把维也纳学派的哲学观概括为："解析的目的是在把思想，把言辞，弄清楚，藉以见出客观的实在。"[④] 其实，这也正是他所推崇的罗素所追求的目标。但他后来并没有对这种哲学给予更多关注，而是仍然钟情于罗素哲学。追究个中原由，恐怕是很快从维也纳留学归国的洪谦在这种哲学方面比他更有权威吧。

1934 年，洪谦在石里克的指导下完成了博士论文《现代物理学中的因果性问题》，荣获维也纳大学的哲学博士学位。随后，他在维也纳大学继续从事研究工作两年。1936 年夏，石里克被一个患有精神病的学生枪杀。1937 年初，洪谦返回北京，担任清华大学哲学系讲师，主要讲授维也纳学派的哲学。这时，张申府因政治原因已经离开了清华大学，张岱年也辞去了在清华的教职，躲进北京图书馆的宿舍完成他的《中国哲学大纲》。七七事变后，洪谦随清华大学的教授们到了云南，在西南联合大学教授维也纳学派哲学。关于他在西南联大的工作情况，有不

①　今年也是张岱年先生（1909 年 5 月 23 日出生）诞辰 100 周年，在此特别表示纪念。

②　张申府，1993，《所忆》，中国文史出版社，第 85 页。

③　张申府，1985，《张申府学术论文集》，齐鲁书社，第 68 页。

④　同上书，第 66 页。

同的版本。有的说他在西南联大哲学系任教授，还有的说他没在哲学系，因为哲学系有教授不喜欢维也纳学派，所以他是在外文系教德文，只是在哲学系讲授维也纳学派的哲学。抗战结束后，洪谦应邀到牛津大学新学院担任研究员，一直到 1947 年。回国后，在武汉大学哲学系担任教授兼系主任。1951 年任燕京大学哲学系教授兼系主任，1956 年改任北京大学哲学系教授兼外国哲学史教研室主任，1965 年起担任北京大学外国哲学研究所所长，直到 1987 年辞去所长职务，但仍担任北京大学教授。①

正如张申府终身以传播和研究罗素哲学为己任，洪谦则"以宣扬石里克的哲学为其终身职志"（贺麟语）。范岱年等人把洪谦在中国介绍维也纳学派的哲学与艾耶尔向英语国家介绍逻辑经验主义哲学作了一个比较，认为"前者比较忠实与全面；后者更多地阐述作者自己的观点。"② 应当说，这个评价还是比较公允的；但这还主要是针对洪谦在 1949 年前的工作而言。事实上，在 20 世纪 70 年代之后，洪谦对维也纳学派的某些思想观点也开始提出批评意见，特别是在知识基础问题和真理问题上不同意石里克、卡尔纳普的观点，明确提出自己的反基础主义思想。这些都使得洪谦在当代中国哲学中的形象，不再是对维也纳学派哲学的一个简单介绍者（无论介绍得如何忠实和全面），而是一个思考维也纳学派提出的哲学问题的真正研究者，一个真正的哲学家。我想，正是由于洪谦对维也纳学派哲学的创造性发展，他才会得到国际哲学界的高度重视，维也纳大学的马特尔院长才会说他"在维也纳学派的哲学上作出了卓越的贡献"，美国《在世哲学家文库》的编者汉恩才会说他的文章是"一个强项"，东京大学才会认为他"对逻辑实证主义和维特根斯坦的哲学都有深刻的认识"。③

说到洪谦对维也纳学派（特别是对石里克）的感情，可以说到了痴迷的程度，正如同石里克对维特根斯坦哲学的痴迷，或者是张申府对罗素哲学的痴迷一样。对石里克本人，洪谦在许多地方都表达了自己的崇高敬意，把他看做自己"心中的偶像"。对维也纳学派的哲学，洪谦也"忠实地"维护这种哲学的尊严，特别是在受到其他哲学家的误解或攻击的时候，他会毫不犹豫地挺身而出，为维也纳学派的哲学澄清误解，④ 或反击其他哲学家对逻辑实证主义的任何

---

① 关于洪谦的生平，可以参考范岱年、胡文耕、梁存秀的《洪谦和逻辑经验论》一文，载《自然辩证法通讯》1992 年第 3 期。该文也收入范岱年和梁存秀编辑的洪谦的《论逻辑经验主义》（商务印书馆 1999 年版）。
② 洪谦，《论逻辑经验主义》，第 333 页。
③ 同上书，第 348 页。
④ 洪谦，1989，《论〈新理学〉的哲学方法》，载《维也纳学派哲学》，商务印书馆。

攻击。① 而在对维也纳学派哲学的这种捍卫中，他也会由于"爱心太切，以至于不加辨析地运用它"。② 尽管如此，洪谦追求真理、追求学术的弃而不舍的精神，曾深深影响和感动了几代中国学者。任继愈先生称"洪谦是向国内学术界介绍维也纳学派的第一人"，③ 汪子嵩在回忆西南联大时说，"在当时哲学系教授中，洪先生是惟一在国外专门学习西方现代哲学流派——维也纳学派的。"④ 杜小真在谈到萨特哲学的魅力时说，"洪谦先生注重逻辑和实证，但他内心的最深处却蕴涵着深深的人文关怀。他的'执着'，他的'傲骨'，连同他对我译介萨特的可贵支持和鼓励，时时会让我在他仙逝多年之后，仍然感到心灵的温暖"。⑤ 靳西平为洪谦先生在"文革"时期的"沉默"而击掌，认为他是"为自己的学术立场而沉默"。⑥ 王炜在回顾北京大学外国哲学研究所的 40 年历史时，对洪谦先生和熊伟先生的"述而不作"给出了自己的诠释："他们大概都属于孔老夫子示范出来的那类典型的中国传统文人——述而不作。他们知道，为学为文的重要和艰难，把能说的说清楚，已属不易，遇不可说的，不保持沉默，即是妄言与僭越；更晓得节省文字，才能让语言把意义显现出来。"⑦ 这些恰恰是洪谦先生的座右铭：他最喜欢的格言就是苏格拉底的"我知我无所知"。根据范岱年等人的统计，洪谦先生生前只发表过 31 篇文章，其中 1949 年前发表 10 篇，1950—1979 年发表 6 篇，1980 年后发表 15 篇。1949 年前发表的文章均被收入《维也纳学派哲学》一书，1949 年后发表的文章则被收入《论逻辑经验主义》一书。⑧ 而在 1949—1979 年漫长的 30 年中，洪谦的主要工作就是编译西方哲学家的著作，因为在他看来，在当时的历史条件下能够为国内学术界提供一些有价值的研究资料就是对中国哲学发展的最大贡献了。的确，在洪谦主持下编译的《西方古典哲学原著选辑》为那个特殊时代的中国哲学界提供了重要的精神食粮，直到今天，这套选辑仍然被看做是了解西方哲学的重要参考资料。后来，洪谦还主持编辑了《西方现代资产阶级哲学论著选辑》，后修订时改名为《现代西方哲学论著选辑》，同样为国内哲学界提供了重要的第一手研究文献。主持翻译

① 洪谦，1990，《逻辑经验主义文集》，香港三联书店，第 43—45、69、257 页。
② 程炼，《洪谦论弗雷格的数的定义》，2006 年 11 月澳门"哲学交流与文化融合"会议论文。
③ 任继愈，《抗战时期西南联大散记》，《北京日报》2006 年 4 月 3 日第 20 版。
④ 汪子嵩，2007，《漫忆西南联大哲学系的教授》，载《不仅为了纪念》，三联书店。
⑤ 杜小真，《应该感谢他——写在萨特百年诞辰、逝世 25 周年之际》，载《随笔》2005 年第 3 期。
⑥ 靳西平，《"海德格尔学案"带来的两个困惑》，载《开放时代》2000 年第 11 期。
⑦ 王炜，2006《外哲所四十年——尊师琐记》，载《王炜学术文集》，上海译文出版社，第 289 页。
⑧ 参见范岱年等人为《论逻辑经验主义》一书所编的《洪谦论著目录》以及《编后记》，该书第 352—355 页。但据何方昱考据，《洪谦论著目录》仍有疏漏，没有收入洪谦的另外三篇文章。见何方昱：《"学"、"术"统一：1940 年代洪谦思想世界的另一面相》，载《科学文化评论》2007 年第 4 卷第 5 期。

这些资料，洪谦都坚持了"信"、"达"、"雅"的基本原则，他对译文的要求都非常严格，哪怕是在当时已经非常著名的翻译家翻译的文章，也要求有校对，有时甚至还要两个人校对；但同时，他也非常鼓励年轻人尝试翻译，手把手地指导他们译文。他对合作者的工作成就从来都是给予最大的感激，反而把自己的工作成绩放到最不显眼的位置。我已经看到不少专家学者撰文对洪谦先生的谦逊品格表达了敬意，他那严谨的工作态度和谦和的待人风格，正是中国老一辈知识分子共有的优良品德。已有学者撰文指出，洪谦先生一生不仅是在宣传阐述维也纳学派的哲学，而且始终以一个中国知识分子的胸怀担负着时代赋予的使命。① 在烽火硝烟的抗战时期，他以审慎的态度对待国家学术事业的建设，他的《释学术》一文就明确地表达了一个学者的时代使命感："当此'胜利在望，建国工作'即将开始之时，吾人对此荣负之重任，似乎宜借既往，以参考未来，戒妄慎思，小心翼翼，共成此建国之神圣大业。否则，不特有负吾人之职责，同时亦将为万世子孙之罪人矣。"② 解放后，他依然对国家的哲学研究事业建议立言，呼吁加强对西方哲学史的研究，他于 1957 年发表在《人民日报》上的文章《应该重视西方哲学史的研究》，被看做老一辈知识分子对国家建设一片热忱和忠心的最好表达。

说到与维也纳学派有关的人，还有一位不能不提，这就是冯友兰先生。他与洪谦在 20 世纪 40 年代发生的一段思想交锋，早已成为当代中国哲学中的一个"学术公案"；在我看来，他们之间围绕维也纳学派形而上学的讨论，不过是反映了当代中国哲学中的传统哲学观念与西方哲学观念之间的交锋。他们之间的那场争论及其思想分歧，我后面再讲，这里要说的是冯友兰对维也纳学派的了解。从目前掌握的资料看，还没有任何材料能够清楚地证明，冯友兰曾与维也纳学派（除了洪谦之外）的成员有过直接的交往，也无法证明他曾读过石里克、卡尔纳普等人的著作。根据他著作中对维也纳学派思想的表述，可以肯定的是，他主要还是从洪谦那里得到维也纳学派的哲学观点。当然，冯友兰曾在 20 世纪 20 年代在美国攻读博士学位，后在 30 年代游历欧洲，并在 40 年代赴美讲学，这些经历可能会使他更加直接地了解维也纳学派。仅从时间上分析，只有他在 1934 年参加的在布拉格举行的第八届国际哲学大会上，有可能见到维也纳学派的成员，因为这次会议正是维也纳学派成员在国际哲学舞台上第一次集体亮相，会议还开设了一个专门的分会论坛，由弗兰克主持，题目为"自然科学的前沿问题"，石里克、卡尔纳普、

---

① 何方昱，《"学"、"术"统一：1940 年代洪谦思想世界的另一面相》，载《科学文化评论》2007 年第 4 卷第 5 期。

② 洪谦，《释学术》，载《思想与时代》1944 年第 31 期。

卢卡西维茨、莱欣巴哈、内格尔、莫里斯等著名哲学家都在这个论坛上发言。① 或许是由于这个论坛主要涉及科学问题，没有任何资料可以表明冯友兰参加了这个分论坛的活动。1946 年他应邀赴美讲学，这时早已移居美国的维也纳学派主要成员的思想已经开始发生变化，如卡尔纳普，他们的早期思想也招致蒯因等人的批评。加之他在美国的时间只有一年，主要精力在忙于讲授中国哲学，所以，冯友兰的此次美国之行也不太可能对维也纳学派有直接的了解。学界最为乐道的是冯友兰与维特根斯坦的会谈，认为这是他获取维也纳学派思想真经的最好证明。但殊不知，维特根斯坦与维也纳学派的思想本身就是同言殊道，这早已在洪谦那里得到了证明。更况且，30 年代维特根斯坦的思想已经开始发生变化，他的早期思想成为他自己批判的对象，所以，冯友兰与维特根斯坦于 1933 年的那次会面并没有使冯友兰得到维也纳学派思想的真义。当然，尽管我们无法证明冯友兰先生与维也纳学派之间有直接的个人联系，但必须承认，正是他在《新知言》中对维也纳学派思想的批评，对于国内学术界了解维也纳学派的思想在客观上起到了重要的宣传作用。

由于维也纳学派所倡导的逻辑实证主义以及维特根斯坦和罗素等人的思想同属于分析哲学的阵营，而他们的共同特征是强调逻辑分析方法在哲学研究中的关键作用，这样，与逻辑分析研究相关的哲学家自然就与维也纳学派有了思想上的血缘关系。在这里，我主要是指金岳霖和他的学生殷海光。

我们知道，金岳霖 1914—1921 年在美国宾夕法尼亚大学、哥伦比亚大学学习政治学，获哥伦比亚大学政治学博士，之后在英、德、法等国留学和从事研究工作。1925 年回国后受命担任清华大学逻辑学教授，通常认为，他"是最早把现代逻辑系统地介绍到中国来的逻辑学家之一"。的确，金岳霖是当代中国逻辑学的奠基者，对现代逻辑在中国的传播起到了关键性作用。我们也知道，卡尔纳普等人在现代逻辑的建立中曾起到了重要作用，维也纳学派的哲学精神正是现代逻辑的精神，在这种意义上，现代逻辑应当与维也纳学派的思想是一脉相承的。但令人不解的是，金岳霖似乎并没有对维也纳学派表现出专门的关注，至少没有资料证明他专门就维也纳学派的哲学发表过文章。其中的原因，分析起来可能有两个：其一，相比较维也纳学派的哲学，金岳霖更倾向于罗素的哲学，因为在他看来，罗素提倡的逻辑分析更是为了对世界有所了解，而不是像维也纳学派的学说那样，只是关注语言逻辑本身。其二，不同于维也纳学派的哲学，金岳霖的思想具有非常强烈的形而上学情怀，他的逻辑学和知识论是与他的形而上学思

---

① F. Stadler, *The Vienna Circle*, *Studies in the Origins*, *Development and Influence of Logical Empiricism*, pp. 358 – 359.

想紧密地联系在一起的。我们知道，维也纳学派是以反对形而上学为其哲学的基本出发点的，他们用来拒斥形而上学的主要工具就是现代逻辑。然而，在金岳霖看来，现代逻辑不过是一种更为普遍的"逻辑"的表现形式而已，他把这种普遍的"逻辑"看做是对"式"的研究，而这种"式"则是一切事物性质的规定，是"唯一逻辑"的逻辑。有学者指出，金岳霖实际上是把他的逻辑学"形上学化了"。① 由此可见，金岳霖的思想并不属于维也纳学派所在的逻辑实证主义，他对维也纳学派知多言少也就毫不奇怪了。

如今，我们对殷海光已经不再陌生，无论是在港台还是大陆，学者们对殷海光思想的讨论已经远远超出了学术的范围。但我在这里更关心的是他对现代逻辑的研究和教学工作。殷海光于 1938 年在金岳霖的大力帮助下考入西南联合大学哲学系学习，4 年后考入清华大学哲学研究所，专攻西方哲学。他毕生热心于现代逻辑的研究、教学和宣传。他认为，中国文化极其缺乏认知因素，主要是由于儒家文化的泛道德主义倾向和中国文化采取的"崇古"价值取向，而这必须依靠西方实证论哲学的输入来补救。于是，殷海光大力提倡"认知的独立"，强调"独立思想"。正是在这种精神的指引下，殷海光终生宣传科学、民主和自由，被看做是一位富有批判精神的自由主义者。虽然他在 50 年的生涯中致力于以科学的精神和批判的态度反思当时的台湾社会生活，但殷海光似乎并没有对以这种精神为核心的维也纳学派哲学做过专门研究，而只是在台湾大学开设过"逻辑经验论"课程。这表明，殷海光关心的并不是维也纳学派的哲学本身，而更多的是这种哲学提倡的逻辑分析方法和严格科学的态度。

如果从张岱年 1933 年的文章算起，维也纳学派进入中国至今已经有 70 多年的历史了。在这个过程中，当代中国的几乎所有重要哲学家都与维也纳学派的思想有过各种各样的关系，无论是赞同宣传还是质疑批判。在一定意义上说，维也纳学派传入中国的历史，就是一部西方现代哲学与中国传统哲学、科学的分析方法与思辨的形而上学相互碰撞的历史，而在这种碰撞中，维也纳学派的哲学始终处于守势和被动的地位。抛开其中涉及的工具化、实用化倾向以及意识形态作用因素不谈，当代中国哲学从维也纳学派哲学中得到的不仅是逻辑分析的哲学方法，更有如何理解哲学性质的深刻启发，以及如何从维也纳学派的哲学看待中国传统哲学文化的另类维度。

二、与维也纳学派有关的那些事

说到与维也纳学派有关的那些事情，首先不得不说 1944 年 11 月 11 日发生在洪谦与冯友兰

---

① 王中江，《金岳霖与实证主义》，载《哲学研究》1993 年第 11 期。

之间的那场思想交锋。①

事情还要从 20 世纪 30 年代说起。1937 年初，洪谦从维也纳返回中国，首先是在清华大学哲学系任教，讲授维也纳学派哲学，后来跟随清华大学南迁至昆明，在西南联合大学外语系教授德语，在哲学系讲授维也纳学派哲学。根据张岱年先生回忆，在清华期间，洪谦与同系的冯友兰、金岳霖等在基本哲学观念上就存在着明显的分歧，主要是洪谦反对任何建立本体论的企图，因此，他不同意冯友兰的新理学和金岳霖在《论道》中的学说。这样，"洪谦与清华哲学系的关系趋于淡化了"。② 正是这种思想上的分歧，导致了洪谦在当时国内的学术环境中并没有得到更多的重视，并由此引发了他与冯友兰等人的思想争论。

我们还要先交代一下这场争论的学术背景。根据贺麟先生的记述，西方哲学在中国开始"生根"，应当开始于 20 世纪 20 年代：1925 年"中国哲学会"成立和 1927 年《哲学评论》创刊，表明"我们研究西方哲学业已超出杂乱的无选择的稗贩阶段，进而能作有系统的源源本本的介绍了，并且已能由了解西方哲学进而批评、融会并自创了。"③ 中国哲学会每年举行年会，在会上宣读的论文都是作者个人研究思索的心得。洪谦与冯友兰之间的思想争论，正是在中国哲学会在昆明举行的年会上发生的。冯友兰曾在 1943 年的《哲学评论》第八卷上发表《新理学在哲学上的地位及其方法》，批评维也纳学派拒斥形而上学的做法并没有取消"新理学"的玄学。洪谦正是针对冯友兰的这个观点提出批评。他认为，冯友兰并没有真正理解维也纳学派对于形而上学的态度，而且他的形而上学也并非如他所言是不可"取消"的。根据贺麟先生的记录，"冯先生本人当即提出答辩，金岳霖及沈有鼎先生亦发言设法替冯先生解围。"但我们今天已经无从查证冯友兰是如何答辩的，金岳霖和沈有鼎又是如何解围的。但有一点是清楚的：金岳霖和沈有鼎是在为冯友兰的观点作辩护。这的确是一个值得琢磨的现象：作为逻辑学研究在中国的第一批哲学家，他们为什么会站在冯友兰的立场上，为他的形而上学辩护呢？虽然冯

---

① 见范岱年、胡文耕、梁存秀发表于 1992 年第 3 期的《自然辩证法通讯》中的《洪谦和逻辑经验论》一文（后作为附录重印于洪谦的《论逻辑经验主义》）。发表于 1946 年 12 月的《哲学评论》第 10 卷第 2 期第 30—35 页上的《论〈新理学〉的哲学方法》一文最后有"一九四四，十二，十五 昆明完稿"字样，并在"附记"中写道，该文是"作者本年 11 月 11 日在中国哲学会昆明分会第二次讨论会中的一个讲演"。但在洪谦收该文于《维也纳学派哲学》中时，取消了"一九四四，十二，十五 昆明完稿"字样，这样，附记中所说的"本年"就容易被理解为该文发表的当年。如胡军在《分析哲学在中国》一书第 196 页上就作了如此解释。其实，贺麟早在写于 1945 年的《当代中国哲学》中，就明确地提到该次思想交锋。而且，洪谦先生在抗战胜利后很快就去了牛津，直到 1947 年才回国。所以，即使没有"一九四四，十二，十五 昆明完稿"字样，从时间上推断，这场思想交锋也不可能发生在 1946 年。

② 张岱年，1996，《回忆清华哲学系》，载《张岱年全集》第 8 卷，河北人民出版社，第 539 页。

③ 贺麟，2002，《五十年来的中国哲学》，商务印书馆，第 25 页。

友兰最初也是由于对逻辑学的痴迷而进入哲学门的，但他对逻辑学的理解基本上属于"一知半解"的状态，他对逻辑分析方法的理解与维也纳学派以及洪谦的理解也有很大的差别。① 这些更使得我们对金岳霖和沈有鼎的做法感到迷惑。我们只能对此作出这样一种解释，即这是由于冯友兰当时的学术地位以及金岳霖和沈有鼎对形而上学的同情。或许也是由于这种学术地位的作用，当时并不受到哲学界推崇的洪谦的说法就受到了一定程度的冷落，虽然学者们都承认他的工作具有意义。

如果说洪谦与冯友兰之间的思想争论还属于学术范围内的讨论的话，20世纪50—60年代国内哲学界对维也纳学派的批评则更多地带有政治批判的色彩。1957年开始的反右运动，在中国哲学界引起了唯物主义反对唯心主义的斗争。在这场运动中，维也纳学派的哲学首当其冲，被看做是"资产阶级唯心主义哲学"的典型遭到批判。当时北京大学哲学系的五个年轻教师以"伍思玄"为笔名在1959年的《北京大学学报》上发表了题为《批判维也纳学派的逻辑分析和证实方法》的文章，认为"所谓逻辑分析并没有像维也纳学派设想的那样，使他们'超越'唯心唯物之外；他们的逻辑实证主义或逻辑经验主义实质上不过是巴克莱主义和马赫主义在一种'新'的方式下的复活而已"，而且，"维也纳学派的证实方法绝不是证明知识之意义和真理性的方法，恰恰相反，乃是一种证明知识之不可能的方法。它是一种反科学、反真理的方法"。文章最后说，"维也纳学派哲学作为一种反科学的哲学，像一切资产阶级的唯心主义哲学一样，其最终的归趋，其客观的、阶级的作用'完全是在于替信仰主义者服役'（列宁）。他们反对'形而上学'的根本目的乃是为了以实证主义和不可知论精神毒害科学，把人类知识限制在经验的此岸，而把那'超越'的'彼岸'的世界留给宗教信仰"。② 这显然是为了迎合当时的政治要求对维也纳学派的无理指责。由于作者们的批判采用的都是具有权威性的第一手资料，因此，这个批判文章在当时的哲学界造成了很大影响，为维也纳学派的哲学受到更多的政治批判提供了"理论依据"。然而，另一方面，正是由于文章采用了大量第一手资料，所以，它也在客观上宣传了维也纳学派的哲学，至少让哲学界更多地了解了石里克和洪谦的思想。

当然，在当时的政治大气候下，不仅年轻的学者难以坚持独立的学术思想，就连经历过战争艰难的老一辈学者也难以逃脱思想上的自我背叛。事实上，洪谦本人就在1955年的《哲学研究》上发表过一篇批评卡尔纳普的文章，完全是按照政治的要求对卡尔纳普的物理主义展开了

① 参见胡军在《分析哲学在中国》（首都师范大学出版社2002年）中对冯友兰的批评，见该书第144—145页。
② 伍思玄，《批判维也纳学派的逻辑分析和证实方法》，载《北京大学学报》1959年第3期。

政治大批判。这篇文章后来使洪谦先生感到自惭，他在晚年曾多次表示了对该文的不满，所以，范岱年和梁存秀在编辑洪谦的文集《论逻辑经验主义》一书时就没有收入该文。① "文化大革命"中，洪谦没有发表任何文章，全身心地投入到编辑和翻译西方哲学史资料上，从 1957 年到 1961 年，在洪谦的主持下，四本《西方古典哲学原著选辑》陆续出版。从 20 世纪 60 年代初开始，洪谦又主编了《西方现代资产阶级哲学论著选辑》，为我国的现代西方哲学研究提供了重要的参考资料。这些工作突显了洪谦在逆境中作为一个学者的道德良心。

改革开放以后，我国的外国哲学研究出现了新的转机，维也纳学派的哲学也重新得到了传播和重视，被看做新实证主义的代表而在 20 世纪 80 年代成为国内思想界最具影响的西方哲学思潮之一。这当然与洪谦先生的工作有着密切的关系。从 1980 年开始，洪谦恢复了停止近 30 年的外国哲学研究，开始在国内外哲学杂志上发表文章，并与国外哲学界恢复了学术联系。其中，对国内哲学界影响最大的是他主持编译了《逻辑经验主义》文集。

正如洪谦先生主持翻译的《西方古典哲学哲学原著选辑》和《西方现代资产阶级哲学论著选辑》（后更名为《现代西方哲学论著选辑》）一样，《逻辑经验主义》文集从一出版就成为国内哲学界了解和研究西方哲学的第一手资料，并且成为国内哲学学术研究的典范。该文集的翻译出版不仅凝聚了洪谦先生的毕生心血，而且培养和造就了国内一代研究人才。当年参加文集翻译的学者不仅有与洪谦先生同辈的长者，如江天骥、王太庆等著名哲学家和哲学翻译家，而且有更多当时正在学术发展中的中青年学者，如洪汉鼎、钟宇人、李步楼、周昌忠、贺绍甲、陈维杭等人，他们其中的大部分如今都已经成为国内外国哲学研究的前辈。洪谦先生在该文集的前言中还特别感谢了杜任之、朱德生和张惠秋三位同志，他们当时分别担任了一些行政职务，对洪谦先生的工作给予了大力支持。② 这些表明，该文集的出版不仅是洪谦先生本人的一项工作，更是我国现代外国哲学研究中的一件大事，标志着我们的现代外国哲学研究开始走向学术的道路。

洪谦先生不仅积极地组织翻译维也纳学派哲学的经典著作，而且身体力行地参与传播英美分析哲学的工作。1988 年夏，中国社会科学院与英国皇家哲学研究所、牛津大学等在北京成立了"中英暑期哲学学院"，邀请洪谦先生担任学院的名誉院长。他不但欣然接受了邀请，而且以他的国际影响力邀请西方哲学家参加学院的活动。暑期学院成立的初衷就是每年邀请来自英

---

① 然而，洪谦先生的闭门弟子韩林合在编辑《洪谦集》时，却把这篇文章收入其中。

② 杜任之时任中国现代外国哲学研究会（后更名为"中国现代外国哲学学会"）理事长，朱德生时任北京大学哲学系领导，而张惠秋则是洪谦先生的学术秘书。

语国家的哲学家到中国讲解和讨论西方哲学的最新发展，强调以分析哲学的方式处理一切哲学问题。正是这种思想指导下，暑期学院每年的学习内容基本上都以英美哲学为主，特别是在最初的几年里更是如此，例如，1988 年第一期的主题为"分析哲学"，1991 年第二期的主题是"科学哲学"，随后各期的主题分别为"心的哲学和认知哲学"、"现代认识论"、"哲学与应用伦理学"、"社会科学哲学"、"政治哲学"、"语言哲学"。进入 21 世纪后，暑期学院的学习主题虽然发生了一些变化，开始关注"生命伦理学"、"康德哲学"、"古希腊哲学"、"法哲学"等内容，但哲学讨论的方式并没有发生改变，仍然强调"有洞察力的阅读"和"清晰的思考"。这些正是分析哲学的训练带来的最有成效的结果。如今，暑期学院已经成功地举办了 20 年，国内越来越多的青年学者参加了学院的活动，接受了分析哲学的训练，他们已经和正在成为国内外国哲学研究和教学的骨干力量。应当说，暑期学院的成功举办为分析哲学在中国的传播作出了不可磨灭的贡献。

正是在暑期学院的积极组织和大力推动下，1992 年在北京举行了"科学哲学中的实在论与反实在论"国际研讨会，1994 年在北京举行了"纪念洪谦：维也纳学派与当代科学和哲学"国际研讨会，这两次会议对于维也纳学派的哲学在中国的深入研究是具有标志性的重要事件，因为这两次研讨会不仅使中国哲学家在真正意义上与西方哲学家进行了纯粹的学术思想交流，而且完全确立了洪谦先生作为维也纳学派传人的国际地位。

在 1992 年的会议上，学者们对维也纳学派的科学哲学给予了最大的关注，并对洪谦先生把逻辑经验主义与中国当代哲学的结合所作的贡献给予了肯定，认为他在中国起到了艾耶尔在英国和亨普尔在美国所起的作用，即向本民族的文化中注入了逻辑经验主义的思想。该次会议论文集后来由美国哲学家科恩（R. S. Cohen）、希尔派尼（R. Hilpinen）和我国哲学家邱仁宗联合编辑，由国际著名的克鲁威尔学术出版社（Kluwer Academic Publlishers）出版发行。科恩在编者前言中这样写道，以科学的方式复兴哲学研究在这次会议上得到了证明。"教条式的习惯或主张所带来的限制，危害了科学的真正进步，也的确危害了哲学理解的进步，但这些已经有望远离我们的时代了（虽然要完全摆脱习惯及其程序还很困难）。"[1] 在《回忆洪谦》一文中，科恩特别谈到了洪谦与维也纳小组的密切联系，同时指出了洪谦对当代中国哲学中的贡献在于给出科学思想的清晰性和严格性，强调了科学推理是人类生活的真正指南。

---

[1]　R. S. Cohen, Preface, in R. S. Cohen, R. Hilpinen & Qiu Renzong, eds. *Realism and Anti-realism in the Philosophy of Science*, *Beijing International Conference*, *1992*, Dordrecht／Boston／London：Kluwer Academic Publishers, 1996, p. xii.

1994 年的会议是完全确立洪谦先生国际学术地位的标志性事件。在这次会议上，来自世界10 余个国家和地区的 40 多位哲学家充分肯定了洪谦先生在研究和传播维也纳学派思想中所起的不可替代的作用。大会名誉主席、时任中国社会科学院副院长的汝信在致辞中这样说道："维也纳学派是科学哲学史和一般哲学史上划时代的里程碑，对世纪的自然科学、人文科学和社会科学均产生了重要的影响。作为维也纳学派成员，已故的洪谦教授在中国当代哲学中担任了一个独一无二的角色。"会议的目的在于，从多个角度重新考察、重新评价维也纳学派所提出的哲学纲领。奥地利研究维也纳学派的专家哈勒作了题为《洪谦与石里克学派》的主题报告，回顾了洪谦先生的求学经过。报告还介绍了洪谦与石里克及维也纳学派其他成员的关系。英国学者尼克·布宁探讨了洪谦与其同时代哲学家胡适、金岳霖、冯友兰、熊十力等人之间的学术关系和争论。范岱年在报告中介绍了洪谦与纽拉特的关系。洪谦的学生们还回忆了在洪谦先生身边学习和工作的情景，着力发掘了洪先生的人格操守和学术追求。关于维也纳学派学术观点的再评价，人们着重讨论了石里克与赖兴巴赫的差别、蒯因对卡尔纳普的批评。[1] 这些观点都引起了与会的国内外学者的共鸣。

1992 年 2 月 27 日，洪谦先生与世长辞，这是中国哲学界的"一个无法弥补的巨大损失"（范岱年语）。这不仅使中国失去了一位卓越的哲学家，而且使世界失去了最后一位维也纳学派的成员。但洪谦先生毕生为之努力的哲学研究事业已经在中国大地得到了生根，分析哲学的方法已经成为中国哲学家们从事哲学研究的重要方法之一。在暑期学院的大力支持下，大陆学者与香港学者于 1999—2000 年分别在昆明和苏州共同举行了两次"分析哲学与中国哲学"研讨会，强调以分析哲学的方式研究中国哲学的重要性，取得了很好的学术成果，在国内哲学界也产生了一定的学术影响。但这两次会议主要以分析哲学研究者为主体，是分析哲学家向中国哲学家发出的对话邀请；2009 年在华东师范大学举行的"中国哲学与分析哲学"国际研讨会则是由中国哲学家向分析哲学家发出的邀请，这更表明了对分析哲学研究方法的诉求已经成为我们从事哲学研究的必需。

三、与维也纳学派有关的那些思想

谈到与维也纳学派有关的思想，首先要说的当然是洪谦对维也纳学派的研究工作。虽然洪

---

[1] 胡奈，《"纪念洪谦：维也纳学派与当代科学和哲学"国际会议在北京举行》，载《哲学研究》1994年第 12 期。

谦先生被看作是维也纳学派思想在中国的权威传播者，但他并非对维也纳学派的所有观点都采取赞同的态度，相反，他对卡尔纳普、纽拉特、艾耶尔等人的思想有不少不同的批评意见，而且对逻辑经验主义的后来发展也提出了自己的独特见解。应当说，正是由于洪谦先生的洞见，才使得他被看作在哲学上做出了卓越贡献的人。

仔细阅读洪谦先生早年的《维也纳学派哲学》和晚年的《论逻辑经验主义》，我们不难看出洪谦先生对维也纳学派思想的忠实阐述和有力辩护，也可以看出他对逻辑经验主义哲学的有效推进，对此，范岱年等人在《洪谦和逻辑经验论》一文中已经作了详尽的介绍和分析。在这里，我只想指出，洪谦先生的思想阐发和观点论述不仅是对维也纳学派思想的传播，更是一个中国哲学家以自己的特殊方式对哲学真理的不懈追求；他的思想不但包含了清晰的逻辑分析，而且饱含了中国学者对哲学智慧的特殊感情。例如，洪谦特别注意石里克对伦理命题的论述，强调伦理学是一门与知识有关的科学，而不是毫无意义的形而上学，这与卡尔纳普等人的观点大相径庭。这恰好反映了洪谦作为中国学者的特殊伦理要求，即能够很明确地认识到伦理学在哲学研究中的价值，并且强调了道德需求对思想阐发的必要作用。而且，洪谦还坚守"师道尊严"，对自己的导师石里克的观点多有辩护，这特别表现在他为石里克在形而上学态度上的辩护。这些都表明了洪谦先生作为维也纳学派中国传人的思想特征。

应当说，洪谦先生在中国的最大哲学贡献是他对维也纳学派哲学的准确阐述，这包括了他为维也纳学派成员观点的辩护和对批评意见的回应等。其中，在国内哲学界最有影响的还是他与冯友兰的思想交锋。我们在前面已经对这场交锋的来龙去脉做了交代，这里要分析的是这场交锋的关键究竟何在。

胡军曾在他的《分析哲学在中国》（2002 年）中对洪谦与冯友兰的思想交锋做了较为全面的分析，但结果却是"各打五十大板"，分别批评了他们的思想具有某种局限性，认为这场交锋的根源是他们都没有真正理解对方思想的真实意义。① 从大的方面来说，我基本上能够接受他的分析，但具体而言，这样的分析似乎并没有找到他们之间分歧的要害，也无法解决他们之间的争端。通过阅读理解他们的著作，我发现，他们之间的分歧其实并不是出于误解，而是由于他们对哲学性质的不同理解，由于他们处理哲学问题的方式有很大不同。

在对哲学性质的理解上，洪谦显然遵循着维也纳学派对哲学的理解，把哲学看做是澄清命题意义的活动，由于哲学的主要任务是为了保障人类知识的确立，因此知识论问题自然就成为哲学研究的主要内容。从认识世界的角度看，西方哲学的这种思维方式显然具有很大的实际效

---

① 胡军，《分析哲学在中国》，第 196—206 页。

用，的确能够帮助人类很好地认识和理解世界的真实面目。即使是在强调石里克伦理学的重要
意义的同时，洪谦仍然是把知识论而不是伦理学作为哲学研究的主要内容。这与洪谦所受到的
自然科学训练有着密切的关系。他在跟随石里克后不久，石里克就要求他先学习物理学、数学
和逻辑学，他深受维也纳学派成员的自然科学背景的影响。这样的哲学背景自然就要求他用自
然科学家的眼光看待世界，以自然科学的研究方式处理哲学问题。这在他的所有文章中都表现
得极为明显。反观冯友兰，则情况有所不同。虽然冯友兰早年也曾赴美留学，并一再强调逻辑
分析对哲学研究的重要性，但他并没有把哲学看做如同科学研究一样的认识论活动，而是坚持
中国传统的思维方式，认为哲学是对人生问题的解决，关乎个人的安身立命之本。他把哲学研
究工作的主要任务理解为追求人生的最高境界，认为只有从"无知之知"中才能得到关于世界
的本体论理解。显然，冯友兰是站在中国传统本体论的立场理解哲学的性质和任务，也是由此
去理解维也纳学派的哲学。虽然冯友兰强调了哲学的本体论意义，但他理解的本体论与西方本
体论还是有重要差别。其中的主要差别是，西方本体论强调的是对世界本原的终极研究，试图
以某个或某些根本原则或原理或基质解释世界万物，这样的根本原则具有超越经验的特征，是
世界万物得以产生发展的最终根据；而在冯友兰看来，本体论就是形而上学，追求的是一种
"经虚涉旷"的天地境界。"形上学的功用，本只在于提高人的境界。它不能使人有更多底积极
底知识。它只可以使人有最高底境界。"① 在西方，形而上学研究与科学研究并不对立，两者相
得益彰；但在冯友兰那里，形而上学与科学是背道而驰的，形而上学的工作是对经验做形式的
肯定，而科学则对经验做积极的肯定，这里的"形式"是指"空"，但又指"灵"，"空"意味
着形而上学命题不对任何经验事实有实质性的断定，而"灵"则是说形而上学命题对于一切事
实都可适用。冯友兰把形而上学的方法分为正的和负的，"正底方法是以逻辑分析法讲形上学。
负底方法是讲形上学不能讲，讲形上学不能讲，亦是一种讲形上学的方法。"② 他强调的是所谓
的负的方法，这就是他所谓的追求空灵的境界，他所谓的正的方法其实不过是用来说明空灵境
界的手段而已。显然，冯友兰对哲学性质的这种理解与洪谦和维也纳学派的理解大相径庭，因
为在洪谦他们看来，逻辑分析并非是哲学研究的一种方法，而是哲学研究的全部；对逻辑形式
的研究并非哲学研究的手段，而是所有知识的本质。因为"任何认识都是一种表达，一种陈
述。……所有这些可能的陈述方式，如果它们实际上表达了同样的知识，正因为如此，就必须
有某种共同的东西，这种共同的东西就是它们的逻辑形式。所以，一切知识只有凭借其形式而

---

① 冯友兰，1986，《三松堂全集》第五卷，河南人民出版社，第 167 页。
② 同上书，第 173 页。

成为知识；知识通过它的形式来陈述所知的实况，但形式本身是不能再被描述出来的。形式的本质只在于知识，其余一切都是非本质的，都是表达的偶然材料，和我们用来写一个句子的墨水没有什么不同。"① 这些与冯友兰对逻辑形式和逻辑分析的理解完全不同。

正是由于对哲学性质的不同理解，他们处理哲学问题的方式也迥然不同。我们知道，洪谦秉承了维也纳学派的哲学研究方法，以逻辑分析的方式讨论科学命题的意义，以语词辨析的方法澄清各种不同观点之间的差异。例如，他认为，康德提出的先天综合判断并不存在，因为如果一个命题必须与现实有关联，那就必须用经验来检验它的真假，反之，如果一个命题的真假不可能从经验上加以检验，那么它就一定不是描述事实的命题；如果一个先天综合命题不是经验命题，那么它就既不能以经验为根据，也不能为经验所驳倒，所以，它就是一个无效的命题。洪谦在批评马赫的实证主义时主要区分了它与逻辑实证主义之间的根本分歧，认为后者虽然继承了前者的反形而上学精神，但在一些根本点上则是截然不同的。同样，洪谦在批评冯友兰的新理学时也是采用了分析的方法，指出了冯友兰在知识分类上的混淆，并澄清了维也纳学派取消形而上学的真实含义，辨析了冯友兰对形而上学的理解。应当说，洪谦对冯友兰新理学的批评在逻辑上是完全站得住的。② 然而，冯友兰处理哲学问题的方式则与洪谦大为不同。虽然他一再强调逻辑分析对哲学研究的重要作用，但正如胡军指出的那样，冯友兰在自己的著作中并没有真正运用逻辑分析的方法，他所理解的逻辑分析主要还是"辨名析理"的方法。③ 我认为不仅如此，冯友兰在他的著作中其实更多地使用的是常识直观的方法，即根据我们的常识判断对他提出的形而上学命题做出肯定，而恰恰缺乏对这些命题的形式论证。例如，他对新理学形而上学的四组主要命题的分析就是建立在常识直观的基础之上的。第一组命题"凡事物必都是什么事物"。逻辑上说，这就是同一律，A = A。但冯友兰把它解释为"某种事物是某种事物，必有某种事物之所以为某种事物者"，这就从同一律进入了因果律，而这个转变是根据常识直观，因为常识中并没有追问同一律的必要，但这种追问却正好是形而上学需要回答的问题。第二组命题"事物必都存在"，这仍然是同一律的另一形式，但冯友兰将其解释为"存在底事物必都能存在。能存在底事物必都有其所有以能存在者"，这就是用存在者解释存在本身的意义，

① 石里克，1982，《哲学的转变》，载洪谦主编《逻辑经验主义》上卷，商务印书馆，第7—8 页。
② 值得注意的是，冯友兰虽然在昆明会议上对洪谦的批评有所回应，但他后来并没有写文章反驳洪谦，进一步阐明自己的观点。分析起来，这里可能有两个原因：其一，洪谦作为维也纳学派的成员，对维也纳学派哲学的理解自然最有权威，或许冯友兰认为在这一点上无法与他相争；其二，由于冯友兰当时处于构建自己新理学的巅峰，认为自己的形而上学就是要与西方哲学决裂，所以并没有把洪谦的批评意见放在眼里。
③ 胡军，《分析哲学在中国》，第 143 页。

符合我们的常识概念。第三组命题"存在是一流行。凡存在都是事物的存在。事物的存在都是其气实现某理或某某理的流行",这些是说明了万物归一的道理,他最后由此得到"道体"、"乾元"成为一切流行之动力。这些观念显然来自中国传统文化,但却穿上了西方本体论的外衣。第四组命题"总一切底有,谓之大全,大全就是一切底有",这里是把"大全"和"一切有"等同起来。如果按照西方哲学的理解,"大全"并非全有,而是在一切的有之外的更大的东西,是决定了一切的有的东西。但这里把"大全"和"一切有"等同起来,其实是符合我们日常的理解,即认为一切存在东西的整体就是"大全"。从冯友兰对每组命题的解释中可以看出,他不断地运用到我们的日常理解,即我们对世界万物的混沌理解,因为他使用的四个观念都是非概念的,就是说它们都是无法言表的,正所谓"道可道非常道"。应当说,这样一种形而上学既于观念的澄清无所帮助,也于我们的日常经验无所帮助。

尽管冯友兰的这种形而上学已经遭到了洪谦的釜底抽薪式的批评,但令人遗憾的是,冯友兰非但没有因此修正自己的理论,反而更为全面地推行着这种新理学在当代中国哲学研究中的传播,使其成为当代中国的主流思想之一。这其中存在一个历史的悖论:冯友兰当年正是认识到中国传统文化中缺乏严密的逻辑并由于学习逻辑而进入哲学之门,他还在自己的著作中大力提倡使用逻辑分析的方法研究中国传统哲学,但在他的哲学中却存在着大量不完全符合逻辑要求的论述,而且他也正是由于这种混沌的思想方式而成为当代中国哲学的一面旗帜。我这样说并非对冯友兰先生不尊重,而仅仅是想说明,新理学的建立与逻辑分析方法的运用之间的矛盾,构成了冯友兰形而上学哲学大厦的基础,同时,这也是导致新理学最终失败的根本原因。

纵观维也纳学派在中国的经历,我们可以明显地感觉到,这种以科学为模式建立起来的哲学观念总是与中国的传统文化处于一种紧张的矛盾之中。更进一步地说,包括了维也纳学派哲学在内的整个西方哲学传统在进入中国的思想语境时也总是处于比较尴尬的境地,总是面临各种各样的"误读",乃至于西学东渐百年之后人们依然在讨论"中体西用"之类的问题,甚至还有人试图彻底否认西学东渐的历史意义。在这种历史和现实的背景下,重新认识维也纳学派哲学的历史价值,重新了解维也纳学派进入中国的历史,对于我们更好地理解西方文化,特别是更为清楚地认识到我们自身的文化,都具有重要的理论和实践的意义。

The Fate of Vienna Circle in China
Yi Jiang

Beijing Normal University

Abstract: Professor Tscha Hung is the key descendant of Vienna Circle in China. However, historically, the first person who introduced the philosophy of Vienna Circle is not him but Zhang Shenfen and his brother Zhang Dainian. Whatever they did, Tscha Hung made a crucial contribution to the spreading of Vienna Circle in China. Feng Youlan also explained the philosophy of Vienna Circle by analyzing metaphysical problems in terms of logic. Jin Yuelin and his distinguished student Yin Haiguang played a role in spreading of Vienna Circle in China by their study in logic. The debate of Tscha Hung and Feng Youlan in 1940s reflects the gap of ways of the West and Chinese thinking. Tscha Hung kept his all life in investigation and development of Vienna Circle, even though it was difficult for him to do the academic in the Cultural Revolution. The debate of Tscha Hung and Feng Youlan also reflects the difference of understandings of the nature of philosophy.

Keywords: Vienna Circle; Western philosophy in China; logical analysis; differences of the Western and Chinese philosophies

缅怀彼得·斯特劳森爵士

——写在斯特劳森诞辰 90 周年之际

◎ 林允清

北京师范大学

摘　要： 在这篇回忆中我主要怀念我在 1995—2004 年间与彼得·斯特劳森爵士之间的交往与友谊。正是由于斯特劳森的鼓励，我才得以前往牛津大学学习语言学和哲学。也正是斯特劳森引导我走上了哲学探索的道路。我希望这篇回忆能够记录他杰出的个性、善良的品格、慷慨的性格以及催人奋进的精神。我还希望能够揭示语言学研究与他的哲学工作之间的密切联系。

关键词： 斯特劳森；牛津；句法学；语义学；逻辑；康德；维特根斯坦

我于 2004 年夏天从伦敦大学回到北京工作，从而结束了长达 18 年之久的旅英生涯。刚回国的日子很忙碌，就没能与彼得·斯特劳森爵士联系。2006 初的一天，一个在伦敦的同事发来电子邮件，告诉我说斯特劳森去世了。我当时很惊讶，也很难过，没想到离开英国才一年多，他就仙逝了。那时我打算写一篇纪念他的文章，然而由于各种原因那个想法一直没能兑现。一晃回国已经 5 年了；炎炎的北京的夏日让我不禁想到英国的清风细雨，想到把我领上哲学之路的彼得·斯特劳森爵士。于是我心中涌起一阵阵强烈的冲动，想把对他的回忆写下来，以寄托我对他的思念和敬意。

斯特劳森的英文全名是 Peter Fredrick Strawson。他于 1919 年 11 月 23 日出生于英国伦敦，生前曾是牛津大学的哲学教授，是国际上公认的 20 世纪最伟大的哲学家之一。1977 年，他因为对哲学作出的卓越贡献被英国女王授予爵士称号。按照汉语的习惯，我们应该称斯特劳森为"斯特劳森爵士"，正如我们说"王先生"、"李教授"、"张老总"等等。但就英国的风俗来说，我们只能称他为"彼得爵士"（Sir Peter）而不是"斯特劳森爵士"（Sir Strawson）。当然我们还可以称他为"斯特劳森教授"（Prof. Strawson）、"斯特劳森先生"（Mr. Strawson），或者干脆直称"彼得"（Peter），如果跟他很熟的话。而在写文章或谈论起他时，我们可以简称他为"斯特劳森"（Strawson）。就这篇文章而言，为了方便起见，我就用"Strawson"来指代他吧。

我在 Essex 大学计算机系读博士的时候才知道 Strawson 这个名字。在此之前我学的是工科，接触到的主要是电子、电机、电脑等等。出国时想读的科目是人工智能，于是就到了 Essex 大学，跟 Raymond Turner 教授读博士。Turner 是逻辑学家，精通数理逻辑和哲学逻辑，曾在这两个领域都拿过博士学位，所以在他的影响下我也搞起逻辑来，后来明确到要研究时间逻辑中的一些问题。剑桥大哲学家 Russell（罗素）曾在时间逻辑上作过很重要的贡献，他提出人们的时间概念是由平时观察到的事件构造出来的。我的研究不可避免地要讨论 Russell 的工作，实际上我的博士论文可以说是完全建立在 Russell 的时间理论之上的。为此我仔细阅读了 Russell 的很多著作，包括啃过他的巨著《数学原理》（Principia Mathematica）。Strawson 以一篇批评 Russell 的文章《论指称》（On referring）而成名于哲学界，我自然也认真地阅读了那篇文章。不过那时并没有读 Strawson 的其他著作，虽然通过广泛的阅读我也知道他是"日常语言哲学学派"的重要成员。

真正觉得 Strawson 的工作与我的研究有密切关系是后来我在 Cardiff 大学做研究员的时候。1990 年我到 Cardiff 大学工作，加入了系统功能语言学家 Robin Fawcett 建立的计算语言学研究中心，一做便是 6 年。研究中心的目标是建造一个智能的人机对话系统，以系统功能语法为核心，研究语句和篇章的结构、意义、生成和理解，并在计算机上予以实现。除了如何建立系统功能语法网络并进行语句生成之外，我思考最多的便是：（1）句子的语法结构（syntax）到底是什么；（2）其逻辑结构（logical form）又是什么；以及（3）推理（reasoning 或 inference）究竟是怎么回事。我之所以觉得语法结构很令人困惑，是因为那几年我们几乎每天都在给句子作语法分析，但经常是今天分析是这样、明天分析又是那样。不光如此，不同的理论对同样的句子所作的语法分析也经常不同，比如 Fawcett 的语法分析跟 Halliday 的就不同，而他们的语法分析跟 Chomsky 的又大相径庭。到底句子的语法结构是什么，这令我百思而不得其解。再来看逻辑结构问题：自从 1905 年 Russell 发表了他的《论指称》（On denoting）一文以来，哲学界及语言学界的一个主流思想就是句子的语法结构和其逻辑结构经常是不同的、因而要去发掘句子的逻辑结构以明确地表达句子的意义。同样，这也给我带来巨大的困惑：对于同样的句子，不同的学者会提出不同的逻辑结构，那到底谁的提法是正确的？再说，对句子的语法结构尚没有明确的结论，那又如何去客观地发现其逻辑结构呢？接下来是推理问题：逻辑（logic）通常被认为是推理的机制，但逻辑跟日常语言有很大的出入，日常语言的逻辑是什么，它跟语法结构有什么样的关系，逻辑本身又是什么，怎么知道一个逻辑系统是客观存在的呢？这样的问题在那几年里也一直困扰着我。慢慢地，我对语法结构问题有了自己的解释，那就是句子的语法结构其实很简单，就是平时我们都知道的一些词的使用方法。比如：It is kind of you to come to see me

这句话的主要结构就是：it is kind of somebody to do something，其次要结构就是：（somebody）comes to do something；而这两者就是关于 kind 和 come 这两个词的正确使用方法。按照这个思路，语法是什么就有了明确的答案，也不会再有对同一个句子不同人会给出不同的语法分析这样的问题。顺着这个思路走下去，就会觉得没有必要提出逻辑结构这一神秘概念；非要有逻辑结构的话，那逻辑结构就是语法结构。再继续走下去，就会觉得日常语言的逻辑也变得清楚了——它跟语法结构，也就是词的使用，是紧密相关的。就在这个时候，我读了 Wittgenstein（维特根斯坦）的《哲学研究》（Philosophical Investigations）和 Strawson 的一些著作。

Wittgenstein 的早期著作《逻辑哲学论》（Tractatus Logico-philosophicus）我在 Essex 大学读博士时就读过了。前面说过我博士做的是时间逻辑研究，确切的说是研究人们的时间观念是怎样由所观察到的事件构建出来的。所以我当时就阅读了很多涉及"事件"（events）、"情境"（situations 或 states of affairs）和"变化"（changes）等概念的著作，其中就包括 Wittgenstein 的《逻辑哲学论》，因为"情境"是这部著作里的一个重要概念。我当时并没有读懂这部著作，它在我的博士论文中也没有留下什么痕迹。但它所表现出来的"逻辑原子主义"（logical atomism）对我在 Cardiff 的前几年里影响还是很大的，因为在那个时期我也非常热心又充满激情地去挖掘句子背后的逻辑结构。但在我对语法、逻辑结构和逻辑有了自己的一些见解之后，我读了 Wittgenstein 的《哲学研究》，感到一种很强烈的共鸣。其中一个共同点就是很多问题（也许）可以通过众所周知的事实来化解，比如我觉得语法问题就可以通过人人皆知的词的使用方法来解释。当然 Wittgenstein 要化解的是哲学问题，而我要对待的是当代语言学的问题；但是语言学问题思考到深处也就成了哲学问题了。另一个共同点就是我觉得日常语言并没有什么毛病和不足，没必要去建立一些人为的理论，比如逻辑理论，去对日常语言进行分析。当然这就是所谓的"日常语言学派"的基本观点——至少很多学者都是这么认为的。于是我想到"日常语言学派"的另一个代表人物 Strawson，便开始读他的一些著作。Strawson 的《论指称》一文指出日常语言的句子并不需要像 Russell 那样去用所谓的逻辑结构来分析，而应仔细看看那些句子在日常生活中是怎样被使用的。Strawson 也不赞成用逻辑来解释日常推理，他指出逻辑和日常推理有很大的差异，并认为日常推理另有解释方法，这一点他在《逻辑理论导论》（Introduction to Logical Theory）、《逻辑和语法中的主谓语》（Subject and Predicate in Logic and Grammar）和《分析和形而上学》（Analysis and Metaphysics）中都有论述。我发现 Strawson 的观点和我的观点有不少重合之处，而且他那时还健在，就在牛津大学，离 Cardiff 也不远，于是我便有了和他交流的想法。

1995 年我将自己对语法、语义及逻辑的想法汇总写成了一篇文章，并在 9 月份召开的欧洲认知系统学会（European Society for the Study of Cognitive Systems）的研讨会上宣读了这篇论文。研讨会在牛津大学的 Wadham 学院举行，我们在学院的宽敞的学生宿舍住宿，在学院的古色古香的餐厅就餐，在学院的庄严的会议室开会，在学院的极具情调的酒吧喝酒聊天。在此以前我曾经去过牛津，不过只是走马观花地看看而已。但这次是在学院里吃住开会讨论，第一次体验了牛津大学的学生生活，真让我对牛津大学的生活羡慕不已，从而萌发了到牛津大学学习深造的念头。

我在那次研讨会上宣读的文章题为"Grammar, semantics, and logic：towards an 'ordinary language' theory of language"，文章深受 Wittgenstein 和 Strawson 的影响。虽然文章题目中的"theory"一词用得不很适当（因为 Wittgenstein 是反对建立任何哲学理论的），对 Wittgenstein 后期哲学理解得不全面，对 Strawson 的哲学思想认识得也不够深刻，但那篇文章毕竟是我几年思考的结果，也反映了我当时那种哲学爱好者的热情。谈到哲学，也许我可以说从在 Essex 读博士起就在做了，因为我的博士论文的内容分三篇文章发表了，其中一篇登在逻辑学期刊（Journal of Applied Non-Classical Logics）上，一篇登在哲学逻辑期刊（Nordic Journal of Philosophical Logic）上（还有一篇收录在一本有关人工智能的书里），而这两个期刊都属于哲学的期刊（至少后者是）。但那毕竟只是对 Russell 的时间理论的扩展和应用，自己的独立思考并不多，而且涉及的哲学问题也不广泛。我很想做有关语言的一系列哲学问题的探讨，比如什么是语法、语义、语用及逻辑推理，但这样的研究光靠我在一个相对偏僻的地方孤立地思考是很难有所建树的，于是我便想到去牛津大学这样一个世界学术中心去学习、参加讨论和进行研究。我想到了 Strawson，便给他写了封长信，描述了我的背景、我对语言的思考以及我对他的著作的看法，并寄去了我的相关文章，同时我还表达了想跟他再做一个博士的想法。我是 12 月 8 日给他写的信，没想到他 12 月 11 日就给我写回信了。他信中说他赞同我对语言的一些想法，也很感谢我对他的著作的评论；但他说他已经退休多年，早已不带学生了，他建议我考虑以其他方式去牛津大学，他将乐意跟我一起讨论我的语言研究。受到 Strawson 的鼓励，我便开始申请去牛津大学学习之事宜，但申请过程有颇多的不顺，以致我几乎丧失了信心，毕竟牛津大学的要求是相当严格的。1996 年的 3 月，在绝望中，我写信给 Strawson 诉说，希望能见他一面，谈谈我今后应何去何从。他回信说他 4 月份会有几天有空，说我可以找一天去见他。于是我在 4 月的一天（具体日期已经无法查找了）去牛津他家里和他长谈了一次。那是我第一次见到 Strawson，他当时已经 76 岁了，但精神矍铄，思维相当敏捷。我和他谈了学术上的一些事，后来便聊到我申请来牛津学习的事情，他说"你为什么不和 James Higginbotham 谈谈呢？他是个很好的学者"。正是 Strawson 的这个建议，我才最终有幸被牛津大学语言学系录取，师从系主任 James

Higginbotham 教授，先做硕士，然后再转成博士。被语言学系录取后，我也被 Somerville 学院接收，成为该学院的研究生，学院也给我安排了宿舍。

1996 年 10 月初我便离开 Cardiff 来到了牛津，住进了 Somerville 学院的学生宿舍，开始了我的牛津生涯。Somerville 学院地处牛津小镇比较中心的位置，1879 年建立，是牛津较为年轻的学院，刚开始是个女子学院，1992 年才开始收男学生。英国前首相撒切尔夫人当年曾就读于 Somerville 学院，牛津大学语言学系主任一般也都是该学院的院士。学院有三个相连的院子。前两个院子很小，院子的四周都是两三层的小楼，是一些办公室和院士们的宿舍。第三个院子大得多，中间是个很大的草坪，终年常绿，周围是院图书馆、餐厅、酒吧、大学生宿舍和研究生宿舍，还有一个小小的教堂。从 Somerville 学院到语言学系只有一二百米的距离。语言学系坐落在细长的 Walton 路上，和中国研究中心（China Centre）共用一栋红色的小楼。小楼有两层，底层是中国研究中心，语言学系在楼上，地下还有一层，是中文图书馆。楼上房间不多，有几间是教师的办公室（一个教师一间，最大的那间是系主任的），另外几间便是教室。教室不大，桌子摆成一个长方形，上课时教师坐在短的一边，学生们便占据其他三个边坐着。教师没有特别的讲桌，所以教师和学生之间的距离就很近，可以说是面对面吧。教师上课也不用投影仪，只是发几张讲义，讲义内容往往是言简意赅，后面附有一大堆参考文献。平时上课时间不多，大多数时间里学生需要自己去阅读和思考。

在英国，大多数的硕士课程是一年的，所得到的学位叫做 MA、MSc、MBA 等等。但牛津语言学系的硕士为期两年，叫做 MPhil；两年内选修四门课，第二年快结束时才有考试，当然到时还得交硕士论文。我第一年选了语法学和历史语言学，第二年选的是语义学和语言哲学。除了历史语言学之外，其他三门 Higginbotham 都教过一部分。因为平时课不多，我便自己疯狂读书或静思冥想。记忆最深刻的地方应该是学院的图书馆吧。它 24 小时开放，学院的每个学生都有一把钥匙，晚间和周末也能自由出入。图书馆里的书可以自己拿走到宿舍去读，只要填一个单子就行了。我白天的时候喜欢坐在图书馆外面的石阶上看书，背靠着石柱，面朝着葱绿的草坪；夜晚我便在图书馆里，占据一个宽敞的位子，打开桌灯，桌子上是一摞摞厚厚的书籍，没有人打扰，直到太累了或太饿了才回宿舍。牛津的宿舍极好，有清洁工每天给打扫卫生，床单枕套也负责给换洗。吃饭也不需自己做，学院的餐厅伙食很好，在那吃饭也很有情调。在牛津，人显得非常地单纯，要做的事无非是这些：上课、看书、吃饭、睡觉、泡吧、蹦迪、划船、聊天等等。心无旁骛，也许这是牛津人能做好学问的一个重要原因吧。

Strawson 对我能来牛津读书很高兴，我也很珍惜能跟他面对面交流的机会。在牛津的日子里，我经常到他家里跟他一起喝茶聊天讨论。从牛津的镇中心往北有一条漂亮的主路叫 Wood-stock 路，路两边是一些学院和居民房，房子一般都是两三层的小楼。Strawson 的家就在 Wood-stock 路边上的一条小路上，名曰 Farndon 路，门牌号是 25 号，是一个三层的维多利亚式的红砖小楼房，最底层是客厅和厨房，楼上是书房、卧室和客房。我每次要见他时，先将我写的东西寄给他，他看完后跟我约个时间，一般是下午 3 点左右，我再去他家，在客厅里谈话讨论，一般会讨论一个半小时。Ann（Strawson 的妻子）总是会端上来泡好的红茶、喝茶要加的牛奶和糖，还有一些饼干之类的小点心。Strawson 一般让我先谈谈我的文章和想法，然后跟我讨论，有时让我更详细地阐述某个想法，有时说说他的看法，有时提出些建议。讨论的时候，Strawson 经常会陷入沉思，客厅里便是一片寂静。当他沉思的时候，我也不去打扰他，就在一旁静静地坐着，思考我自己的东西。Strawson 是一个标准的英国绅士，总是显得那么雍容大度。如果他觉得我的某个想法有问题，或者他不同意我的某个观点，他会明确地表达出来，但会鼓励我去考虑他还有其他人的反对意见以便修改和完善我自己的想法和观点。同 Strawson 谈话，我从来都没有感到过紧张，从来都没有觉得自己所说的东西太幼稚，从来都没有感到自己在一个哲学伟人面前抬不起头。他没有架子，脸上总是挂着微笑，声音总是那么柔和。他总是能让我言所欲言，总是能让我觉得自己在做有意义的思考，总是能让我高兴而来又高兴地离去。他从没有说：你是对的，就应当这么干。他总是说：你这样想有道理，你再去认真思考研究，从多个角度去考虑看看有什么不妥的地方。就是通过这样面对面的交流，我见识到了一个伟大哲学家做学问的方式，也学到了怎样进行哲学思考。Strawson 虽然不是我的正式的指导老师（tutor），但我从他那得到的指导并不比从正式的指导老师那里得到的少。单从这种面谈次数来说，我和 Higginbotham 还是经常面谈的，但见其他指导老师的次数就寥寥无几了，然而我见 Strawson 的次数倒是很多的。况且，只有 Strawson 能够让我在思考的空间里自由翱翔，只有他能让我把想像的能力发挥到极限。

读硕士的两年中，我受 Wittgenstein 和 Strawson 的影响很大。Wittgenstein 和 Strawson 都强调日常语言的重要性。不过，那时 Wittgenstein 给我影响最大的是要用众所周知的事实来化解哲学问题。我试图用一些为大家所熟知的词的使用方法，我称之为"句子框架"（sentence frames），来解释 Chomsky 所想解决的语法问题，为此我写了一篇长长的文章《乔姆斯基评日常语言学派的语言观》（Chomsky on the "ordinary language" view of language），投到哲学期刊 Synthese，被接收了。文章叙述了日常语言学派的一系列关于语言的观点，回顾了 Chomsky 对这些观点的批判，提出这些观点可以从词语及其使用的角度给以较满意的解释。文章的结论是日常语言学派的语言观是可行的，我们可以在这个框架下解释语言的诸多现象，而不必像 Chomsky 那样摒弃日常语言学派的语言观而另创一个完全不同的理论。Synthese 是国际哲学界最好的期刊之一，这篇文章能被 Synthese 接收并将发表，对我是一个不小的鼓舞。Strawson 也很高兴，他向我表示祝贺并鼓励我继续研究下去。

硕士期间所受 Strawson 的影响在于他的康德式的哲学。Strawson 在讨论的时候对我说，他同意我用"句子框架"来解释语法现象，而且认为这样的解释有很大的说服力；但他觉得人类应该有一些普遍的认知能力，比如人们有形成各种概念的能力，这些能力也许可以解释人类为什么会有语言，关于这一观点 Strawson 在他的《个体》（Individuals）和《逻辑和语法中的主谓语》中都有一定的论述。Strawson 的哲学观点很大程度上受了 Kant（康德）的影响，Kant 认为人类需要有一些先天的概念才能有后天的经验，为此他在《纯理性批判》（Critique of Pure Reason）中探讨了一系列他认为是先天的概念。在我看来，Strawson 所关心的问题就是语言习得机制问题。为此我专门研究了 Kant 的《纯理性批判》、Pinker 的《语言本能》（The Language Instant）、Skinner 的《言语行为》（Verbal Behavior）、Jespersen 的《分析语法》（Analytic Syntax）和《语法的哲学》（Philosophy of Grammar）等著作，当然还有 Chomsky 的诸多论著。我的结论是语法可以用"句子框架"来解释，而"句子框架"的习得可以用 Kant 和 Strawson 所提出的先天基本能力来解释，比如领会空间和时间的能力、区分数量和质量的能力、辨别共性和个性的能力、区分个体和发现个体的能力等等。而 Jespersen 刚好在这两方面都有论述：在《分析语法》中 Jespersen 讨论了一系列"句子类型"（sentence types）并以此来解释人们创造性地说话的能力，而这些"句子类型"和我所说的"句子框架"是有许多共同之处的；在《语法的哲学》中 Jespersen 对人类语言的基本能力也作了探讨，并认为这些基本能力就构成了"普遍语法"（universal grammar）——当然，Jespersen 的普遍语法和 Chomsky 的是完全不同的。在和 Strawson 面谈时，我和他讨论了 Jespersen 关于人类语言基本能力的工作，Strawson 认为他和 Jespersen 的思路是相似的（用他的原话就是"similar"、"closely related"）。当然，Strawson 和 Jespersen 因为领域不同，彼此并没有任何学术上的联系或影响。我打算将 Kant、Strawson 和 Jespersen 的理论结合起来，认为语言学界应该去探讨以上所述的人类先天的语言基本能力，于是我便提出"康德式语言学"（Kantian Linguistics）这个概念。

我的硕士论文就是以上这些内容，由三篇文章构成："Chomsky on the 'ordinary language' view of language"，"Jespersen, Skinner, and Chomsky on language"，和"Language and evolution"。每一篇文章都和 Strawson 进行过深入的探讨。硕士论文定名为"语言能力的本质：观念和争执"（The Nature of Linguistic Competence：Conceptions and Controversies）。除此之外，我还对"意义"（meaning）进行了大量的思考，花了很多心血写了篇《对意义的沉思》（Meditations on meaning），是仿照 Descartes（笛卡尔）的《第一哲学的沉思》（Meditations on First Philosophy）而作。文章充满自问自答，不给思绪以任何约束，任之自由飞翔。但由于内容太多，而且思考得很不成熟，就没有纳入到硕士论文里去。Strawson 认为我那两年在哲学研究上进展很快（用他的话说就是"considerable advance"），他感到很欣慰，我也很兴奋。

当硕士课程进行到第二年时，我们需要考虑申请继续读博士。我从 Higginbotham 那学到了很多东西，不仅是先进的知识，还有做学问的严谨态度。我很想跟 Higginbotham 继续做博士研究，但我想去哲学系，因为我觉得更喜欢对哲学问题的探讨。在哲学系读博仍可以拜 Higginbotham 为导师，因为他也是哲学系的教授。我特别想探讨的问题是人类的语言能力究竟是由什么构成的。诸多的原因使得 Chomsky 认为人的大脑中一定有一个普遍语法，并推断它是由少数几条语法原理组成而且这些语法原理是基因所决定的。Chomsky 的理论非常有革命性，而且他的论证鲜明、流畅、有很强的号召力。然而，我认为 Chomsky 的论证是有严重漏洞的，因而他的结论也就不完全正确了。我觉得人类的语言能力可以另加解释：人类之所以能够使用语言，是因为人有一些基本的、先天的能力，对于这些基本能力 Kant、Strawson 和 Jespersen 都有过探讨。我打算将"康德式语言学"作为我在哲学系读博的研究课题。当然，提出这样一种语言学研究，也是为了和 Chomsky 的"笛卡尔式语言学"（Cartesian Linguistics）相对应，目的是想打造另一个有着深厚哲学基础的语言学理论。

Strawson 对我的研究计划很欣赏，毕竟他多年来一直从事这方面的思考，并出版了以上所提到的两本书。他的《个体》一书名扬四海，可是他的《逻辑和语法中的主谓语》却几乎无人问津，但 Strawson 本人却对它钟爱有加。我的"康德式语言学"，如果做下去的话，将能把他在这两本书中的所表达的思想发扬光大，并在此基础上进行更深入和广泛的研究。申请读博得需要推荐信，我问 Strawson 是否能够做我的推荐人之一，他很爽快地答应了，并很快把推荐信给了大学招生办公室。然而，结果并不如我所愿：我并没能被哲学系接收。哲学系给我解释说，系里每年只收几个博士生，想把机会留给那些没有读过博士的学生。这个解释很说得过去，我也没有怎么受影响，就继续留在语言学系跟 Higginbotham 做博士。然而，我的研究计划需要有所改动，因为"康德式语言学"在语言学系就显得有些太哲学了。但和具体语言的具体分析相比，我对语言学中的哲学问题更有兴趣。于是我便打算更深入地研究 Chomsky 的语法理论、并研究 Davidson 的语义理论，尤其关注这两个理论的哲学基础。其实这和我提出的"康德式语言学"并不冲突。"康德式语言学"想揭示人类的语言的基本能力，是一个宏大的计划；而我此时想做的是人类语法和语义的基本能力，这可以说是前者的一部分。经过认真思考，我最后确定研究课题为"语法、意义和理解：语法能力和语义能力之探究"（Grammar, Meaning and Understanding: An Inquiry into Syntactic and Semantic Competence）。这里的小标题是有意模仿 Russell 的《意义与真理之探究》（An Inquiry into Meaning and Truth）的。

1998 年夏天，两年的语言学硕士结束了，我顺利地通过考试，拿到了硕士学位，并取得了继续跟 Higginbotham 做语言学博士的资格。我还从 Somerville 学院转到了 St. Hugh's 学院，因为我得到了该学院的"优秀华人学生奖学金"。St. Hugh's 学院和 Somerville 学院相似，都是比较年轻的学院，学生的学习和生活气氛很轻松。St. Hugh's 的院子更大，院子里有一个很大的草坪，草坪里种着各种各样的花，花开的时候，五彩缤纷、花香四溢。躺在如茵的草地上，闻着幽幽的花香，晒着暖暖的太阳，或读书、或思考、或者只是在那躺着，真是非常地享受。读博期间不需要再去上课，也没有作业了，自己读书和思考的时间就更多了。St. Hugh's 学院离 Strawson 的家更近，走路也就几分钟吧。因为离得近，我有信也就不寄了，而是直接走去他家，把信从他家门上的信孔塞进去。（英国人家里的大门上一般都有一个孔，专门是送信用的。）

在一次交谈中，Strawson 谈到中英暑期哲学学院，他告诉我说他是名誉院长，中方负责人是中国社会科学院哲学研究所的江怡研究员，英方负责人是牛津大学中国研究中心的 Nick Bunnin 博士。由此我便结识了江怡教授和 Bunnin 博士。Bunnin 博士的办公室就在语言系的楼里，我见他很容易。我回国探亲时，去拜访了江怡教授，建立了学术上的联系。中英暑期哲学学院后来发展成为中英澳暑期哲学学院，直到现在的中英美暑期哲学学院。

在我的硕士论文里，满是对 Chomsky 的批评；博士研究中又对 Davidson 的语义理论进行了深入的批评。我敢对这两个大家进行批评挑战，一个方面是由于我喜欢追根朔源吧。我想知道人类语法功能和语义能力是怎么回事，我便去学习 Chomsky 和 Davidson 的解释，但我不完全同意他们的论证和结论，于是我就想指出他们的问题，并提出我自己的观点。我敢于挑战这两个权威的另一个原因就是 Strawson 的鼓励。他虽然没有说 Chomsky 和 Davidson 是错的而我是对的，但他觉得我说的有价值、值得去探讨。那时我的处境应该说是很艰难的。Higginbotham 曾是麻省理工学院语言学和哲学系的教授，和 Chomsky 曾是同事。他是 Chomsky 理论和 Davidson 理论的专家，他推崇这两个理论并把它们结合起来，在理论语言学界占有重要的地位。1993 年他被牛津大学挖过去做普通语言学教授并担任语言学系主任，因而牛津大学的生成语法和形式语义学就成了研究的重点。在这样的环境中去做批评 Chomsky 和 Davidson 的研究，并想拿到博士学位，而且头上是 Higginbotham 这样的导师，肯定是要做出些东西的，否则无法通过博士答辩。不过我当时就想找 Higginbotham 做导师，因为我就想跟 Chomsky 和 Davidson 的学者们直接交流对话，这样才能使我想说的话更有说服力。在此，我也很感谢 Higginbotham 收我为学生。我由衷地敬佩他，他能允许他的学生和他唱反调，真的显示了他在学术上的大度。

如果说我的硕士研究主要是受到了 Wittgenstein 和 Strawson 两人的影响，那我的博士研究受到的影响则主要来自 Wittgenstein 一个人。虽然我的文章《乔姆斯基评日常语言学派的语言观》于我读博第一年在哲学期刊 *Synthese* 上发表了，但我意识到这离让 Chomsky 一派同意我的观点还差得很远，其中一个原因就是他们不会认为他们那样做有什么错误。Wittgenstein 说：你必须彻底理解哲学家为什么觉得那些哲学问题是问题，你必须帮他分析他的思路，你的分析必须得让他本人承认，这样他才能认清他所犯的思维上的错误，才能使他意识到原来困扰他的哲学问题并不是真正的问题。于是我便潜心地去研究 Chomsky 为什么非得提出个"普遍语法"理论，研究他的思维过程并指出他在思维过程中所犯的错误，为此我读了 Chomsky 几乎所有的语言学著作，研究结果总结在《转换之转换》（The transformations of transformations）一文中，此文发表在国际期刊 Language and Communication 上。我个人认为，这篇文章比我那篇 Synthese 文章无论是从语言学角度还是从哲学角度都深了一个层次。此后，我又用这个模式对 Davidson 的语义学理论进行了深入的分析，写了 "The meaning of Davidson's truth theory" 一文。这三篇文章便构成了我的博士论文。

博士论文初稿出来后，我开始考虑以后的工作问题。我很想去美国的著名大学工作，以便和那里的 Chomsky 或 Davidson 的专家学者们进行直接的交流，并顺便了解和体会美国的教育系统。我跟 Strawson 谈了我的想法，他很赞同，并同意为我写推荐信。我申请了美国包括哈佛、普林斯顿等十几所一流大学哲学系或语言学系的教职。为了节省 Strawson 的时间，我把十几个信封上都写上地址，然后到 Strawson 所在的 University 学院的办公室把那些信封交给他，他会把推荐信给学院的传达室，传达室会帮他寄出去。当我把那叠信封交给 Strawson 的时候，心里真是很歉疚，要知道 Strawson 是老一辈人物，不会使用电脑，写信全都是用手写，要他写那么多份推荐信，该是多么大的麻烦啊。后来我在美国遇到一个教授，他就在我所申请的一所大学里工作，他对我说他是生平第一次见到 Strawson 写的推荐信。这让我很感动，是啊，Strawson 给多少人写过推荐信呢？可是，我并没有得到美国的工作，其中一个原因是在美国申请大学教职一般必须已经得到博士学位，而我当时博士还没有到手。在英国申请大学教职倒不要求博士必须已经到手，于是我便申请到了伦敦大学的教职，2000 年秋天就去了伦敦。

我在伦敦大学一边工作，一边修改我的博士论文，一边写些文章。伦敦到牛津的交通很发达，每十分钟就有一趟公共汽车，一个半小时就能到。我经常会回牛津，或者去见 Higginbotham，或者见 Strawson，或者只是和我的一些朋友聚会。在伦敦期间我写了两篇主要文章："Davidson's interpretive trilogy" 和 "Wittgenstein and theoretical linguistics"，这两篇文章我都寄给 Strawson 看过，它们更偏向于 Wittgenstein 的后期语言哲学。

2003 年 7 月我参加了牛津大学的毕业典礼，穿上了梦寐已久的牛津博士袍。我开始考虑自己的将来。当然，我可以一直在伦敦大学任教，也可以再争取去美国的大学工作。但我自出国起一直有回国工作的想法，现在博士做完了，该是回国的时候了。2003 年 12 月至 2004 年 3 月我到香港大学哲学系做访问学者，同系主任 Laurence Goldstein 教授还有其他学者进行了密切的交流，收获颇丰。2004 年夏天我便来到了北京师范大学工作。临离开英国时，我给 Strawson 写了封告别信，他回信说理解我的决定，并勉励我在学术上继续努力。没想到那竟是和 Strawson 的最后一次交流！

转眼 5 年过去了，想到 Strawson 对我的抬爱，想到自己还没有做出什么成绩，真是很惭愧。但是，我知道他就在天上——他就是天空中某颗闪烁的明星。也许他正在微笑地注视着我，正在默默地鼓励着我。于是我觉得有一种庄严的义务感，觉得应该好好地做一些事情，至少应该尽自己的努力，这样才能在每次想到他时不至于内心惶惶不安。Strawson 虽然不在了，但我眼前依然会经常浮现他那慈祥的面容、他那睿智的眼神和他那深沉思考的样子。这位哲学巨匠曾给哲学带来了莫大的繁荣，我希望也相信哲学不会因他的离去而萧条枯萎。我们这些哲学后辈们会沿着他留下的足迹，披荆斩棘，去探索哲学的真谛。

In Memory of Sir Peter F. Strawson
——written on the 90th anniversary of his birth
Francis Yunqing Lin

Beijing Normal University

Abstract: In this memoir I recall my interactions and friendship with Sir Peter F. Strawson during the years 1995 – 2004. It was due to the encouragement from Strawson that I went to Oxford to study linguistics and philosophy. It was also Strawson that led me onto the path of philosophical exploration. In this memoir I hope to report his outstanding personality: gentle, kind, generous, and ever encouraging. I also hope to reveal the close connections between linguistic research and his philosophical work.

Keywords: Strawson; Oxford; syntax; semantics; logic; Kant; Wittgenstein

中山大学分析哲学读书会状略

◎ 刘小涛
　中山大学

本文报道的是中山大学哲学系"分析哲学读书会"近三年里的活动情况。这个群体并不广为人知，但却令人诧异地富于成效。尤其是，它的许多方面都折射出我国分析哲学研究的现状和动向。

主要归功于张华夏和林定夷先生的努力，自改革开放以来，中山大学哲学系一直保持着对科学哲学和科学方法论的核心问题进行研究的浓厚兴趣。亨普尔的《自然科学的哲学》、内格尔的《科学的结构》、卡尔纳普的《科学哲学导论》、波普尔的《猜想与反驳》、拉卡托斯的《证伪与科学研究纲领方法论》、库恩的《科学革命的结构》等历来是最基础的读物。通常，两位先生还会要求自己的研究生选修数学，或者物理学、生物学等自然科学的专业课。好几位出身于这个培养基地的长辈都已取得不俗成就。

2003 年，中山大学哲学专业获得博士学位一级学科授予权。因为《因果观念与休谟问题》和《反本质主义与知识问题》的广泛影响，张志林先生担任了科学哲学方向学科带头人。分析哲学注重的方法与科学哲学针对的问题得到很好的结合，成为研究生训练的基本导向。

我于 2006 年秋季入学，那时候，周燕、黄敏、胡浩、王静、闫坤如、袁继红等人俱已在张志林先生的指导下完成博士论文，在各自的研究领域取得了某些见识（包括分析哲学、科学哲学、语言哲学、认知科学、社会科学哲学等）。未毕业的博士研究生里，除几位倾向于默默工作的学长外，沈健在探究量子力学革命中的理论还原问题，刘钰森为知识的限度问题所累，朱诗勇忙于考虑科学准实在论的相关哲学问题，肖健在关心医学伦理，李田在考察科学争论的机制问题，梁礼宏在探索科学解释的语用问题，王晓阳刚做好从神经生物学的视角研究意识的打算。

按照培养计划，我们几个新生（包括舒国萱、夏代云、谭力扬、何睿、倪明红、以及我）第一学期应该修认知科学哲学（李平主讲）、分析哲学（黄敏主讲）以及数理逻辑（任远主讲）等专业课。当代哲学研究领域知识专门化的程度越来越需要集思广益，加上为了配合教学以及训练文献阅读能力的必要，我们几人商定，应该举行定期的聚会（两周一次，通常在周五晚上），通过专门讨论某个经典文献以促进理解和思想交流。

作为一项学生的学术活动，这些最初的动机得到张志林、李平、黄敏几位老师的支持。这样，以分析哲学研究所和科学哲学与认知科学研究所为依托，读书会得以成立。在几位老师的指导下，我们围绕弗雷格、罗素、维特根斯坦、卡尔纳普等早期分析哲学家的著述展开阅读和讨论。除这几位老师外，参加成员主要是哲学系在读的科学哲学专业研究生，以及外国哲学专业的部分学生。

形成惯例后，它的影响逐渐得以扩大，吸引了哲学系各个专业的学生参加。尤其，于2007年，张志林老师开始授课（上半年讲科学哲学、下半年讲语言哲学），借此良机，读书会取得长足发展。先生一些已毕业的学生成为读书会的常客，并自发筹集了些经费，后来又得到了冯达文先生提供的经费支助。因为研究趣向接近，我系朱菁老师和任远老师也成为读书会指导老师。慕张老师之名而来听课的外系学生（如现执教于武汉大学社会学系的张杨波先生）以及其他社会成员也壮大了读书会的阵容。

考虑到核心成员已具备分析哲学的基本训练，读书会讨论的范围相应得以扩展。一些个人研究成果、最新研究动态报告也成为讨论的主题。比如，在没有酬劳的情况下，林定夷老师作过《论科学与非科学的划界问题》的报告、任远老师作过《Belief Ascription and De Re Communication》的报告。学生的系列报告包括：《量子革命与问题还原》（沈健）、《知识的限度——迪昂蒯因论题研究》（刘钰森）、《上帝的本体论证明》（宣庆文）、《塞尔的心灵哲学》（李珍）、《社会怨恨与宗教伦理——关于〈17世纪英格兰的科学、技术与社会〉的思考》（张杨波）、《概念构架：戴维森与帕特南之间的分歧》（刘小涛）、《经验反常、创造性溯因推理与科学发现》（夏代云）、《论私密性——针对感受特质（quale）及其相关问题的一项研究》（王晓阳）、《论社会科学规律的可能性》（袁继红）等。

最值得记忆的事发生在2007年12月间，北大哲学系程炼先生和邢滔滔先生赴粤，为读书会作了九次讲演（费时一星期）。程炼的讲演几乎是一门心灵哲学课程，内容包括：心灵哲学概述、意向性的自然化、意识与物理主义、依随与物理主义、计算主义；邢滔滔的讲演内容主要涉及上帝存在的本体论论证，内容有：哲学论证、Anselm与Gaunilo、笛卡尔与康德、莱布尼茨的模态分析、哥德尔的"莱布尼茨式"证明、Plantinga的模态证明。这一星期，宛然一场分析哲学的盛宴。期间，程炼、邢滔滔、张志林、李平、朱菁、黄敏几位老师，以及读书会的成员，围绕心灵、语言、世界、上帝存在的本体论证明等议题展开激烈争辩。

2007年11月底的一次读书会也值得提及。其时，任远正与我们讨论信念归属的问题。美国佛罗里达大学哲学系刘闯教授闯了进来（他上午在系里作了题为"量子世界与自由意志"的讲演），旋即参与讨论。后来，他告诉我们说，这个读书会他耳闻已久。

仿佛在 2008 年元旦后的一个寒夜，张志林老师透露说——他可能将调任复旦大学。这个消息伴随着惊讶在师生中流传的时候，我以及我的朋友们都有一种担忧，担忧这个学术共同体会因此解散，就如同失去了精神领袖的维也纳小组那样。

因为社会体制的原因，张老师的调动并不顺利。他滞留广州一直到 2009 年 3 月，尽心指导读书会成员的研究工作。期间，除了针对某些论著的讨论外，学生在读书会上所作的研究报告包括：《论现象概念》（王晓阳）、《乔姆斯基的"学习理论论证"与模块性假设》（刘小涛）、《库恩概念学说的认知分析》（倪明红）、《科学实在论的因果机制指称理论》（谭力扬）、《他心与上帝存在——谈他心问题在普兰廷格思想中的流变》（陈思敏）、《拥有一种命题知识时，我知道什么？——一个对 Gettier 反例的尝试消解方案》（何朝安）、《一个温和物理主义者眼中的"黑白玛丽"》（王晓阳）、《语言知识：我们知道什么？——对达米特的批判性考察》（刘小涛）、《宇称不守恒和判决性实验》（舒国萱）等。

事实表明，作为哲学训练的辅助性建制，分析哲学读书会有力地推动了共同体成员的研究工作。单就 2008 年而言，以下成果发表前俱经读书会讨论：

1. 朱诗勇，《观察理论化的困境与根源》，载《自然辩证法研究》2008 年第 1 期。

2. 刘小涛，《不融贯的概念构架观念——戴维森的先验论证及其缺陷》，载《自然辩证法研究》2008 年第 4 期。

3. 黄敏，《维特根斯坦〈逻辑哲学论〉的入口》，载《哲学研究》2008 年第 5 期。

4. 王晓阳，《论意识的认知神经科学研究及哲学思考》，载《自然辩证法研究》2008 年第 6 期。

5. 袁继红，《论社会科学规律之可能性——从当代自然主义和反自然主义的角度看》，载《自然辩证法研究》2008 年第 7 期。

6. 夏代云，《创造性溯因推理与科学发现——以现代原子模型的早期发展为例》，载《自然辩证法研究》2008 年第 7 期。

7. 刘小涛，《乔姆斯基的"学习理论论证"与模块性假设》，载《哲学研究》2008 年第 10 期。

8. 舒国萱，《迪昂—蒯因论点对判决性实验的意见》，载《自然辩证法研究》2008 年第 12 期。

另外，在一些重要学术会议上，读书会成员的表现也非常抢眼。例如，在 2008 年 9 月上旬由山西大学承办的全国科学哲学专业博士生论坛上，李珍的论文《意向性与因果性——基于干预主义因果论进路的意向因果性的研究》获得一等奖，拙文《学习理论论证与模块性假定——乔姆斯基的二难》获得二等奖。

2008年6月上旬，读书会有幸请到浙江大学的盛晓明先生作讲演。先生指出，哲学研究中，有两种完全不同的精神倾向：一种是自康德以降（或者更早）的先验主义态度；另一种是经蒯因的倡领而来势汹汹的自然主义态度。这两种精神倾向分歧在读书会成员内部也有体现。我们的成员教育背景不一，有些经过严格的自然科学训练，有些则受过良好的人文学科熏陶；又因性情各异，彼此关心完全不同的哲学问题。因此，通常并没有完全一致的哲学立场。有些人，坚定地采取了极端物理主义立场；有些则温和得多，尽管对方法论的自然主义报有同情；也有些人，仍然觉得逻辑分析和语言批判是哲学分析的真正要义。

虽如此，除了地域、社会建制上的原因外，似乎在精神上，也能在核心成员身上发现某些共通之处，得以把读书会标识为一个学术共同体。

首先，作为哲学中最核心的理念之一，思想自由为我们所推崇。我们都认为，接受或评价一个哲学主张、一个哲学论证、一个哲学理论，应该完全出于自己的独立思考，而不是出于独断或听命于权威。

其次，深受张志林先生感染，我们大抵都对学术抱有赤诚而热烈的追求。在研究工作中，这种追求体现为对某些哲学问题的严肃思考以及孜孜不倦的探究。先生每每鼓励："要敢于思考哲学大问题。""取法乎上"，这几乎塑造了每一个读书会成员的思考格调。

再次，读书会强调分析哲学中"做哲学"的精神。以一种理性的冷静态度来研究哲学，并以清晰的语言表述和严格的哲学论证作为最基本的评价标准。而且，我们都不太愿意从事哲学史的考据，也不太愿意阅读那些概念性诗歌（不管它是富于想像力还是晦涩不堪）。前者或许能发现一些历史事实，后者也许对某些个人而言更为有趣。不过，我们以为，它们都不是做哲学之根本。

并非所有的优良哲学品质我们都已具足，也并非我们所认可的优良品质都已得到国内同行承认。如今，张志林老师已就任复旦大学。而中山大学分析哲学读书会的活动仍在继续，因张老师的榜样示范力量塑造形成的传统也在延续。消除了多余的担忧，我们希望，中大的分析哲学读书会将继续办下去；我们也希望，因张老师的努力，更多理智成熟的标志性品质也会融入复旦大学的哲学追求之中。

编后记

　　《中国分析哲学》终于正式出版了！在这里，我们首先要向为中国的分析哲学事业作出了重大贡献的老一辈哲学家表示崇高的敬意！还要向多年来勤奋耕耘于这个领域的学者们表示衷心的感谢！也要向正在或准备在这个领域里努力钻研的青年学子表示全心的鼓励！

　　本系列出版物由中国现代外国哲学学会分析哲学专业委员会主办。该专业委员会自 2005 年筹备之日起，就开始组织全国性的分析哲学研讨会，2006 年委员会正式成立，致力于组织国内的分析哲学研究和传播工作，推动分析哲学在当代中国哲学中的研究和发展。截至 2009 年，分析哲学专业委员会组织的"全国分析哲学研讨会"已经成功举办了五届，在国内外哲学界都产生了很好的学术反响，参加者从最初的 20 余人增加到 80 余人。北京大学哲学系、中山大学哲学系、武汉大学哲学院、浙江大学人文学院哲学系和语言与认知研究中心积极支持并承办了各届研讨会。几乎每次研讨会都邀请到了来自英、美、澳大利亚等国的哲学家参加，扩大了中国分析哲学研究在国外哲学界的影响。正是在分析哲学专业委员会的大力推动下，国际著名的分析哲学杂志《综合》于 2009 年组织出版了《分析哲学在中国》专栏，发表了国内学者的研究论文，反映了中国分析哲学的研究现状，得到了国际学术界的关注。

　　在 2009 年 4 月浙江省建德市梅城镇举行的第五届全国分析哲学研讨会上，分析哲学专业委员会决定编辑出版《中国分析哲学》，并确定了论文编选工作的基本原则和主要程序。随后，专业委员会在哲学专业杂志和网站上对外发布了公示，广泛征求论文，并从第五届全国分析哲学研讨会论文中选取了部分论文，采用双向匿名评审的方式，评审专家对来稿进行了严格审读，最后确定了入集的论文。根据专业委员会的意见，《中国分析哲学》将每年出版一辑，收入的论文将主要来源于每年度的全国分析哲学研讨会，并坚持采用双向匿名评审的方式。

　　本期《中国分析哲学》由浙江大学人文学院和语言与认知研究中心（CSLC）鼎力资助，分析哲学专业委员会在此表示衷心感谢和崇高敬意！最后还要感谢浙江大学出版社的大力支持，感谢北京启真馆文化传播有限责任公司的积极合作，特别感谢本期编辑朱岳先生大量细致的工作。

《中国分析哲学》编辑委员会

2009 年 9 月 30 日

图书在版编目（CIP）数据

中国分析哲学：2009/中国现代外国哲学学会分析哲学专业
委员会编 . —杭州：浙江大学出版社，2010.5
ISBN 978 – 7 – 308 – 07494 – 0

Ⅰ.①中…　Ⅱ.①中…　Ⅲ.①分析哲学 – 中国 – 文集
Ⅳ.①B089 – 53

中国版本图书馆 CIP 数据核字（2010）第 062164 号

中国分析哲学：2009
中国现代外国哲学学会分析哲学专业委员会　编

策　　划	朱　岳
责任编辑	王志毅
装帧设计	王小阳
出版发行	浙江大学出版社
	（杭州天目山路 148 号　邮政编码 310007）
	（网址：http：//www.zjupress.com）
排　　版	北京京鲁创业科贸有限公司
印　　刷	杭州杭新印务有限公司
开　　本	787mm × 1092mm　1/16
印　　张	27
字　　数	531 千
版 印 次	2010 年 6 月第 1 版　2010 年 6 月第 1 次印刷
书　　号	ISBN 978 – 7 – 308 – 07494 – 0
定　　价	75 . 00 元